Gondar

Nicholas Luard, who lives in London with his wife, Elisabeth, is the author of several thrillers, including *The Orion Line* and *The Robespierre Serial*. He has also written non-fiction books, *Andalucia, The Last Wilderness*, and has lived and worked in Africa. In *Gondar*, for the first time, he has married his genius for storytelling with his knowledge of and passion for that continent.

Gondar

Nicholas Luard

ARROW BOOKS

Arrow Books Limited
62–65 Chandos Place, London WC2N 4NW

An imprint of Century Hutchinson Limited

London Melbourne Sydney Auckland
Johannesburg and agencies throughout
the world

First published in Great Britain in 1988
by Century Hutchinson Limited
Arrow edition 1989
© Nicholas Luard 1988

Photoset by Deltatype Ltd, Ellesmere Port
Printed and bound in Great Britain by
Anchor Press Ltd, Tiptree, Essex

ISBN 0 09584409

For Casper Luard

— Prologue —

The priest had been lacerated from his scalp to his ankles by at least nine different leopards. Ras Michael could tell that from the spoor of the pug-marks in the dust round his body.

Ras Michael gazed down at him from his horse.

The man was lying pegged out naked on his face with his priest's robe rucked up round his shoulders. The blood from the wounds was still dark and wet. Ras Michael dismounted stiffly and prodded him with his foot. A groan lifted into the early morning air on the little plateau high in the hills above the Abyssinian city of Gondar.

The priest was still alive.

Behind the Ras — the word meant a great chieftain — the officer commanding the squadron of bodyguards, who had ridden with the old warlord up the mountain track, heard the groan too. The officer swung himself out of his saddle. He whistled as he saw the mutilated flesh. Then he drew his sword.

'He's been well-serviced, Ras,' the officer said, chuckling. 'Shall I cut him free or put the blade in him?'

Ras Michael thought for a moment as the sword flared in the sunlight.

The priest had been arrested and convicted the day before. His crime was corruption. Ras Michael's men had caught him redhanded in the act of taking bribes from the Arab merchants who were trying to establish a monopoly over Gondar's trade with the coast.

Ras Michael had pronounced sentence himself. In committing treason the priest had defiled his cloth. In turn he would be defiled.

The punishment, the harshest in Gondar's code, was immensely old. The priest had been brought up to the plateau. There he had been daubed with spots and staked out on the ground. Then the guards had found and killed a leopardess in heat – the hills above Gondar abounded with the creatures. They rubbed the man's skin with a mixture of the leopardess's vaginal fluids, and crushed leaves of the herb valerian.

Afterwards they left him to the night and the waiting males.

The leopards started to gather even before the guards had ridden away. Inflamed by the mating odours lifting on the night breeze they sprang down, quarrelling and snarling at each other as they used their talons to savage at the puzzle of the priest's body – its rank enticing scent familiar but its shape unknown. Each time their claws raked him in exploration, more of his flesh was ripped away.

By now they had almost skinned him alive.

The leopards had scattered at Ras Michael's approach but he knew they would be waiting to return hidden in the rocks above, their cold agate-coloured eyes gleaming in the shadows.

'Leave him as he is!' Ras Michael answered curtly. 'Let the cats finish their work. Afterwards the birds can take the scraps – '

The officer glanced at him in surprise.

If a criminal sentenced to the leopards survived the ordeal of the night, he was traditionally cut free or put out of his agony next morning.

'He wasn't filling his own purse,' Ras Michael went on. 'He was lining his master's. One day, so help me God, we'll spread the Acab Saat's own legs for the leopards. Meanwhile this one can pay for his master too.'

The thought of the royal bishop made Ras Michael's face darken with anger. He turned away and reached for his horse's bridle.

'Help me up!' he snapped.

The officer ran forward. He heaved the white-bearded

Ras into the saddle and vaulted back onto his own mount. Bridles and stirrups jangled, and the riders set off back down the track towards Gondar.

Behind them the musty smell of the waiting leopards coiled out over the baked earth, and vultures began to flap forward across the stones.

— 1 —

It was a very important day, the most important day in her life.

Ozoro Esther – the Abyssinian title 'Ozoro' signified a princess of the royal blood – had known about it for three months. Now the morning had finally arrived, she found to her surprise she wasn't nervous. She felt intrigued. More than intrigued, she felt physically and mentally excited. Her cheeks kept flushing. Her breast lifted and fell more swiftly than usual. Her nipples were hard, and a strange hollowness in her legs came and went with a recurring dampness between the top of her thighs.

Very soon the preparations would start. Meanwhile she wanted a little time on her own. It was the last chance she would have until long after nightfall.

'Kalima!' she called out.

The old servant woman hurried towards her across the courtyard.

'I'm going outside,' Esther went on. 'When you're ready for me, I'll be in the nightingale garden.'

Kalima bowed.

As Esther headed for the park she caught a glimpse of the mountains above the palace roofs. A tiny plume of dust hung over one of the tracks that crossed the mountain flanks. A group of horsemen was winding down towards Gondar. She paused. They were probably late guests for the feast her father was giving that night.

Esther walked on.

Gondar's royal palace was a low rambling castle of weathered golden brick. There had been a fortress on the site for centuries, but most of the palace had been built over the past hundred years. By then the kingdom had long been influenced by the Arabs. One of the early European travellers to Abyssinia had likened the building to the Alhambra palace in Granada.

It was full of little hidden courtyards where fountains glittered in the hot light, and ferns and flowers spilled down from the battlements. Between the courtyards long shadowy passages wound through cool halls and chambers. Mosaic tiles glowed against the dusky walls and richly woven oriental carpets shone in islands of colour on the stone-flagged floors. There were arches and fretted colonnades, terraces and towers, domes and great barred gateways.

To Esther the palace was more than the home she had known all her life. It was also a place of magic and enchantment.

The air was always thick with scent. In summer with the fragrance of blossoms, in winter with the warm aroma of the herbs tossed on the blazing fires. Even on the days of the fiercest mountain heat the rooms always chimed with the sound of falling water outside. The corridors were always thronged with people. The royal guards in their scarlet cloaks. The silent barefooted slaves. The family servants like old Kalima. The noisy arguing courtiers. The court musicians and scribes. The visiting merchants and travellers, with their magnificent robes and turbans.

Vibrant with life, ancient, sumptuous, elegant and sometimes to her, as a child, frighteningly mysterious, the palace was an unending treasure chest of delights. Yet if there was one corner of it Esther loved more than any other, it was the garden of the nightingales.

She crossed the tree-shaded park and climbed the flight of steps that led up to it.

The garden lay at the furthest end of the park from the palace. Paved with brick and thickly planted with lavender and roses, it jutted out from the walls over the plain like a stone raft moored between the earth and sky. It was called the nightingale garden because in the spring nightingales always nested in its bushes. Their liquid soaring song filled the air on every side now.

Esther edged round the single tree that shaded the garden. She pushed her way between the banks of scented plants, and wriggled up into a narrow opening in the outer parapet.

There she sat swinging her legs over the edge.

The year was 1836. Esther, the only child of the emperor of Gondar, was fifteen. She was tall and slim, with a finely-modelled face, pale coffee-coloured skin, and dark long-lashed eyes. Her straight black hair was coiled on top of her head and held in place by a jewelled turban. She was wearing a soft calico tunic that fell from just above her breasts to her ankles. On her feet were leather sandals. By Abyssinian standards she had been a mature woman for the past two years – if she hadn't been the emperor's daughter she would have been married long since. But for the daughter of Gondar's ruler it was very different.

Esther plucked a twig of myrtle and chewed on it thoughtfully as she gazed down. The plain was spread out beneath her, as gold and tawny as the palace under the haze of the morning sun.

From the very beginnings of human settlement, the rich Abyssinian plains and uplands had played host to a myriad changing tribes and peoples. By 1836 the tides of invasion and warfare across the ages had left the country under the domination of three main kingdoms. Gondar was the oldest and most powerful. Both the kingdom and its capital took their name from the hill on which the palace and the town were built, a precipitous rib of rock running southwards from the towering Mountains of the Moon.

If Esther turned her head and looked back she could see the mountain peaks shimmering in the far distance.

From where she sat perched at the prow of the ridge, the ground appeared to fall sheer below her in an immense vertical drop for almost a thousand feet. In fact the cliff sloped slightly outwards. It was lined with rocky shelves. Each shelf contained a cluster of tiny mud-brick houses, clinging to the edge like swallows' nests. The groups of houses were linked to each other and to the city above by a warren of steep and narrow paths. Overgrowing the paths and ledges was a grey-green mantle of fierce razor-thorn acacia bush. Deliberately left uncut, except where the tracks climbed upwards, the thorn bush and the towering wall of the cliff made Gondar a virtually impregnable fortress.

For over two thousand years Gondar, the fabled kingdom of Prester John as the remote Europeans named it, had survived almost unchanged since the days when it was ruled by the Queen of Sheba. The young Esther couldn't measure the past in centuries, let alone in millennia. For a fifteen-year-old girl time on that scale had no meaning. To Esther the past was last Christmas, the feast of the Kings twelve days later, and her birthday in April – and, more importantly, the presents she'd been given on each occasion. The coral bracelet from her father, the white doves in the nest from Kalima, the sack of sugared almonds from the Arab merchant who'd arrived at court the week before.

Yet the Queen of Sheba was also part of Esther's past – and she was as real and familiar to the girl as the two doves which now perched every night above her bed. So was the queen's long-ago lover, the great King Solomon. Esther had been taught about them both all her life. They were not merely her ancestors. They were part of her being, the source of her blood.

Only the river, she'd learned, was more important.

The river.

Craning her neck, Esther could just see the point where it gushed out of the rocks midway down the cliff and began to plunge towards the plain. At that height it was a supple and shining torrent, a wind-plucked fountain of water that leapt and cascaded over the boulders in its path.

When it reached the plain its speed suddenly slowed and its colour changed. It became heavy and lethargic.

The cold silvery cleanness turned to a muddy camel-hide brown, its translucent feathers of spray to flecks of dirty yellow foam. With every mile it flowed north the river's texture thickened even more with silt, and its coiling eddies grew deeper and darker.

Compared with the wild soaring stream that erupted from the cliff, the river then was drab and monotonous. Esther had never seen it in its lower reaches. She only knew that however far from its source it flowed, however deep and turgid its waters ran, it was always, in the words of the people of the plain, the river of life.

They referred to it by the name of Nile. It nourished the kingdom of Gondar. It nourished fifteen other kingdoms between the mountains and the distant Mediterranean sea. Its liquid wealth supported more than ten million people, over half of Africa's entire population.

It was the most vital, the most precious, artery on earth. Esther did not know that. The girl knew only that it was her river. She thought of the emperor, and addressed him, as her father. He was not.

Esther was the river's child.

Narrowing her eyes into the sun, she squinted down at the arch of water tumbling far below her. Then she drew back into the tree's shadow. She pulled the skirt of her tunic up over her thighs. She spread her legs apart, and reached down with her hand. Over the past three months she had been examined every week by the court physician and the group of old women who acted as ladies-in-waiting and advisers to the emperor's wife, Esther's stepmother – Esther's own mother, the emperor's first wife, had died when Esther was five.

Esther parted the lips of her vulva and pushed her fingers inside. She knew exactly what she was feeling for – the fragile band of membrane barring the entrance to the womb. It was what the physician and the old women had inspected again and again since the spring, reassuring themselves every time that it was still unbroken. Esther touched it.

The membrane felt moist and springy and resilient.

Esther withdrew her hand. She lifted her fingers to her nose and sniffed. The scent on her fingertips was musky and curiously fragrant, reminding her of the odour of almonds. She licked her fingers delicately, like a cat cleaning itself. Then she put her hand back under her tunic. She half-closed her eyes, and fondled herself again.

By dusk the virginal membrane would have been ruptured.

Vaguely Esther wondered what it would feel like when the thrust came. There would be a brief moment of pain, Kalima had warned her of that. But the pain would pass almost instantly, old Kalima said. Afterwards she would only experience pleasure.

What preoccupied her now as she rocked backwards and forwards in the shade, her hand moving rhythmically between her legs, was who would be the man who came to break the membrane. She was the child of the river and she would bear the river's child.

In what form – the question obsessed her as it had done for months – would the river come to her to plant its seed?

— 2 —

'You!'

The voice cut through the smoke like the crack of a cobra-skin whip. On the far side of the fire the line of men shuffled and stared at each other nervously.

'You!' the voice repeated. 'The one with the pale skin near the boma gate.'

The tall man in the heavy woollen cloak raised his staff and levelled it like a lance above the flames. Behind him the detachment of soldiers were standing shoulder to shoulder.

Raghe glanced to his left and then to his right. The villagers on either side were gazing uncertainly into the torch-lit square of earth where the stranger was standing. Raghe swallowed. The staff was unmistakably pointing at him.

'Me, baku?' he asked, using the dialect word of the plain for a priest.

'Come here!'

Raghe stepped round the fire and walked hesitantly up to the man. As he stopped in front of him the stranger gestured to one of the soldiers. The soldier seized the hem of Raghe's cotton wrap and ripped it away, leaving him naked.

'How old are you, boy?' the priest asked.

Raghe was silent. He stared at the earth, his forehead furrowed in embarrassment and worry. He had no idea. An older man in the line beyond the fire leant forward.

'He was baptized in the summer after the second of the five big rains,' the old man said. 'I remember because his father held the river pasture by the Kwale pool and I stood for his witness.'

The priest nodded. The children of Gondar were christened in the first six months of their lives. The great five seasons of rain had ended twenty years ago. It meant the young man was seventeen.

The priest revolved the staff in his hand. Then he prodded out its tip, and lifted the young man's penis.

'What have you been doing with this?' he demanded.

'I don't understand, baku,' Raghe stammered.

'Well, have you been putting it into goats or cattle?'

'No, baku.'

The priest suddenly drew the staff back and slashed it against Raghe's stomach. Raghe doubled forward.

'Tell me the truth!'

He struck Raghe again. Raghe gasped and clutched his belly.

'Baku, I promise you' – the words came out choked – 'I've played with the girls inside the boma. But I've never put it into them or into anything else. That's my word.'

The priest inspected him again. The youth was tall and strongly muscled, with a handsome open face and wide well-set eyes, blinking now with pain. Close at hand the smoothness and paleness of his skin were even more noticeable. In the firelight he could almost have been white.

'Take him to the waggons!'

As the soldiers seized Raghe and hurried him away, the priest turned on his heel. He would need to interrogate the boy further and examine him in daylight, but he had little doubt he had found what he had been looking for. He strode off after the soldiers.

The waggons which had accompanied the party across the plain were drawn up a hundred yards beyond the village. Beside them the soldiers had pitched the priest's large oxhide tent. As he approached it he shouted for a pitcher of wine. Then he ducked under the flap. He threw himself down on the mound of tapestry cushions, and waited impatiently for the wine to arrive.

It had been a long day and he was hot and thirsty.

The priest's name was Abba Salama. Although the

country people addressed him as baku, in Gondar he was known by his title of the Acab Saat – 'the guardian of the fire'. Like much of the rest of Abyssinia, and uniquely in Africa, the kingdom of Gondar had been Christian for well over a thousand years. During that time the religion had evolved into a very different form of Christianity from the one practised in Europe. Gondar's church still clung to many of the ancient rituals from the country's past. Worship of the holy fire was one of them. Salama was both a Christian priest and the guardian of a pagan tradition.

As the Acab Saat he not only occupied the third most important position in the church. He was also the royal bishop and the emperor's personal religious adviser. It made him one of the most powerful men in the kingdom.

'Jacob!' he shouted. 'Bring that wine!'

Cursing his servant's slowness, Salama kicked off his boots and loosened the belt round his cloak. Then he lay staring irritably at the slit in the tent.

At thirty-seven Salama was a tall heavily built man with powerful shoulders and bulging thighs, a legacy of his passion for horse-riding and falconry. As with many Abyssinians, Arab blood had entered his ancestry on several occasions. He had cropped mustard-coloured hair, usually hidden by the cowl of his cloak, coppery skin and a coarse brooding face with a curving hawk's-bill nose. His eyes were hard and unblinking while his mouth, in complete contrast, was soft and moist with full, almost feminine lips.

As many like Raghe had found, the combination of the two, the cold piercing eyes, predatory and sadistic, and the opulent mouth, could be chilling.

The effect was not misleading. As well as being one of the most powerful men in Gondar, Salama was also one of the most feared and hated. Greedy, vengeful and ruthless, he had already used his position to amass a personal fortune that would soon rival the emperor's. In Salama's view that was only a start. Intensely ambitious, Salama was after nothing less than Gondar itself. It

18

would take time, he knew that, years perhaps, but he could afford to be patient. At thirty-seven, after all, time was on Salama's side.

'Where the hell have you been?' Salama snapped as his servant came into the tent.

Without waiting for Jacob to answer, he seized the pitcher and drank from the spout, pouring the wine into his mouth until it spilled over and ran down his chin. Coughing and spitting, he brushed it away. Then he drank again. A few minutes later with the pitcher empty he settled back on the cushions.

For the first time that day Salama felt content.

After three weeks of dusty and uncomfortable travelling, the search was over and he could return to Gondar. He could exchange the heat of the plain and the fly-blown tent – even now the air round the tallow lamp was thick with insects – for the cool airy chambers of the bishop's house. The bishop's house had other pleasures too. Suddenly Salama was reminded of them.

He scratched his groin reflectively.

'A woman, Jacob,' he said.

'Yes, Acab. I have looked at the headman's wives.'

Like all Salama's servants Jacob was well familiar with his master's tastes and his almost insatiable appetite.

'And?' Salama prompted him.

'They were at food,' Jacob answered. 'I could see them only from the waist up. The younger ones are thin, without meat on them. But there was one of perhaps twenty-five. She is old I know, Acab, and she will have dropped children. But she still has body and firmness to her.'

Salama thought for a moment.

The village was almost two hundred miles from Gondar. He had little idea what the local women were like – he'd been too hot and preoccupied as they travelled to pay any attention to them. Normally he liked young girls, smooth and fresh and unbroken. On the other hand Jacob knew his preferences. The headman invariably bought the pick of the local crop. If Jacob thought the twenty-five-year-old was the choicest, he would take a look at her.

'Tell her I'll hear her confession,' Salama said.

'Yes, Acab.'

Jacob went out. Five minutes later the tent flap parted again and a woman stepped hesitantly inside. Pulling her skirt across her hips with one hand, she gazed at Salama wide-eyed.

'You asked for me, baku?' she said.

Salama stared at her.

She was magnificent – tall and firm with a bold carriage to her head and a helmet of braided hair that fell in shining waves over her shoulders. If she had dropped children, and it was inconceivable she hadn't, they had left no trace on her body. Her breasts rose sharply under the cotton halter and her waist angled in above her hip like a girl's. Not for the first time Jacob's judgement had been impeccable.

'What is your name, my daughter?' Salama asked.

'Vimarad,' she answered.

'I am glad you have come, child,' Salama said. 'I know you will welcome the opportunity of making your confession.'

Desire and the sudden flood of blood to his groin made Salama's voice husky. The woman noticed. She drew back instinctively.

'I confessed to the baku from Ovamba when he came by here only yesterday,' she said.

'The Mother Church instructs us all that none of her children can confess too often.' For a moment Salama's tone was ingratiating. Then his voice hardened. 'Kneel, daughter, and confess.'

Frightened, the woman dropped to her knees.

'I have sinned, father,' she stammered. 'This morning I wished my husband would stop bringing copper bracelets to Malu, the wife he bought in the winter. I wished he would give his time and some of his wealth to old Benzama who he married first. She is sick and with the copper he could give her a fire all day and all night – '

She hesitated. 'I think my wish was a sin. Perhaps the sin of jealousy.'

'And that is all?' Salama demanded.

'Yes, father.'

'Then I absolve you.' Salama made the sign of the cross. 'Stand, my daughter, go and sin no more.'

Gratefully the woman got to her feet, pulling her skirt round her again.

'Thank you, father.' She forced a quick smile. 'May I leave now?'

'Not yet – '

Standing above her as she knelt, Salama had seen her body ripple beneath the light cotton. When she bowed her head he had almost been able to peer down to the cleft between her legs. Now his breath was coming in quick shallow gulps.

'I want you to come and rest with me, child.'

As the woman shrank back Salama reached out and gripped her arm, digging his fingernails into her flesh until she moaned.

'You will do as I say,' he said quietly and menacingly. 'I am a bishop of your church, the royal bishop of your church, and it is your Christian duty to obey me. If you do not – '

Salama paused. Then he added, almost whispering now, 'I will excommunicate you.'

He slipped his hand inside the woman's halter-top and cupped her breast. Then he made a pyramid of his fingers, drew them up to her nipple, and squeezed it, digging brutally at the surrounding flesh with his nails until her breath jetted out involuntarily in pain.

'Do you understand?'

The woman shuddered and nodded.

Salama smiled.

It was a threat he had used many times and it had never failed him – not with children, not with wives, not with mothers, not even with the occasional adequately fleshed grandmother on whom more than once, and in the absence of anything better, he'd been forced to slake himself. The Abyssinians, he knew, were a cunning, childlike and often dangerous people, but they had been in thrall to their church, the Christian church, for centuries. No one, not even the boldest, was prepared to challenge its laws and the commands of its bishops – least of all the superstitious people of the countryside.

'Good,' Salama said.

Until then he had been smiling. Now the smile left his face. The woman had been stubborn and provocative. For a few moments he had almost thought she was going to defy him. She had finally capitulated, but she was going to pay for her defiance.

Suddenly Salama ripped away her halter-top.

The woman crossed her arms over her breasts. Salama seized them and dragged them apart. Then he tore off her skirt. Now she was standing naked in front of him. He smiled again as he surveyed her body. She was quite unprepared when his hand lashed out and struck her across the mouth. Her face tensed in pain and fear, and a trickle of blood ran down from her lips.

'Down on your knees again, my daughter,' he instructed.

As the woman dropped to her knees Salama hitched up his gown.

'Taste me,' he said. 'Taste me with all your skill and care. Because if your tongue stops even once, I will burst your eardrums.'

Weeping, the woman pushed her mouth against his groin.

At midday a week later the waggons, with Salama riding ahead and the soldiers marching behind, reached the ridge on which Gondar was built.

Salama ordered the little column to halt at the foot of the cliff. There he divided the column into two. He sent one party, consisting of two of the three waggons and most of the soldiers, on ahead to the city by the winding road that climbed up the ridge's flank to the west. The third waggon, a sergeant, and six hand-picked soldiers he kept with him.

Salama waited until dark. Then when he decided it was dark enough, he made ready to move.

'Get him out,' he instructed the sergeant.

The sergeant vaulted up on to the waggon.

Unlike the other two waggons the one Salama had kept was covered with tightly sewn hides, which made it impossible for anyone either to see in or out. The sergeant cut a hole in the sides and the youth, Raghe, clambered down blinking. As his feet touched the ground he stumbled. The sergeant gripped him by the arm and dragged him over to Salama.

Salama looked at him in the starlight.

Raghe had been kept sealed away in the waggon ever since they'd left the village. Apart from a certain un-steadiness in his movements, which would quickly pass, the experience didn't seem to have done the youth any harm. Salama turned towards the cliff. It reared up above them in the darkness like a vast black wall, studded with pinpricks of light from the lamps in the clusters of houses high on the ledges.

'Where's the guide?' he asked over his shoulder.

'Here, Acab,' a voice answered.

One of the soldiers trotted forward.

'We'll leave now,' Salama said. 'I will be behind you. Sergeant, you follow me with the boy. Keep a tight hold on him until he's found his legs again.'

With the guide leading, the group set off towards the cliff. A few minutes later they were inching their way up a path running in impenetrable blackness through a tunnel of razor-thorn acacia.

To their right as they climbed Salama could hear the sound of the river as it tumbled down the cliff's face. The noise faded and swelled according to the folds in the rocks. Sometimes it was a faint distant murmur. At others it was so close and loud the roar was almost deafening.

Panting and sweating, Salama heaved himself up-wards.

Choking dust from the guide's heels spewed over his face. The thorns slashed rents in his gown and tormented his skin. Once they collided with a villager herding a flock of goats down the same path. There was an angry exchange. The frightened animals butted past them, knocking Salama's legs away and forcing him to cling to the roots of a bush to avoid being swept down with the flock.

Then they climbed on.

Finally they emerged on to a level platform. The guide turned to the right. He reached back for Salama's hand, and led him through a tangled maze of thorn, trees and creepers so thick Salama doubted they could even be following a path any longer. Ten minutes afterwards everything suddenly changed. The clouds of dust vanished, the vegetation melted away, the air was cool and clear.

'Here, Acab,' the guide said.

His voice seemed to echo slightly.

He let go of Salama's hand and moved away. There was the rasp of steel on flint. A spark ignited a lantern's wick, and a pool of light seeped out. Blinking, Salama shook his head and stared round. A moment later he recognized where he was.

Behind its almost sheer face the porous limestone of the Gondar cliff was honeycombed with caves, passages and caverns. They had been carved out of the stone over the centuries by the passage of the river. At some stage, thousands of years before, it had bored out the chamber where Salama was standing. Then the river had found another release from the rock higher up the cliff at the point where Esther, gazing down from the garden of the nightingales, could see it erupt into the air in a bright sparkling stream.

When the river changed its course it had left the cavern dry and abandoned. Salama recognized the cavern because he had been there before. On that occasion he had reached it by the tunnels that led down from the city rather than up the steep sinuous path of the cliff's face. This time his visit had to be secret.

Like his predecessors since the time of the great Queen

Sheba, Salama was carrying out the most sacred of his duties as the Acab Saat.

The lofty chamber of rock was the anteroom to the river's birthplace in the stone above. From the time of Solomon on it was where the husbands of the river, the fathers of the river's child, had spent the night before they sowed their seed.

'You!' Salama snapped. 'Come here!'

He beckoned and the sergeant pushed Raghe forward. The young man's face was still drawn and pallid, but he had recovered from the trembling that had seized him after he climbed down from the waggon.

'From now on this is where you'll be living,' Salama said. 'The sergeant and the men will stay with you. There's food, bedding, fuel for a fire, everything you need. Understand?'

The young man nodded. 'Yes, baku.'

Salama glanced at the sergeant. 'He starts in the morning. The girls will be here early to get him ready. I will be down later myself.'

'Very good, Acab.' The sergeant paused, then added, 'How long will we be here, Acab?'

Salama gave a cold smile. 'That depends entirely on how the young man performs.'

He turned and crossed the floor of the cavern.

The guide was waiting for him with a lighted flare by a natural arch on the far side. Salama followed him through the arch and they began to climb up a flight of roughly hewn steps. Half an hour later, after ascending a labyrinth of tunnels, they emerged into the open air by a guardhouse in the royal park on top of the hill.

Salama glanced at the sky.

From the position of the crescent moon it was approaching midnight. He dismissed the guide and set off for his house on the other side of the park. After three weeks travelling through the heat and dust of the plain he wanted a bath of hot water and a change of clothes. Most of all he wanted some sleep.

Tomorrow was going to be a busy day.

— 3 —

'Haven't you finished yet?' Esther asked irritably.

'Not quite, my child,' Kalima, the old womanservant, answered. 'Have patience. It is almost done.'

Esther frowned and drummed her fingers on the tiles. It seemed to have been hours since she'd been called in from the garden of the nightingales.

As Kalima approached her again Esther held up her arm resignedly.

Esther was sitting cross-legged on the floor of her bedroom in the palace. It was a dusky high-ceilinged room with narrow windows against the sun and tapestry hangings on the walls. Apart from the low bed the room was furnished with two large Kuwaiti chests, ornately decorated in beaten copper, a leather-seated stool, and a washstand with a pottery jug and bowl.

Sheepskin rugs were scattered over the tiles and in spite of the heat a fire was burning in the heavy iron brazier.

As well as Kalima there were seven other women in the room. It was early afternoon now and Esther's eight attendants had been there from the start. During the morning other visitors had come and gone. The emperor had looked in, inspected her proudly, and patted her cheek. The great warlord Ras Michael, the emperor's protector, had passed by to greet her. Her stepmother had come in twice, fussing and scolding Kalima who listened to her patiently, waited until she left, and then continued as before.

Once the Acab Saat, Abba Salama, had knocked and entered. His visit lasted barely two minutes. He studied Esther, congratulated her, cast his eye, as he always did, over the other women in the room, made a benediction, and left smiling. Until his appearance Esther had been relaxed and happy. Afterwards she felt tense and on edge. She was still on edge two hours later – it was why she had snapped at Kalima.

For reasons she had never been able to work out, Esther was frightened of the Acab Saat.

Sitting on the floor she puzzled over it again. The priest had always treated her, on the surface at least, courteously and solicitously. Somehow it had to do with the way Salama looked at her. The Acab's hunger for women was a by-word at court. As a priest he had, of course, taken a vow of chastity. In Salama's case the vow seemed to have acted like an itching aphrodisiac. He coupled with every woman who took his eye – and everyone knew how he coerced them into submitting.

Esther was well aware that he coveted her. She didn't mind that. There were any number of men at court, many of them much younger than Salama, whose eyes filmed with desire as they looked at her. She enjoyed it. She found it funny and exhilarating and warming. It was so natural, a confirmation of her body and her identity. More than once she'd longed to beckon to one of them, lead him aside in private, and explore his body just as eagerly as he wanted to explore hers.

Salama was different.

His eyes were chill and brutal. When they assessed her, Esther never felt he wanted to hold and touch and embrace her as the others did. She sensed he wanted to humiliate her, to cause her pain, to bruise and gouge and tear her skin. He was driven, she felt, by cruelty and contempt. More frightening still, there were moments when Esther believed he even wanted her dead.

Esther shuddered. Then she realized that Kalima was returning to her across the floor for what seemed like the thousandth time.

'This is the last one, child,' Kalima said.

Behind Kalima was one of the women who'd been helping her. The woman was holding a brass pan by its long iron handle. Kalima dipped her fingers into the pan and stroked them lightly under Esther's chin.

All morning two of the other women had been kneeling near the fire. One had a metal rasp and a rush basket filled with green twigs, the other a pestle and mortar. The twigs came from a myrtle bush — cut close to the ground at dawn that morning and still oozing sap. Periodically the first woman picked a twig out of the basket, and rasped at it until a little mound of resinous sawdust accumulated beside her.

The second woman scooped up the sawdust, poured it into the pestle, and pounded away until it had been reduced to a fine powder. Afterwards a third woman took the powder, stirred it into a panful of palm oil, and heated it over the fire. Finally Kalima applied the mixture to Esther's skin. The combination of the two scents, myrtle and palm oil, created a strong sweet fragrance that lasted for hours.

It swirled through the room now, mingling with the heady smell of roses produced by a handful of sieved red earth which had just been tossed on the fire.

'Now, stand up and let's look at you,' Kalima said, stepping back.

There was an intake of breath and murmurs of astonishment as Esther got to her feet.

Esther stretched her limbs like a cat. Then she walked across the floor and studied herself in the long ebony-framed mirror by the bed.

She was dressed in a light, almost sheer cotton gown dyed a pale indigo blue. The gown was unbelted and she was wearing nothing beneath. With the light falling from the windows behind her it looked as if her naked body were wreathed in sea mist. Round her neck were four bands of beaten gold chain hung with sequins glittering on silk threads. Gold rings dropped from her ears, and her hair, braided and twisted into a crown on top of her head, gleamed with rows of little crimson beads and tiny white cowrie shells — the shells Esther had known since childhood as blackamoor's teeth.

Esther tilted back her head and arched her neck.

She raised her arms and pirouetted once, twice, and then a third time. The dress billowed out and swirled round her. It was so fine she could barely feel it. She might have been clothed not even in mist but in air. In the glass the gold, the crimson beads and the little toothed shells sparkled and glittered.

Esther laughed. 'Am I ready?' she asked teasingly.

'You are not only ready, child,' Kalima answered softly. 'You are beautiful.'

Kalima's eyes were moist. Behind her the seven other women, all of them standing now, cupped their hands and applauded. Several were crying too.

'Then can we go?' Esther said.

Kalima nodded and took her hand.

A detachment of the royal bodyguards was waiting for them at the foot of the stairs which led down from the bedchamber. The soldiers were wearing ceremonial cloaks of scarlet silk. As they turned and marched ahead into the courtyard the cloaks billowed and flared in the sunlight like mountain poppies.

Then Esther heard music. She glanced up.

The galleries round the top of the courtyard were filled with the emperor's musicians. At her appearance they had all started to play. The fluting of pipes and the beat of goatskin drums lifted into the air and seemed to hang like a canopy over her.

Esther smiled and waved and walked on.

The music followed her as the procession travelled the length of the palace. Everywhere there were great mounds of flowers, more flowers than Esther had ever seen, and throngs of onlookers. Slaves clustered together in awed whispering groups as she passed. Guards raised their spears in salute. Servants and courtiers cheered and applauded. Members of her family, laughing and crying at once, reached out to touch and embrace her.

The daughter of the river was returning to the river as a woman.

By tradition her return was a private occasion, but the

event was so significant and momentous in Gondar's life that everyone in the great throbbing beehive of the palace wanted to witness and take part in it.

Finally the procession came out into the park. There were more soldiers here, drawn up in two facing lines that formed an avenue which led away across the parched earth beneath the trees to the vault by the palace walls where Salama had emerged into the darkness the previous night. Esther walked slowly between the soldiers until she reached the vault. Then she stopped.

Another crowd was gathered by the entrance that led down to the river's caverns. There were more pyramids of flowers and more musicians. As the drums and flutes rang out again and the scents swirled round her, Esther picked out the faces of the emperor, her stepmother, Ras Michael, the Acab Saat, and almost every other important member of the court she'd known from childhood. In turn she greeted them all. Then she turned back to Kalima.

The old woman was weeping openly now. Esther threw her arms round her. Kalima protested and tried to break away.

'Don't, child,' Kalima said. 'Remember your hair.'

'My hair?' Esther laughed. 'What is my hair compared to my mother?'

'I am not your mother, as you well know,' Kalima answered.

'Well, my mother was not my mother either,' Esther said. 'I'm the river's child. You've taught me that all my life. The child of the river has neither father nor mother. So since I haven't got a mother, and anyway she's dead, I've chosen you – '

Esther paused. Suddenly she burst into tears. 'I love you, Kalima, mother of my heart,' she said.

'Daughter of my own heart, I love you too,' Kalima replied. 'Come back to me.'

'Of course I'll come back. I'll come back tomorrow. And then – ' Esther couldn't control herself any longer. She began to weep helplessly.

Kalima held her for a moment, pressing the girl against her chest. Then she lifted her head resolutely and nodded at the guide who'd been waiting under the arch's shadow. The guide came forward and took Esther's arm.

'Kalima!' Esther called out in anguish.

Kalima's face was stern now. She watched expressionlessly as Esther was led into the vault and disappeared.

Esther would indeed be back in the morning. Kalima would hold her and pet her again. They would discuss what had happened during the night, and they would laugh and scold each other and everything would be as it was. Except it would also be changed, changed utterly. Esther would no longer be a child, her child. She would be a woman and she would be carrying the river's child.

Life and death and the generations would have passed on, casting them both aside in their wake.

As the little crowd began to drift away, Kalima sat down on the scorched grass and wept again.

— 4 —

'Come here where I can see you.'

With Raghe following him nervously, Salama strode over to a torch mounted on a bracket in the cavern wall.

Salama turned and inspected the youth.

The two girls Salama had sent down from the palace early that morning had been working on Raghe ever since. Escorted by the soldiers, they had first taken him back to the cliff face and along a path to one of the river's hidden pools. There he had been bathed and washed. Returning to the cavern they had trimmed, curled and oiled his hair. Next they had rubbed his entire body with the same aromatic mixture of myrtle and palm oil that old Kalima had applied to Esther. Finally they had dressed him in a plain white gown and a pair of leather sandals with elaborate gold buckles.

Salama grunted in approval. They had done well. The youth, simple peasant boy as he might be, looked magnificent.

'No more questions?' Salama asked.

'No, baku.'

Salama nodded. Raghe had been carefully briefed, not that his task was difficult. It was one every full-blooded male in Gondar would have envied.

'Bring the lamp!' Salama called out.

A soldier ran over with a small earthenware lamp, its oil-fed wick already burning, and handed it to Raghe.

'You will only need it for the first hundred paces,' Salama said. 'Afterwards there's light from holes in the rock. Put it down as soon as you can see, but leave it burning – you'll want it on the way back. Stay until you're told to go. Then return here. Understand?'

'Yes, baku.'

'Acab – '

A voice was calling behind him. Salama turned. It was one of the girls. She came forward holding a single white acacia blossom on a stem barbed with thorns.

'He should take this, Acab,' she said.

'I had forgotten.' Salama beckoned and she handed the flower to Raghe. 'You may go now.'

For a moment the youth stood transfixed. He was trembling. Then, holding the lamp in one hand and the flower in the other, he turned and entered the tunnel at the upper end of the cavern.

The tunnel curved upwards through the darkness, twisting first to one side and then to the other. At times the roof was so high it was beyond the lamp's reach. At others it pressed down to within a few feet of the ground and Raghe had to crouch, shuffling forward with bended knees. Occasionally the passage opened into a cavern like the one he'd left. Stalactites hung down from above and piles of ancient bones littered the floor. Then the tunnel would close in again.

After a while Raghe noticed that stretches of the walls on either side were covered in paintings.

He stopped and examined them. The paintings were very old. The colours were faded ochre, indigo and terracotta, but the figures were drawn with a vivid, childlike energy. There were scenes of feasts and hunts and battles, and a recurring image of a woman in a pale blue robe with a group of warriors behind her. In one of the paintings a warrior lay killed with a spear through his heart. A group of soldiers was standing above the dead man, and the moon was rising over a river behind.

There was something strangely ominous about the blank implacable expressions on the soldiers' faces. Raghe shivered and hurried on.

Finally the passage came to an end and the darkness lightened. He had reached an immense cavern. Much larger than any before, it stretched away in front of him as far as he could see. The light was filtering down from a series of holes in the roof, and the air was fresh and cool. At the same time Raghe suddenly smelled the scent of lilies and heard a distant murmur. Puzzled, he put down the lamp and continued. With every step the scent grew stronger and the murmur louder.

Ten minutes later Raghe stopped abruptly. He gazed forward astounded.

Swinging sharply to the right, the cavern had opened into a vast natural chamber. High at the back a stream cascaded out of the rocky wall. The stream tumbled in an arc down to a pool from where the water flowed away underground. A single dazzling shaft of sunlight fell from the roof, piercing through the green thorn bushes outside. Carrying the leaves' reflections with it, the light glittered off the pool and the waterfall, and filled the whole chamber with a luminous green glow.

The murmur Raghe had heard came from the falling water. Close at hand and echoing off the walls, it sounded like the chiming of thousands of bells. The scent of lilies, overpowering now, was swirling out from banks of pale gold flowers growing round the pool. Its surface rippled and gleamed with the dancing reflections of their petals.

Raghe blinked uncertainly in the unexpected brilliance.

Then, standing in the middle of the lilies on the far side of the pool, he saw a young woman. She was as beautiful and slender as the flowers themselves. Like the images of the queen in the paintings on the passage walls, she was wearing a pale blue gown. She raised her hand and beckoned to him.

In a trance Raghe crossed the stream.

'I am Esther,' she said.

She smiled. She had even white teeth, dark hair, shining black eyes, and a skin even paler than his. She was the loveliest woman Raghe had ever seen.

As he stood dazed in front of her she reached down. She caught the hem of her gown, pulled it over her head, and tossed it away.

She was naked.

Irresistibly Raghe's eyes were drawn downwards from her face. He saw her neck, the swell of her breasts, the flatness of her stomach, the triangle of hair between her thighs, the slender fall of her legs to her straight narrow feet. He heard the chiming water and smelt the lilies and then other scents, warm musky scents, that were coming off her skin.

Suddenly everything changed.

His fear, his bewilderment and apprehension, vanished. He was no longer a confused peasant boy, a stranger far from home caught up in an ancient sequence of events he couldn't begin to understand. He was simply a young man face to face with a young woman who was naked and smiling.

Desire poured over him like a wave.

It plucked at his groin, hardened, and speared out towards her. He dropped the blossom he'd been carrying and tore off his cloak. He reached for Esther and pulled her against him. Almost frantically he explored her body with his hands and mouth. Then, trembling and panting, he drew her down with him on to the bank. As he sank to his knees he felt a needle-sharp pain.

Raghe had fallen on the thorn-barbed stem he'd just cast aside.

Somehow, as he rolled on top of her a moment later, the pain made the explosion of pleasure even more intense.

—— 5 ——

Two months later old Kalima left the palace.

She crossed the park and presented herself before Salama in the hall of the bishop's house.

'She has missed her time twice,' Kalima said.

'You are sure?' Salama asked.

'I may be old,' Kalima answered. 'But I know the ways of a woman's body and I can still count sunsets.'

That night Salama went down to the lower cavern in the cliff face.

'You have done well,' he said, smiling at Raghe. 'The seed is planted. I hope the experience was enjoyable.'

Raghe twisted his hands together and smiled back uncertainly. After two months he had become friends with the sergeant and the other soldiers who had shared his quarters there, but the priest still terrified him.

'Thank you, baku,' Raghe said. 'Is it finished?'

'Yes, it is finished. We will take you home now.'

Salama snapped his fingers and the sergeant ran up.

Salama spoke to him briefly and the sergeant nodded. He turned away, grinning happily. For the sergeant the two months in the cavern had been monotonous and claustrophobic. He was delighted that they were over.

Half an hour afterwards the same party that had climbed the cliff face eight weeks before set foot on the plain again – the journey down had taken them only one third as long as the wearying climb up. It was dark as it had been then and the covered waggon was waiting in the same place. Once again Raghe was ordered to climb inside. He hid himself away and they set off south.

Four hours later Salama, who was riding ahead, ordered them to halt.

They had reached a broad pool in a lonely stretch of the river whose course they had been following since leaving the cliff. Below the pool a ladder of rock-strewn rapids carried the waters north. Salama told the sergeant to bring Raghe out of the waggon.

'I expect you could do with a good cool wash before we go on,' Salama said cheerfully. 'It must be hot in there.'

'Yes, baku.' Raghe smiled appreciatively.

'Come with me.'

They walked together to the bank above the pool and scrambled down to the water's edge.

'Take off your cloak,' Salama instructed. 'I will keep it dry for you here.'

As Raghe stripped, Salama stepped behind him and drew out his rhino-horned dagger.

'You are very kind, baku.'

Raghe turned and held out his garment.

As he did Salama gripped him by the hair from the back and slashed the dagger across the youth's throat, sawing it backwards and forwards. Blood spouted into the air. Raghe's back arched and he twitched convulsively like a dying fish. Then he choked and went limp. Salama held him by the hair until he was still. Afterwards the Acab Saat pitched him forward into the water.

Salama ripped up a bunch of reeds. He wiped the dagger's blade clean, and gazed across the pool.

Drawn by the stream's flow, the body was being carried towards the rapids. Behind it a broad stain, black under the moonlight, was spreading out over the pool's surface. As Salama watched there was a splash and a V-shaped ripple arrowed away from the far bank. Set back from the ripple's point was a pair of gleaming scarlet eyes.

Salama nodded contentedly.

The river had sired a child and the child's father had been returned to its waters. The river would take care of the remains of its own.

The unborn child, Esther's child, was another matter. He or she would be the heir of the kingdom. Once the royal family's protector, the great warlord Ras Michael, was dead, only the child would stand between the Acab Saat and all Gondar.

Salama turned and climbed the bank as the crocodile reached the youth's body.

'Gondar!' he called to the sergeant.

He kicked at his horse's flanks and galloped back across the plain.

— 6 —

'I want it filled right to the top, Jamie.'

Jamie nodded as he picked up the wooden pail.

'And ye mind the rocks off Eilean point when the tide turns,' his grandmother went on.

'Och, I can swim,' Jamie said scornfully. 'I've swum across the sound often enough.'

'Ye be careful, laddie!' the old lady said. 'I'm not having your father coming home to be told you're supping with the mermaids. Now away with ye and be sure you're well back in time for me to make the dinner.'

Swinging the pail beside him, Jamie went out and climbed the low hill behind the little cottage.

At the top Jamie paused.

It was a clear bright morning in early May in the spring of 1842. Six years earlier Ozoro Esther had been made pregnant with the river's child in the cavern beneath the citadel town of Gondar. Gondar was one-third of the way round the world from Scotland. Jamie had never heard of the mountain kingdom. He had never even heard of the continent of Africa.

Jamie's entire physical world was bounded by the island, the sacred island of Iona, which lay spread out beneath him now in the sunlight.

Only four miles long and barely two miles at its widest, Iona lay off the west coast of Scotland in the group of islands known as the Hebrides. Immediately to the east was the much larger island of Mull. Mull was separated from Iona by a narrow channel – the sound Jamie had swum across so often on expeditions with his father and elder brother to gather gulls' eggs from the birds' nests on Mull's Gribun cliffs.

From where Jamie was standing he could see the cliffs and above them the flanks of Ben Mor, the great 'brown hill' with its peak still veiled in morning cloud.

Spread out across the sea to the north was a chain of other Hebridean islands. Staffa, Coll and Tiree, Muck, Eigg, Rhum and Canna, all of them lying like sleeping seals in the water. Sometimes, when the weather was particularly clear, Jamie could even see the crests of the great dark Cuillins on the distant isle of Skye.

Westwards there was nothing – nothing except the immensity of the grey Atlantic stretching three thousand miles to the coast of Canada.

Jamie half-closed his eyes.

In winter when the Atlantic storms came raging in over the flat little island, Iona could be grim and desolate. On a sun-filled May morning like today Iona was, in the words of Jamie's grandmother when spring returned each year, 'The Lord's whisper of paradise'. The air was fresh and sweet. Drifts of wildflowers covered the warm springy turf. The white sands of the island's coastline gleamed in the light. A sea eagle's shadow skimmed across the grass. Otter cubs tumbled along the shore and the plaintive cries of curlews lifted on the breeze.

Jamie gave a shout of pleasure.

He dropped the pail, and set off at a run for Camas Corra-ghritheach, Heron's Bay. Reaching the edge of the sea, he unbuckled the length of oily grey plaid round his waist and kicked off his boots. Gasping at the shock of the icy water, he plunged into the waves and struck out into the bay.

Jamie Oran – no one ever called him James – was nine.

A spare sinewy boy of above average height for his age, he had curling red hair, vivid blue eyes, and a strong face with high, slightly flattened cheekbones. He was the second of the family's four children, with an elder brother and two younger sisters. The previous November the family had been riven by tragedy. November was often a dank and chill month on Iona. The children's mother had contracted pneumonia and died in their midst after a short illness.

Jamie adored her and her death left him distraught.

For weeks on end he seemed to wall himself away from the world, retreating silently for hours into some remote and lonely area of his mind. Only now months later was he occasionally able to forget the pain, and respond to the island's pleasures as before.

The experience of those months had changed Jamie profoundly. Before, he had been a cheerful outgoing boy. Now he was solitary, tactiturn and restless. Some malign fate had wantonly snuffed out the warmth and light in his life. It had left Jamie bewildered and embittered. Most of all, although he was too young to be aware of it yet, it had hardened him. The world would never again be safe. It was full of menace and danger.

Somehow, Jamie knew, he could meekly bow down before whatever life brought him, as his father did. Or he could brace himself. He could stand up and fight. His mother had fought. To the very last she had battled against the racking wasting illness. She had died holding her children's hands, still smiling defiantly.

Jamie would fight too. He would do more. He would not let the dangers come to him. He would go out and find them for himself. He would face and overcome them on their own ground. Only then would he repair the terrible damage that had been done to him, and recover something of what he had lost.

Unwittingly his sisters had helped Jamie as he tried to come to terms with his grief.

Jamie's father, Hamish Oran, was a weak and feckless man with a fondness for the coarse locally distilled usquebaugh. Jamie's brother, Duncan, was cast in the same mould. As the winter passed Jamie realized that, apart from their grandmother, he was the only person the little girls could depend on. He transferred to them his deep affection for his mother, and tried to fill something of the gap her death had left in his sisters' lives. Somehow the responsibility he'd shouldered was starting to blur his own sense of loss as he attempted to heal theirs.

In the middle of the bay Jamie turned and floated on his back.

The sun was warm on his face and the scents of the spring growth drifted out across the sea. He sniffed contentedly. Then he wrinkled his nose and frowned.

Another smell was seeping out from the shore. Sweet and smoky, it was burning kelp. The kilns had been lit. The smell had been familiar to Jamie all his life, but for once he found it offensive. It jarred with the freshness of the May morning.

Jamie rolled over and jack-knifed down into the blue-green waters, shutting it out of his nostrils.

Kelp was the Gaelic name for the tawny-gold seaweed that grew prodigally along almost every inch of the western isles' rocky coastline. By 1842 it had been the mainstay of the Hebridean economy for half a century, causing the islands' population to more than double in the time. The reason lay on the mainland far to the south. As the numbers of the inhabitants in the English towns and cities grew, so inevitably did their demand for food. With the southern farms being called on to produce larger and larger crops, the landowners found out the soil had to be fed too.

The answer was fertilizer – and the cheapest, most efficient fertilizer was Hebridean kelp.

Kelp required no cultivation. It flourished as abundantly round the Scottish shore as the dandelions, thistles and nettles of the inland meadows. All that was needed to harvest it was an army of unskilled labour. After being dried over peat fires in simple brick kilns, the weed, by now reduced to marble-coloured powder, was shipped to wholesalers in the southern ports.

Jamie's father, Hamish, was one of the many who'd been lured to the isles by the promise of work as a kelp-gatherer. He rented a cottage and some land on Iona, and settled down to a life in which, as he thought, kelping would occupy him for four days a week. The rest of the time could be devoted to raising cattle.

If it worked out as he planned, Hamish would have a very comfortable existence.

It did not work out as Hamish planned. He had reckoned without his own incompetence and the landlord's greed. His cattle failed to produce the expected revenue – Hamish was a poor stockman and in any event the holding was too small. As he fell behind with his payments, the landlord raised his rent. To settle the arrears Hamish was forced to spend the entire week as a kelper. It was exactly what the landlord, who was also the kelp merchant, intended.

In Hamish's case even that wasn't enough. He got deeper and deeper into debt, until the only way he could save himself from eviction was to go south each summer and sell his labour to the English farmers for the harvest – work which paid double a kelper's wages.

Hamish Oran had left for the south two weeks earlier. With him he'd taken Jamie's elder brother, Duncan. At thirteen Duncan was well capable of a man's work and hire. It would be the summer's end before Jamie could expect to see either of them again. Meanwhile he would be left on Iona with his grandmother, the two little girls, and the still-aching void in his life.

As he arrowed up to the surface, Jamie felt the hurt clench at him again.

Last summer his mother would have been standing on the shore encouraging him, and calling out in her clear vibrant voice. He would have cut furiously through the waves towards her, heaved himself out of the sea, raced across the sands, and thrown his light hard-muscled child's body against hers – burying his face in her neck as she protested about his wetness while she bent laughing to kiss him.

There was no one on the shore today.

The sands of the bay were white and empty. Jamie stared at them over the waves. The tears came less often now, but for a moment his eyes were blurred. Then he shook his head grimly and scowled. The girls needed their dinner. The pail had to be filled. That was what was important.

He struck out for the shore where the rocks were thick with mussels.

A mile away across the island, hidden from Jamie's sight by the whalebacked hump of the hill, the Iona ferry was pulling into the little stone jetty across the sound from Mull.

The ferry was an ancient open-decked rowing boat. It had space for six passengers, a quantity of baggage, and two oarsmen. Normally one oarsman was enough. A second was needed only on winter crossings, or when a troublesome cow being sent to the Oban market refused to swim behind, and had to be towed in a second boat. No cattle were being moved that morning and only the ferryman, old Dougal Maclean, was at the oars. As they reached the jetty he shipped the oars and clambered out.

Holding the boat's mooring rope, Dougal watched his passengers disembark.

There were five of them. One, Fergus Colquhoun, he had known by sight for twenty years although he must have spoken barely as many words to him in the time. A big raw-boned man with a sunken slate-coloured face, Colquhoun was the Campbell's factor in the isles.

In common with large parts of Mull and several other Highland and island estates, Iona belonged to the Duke of Argyll. Like all Highlanders old Dougal never thought of Argyll as a 'duke', that strange foreign title borrowed from the French. As head of the clan whose name he bore, he was simply 'the Campbell' and Colquhoun was his 'man' – the servant who managed his affairs in the Hebrides.

Colquhoun was the first to land. Then the other four climbed on to the jetty. Leading them was a small and furtive-looking man with a narrow ferret-like face and the brass badge of a Principal Sheriff-Substitute on his jacket. Behind him were three strongly built men in police tunics.

'We'll be back by six,' Colquhoun said. 'Make sure you're not away.'

Old Dougal didn't answer. His face expressionless but his mind heavy with foreboding, he watched the party move off.

Less than a hundred yards from the jetty was Iona's one village, a narrow straggle of little reed-thatched cottages with a row of fishing boats drawn up on the shore and the silhouette of the ruined abbey rising above the roofs. At the entrance to the village a heavy stake had been hammered into the ground. Nailed to it was a crudely printed poster.

Colquhoun, who was leading the group, stopped in front of the stake and jabbed out his finger.

'The law requires three weeks,' he said. 'And three weeks it's been up. There's none as can complain.'

The little sheriff-substitute peered up at the poster. He narrowed his eyes and began to read.

'The said Defenders are hereby ordered,' the poster stated, 'to flit and remove themselves, Bairns, Family, servants, sub-tenants, cottars, and dependants, Cattle, Goods and gear, forth and from possession of the said Subjects above described with the pertinents respectively occupied by them, as aforesaid, and to leave the same void, redd and patent, at the respective terms of Removal above specified, that the Pursuer or others in his name may then enter thereto and peaceably possess, occupy and enjoy the same in time coming – '

'But it's all in English,' the little man objected. 'They won't have understood it.'

'For God's sake, man!' Colquhoun snapped. 'Do ye think they'd have understood it any better if it had been in the Gaelic? You're in the western isles, not in some fancy Glasgie academy.'

'Then why – '

'Why put it up if they can't read?' Colquhoun finished the question for him. 'That's not for ye or me to question. It's what the law says and we both know the law's always right, don't we? Christ, man, at least ye should – it's the law that's bluidy paying ye!'

The sheriff-substitute flushed and rubbed his hand nervously across his chin.

Colquhoun stared down at him with a mixture of anger and contempt. Anger at the bad luck which had caused the sheriff to break his leg the week before; contempt for the substitute who'd been sent in his place. The sheriff was a man after his own heart – firm, blunt-speaking, and realistic. His deputy was pathetic, a timid quibbling nonentity. Colquhoun had realized that as soon as he'd met him on the Mull pier an hour before.

'Is it the first time ye've been out on one of these?' Colquhoun asked pleasantly, suddenly changing his tone.

The little man nodded.

'Then mebbe I can explain the procedure – '

Colquhoun had decided to control himself. There was a job to be done and he wanted to get on with it. He'd be better off humouring the man than abusing him.

'The properties belong to His Grace the Duke,' he went on. 'No one disputes that. They have been let to tenants, but His Grace now wishes to take the land back and put it to a different use. The law naturally allows him to do so. All it requires is fair warning and a decent period of notice. His Grace has given the tenants both. The time has come to remove themselves. Ye and your constables are here to see the law is obeyed. I am here on behalf of His Grace to take possession of the vacated properties. It's as simple as that.'

Colquhoun smiled as he finished. Blinking in the bright sunlight, Fraser, as the sheriff-substitute was named, gazed up at him.

He disliked Colquhoun intensely. The man was a coarse and sardonic bully. Fraser had guessed as much the moment he saw him. The impression had been reinforced by everything Colquhoun had said since. Unfortunately Fraser knew Colquhoun was right. Fraser's protest about the language of the poster had been naïve and absurd —and in any event the poster was no concern of either of them. The law was the law. Under it the eviction of a landlord's tenants was indeed a straightforward process.

Fraser swallowed.

He felt trapped, humiliated and ashamed. Trapped by his position. Humiliated by Colquhoun's evident contempt for him. Most of all he felt ashamed by his own fear.

'Are ye expecting any trouble?' he asked, trying to keep the nervousness out of his voice.

'Trouble? From these folk?' Colquhoun chuckled scornfully. 'Ye don't know the islanders, sir. They're simple and unlettered, but they're honest and harmless. They may bluster a wee bit, but they've no claim on the land and they know it – '

Colquhoun clapped an arm round his shoulder.

'Dinna ye fash yourself, Mr Fraser. We've got nine crofts to possess today. Just ye stand back and I'll take care of them.'

Leading the party again, Colquhoun headed off across the island towards the columns of smoke lifting into the air from the inland kilns.

Although none of Iona's inhabitants that morning were aware of it, by 1842 the green treasure trove of the isles had been losing its value for thirty years. Kelp's decline started at the end of the Napoleonic wars. Until then heavy import taxes had kept fertilizers from continental Europe out of Britain. After the French defeat the taxes were lifted. Cheaper to produce than kelp and much less costly to transport – the English Channel was only twenty miles across – foreign substitutes quickly began to pour into the country. Soon they were dominating the market.

To the great Highland landlords, who for all their proud titles had become nothing more than immensely wealthy seaweed farmers, the collapse of the kelp industry spelt disaster.

For years they had enjoyed the incomes of millionaires. Now, it seemed, their vast estates were worthless and they themselves were ruined. They were saved by what appeared to be a miracle – the discovery that the hardy Cheviot breed of sheep could thrive on the desolate Highland hills and moors which only the wild red deer had been able to colonize before. In fact raising Cheviots, it soon emerged, could be even more profitable than gathering kelp.

To a man the landlords began to turn over their estates to sheep.

Sheep farming was a very different business from the kelp industry. Kelp needed huge quantities of labour, both for the gathering and the firing. The Cheviot flocks on the other hand required only a few shepherds. The kelpers had to be housed. Their houses, the little stone-built crofts, were invariably encircled by smallholdings supporting livestock.

Now those buildings, smallholdings, animals, and even the human inhabitants became an unproductive liability – they occupied land that could otherwise be used by the flocks.

What followed the Cheviot's appearance in the Highlands was the most tragic and infamous event in Scotland's history – the Highland clearances. The clearances had begun on the mainland estates years before. That May morning they reached Iona.

Striding up the hill in the sunlight with Fraser panting behind him, Colquhoun was utterly uninterested in the consequences of what he was about to do. As the Duke of Argyll's factor he was what the highlanders called a 'laird's man'. He was a paid mercenary, and his fortunes depended on his master's. When Iona's crop had been kelp, Colquhoun had bullied and harassed the islanders until every one of them had been forced into working for the industry.

Now the duke had decided to turn Iona over to sheep.

To Colquhoun that meant first evicting the people. He had no scruples about it. The law, as he'd painstakingly reminded Fraser, was four-square on the landowner's side, and it was being used all over the Highlands.

Furthermore Colquhoun had heard the Cheviot was proving a very handsome investment. When things went well His Grace was a generous employer, not reluctant to hand out a substantial bonus.

Colquhoun hurried on.

He'd told Fraser the islanders were a quiet and honest group. It was true – but not the whole truth. Desperate and faced with what they believed was a patent injustice, they could prove remarkably stubborn. That didn't bother him. In fact it might well add a little entertainment to the day.

As Fraser struggled up to join him, Colquhoun paused at the top of the hill and gazed over the glens running down towards the shore.

— 8 —

'Jeannie, will ye fetch me my shawl?'

As her granddaughter nodded and ran into the croft, old Mrs Oran lowered herself carefully on to the simple bench, made from a driftwood plank and two sawn-off pieces of a rowan trunk, outside the door.

'Here, gran. Shall I put it round ye?'

The little girl reappeared with the black wool shawl and arranged it carefully over the old lady's shoulders.

'Is there anything else ye need?' the child went on. 'Or can Morag and I go over to the burn?'

'Ye can go to the burn – but mind ye take good care of your wee sister.'

Morag, at five a year younger than her sister, skipped with delight. The peat-brown stream with its pools and rocks, its tiny darting trout and secret hollows in the rushes, was their favourite place on the island.

The two little girls ran off and Mrs Oran leant back against the croft wall.

She was sixty-seven, a tall fine-boned woman with white hair, clear almost translucent skin, and keen harebell-blue eyes. On the whole, the old lady thought as she looked down to the sea, the years had been kind to her. True, at the end of each winter now she moved painfully slowly and her hips and shoulders often ached. But that was the Hebridean damp.

As soon as the sun returned, and today for the first time in months the sky was cloudless, the warmth seemed to dissolve the cramping stiffness in her muscles. Within a few weeks she'd be able to walk to the burn with the little girls and sit watching them play in the rock-strewn pools.

Mrs Oran smiled at the thought.

In their different ways all her grandchildren were a pleasure to her. Of course Duncan, the eldest, was sometimes a problem. He took overmuch after his father, and it pained her to smell usquebaugh fumes on the breath of a thirteen-year-old. But even Duncan had his virtues. He might be weak-willed and easily led astray, but he had a ready smile and a generous heart. The two little girls, in contrast, were an unalloyed delight – sturdy, enchanting, and in spite of their years constantly, unfailingly, concerned about her.

The fourth, Jamie, was a puzzle.

Solemn and taciturn, at times showing a sense of responsibility far beyond his age, at others erupting in rages that were almost frightening in their intensity, he seemed to come from a different breed. She loved Jamie most of all and yet she often felt the boy was haunted – a child driven by a daemon. But then Jamie, far more than the other three, was his mother's child. He had her blazing red hair, her strong-jawed face, her relentless determination.

Perhaps, although the old lady had seldom seen it since her daughter-in-law's death, Jamie had her laughter too.

Mrs Oran could only hope so. To be stamped from the tempered-steel mould of Katie and not to be able to laugh or, worse still, to love – and Katie, God bless her, had done both in prodigal measure – would be to be confined to a chilling existence.

Mrs Oran closed her eyes and shook her head slowly.

It was strange. Hamish Oran was her child. Katie, his wife, was not. Yet from the moment Hamish first brought Katie to the croft, she knew the woman was closer to her than her son would ever be. The one was the child of her body. The other, the stranger, the child of her heart. So it had proved over the thirteen years that followed. Now Katie was dead the pattern was being repeated. Duncan and the little girls belonged to her son.

Jamie, silent, troubled Jamie, belonged to Katie – and because of that he belonged to her.

Well, she had done her best for him. Old Mrs Oran had a skill that was rare in the western isles. She was lettered. At the age of twelve she'd been sent as an under-nursemaid to the big house of Kilfinichen on Mull to help look after the laird's six children. The elder children were almost her contemporaries. As their companion she'd been expected to attend the lessons they took from their tutor, a stern but enthusiastic young scholar from Glasgow Academy.

Alert and quick to learn, she was soon able to read and write as well as any of her charges.

She left the laird's employ when she married Hamish's father, but the skill didn't desert her – nor did its accompanying passion for stories, books, poems and ballads, all the 'songs of the Gaelic spirit', as the tutor had termed them in the Kilfinichen classroom. When her husband, a fisherman, was drowned and she went to live in her son's house on Iona, she set about teaching her grandchildren.

Duncan had little aptitude and the girls were still very young, but Jamie was remarkable. At eight he could not only read and write fluently, he had acquired her own passion for ballads and stories.

Every evening when they'd finished reading the bible, the only book in the croft, old Mrs Oran would recite to him from memory. She told him how the great Saint Columba had come to Iona, bringing Christianity to Britain. How the ancient Scottish kings were brought to the little island to be buried in the royal graveyard beside the abbey. She described the battles fought by the lords of the isles, and she recited the ballads that chronicled the triumphs and tragedies of Hebridean life across the years.

'And never forget, Jamie,' she always finished, 'ye come of the same line and ye bear the same bluid. You're the match and equal of any that ever wore a crown.'

'That's because of mam, isn't it?' Jamie would cry. 'She takes her bluid from the kings.'

The old lady nodded.

Katie, sitting across the fire and smiling at her son, was

a fisherman's daughter. Fisherman he might have been and poor at that, but Katie's father bore the proud doomed name of Stuart. Like him Katie was descended from the ancient royal line.

'Does it mean I can have a queen for wife, too?' Jamie used to demand breathlessly.

His grandmother would laugh.

'If she's bonny and canny and true, take her for woman whoever she is,' Mrs Oran answered. 'But aye, laddie, if she comes a queen she'll have met her rightful match in ye. And if it was your own destiny I had to hazard, then I'd no be surprised if it were a queen that was sent to bind ye.'

Jamie was enthralled.

When she finished he had to be dragged to bed clamouring for more. He went to sleep with his head full of images of galloping horses and flashing swords, of golden crowns and queens dressed in white silk, of drum-beats accompanying the funeral ships to the shore, and the royal coffins being carried inland to be laid at rest beside the ancient abbey.

The entire island was changed for him. It was no longer just a space of rock and white sand and green meadow. It had another dimension, a hidden but vivid world in which the present and the turbulent pageant of the past, threaded through with bitter dynastic quarrels, acts of unimaginable valour and daring, and the constant haunting refrain of the pipes, as mournful as the cries of Iona's curlews, existed together.

Mrs Oran nodded contentedly.

Yes, she had done her best for Jamie. God willing, she would continue to do so. Jamie was like a young plant. His mother's death had cut off his deepest roots. Time and care and patience were needed to allow him to grow others.

The air was still and the sun warm. The old lady's eyes closed and her head began to drop to her chest.

Suddenly she sat upright. Mrs Oran thought she had heard someone calling. Puzzled, she climbed stiffly to her feet and peered round. She stiffened. She was right. It was little Jeannie. The child was racing towards the croft from the direction of the glen.

'Gran! Gran!'

The little girl's voice was shrill with fear. For an instant Mrs Oran thought in anguish that something must have happened to the younger sister. Then she saw Morag running behind Jeannie.

'Calm yourself, child,' she said as Jeannie reached her and hurled herself against her legs. 'What is it?'

'Oh, gran, there's men and they're burning the crofts and it's terrible!'

Jeannie buried her face, weeping, in her grandmother's skirt.

'What do ye mean, lassie?'

With an effort Mrs Oran bent down and gripped Jeannie by her arms.

'It's true, gran.' The words came out half-choked between the sobs. 'We climbed up from the burn over the glen and Jimmy Cowie's croft, it was on fire. So is Mrs Maclennan's up the brae. There's men doing it. They're throwing things out and breaking things and it's terrible.'

'It's true, gran,' little Morag echoed, her face white.

Mrs Oran peered horrified across the heather.

For months stories and rumours had been filtering across the island. Some of the Highland lairds, it was reported, were throwing out their tenants and turning their lands over to sheep. Few on Iona had believed the tales. The lairds made their money from kelp. Anyway everyone knew it was impossible to run sheep on the hill, as the Highland moors were known. The beasts starved. Perhaps a few eccentric landowners on the mainland were experimenting with the Cheviot. The animal would never come to little sea-bound Iona.

That had been the old lady's view.

Now, with a chilling certainty, she knew she'd been wrong. The Campbell had sent in his men. They were removing the tenants and burning the crofts. Like

everyone else on Iona, the Orans held their land from
Argyll.

Mrs Oran stared round helplessly.

If the dauntless Katie were alive and Hamish at home,
perhaps together they might have been able to do
something. But Katie was dead and Hamish away south.
She was alone, an old woman with two little girls.

She closed her eyes, her head dizzy. She couldn't afford
to panic, not while her grandchildren were in her charge.
She gazed at Jeannie again.

'Did ye see Jamie anywhere?' she demanded.

Jeannie shook her head.

Mrs Oran closed her eyes in relief.

Jamie was almost certainly still down on the shore.
That at least was something. There was only one way to
save the croft, it had come to her, and that was to make it
appear abandoned. She glanced up at the ridge above the
glen. It was still deserted.

'Jeannie, Morag, listen to me,' she went on. 'We're
going to play a game. Ye ken the wee store below the
chest?'

The children nodded.

Like most crofts the Oran cottage had an underground
chamber where the summer-salted beef and fish was
stored to support the family through the winter months.

'We'll hide in there,' the old lady said. 'Then, if the bad
men come, they'll think there's no one here and they'll go
away. Ye'll have to keep verra quiet, but ye can do that,
Jeannie, and ye too, Morag?'

The children nodded again.

'Of course ye can.' Mrs Oran heaved herself to her feet.
'Now first we'll put out the fire and then we'll tuck
ourselves away.'

She limped into the croft.

'No,' one of the constables said, bending as he stepped
out through the door. 'There's nae one.'

Colquhoun looked in and frowned.

He had never known a crofting family abandon a croft

without a struggle or at least a desperate plea to be allowed to stay. They had nowhere else to go. The inhabitants of this one must have fled in terror and were probably hiding down by the shore. Well, it just made the job easier.

'Stand back,' he said. 'I'll put the torch to it.' He reached for his flint and a taper.

Standing behind him, Fraser suddenly shouted, 'Stop!'

The little sheriff-substitute was sickened.

All day he'd been forced to watch as terrified and weeping families had been evicted and seen their homes burned before their eyes. It was the law and there was nothing he could do about it. But this one was different and he'd had enough.

'If there's no one here,' Fraser went on, 'there's no one to offer resistance. The law says if the folk go quietly the crofts are to be boarded up.'

'For Christ's sake!' Colquhoun swung round. 'They're not folk – they're rats. Leave them their holes and they'll come scampering back as soon as we've gone.'

'I'm here to see the law's carried out,' Fraser said stubbornly.

Colquhoun glowered down at him.

As even a plea was considered resistance, providing an excuse to destroy the crofts, the problem had never arisen before. If the sheriff had been there it wouldn't have come up now. The sheriff knew as well as anyone the dwellings had to be smashed or the crofters simply returned. Yet technically Fraser was right.

Colquhoun glanced at the sun. The day was advancing and they still had three evictions to make. It wasn't worth arguing. He'd send a couple of men over from Mull tomorrow to do the job then.

Colquhoun swung round and bellowed at the waiting constables.

'Get that plank across the door and nail it down!'

The sound of hammering drowned out the patter of feet racing towards them across the turf.

Jamie had first realized something was wrong half an

hour earlier while he was collecting mussels on the shore. Glancing up, he saw seven thick columns of smoke on the skyline. Iona had only five kilns in use. The other columns could only be coming from burning crofts. For one croft in the little community to catch fire was always a serious matter. For it to happen to two at the same time was a disaster. Jamie knew everyone would have gathered to help.

Leaving the pail by the rocks, Jamie started inland to join them.

He reached his home glen and glanced across the meadow at the Oran croft. There were five men gathered round the door. Three were in uniform. The other two, one very tall, the second short and thin, seemed to be arguing. As he watched the tall man called out and the men in uniform wrenched away the seat of the bench, and began nailing it over the door.

A mingled wave of fear and fury swept over Jamie — fear for his sisters and grandmother, fury at what the men were doing.

Jamie began to run forward. As he reached the croft the nearest man to him was the little sheriff-substitute. Jamie lowered his head and hurled himself at the small man's back. Fraser yelped and tumbled forward on to the grass. The other four whirled round, startled. Jamie didn't hesitate. The next closest was the tall man.

Jamie sprang at him. The man's arm swung out to ward him off. In a blind rage Jamie gripped his arm with both hands and sank his teeth into the man's wrist.

'Ye wee devil!' Colquhoun bellowed in pain.

He hurled Jamie from side to side as if he were trying to shake off a maddened rat. Jamie clenched his jaw and bit deeper as blood spurted out over his face. He barely felt the blow which knocked him away. There was a short stab of pain. Then Jamie went limp.

Jamie's jaw slackened, and he dropped unconscious on the turf.

'Bastard!'

Twice Colquhoun kicked Jamie's body viciously.

Then, holding his wrist with his other hand to check the bleeding, he stumbled over to Fraser.

'Is that resistance enough for ye?' he shouted.

Colquhoun's face was an ugly mask of anger.

Instinctively Fraser backed away. The ferocity and unexpectedness of the boy's attack had left him trembling. His back was bruised and he felt exhausted. All he wanted was for the day to be over so he could leave Iona for ever.

'Ye can fire the croft,' he said numbly.

— 9 —

Jamie stirred and opened his eyes.

His head was throbbing and his ribs ached. He blinked and explored the turf with his fingers. The sky above him was paling and there was dew on the grass. Evening was approaching.

He tried to concentrate. Random images drifted back into his mind. The columns of smoke in the still air. The men gathered round the door of the croft. His surging anger and the drum of his racing feet. The sudden violence and the taste of blood in his mouth. It was all vivid and yet somehow remote. He wrinkled his nose. For the second time that day he could smell burning.

There was the scent of fire on the breeze.

Jamie leapt to his feet. He was only a few yards from the croft, except it was a croft no longer – merely a gutted square of open-roofed stone with small flames still flickering round the charred beams. He approached the gaping doorway but the heat of the walls drove him back. He turned. As always the burn which provided the croft with water was cascading through the meadow.

Jamie picked up a wooden pail and ran blindly to it.

For the next hour he struggled frantically backwards and forwards between the stream and the croft, dragging pailfuls of water behind him and heaving them over the walls and floor. Clouds of steam rose hissing into the air. Jamie had no idea what he was doing or why. All he dimly knew was that he had to get into the croft.

Eventually the walls and floor had cooled enough for him to enter.

He stepped inside. The cottage was an empty shell. The

fire's heat had reduced everything to ash – even the iron tools that had been used to work the smallholding were no more than little puddles of molten metal.

Jamie crossed the floor and stopped above the underground storeroom. He bent down and levered up the stones that formed the storeroom's roof.

His grandmother was lying on the hollowed-out space of earth beneath. On either side of her, curled up in her arms, were Jeannie and Morag. The three of them had been suffocated. While the blaze had sucked out the oxygen from the storeroom, the heat hadn't penetrated the stone covering. The faces of the old lady and the two little girls were unmarked. They lay there as still and tranquil as if they were asleep.

Jamie gazed down at them.

He reached out and touched his grandmother's forehead. He rested his fingers on the cheeks of his two sisters. The girls' skin was still warm. He lifted his face towards the sky, thickening now with stars, and wept, the tears streaming down his face as his body heaved and shook.

Then he controlled himself and set to work.

The knocking went on and on.

Old Dougal, the ferryman, rolled off his straw pallet. He opened the door of his cottage, and peered sleepily into the darkness. After a moment he made out the silhouette of a child standing outside. Behind the child was a rough-coated highland pony.

'Who is it?' Dougal asked, puzzled.

'Jamie,' a boy's voice answered. 'Jamie Oran.'

'Jamie! What are ye doing here at this hour?'

Old Dougal knew the Oran family well. Young Jamie passed by the ferryman's cottage at least twice a week on his wanderings round the island.

'My gran and my sisters,' Jamie said flatly. 'They're dead.'

'Dead?' Dougal stared at the boy. 'What happened, laddie?'

Jamie told him.

As he listened Dougal nodded grimly. It had been a terrible day for the island. The sheriff-substitute and the Campbell's man had evicted nine families. The Orans lived at the other end of Iona. For some reason no one from the village had thought to check what had happened to them.

'Ye'd better come in and sleep, laddie,' Dougal said as the boy finished.

Jamie shook his head. 'I want the loan of a spade, Dougal.'

'A spade? Why?'

'To dig their graves.'

'Their graves? Whisht, Jamie, we'll do that tomorrow. We'll bring them over from the croft – '

'They're here now,' Jamie interrupted him. 'I used the beast.'

Jamie gestured at the pony.

'Ye've brought them here on your own?' Dougal asked.

Jamie nodded. Dougal's eyes widened in astonishment. Somehow the boy must have loaded the three bodies on to the animal's back, and trudged beside it through the night to the village.

'Where have ye set them down?'

'In the auld ground,' Jamie said.

Dougal paused.

The old ground was the royal cemetery beside the abbey. The islanders buried their own kind in the meadow plot next to the abbey. He looked at Jamie again. Now that his eyes had adjusted to the darkness he could see the boy's face more clearly. It was pale and drawn, but resolute.

'Verra well,' Dougal said. 'I'll give ye a hand, Jamie. We'll move your folk down to the meadow and dig their places there – '

'No,' Jamie cut him off again. 'My gran and my wee sisters, they'll sleep where they belong – aside my mam with the kings and the queens. If ye dinna fancy digging their beds, then give me your spade, Dougal, and I'll make them alone.'

The old ferryman was silent.

He remembered that Jamie's mother, Katie, had been buried in the royal graveyard. When she died the minister, who was a stickler for the old ways and knew she had been born of Stuart blood, insisted she was laid to rest there. The minister too had passed on since then. Old Mrs Oran wasn't of the same line but her granddaughters were. Dougal didn't think the minister would begrudge the old lady resting space beside the wee girls.

Dougal stared at Jamie once more. Then he stepped into his boots. He picked up the shovel he kept by the door, and went outside.

'We'll set their beds together, laddie,' he said.

With the laden pony following behind, the old man and the boy walked through the night to the graveyard by the abbey. There they started to dig.

Dougal did most of the work, although from time to time he rested and passed the spade to Jamie. Each time he did Jamie gouged at the earth so fiercely that the child's skin ran with sweat and his breath came in great heaving gulps. When old Dougal asked for the spade back, he almost had to wrestle it from the boy's hands.

Eventually they were finished. Beside the ancient graves of the kings and queens there were three new trenches.

They lowered the bodies of Jamie's grandmother and sisters inside, and shovelled the earth back on top, piling it up in ridges which the next winter's rains would press level to the ground.

'They'll sleep sound the noo,' Dougal said as he stepped back from heeling down the soil on the last of the three graves. 'Come ye back to the croft, Jamie, and rest yourself.'

'I'll bide with my kin for the sun,' Jamie replied.

The old ferryman shrugged. There was no arguing with the child. He shouldered the spade and left the graveyard.

Jamie knelt by the mounds of newly turned earth.

There was no moon and the night was black. The only light came from the wheeling, tumbling stars. Occasionally, as the constellations turned, the starlight touched one of the ancient Celtic crosses that stood like guardian sentinels above the graves. Briefly the stone cruciforms would glow as if they had been dipped in phosphorescence. The gleam the stars threw across the darkness lingered in Jamie's eyes long after the constellations had revolved and passed.

Jamie was a Celt.

Like all Celts, and particularly one whose vivid imagination had been nurtured from his earliest childhood by the songs and stories of his grandmother, the night held no fears for him. Starlight and darkness were the stage for visions and dreams. They were the hidden landscape inhabited by the ancient spirits who stood guard now with the Christian crosses above the graves of his kin.

Just before dawn, at the night's darkest pitch, the spirits came to visit the exhausted and grieving child.

They came in the shape of a woman. Jamie's chin was drooping on his chest, but his head sprang up and his eyes opened wide the moment he saw her. At the same instant all the tiredness vanished from him.

Jamie gazed at her calmly and unafraid.

The woman was walking towards him. As she came forward she kept turning slowly and gracefully between the graves. Each time she turned she changed. At one moment she looked like Jamie's mother, Katie, with tumbling red hair, a laughing face, and a slender body. The next she resembled his grandmother, grey-headed and leaning on a stick, her features wrinkled and drawn but her eyes alive and bright with the songs she had sung to Jamie so often.

The woman came to the last of the graves that separated her from Jamie. There she stopped. Between them were only the three newly shovelled mounds of earth. The grave she had reached was the resting place of the driven and fated King Macbeth. Macbeth, Jamie knew, had been visited by witches. But it was no witch who faced him now across the tormented king's tomb.

It was a young woman.

She no longer looked like either his mother or his grandmother. She was barely his own age. Her eyes were black and her skin was the palest shade of umber, the colour of Iona's sands after the tide and the sea-wrack had stained them wet from their sun-burnished brightness. She was wearing a long gown of indigo blue. The gown was so soft and sheer it stirred round her body like a current of sea air. Her ears and neck were hung with golden jewellery. On her head was a circle of white flowers nestling in thorns.

She was a queen, Jamie had no doubt of that. The thorns and flowers were a crown, the gold jewels a queen's adornment. But a queen of a kind and a country of which he had no knowledge, of which he had never heard.

Jamie stared at her, transfixed.

The girl was holding something. Jamie lowered his eyes from her face. In her hands was a casket. The casket was made out of wood, a heavier blacker wood than Jamie had ever seen. As he watched she opened it and drew out a number of objects.

The first was a golden brooch in the form of a snake. The snake, climbing vigorously, was twined round the trunk of a tree. The second was a tiny wooden carving of an elephant with a little fortress-tower perched on its back. The third was an ebony bracelet. The bracelet, oiled and polished, glittered with emeralds as green and vivid as the turf that coiled round Iona's bays.

The last was a jewelled dagger with a worn sharkskin handle. Jamie had no need to touch it to know the blade was razor sharp. The dagger was no ornament. It was the weapon of a fighting man for use in battle.

The girl gazed at Jamie.

She was bold – only a brave young woman would have walked alone through the graveyard of the kings at night – but she was also grieving. Jamie sensed she too had lost something. She held out her hand as if asking for his help.

Jamie got to his feet and reached towards her. His

fingers were almost touching hers when suddenly she was gone.

Jamie stood alone in the night. With the absolute sureness of a child he knew that in the midst of his tragedy, the ancient spirits of the isles had sent a message to him.

'Are you ready?' Toomi called.

Mamkinga half-bent his knees. He balanced himself tensely on the balls of his feet, and held out his hands in front of him.

It was searingly hot in the courtyard. The sun, dazzling off the baked earth wall in front of him, made Mamkinga's eyes blink. He waited. The wall wasn't straight. It angled round two buttresses, cut away to the west, and then ran back to form the shape of a broken V. Mamkinga was crouching at the mouth of the V.

'I am ready!' Mamkinga shouted back.

Toomi, his twin sister, was standing five paces behind him. She was holding a ball the size of a small gourd. The ball was made out of melted resin and covered with strips of calico. Toomi bounced it twice on the bare hard earth. It leapt up from the ground into her hand.

Toomi drew back her arm and hurled it over her brother's head.

Mamkinga heard it whistle above him. He narrowed his eyes like a cat. The ball struck the side of one of the buttresses and ricocheted across to the other. He watched it cannon backwards and forwards. It escaped from the buttresses, struck the wing of the wall, bounced off the ground, and soared back towards him, climbing as it went.

Mamkinga hurled himself off his haunches and jumped like a leaping gazelle. His outstretched arm reached high into the air. The ball slammed into his open palm, and his fingers tightened round it.

He tumbled back to the earth triumphant and laughing.

'You were watching where I was going to throw it!' Toomi shouted.

'I never looked back once,' Mamkinga protested.

'It was not so,' Toomi accused him again. 'You used the eyes of the hunting mongoose. You were looking everywhere.'

Toomi threw herself angrily at her brother. Mamkinga tried to sidestep but the swiftness of her attack caught him off balance. He tripped and tumbled, and they struggled together in the dust.

The fight was brief and bloodless. After a few moments they rolled apart and lay sprawled, panting in the heat. Toomi propped herself up on one elbow and scratched her chin.

'Why don't we see if the figs are ripe?' she suggested.

'Where?' Mamkinga replied.

Toomi thought for a moment. Then she grinned mischievously.

'Let's try the trees in old Kakaba's ground,' she said. 'You keep watch and I will climb.'

'No, Toomi. You were catching. It is my turn to climb.'

They got to their feet. Still arguing, but good-naturedly now, they moved away across the compound and went out through the gate into the main street of the village.

In fact Malinda, as the settlement was named, was considerably more than a village. By the standards of the time – it was the same year of 1842 – it was a town, almost a city, and it had given its name to the country which surrounded it.

Malinda was the second of the three main kingdoms with loose, often overlapping borders that made up nineteenth-century Abyssinia. The richest and most powerful was its neighbour to the south, Gondar, the home of Ozoro Esther. To Malinda's north lay the lands of the nomadic and warlike Galla under their ferocious king, Culembra. Further north still were the territories of other smaller tribes.

Like Gondar, Malinda reached from the plain up into the Mountains of the Moon. Several of Africa's mountainous regions were called by the same name, most notably the ranges far to the south, but the Abyssinians insisted that only their towering uplands truly deserved the title. They had been known by it for centuries, perhaps even for thousands of years.

No one was entirely sure how the mountains had acquired their name. Some said it was because of the high clear air which allowed the moon to shine more brightly than anywhere else in Africa. Others claimed the lofty barren flanks were a reflection of the moon's own surface. Others still, the older generation of Malinda's inhabitants, believed Malinda was a place of portents — the site chosen by the spirits to transmit their messages from the galaxies through the shining moon to the earth below.

To them the entire upland landscape was sacred.

Toomi's and Mamkinga's father was Malinda's heredit-ary embrenche, the chief and virtual sovereign both of the town and the kingdom. The compound he had built for his family at Malinda's centre was almost a village in itself. Covering several acres, it was surrounded by a wall of baked red earth. Within the wall were about fifty single-storey houses with wooden frames and thatched reed roofs. The two largest were used by the embrenche himself.

One was his day house, the other his night house. The open-walled day house was used to entertain the embrenche's friends and guests. The night house, where the embrenche slept, was enclosed by walls of plaster into which a blend of herbs and cow dung had been mixed to keep off the insects that swarmed towards the light of the oil lamps.

On either side were the living quarters of his three wives. Each had day and night houses too. Beyond were rows of other buildings for the more distant members of the embrenche's family, his servants, and his slaves. In all the compound was home to some two hundred people. Malinda was made up of many more family compounds like it. The compounds grew smaller and more crowded the further away they were from the embrenche's.

Like Gondar, although much lower in the foothills, Malinda was built on a ridge. Apart from prosperity it was all the two towns had in common. The ancient fabled city of Gondar was sophisticated and cosmopolitan. Malinda was smaller and quieter, a remote country cousin of the bustling metropolis to the south. In Gondar, where the golden palace soared above the city and the streets were thronged with merchants and visitors from every quarter of the continent, the lofty fortifications seemed to wall out the African landscape.

In Malinda the rawness, the bounty and the savagery of Africa pressed in on every side.

Except for the tongue of fertile plain that lifted towards the town, the countryside round Malinda was wild and harsh. One of the twins' earliest memories was of climbing up into the gallery that ran round the top of their father's day house, and watching the great herds of antelope and giraffe grazing the hill slopes beyond the compounds. When the storm clouds gathered, when thunder roared down from the mountains and forks of lightning ignited the grass, the herds would scatter and race before the fires with a drumming of hoofs that shook the piles on which the house was anchored.

Often the twins would see prides of lion prowling outside the wooden stockade that ringed Malinda. The lions seldom entered the town but the hyenas were bolder and more aggressive. Barely a week went by without a hyena leaping the stockade at night. Many an unwary Malindan child had been seized and eaten alive in the streets. Jackals were even more common. In winter the embrenche would corner them against the compound walls. The twins would watch, fascinated, as their father slaughtered them with an axe.

As they walked out of the compound that morning Toomi and Mamkinga were nine years old.

They were not identical twins – one was a girl and the other a boy – but in every other way they were virtually indistinguishable. Both had the same lithe bodies, the same shining brown skin, the same dark and steady eyes, the same Abyssinian features, even and fine-boned and graceful. Standing face to face they were like mirror images of the same person. Their voices, their gestures, even their unconscious mannerisms, were a perfect echo of the other's.

As babies only the marks of their different genders told them apart, but as they grew older the differences had become more noticeable. Mamkinga had broader shoulders and a wider neck than his sister. Toomi's hips were a little fuller than her brother's and her arms more slender. In every other way the twins still appeared identical. Wearing as they always did the same clothes – blue calico wraps knotted at the waist – it was still almost impossible for anyone who didn't know them to tell the two apart.

For those who did know them, their family, servants and slaves, Toomi and Mamkinga were as different as night and day.

Toomi, the girl, was thoughtful, considerate, decisive and gregarious. She delighted in company. She loved looking after the smaller children in the household. She was a natural leader who made up her mind swiftly and never hesitated in following the course she had chosen.

In contrast Mamkinga, her brother, was moody and irresolute. Where his sister was open, affectionate and impetuous, Mamkinga was diffident and withdrawn. Easily upset, he would often sulk for hours on end; Toomi's childish flashes of anger passed within minutes. Unlike his sister, who made friends with anyone from a visiting chief to one of her father's new slaves, Mamkinga was wary with strangers.

Confronted with a choice, Mamkinga would prevaricate endlessly. It was Toomi in the end who usually took the decision for him.

Once when they were younger Malinda was visited by a group of Arab traders from Zanzibar with salt and cloth to sell. As was traditional their leader brought presents for the embrenche's children. The Arab merchant had mistakenly been told there were three of them –

in fact the twins had no brothers or sisters. Accordingly he came with three gifts.

When the Arab had set out the three offerings, the embrenche called Toomi and Mamkinga into his day house.

'Look at what this kind stranger has brought you,' the embrenche said.

Wide-eyed and entranced, the twins gazed at the table where the presents were displayed.

The first was a tiny seahorse, dried and dipped in clear mastic varnish so that it glittered like a miniature golden mermaid. The second was an intricate carving in green jade of a bridge thronged with oriental peasants. The third an Egyptian glass drinking cup with a chased silver phoenix for a handle.

'You may choose one each,' the embrenche went on, 'but you must make your choice swiftly – '

He glanced up at the trees which shadowed the compound.

It was late in the year and the leaves were falling. The embrenche pointed at a high branch with a single yellow leaf still clinging to its tip.

'Before that leaf reaches the ground, each of you must decide,' he said. 'If not there will be nothing for you.'

As he spoke a gust of wind plucked the leaf from the branch, and it began to spiral down.

Toomi didn't hesitate. From the moment she had set eyes on the seahorse, Toomi knew she wanted it more than anything in the world. She reached out and seized it. She cupped the strange glittering object delightedly in her hand. Then she looked at her brother.

Mamkinga's gaze was switching irresolutely between the jade carving and the glass goblet. He stretched out his hand towards the little bridge. Then he checked and switched to the goblet. He frowned and hesitated. His hand moved back to the jade and hovered above it again. His face was clouded with indecision. The choice between the two was beyond him.

Toomi glanced outside.

Tossed from side to side on the swirling currents of air, the leaf was inexorably approaching the ground. Out of the corner of her eye she could see that her father and the Arab merchant, both of them smiling, were watching its descent too.

At any moment the leaf would reach the earth.

Her eyes swept back to her brother. In an agony of impatience and frustration Toomi watched as he continued to hesitate. Any second and the chance would be gone. Toomi could bear it no longer. Just before the leaf settled in the summer-baked dust of the compound, her hand darted out and gripped the goblet by its silver handle.

'Mamkinga has chosen this,' she announced to her father.

Toomi placed the goblet in her brother's hands. Mamkinga looked down at it first in surprise and then with growing delight.

'I said each of you must choose,' the embrenche replied, 'not you alone. What you have done for Mamkinga is forfeit.'

He reached for the goblet.

Toomi pulled her brother protectively towards her. She shook her head as she shielded the glass with her arm.

'The choice was his,' she said stubbornly. 'He made it on his own and he told me in silence what he had done.'

As Toomi finished speaking, Mamkinga nodded in confirmation of what his sister had said. The embrenche stared down irritably at the two of them. As so often, the silent communication between his two children baffled him.

Then behind his back the Arab merchant began to laugh.

'Let the girl speak for the boy, embrenche,' the Arab said. 'However the choice was made, they are both welcome to the small tributes we bring them.'

As the embrenche turned to answer him, the twins scuttled away.

They hid the Arab's gifts in a remote corner of the

73

compound. For years afterwards the seahorse and the goblet were their most treasured possessions.

The gulf in temperament between the two was vast.

In spite of that the twins were inseparable. Often they seemed to inhabit two halves of a single body and a single mind. If Mamkinga fell and hurt himself out of Toomi's sight, Toomi would start to cry in pain too. Toomi would open her mouth to say something and Mamkinga would speak the same sentence at the same moment. Sometimes without exchanging a word they would simultaneously get to their feet. They would head off in silence across the compound. Then, still without speaking, they would embark on some elaborate joint activity like building a model fortress in sand or playing a complicated game.

Until they were five they slept together in the night house of their mother, the embrenche's youngest wife. Then Mamkinga, as Malindan tradition required, was told to sleep in his father's night house.

The first night of their separation neither he nor Toomi slept at all. They lay awake crying for hour after hour. When morning came and the houses were opened they ran together. They put their arms round each other and lay down in the dust in the shadow of one of the compound's trees.

Then, locked together, they slept all day.

In Malinda twins were rare and considered highly favoured by the spirits. After a week had passed with the children still unable to sleep at night, the embrenche called the other village chiefs to the compound. Everyone agreed an exception had to be made to tribal custom. The twins were of different sexes, but they belonged together. To separate them, as their night-long misery had shown, was wrong.

For once a brother and sister must be allowed to share the same sleeping quarters.

The next day the embrenche had a new night house built just behind his own. It stood apart from the other houses and it was for the twins alone. Afterwards Mamkinga and Toomi slept there together with only an

74

old servant lying by the door for company. The very first possessions the twins installed in the night house were the seahorse and the glass goblet.

Not long after they moved into their new quarters a minor chief from one of Malinda's outlying villages came to visit the embrenche. With him he too brought a gift. It was a pearl-spotted owl. In Malinda every owl was a symbol of good fortune, but the little pearl-spotted owls, with their bright orange eyes, their speckled chests and their ferocious behaviour – they seemed to challenge their great cousins, the eagle owls, as they puffed out their feathers and stamped imperiously on their perches – were the most favoured of all.

The embrenche gave the owl in its plaited rush cage to Toomi.

Toomi adored the bird. For a while it even supplanted the seahorse in her affections. She kept the owl's cage by her bedside, and fed the bird night and morning with insects and little scraps of meat she stole from the embrenche's kitchen.

One evening Mamkinga produced a lizard he had trapped on the common outside the town. As he opened the cage door to place the lizard inside, the owl sprang past his hand. It circled the room and flew out of the open window into the darkening air.

Toomi, who was watching her brother, was enraged. 'You did it deliberately!' she screamed. 'You were jealous and you let the bird go free!'

She sprang on her brother and began to beat him with her fists.

Mamkinga backed away. He had indeed envied their father's gift to Toomi, although he hadn't intended to free the bird. As his sister continued to attack him he ran from the house.

Outside, Mamkinga crouched under the stars on the baked earth of the roadway. Finally, seething with a mixture of resentment and guilt, he crept out of the embrenche's compound. He gained the street. Then he ran blindly through the town and out into the forest that surrounded it.

That night, for the first time in her life, Toomi slept alone.

When she woke at dawn there was no print on the fern-filled calico mattress that lay beside hers. Frantically she searched the compound. There was no sign of Mamkinga. All of her anger against her brother and his clumsiness had gone. In its place she felt grief and desolation.

Somehow she managed to conceal Mamkinga's disappearance from the rest of the embrenche's household.

'He left early to hunt,' she explained when his absence at the communal breakfast was noted. 'He will be back before darkness.'

Toomi smiled brightly.

Then she retired to the night house. She remained there distraught as the sun rose. As the day passed the sun wheeled across the sky. It came to its fiercely burning peak, and sank into dusk again. All the while Toomi paced restlessly round the room she shared with Mamkinga. She no longer had any interest in the bold little owl she had lost. All she wanted was for her brother to return.

Mamkinga finally came back as the stars appeared.

He stumbled wearily into the compound. He was exhausted, and his body was streaked with sweat and dust. Perched on his shoulder, its little talons struggling for a grip on his skin, was another pearl-spotted owl. It had been trapped with a resin-based lime, and its feathers were clogged and bedraggled.

'Here,' Mamkinga said as he passed the owl to her. 'I give you back your bird.'

Toomi settled it down, hissing and snapping forlornly, on her wrist.

'Where did you find it?' she asked.

Mamkinga slumped down on his bed.

'There are dwellers in the forest,' he answered. 'They snare owls as bait for sand grouse. They put the owls out on branches. When the grouse come down to mob them, they shoot the grouse with arrows. When the hunt is over, they kill and eat the owl, too.'

'And they gave you this one?'

Mamkinga shook his head. 'I had to barter for it. I took the goblet the Arab gave us. I showed it to them and they said it was worth an owl.'

'You changed the goblet for the bird?'

Toomi gazed at him appalled.

There were owls everywhere in Malinda – their calls filled the streets each night – but the chiselled glass with its silver phoenix handle was a treasure beyond price. Now it had gone.

Numb with exhaustion, Mamkinga nodded. 'I thought it was what you wanted,' he said dully.

For an instant in fury at his stupidity Toomi raised her hand to strike him. Then she stopped and burst into tears. She threw her arms round Mamkinga's neck and wept. They went to bed and slept, holding each other by the hand.

All night the owl hopped angrily and uncomfortably between the children's sleeping bodies, prevented from flying by its lime-clogged plumage.

In the morning Toomi consulted the embrenche's senior huntsman. The owl's feathers could be cleaned, the huntsman told her, with citric acid. He showed her how to extract the acid from the shaven peel of lemons. Toomi worked on the owl's plumage for a week. When the delicate fibres were eventually restored to health, she carried the bird outside and launched it into the evening air.

The owl circled the compound and settled back on the ledge beside Toomi's head. By then it had become too devoted to the rich diet of insects that swarmed to the compound's lamps to want to leave.

The owl snapped at Toomi's ear. It puffed out its chest, clattered its bill, stamped from one foot to the other, and settled down contentedly and hungrily for nightfall.

Watching the bird, Toomi laughed with delight. Her brother was standing beside her.

'You loosed an owl from a cage,' she said to Mamkinga. 'And then you gave me back one that is free.'

Mamkinga shuffled awkwardly and smiled.

'Now!' Toomi said.

Toomi was bending down.

They had left the embrenche's compound, threaded their way through Malinda's straggling lanes, and reached the house of old Kakaba. Mamkinga put his foot into the cup made by her interlaced fingers and sprang upwards as she heaved from below. He gripped the rim of the wall.

Mamkinga wriggled on top, and peered over the other side.

'Come on!' he called back softly.

He worked his way round on his stomach until he was facing the street, and reached down. Toomi backed away. Then she ran forward. She jumped and Mamkinga pulled her scrambling up beside him.

They both lay for a moment on the wall, gazing down at the compound of old Kakaba below.

Kakaba was the uncle of one of Malinda's sub-chiefs. For years he had been headman of a village high up in the Mountains of the Moon. When the last of his five wives died he decided to retire to Malinda itself. Normally he would have moved into his nephew's compound, where a day and night house would have been built for him. But Kakaba was a proud and independent old man. He had demanded his own compound.

He put his case to the embrenche, and the embrenche agreed. He allocated Kakaba a space on the edge of the village. By then Malinda had spread out to the surrounding woodland. The area given Kakaba contained a group of tall and ancient fig trees.

'There doesn't seem to be anyone,' Mamkinga whispered as they studied the ground below.

'Of course there isn't,' Toomi said scornfully. 'They're all out at the common.'

Mamkinga wrinkled his face in doubt. 'Well, Kakaba might have left someone behind.'

'In the last of the full summer moons? When it's

harvest?' Toomi snorted. 'Kakaba's taken all his people, just like everyone else has done.'

Mamkinga frowned. He knew his sister was almost certainly right but still, endlessly cautious, he hesitated.

Malinda depended for its existence on agriculture.

Six miles away the land flattened into an irrigated plain and became extraordinarily rich and fertile. The plain was Malinda's granary. It produced everything from fruit to corn, tobacco to cotton, honey to herbs.

Every morning a large proportion of Malinda's inhabitants would leave the village and make the two-hour walk to the plain, the common as they referred to it, to tend its crops. They took with them all their children over the age of eight and they returned to the village at night. By day during the annual harvest Malinda was virtually deserted. Everyone, from the oldest to the very youngest capable of helping, was needed to gather the crops.

The only people left behind were the smallest children and a few slaves to look after them.

Most of the work of the harvesting was done by Malinda's women, but the men's presence alongside them was essential. The lands of the Galla to the north were much poorer. The Galla raided Malinda's commons whenever and wherever the chance occurred. Malinda's menfolk accompanied their women and children to the fields to protect the kingdom's green and golden wealth.

'You had better stay up here in case old Kakaba sends anyone back,' Toomi said. 'I'll see if the fruit is ripe.'

The clump of fig trees was fifteen yards away.

Toomi dropped down inside the compound. She ran over to the trees, and started to climb. A few moments later she disappeared in the leaves. Mamkinga waited. Then he heard a squeal of delight.

'Mamkinga, they're wonderful!' Toomi called unseen. 'They're sweet and juicy and there are thousands of them. Come and see!'

Mamkinga barely hesitated.

Figs were the twins' favourite fruit and the temptation was irresistible. Forgetting Toomi's injunction minutes before, Mamkinga jumped down and ran to join her.

'Stay on the ground,' Toomi said. 'I'll throw them down to you.'

Toomi was right.

Mamkinga had never seen so many figs in his life. As Toomi dropped them through the branches Mamkinga caught them and piled them at his feet. Then his sister climbed down. They squatted on either side of the pile. Talking excitedly, they began to eat.

They were so busy cramming the sweet honey-flavoured fruit into their mouths, they were unaware of the danger until it was too late. Mamkinga was sitting with his back to the wall, so it was Toomi who saw the man first. As Toomi's eyes widened in fear, Mamkinga felt the hairs on the back of his neck prickle.

Mamkinga's head jerked round.

There was a man on top of the wall. Like the twins he had climbed it from the road. He leant over and pulled a second man up beside him. Neither of the men had anything to do with old Kakaba. They were not even Malindans. They were thickly built, with mahogany-coloured skin, coarse blunt features and wiry close-curled hair. They were both wearing tattered shorts and one of them had a coil of rope over his shoulder.

'Oye-Eboe,' Toomi whispered.

The Oye-Eboe – the word meant 'the red men from a distance' – were a tribe of nomadic merchants and traders who lived to the south-west of Malinda. In general their relations with Malinda were good. The twins had often seen men of the Oye-Eboe in Malinda's market bartering guns and dried fish for grain and salt.

The Oye-Eboe were also notorious dealers in slaves. Usually the slaves they marched through Malinda on their way to the coast had been taken outside the country. But when slaves from elsewhere were in short supply, the Oye-Eboe were quite prepared to abuse Malinda's hospitality and capture its own people.

Their favourite time was when, as now, the harvest was being gathered from the common. They would enter the compounds of the almost-deserted villages and seize any children who had been left behind. Toomi and Mamkinga had been warned against them since they could speak. Normally, as the embrenche's children living in the central compound and under the care of his servants, they were in no danger.

That day in slipping out to raid old Kakaba's figs, they had unwittingly made themselves vulnerable.

Old Kakaba's house was set among the poorest and worst-protected compounds. Prowling through the deserted streets on the outskirts of the town, the Oye-Eboe had heard the twins' voices. The men had scaled the wall and spotted them.

To the Oye-Eboe there was nothing to distinguish the twins from any other pair of poor Malindan children. The men leapt down from the wall.

'Run, Mamkinga!' Toomi shouted, her voice rising in terror. 'Run!'

She leapt up. Catching her brother's hand, Toomi dragged him after her.

Toomi ran blindly, screaming as she went. Dimly she thought of trying to reach Kakaba's night house and somehow barricading herself and her brother inside.

It was hopeless. The two men, much taller and swifter than the children, raced after them. The Oye-Eboe caught up with the twins at the night house door. There was a brief struggle as they seized one each. Wads of cloth were stuffed in Toomi's and Mamkinga's mouths to stop their cries. Their arms were roped behind their backs. Then, twisting and straining, they were propelled back to the compound wall.

One of the men scrambled on top. The other heaved the children up to him. Toomi was the first. On the far side she glimpsed an Oye-Eboe woman waiting to catch them. The woman had the same pug features and cold greedy eyes as the men. As Toomi tumbled down she managed to spit the cloth from her mouth. The woman gripped her round the waist.

Toomi screamed again and sank her teeth into the woman's arm.

Toomi heard a quick intake of breath and a sharp cry. The woman dropped her and Toomi fell to the ground. Then the woman bent down and clubbed her in fury across the ear. Toomi's head rang and waves of dizziness rippled over her. At the same moment she was aware of Mamkinga crashing down beside her.

Afterwards Toomi lost consciousness.

— 11 —

'Toomi! Toomi!'

A voice was whispering in her ear. Toomi shook her head and opened her eyes.

'What is it?' she asked, blinking in pain.

She tried to concentrate. The voice was Mamkinga's. Toomi peered upwards.

Her hands were tied behind her back. Above her there were trees. She could see branches and the shapes of leaves, shot through with sunlight and stirring as the breeze moved them. The ground was springy and cool.

She turned her head. 'Where are we?' she whispered back.

Toomi could see Mamkinga now.

Her brother was lying with his head close to hers and his arms were also tied behind him. Toomi shuddered. For an instant she struggled against the bonds. Then she fell back on the earth and began to sob.

'Quiet, little sister!'

Mamkinga jack-knifed himself forward and pressed his face down on hers, stifling Toomi's cries.

'You must not let them know – '

Mamkinga glanced anxiously over his shoulder. The three Oye-Eboe, the two men and the woman, were squatting a few yards away in the shadow of another tree. None of them seemed to have noticed Toomi's sobs.

'They're trying to take us away from home,' Mamkinga whispered. 'We've been walking and walking. One of them carried you over his shoulder. They made me follow behind.'

'Did you not tell them our father is the embrenche?'

Mamkinga nodded. 'I shouted at them. I said he would come and find us, and they would be killed. They just laughed. They do not believe me. Because of where they caught us, they think we must be a herder's children from the edge of the town.'

Toomi managed to stop her tears. She thought for a moment.

Old Kakaba's compound was in the poorest part of Malinda. She and Mamkinga dressed exactly like every other Malindan child. There was nothing to associate them with the embrenche's household at the centre of town. With a sickening shock Toomi realized no one would believe they were the children of the country's ruler.

'Where are we going?' she whispered.

Mamkinga wrinkled his face.

Almost as soon as he could walk, Mamkinga had been taught how to orient himself in the countryside by the angle of the sun. The slave caravans of the Oye-Eboe always headed east towards the distant sea. For some reason they had been travelling the opposite way, directly westwards into the sun's already declining light.

'I'm not sure,' Mamkinga replied. 'They seem to be taking us towards where Mama Okota's father used to live. We went there once in the winter moon, remember, Toomi?'

Toomi nodded.

Mama Okota was the embrenche's oldest wife. They had once been taken to visit her father's village in the quiet time between the harvest and the sowing.

'It doesn't matter,' Mamkinga went on. 'We're going to escape, wherever it is. Just lie still and pretend to be asleep. If you do, they will have to carry you and you will save your strength.'

'How can we escape?'

'I don't know,' he answered dully.

Toomi stared at him.

A moment ago Mamkinga for once had sounded confident and decisive. Now her brother had lapsed back

84

into his usual mood of doubt and uncertainty. Her head still aching from the blow, Toomi knew that if they were to escape, it would have to be her who found a way to do it.

She heard a rustle as the Oye-Eboe stood up. One of the men tramped over towards them. Toomi closed her eyes and lay back on the earth.

A moment later she felt herself being lifted and swung over the man's shoulder. Bumping and rocking, she knew they were on their way again. She looked cautiously behind. Mamkinga was stumbling wearily after her. Then the woman approached and peered at her suspiciously. Toomi shut her eyes again and let her head fall lifelessly against the man's back.

They walked until darkness fell.

Finally they halted in a clearing in the forest. Toomi was dumped on the earth and Mamkinga lay down protectively beside her. Neither of the twins had any idea where they were. All they knew was that they had been travelling west from Malinda and they had been on the move since mid morning. The Oye-Eboe lit a fire and cooked a meal of maize gruel.

Toomi's and Mamkinga's hands were untied and the woman gave them a bowl each.

'Our father is the embrenche!' Toomi shouted. 'Even now he will be sending out the warriors of our country to find us. Let us go or you will surely die!'

It was as futile as Mamkinga had told her. The woman chuckled scornfully.

'And my father is the Emperor of Gondar,' the woman said. 'Eat, you little bush rats! It does not matter who sired you. Where we are going, no one will come looking for you.'

In spite of their hunger the twins hurled the bowls away without touching the gruel.

Their hands were bound again and they slept together, pressed against each other and tossing miserably all night.

The next day the group went on. Now Toomi was

made to walk too. She trudged beside her brother with the two men in front and the woman bringing up the rear. The Oye-Eboe used a dialect of the same language as the Malindans, but it was broad and difficult to understand. As they spoke little among themselves anyway, the twins learned nothing of their plans.

Since the morning they had been travelling through tall grass and scattered acacia thorn bush. At midday, with the sun at its highest and hottest, they reached a dust road. They stopped for a while beside it. The twins were offered further bowls of gruel, the leavings from the night before and cold now, but once again they refused to eat. Then they headed on.

An hour along the track they saw a party of people heading towards them. As the party came closer Toomi peered intently at them through the dust. The people had the same brown skins as herself and Mamkinga, and they were wearing the same calico wraps.

They were fellow Malindans.

Toomi gave a low fluting whistle. Mamkinga glanced at her. She nodded, urging him silently with all her power not to move until she gave the word. Mamkinga understood. He lowered his head and plodded on beside her until the approaching group were only ten yards away. Then Toomi looked up and started to shout.

'They have caught us!' she bellowed frantically. 'Save us, save us!'

As she hurled herself forward, Mamkinga raced after her. He joined in Toomi's frenzied cries. For a moment they both broke loose of their captors. Then the Oye-Eboe plunged after them.

The twins' attempt to escape was doomed.

With their arms lashed behind their backs, they could hardly run. Within seconds the men had caught up with them. They hurled the twins into the long grass beside the track. As the woman screamed abuse at the approaching group of bewildered Malindans, the two Oye-Eboe men drew their daggers and waved them menacingly. The

Malindans circled the three in fear and hurried away up the road.

Like stunned and trapped gazelles, Toomi and Mamkinga lay bruised and breathless in the thick waving grasses.

Before they could even call out again, the men seized them by the hair and pulled them violently to their feet. The woman came up and shrugged off a pack she had been carrying on her shoulders. Inside were two thickly woven hemp sacks. She held the mouths open and Toomi and Mamkinga, their wrists still tied, were dropped inside.

The necks of the sacks were lashed tight. The Oye-Eboe men took one sack each and threw them up on their backs. Then they set off again.

Inside the sacks, terrified and choking with dust, Toomi and Mamkinga wriggled like trussed mongooses.

—— 12 ——

The twins were carried on the men's shoulders throughout the afternoon. Clouds of dust rose from the track and
seeped through the hemp. The coarse weave grated
against the twins' skin, and their bodies jolted painfully
on the men's backs. Gasping for breath, blinded and
bruised, all they could do was listen helplessly to the
sounds of the bush outside.

Several times they trembled as elephants suddenly
trumpeted somewhere close at hand. Once the Oye-Eboe
came across a pack of hyenas lying up in the acacia thorn.
The hyenas must have leapt up startled, and a terrible
snarling clamour filled the air as the pack confronted the
humans. The men shouted and dropped the sacks.

For an appalling moment Toomi thought they had
been abandoned to the animals.

She rolled herself into a ball and closed her eyes in
terror, expecting at any instant to feel the hyenas' foul-
smelling teeth slash through the hemp into her body.

Then the hyenas backed away and ran off into the
scrub. The Oye-Eboe heaved the twins up again and the
journey continued. When they were eventually dumped
on the ground and the sacks' mouths untied to allow
them to crawl out, it was approaching dusk.

Toomi and Mamkinga emerged aching and weak from
the stifling heat and the lack of oxygen.

For several minutes they lay exhausted beside each
other. Then Mamkinga forced himself to sit up. The
African night fell swiftly and the last of the light was
already fading. In a few moments it would be too dark to
see their surroundings. The dust in the sack had mixed

with their sweat and dried into a hard painful film over their skins.

Mamkinga rubbed the flakes from his face and gazed round.

They had stopped in another clearing, this time on an open tree-studded plain. All round them was the familiar grey-green acacia scrub. Somewhere close at hand was a stream – Mamkinga could clearly hear the splash of falling water. On every side there were the shadowy silhouettes of the elephants they had heard screaming and trumpeting earlier. The huge creatures seemed to float menacingly in utter silence now above the bush. Occasionally light from the rising moon caught the yellow-white curves of their tusks.

A lion called with a deep grunting roar. Vervet monkeys scrambled, chattering nervously, among the tree branches. Nightjars churred and dipped their wings in the sand. A marsh owl swooped low over the fire the Oye-Eboe had just lit, hawking for the insects drawn to its flames. The tangled scents of the African day sharpened briefly and then lost their fragrance with the onset of night.

Mamkinga stretched his neck upwards.

Over the scrub in the opposite direction from the setting sun, he could see the distant flanks of hills. He guessed the hills were the sprawling lower ribs of the Mountains of the Moon. They looked immensely far off.

Mamkinga's heart sank as he stared at them.

It was almost two full days since they had been captured. They had been travelling all the while. Apart from the intervals between sunset and sunrise Mamkinga had no means of measuring time, and none at all for calculating distance. But the hills' remoteness in the darkening air confirmed what his instinct had already told him.

They were far from home and moving further away still.

Mamkinga didn't know how far Malinda's borders stretched. The very idea of a border had no meaning to him. He only knew there was a space of country where the authority of his father ran, and beyond that other embrenches ruled. He knew too that in Malinda the slaving activities of the Oye-Eboe were strictly controlled.

Every slave the Oye-Eboe wished to transport through the country had to be described and accounted for. Prisoners taken in war, civil murderers and other wrongdoers were considered legitimate stock for sale – Malinda sometimes sold its own criminals to Oye-Eboe traders.

But the unjustly taken, the innocent, whether men, women or children, were not only refused passage. Malinda insisted they were released to make their way home in freedom. When the Oye-Eboe wished to sell slaves they could not account for, they crossed the country by night. And when they captured Malindan children in raids on the village compounds, they hurried them out of the country as quickly as possible to sell them elsewhere.

Mamkinga was only nine. Even at that age he had been taught enough to have little doubt about what was planned for him and his sister. They were being taken away from Malinda to be offered for sale beyond the embrenche's rule.

'Stand up!'

The command came from one of the two men.

The man dragged Mamkinga and Toomi to their feet. Then he untied the ropes that bound their arms behind their backs. As they rubbed their numb and bleeding wrists the woman came over. Like the night before, she was carrying two charcoal-baked gourds.

That morning the Oye-Eboe had stalked and killed a gazelle.

They had spotted a young doe with a damaged tendon trailing behind one of the herds that rippled round them in the bush. The two men ran forward. They separated the doe from the rest of the herd and drove her back into the gully, where the woman was waiting hidden. As the limping gazelle came towards her, the woman leapt out to bar its passage.

Terrified, the animal tried to scale the gully's walls. With its wounded leg dangling behind it, the doe could only scrabble ineffectually at the steep sandy slope. The men raced up. They threw themselves on the gazelle and slaughtered it with their knives.

The gourds the woman was carrying were filled with spit-roasted chunks of meat from the animal's haunches.

'Tonight you will eat,' the man behind her said. 'If you do not, you will be whipped.'

The man had cut a switch from a sapling. He flexed the switch, making it whistle in the air. Then he jerked Toomi round and slashed it against her buttocks.

Mamkinga leapt forward to protect his sister. The man hit him too. Mamkinga felt a sharp spasm of pain. It must have shown on his face because as he sucked in his breath the man chuckled. As he lifted the switch again, the woman spoke.

'Stop!' she snapped. 'You will only damage them.'

She put the gourds down on the ground and pointed. 'Eat!'

The twins gazed at each other.

After thirty-six hours without food they were both weak from hunger. Refusing to eat had been the one act of defiance available to them. They had vowed to continue until their captors realized they would sooner starve than submit. Then, Toomi believed, the Oye-Eboe might let them go.

Now she shook her head.

The man was still making the switch whistle. It was hopeless. She might have been able to endure the pain herself, but Toomi couldn't bear the thought of watching her brother in agony. As so often the same thought was going through Mamkinga's mind about his sister.

At the same instant they both dropped to their knees and started to eat ravenously.

Early the next morning they set off again. This time the twins' hands were left untied and they were allowed to walk. Discussing it quietly together, Mamkinga and Toomi guessed there was no Malindan village near and the Oye-Eboe were unconcerned about meeting anyone.

They walked for the next eight days.

Whenever they stopped at nightfall the setting sun was always immediately in front of them. The twins knew they were still moving west. Before they set out on the twelfth day their hands were tied once more. Three hours later they reached a village. By then they had travelled over two hundred miles from Malinda.

The Oye-Eboe led them along a track of dried mud between rows of low plaster-walled houses and into the market square. There the twins were forced to wait for what seemed like an eternity in the middle of a crowd. The heat was intense. Strange figures jostled and clamoured round them. Sweat poured down their bodies and harsh unfamiliar smells swirled into their nostrils.

Finally one of the Oye-Eboe men gripped each of them by the hair.

The man shouldered his way through the throng, tugging the twins behind him, and came out into a small open space at the centre of the radiating lines of market stalls. Lengths of tree trunk had been embedded in the earth to form pedestals above the ground. The man seized the twins in turn and lifted each of them on to one of the trunks.

Mamkinga blinked in the brilliant sunlight.

Perched precariously on the trunk, he could look down on the crowd. It was even thicker here. Pressed shoulder to shoulder in a circle, men and women surged backwards and forwards, shouting, arguing, pointing and muttering. A bearded man in a dirty cloak came up. He pinched Mamkinga's calf muscle, and retired shaking his head. Another man did the same. He thought for a moment, and went away too. A woman reached up with her hand and pulled down his lower lip. Then she also vanished.

With a sickening shock Mamkinga realized his worst fears had been right. He and Toomi, the children of the great embrenche of Malinda, were being displayed for sale as slaves like common criminals.

Mamkinga cast an agonized glance at his sister.

As Mamkinga looked at her a man approached Toomi. He ripped off her skirt, and pushed his fingers between her legs. Toomi spat violently down at him. The man lifted his arm to hit her but one of the Oye-Eboe pulled him away. The Oye-Eboe dragged Toomi off the block, and hit her savagely himself. Then he heaved her back again.

Blood trickled down from Toomi's lip.

Mamkinga strained against the ropes which bound him, his teeth clenched with anguish and rage. Suddenly the other Oye-Eboe man turned towards him and tugged him off his block. Mamkinga thought he was going to be struck too, but the man gripped Mamkinga's chin and jerked his head up.

His eyes watering and his neck wrenched painfully round from his shoulders, Mamkinga made out that there was a woman standing above him.

'It's for my son,' the woman was saying. 'A servant of course but also a companion.'

'He is all the great lady has been looking for,' the Oye-Eboe replied. 'The boy is clean and firm and without sickness. He will grow shoulders to the span of an ox. There is a lifetime of labour in his limbs.'

'Where is he from?'

'He was born to a herder in the mountains.'

'It is not so!' Mamkinga shouted. 'My father is the embrenche of Malinda. He will – '

Mamkinga got no further.

The man struck him a violent blow across the head. Mamkinga's ears rang and his knees buckled. He reeled dizzily and clutched the tree trunk for support.

'All the mountain children say the same,' the Oye-Eboe remarked to the woman, twisting Mamkinga's ear viciously as he spoke. 'It means only there is good stock in them. The great lady will surely discover that for herself.'

Mamkinga was silent.

The pain and humiliation were too much. His eyes blurred with tears, he waited while the woman inspected him. Dimly he saw that she was immensely fat. Her face was swollen, her neck vast, and great bulges of flesh strained against her black gown from her shoulders to her feet. She was laden with gold rings and bracelets, and her breath reeked of spices.

'How much?' she asked.

The Oye-Eboe named a price. The woman snorted derisively and waddled away. The man, still holding Mamkinga by the ear, ran after her. They haggled furiously for a long time. Then they reached agreement.

The woman produced a bead-embroidered purse and counted out a number of copper coins, licking each one with her tongue to raise its brightness before she passed it over.

The Oye-Eboe knelt and scrawled crosses in the earth as he counted them. When he was satisfied he stood up and dropped the coins into a pouch at his belt. Another man appeared then, a tall ebony-skinned figure who was evidently one of the woman's servants. He cut Mamkinga's bonds and led him away behind the woman, who was pushing ahead through the crowd.

As they went Mamkinga looked back despairingly over his shoulder, searching for his sister.

Toomi was still standing on the tree trunk. She was naked and blood was still running down her chin. The crowd surged round her. Toomi looked frail and vulnerable, but her head was still held high in defiance.

Tears streaming down his face, Mamkinga called out to her.

Toomi didn't hear him. Clasping her hands in front of her groin, she was gazing bitterly at the throng below. The fat woman's servant tugged him away. Mamkinga stumbled on.

It was to be eleven years, the years of what remained of their childhood and adolescence, before Mamkinga saw his sister again.

— 13 —

Jamie's vigil in Iona's royal cemetery above the newly dug graves of his grandmother and sisters ended when day broke.

As dawn approached, the weather changed. The brilliant starry sky filmed over. When the sun eventually rose it did so behind heavy banks of cloud. A chill rain was falling. Jamie got up from his knees and stumbled out of the graveyard.

By then Jamie hadn't slept for twenty-four hours. He was cold and wet and so tired his bones ached, but he knew he couldn't sleep yet.

Apart from his father and brother, Jamie had lost his entire family. Now Hamish and Duncan were all he had left. Jamie had to find them to tell them what had happened. He didn't know where they were now but he knew where to start looking.

When Hamish and Duncan Oran set out for the south two weeks earlier they had booked passage from Oban aboard a ship named the *Hercules*. Jamie knew that because he had been sent over to collect their tickets from old Dougal, the ferryman. Oban was the port on the Scottish mainland, just across the water from Mull, which serviced much of the western Highlands. The *Hercules* belonged to the Highland and Island Emigration Society.

Ostensibly a charity, the society was in fact a commercial concern which made its money from transporting families evicted by the clearances to the New World.

The *Hercules* was sailing out of Oban for Canada. On

its way it was putting in at Liverpool. Hamish and Duncan were leaving the ship there to continue their journey south. Before they sailed from Oban, Jamie was certain, his father would have told someone where they were heading.

Jamie's search would start on the Oban quay.

To reach Oban meant travelling the width of the neighbouring island of Mull and then crossing the channel to the mainland. Before that Jamie would have to cross the sound that separated Iona from Mull. He had swum the narrow channel of water many times before. Never had it looked so cold and daunting as it did that dawn.

On the white Iona sand Jamie shivered. Then he strode into the icy white-capped waves and struck out for the far shore.

It was the bleakest, most difficult crossing he had ever made. The swift Hebridean tide was running against him. Sheets of rain lashed down across his face and the wind-driven spray stung his eyes. His muscles kept cramping with tiredness and he was ravenous with hunger. Only rage drove him on, a bitter fury at what the obscene strangers had done to his family and his home. But every surge of adrenalin that his anger pumped through his aching body was countered by the chill and battering assault of the waves.

Once in mid channel Jamie almost gave up.

He had been measuring his progress by a line of foaming rocks that rimmed the Mull shore to his left. As the tide swelled to its full force, Jamie saw the rocks retreating. He was being swept back. Despairingly he lifted his head. A breaker reared and crashed over him. Salt water cascaded into his mouth and throat, and poured down into his lungs. Choking and unable to breathe, he somehow heaved himself above the surface. He spat the water out. Dizzy with exhaustion, he rolled on to his back.

He could not go on.

It was better to abandon the attempt and surrender

himself to the churning waves. They would carry him into the ocean and leave him to rest among the seals and the keening gulls. At least he could sleep there. His mother, his grandmother, his sisters, his home, all had been taken from him. There was nothing Jamie could do to bring them back. Hamish and Duncan would survive without his help.

Jamie closed his eyes. For an instant he let himself be rocked by the tumbling sea. As he began to drift into unconsciousness an image suddenly crossed his mind.

He saw again the young woman in the indigo-blue gown stepping between the graves in the royal burial ground.

Jamie stiffened and blinked. He brushed the spray from his face and licked the rain from his mouth. Frowning, he remembered he had made promises. Jamie no longer knew what the promises were or who they had been made to, but he did know they had to be kept.

Jamie emptied his lungs and took a vast heaving breath. He turned on to his face again and struck out once more for the shore. As his arms cut through the water he was aware that the fierce press of the tide had slackened.

Very soon the sea would be running with him.

Half an hour later Jamie crawled up on to land. He was on Mull. He had completed the crossing, but the effort had cost him the last reserves of his strength. He was dizzy with hunger and chilled to the marrow from the icy battering of the waves. Most of all he was drained from exhaustion. He had to sleep.

He hauled himself up into the rocks and fainted.

When Jamie woke again it was dusk. Pushing himself to his feet, the boy realized to his horror that he must have slept for fifteen hours. He should have been on his way long ago. With every hour that passed the trail of his father and brother would grow colder. Yet before he set out Jamie knew he had to eat. He was so famished now he felt light-headed.

As he stared back at Iona he kept swaying. The white sands across the sound drifted in and out of focus. At least there was food at hand. Jamie stumbled back to the rocky shore.

All over the Highlands and islands that year families of evicted crofters were surviving as Jamie did then – scavenging the rocks like animals and living off their clusters of limpets, mussels and clams. All the Hebridean shellfish were a traditional part of the Highland diet, but all were usually eaten cooked. Jamie had neither the time nor the materials to build a fire and cook. He simply picked up a stone, smashed the shells where he found them, and greedily ate whatever was inside.

When his stomach was full and the dizziness had begun to fade, he drank deeply from a burn. Then he set out.

The thirty miles across Mull took the boy two days. It was a grim and frightening journey. The cloud gave way to relentless driving rain. Normally Jamie would have been able to find shelter and food at any croft along the way. But Mull had been cleared, the people had gone, and the crofts, like the Orans', were open-roofed ruins – occasionally at night Jamie would see the flames still burning on some distant ridge.

Several times on the road he came across groups of uniformed men like those which had come to Iona. Whenever he did Jamie ran in terror and hid in the hills, burying himself in the heather like a mountain hare until they disappeared.

He slept under storm-felled rowan trees, huddling beneath the upturned roots for shelter against the rain. He drank from the many burns that criss-crossed the hill flanks. He ate whatever he could find. There were no shellfish once the long sea loch, Loch Scridain, was behind him, but on the moors there were patches of blaebush and rowan. It was too early in the year for the berries to have ripened, and he had no choice except to eat them green – ravenously sucking out the juices and sharp tangy fibres, and spitting away the skins and seeds.

Soon after dawn on the fourth morning Jamie arrived at Grass Point at the south-eastern corner of Mull.

The Scottish mainland and the port of Oban lay five

miles away across the water. Most of the ancient drovers' roads across Mull led to the headland. For centuries it had been the departure point for livestock from the island on its way to the mainland markets. Some of the animals were shipped across the sound in boats, others were made to swim.

As Jamie came down towards the little pier, he saw he was in luck.

A herd of cattle was gathered by the shore and one of the new steam-powered ferries was approaching the island. The cattle were probably sequestered stock belonging to evicted crofters. The ferry was coming to collect them for auction at the Oban market – the money they fetched would be taken against the crofters' rent arrears.

Jamie broke off a switch of ash and walked up to a group of boys standing herd over the cattle. The tallest of the boys, a narrow-eyed child of eleven in a ragged oatmeal kilt, examined him suspiciously.

'For what are ye doing, loon?' he demanded.

'The man told me to gie ye a hand,' Jamie answered. 'He wants his beasts safe to market.'

He flicked the switch casually and stared at the cattle.

The 'man', meaning the laird's man, might have been any one of the dozen factors on Mull who, Jamie guessed, had gathered in the cattle to settle the debts due to their masters. They would have hired the boys to look after the animals they had claimed. It was quite plausible that one of them had hired Jamie too.

The narrow-eyed child scowled at him. Then he shrugged and spat.

'We're together,' he said. 'Any freelish at Oban pier and it's cut between us, ye understand?'

Jamie nodded. 'I'll divide with the rest of ye.'

A few minutes later the ferry nudged into the pier. The ramp at its stern was lowered. The boys lashed the cattle into the water and drove them into the hold. Then the ramp was raised again and the boat backed away.

On board Jamie crouched with the others by the stern.

The driving rain and the sea-spray blowing back from the bows soaked and chilled him again.

Jamie didn't mind. He had got what he was after – a free passage across the sound.

As the ferry approached Oban it had to give way to another larger vessel that had just left the quay and was making for the open water beyond the harbour mouth. Jamie watched it go by through eyes half-shuttered against the wind and rain. If the weather hadn't been so bad he would have been able to read the ship's name spelt out in white letters on its stern.

The ship was the *Hercules*, putting to sea at last almost three weeks after its scheduled sailing date.

All Jamie saw was a grey blur and the sails filling and billowing like clouds as they caught the wind in the sound. Jamie's glance turned away. He looked back at the cattle stamping and bellowing nervously in the hold.

Ten minutes later the ferry docked at Oban pier.

The cattle were unloaded and the boys drove them across the quay into the pens beside the market on the far side. As the pen gates swung shut a number of men in tweed jackets walked down the gangway from the ferry's saloon, and distributed coins to the boys. Most of the money went to the tall oatmeal-kilted lad who had challenged Jamie at Grass Point.

The boy gathered the others round him and divided the coins between them. Jamie was ignored both by him and by the factors who were paying off the boys. Then the last of the tweed-jacketed men spotted him standing apart from the rest.

'Was it ye who was caring for the Quinish herd?' the man demanded.

'I was helping with all yon beasts,' Jamie answered truthfully.

He had helped to drive all of the cattle on to the ferry and then off it again into the Oban pens.

'Well, here's this for your pains, laddie.' The man tossed him a penny and walked away.

Jamie reached out his hand to catch the coin but it fell

short of his fingers on to the quay. He knelt to pick it up. As his fingers touched it, a barefoot heel stamped down on his hand. Jamie's head swung up.

The boy in the oatmeal kilt was standing above him.

'Gie that to me,' the boy said.

For a moment Jamie was too startled to be angry.

'It's nae but a penny,' Jamie protested. 'Ye said we'd share the freelish. Ye've given three times as much to the others and nae doubt ten times to yourself. This is all I've had.'

'Ye wasna in my gang,' the boy answered. 'Only them that's with me divvy up the freelish. Is that nae so, loons?'

The boys gathered in a ring behind him gave a chorus of agreement.

'But I drove the beasts and did the work as fair as ye,' Jamie said.

'Is that the truth, wee man?' The boy grinned. 'Then why don't ye fight me and prove it?'

He ground down his heel on Jamie's fingers. As the pain coursed up through his arm Jamie tore his hand away.

He jumped to his feet. For the first time in his life anger flooded over him in a dark dizzying wave. He had never fought anyone before. On Iona there had been no need. Now rage filled him until he felt he was going to choke.

His sporran was empty. He had nothing in the world apart from the penny idly tossed him by one of the lairds' factors. He had worked for it as hard as any of the others. Suddenly the penny – it lay between them on the quay still – was vitally important. If he was going to find his father and Duncan, it might be crucial to him.

Jamie looked at the boy's grinning face and lashed out blindly, furiously, with his fist.

The boy swayed to the side. Jamie's blow swung harmlessly into the air beside his head. The boy laughed. He clenched his own hand and drove it into Jamie's stomach. Jamie coughed as the breath was driven from him. He lurched forward. As he did the boy jolted his other hand into Jamie's face.

Blood spurted from Jamie's nose. He staggered back, trying to regain his balance. The boy sprang after him and began hitting him mercilessly on his body, his head, his arms – anywhere he could find a target.

Jamie was driven further backwards.

Blood and tears were running down his face. He was breathless and tired. He tried to hit back but he was helpless. He felt pain, he felt anger, he felt frustration. But most of all he was humiliated. The boy in the oatmeal kilt was two years older but no taller or better-muscled than Jamie. As his blows thudded against Jamie's body and Jamie found himself powerless to avoid them, he knew the boy was winning because he had something that Jamie didn't.

Jamie didn't know what it was. All he knew, as step by step he gave way, was that the boy was making a mockery of him. He was stealing Jamie's penny and the boy's companions were braying their approval as he did.

The two were on the quay now.

Jamie's face was sheeted in blood and he could barely raise his arms to defend himself. The boy stepped back. He gazed at Jamie for the last time and laughed. Then he swivelled from the hip and hammered his clenched fist against Jamie's chin. Jamie's legs buckled and he fell.

As he crumpled to the ground his head struck the metal rail that carried the wheeled cargo-billies across the quay. Jamie lost consciousness.

The boy in the kilt looked down at him.

He raised his arm in triumph. He turned. He walked back and picked up the disputed penny from where it was still lying by the gates to the cattle pens. The boy held it up laughing to the band of his fellow urchins who had followed the fight. Then, as they clustered admiringly behind him, he walked away.

On the quay Jamie lay huddled in a pool of blood.

— 14 —

Dr Cameron was tired, frustrated and angry.

The Highland and Island Emigration Society had announced his appointment as their 'medical adviser and superintendent' on the posters advertising their sailings well before they had even agreed his terms of reference – let alone a fee for his services. A responsible and conscientious practitioner of medicine for some twenty years, Cameron considered the fee much less important than the public's expectations about what he could do.

The *Hercules*, whose departure from Oban had been delayed for nearly three weeks because of arguments about the ship's safety, had sailed twice before under the society's auspices. On both occasions the voyages had been a disaster.

On the first, nine passengers had died of an unidentified fever before the ship reached New York. On the second, no less than half of those aboard had gone down with cholera within days of the *Hercules* leaving port. The ship had been forced to put in at the Irish port of Cork, where many of those infected had succumbed. The Irish authorities had eventually refused it permission to continue and the voyage was cancelled.

Now Cameron was somehow expected to guarantee it a clean bill of health across the Atlantic.

Well, he could not and he would not and he had told the master as much bluntly face to face. While the passengers were penned away by the hundred on stacks of bare pine shelves barely two feet apart between damp and rotting beams, no doctor on earth could ensure disease wouldn't break out. They had nowhere to wash, nowhere to exercise, and only one reeking privy on each deck. Their conditions were worse than those of cattle on the old island ferries.

The master had been sympathetic.

He was a humane man and he disliked the society's arrangements almost as much as Dr Cameron did. On the other hand he had been lucky enough to get the command of the *Hercules*, and if he wasn't prepared to sail it, there were plenty of others eager to take his place. Tight-lipped and angry, Dr Cameron had left the wheelhouse only minutes before the mooring ropes were cast off. Now he stood on the pier watching the ship draw away and wondering bitterly how many of those on board would still be alive when it docked six weeks later at Boston.

With the tide and the wind behind it, the *Hercules* cleared Oban bay and slipped behind the rain-drenched slopes of the little island of Kerrera on its way to the open sea.

As the ship vanished from sight the crowd on the pier broke up and drifted away. Dr Cameron rubbed his chin and waited as the Mull ferry came in and berthed in the *Hercules*'s place. Cattle streamed off the ferry. Small boys chased them into the market pens and clustered together, waiting to be paid off for their work. Two of them seemed to be scuffling.

His mind still on the society, Cameron was barely aware of the fight.

It was Saturday, Cameron remembered. There would be no one in the society's Glasgow offices until Monday morning. As soon as the offices opened at nine he would be there. He would demand to see the secretary, and tell him what he thought about the society's arrangements for transporting its so-called members. Then, having resigned his position, he would write an open letter to the government.

Taut and bristling, Dr Cameron turned and strode away.

A few moments later as he passed the cattle pens his foot caught something and he stumbled. Cameron regained his balance and glanced down. Lying on the pier was a small sodden bundle. For an instant Cameron thought it was a sack destined for the *Hercules* and accidentally dropped by one of the dock-hands carrying it aboard. Then the bundle stirred.

Cameron peered at it again.

It wasn't a sack. Lying at his feet was a child. The child was a young boy with a grey Highland blanket strapped round his waist. The boy was clearly cold and sick, and his face was covered in blood. He had suffered some accident, Cameron guessed. Judging by his hollowed cheeks and sunken eyes, he was starving too.

As Cameron stared down at him, the boy opened his eyes and blinked. He registered Cameron's face. Then he tried to struggle upright, gazing frantically round the pier.

'It's my dad and Duncan,' the child said. 'I have to find them. Do ye know where they are, sir?'

Almost before the words were out of his mouth the boy lapsed into unconsciousness once more. His head dropped back on the cobbles and his thin arms spilled out wide under the rain.

Throughout the Highlands that year, as for many years before, human refuse had been tossed up by the clearances into every village, town and port. The child, Cameron guessed, was no doubt just another victim of the Cheviot. In the course of his work Cameron had seen hundreds of the dispossessed Highlanders. Bitterly as he disapproved of the law which had made them homeless, there was nothing he could do to help them. The problem was far beyond the resources of any one individual.

Cameron began to turn away. Then he hesitated.

From what the boy had said he must have intended to sail with his father and his brother on the *Hercules*. Missing the ship had most likely saved his life – the highest mortality rate on board was always among the children. Yet the savage irony was that his life had been saved at sea only to be almost certainly lost ashore. No abandoned child in his condition – thin, famished and fever-racked – was likely to survive for long.

Cameron looked at him again. The boy's eyes were closed now. Open briefly when he sat up, they had been blue and level and dauntless. There had been no fear or self-pity in them – only a stubborn determination to join his father.

'Driver!' Cameron suddenly called out.

He had rented a horse and trap for the day when he got off the overnight stagecoach from Glasgow that morning. The driver ran over from where the trap was waiting at the foot of the pier.

'Pick the child up,' Cameron instructed. 'Put him inside on the seat. Then take me somewhere I can get him a dry plaid. Afterwards we'll go back to the coach stop.'

By nature and temperament Cameron was a cautious man. Impetuous decisions were alien to everything he believed in. Yet the decision he'd taken now had been made on the spur of the moment – and he had no idea why he'd done it.

Perhaps it was anger against the Highland and Island Emigration Society whose victim the child had so nearly become, and whose greed had driven Cameron to rage. Perhaps it was simply the boldness and questing courage in the boy's eyes during the brief moment he'd recovered consciousness.

Cameron didn't know. All he knew was that he was taking the thin-ribbed waif home with him to Blantyre.

— 15 —

The fat woman who bought Mamkinga as a slave-companion for her son was a widow.

She was named the Widow Okuma and she lived in a large house near the centre of the village, only a hundred paces from the market square where the twins were put up for sale.

The village, Nasir, was a trading post on the border between Abyssinia and the Sudan. As a girl Widow Okuma had been a famous beauty. At thirteen she married a successful merchant, much older than herself. She had borne him one son. Then her husband died, leaving her an extremely rich woman.

Until the merchant's death she had been an exemplary wife – loyal, obedient and hard-working. Afterwards she embarked on a life of self-indulgent pleasure. She had the merchant's fortune and she was answerable to no one. She gorged herself. She took as a lover any youth in the village who caught her fancy. She tippled the fiery local palm wine from the moment she woke until she slumped unconscious over her bed at night. She abused and bullied her servants mercilessly, and she allowed the management of the house to disintegrate.

Gross and wanton, Widow Okuma was regarded in the village only in part as a jest. Much more she was an object of admiration. In the Sudan, as in most of Africa, fatness in a woman was attractive, and wealth a sign of virtue. Widow Okuma had both in ample measure.

To the inhabitants of Nasir, Widow Okuma was an adornment to their community.

When she finally tired of Nasir's youths and took a

permanent companion to live with her, it was no surprise to anyone that her choice was unusual and entirely in character. The man she chose was a European. A failed jute merchant from the Ivory Coast, he was an expatriate Scotsman named Alexander Butter. After the collapse of his business, Butter – a wiry little man with red-veined eyes and thick white hair that stood up on his head like a cock's comb – had drifted across Africa until he reached Nasir – one of the first Europeans to do so.

In Nasir he met the Widow Okuma. The affinity between the two was immediate. Both drank heavily. Both enjoyed food and song and laughter. The penniless Butter was a born entertainer. The rich but lonely Widow Okuma was hungry for entertainment. She had a large house and the servants to staff it. It was exactly what Butter was looking for.

Butter moved in with the Widow. Within weeks they were both as contentedly and drunkenly familiar with each other as if they had been married for years.

On Widow Okuma's side there was another reason for welcoming Butter's arrival. The inhabitants of Nasir might sometimes mock her. What no one doubted was her devotion to the child of her marriage, her son Timba.

Timba was eight. Born only a few months before the merchant's death, he was a pleasant outgoing boy who remembered nothing of his father and adored his mother. As Timba grew up the Widow Okuma knew he needed the presence of a man in the house. As well as being a companion to herself, Butter was going to be a substitute father to her son – and one who would teach him the ways of the northern world which, the Widow Okuma was shrewd enough to guess, was becoming an increasingly important presence in Africa.

After Butter's arrival all that Timba needed was a playmate. The Widow Okuma had been searching for a suitable one for months. Slave-boys of the right age were not easy to find. When she saw Mamkinga in the market square, it had taken her only minutes to make up her mind.

Butter was the first person Mamkinga saw when he arrived at the Widow's house on the day the Oye-Eboe sold him.

The one possession the little Scotsman had taken with him on his wanderings across Africa was an old rocking chair. He had installed it on the house's front verandah overlooking the street. Every morning until the heat drove him inside he would sit on the chair, a horn mug of cane spirit in his hand, rocking backwards and forwards as he watched the villagers of Nasir going about their business.

He was there when the Widow Okuma returned from the market. Holding Mamkinga tightly by the arm was the Widow's senior slave, a tall and gaunt Sudanese from the desert named Toko.

'What have ye bought in the market, then?' Butter remarked, patting the Widow on her rump as she waddled by him.

'A friend for Timba,' she replied. 'And the gold I had to pay for him! May the river's spirits sleep, but my son will ruin me yet.'

Waving her hands as if she were on the brink of penury, she disappeared inside, calling over her shoulder to Toko as she went.

'Get the smith!' she shouted. 'I want the boy bangled.'

'Yes, Widow,' Toko answered.

The gaunt slave had a long leather thong draped over his shoulders. He removed it and tied one end round Mamkinga's neck. The other end he knotted to one of the verandah's posts. Leaving Mamkinga tethered, he vanished in search of Nasir's village smith.

'So who are ye, wee laddie?'

Butter had pushed himself to his feet and walked forward to inspect the Widow's acquisition.

From the dust below the verandah, Mamkinga stared up at him.

Mamkinga had no idea what he had said. He had seen Europeans before – Portuguese and British traders occasionally found their way to Malinda – but never one so close. This one's white skin – to Mamkinga its paleness was almost dazzling – was blotched with red lumps. His breath reeked and his eyes, screwed up tight behind their mottled lids, seemed to have difficulty in focusing on him.

'Do ye have a name?'

Butter clambered unsteadily down the steps. He plucked at the leather thong and pulled Mamkinga towards him. Then he peered at the boy again.

'Madainn Mhath,' Butter said. 'Know what that means, laddie? Well, I'll tell ye. It's the Gaelic for good morning. And a fine morning it is, too – '

The horn mug still in his hand, Butter waved expansively at the sky.

'And when evening comes,' he went on, 'we say "Feasgair Mhath". Got that, laddie? Faisgair Mhath. Furthermore – '

Swaying, the little Scotsman took another gulp.

'Should ye be escorting a lassie hame at the time, we say "Oidhche Mhath, mo ghaoil". Understand?'

Mamkinga stared at him expressionlessly.

For all he knew Butter might have been addressing him in the language of the giraffes that roamed Malinda's plains.

'Och, you're as ignorant as the rest of your folk, ye wee black bastard – '

Butter cuffed Mamkinga hard across the head. The little Scotsman turned away. He swallowed what was left in the mug. As the fiery liquid ran down his throat, he paused. He wrinkled his face in thought, and glanced back.

The Widow Okuma's son was amiable but simple, Butter had discovered. This child, the boy she'd bought in the market, had something about him that was different. His face was sullen but his eyes were alert and inquiring.

'Madainn Mhath.' Butter repeated the words twice and pointed encouragingly at Mamkinga.

The white man was trying to make him say something, Mamkinga realized. The first time Mamkinga hadn't understood and the man had hit him. The blow was still ringing in his ears. Mamkinga learnt quickly.

'Madainn Mhath,' he said, fumbling over the unnatural sound.

'Again!' Butter ordered him.

There was no mistaking the instruction. Mamkinga repeated the word.

'Good laddie.' Butter beamed at him. 'Gie us a month and we'll have ye speaking like a white man born – and in the old tongue, too.'

Toko, the tall slave, reappeared then with the village smith, and Butter stumbled back into the house.

The smith was carrying two bracelets made of heavy copper links. Mamkinga was made to place his arms on a wooden block while the smith hammered the bracelets round his wrists. When Mamkinga stood up again the copper links jangled and tugged uncomfortably at his skin.

The smith went away. Mamkinga was left standing alone, still tethered by the neck like an animal to the verandah post. The hot morning sun flashed off the copper and the dust rose to his nostrils. Mamkinga didn't need to be told the bracelets were the Sudanese way of identifying a slave. He bit his tongue until the blood ran into his mouth.

No one was going to see the son of the Embrenche of Malinda weeping.

Mamkinga stayed in the Widow Okuma's house for a year and a half.

In many ways his time there was undemanding. Widow Okuma was good-natured and indulgent. From the beginning her son Timba, thrilled to have a playmate for the first time in his life, insisted on treating Mamkinga like a brother. The evening of Mamkinga's arrival, Timba took him down to the river to bathe.

The river was a hundred paces from the back of the Widow's house. The far bank was steep and topped with a towering wall of trees which marked the rim of the forest on the other side. The waters at the centre were broad and deep, but on the near side where the village stood the river bed sloped up into shallows.

The villagers bathed there once a day, the men in the morning, and the women and children in the evening, although like most Africans no one ever ventured more than waist-deep from the shore. Only the boldest went even as far as that. The river was dark, mysterious and dangerous. Beyond where feet could touch the bottom it was a place of portents, the abode of spirits and terrifying man-eating creatures like crocodiles.

The evening gathering was a social occasion. The women laughed and gossiped and smoked their corn-cob pipes as they did their washing, while the children played in the reed-fringed pools. It was Timba's favourite event of the day. Now he had a companion to share it with.

He ran down the bank and waded into the water, shouting for Mamkinga to follow him.

'We'll make reed canoes and race them against each other,' Timba called. 'Come, Mamkinga, come!'

Mamkinga walked slowly to the foot of the bank. He dropped sullenly to his haunches and squatted there motionless, ignoring Timba's shouts.

A moment later something lashed down across his shoulders from behind. Convulsed with pain, Mamkinga was thrown forward on to his face. He spat the sand from his mouth and twisted his head back. The gaunt Toko was standing behind him, a heavy knobbed stick in his hand.

Toko raised the stick again and pointed grimly at where Timba was splashing in a pool.

Mamkinga scrambled to his feet and ran forward. Then, his back aching, he listlessly began to copy Timba and fashion a tiny canoe out of the reeds. Afterwards the two boys played together in the shallows every evening.

Butter, the drunken little Scot, made a hobby of teaching the boys English and a smattering of Gaelic. Timba was a poor student but Mamkinga had a gift for languages, and Butter was constantly calling for him. Very soon, and almost without realizing it, Mamkinga could speak English.

'For an ignorant black savage, you're a wee marvel – !' Butter said proudly one morning when Mamkinga delivered his first full sentence in the new language without the little Scotsman's prompting.

He patted Mamkinga on the head and waved his mug. 'Now try it in God's own tongue.'

As Butter spoke the phrases in Gaelic, Mamkinga struggled to repeat them after him.

Within weeks of his arrival Mamkinga was living almost like a member of the family. The chief cause was neither Butter nor the lonely little Timba, but the Widow herself. Widow Okuma had taken a liking to Mamkinga.

The initial reason was her toilette.

Like most of Nasir's villagers, the Widow's ample body hosted a flourishing community of lice. Twice every week the parasites had to be removed. The task required small nimble fingers. Until Mamkinga's arrival it had been carried out by the daughter of one of her neighbours, who, in the Widow's view, was paid exorbitantly for the job.

As soon as Mamkinga was installed Widow Okuma decided he could do the task just as well – and much more economically.

'Come here!' she called to him one morning. The Widow handed Mamkinga a fine-toothed ivory comb.

She waddled into her sleeping chamber and sat herself down on a high-backed stool. Leaning her head back against the padded leather rest, Widow Okuma gestured with one of her plump hands at her woolly black hair.

'Go through it strand by strand,' she instructed Mamkinga. 'If you miss even one louse, you will go without dinner tonight.'

Mamkinga's fingers parted her hair and began to search her scalp. Widow Okuma closed her eyes and settled back luxuriously.

Half an hour later Mamkinga had finished. Widow

Okuma struggled to her feet. She ran her own hands through her hair, gazing in the mirror as she did so. Her scalp felt clean and fresh. She grunted in approval. As far as she could tell the boy had done the job quickly and well. The Widow straddled herself over the stool again.

'Now for the rest of it,' she said.

She heaved her tunic up to her waist, parted her bulging thighs, and pointed at her groin.

Mamkinga knelt in front of her and began to comb through her thick and curling pubic hair.

De-lousing his mistress was not the only task in her toilette Widow Okuma entrusted to Mamkinga. As soon as she discovered how adept he was, she made Mamkinga responsible for the weekly impregnation of her body with scented herbs. The ritual was long and complicated. It took place in a special room next to her bedchamber.

The room was small and bare.

In the centre of the floor a hole had been dug in the ground. Hours before the ritual began Mamkinga had to fill the hole with charcoal and light a fire. When the fire had burnt down to glowing coals, he sprinkled the ash with a mixture of dried herbs and other ingredients. The mixture was stored in a glass jar on a shelf by the door. It included frankincense, myrrh, sandalwood, seaweed from the Red Sea and a powdered extract from the glands of the African musk cat.

As soon as the scents of the herbs began to fill the room, Mamkinga had to call for his mistress. The room was named the honey-pot.

'The honey-pot is ready!' he would shout.

The Widow Okuma came through from her chamber. She was wearing a loose and billowing cotton shift. She removed the shift and handed it to Mamkinga. Underneath she was naked.

The Widow, a mountainous mass of dark flesh with huge sagging breasts and ripples of fat enveloping her arms and legs, squatted down above the embers. Mamkinga rearranged the shift round her so that it enclosed her body like a tent. Then, snuffling contentedly as her pores opened and she began to sweat, the Widow would wait while the scents of the herbs permeated her skin.

Sometimes she would remain above the smouldering coals for several hours. As she crouched there, Mamkinga brought her horn mugs of palm wine and occasionally lifted the rim of her shift to throw more herbs on the ashes beneath her haunches.

When Widow Okuma finally decided her skin had absorbed enough, she would bellow for Mamkinga. Mamkinga ran into the room and levered her to her feet. Then she waddled back into her bedchamber and collapsed on her bed.

One day when Mamkinga escorted her to her bed, the Widow had drunk even more wine than usual. She rolled back on the mattress, belching contentedly. As Mamkinga turned to go she caught his wrist and pulled the child towards her.

'Come and lie with me,' she said, smiling drunkenly at him.

Mamkinga was wearing a calico wrap. The Widow tugged it away. A moment later Mamkinga was lying naked beside her beneath the cotton coverlet.

Widow Okuma nuzzled his ear.

Then she reached down and began to play with his testicles. The movement of her hand was slow and drowsy. After a while as she continued to tickle him Mamkinga felt the blood heat in his groin. The Widow felt him hardening and her fingers became more insistent. Suddenly she turned on her back. She spread out her legs, pulled Mamkinga on top of her, and guided him inside her.

Mamkinga gasped and spent himself almost instantly. His head reeled and he fell forward shuddering and panting on the Widow's breasts.

'Too fast, child, too fast,' Widow Okuma reproved him. 'You must learn to be patient. Recover yourself and we will start again.'

She held Mamkinga in her arms and crooned to him

until his breathing slowed. Then she started to play with him again.

This time when his erection came, Mamkinga held it for longer. He perched on top of the Widow while she heaved and wriggled happily beneath him. When he finally spent himself again, Widow Okuma had also brought herself to orgasm. She shivered and let out a great moaning sigh. Then she rolled away and fell asleep.

As she began to snore Mamkinga slipped out of the bed and crept away.

Mamkinga's body was dripping with the Widow's sweat and his skin reeked of the scents she had absorbed from the fire. He sluiced himself with water from the jug by the kitchen door. Then he went out into the yard behind the house. Timba, Widow Okuma's son, was waiting impatiently for him.

A few minutes later the two boys were playing together in the dust.

Afterwards the Widow often took Mamkinga to her bed. Sometimes they would be joined there by Timba and occasionally by Butter too, although the little Scot had usually drunk too much cane spirit to be interested in what happened beneath the cotton coverlet.

The first time Timba was called to the bed, he had wandered into the bedchamber by accident while Mamkinga was straddled across his mother. Widow Okuma heard the swish of the hangings in the doorway and glanced round. She saw Timba standing there puzzled, and beckoned him across the floor.

'You must watch what your little friend is doing,' the Widow said, gathering Timba in her arms and pulling him in beside her. 'One day you will have wives. I will buy them for you and they will be good wives. But to keep them good you must also keep them happy. Learn from Mamkinga how to do that.'

Accepting without question anything his mother told him, Timba lay earnestly watching.

Mamkinga's experiences in Widow Okuma's bedchamber affected him little. As his sister Toomi was to find, sex was a natural if puzzling part of adult life. As he rocked and bounced between Widow Okuma's thighs, he knew he was giving her pleasure. When the Widow was content, she treated him well.

For Mamkinga that was enough. Even at the moment of discharge his mind was planning and calculating.

— 16 —

Eighteen months passed. Then one afternoon, as so often before, Mamkinga slipped out of Widow Okuma's bed.

It was the day of the Widow's weekly scenting ritual. She had spent several hours squatting over the fire, and Mamkinga had brought her more mugs of wine than ever. Moments after she pulled Mamkinga into bed, she rolled over and began to snore.

Mamkinga knew she would sleep for the rest of the day. He swung his feet on to the floor.

As he tried to move away Mamkinga found his wrist was caught. Several times in the past Widow Okuma had fallen asleep lying half on top of him. Always before he'd been able to free himself by lifting one of her limbs. This time his wrist was wedged against the bedpost, and her body was resting on his forearm.

There was nothing for it except to pull violently and hope she was too deeply asleep to notice. Mamkinga braced himself and pulled. To his astonishment his arm came free – but the copper bracelet remained where it was. An instant later there was a clatter as the bracelet dropped to the floor.

Mamkinga gazed at his wrist in disbelief.

For the first time in a year and a half it was without a shackle. Hardly daring to breathe, he reached under the bed and recovered the bracelet. Then he tiptoed from the room.

Outside, it took Mamkinga only seconds to realize the explanation. His skin was coated with Widow Okuma's scented oils. The oil had made his wrist so greasy that when he pulled hard, the bracelet had simply slipped off.

He experimented with the bracelet on his other wrist. Narrowing his hand, he found he could remove it too.

The second bracelet was halfway off when Mamkinga heard footsteps in the passage outside. It was almost certainly the gaunt Toko. He frenziedly replaced both manacles and ran outside to the back yard.

Mamkinga, his mind churning, sat down panting below the gnarled old fever tree which shaded the yard. Then he began to make his plans.

When the Widow scented herself the following week Mamkinga was ready. The fever tree had a hollow trunk where he and Timba sometimes hid themselves when they were playing. Over the week Mamkinga had managed to steal from the kitchen a short ebony-handled knife, a small bag of ground maize and a length of hemp twine. They were all hidden inside the tree.

That day Mamkinga needed no grunted promptings from Widow Okuma as she spread her immense thighs over the coals. Carefully he made sure that every inch of her skin was covered with her precious oils. When Mamkinga joined her in bed he rolled on top of her so enthusiastically that she blinked in surprise.

'Are you learning at last to enjoy it, too, little man?' the Widow demanded.

Mamkinga gave her one of his rare smiles.

Thirty minutes afterwards Widow Okuma was asleep. Mamkinga slid out of bed. He took a quick glance at his body. His skin was dripping with oil and sweat. He crept from the room.

It was early afternoon, the hour of the day when the heat was fiercest and everyone rested – Widow Okuma in her bed, Butter in his rocking chair, Toko and the other slaves in their quarters, Timba in his own hut. Holding his breath, Mamkinga lifted one wrist. He narrowed his hand, and pulled at the heavy copper bracelet. It slipped off almost without effort. So did the manacle on his other hand.

For an instant Mamkinga closed his eyes, hardly daring to breathe. Then, carrying the two manacles, he set off along the passage.

There were two ways out into the yard, one through the kitchen and the other through a dark little storeroom beside it where the cane spirit was kept. In spite of the hour it was just possible one of the slaves was still in the kitchen. Mamkinga tiptoed towards the storeroom. He paused and listened. He could hear nothing.

Mamkinga stepped through the darkened doorway. As he did he collided with someone coming out.

It was Butter. The little Scotsman had woken with a parched mouth, and lurched through to fill his mug. Mamkinga stared up at him, frozen with surprise and fear. Butter gazed back through bleary eyes. He saw the bracelets in Mamkinga's hand.

'What the hell are ye doing – ?'

Butter stopped with the question unfinished. Suddenly in spite of his befuddled brain Butter realized what was happening.

The slave-boy was trying to escape.

'The devil ye will – !'

The two moved at the same instant.

Mamkinga hurled away the copper bracelets and dived past the Scotsman. As he did Butter crashed the mug down on Mamkinga's head. The mug had a heavy iron rim at its base. The rim caught Mamkinga a jarring blow on the back of his neck. His knees buckled and his head swam.

Muzzily he groped for the storeroom door and heaved. The door yielded and he reeled out into the yard.

'Treacherous wee bastard!' Butter shouted.

By then Butter considered Widow Okuma's goods were almost as much his own property as hers. Inflamed by the cane spirit and bellowing in fury, the Scotsman ran after him.

Normally Mamkinga would have been much faster than his pursuer. Now stumbling painfully, his legs weak and his head dizzy, he knew Butter was gaining on him with every stride. The only chance was the knife in the tree. Dimly Mamkinga knew he had to kill the drunken little Scotsman, and escape before the rest of the household was raised.

Mamkinga cannoned against the trunk.

He plunged his hand into the hollow and searched frantically. His fingers closed on the metal shaft as the Scotsman caught up with him. Mamkinga began to pull out the knife, but it was too late. Butter scythed Mamkinga's legs away from behind and kicked him brutally with a heavy boot as he fell.

Mamkinga's head struck the tree's great twisted roots and he passed out.

By the time he returned to consciousness the yard was in uproar. Widow Okuma had waddled out of the house, screaming and waving her hands, with Toko and the other slaves gabbling excitedly behind her. They all streamed over and gathered round the tree.

The Widow took in the scene at a glance.

'I treated him as my own family,' she wailed. 'I fed him at my table. I took him to my bed. I gave him to sleep with my son. And he repays me with this –'

Suddenly her anguish turned to rage.

She leant down and hit Mamkinga again and again across the face, screaming at the top of her voice until, breathless, she was forced to stop.

'The cunning wee devil's been planning it for days,' Butter said as she heaved herself up. 'Will ye look at these?'

Butter had been searching around in the trunk, and found the twine and the maize. He held them out towards her with the knife in his other hand.

Widow Okuma screamed again. 'He was going to bind and murder us all before he ran away! I shall have him killed! I shall kill him with my own hands –'

She broke off. For several moments she stood panting and gasping for air. Then her swollen face hardened in anger and her eyes glittered venomously.

'He had hidden them in the tree?' the Widow demanded.

Butter nodded. 'Aye.'

'Then let the vultures peck through the bark,' she said grimly, 'for the tree is where they will find him.'

Widow Okuma turned. She shouted some orders to Toko and lumbered back to the house.

Soon afterwards the smith appeared. A link was removed from each of the copper bracelets and they were hammered back on to Mamkinga's wrists. This time there was no chance of them slipping off. The gaunt Toko spoke curtly to two of the slaves. They seized Mamkinga, lifted him off the ground, and thrust him inside the hollow trunk.

Finally Toko came forward with a hardwood plank. He hammered it firmly over the entrance to the trunk so that only a small slit was left open.

'I trusted ye, too, ye wee black devil, and ye betrayed me – !'

Butter had placed his face to the slit. Looking up, Mamkinga could see his red-veined eyes gleaming angrily in the shadowy light.

'Well, ye heard what the Widow said. Ye'll bide there without food or water until you're ready for the birds!'

Butter's face vanished.

Mamkinga looked slowly round. He knew from his games with Timba that there was enough room for him to turn, to move his arms, even to squat at the base of the trunk. But that was all. Not far above his head the hollow narrowed into a small funnel which ended in a scrap of light high in the leaves.

Mamkinga reached up and tapped the board Toko had nailed over the hole. It was as hard and unyielding as rock. There was no way out. He would stay there until he died from hunger and thirst. Then the plank would be removed and the vultures would find their way to him.

Mamkinga had vowed never to cry. He wept then. His tears were not of fear or pain, but from a terrible aching frustration.

He had been given his one chance of freedom and he had thrown it away.

*

The afternoon eventually gave way to evening.

With dusk the air cooled in the yard. Inside the trunk it remained stiflingly hot until after night fell. Mamkinga had spent the hours squatting on his haunches. When darkness came he stood up. Pressing his feet against the rotting ledges of wood, he found he could raise his head to the level of the slit.

Mamkinga peered out.

The lamps were burning in the Widow's house. The hangings in her bedchamber had been drawn against night-flying insects, but the door to the kitchen was open. Through the doorway Mamkinga could see one of the slaves stirring a cauldron on the fire.

A gust of air brought the smell of simmering gruel to his nostrils and his stomach rumbled.

In a sudden fit of rage and hunger Mamkinga hurled his light body from side to side, trying to break through the walls of the trunk. It was hopeless. Outside its hollow centre the tree was as hard and strong as ever. Trembling from his futile effort, Mamkinga opened his mouth to shout. He stopped himself before any sound came out.

He would not plead, nor would he allow himself to die. For Toomi's sake he would survive.

Mamkinga dropped back on to his haunches. He spent the night sleeping fitfully, waking every half hour to stand for a moment so that the blood could circulate through his legs. Once he woke to hear an owl calling at the top of the tree. He gazed up at the scrap of starlight far above him, hoping – he did not know why – to see the bird.

He failed to find it and the owl did not call again.

'Mamkinga – !'

It was dawn. Mamkinga opened his eyes. A voice was calling softly. Mamkinga clambered up stiffly and pulled himself up to the level of the slit.

'I have brought you some water – '

Timba was standing on the earth below. He glanced nervously round. Then he handed up a leather water carrier. Mamkinga reached up and caught the strap in his fingers. The leather was soft enough to allow him to work it in through the slit.

'I rose before anyone woke,' Timba whispered. 'Mama Okuma is so angry I think she would beat me if she knew. She says she is going to leave you there until you die – '

Timba peered at Mamkinga with a mixture of awe and curiosity. 'Were you really going to run away?'

'Yes,' Mamkinga said flatly.

'But why?'

Before Mamkinga could answer there was a shout from the house.

Terrified, Timba turned and raced away. From the shouting that went on for several minutes afterwards, Mamkinga guessed the boy must have been seen. He heard Timba screaming. Then there was silence.

Mamkinga squatted and examined the water bag.

It was the size of those the slaves carried when they went out to work in the fields. The water was enough to last them a day. Mamkinga knew he would have to make it last him for as long as he could. Unless Timba plucked up enough courage to visit him again, it was all Mamkinga would get. When it was finished he was doomed.

Mamkinga drank a few mouthfuls. Then he settled down again.

The second day passed. By nightfall hunger was beginning to make Mamkinga light-headed. He found himself singing the hunting and harvest songs he and Toomi had been taught by their father's herders. Twice he was sure he was back in the compound at Malinda. On one occasion he was playing the African game of ojukla with Toomi. He reached out to move a pebble from one scoop of sand to another, and was astonished when his hand struck the wall of the trunk.

Eventually, exhausted, he fell asleep.

The owl came back that night. Mamkinga woke to hear it hooting much closer than before. He stood up and saw the bird perched on a branch just beyond the slit. The owl's breast feathers gleamed with translucent speckles of silver in the starlight. Mamkinga realized it was a pearl-spotted owl, like the one he had once accidentally let free from Toomi's cage and then replaced with another he acquired in barter from the forest hunters for the crystal goblet.

Mamkinga's heart lifted as he watched it.

The owl reminded him so vividly of his sister, for a few moments it was almost as if Toomi were there with him. In his hunger and loneliness Mamkinga reached out longingly towards the bird. The owl turned its head, first to one side, then to the other, looking at him with clear bright eyes. Then it flew away.

When Mamkinga slept again he felt Toomi's arms around him.

On the third day Mamkinga caught a lizard. It was a little green ghekko a handspan in length. He saw its head silhouetted against the slit and he waited until it had begun to crawl down inside. Then Mamkinga seized and ate it. The lizard was his first food in three days. He devoured it all, spitting out only the hard-edged jaw bone.

For a while afterwards he felt stronger and more lucid. By darkness the ravenous hunger had returned and he was light-headed again.

That night the owl came back.

Mamkinga was dozing fitfully when he heard a scuffle on the branch outside. There was a rustle as something seemed to drop down through the slit. Painfully Mamkinga climbed up. As he gazed out, the owl spread its wings and flew off.

Puzzled, Mamkinga felt around at the base of the trunk. He was right. The owl had dropped something. His fingers touched the small and still warm body of a bird. Mamkinga picked it up. In the starlight he saw he was holding a half-grown sand grouse.

Mamkinga ate it ravenously, not even bothering to pluck the feathers first. Before daylight the owl returned twice more. Once it brought a small grass snake and the second time a plump cane rat. The owl nudged them both through the slit with its beak. It hooted softly and vanished.

Mamkinga ate the two animals as hungrily as he had eaten the lizard and the grouse. When the sun began to rise, he squatted once more.

Mamkinga was dazed.

This time it was not from light-headedness but with a wild soaring sense of comfort and hope. The bird that had come to him out of the night was not an owl. It was Toomi. Toomi knew what had happened to him. She had called on the ancient spirits of the mountains. She had spoken to them and they had given her wings and she had hunted the darkness to feed him.

While Toomi was alive he would never starve.

Mamkinga looked up at the fading stars. Silently he thanked the spirits in prayer for what they had granted his sister to do.

That day Widow Okuma visited the tree. She was not tall enough to reach the slit so she stood beneath it, screaming bitter curses at Mamkinga and kicking the trunk with her foot.

'You think I will relent?' she shouted. 'Never! I paid gold for you, gold, you wicked thieving child of darkness! After all I did for you, you chose to try and murder us all and then run away. Now you know what happens to such as you!'

She spat at the tree. Then she heaved her way back to the house.

Mamkinga knew she had been drinking, but there was a malevolence in her voice he had never heard before. Helpless but still defiant, he huddled at the base of the trunk.

During the day Mamkinga trapped a second lizard. He was dozing and he woke to see it feeding off a line of ants crawling over the inside of the trunk on a level with his head. He ate the lizard without standing up. As he finished, his eye was caught by a tiny flicker of sunlight.

Mamkinga peered forward.

The ants were entering the trunk through a hole in the wood no bigger than a needle's puncture. The hole was also letting in the sun. Mamkinga put his hand over it and pressed gently. The wood seemed to yield slightly beneath his fingers. The winter rains must have eaten deeper into the trunk here than higher up, and the hollow wall was thinner.

Mamkinga raised his knees. He braced his back and kicked out. There was a creak and the wood seemed to give a little more. He kicked again and again, but however much he strained the trunk wall stubbornly refused to part.

Eventually, limp and sweating, Mamkinga gave up. He leaned back to wait out the day's heat.

Toomi – as Mamkinga thought of the owl now – visited the tree again three times in the hours of darkness. She brought him another sand grouse and two baby mongooses. On the third visit the owl remained on the branch for a long time. The bird snapped its beak and gazed steadily at the slit through its shining yellow eyes, as clear and brilliant as the lemon-petalled waterlilies that starred Malinda's mountain streams.

Staring back, Mamkinga knew the owl was trying to tell him something. Anguished, he didn't know what it was.

At last the owl spread her wings and glided away into the darkness. In a sudden spasm of terror Mamkinga sensed he had seen the bird for the last time. His mouth dry, he gulped from the water bag. Then he crouched and tried to sleep.

The fifth day was hotter than any of the others.

By mid morning Mamkinga's body was sheeted in sweat. His lips were puffy, and his mouth was so raw and parched that his tongue bled as it rubbed against it. He had hoarded the water from the moment Timba had given it to him, rationing himself to a few mouthfuls at dawn and sunset. Now he had to have a sip.

Mamkinga reached for the leather bag.

It felt strangely light. He tilted its spout against his lips.

Nothing came out. Puzzled, Mamkinga shook it. Slowly he realized that when the owl flew away he had unthinkingly gulped down all that remained.

There was nothing left.

By the time darkness fell Mamkinga was almost delirious. For five days he'd been imprisoned in the narrow stifling hollow of the tree trunk. Now he could feel his head rolling. His arms and legs quivered uncontrollably, his body felt as light and soft as a wandering current of the river's air, the space before his eyes drifted sickeningly in and out of focus.

'Why did ye desert me, ye wee black savage – ?'

It took a moment for Mamkinga's fevered mind to recognize the voice as Butter's.

Giddy and shaking, Mamkinga slowly struggled up until he could see out through the slit.

'Ye were my friend and companion. For Christ's sake, didna I teach ye the old tongue? Didna I look after ye fair – ?'

The little Scotsman was sitting cross-legged on the ground beneath the tree. Stuck in the earth beside him was a burning torch he had used to light his way from the house.

Butter had the inevitable mug of cane spirit in one hand and a large stoppered leather flask in the other. He was drunker than Mamkinga had ever seen him. He was swaying from side to side in the torch's wavering glow, and his words were so slurred they were almost incomprehensible.

'Ye've taken yourself away and it's left me sore lonely,' Butter whined. 'I've nae one to converse with, nae one but ignorant niggers to tell my tales to – '

Drunken tears filled his tiny scarlet eyes. Butter hiccuped and brushed them away. Then he waved his mug in the air.

'Yet I'll nae be stopped. There's nae a jock or a jeannie alive as can hold Alexander Butter when the tale-telling mood's on me. I'm going to tell ye a story whether ye're there or not.' The Scotsman paused, frowning. 'Are ye there, ye wee devil, or have ye gone to the widow-making waves?'

Numb and trembling, Mamkinga remained silent.

'Nae bother. I'll give ye the tale either way. The tale of the seal-man. Do ye ken what a seal is, ye puir nigger? A seal's a warm-blooded creature just like ye or me except the beast has grey fur and swims in the sea. Swim, do ye understand, swim – ?'

Butter cupped his hands and cleaved the air as if he were pulling himself through water.

'Now, seals have a verra strange ability. They can turn themselves into men. And this seal, he sees a wee lassie walking by the shore. She's the bonniest wee lassie that ever stepped and the seal falls tail over whisker in love with her. So he turns himself into a man and swims through the waves to the land – '

The Scotsman's voice hiccuped on.

Inside the tree trunk Mamkinga was swaying almost as much as Butter. He could smell the fumes of the cane spirit and his head was reeling.

Yet for some reason, racked by hunger, exhausted, dehydrated and giddy, Mamkinga went on listening as if he were hypnotized. Again and again across his brain there flashed a picture of the creature at the centre of Butter's story.

Half man and half animal, it was somehow borne up on water and moving with cleaving arms through the swirling eddies.

'And then on the verra night they were married,' Butter finished, 'it came to the seal-man that if he lay with the lassie, he would never be able to swim again. So the seal-man leaves her. He walks back down to the shore. The lassie follows him. She sees him step into the waves. Then all she can see is a seal swimming away from the land – '

The mug fell from Butter's hand.

He clutched his stomach and vomited. Cursing, he peered muzzily into the darkness round the tree.

'Did ye enjoy that, then?' he bellowed. 'Och, have a

drink with your old friend, ye wee bastard! It's nae often ye'll hear the auld tales.'

Butter clambered to his feet.

He stumbled over to the tree and forced the leather flask through the slit. As he did the stopper came out.

A gush of cane spirit poured down Mamkinga's body. He gasped. In the cramped space the stench was overpowering. As the fumes filled his lungs and the liquid stung his skin, Mamkinga suddenly came back to life.

He grasped the flask and thrust it back. The flask bounced off Butter's head and fell to the ground, emptying its contents round the trunk. As the flask fell it sprayed a few drops into Butter's eyes.

The little Scotsman put his hands to his face and screamed in pain.

'Ye devil!' he shouted. 'Ye've upped and blinded me!'

In fury Butter seized the torch and threw it into the pool of spirit. Instantly a sheet of flame leapt up round the trunk.

Inside the trunk Mamkinga could feel the air being sucked away from his face. He fell to his haunches, trying to breathe. It was no better. The fire was drawing all the air from the hollow. Mamkinga began to choke. He pulled his legs back. Desperately he kicked out with all his remaining strength at the wall of the trunk where the ants had crawled in.

Mamkinga kicked once, twice, and a third time.

The wood creaked and caved outwards but didn't break. His head clouding dizzily, he lashed out once more. There was a splintering sound. A section of the trunk gave way. Mamkinga gasped as air flooded in. He heaved for breath. Then he knelt and stumbled out.

The fire was blazing everywhere. Butter was weeping and howling, and shouts of alarm were lifting from the house.

Mamkinga threw himself through the flames and began to run.

Ahead of him in the darkness was the river. Blindly he raced towards it. When he reached the bank he plunged downwards. Forcing his way through the reeds, he waded out into the shallows. A moment later the bottom dropped beneath his feet.

Mamkinga had never swum in his life, but in his mind – encouraging him, beckoning to him, calling him on – was a bright clear image of the grey creature which could cleave its way through water.

Unhesitatingly Mamkinga struck out for the far bank.

— 17 —

Mamkinga reached the opposite bank as the moon rose over the trees.

He pulled himself out of the water and stood for a moment listening. The air was full of the sounds of the approaching African night. A pack of baboons was chattering on the shore. Behind him in the river hippos were grunting. A crocodile lurched off the bank and arrowed out into the depths. Somewhere hidden close at hand a lion roared, the great menacing rumble briefly silencing all other noises.

Mamkinga shivered as the roar died away. Then he shook himself dry and hurried up into the towering hardwood forest that curled down over the bank like an immense green wave.

His body was weak, emaciated and exhausted. His skin was charred from the flames of the fire. His eyes were blurred and his wrists still shook. It did not matter. Nothing mattered any longer except that he was free. His freedom gave Mamkinga's steps a soaring strength, a buoyancy and an urgency that a dozen years of rest and food could never have provided.

Mamkinga strode confidently on.

There was still just enough light from the setting sun to give him his direction. The ten-day journey he and Toomi had made as captives of the Oye-Eboe had taken them due westwards from Malinda. All he had to do to find his way home, Mamkinga knew, was retrace his journey for the same distance in the opposite direction. He followed the bank north for almost a mile. Then as night fell he turned west by an immense baobab tree and headed inland along a game track.

Fifteen minutes afterwards something brushed against his leg.

Mamkinga was walking slowly and warily. He checked and glanced down. In the darkness he could see nothing except a tangle of vines over the path. He lifted his foot and stepped forward. There was the snap of a breaking branch. Something gripped his ankle. At the same instant he was suddenly upended. A net closed round him and Mamkinga felt himself being plucked into the air.

A moment later he was dangling helplessly high above the track.

Silently in the darkness Mamkinga struggled desperately to free himself. There was nothing he could do. Gradually it dawned on him, as he fought against the fibre strands of the net, that he had been caught in a snare. With the blood pumping inside his head and his arms trapped by his sides, he swung slowly upside down among the branches.

Mamkinga hung there all night.

Animals passed below on their way to drink. Insects, drawn by the warmth of his body, clustered round him. Mamkinga heaved helplessly as they swarmed over his skin, biting into it and sucking out his blood. Two bats roosted for a while on the netting. A tree mongoose ran down from the branch above. It licked his face exploringly, and scampered away. A pack of wild hunting dogs caught his scent as they scavenged the river's game tracks.

They gathered beneath the tree, baying hungrily as they pawed upwards against the trunk.

Mamkinga shrank, trying to hide himself in his own skin, but he was far beyond the dogs' reach. After a while the pack moved on and their calls slowly faded along the river's banks.

Then towards morning as a shell of light spread over the horizon, Mamkinga heard a rustle above him. He peered into the leaves and his body convulsed in terror. A huge male leopard had climbed the tree and was padding out along the branch towards him. The leopard came to the end of the branch. It reached down with its paw and tugged at the netting of the snare, nudging the dangling bag to and fro with its talons.

Inside the netting, his arms and his legs pinioned and his face glazed with fear, Mamkinga stared up at the animal.

As it crouched above him in the half-light, the leopard's eyes were pale and hungry. Its bunched muscles rippled under the spotted sheen of its fur. For a moment the animal was uncertain. It could smell the boy but it was confused by the cords of the net. Puzzled, it patted the bag from side to side like an immense cat playing with a mouse. Then its brain registered the shape of Mamkinga's body inside.

There was prey trapped within the netting.

The leopard drew back its head. It opened its mouth and gave a chilling roar. Mamkinga glimpsed the curve of its yellowing fangs and the pink flicker of its tongue. The leopard's talons slashed out at the bag again and hooked it up on to the branch. The animal started to tear at the cords with its teeth and claws as it struggled to get at the child.

Mamkinga screamed.

He arched his back and scrabbled for the branch with the soles of his feet. Frantically he kicked out. The force of his legs against the wood tore the bag from the leopard's grasp. Mamkinga was sent plunging down. He came to a stop with a jolt that almost snapped his neck. Above him the animal roared and snarled. It reached down with its paw and savaged the netting again.

Swinging below the leopard, Mamkinga went on screaming.

He had no idea for how long he screamed. When at last he stopped, breathless, trembling and drenched in sweat, he looked up. The leopard had vanished. As he gasped for air, he became aware of another sound. There were voices speaking beneath him.

Mamkinga twisted his head and peered down.

It was still too dark to see the ground, but long before the leopard's arrival Mamkinga had realized that the snare which had trapped him had been set either for antelope or goats. Now the hunters who set it had returned to check their traps before morning. Their return had frightened off the leopard.

Almost certainly, Mamkinga knew, they were poachers.

He was right. There was a tug on the rope. Then he felt himself being lowered. He bumped against the earth. The folds of the net settled round him and he stretched his cramped limbs. As he did Mamkinga was aware of faces staring down at him. The faces belonged to a group of men. They were wearing foul-smelling leather cloaks and carrying spears. Puzzled and excited, their voices rose. They had been expecting an animal in the net. Instead they had found a boy.

The drawstring at the net's mouth was loosed and Mamkinga crawled out. A hand grabbed the copper manacles round his wrists.

'Dekumbu!' Mamkinga heard a voice say.

Since his capture Mamkinga had been able to understand everyone he had encountered. The Oye-Eboe spoke a dialect of the Malindan tongue, so did the inhabitants of Widow Okuma's village.

These people were different. Since he'd first heard them below him, Mamkinga hadn't understood a word they'd spoken. But he knew the meaning of dekumbu. Throughout central Africa it was a lingua franca term for slave. The hunter had recognized the significance of the bracelets. The man knew too how Mamkinga had come to be caught in the trap.

Mamkinga was a slave who was trying to escape.

A moment afterwards Mamkinga was hauled to his feet. His hands were bound behind his back and he was propelled forward into the trees. With one man striding out before him and three others following, one of them prodding him with a stick, he headed away from the now rising sun.

The sun, as Mamkinga knew well, rose in the east, his intended direction. He was being taken even further away from the Mountains of the Moon.

The men were Waziri, a poor nomadic tribe who lived off flocks of goats on the western borders of Abyssinia and periodically raided the smaller villages for livestock.

It was a goat that the snare had been set for, but a young escaped slave was an infinitely richer prize. Mamkinga was worth almost an entire flock. The Waziri marched him across country for ten days, killing birds and small wild animals for food. For the first week they travelled by night, lying up during the daylight hours in case they were challenged about Mamkinga's ownership.

When the men were finally clear of the area where they had caught him, they moved by day.

Frightened and dejected, Mamkinga trudged wearily along with them. At least on his first journey Toomi had been with him, and the Oye-Eboe had spoken the same language. Now he was entirely alone. His one chance of freedom had been thrown away, and he had no means of communicating with these grim-faced men with their menacing spears and their leather capes that reeked of carrion and putrid flesh.

On the eleventh evening the Waziri came in sight of a village.

Larger than Nasir, it was named Bala. Bala was the market town for the surrounding district. By the time they approached the village centre it was dark and the market had long since closed. The Waziri hurried through the streets until they came to a large sprawling building constructed round an open courtyard. They entered the courtyard through an arched gateway. In the light of a fire Mamkinga could see groups of men and women sitting or lying on the ground.

Three of the Waziri disappeared. The fourth remained behind, holding Mamkinga by the arm. Half an hour later the others returned. They were accompanied by an Arab. The Arab was tall and angular, with a deeply trenched face and narrow ash-coloured eyes. He was wearing a long yellow jellabah, and a black turban was wound round his head.

For several moments he inspected Mamkinga in silence. Then, speaking in Swahili, he asked, 'Where do you come from, boy?'

Swahili was the simple common language used by many central African peoples to communicate with others who didn't speak their own tongue. Mamkinga had learned it in his first years.

'Malinda,' he said.

The Arab said something to the Waziri beside him.

The man pulled Mamkinga closer to the light of the fire. The Arab walked slowly round him. Even when the Arab was behind his back, Mamkinga was aware of a cold assessing gaze travelling over his body.

'From where in Malinda and how were you taken?' the Arab demanded as he stood before Mamkinga again.

This time he spoke not in Swahili but in Malindan. Mamkinga started. It was the first time in eighteen months anyone had addressed him in his own language.

Mamkinga opened his mouth to answer. Then he hesitated.

At the sound of Malindan, Mamkinga had been about to say once more that he came from Malinda itself and was the embrenche's son. He suddenly changed his mind. Somehow, Mamkinga sensed, if this man knew the truth it might make him an even greater prize. Even worse, it might lead to questions about Toomi. Mamkinga knew that if Toomi fell into the man's hands something terrible would happen to her. The others, the Oye-Eboe and the Waziri, might have been harsh and greedy but they were still only traders selling a commodity.

The Arab was different. Like the black and gold snakes Mamkinga had been warned against as far back as he could remember, the Arab was evil.

'I lived in a small village in the mountains,'

Mamkinga replied instead. 'I was taken by the Oye-Eboe when the people were harvesting the common. They sold me to a woman in Nasir. I ran away.'

As the Arab continued to stare at him, Mamkinga's mouth dried. He could feel his hands starting to shake. Happily his arms were lashed behind his back and the man couldn't see them.

After an interminable time the Arab, apparently satisfied, nodded. He turned and spoke to the Waziri. The Waziri answered and what seemed to be an argument broke out.

Mamkinga couldn't follow what was happening, but he guessed they were haggling.

He waited. In the occasional intervals in the argument he could hear a spasmodic jangling sound which seemed to come from every side of the courtyard. Mamkinga looked over the flames and saw what was causing the noise. The men and women lying on the ground were all manacled to each other by heavy iron chains. Each time one of them moved the metal links grated and the ugly rattle lifted into the air.

Mamkinga clenched his jaw and gritted his teeth.

'Etoshi!'

The argument had finally ended and the Arab was calling.

A heavy-shouldered man bearing a basket of metal tools ran forward. The Arab gave him some instructions. Round the man's wrists were the same copper insignia of a slave that Mamkinga was carrying. The Arab paid off the four Waziri. Without glancing at Mamkinga again, he strode away towards the house.

As he disappeared the heavy-shouldered man prodded Mamkinga towards an anvil on the far side of the fire. He made Mamkinga kneel. Then he set about heating his tools in the flames.

An hour later Mamkinga found himself shackled by a chain running from an iron neck-collar to the last in a group of women gathered at the back of the courtyard. His hands were manacled too and so were his ankles, although the lower chain was long enough to allow him to walk. All the women were tied in the same way.

Mamkinga had been put with the women because of his age – at barely eleven he was closer in height to them than the bands of men.

He settled down in the dust beside his neighbour. She was a plump passive girl, a few years older than himself, who was already asleep. Beyond her was an older woman who kept shifting fretfully. Mamkinga watched the older woman as she tossed and heaved and muttered to herself. Then, when he heard her say something to the woman beyond her in Malindan, he plucked up his courage and spoke.

'Where are we going?' Mamkinga asked.

The woman peered at him suspiciously over the shoulders of the sleeping girl.

'Who are you?' she said.

'I am from the mountains,' Mamkinga answered.

'Ill fortune took you from there, child, as it did me from Koneng.' She shook her head bitterly. 'The Arab, Ben-Alu he's called, he's the worst in the countryside. He's taking us to the coast.'

'What is the coast?' Mamkinga asked, puzzled.

The woman didn't answer. Either she didn't know or she had lost interest in replying. She turned on to her stomach and began to mutter to herself again.

The night air was cooling swiftly. Mamkinga rolled himself into a ball, clutching his knees against his chest for warmth. As he moved, the chains bit painfully into his skin.

Mamkinga gazed up at the stars.

The coast. The word meant nothing to him. All he could imagine was that it was the name of another village where he would be sold again. Maybe it would offer him another chance to escape. Closing his eyes, he was sure that would be so.

With a child's resilience Mamkinga went to sleep.

'It is *irresponsible*,' Mrs Cameron repeated for the third time. 'Irresponsible, unhealthy and dangerous.'

'I am a doctor, my dear,' Cameron replied patiently. 'A doctor's first duty is to save lives. In my profession the chief irresponsibility would be to neglect that duty. As far as health is concerned, cold, misery and hunger are not diseases – they are the sad conditions of many which happily can be alleviated by the more fortunate. And as for dangerous – '

He paused. 'Flora, dear, I really do not believe a small starving child can pose a serious danger to two adult Christians.'

If the reference to Christianity struck home, Mrs Cameron, a devout and regular attender at kirk, did not show it. She continued to stare stonily at her husband.

Cameron sighed.

His wife had changed greatly over the twenty years of their marriage. From an attractive if always somewhat unimaginative girl, she'd developed into a harsh and bigoted woman. Somehow any generosity she once had had fallen away with her looks. At forty she was gaunt, grey-haired and constantly, obsessively suspicious – so ready to attribute the worst possible motives to other people's actions that at times Cameron thought she might perhaps be afflicted with a sickness of the mind.

He often wondered if it wasn't a consequence of her failure to bear children. For many years it had saddened him greatly that they were childless. Much more often now he was thankful.

'The boy was on the point of death, my dear,' Cameron

went on. 'He is still obviously very ill. God willing, he will recover. I can then trace his family and return him to them. Flora, is it not possible it was what the Lord intended when he placed the child at my feet?'

Mrs Cameron said nothing for a moment.

Then her nostrils flared. She sucked in her cheeks. At the same time the pupils of her eyes seemed to dilate. It was a habit, or maybe an instinctive reaction under stress, which Cameron had noticed more and more of late.

Cameron found it puzzling and unnerving.

'If our home is to be made a haven for the unregenerate,' she snapped, 'I suppose I must be grateful you have thrown its doors open first to your dear cousin. No doubt she and this waif will find much in common. Let her minister to the creature.'

White-faced, Mrs Cameron left the room, slamming the door behind her. Cameron shook his head wearily. Then he followed her out and started up the stairs towards his study. On the landing he paused and glanced in at the room where he'd put the boy to bed. The child was still tossing feverishly between the sheets. He hadn't recovered consciousness again since they'd left the Oban pier. That was almost forty-eight hours ago now.

Cameron went over to the bed and touched the boy's forehead.

It was hot and filmed with sweat. He raised the boy's head and picked up the glass by the bedside. Cameron parted Jamie's lips with his fingers, and trickled some water into his mouth. Instinctively and without waking the boy swallowed thirstily. Afterwards Cameron stared down at him. Until the fever passed the child clearly needed nursing round the clock. He had no time to do it, and there would be no help forthcoming from his wife.

Standing there, something his wife had said a few moments before came back to him. 'Let her minister to the creature,' Mrs Cameron had suggested, referring to his cousin. She had spoken the words in bitterness and contempt, but Cameron suddenly realized she was right. His cousin was the ideal person to look after the boy. She had nothing to occupy her and she was well used to dealing with the sick.

Furthermore, as the wife and companion in his travels of the great missionary and explorer, Dr David Livingstone, she must have treated more cases of fever than Cameron had done.

Cameron left the room. He crossed the landing and knocked on the door on the far side.

'Mary, my dear,' he said, 'could I come in and have a word with ye?'

Mary Livingstone listened.

The boy's breathing hadn't changed in the thirty minutes she had been out. Limping slightly, she crossed the room and sat down in the chair again.

She had been there for two days now and much of the intervening nights too. Mary didn't mind. At least no one disturbed her and she could rest. It was all she wanted. Sometimes she even wished she were lying in one of the graves in Blantyre churchyard outside. For a missionary's daughter it was a sinful thought. Although Mary did her best to conceal it, her faith as well as her body had been a casualty of the past few years.

She crossed her hands in her lap and gazed through the window, a small plump woman with a homely face, little sun-faded eyes, and dark wiry hair over which she invariably wore a white bonnet.

Mary Livingstone had been born twenty-seven years earlier in Africa at the mission post established by her parents, Robert and Mary Moffat, in the village of Kuruman on the edge of the great Kalahari desert. The first seventeen years of her life were happy and untroubled. Then one day in 1838 a young man arrived at the mission. His name was David Livingstone and he'd been sent out to Africa by the Church Missionary Society in London.

The young man was strongly built, with thick black hair and curiously intense eyes that always seemed to be fixed on some point in the remote distance. After the novelty of his arrival wore off Mary paid little attention to him. One day everything changed. Livingstone was carried into the mission in a litter. He had been terribly mauled by a lion. Mary's mother charged her with nursing him back to health. For the next six weeks he was seldom out of Mary's sight.

Mary sighed.

In retrospect what happened was all too predictable. An impressionable seventeen-year-old girl, Mary fell deeply in love with her patient. When Livingstone asked her to marry him she had no doubt he was equally in love with her, although more than once later she was to reflect on the way he made the proposal.

'I am determined to cross the Kalahari desert, the Great Thirst as the natives call it,' Livingstone said. 'Afterwards, if God permits, I will travel further, much further. I intend in His name to unlock the doors to this entire continent, to penetrate its mysteries and bring to them the light of the Word. And I would like to marry you, Mary.'

It was to prove a chillingly accurate list of his priorities.

At the time Mary merely heard the few words almost casually tacked on to the end. The handsome young servant of God – in her infatuation Livingstone had become a paragon – had asked for her hand in marriage.

They were wed in Kuruman's little wooden church. Six months later Livingstone, true to his promise, left the mission and set out to cross the desert. At his insistence Mary, already heavily pregnant, went with him in the waggons he'd prepared for the journey.

Sitting by the window Mary closed her eyes and shuddered. The attempted crossing was the start of an unending nightmare.

Four weeks after they set out they were forced to turn back. The heat of the great stone plateau was too savage. Their oxen were dying and they themselves were hallucinating from exhaustion and lack of water. Undeterred, Livingstone was adamant they should try again. The following year they did. Again, having been even closer to death, they were beaten back. It made no difference.

All Livingstone was interested in was another attempt.

By then Mary was stripped of her illusions. She wasn't married to an ordinary man or even an ordinary missionary. Her husband was haunted, possessed, driven by a daemon that for all his elaborate protestations had little to do with God. Livingstone, she began to feel, was impelled by something much darker and lonelier – a blind obsession to besiege the citadel of Africa and test his own body and spirit against its defences. Triumphing over the Kalahari was only the first, if the most challenging, step on a lifelong crusade.

They finally conquered the desert on the fourth attempt.

On the way, driven crazy by thirst, the oxen drawing Mary's waggon bolted. The waggon overturned. Mary was hurled out and suffered a heart attack. It left the right side of her face permanently paralysed and caused her to limp ever afterwards. At the time she was once again pregnant – four children had been born over the past four years in the intervals between Livingstone's restless wanderings. Soon after the accident Mary gave birth again. The baby was a girl whom she named Elizabeth.

The Kalahari's heat and mosquitos proved too much for the child. Elizabeth survived only a week. When she died Livingstone buried her without ceremony near the shores of Lake Ngami. Then he pressed on. He had more important matters on his mind than a grief-stricken wife or a dead child, even though it was his own, or indeed than the Lord God Almighty to whom all three were answerable.

Livingstone had his personal obsession to satisfy.

For a while longer Mary had no choice except to travel with him. Then when the desert was crossed and they returned to the south, she rebelled. She demanded to go 'home' to Britain. It made no difference that her only real home was at Kuruman, she'd only visited Britain once before in her life, and she had nothing to return to – not a house, not even relatives who might give her shelter. She wanted to be somewhere else, anywhere else providing it wasn't Africa.

Livingstone agreed.

She could take the children, he said. She could stay with his own relations in Scotland – he would write and arrange it. Then, when she had rested and recovered, she could bring the family back. Meanwhile he had other journeys to make.

Livingstone patted her disinterestedly on the cheek and returned to his maps.

'Mam! Where are ye, mam?'

Mary started. The words were the first the boy had spoken since she'd been watching over him. She stood up and went over to the bed.

The child was still lying on his back but his eyes were open now. He stared up at her. He blinked and frowned.

'Who are ye?' he asked.

'I'm looking after you,' Mary answered. 'You've been ill. I think at last you're getting better.'

'Where's my mam – ?'

The boy broke off. He lay for a moment in silence. Then he quivered and tried to heave himself into a sitting position.

'Where's dad and Duncan?' he shouted. 'They had tickets for yon boat – '

The effort was too much. His voice trailed away and he slumped back on the pillow. Mary tried to soothe him.

'What's your name, child?' she asked.

The boy, Jamie, looked at her. His deeply shadowed eyes were narrow with suspicion.

'What's that to ye?' he demanded.

'I want to help you.'

'I dinna need help. I have to find dad and Duncan. That's all I need.'

'Well, if you tell me who you are, at least I can start looking for them until you're well enough to do it yourself.'

Mary smiled. Jamie lay for a moment in silence. Then he said bleakly, 'I'm Jamie. Jamie Oran.'

'And who's Duncan?'

'My big brother.'

'Jamie,' Mary said, 'I don't know about any of your family. If you tell me where you come from, maybe we can find your mother.'

'My mam's dead,' Jamie answered flatly. 'I wasna thinking straight. She passed in the winter.'

'Is there anyone else we might find?'

Jamie made a tired movement with his head. 'My gran and my two wee sisters, they're gone too. The men's fire smoked them away. Yon Dougal and me, that's auld Dougal from the ferry, we laid them in the kings' and queens' yard. There's nae one else —'

He paused and added abruptly, 'I've a terrible hunger on me. Would there be a wee scone or some mealy, mebbe?'

'I'll get you something,' Mary said.

She left the room.

Five minutes later she returned with a bowl of barley gruel. She propped Jamie up in bed and handed him the bowl. Jamie was too weak to hold it, so she took the bowl back and began to spoon the gruel into his mouth. When the bowl was empty, Jamie's head fell back and his eyes closed again. Seconds afterwards he was asleep.

He woke again at dusk. He was still hungry and Mary fed him with another bowl of barley. This time his eyes remained open when he'd finished eating.

'You were going to tell me about yourself, Jamie,' Mary said as she sat by the bed.

'I wasna so. It's no telling I'm after. It's finding my dad and my brother —'

Jamie paused. 'Where am I?'

In his hunger and exhaustion it had barely occurred to Jamie until then. He remembered driving the cattle across the Oban pier. He remembered his fight with the tall gloating boy by the pens — and the bitterness of the recollection made him even more suspicious of the woman beside him. But after that, nothing.

Mary Livingstone told Jamie what had happened after Dr Cameron found him unconscious on the cobbles.

'So he brought you here to his home near Glasgow,' she finished. 'The doctor's my cousin. He wants to help you. I do too. Won't you tell me where you're from?'

'Glasgie?' Jamie frowned. It was almost all he'd registered. 'Glasgie's no bluidy use to me. Yon's to the south. Dad and Duncan, they were sailing out of Oban. I canna bide here. I maun go – '

Jamie made another effort to get out of bed.

Mary tried to restrain him. The ferocity with which the child struggled against her astonished her. In Africa she'd nursed grown men hallucinating with fever, but never anyone who'd fought as stubbornly and frenziedly as Jamie Oran did then. It was like holding down a wild leopard cub.

They wrestled across the bed as he shouted and kicked and swore. Once he lashed out with his hand and raked her face, drawing blood from her cheek. Then the boy fell back helplessly again. He was too weak. He gazed at her with bitter unforgiving eyes.

'If I tell ye what ye want to know, will ye let me part?' he demanded, his voice a whisper.

They were both panting. Mary, her chest heaving, smoothed down her rumpled dress and straightened her hair. She dabbed at the bleeding scratch on her face with a handkerchief and nodded.

'Of course,' she replied. 'You're not a prisoner here. But your father's and Duncan's ship has sailed, and you're sick. You must be strong again before you start looking for them. You know that as well as I do.'

The intensity of Jamie's stare as he listened to her was frightening. When Mary finished he lay in silence. Then in a cold hostile voice he began to talk.

— 19 —

'He comes from the island of Iona,' Mary Livingstone said to Dr Cameron later that evening when Jamie was asleep again.

They were standing on the landing out of earshot of the doctor's wife, who was sitting in the parlour below. Cameron listened as Mary told him what she had learned.

'It is a terrible story,' he said, shaking his head as she finished. 'His mother, grandmother, his sisters, and now this.'

'At least his father and brother are still alive,' Mary said. 'He says they sailed on the *Hercules*. There must be some way of tracing them when they disembark.'

'Aye,' Cameron replied doubtfully, remembering his forebodings about the ship. 'But that's going to take time. Meanwhile the bairn will have to regain his health. How long do ye reckon that will take?'

'He's had a sore fever,' Mary answered. 'With that and no food the child must have lost half his weight. He's nothing but skin and bone. He should be in bed for a month.'

'Aye, I fear that's my view,' Cameron agreed.

He frowned.

Cameron had brought back the child on impulse. He'd anticipated his wife's reaction would be hostile, although never as vehemently so as it proved. At worst, Cameron had thought, they might have to look after the boy for a few weeks. Then Cameron assumed he would have been able to trace some members of Jamie's family, and return him to them restored to health, with the gift of a little money to help them all over the weeks ahead.

Now he had to confront a situation where his wife was implacably opposed to the child's presence in the house, the boy would be in bed for a month, and it might take several months more to find his father. Short of the inconceivable step of throwing him out on to the street, Jamie could be there for half a year.

Cameron put his hands to his head in anguish. Mary reached out her hand and caught his wrist.

'Charles, I'll look after the child until he's well again,' she said. 'At least that will lift the burden from Flora.'

Cameron lifted his head and gazed at her in gratitude.

'But what will ye do with him, Mary?' he asked.

Mary smiled. 'I've discovered Jamie's lettered. I'll read to him.'

'The gentleman who wrote this was called Mr Mungo Park,' Mary said. 'He ventured into parts of central Africa, that's many miles to the north of where my husband is at present, over thirty years ago – long before you were born. He titled his book *Travels in the Interior Districts*.'

She opened the book and started to read. Jamie propped himself up and listened intently.

It was over three weeks since he'd opened his eyes and seen the plump little woman in her white bonnet and severe black dress leaning over him. He remembered little of the days which followed. The fever kept returning and for long periods he was unconscious. Then suddenly the fever ended. Afterwards, with the resilience of a naturally healthy child, Jamie began to recover. Now he was allowed up to walk round the room, still a little unsteadily, for ten minutes each day.

Mrs Livingstone, as he'd learned the lady was named, said that soon he would be able to go down into the garden.

Apart from Mrs Livingstone Jamie had only had two other visitors. The first was Dr Cameron. The doctor was a kindly worried-looking man who came in to see Jamie for a few minutes every evening when he got back from his rounds. Jamie knew Dr Cameron was married but he had never seen his wife, although once or twice he had heard a voice on the stairs which he guessed was hers. The voice always sounded sharp and angry. Mrs Livingstone told him Mrs Cameron was in poor health and was forced to lead a quiet life.

Somehow Jamie didn't find the explanation wholly convincing.

It was the only time he doubted Mrs Livingstone. In every other way he had come to trust her completely.

The change in their relationship had not been quick or easy. For days after they had struggled together on the bed and he had scratched her face in anguished fury, Jamie's attitude had been one of childish hatred and resentment. She was keeping him a prisoner. She was preventing him from finding his father and Duncan.

Even more than the brutal men who had fired the croft, she was responsible for all his misery.

Yet Jamie was a pragmatic child. Gradually he began to accept that the sailing of the *Hercules* was a fact. Another fact, it dawned on him, was his illness. Until the ship berthed and he was well, there was nothing he could do. And the one person who seemed determined he regained his health was the patient little woman with the lopsided face.

There was something else. All his life Jamie had been used to affection – from his mother first and then from his grandmother. Like a young animal he took for granted the touching, the holding, the comforting warming sounds of a concerned voice, the provision of food and laughter, advice and admonition. Almost unconsciously Jamie started to realize that Mary Livingstone was providing them too.

Finally he discovered that, like himself, she was a guest in the house. Her husband was a cousin of Dr Cameron and she'd come to stay there with her children for a few months on a visit to Britain from Africa. The double bond became a triple one. She told him the truth. She looked after him with love. Most of all they shared the same position in the household.

Both of them – the waif from the Oban quay and the wife of the great African explorer – were strangers in the gaunt Blantyre mansion.

In Jamie's eyes it made them equal as nothing else could ever have done.

One of Mrs Livingstone's children had been Jamie's other visitor. The children had been forbidden to enter his room in case the infection had lingered and they picked it up, but the morning Jamie began to recover, the door was pushed open and the head of a small boy appeared round it.

'Have you ever seen a lion?' the boy demanded aggressively.

He was a sturdy child of no more than four with dark curling hair and a determined square-jawed face.

'Nae.' Jamie shook his head.

'Well, I have. I'm Tau and I'm a lion. That's what my name means. I'll show you – '

The little boy wrinkled up his face. He bared his teeth and gave an ear-splitting roar.

'That's what lions do,' the boy went on. 'A lion tried to eat my dad. My dad killed it with his gun. That's why I'm called Tau. My dad's got a hundred guns. I bet you haven't.'

Jamie stared at him.

The boy chuckled and gave another roar. Then there was the clatter of footsteps on the stairs. Mrs Livingstone appeared and chased Tau out of the room. As the boy ran away Jamie heard him shouting, 'He hasn't got a gun and he's never seen a lion! He hasn't got a gun and he's never seen a lion!'

The triumphant litany went on and on until Tau's voice faded in the garden.

Jamie lay back frowning while Mrs Livingstone fussed round him. Then he said, 'Did a lion really try to eat your man, miss?'

Mary nodded. 'Dr Livingstone fired at the creature when it attacked him. The lion eventually dropped dead, but before it did it caused him fearful injuries.'

'What does a lion look like?' Jamie asked, puzzled.

Mary gazed down at the bed. 'Well, I could describe it to you, Jamie, but I can do better than that. I'll show you a picture of the animal. It's in a book. We'll look at it together this afternoon. Then I'll start to read to you about Africa.'

Africa.

For almost three weeks Jamie had heard about little else. Mary had started with her own father's book, Robert Moffat's *Missionary Travels* which, she told Jamie proudly, had been published five years before to public acclaim. She followed that by reading him the English translation of Renée Caillé's *Travels through Central Africa*. Afterwards she'd gone back in time to Richard Lander's *Record of Captain Clapperton's Last Expedition to Africa*.

Now she was embarking on an even earlier work, the journals of the great Mungo Park.

The names of the explorers and the dates of their expeditions meant nothing to Jamie. They floated vaguely through his head like the summer butterflies which migrated across Iona – appearing and vanishing with the sun and clouds. But the words they used, the images they evoked, the landscapes, peoples and animals they described, the customs and beliefs they recorded – all of them made an impression as vivid and indelible as the stories his grandmother had told him of Highland folklore.

Another world, an entire planet, took shape in Jamie's mind.

It was vast and remote, as huge and far and mysterious as the moon. It was full of terrifying dangers, of jungles and scorching deserts, of icy mountains and raging rivers, of deadly diseases and wild creatures of an unimaginable size and ferocity, of men with black skins who had never heard of God, who ate human flesh, and casually slaughtered each other in thousands as the whim took them.

Yet unlike the world of his grandmother's ballads and

fables, it was a world that existed now. At that very moment men like Mrs Livingstone's husband were exploring it.

'He must be a true hero, miss,' Jamie remarked thoughtfully one evening after she'd told him again, at Jamie's insistence and for perhaps the twentieth time, the story of Dr Livingstone and the lion.

A hero, in the vocabulary of Jamie's grandmother, was one of the ancient Highland warrior chieftains whose feats had passed into ballad and fable.

'In a way I suppose he is,' Mary sighed. 'But then every white man who goes to Africa on a quest like my husband's is a hero. Unfortunately, heroes aren't always the easiest of souls for us mere mortals to live with.'

Mrs Livingstone smiled wistfully.

Jamie barely heard the second part of her reply. He was staring intently through the window. His eyes were fixed on somewhere much more remote than the slate roofs of the Blantyre houses outside.

20

The contractions were gripping her at shorter and shorter intervals. Ozoro Esther could feel one starting now.

She arched her back. Sweat was pouring off her and she was trembling uncontrollably. Nothing she had been told had prepared her for the pain. Each time it came it was as if her stomach and hips were being wrenched apart by an immense pair of metal tongs.

Esther closed her eyes and screamed.

'Keep pushing, child,' she half-heard old Kalima saying. 'It will not be long now.'

The spasm passed and she slowly relaxed, sobbing. Kalima wiped her face with a damp cloth.

'Not long, I promise you,' the old servantwoman repeated.

Esther reached for Kalima's hand. Then she lay waiting in dread for the next agonizing assault on her body.

Esther was lying in one of the upper-floor chambers in the palace. It was a night in late summer and the candle-lit room, its air heavy with the scent of cedar-wood smoke, was stiflingly hot. The heat was made worse by the number of people there. The chamber had been divided in two by a tapestry curtain two-thirds of the way along its length. The smaller space had been set aside for the birth. The larger area beyond was intended to accommodate everyone waiting to learn the outcome. Yet so many people had arrived during the hours of Esther's labour, the throng had long since pushed its way through the curtain into the delivery area.

From time to time Kalima would leave the couch and beg them to retire.

It was a hopeless task. The crowd was too big, and the birth of an heir to the kingdom of Gondar too momentous an event for anyone to pay attention to the pleadings of an old woman.

Esther was left lying pain-racked and exhausted with the throng milling round her. Occasionally she was aware of faces she recognized.

Her grandmother, Iteghe, the old white-haired dowager empress of Gondar, came in and out accompanied by her ladies-in-waiting. So did Iteghe's daughters, Esther's aunts, and their children, friends and companions. The leaders of the church, including the brooding Salama, were constantly entering with their retinues of priests. Then there were the various dignitaries of the court, the chamberlains, ministers, secretaries and physicians. Finally there were the attendants, guards, musicians and entertainers – all of them infected by the drama of the occasion and all as anxious about the birth as the highest in the land.

'Push, child, push! Only a few more and it's over.'

It was another agonizing hour later.

Esther was squatting on the floor beside the couch now, with her legs parted and her hands gripping her knees. The pain of the contractions had become so violent it was almost unendurable.

She heard Kalima's voice as if the old woman were calling to her from an immense distance away. Esther shook her head weakly. She gathered herself and gave another frantic heave, trying desperately to rid herself of the tearing burden lodged inside her. Suddenly it began to move.

Screaming and weeping she heaved again and then again and then once more.

'There, lie easy, child.'

Inexplicably Kalima's voice was no longer urgent but soothing and comforting. Bewildered, Esther tried to look at her. She had been lifted back onto the couch. Figures were surging round her and the chamber echoed with a deep murmuring clamour.

Then she understood. There were no more contractions. The pain had ended and the weight had gone. It was over.

'What do I have?' she whispered.

'A daughter,' Kalima answered. 'The loveliest little girl I have ever seen.'

'Can I hold her?'

'Soon, child, soon,' Kalima said. 'There is something to be done first.'

Kalima had been kneeling beside her. The old woman stood up with the baby in her arms. The naked infant was pink and wrinkled and bellowing fiercely. Kalima wrapped it in a shawl and set off across the room.

The crowd fell silent and stood back to let her through.

Kalima crossed the floor and went out of the door at the far end. In the vaulted passage outside she turned right and headed for the apartments of Ras Michael.

It was nine months almost to the day since Esther had been taken down to the river cavern. The intervening time had been the most eventful of Esther's life. As soon as her pregnancy was certain she was married. Her husband, Georgis, the son of one of Gondar's great families, had been chosen for her by Ras Michael. Although Esther's father, the emperor, nominally ruled Gondar, the real ruler and the most powerful man in the kingdom remained the great white-bearded warlord.

It was entirely due to Ras Michael that the ancient royal dynasty still occupied the throne. The old emperor, Esther's grandfather and Ras Michael's contemporary, had been killed in a palace rebellion. Ras Michael, then a young country chieftain, rescued the son and began a campaign to put him on the throne. The campaign was long and bloody. Ten years after it started Ras Michael finally recaptured Gondar from the rebels and restored the line of Sheba to the palace.

Ever since he had been emperor in all but name.

During Esther's pregnancy her father had died. It meant that within nine months she had conceived, married, become empress in her own right, and had now given birth to her successor. Yet, as before, Ras Michael remained the true ruler of Gondar.

It was towards the Ras's apartments that Kalima hurried now with the infant.

Squatting between the guards outside the ageing warlord's door was Ras Michael's favourite servant, the dwarf Doho. Doho, a tiny misshapen figure with bandy legs, a huge head and an alert inquiring face, had served Ras Michael all his life.

He was waiting now for news from the birth chamber almost as anxiously as his master. When Kalima came into sight, Doho leapt to his feet. He took the baby from her and studied it intently. He conferred briefly with the old woman. Then he scurried into the room beyond.

Ras Michael was striding impatiently up and down.

'A girl-child, Ras,' Doho said.

'Uncover her,' the Ras commanded.

Doho pulled back the shawl and Michael peered down. Doho stared intently at the baby again.

'She appears to have everything,' Ras Michael ventured.

'Much more than that, Ras,' Doho said confidently. 'Believe me, this one's the perfect seed. Old Kalima delivered her. She has never seen an infant so well formed. The baby will grow into a flower.'

'You should know, you lecherous little creature. You've left your seed in enough of Gondar's blossoms.'

As Doho chuckled – his sexual exploits were a legend at the court – Ras Michael turned.

Hanging on the wall behind him was a huge ceremonial shield. It was made of old and intricately worked bronze, its curved outer surface set with panels of jewels. As Ras Michael took the shield down it flared and glittered in the light of the oil lamps. He balanced it in his hands and held it out towards Doho. The dwarf folded the robe round the baby again and laid her carefully inside.

Ras Michael carried the child towards the door that led to the balcony. Then he paused.

'What do we name her, Doho?' he asked.

The dwarf stood in silence for a moment, his face wrinkled in thought.

'When she comes to rule,' Doho said eventually, 'she will be a great beauty. It has always been said one day a queen would come lovelier than the great queen herself. When that day came she would be named with Sheba's own name, the name of the first mother of the river's child. Rachel. None has been named so since Sheba. This is the child, Ras.'

Ras Michael nodded.

'Call in the guards,' he said.

Doho shouted. The armed men who had been waiting outside ran into the room. Flanked by them Ras Michael stepped out on to the balcony.

The palace stood in the centre of Gondar overlooking the town's main square. From the square radiated avenues, streets and alleyways, reaching in every direction to the high walls that circled the town. Like the palace itself most of the houses and buildings were made of baked clay brick. By day, from the mountains above, Gondar looked like a great tapestry of tawny gold and ochre, draped over the ridge on which it was built and shot through with the silver threads of the glittering skeins of the river's waters.

At night the mountain colours vanished. Then it became a raucous bustling metropolis, flaring with torchlight and vibrating with music and clamour. The streets were always thronged after dark. That night they were more crowded than for years.

Since dawn the day before, when news ran through the town that the empress, as Esther now was, had gone into labour, Gondar's inhabitants had started to pour into the square. Now, in the early hours of the following morning, thousands of people stood there, jammed shoulder to shoulder. The heaving press of bodies had forced the crowds to spill back from the square, and fill the streets and alleys behind.

Drums were beating and flutes playing. Blazing tapers

cast their light over the upturned faces of the multitude. Packs of half-wild dogs howled and the horses of Gondar's nobility, each waiting with his own retinue of guards and servants, whinnied and jangled their bridles.

When the shutters opened and Ras Michael appeared, a vast expectant cry went up. Word had already reached the throng that something had happened, although no one knew exactly what.

The Ras walked forward to the stone balustrade and lifted the shield into the air above his head. The throng fell silent.

'I bring you Ozoro Rachel!' he shouted. 'I show you the daughter of the empress, and Gondar's future ruler. I give you the river's child!'

The shield gleamed with the reflections of thousands of lights from below. The soldiers beside him raised their spears and shook them in the darkness. A great roar lifted from the crowd.

'Ozoro, Ozoro, Ozoro Rachel!' they called. 'Hail to Rachel, child of Solomon and Sheba! Hail to the child of the river!'

The shouts rang out tumultuously for minutes on end. Long after Ras Michael had left the balcony with the baby and the shutters had been closed, the cheers were still rising into the summer night.

Ras Michael returned the child to Doho who in turn handed her back to Kalima. The old woman carried the infant back to the delivery chamber.

By then everyone, apart from a few servant girls who had helped Kalima with the birth, had gone. Kalima ordered the remaining few out of the room and approached the couch. There, for the first time, she laid the baby in Esther's arms. Esther took her wonderingly. She touched the child's face. Then she settled her against her cheek.

'Is she named?' she asked.

Kalima nodded. 'She is to be called Rachel after the great queen whose blood is hers. Long after both of us are gone, my child, your daughter will rule Gondar as her ancestor once did.'

The old woman gazed at the much younger one.

The baby was lying howling on Esther's breast. Kalima put her arms round Esther. The old servant and the young queen-empress both began to cry. Their tears had nothing to do with the past or the future, the kingdom or its inheritance.

They were simply tears of relief and happiness at the linking presence between them of a new life.

21

The wooden top was painted in brilliant bands of colour.

It had a long neck, a swollen centre like an evenly shaped ripe gourd, then it narrowed at the base to the sharp tip of its balancing point. Doho the dwarf wound the cord round the groove that years of use had worn down in the neck. He rubbed the two strings furiously between his flattened palms and suddenly jerked them away.

The top throbbed and began to move across the stone terrace, gathering speed as it went.

'Wait!' Doho said. 'Don't move until I tell you!'

Behind him Rachel hitched up the skirt of her shift so it wouldn't tangle with her legs. She followed the top's progress with a child's intent frowning concentration. The top skipped a gap in the flagstones and approached the step down to the grass beyond.

'Now!' the dwarf called. 'Run like the wind!'

Rachel threw herself forward.

The top, a whirling humming rainbow, was racing away. She dodged round the little fountain, scampered over the last few yards of the terrace, and stretched out her arm. Her hand folded round it just before the top tumbled on to the ground below.

'Wonderful!' Doho was applauding wildly. 'I couldn't have done it better myself. We'll make a tumbler of you yet, young lady. Shall we do it again?'

Her cheeks flushed with pride, Rachel nodded.

She retired behind the line Doho had chalked on the stones and waited while he re-wound the cord round the top's neck. Then she gathered up her skirt ready to sprint forward once more.

Rachel was five.

In the years since Doho had first seen her as a bellowing infant with a crumpled scarlet face and tightly closed eyelids, she had developed into an extraordinarily beautiful child. She had Esther's pale skin, her slender well-made body, and her long black hair, lustrous and straight. Her eyes were her mother's too, clear and dark and shining. Everything else was her own — or perhaps came from the line of the father she had never known.

Rachel was taller than Esther had been at the same age. Her face was finer and bolder. Even at twenty-two Esther's cheeks were already beginning to thicken. Rachel's features in contrast, as Doho remarked to Ras Michael one day, looked as if they had been carved out of the mountain air.

'The snow and the winds must have made them,' the dwarf said.

The old warlord studied the child. He grunted gruffly in agreement at Doho's assessment. Then Ras Michael stumped away.

In temperament Rachel was even more different from her mother. Esther was placid and outgoing. She was given to laughter. She made friends quickly. Apart from a lazy easily satisfied curiosity, Esther questioned nothing. Rachel, in contrast, was a reserved and private child. She lacked the ready gift of laughing, although on the rare occasions when she did laugh the sound welled out in a joyous cataract of happiness.

But the biggest difference between mother and daughter was in Rachel's intelligence. Alert and quick, Rachel asked questions constantly. The child was passionately interested in the world around her. She wanted to know everything, to have everything explained.

'Why do the swallows go when the leaves fall?' she demanded one evening as the summer ended, and she and Doho were walking in the park. 'And where do they go to?'

Doho glanced at her in surprise. 'How do you know they go?'

'Because I can see them, of course,' Rachel replied. 'One day they're here, the next they're not. Look, they're getting ready to leave now – '

She pointed. A flock of swallows preparing to migrate was circling and twittering anxiously above them in the fading light.

'You know where you take me to watch the caravans come in?' Rachel went on.

Doho nodded.

Beneath the eastern walls of the palace was a large open courtyard, where the Arab caravans from the coast had to report when they arrived in the city. There the loads were examined and taxed by the royal chamberlains, before the merchants were allowed to proceed to Gondar's great covered market.

The courtyard was one of Rachel's favourite places in the city.

She made Doho take her there as often as she could. She loved the colour and excitement of the caravans' arrival. The little Nubian boys who darted ahead through the clouds of dust screaming to clear the way. The cracking of whips as the huge lumbering camels came into sight. The creaking laden carts, each flying the banner of Islam. The proud hawk-nosed merchants in their brilliant cloaks riding their glossy horses. The beating drums and the rockets fired into the sky that announced the last waggon had passed beneath the entrance arch.

'When we went there yesterday,' Rachel said, 'I saw some of the birds fly down and perch on a waggon. I thought they might stay there and ride back with the caravan to the sea.'

She looked uncertainly at Doho.

Doho chuckled. 'You're a very observant young woman but, no, the birds don't ride on the waggons to the sea. Swallows are rather like you. They've got sharp eyes and they need to eat. When they see winter's coming, they fly away to somewhere it's warmer and there's more food.'

'Where's the somewhere?'

Doho rubbed his chin. 'Far away.' He gestured vaguely towards the north.

Rachel glanced at him through her wide level eyes.

The first part of the dwarf's answer satisfied her. The second did not. She sensed Doho didn't know where the swallows went in winter. It didn't matter. One day she'd find out for herself.

On another occasion they passed a detachment of the royal bodyguards. There were hundreds of guards all over the palace – so many, it seemed to Rachel, that sometimes they were like a great living rope of scarlet that twisted from one end of the building to the other.

Rachel looked at their dazzling red cloaks billowing out behind their shoulders as they marched. She paused frowning by Doho's side.

'Why are the soldiers' cloaks red, Doho?' she demanded.

The dwarf thought for a moment. 'Because it's a lovely colour,' he said.

'Blue's even better,' Rachel replied. 'That's what my mother and the emperor wear. So why don't their soldiers wear it, too?'

Doho wrinkled his face in thought.

It had never occurred to him before, and he didn't know. Sometimes, the dwarf reflected with affectionate irritation, the child was almost too alert and inquiring.

'I will find out,' he answered shortly.

That night he consulted his master, Ras Michael. The Ras told him the royal bodyguards were deemed to be invincible. They had always worn red cloaks so that the emperor's enemies would never know whether or not they had been wounded in battle.

Doho told Rachel the reason the following day. She nodded and smiled mischievously as she listened to him.

'When I'm empress,' she said, 'I'll make you wear a red cloak, Doho. Then when you're wounded defending me, you can bleed and bleed and no one will know either.'

The dwarf snorted and lifted his hand to cuff her, but Rachel ran away laughing. Cursing under his breath, Doho watched her. Then he burst into laughter too.

Doho adored the child in every way. Most of all, with his own quick brain, he loved her for her mind. With Ras Michael's tacit approval the dwarf had made himself her tutor. Rachel had her own retinue of nursemaids, instructors and servants, and children of her own age were often brought to the palace for her to play with. But Doho was her favourite companion.

The dwarf knew it had given him a matchless chance to become the most important influence on her childhood. It was an opportunity he was determined not to waste. He set out to teach her everything he knew.

'Right,' Doho said after he'd spun the top a further dozen times. 'Now we're going to do something different, something quite new.'

Rachel gazed at him, her eyes bright with interest. 'What is it?' she demanded.

'It's a game called the naming of the plain,' he answered. 'It's about remembering the names of all the villages, hills and streams you can see from the walls. If you remember enough you get a prize. If you get them all right, it's a big prize. Come on and I'll tell you how it's played.'

With Rachel trotting excitedly behind him he set off through the park towards the garden of the nightingales, where Esther had sat looking over the plain of Gondar on the day she went down to the river.

The kingdom of Gondar was never entirely tranquil.

The ceaseless tides of dispute, war, conquest and retaliation that plagued all the countries of the Mountains of the Moon, and the lands far beyond Abyssinia, prevented that.

Yet during Rachel's childhood Gondar enjoyed a period of remarkable peace and prosperity. The natural riches of the countryside depended on rain. For an unusual number of years in succession the rains were good. Food was abundant. Even in the remotest villages the inhabitants thrived. The excellent harvests inevitably attracted raids from beyond Gondar's borders, but in Ras Michael the kingdom had a powerful and resolute protector.

By inclination and experience the great warlord was a soldier.

The Ras believed utterly in the primacy of the army. Over the decade before Rachel's birth he had built Gondar's army into the best-trained and most effective in Abyssinia. It was his personal weapon and although the Ras was starting to show signs of age – his hair was whitening fast and he could no longer jump into the saddle from the ground when he rode – he still used it with the vigour and decisiveness of a much younger man.

The kingdom's borders were stoutly defended. Marauding bands were chased out of the country and punished mercilessly if they were caught. All of settled Africa knew, for the intelligence travelled swiftly everywhere along the far-flung routes of the caravans, that Sheba's ancient lands were in firm and resolute hands.

The river's child, it came to be said, slept as safely in her bed as the sun when it dipped into the cradle that the spirits held out below the western horizon.

At the same time Ras Michael used the army to keep order inside Gondar. The justice it dealt out was swift, rough and often brutal. Yet compared to the violence and lawlessness of other African nations at the time, Gondar was stable and safe for citizen and traveller alike. The royal family were more than happy to leave the country's affairs in the Ras's capable hands. So too were Gondar's other great landowning families, its powerful merchants, and the citizens of the capital.

For all of them those years would be remembered nostalgically for as long as they lived as a time of unprecedented good fortune.

Only one faction in the kingdom was unhappy with the combination of good harvests and Ras Michael's iron rule – the church. Based largely on superstition and secret ritual, Gondar's ancient church, as it had long ago discovered, fared best in times of famine. The people needed it urgently then to intercede for them and placate whatever God or spirit was denying them their crops and killing their stock.

When the crops came home in laden waggons and the cattle wintered with glossy coats, the church was worth at most token acknowledgement – at worst it became an irrelevance.

The church's unhappiness was compounded by the role Ras Michael had created for the army. In the past, even in times of plenty, the church had been able to use its traditional authority to regulate matters in Gondar's towns and villages. Now the army had taken over that task. When disputes needed settling, the villagers no longer went to their local priest – they turned instead to the area's military commander.

They had learned he was certainly no worse a judge than the priest and he cost no more to bribe. But unlike the priest, he could enforce his judgement on the spot with his sword.

To the country people any decision had always been better than no decision – and the army's decisions had teeth.

The disquiet was felt at every level in Gondar's priestly hierarchy from the lowliest country curate to the great bishops in the capital. No one experienced it more keenly and bitterly than the Acab Saat. For the intensely ambitious Salama they were years of almost unendurable frustration.

Salama wanted nothing less than control of the entire kingdom.

He had always done so. Even that was only a beginning. With Gondar in his power he was certain he could subdue Malinda to the north and the country of the Galla beyond it. It would give him all the central highlands of Abyssinia. With them as a base he could start to move out into the rest of Africa. Beyond the

Mountains of the Moon the horizons stretched out almost to infinity. However far they reached, Salama was determined to cross and conquer them.

Like the young Alexander he saw no limits. The empire he was going to create would span the entire continent.

Salama's time would come. Until it did he would have to wait. The rains monotonously continued. The grip of Ras Michael and his army remained as tight as ever on the land. Salama loathed the ageing white-haired warlord, but there was nothing he could do to dislodge him. So he kept his counsel and his pride. He joined the Ras in his weekly meetings with the emperor. He was cordial and frank in giving his views, the views of the church. He argued vigorously in defending the church's position.

Then, when he was overruled as he invariably was, Salama left the chamber smiling good-humouredly. Georgis was weak and inept. The Ras was stiffening with every passing season. The rains could not last for ever. Time was the Acab Saat's ally. He could afford to be patient.

Salama continued to be patient in every way but one – the exercise of his lust.

With one exception every woman in Gondar was available to him. The exception was Esther. As Gondar's queen-empress she was untouchable. Highly charged, bored, restless and frustrated, but most of all driven by a sexual desire that eventually became obsessive, Salama decided he must possess her.

It was the only reckless decision he ever took and it proved to be fateful both for the course of his own life and the history of Gondar.

— 22 —

Salama was physically attracted to Esther even before she reached maturity.

There was something infinitely sensual about the graceful long-legged child which, try as he might, he could not find in any of the village girls of her age he ordered to be brought to his room.

When her body changed to a woman's the desire became even stronger. In part it was simply the response he would have had for any flawlessly made young woman just after she'd passed through puberty. She was like one of the first perfect fruits of early summer – ripe and fresh and rounded, with the bloom untouched on her skin and the juices thick in her.

Yet that was only one part of her attraction. It had another, far more provocative and insidious dimension.

Esther was inviolable to any except the man chosen to be father to the river's child, and then later to her husband. To penetrate her was sacrilege. It was also treason. It gave Esther an extraordinarily enticing allure. Somehow, with the instincts of someone who had barely left childhood, she was aware of it – and the power it conferred on her.

Esther flaunted herself, it seemed to Salama.

Whenever the heat bore down on Gondar she would wear a shift that was almost transparent, with nothing beneath it. He would see the guards staring at her wide-eyed and bemused as she passed. If Salama met her in the park or the palace corridors, she would slow her pace and smile at him beguilingly. Sometimes she would sit on one of the carved stone benches. She would pull up her skirt, and examine her leg for a mosquito bite. Once the light cloth slipped back from her bent knee and Salama glimpsed a tunnel of sunlit flesh leading to the cone of shadow at her groin.

He stared transfixed at the dusky triangle between her legs.

Sweating, he smiled and nodded at her, and moved on. To Salama she was, as always, teasing and humiliating him. By the time he reached Ras Michael's audience room he was hot not just from the sun – but with a tangled charge of lust and anger.

It never occurred to the Acab Saat that Esther wore the lightest shift she could find because of Gondar's summer heat. That she was still in many ways a child. That for reasons she couldn't define, she disliked and feared the powerful bearded bishop, and the searching way he stared at her each time they met. That she sat and pretended to look for insect bites in the hope that he would continue on his way and leave her alone. That she had no interest in him whatever, and all she wanted to do was to be left alone to play and laugh with the servant girls she had known all her life.

The relationship between them began to change after Salama delivered the young man, Raghe, into the cavern at the river's source.

Angry and jealous, Salama had sent the youth up the passage to Esther. Raghe, an ignorant village boy, was on his way to do what was denied even the Acab Saat – to plunge down between Esther's thighs and feast on the pale-skinned princess.

When Salama drove his dagger into Raghe and tossed him to the crocodiles, the Acab Saat was doing more than simply following tradition – he was vindictively taking his own revenge.

With Raghe, Ozoro Esther experienced sex for the first time. She found it simple, exciting and immensely enjoyable. After Raghe vanished she missed him acutely, partly as a young man she'd become fond of but much more for the loss of the physical pleasure he had given her. During the later stages of her pregnancy the absence of sex mattered less. A few months after Rachel's birth her yearning for it returned even more strongly than before.

By then she was married to Georgis – and Georgis was a homosexual.

For several weeks the amiable but weak and selfish young man managed to avoid sleeping with Esther. Then one night he drank a great deal of wine and nerved himself to go to her room. The result was a humiliating failure. Georgis fumbled and lunged at her for almost half an hour, but in spite of the wine and all Esther's encouragement he could do nothing.

Furious with himself and disgusted at what he'd been through, Georgis left her chamber and went on drinking until he lost consciousness.

'I'm sorry,' Georgis said to her next morning, flushed with embarrassment but determined he would never undergo the revolting humiliation again. 'I am made differently, and there is nothing I can do to change it. You have your child and the kingdom has an heir. That's enough. Except in public from now on we will live separately. I hope you will be happy.'

Bewildered and tearful, Esther watched him walk away.

Later, still in tears, Esther consulted Kalima. The old woman comforted her but said it was the way of the world and that as the king's wife she would have to accept it. Besides, she added, echoing Georgis, she had Rachel – was not that enough?

Rachel was not enough.

As a start, once Rachel was weaned the baby was given her own quarters, where she was so hemmed in with nurses and servants it seemed to Esther she barely saw her. But even if the child had been with her, Esther knew it would have made no difference. What she was missing was something no baby could provide. She was a healthy and uninhibited young woman, and she wanted what the naked Raghe had given her.

Bored, restless and unhappy, she began to roam the halls and gardens of the palace again. Inevitably she often came across the Acab Saat.

In the past Salama's hot searching glances had not only frightened Esther – they had bewildered her too. Now she understood what provoked them. She had seen the same hungry look in Raghe's eyes when he visited her. The realization was intriguing. It somehow reduced Salama from the status of a fearsome ogre to a normal, if still awesome, human being.

Esther remained scared of the Acab Saat and she hadn't yet conquered her instinctive dislike of the powerful brooding priest, but she no longer froze inside and turned away when he approached. Now she could look him levelly in the face.

There were other things about Salama which intrigued her.

After a while she sensed that almost every man in the palace, from Ras Michael's grey-bearded ministers to the young guards, responded to her in the same way as Salama did. But they all took great care to conceal what they felt. They lowered their eyes or coughed and turned away when she came by. Not the Acab Saat. He looked at her if anything even more boldly than before, and he didn't hesitate to let his eyes travel deliberately up and down her body.

Salama wasn't slow to notice the change in Esther.

At first he put it down to an increase in her confidence after the child's birth. It allowed her to be even more provocative and taunting – increasing both his anger and his lust. Then Salama began to wonder. Georgis's tastes were common knowledge. He was unlikely to be satisfying her. Certainly no one else in the palace would dare take his place in her bed.

Perhaps Esther was trying to convey an entirely different message to him.

Salama started to study her more closely. He couldn't detect anything approaching an invitation in her behaviour. Equally there was no sign of rejection. Once or twice he even thought there was a speculative look in her eyes when she stared at him.

Salama's excitement mounted each time they met. Finally the temptation to satisfy it became irresistible.

Esther slept in a room in the western wing of the palace. Next to her and linked by a communicating door was the baby Rachel's bedchamber. The only acknowledgement that she was the child's mother, Esther often reflected ruefully, seemed to be that Rachel was allowed to sleep in the adjoining room. A little further along the corridor, and again linked to Rachel's bedroom by a door, was the room where her two nurses slept – ready to come through and attend to her if the baby woke during the night.

There were guards at either end of the corridor but a large number of other chambers led off it, including those the king used as his private quarters.

Salama's plan was simple.

He would visit Georgis after supper, as he often did, and stay talking to the young man until it was late. Then he would leave. By then Esther would be in bed. He would walk down the corridor, enter her room, and approach her. If she rejected him and even called out, the only people likely to hear were the nurses. They were simple and uneducated women from the plain. If they appeared, Salama would say he was there to give the queen a blessing before she slept, and sternly order them away.

Given his familiar presence and his chilling authority, Salama was certain they would leave instantly. Esther might continue to scream, but he very much doubted it. The situation would be too ambiguous and compromising, and she had, he guessed, enough sense to know it.

If the worst happened Salama would retire and the matter would be ended.

Yet the more he thought about it, the more he watched Esther when they met, the less he believed it would finish like that. She wanted a man, he became increasingly sure. There was only one man available at the court, one man who was bold and experienced enough to give her what she wanted, and it was the Acab Saat.

Salama chose his night with care.

He waited until the height of the summer when the palace was at its quietest. To avoid the worst of the heat, many of those who lived there during the rest of the year had retreated to their houses higher up in the mountains. The king had to stay behind, so did Esther, and so too did Ras Michael.

Salama went to the king's room after supper. Georgis, who had a young man with him, was listless and irritable. Salama spun out their conversation for as long as he could. Then, with Georgis yawning, he left.

Esther's room was fifteen paces down the corridor on the left.

Salama entered swiftly but quietly. The room was in darkness but in the gleam of the starlight from the open window Salama saw she was asleep. He went over to the bed and drew back the thin cotton coverlet lying rumpled over her. Beneath it she was naked.

His breathing quickening, Salama reached down and fondled her breasts.

Esther opened her eyes and stared up at him. She didn't react to his touch, she simply lay there passive and silent. Salama smiled. He was right. Whatever she was feeling, and in a moment he'd make her feel exactly what he wanted, she wasn't going to reject him.

Salama stroked the mound of hair between her legs.

As desire suddenly flooded over him, he stepped back. He lifted his gown and pulled it over his head. He was going to savour every inch of her. He was going to enjoy the young woman naked. But before he did he was going to arouse her too.

Salama lowered his head over her parted thighs and thrust out his tongue.

Doho the dwarf was hot and restless.

He shifted uncomfortably on the little straw-filled mattress. Then he sat up and rubbed his neck. Ever since Ras Michael had moved into Gondar from his fortress in the hills years ago, Doho had slept at the door of the room the old warlord had taken for himself inside the palace. The Ras had often offered him quarters of his own, but Doho was happy where he was. There was a roof over his head. Apart from that Doho was occupying the same space that had been his at the entrance to Michael's tent during the long years of campaigning.

Like the old Ras, Doho slept less now than he did then.

When Gondar's heat was as sticky as it was tonight, Doho sometimes found it difficult to sleep at all. Thinking wistfully of the breezes that used to cool him in the mountains, he decided to go out into the park. All the palace doors were locked and guarded after dark, but as the Ras's dwarf Doho was one of the few people free to go anywhere at any time.

He stood up and walked down the long passage.

As he passed the door to the king's apartment the light inside went out. The low murmur of voices continued and he could hear the sound of a man giggling. Georgis was obviously entertaining another of his 'friends'.

Doho sniffed contemptuously. Then he scuttled on. Further along the passage, opposite the door to Rachel's bedroom, he paused. Whenever he roamed the palace at night, Doho always liked to look in and see that all was well with the child. She had her nurses of course but with his fiercely protective attitude towards the future queen-empress, Doho was never satisfied until he'd checked for himself.

He crossed the corridor and tiptoed in.

Rachel was sleeping quietly on her wood-framed bed, its calico-covered mattress filled with fresh springy plantain. Smiling, Doho gazed down at her. He bent over the bed and kissed her gently on the forehead. As he turned to go, he heard a noise from the room beyond. Doho stopped. It was the room where Esther, the child's mother, slept. He listened and heard the sound again – a panting followed by a moan.

Puzzled, Doho crept across the floor. He opened the communicating door a crack, and looked through.

Instantly the dwarf froze.

Esther was lying naked on her back with her legs parted. Kneeling on the bed above her was the burly figure of a man. He too was naked. The man's head was lowered between her thighs and his tongue was pumping at her groin. The starlight wasn't strong enough for Doho to make out the man's face, but the dwarf knew he wasn't Georgis.

As Doho crouched, shocked and astounded, Esther moaned again. The sound was louder than before. For the dwarf it was enough. He didn't pause to wonder whether it was a cry of fear or pleasure. He simply assumed she was being raped. In his belt was a short curved dagger. Doho plucked the dagger from its sheath.

Doho hurled open the door, and leapt into the room.

'Stop!' he shouted.

Salama's head jerked up.

The Acab Saat's chin glistened wetly with his own saliva and the juices from Esther's body. Before he could jump down from the bed the dwarf was on him. Salama saw the dagger flash in the air and threw up his arm. The blade slashed across his elbow.

Grunting with pain, Salama managed to kick Doho in the chest.

As the dwarf reeled back, Salama scrambled off the bed. His eyes swept the room. He spotted a heavy iron poker by the fireplace and seized it. Doho, recovering his balance, vaulted the bed and ran along the wall on the far side.

Filled with murderous rage, Salama set off after him.

Salama's loathing for Ras Michael extended to his retinue. He had always hated this malign little creature more than any of the Ras's servants. Now he was going to beat him to death. His knuckles white with fury as they tightened round the iron bar, he circled the bed towards the dwarf.

Salama would certainly have done what he intended. He half-caught Doho once with a vicious blow that glanced off the bedpost. The dwarf, almost stunned, managed to pull himself under a chair. Then, as Salama tried to drag the chair away, the room suddenly filled with noise and light and people.

Doho's shouts had reached the guards. It had also woken Rachel, her nurses, and almost everyone else along the corridor. Rachel began to cry. The nurses rushed through. The guards poured in with their lanterns and their spears.

A moment later Ras Michael and his attendants appeared.

As the Ras surveyed the scene Esther, still naked and weeping now, ran out to comfort her daughter. Salama dropped the iron poker. He caught up the bedcover, wrapped it round him, and stared aggressively across the floor.

'Pick up the little man,' Ras Michael said quietly.

Two of his attendants ran forward. They lifted Doho, limp and bleeding from the head, and carried the dwarf away.

'Return to your house, Acab,' the Ras went on. 'It does not need an old soldier's eye to understand what was attempted here. The simplest man in Gondar could see it plain. You will attend the king's council in the morning.'

Silent but still furious and defiant, Salama strode from the room.

Ras Michael waited until the sound of his footsteps

faded in the passage. Then he ordered everyone else out too. Afterwards he walked through to Rachel's bedroom.

The nurses had retired, leaving a small oil lamp burning on the table by the bed. Esther, huddled in a cloak now, was sitting on the bed cradling her daughter in her arms. The child was asleep again. Esther's cheeks were still bright with tears and she glanced up fearfully as the Ras came in.

The old warlord walked stiffly over and stood looking down at her.

'I have three questions to ask you, child,' Ras Michael said. 'The first – was that the first time this has happened?'

Too frightened to speak, Esther nodded.

'The second is this,' the Ras went on, 'is there any chance you may be with child after tonight?'

Still without speaking Esther shook her head.

Ras Michael stared at her for a long time. Then, apparently satisfied, he nodded.

'The third question would have been – did you invite him to your room?' Ras Michael paused. Before the terrified Esther had even understood what he was saying, the Ras continued. 'I will not now ask you to reply. What you have said is enough. But I tell you this – '

Ras Michael stopped again. When he went on his voice was suddenly chill and menacing.

'You are mother to the child of the river,' he said. 'Never forget it. Never forget that unless your husband seeds you, the river's child is all you will ever be mother to. And I mean ever. You are innocent tonight, young woman, because it is seemly and prudent you should be so. But if this ever happened again you would be required to answer the third question – and God help you if your answer was not accepted.'

He left the room. For a long time afterwards Esther sat on the bed shivering and sobbing.

The council chamber was a large vaulted room on the ground floor of the palace. At one end was a raised alcove screened from the body of the room by a curtain. Behind the curtain the emperor sat hidden, listening to the deliberations of his ministers on the floor below.

Apart from the emperor's appointed ministers the council was composed of Gondar's noblemen, the country's great landowners, its generals, bishops, and the richest and most powerful of its merchants. Salama presented himself before them the following morning. Ras Michael himself put the case against the Acab Saat.

The Ras's speech lasted barely five minutes.

The Acab Saat, he said, had attempted to violate the queen. There could be no disputing the facts. He had been discovered naked in her bedroom late at night by a dozen witnesses. Even ordinary adultery was among Gondar's most serious crimes. Any citizen convicted of it was liable to be sold into slavery. The attempted rape of the country's queen was infinitely graver.

There could only be one punishment – death.

Salama's defence was bitter, furious and rambling. Apart from his presence in Esther's room, he denied everything. He had visited the queen at her request to hear her confession. It was a normal part of his duties as the royal bishop. He had been fully dressed throughout and nothing else had happened. Anyone who claimed otherwise was a perjurer.

The charges against him were a vile conspiracy by his enemies at court.

'Furthermore,' Salama finished, 'as the Ras knows well there is no penalty of death for the bishops of the church. We are not answerable to Gondar's law, but to another higher law. If such a sentence was pronounced against me, sacrilege would be committed by the entire country. From that moment on while breath remained I would excommunicate every man, woman, and child who came within my sight – '

Salama stabbed out his hand and extended his finger. His eyes blazed with fury beside the curving hawk's-bill of his nose.

'Starting with this assembly here, each and every one

will be severed from the grace of the Almighty and cast for ever into darkness.'

Glowering and unrepentant he stared round the chamber.

Excommunication was a chilling threat. Its effect was exactly what Salama intended. With the exception of the Ras, everyone in the gathering backed nervously away.

'The king will give his judgement,' Ras Michael said imperturbably.

He crossed the floor and climbed the steps that led to the alcove.

As the Ras parted the curtain there was a rare smile on his lined and scarred face.

Ras Michael was well satisfied with the events of the past twelve hours. He had wanted to be rid of the Acab Saat for years. In being discovered naked in Esther's room, however he had come to be there, Salama had played into his hands. There had of course, unfortunately, never been any question of executing him. The Ras knew that Salama would threaten excommunication, and he had demanded the death penalty only to frighten the others present.

But there was another penalty which would suit Ras Michael's purposes almost as well.

The old warlord bent over the emperor and whispered in his ear in a pretence of consulting him. As everyone out of sight on the far side of the curtain knew, it was a charade. Ras Michael and not the emperor would decide what happened to Salama, just as the Ras decided everything else in the kingdom.

The Ras reappeared. He climbed down the steps, and walked to the centre of the chamber where he stood facing Salama.

'The king has found you guilty of the charge against you,' Ras Michael said. 'But in his wisdom and mercy and out of his deep respect for the church, he has decided you shall not be executed. Instead you will be exiled from Gondar for life. You have until dusk, Acab, to deal with your affairs. Then you will start your journey to the kingdom's borders.'

For the briefest instant Salama seemed to waver.

The colour left his cheeks. Then the Acab Saat stiffened. His face flushed with anger and his eyes blazed again.

'You and all those in this chamber today,' he said, 'will regret this until your last hours and in the darkness that lies beyond them. I shall return to Gondar – and may God have pity on you when I do, for I will not!'

Two weeks later Salama crossed the kingdom's borders.

With a small company of retainers, Gondar's former royal bishop and Guardian of the Holy Fire rode in bitterness and vengeance as an exile into neighbouring Malinda.

— 24 —

'Please, miss, I'm no tired the yet,' Jamie pleaded. 'A wee bit more and I'll sleep straight, I promise ye.'

Mary Livingstone shook her head. It happened every evening now. The child's appetite to learn about Africa was insatiable.

She smiled indulgently as she looked down at him.

Jamie came from Iona. Mary had never seen the island, but her husband had. He had grown up within daily sight of it – or so he claimed. Dr Livingstone, already famous and a household name in the educated world of the west, had taken publicly to describing himself as an 'Ulva man'. Ulva was another, even tinier, rocky Hebridean island just to the north of Iona and lashed by the same Atlantic gales.

Dr Livingstone, Mary knew, was lying. He had never even seen Ulva, let alone set foot on it.

Why her husband laid claim to Ulva as his home, Mary had no idea. Possibly it gave him the roots he had never had, possibly its very nearness to the sacred isle satisfied some unfulfilled childhood yearning. Mary didn't know. What she did know – and she was one of the very few who did – was that David Livingstone was born and had grown up in Blantyre on the outskirts of Glasgow. His father came from Ulva, that was true, but David himself had never as much as visited the Hebrides.

Dr Livingstone's passionate allegiance to an island he had never cast eyes on was just another of the troubling enigmas in the tormented mind of the man she had married.

Jamie was different. Jamie was neither her husband

nor her son. He didn't beget David's difficulties, nor did he stand to inherit them. Jamie stood alone. Yet the lean sparely built boy with his tumbling red hair and his keen Hebridean eyes, as fathomless as the blue-grey waters that tumbled over Iona's rocks, did unquestionably come from the sacred isle.

Jamie's true home was the island her husband now pretended he had grown up in sight of.

Mary Livingstone sighed. It was all very complicated.

Mary made no pretence of understanding the complications. All she knew was that they stemmed entirely from her husband. All the troubles in her life always had. David had driven her almost distraught. He had broken her health, destroyed her faith, killed – it was not too strong a word – one of her children. Yet she loved him still. And in loving him, she accepted his fantasies.

Dr Livingstone had a dream-like allegiance to Iona.

The freckle-faced boy Jamie, with his fierce and troubled features, was a true child of Saint Columba's island kingdom. Somehow in Mary's mind and emotions the two, her gaunt haunted husband and the starving fevered lad that Dr Cameron had picked up on the Oban quay, became entwined. Mary would give Jamie more, allow him more, than the children of her own body – she would even chase her beloved but mischievous son Tau from the room when she was reading to Jamie.

She turned the page.

'Just five minutes then,' she said.

As Mary Livingstone read on, Jamie listened with total absorbed concentration.

The men whose lives and adventures Mrs Livingstone read out to him – the heroes of Jamie's thoughts and dreams – were taking the word of God to the heathen. At the same time they were also waging war against the institution of slavery. That much had been clear almost from the start.

Yet as Mrs Livingstone went on, it came to Jamie that the great heroes of her stories were also searching for something. They were all in their different ways engaged on a mighty quest – even Dr Livingstone, the greatest of them all, was in his wife's words embarked on a 'noble inquiry'.

What gradually emerged was that they were all pursuing the source of a river. The river was called the Nile. It was the longest and largest river in the world – so wide at its mouth that it was difficult to see from side to side. In his mind Jamie tried to compare it with the tumbling burns on Iona, the only streams he had ever known. It was impossible.

According to Mrs Livingstone the Nile could have accommodated ten Ionas in a line and still left space for its waters to pour through between them to the sea.

Even harder to understand was why the men were so anxious to find the river's source. For days Jamie puzzled over the question. Then he asked Mrs Livingstone.

'Why?' Mary thought for a moment. 'Do you remember from the bible, Jamie, about the river of life?'

'Aye,' Jamie nodded. 'I mind it well.'

His grandmother had often read that part to him.

'Well, in a way all rivers are rivers of life,' Mary went on. 'Think of the streams on Iona. Didn't they nourish fish? Wasn't the grass thicker and richer on the banks where they ran? Didn't cattle go to them to drink and people build their houses nearby for the same reason?'

Jamie reflected. It had never occurred to him before, but Mrs Livingstone was right. He nodded again.

'Aye,' he said. 'Ma sisters and me, we used to guddle the wee burn for trout.'

'Then think of the biggest river in the world,' Mary continued. 'A river supporting not just a few crofts like yours, but millions of people. A river that somewhere has its secret beginning. Imagine what it would be like to find where that was. Perhaps the Nile is the real river of life. Perhaps the Garden of Eden lay at its source – '

She paused. 'The man who discovers it will be famous for ever. But much more than that, think what he might find there. He might find the fount of life itself.'

Jamie looked reflectively at the sky over the slate roofs of Blantyre. The air was heavy with dust from the coal-yards at the edge of the town, and the gathering evening clouds were blurred and hazy.

An African sky, Jamie guessed, would glow with the bright scintillating brilliance of the bay at Camas Cuil when the sun was high, the western wind was still, and nothing troubled the island's shining waters. What the still dark pools of the river of life would throw back to the African air, Jamie couldn't even begin to imagine.

'Do ye reckon your husband will get there first, miss?' Jamie asked.

'That is in God's hands, young man, not mine or his,' Mary answered.

'Well, if he doesna,' Jamie said, 'mebbe I'll be the one.'

Mary looked across at the still pale-faced and hollow-cheeked child with his determined blue eyes and rumpled red hair. She smiled.

Mary Livingstone went on reading.

Jamie would have been happy if she had continued to read to him for months. It was not to be. That Tuesday morning he had exactly five days of her company left. On Saturday she finished Mungo Park's *Travels*. When she turned off the lamp and said goodnight, Mary promised that the following day she would start on a new volume after the Sunday morning service.

Sunday morning came.

The hour for the service arrived and passed. Still Mary did not arrive. Jamie shifted restlessly in his bed. Finally he heard the murmur of voices below. He swung himself down to the floor and tiptoed across the room.

Opening the door, Jamie tried to make out what was being said in the hall below.

— 25 —

'Not one moment longer!' Mrs Cameron's voice was bleak and determined.

Standing in front of her in the parlour, Dr Cameron rubbed his hands together and creased his face unhappily.

'Flora, it is only supposition – ' he began, but his wife cut him off.

'Supposition?' she snapped. 'Do you really believe I cannot tell the smell of alcohol on a person's breath? It was sickening, Charles. And what about the so-called "headache"?'

'You may have confused the smell with some medicament, my dear,' Cameron said. 'Surely, if Mary had a headache it would be quite normal for her to take a restorative.'

'In which case, did she consult you first?' Mrs Cameron demanded.

Cameron shook his head. 'No, I agree she did not. But then of course her husband is also a doctor. Perhaps David prescribed a medicine before she returned home,' he finished lamely.

'Your cousin, David Livingstone, is mad,' Mrs Cameron said brutally. 'His wife, to whom you have so graciously made available our house quite regardless of my convenience, is a tippler – '

Her face tightened with disgust as she spoke the word.

'That is not all. There was no "headache" this morning. Quite deliberately she chose not to attend the kirk. And furthermore you may be interested to read this – '

Mrs Cameron produced a letter from a drawer in the mahogany escritoire she used as a desk. She handed it to her husband with a flourish.

'What, I am entitled to ask, were you and your cousin's wife doing on the stairs last night when I chanced on the two of you as I went to bed?'

Cameron stared at her, appalled. 'Flora, what are you suggesting? Mary had just turned off the child's lamp. We were discussing his progress – '

'Really?' Mrs Cameron interrupted him again. 'Please read the letter, Charles. After all, it is from another of your cousins.'

She gave a thin triumphant smile.

Cameron took the letter and began to read. As he did a chill spread over him. The letter was in reply to one from his wife. It was written by his sister-in-law, Sara Carnegie. Mary Livingstone had been staying with the Carnegies in Edinburgh before she moved on to the Camerons. According to his sister-in-law Mary Livingstone was becoming notorious as a drinker, a non-believer, and a flirt – Sara said that on no less than three occasions in the past she had tried to 'beguile' men, all of them married, with whom she had come into contact.

Cameron finished the letter and looked up at his wife, stunned and shaken.

He knew Mary, and he knew that what had been written could only be lies. Mary was a kind and honest woman, a loving mother to her own four children and a diligent nurse to the waif he'd found on the Oban docks. The idea of her drinking, let alone of her abandoning her faith and making approaches to other men, was incredible. On the other hand the letter had been written by his cousin by marriage, Sara, and could not be ignored.

White-faced, Cameron said, 'I wish to speak to Mary in private.'

Without waiting for his wife to reply he walked out of the room.

Mary Livingstone was waiting in his study across the hall. Dr Cameron closed the door behind him as he entered. One by one, he put the accusations to her, his voice unsteady as he spoke. Mary listened to him with her head lowered. Then she looked up. For several moments she was silent.

'Yes, Charles,' she said finally. 'Much of what you have been told is true. I do drink. I find it comforts me. I have great difficulty with my faith. It no longer gives me the support it once did. For the rest, no, I have never considered another man, nor made the smallest approach to one – '

She wrinkled her face and smiled. 'I'm little and plump and rather less than well favoured. As a houri I would not invest in my success. Would you not agree, Charles?'

Cameron said nothing.

'I am married to a man I do not, in truth, like very much,' Mary continued. 'Your cousin David is strange and haunted. Often, I think unintentionally, he is cruel. Yet he is my husband and I have borne his children. I love the children and, maybe, I still love him. I will never desert any of them.'

Cameron stared at her in anguish as she finished. He felt a profound sense of shock coupled with an even greater feeling of pity. Shaking his head sorrowfully, he put his hand on her shoulder.

'God knows what you must have been through for this to happen, Mary,' he said. 'You have my deepest sympathy. On the other allegations I believe you utterly. They are baseless lies and shall be nailed. I will write to Sara myself. Yet I fear you must leave my house. Flora holds strong opinions and your continued presence would be a source of constant aggravation.'

Mary nodded. 'Of course. I did not expect otherwise. You have been most kind to me and I greatly regret the distress this must have caused you. I shall go to my room now and start making the necessary arrangements – '

She turned away. Then she hesitated and glanced back.

'Jamie is well on the way to recovery,' she said. 'Please

do what you can for him. For a crofter's child he is a boy of rare qualities. Given the opportunity, I would not be surprised if he achieved great things.'

'I will take care of him,' Cameron said. 'You have my promise.'

It was late in the evening when Mary eventually went to Jamie's room. He was already half-asleep and he blinked drowsily as she appeared by his bed with a lamp.

'Hullo, Jamie,' she greeted him.

Her voice was bright but Jamie could see she had been crying. Her eyes were red and there were blotches on her cheeks. He lay gazing up at her.

'I have to leave in the morning,' Mary went on. 'I have another cousin I must visit before I return to Africa and I will be away before you are awake. It is rather sad, as we were just beginning to get to know each other. I will miss reading to you – '

Her voice faltered. Then she controlled herself. She picked up a basket she had brought into the room, and continued.

'I'm leaving the books we didn't have time for,' she said. 'I hope you will read them after I've gone. You may not understand all the words at first, but I'm sure Dr Cameron will help you. One day perhaps you'll go to Africa yourself. I hope so too. It has broken many good men, but I do not think it will break you, Jamie – '

Mary smiled. 'Maybe you'll even find the source of the great river.'

'Aye, that would be a prize worth the winning, would it not?' Jamie said.

'The greatest prize of all,' Mary agreed.

'And queens mebbe would marry me for that.'

Mary laughed. 'Any queen worth her salt at the table, Jamie, will marry you for yourself alone. But, yes, to find the river's source would be a gift to lay at any lassie's feet.'

She hesitated.

Africa was all she had been able to give Jamie, all, she

realized now, she was leaving him with. The dark continent had enslaved her husband, wrecked their marriage and her faith, and caused the death of her last child. Suddenly she was filled with fear that she might have placed Africa's snare round Jamie's neck, that unwittingly she might have saddled him with the daemon that rode her husband.

'Never let it be everything in your life, Jamie,' she said. 'Africa's full of darkness and mystery. You'll need the sunlight and simple things too. Queens are like the rest of us. They like the day better than the night.'

'Dinna fash yourself, miss,' Jamie answered. 'I'll wed in the sun – or I'll no wed at all. But if your husband doesna' get there first, I'll find where yon burn rises.'

Mary was silent again.

'Well, if you decide to try, this may be helpful.' She reached into her purse and pulled something out. 'You remember my telling you about the Royal Geographical Society in London?'

'Aye. The folk that aid your husband and such in their travels?'

'That's right,' Mary said. 'This is a letter to the society's president. It introduces you. It says you're a worthy young man who merits their support. Keep the letter safely. It may be years before you need it, but one day it could be very useful to you. However long you wait, I very much doubt if they will have forgotten the name Livingstone.'

Like every Highland boy Jamie carried a sporran, a leather pouch attached to the belt round his waist which supported his plaid. Unlike the sporrans of the lairds, which were made from elegant badger or pine martin pelts, Jamie's sporran was stitched out of raw cowhide. It was the only possession he'd brought with him from Iona and it was lying on the table by his bed.

Jamie reached out for it. He carefully tucked the letter inside and drew the buckle tight.

'It'll nae get lost there,' he said.

'Sleep well, Jamie,' she said. 'Sleep well wherever you go.'

Mary looked down at him for a moment longer. Then she leant forward and kissed him on the head. She went out and closed the door, leaving the room in darkness.

Jamie lifted his head and touched his skin.

It was damp. Mrs Livingstone must have been crying again. He closed his eyes. Hanging in the air was a faint elusive smell. Jamie sniffed. He realized what it was. It was the smell of usquebaugh, of whisky, the same smell that had always clung to his father. Strangely, he found it comforting.

Jamie turned over. He took the sporran from the table, and put it under his pillow. Then he drifted back into sleep.

Mary Livingstone and her children left the Camerons' house at seven the following morning. They were bound for another cousin of her husband, the Reverend Robert Mackenzie, the minister of the nearby village of Tomintoul. Dr Cameron took them down to the coach that would carry them there. Then he returned home.

As he entered the hall he realized from the clatter of dishes in the dining room that his wife was already at breakfast. The meal, Cameron knew, would be a difficult one. For Mrs Cameron, Mary's swift departure had been a personal triumph. It was not an event she would let pass without a torrent of vindictive comment.

Trying to delay the moment when he would have to confront her across the table, Cameron picked up that morning's *Glasgow Herald*. He glanced at the front page. Midway down he froze. Ten days earlier, he read, a naval frigate out of Bristol had picked up a lifeboat. The lifeboat contained five survivors, all crew members of a passenger ship which had foundered and sunk in a heavy storm weeks before, on its journey from Oban to Liverpool. No one else, it appeared, had survived.

The ship was on charter to the Highland and Island Emigration Society. Its name was the *Hercules*.

Jamie was truly alone in the world now.

— 26 —

When Mamkinga and Toomi were put up for sale in the village market on the borders of Abyssinia, Mamkinga's fate was to take him eventually to the distant western side of the continent.

Toomi's, in contrast, was to lead her in directly the opposite direction – back almost to where she had come from.

For two hours that day after Mamkinga had been led away she was forced to stand on the hewn-off trunk in the morning's heat. Intermittently someone came up to inspect her, to pinch her thigh muscles, to drag down her jaw and peer at her teeth, or to probe in her vagina. Each time the Oye-Eboe clustered round her, grinning and chattering encouragingly. Always the would-be buyers shook their heads and wandered off.

Toomi was too tall and slim and wiry.

She lacked the bulk, even the promise of bulk, the buyers wanted. In a young girl they were looking for flesh and stamina and poundage. If her strength didn't match their expectations when she grew to maturity, at least she could warm her owner's bed and maybe whelp better labourers. Toomi failed on every count. She looked inadequate for the field and worthless as breeding stock.

'How much?'

It was almost midday and most of the market crowd had gone.

Twice in the past half-hour Toomi had reeled with exhaustion and almost toppled off the stand. On both occasions one of the Oye-Eboe had jabbed her in the back of the knee with a sharpened stick. The stab of pain had jolted her upright again.

'How much?' the voice repeated.

The question was in Ewhelo. Toomi knew what the words meant – the Ewhelo dialect was almost as familiar to her as her own Malindan – but the Oye-Eboe clearly had no idea what the questioner was asking. They gathered round the stake like hungry crows, jabbering Toomi's virtues in their own tongue as they prodded her once more.

'Can anyone speak for these people?' the voice called out.

The sun was directly overhead and the dazzle from the pale baked-earth ground was blinding, but narrowing her eyes and peering down, Toomi could just see the figure who had spoken.

The voice was husky and deep. To Toomi's surprise it belonged to a woman. She had tightly curled black hair, a strong-jawed face, and penetrating eyes. She was wearing a rough country hide skirt with a wool cape slung over her shoulders, and two male slaves were standing in attendance behind her.

'May I be of assistance, Maigri?'

A plump Indian in a turban and an ankle-length gown shuffled forward. He bowed obsequiously.

'I was hoping for almost anyone else,' the woman said coldly when she saw him. 'If you cheat me again – '

The Indian giggled as she paused. 'I am no more than the grease on the axle of your business, Maigri. What do you wish?'

'The sun is high, the market is over, all that's left is offal,' the woman replied. 'By tomorrow the girl will be worth less than a basket of dry yams. I will buy her now for five shells weight of gold – and that's worth double her true price. Tell these savages that and buy her for me, Raman.'

Without waiting for an answer, the woman walked away. Toomi watched as the little Indian beckoned the Oye-Eboe towards him. Speaking in their own language, he started to bargain with them.

Ten minutes later Toomi was pulled down from the post and propelled across the market yard to an ox-waggon. The two male slaves, who had accompanied the woman, were sitting on the driving bench. The woman herself was reclining on the boards behind. Toomi was tossed up by the Oye-Eboe into the oxen's feeding store at the back, and her arms were lashed to the cross-bar. Then they set off.

As they rumbled out of the now almost empty town Toomi strained her head round in the direction where she had last seen Mamkinga. There was no sign of him. The waggon was heading the opposite way.

Toomi wept.

They travelled until dusk. Then on the outskirts of another village the woman ordered the slaves to halt for the night. The oxen were outspanned and the men made a fire. They cooked some gruel and Toomi was brought over to the flames.

'Walk round,' ordered the woman, who was sitting cross-legged by the fire.

When Toomi had been taken out of the waggon, the slaves had attached a length of chain to her ankle. It allowed Toomi to move but the weight of the chain stopped her from running away.

Dragging the chain behind her, Toomi stumbled round the fire.

Apparently satisfied, the woman nodded. 'Sit down and eat.'

Toomi had had nothing all day and the separation from Mamkinga had drained all the defiance out of her. Hungry, weary and miserable, she squatted and started to gulp down a bowl of gruel.

Across the fire the woman continued to inspect her.

The lantern-jawed woman, Maigri, was a native of the land of the Galla, the third of Abyssinia's main kingdoms. Maigri was a widow. Her husband had been a captain in the royal bodyguard of the Galla's king, Culembra. Five years before he had been killed at Culembra's side in battle. Afterwards Culembra asked

Maigri what she would like as a reward for her husband's bravery. Maigri, a cunning and resourceful woman ambitious for her two sons, requested the post of chamberlain to the Lendama, Culembra's women warriors.

It was a bold request – the post was an important one and traditionally given to a man – but Culembra agreed.

Since then Maigri had done handsomely out of the king's gift. As the Lendama's chamberlain, Maigri was responsible for providing them with almost everything from food and shelter to horses and weapons out of a budget from the royal purse. Shrewdly handled, the budget could accommodate all the women's needs and still leave a healthy surplus at the end. Maigri was very shrewd. Five years later she was a rich woman.

Buying Toomi that day was part of Maigri's business.

Like every warrior chieftain, Culembra rewarded his soldiers with the spoils of war. Occasionally there were periods when, for one reason or another, he had made no successful raids out of the Galla's lands and there were no spoils to be distributed. When that happened Culembra had to pay his soldiers out of his own pocket. After land, the most favoured gift was slaves.

Most of the Galla's lands had long since been pledged. But in the plains and forests to the west slaves were always available.

'Where do you come from, child?' Maigri suddenly demanded.

Across the fire Toomi's head jerked up. She felt better now after the gruel but she was still too lonely and dispirited to defy the woman.

'Malinda,' she said dully.

'So you understand me?'

Toomi nodded.

'From where in Malinda?' the woman went on. 'Who were your parents and who took you?'

As desolate as she was, Toomi didn't hesitate before answering.

She and Mamkinga had impulsively told the Oye-Eboe

they were the embrenche's children. They hadn't been believed. As soon as Toomi saw the woman who had bought her from them, she suddenly realized she and Mamkinga might have been fortunate. The Oye-Eboe were coarse and simple. In contrast the woman, Toomi knew immediately, was shrewd and formidable.

The woman might well have believed the truth – and it could have redounded terribly on Toomi. Toomi had been told of chieftains' children being stolen and held for ransom. Sometimes they were kept captive for years. The woman, Toomi sensed, was just the sort of person who would exploit their plight ruthlessly if she knew the truth.

Toomi had been a prisoner for barely two weeks. The prospect of years of captivity was chilling almost beyond her capacity to grasp it.

Like Mamkinga, Toomi thought only of escape. Her best chance of that, it had come to her, was to be as docile and anonymous as possible. From now on she was no longer the child of the Embrenche of Malinda. She was the daughter of a poor mountain villager.

'I come from Katalo-pila,' Toomi said, naming the 'grass village' that could have been any one of hundreds across the country. 'My father is a herder. The red men took me from the field after the mothers moved forward to glean.'

Maigri frowned. 'You speak very elegantly for a villager's daughter. Why?'

Toomi thought for an instant.

The possibility that her voice might betray her had never occurred to her. Until then she hadn't even been aware she had an accent -- she simply spoke as she had been taught to speak, knowing the country people slurred their words and were sometimes hard to understand.

'The embrenche sends teachers out from Malinda,' she replied. 'I learnt to speak from such a one.'

Maigri said nothing. She stared at Toomi thoughtfully over the flames. Toomi looked back at her, wide-eyed and unafraid. Maigri nodded.

'Get into the waggon,' she said.

Toomi stood up and limped towards the cart, dragging the chain. Almost unconsciously her last reply to the woman's questions had been in the drawl of a country girl.

Maigri sat by the fire.

In spite of the child's answers, there was something about Toomi that puzzled her. Her accent was strange. In addition she lacked the sullen indifference that in Maigri's experience characterized slave-children. Even standing tearfully on the trunk-post she had somehow been aloof and defiant. Her eyes, too, were unusual – steady and watchful rather than apathetic like the other girls Maigri had bought.

Maigri gathered her robe round her and headed for her pallet.

Skinny and strange the child might be, but Maigri hadn't bought her as breeding stock. She was buying for Culembra's Lendama and they, in particular the one she had in mind for the girl, had different concerns.

For Tamule, as the woman she was thinking of was named, Toomi –even with her oddly educated accent – would do very well. And she was a bargain too.

Maigri thought of her sons, and slept well.

In the back of the ox-waggon Toomi barely slept at all. She was tired almost to the point of fainting, but as the stars wheeled across the African sky she thought only of the other half of her mind and body. Mamkinga. Her brain insistently pounded out his name and her hands reached yearningly for him in the darkness.

Toomi's fingers touched nothing but the chill and dew-laden night air.

—— 27 ——

They travelled for three weeks.

For the first two weeks Toomi had the luxury of riding in the back of the waggon and being fed each evening from the meal the slaves cooked at the fire. Then one night they reached another village and everything abruptly changed.

Maigri had been away on a buying journey for almost four months. The market village on the borders had been the last stop on her trip. By then she had already acquired most of what she wanted. She had left the rest of her purchases, some seventy slaves – most of them women or girls – to await her return with the rest of her escort.

Now Maigri was on her way home.

Toomi became just one more unit in a small human herd being driven on foot towards the hills. The anklet and chain were removed from her leg, and instead she was manacled to the group of slaves Maigri had already bought. Like her brother, Toomi was forced to trudge in swirling dust behind the ox-waggons that led the way.

By the standards of the slave traffic criss-crossing central Africa that year, they amounted to no more than a tiny group – an easy prey for any of the predatory bands that prowled the slave routes. Maigri had few guards to protect her, but she was unafraid. She had Culembra's warrant. The fearsome reputation of the Galla's king reached far beyond the Mountains of the Moon.

Any bandit who tried to halt and raid her troop would bring a terrible retribution down on his head.

As well as slaves, Maigri had bought sixty head of cattle. When they stopped to camp for the night the cattle were penned in a circular stockade of thorn bushes to protect them against attacks by lions. Every evening the first task of Toomi and the other slaves was to cut the bushes and build the stockade. It was back-breaking work at the end of the long day's march. By the time they finished Toomi's hands and arms were always sheeted in blood from the needle-sharp thorns.

When the stockade was complete the cattle were driven inside, accompanied by two of the slaves, and the entrance was sealed with more bushes.

The slaves' job was to frighten off any lions. They built a large fire at the stockade's centre and kept it blazing until dawn. If a lion approached they would be alerted by the frenzied behaviour of the cattle. They seized fire-brands from the blaze and hurled them over the wall of thorn, pelting the animal with burning branches until it ran off.

The job involved staying awake all night, and every day Maigri assigned two different slaves to it. Toomi's first turn came a week after they left for the hills. She and her companion, a big male Yoruba, one of two brothers Maigri had bought, built the fire. Then they settled down beside it as the cattle milled round them. Until then the column had encountered few lions.

That night it was very different.

The lioness paused and checked in mid stride, her forefoot poised in the air.

She wrinkled her nostrils and sniffed the night breeze. Behind her the other members of the pride did the same. They too had caught the scent that was drifting towards them through the darkness. In the distance there was a flickering glow. The rank enticing smell grew stronger every moment.

The lioness lowered her head and snarled. Then she set off again. Before, she had been travelling at a steady trot. Now the great cat moved at a swift lithe gallop.

There were seven lions in the pride — five adult females and two young males. The lioness at its head was the pride's matriarch and leader. An immense tawny-skinned creature with a scarred face and black-tipped ears, she was at the height of her powers as a hunter. Normally under her leadership the pride fed well. But for several weeks the game on the plain had been widely scattered, and it was three nights since they had killed.

As they approached the corral all seven animals were tormented by hunger. The leading lioness felt the pangs even more acutely than the rest. Two of the females behind her had cubs. As the pride matriarch she, in the end, was responsible for their survival.

Silent, implacable and deadly, the lioness bounded forward beneath the stars.

Toomi was dozing inside the ring of thorn bushes when the cattle started to crowd together and bellow in terror. She and the Yoruba leapt to their feet. It was midnight. They piled wood on the fire until the flames soared into the air. Then they picked up burning logs, and stepped cautiously to the thorn wall. There were gaps in the thorn and it was possible to spot a lion outside by the reflection of the firelight in its eyes.

To her horror Toomi saw not one pair of eyes but seven.

In the fire's glow the eyes were huge and amber and hypnotic. She could smell the raw stench of the lions' bodies. As Toomi stared at them transfixed with fear, one of the lions opened its jaws and roared. At a distance of only a few paces the sound was terrifying.

Trembling, Toomi jumped back.

'Throw!' the other slave shouted.

The Yoruba tossed his branch over the bushes into the middle of the pride. Toomi did the same. As the two firebrands fell, trailing sparks behind them, the lions snarled and scattered. A moment later they were back. This time they were all roaring.

'More!' the Yoruba called.

With Toomi behind him he raced back to the fire. Sweating, they started to run backwards and forwards between the flames and the wall of thorn.

Instead of driving them away, the hot coals and the showers of sparks only seemed to enrage the lions. They paced backwards and forwards, roaring hungrily and lashing at the bushes with their paws. With the cattle stamping and bellowing the tumult was deafening.

The pride matriarch reared up and tried to claw a hole in the stockade. A thorn lanced into one of her pads. The lioness grunted in pain and anger, and dropped back. She brushed her paw against the earth until the thorn had been dislodged. She lifted her head and gazed at the wall. Then she whirled away and vanished.

For an instant Toomi thought the animal had finally been scared off. Then there was another roar, even louder and more chilling than the ones before. A moment later something erupted out of the darkness and soared over the thorns into the stockade.

Ferocious and cunning and goaded into desperation by the emptiness in her stomach, the lioness had realized that the danger lay not in the firebrands or the two forked shapes hurling them, but in the stockade wall. Beyond that the cattle were defenceless.

The lioness landed inside the corral in front of one of the forked figures. It was the Yoruba. Before the stupefied slave could move, the lioness sprang at him. Snarling and grunting, the animal broke his neck with a single blow of her forepaw and tore out his throat. She savaged his body with her claws and nudged him aside.

Then the lioness lifted her head.

She was after the cattle beyond the fire. Between her and them stood a small two-legged figure holding one of the painful and irritating sticks of flame. To the lioness the tiny fragile shape, as insubstantial as a fluttering bird, was haloed by the fire's glow. The lioness crouched and flicked her black-tipped tail. In the firelight it was like a snake's tongue snapping from side to side.

Toomi watched it, mesmerized.

She could see the Yoruba's blood smeared over the lioness's head and the long yellow incisors curving down from its upper jaw like ivory daggers. The animal's eyes were no longer amber but deep red-brown and glittering. They seemed to be gazing into hers with the terrible cold intensity of the mountain starlight.

The movement of the tail stopped. The lioness roared once more. Her ears flattened and the black tips vanished. A blast of warm foetid breath, reeking of carrion, reached Toomi's face. The animal began to pad towards her, moving faster and faster with every step.

As if she were in a dream Toomi lifted the glowing branch and held it out. Her arm moved so slowly it might have been weighted down with rock. She felt faint and sick and disembodied. The lioness was only two paces away. Toomi saw it begin to rise in an arc from the earth, its jaws open and its unsheathed claws stretching out towards her.

Suddenly there was a shattering explosion.

The lioness was jolted sideways in mid air as something smashed into its shoulder. The animal seemed to collapse. It crumpled limply to the ground, knocking Toomi on to her back. Twisting away as she fell, Toomi glimpsed Maigri behind her. The bushes at the entrance to the stockade had been dragged aside, and Maigri was standing in the gap. In her hands was a heavy long-barrelled musket.

Toomi saw a plume of smoke lifting from the gun. Then she lost consciousness.

When Toomi recovered she was lying in the back of the waggon. The sun was high and they must have been travelling for several hours. Maigri was seated on the cross-bench at the front. She heard Toomi stir, and glanced back.

'I paid good money for you,' was all Maigri said. 'Do not think I would ever let the lions rob me.'

Maigri cracked her whip and the waggon rumbled on.

Toomi was allowed to remain where she was all day. But that evening when they halted, Maigri handed her a machete and told her to get out.

A few minutes later Toomi was hacking at the wiry

recalcitrant bushes for the night's stockade, and her skin was being torn again by the painful thorns.

The column finally reached the Galla's lands at the end of October.

Toomi had known from the start of the journey that she was travelling in the general direction of her home. She had the sun to orient her and she remembered several of the villages they passed through from her travels with her brother and the Oye-Eboe. But none of her new companions, the slaves she was yoked to, knew where they were heading, and it was hard even to communicate with them.

On the edges of the kingdom of Gondar they turned north to skirt both Gondar itself and Malinda. A day later Toomi was lost. The sun no longer rose in front of them at dawn, but to their right.

A week afterwards they swung east again and the sun returned to its former position. They had left the plain and were climbing through the foothills of the Mountains of the Moon. At night the air was chill and by day the sky's rim was broken by ridges and crests. For a while Toomi had the comfort of walking through countryside like the one in which she'd been raised. There were the familiar aloes, the familiar flowers, the familiar trees and birds and animals.

Then they too changed and the mantle over the rising landscape became increasingly sparse and alien.

A few days before the journey ended the waggons paused one morning at a hill village. A lumpy young woman was pushed out of a hut. Maigri examined the girl and gestured her to join the other slaves. Vacant-eyed, the girl padded back to take up her position in the dust.

When they stopped that evening Toomi saw the girl wandering among the other slaves. She was calling out, 'Pula! Pula!'

Pula, the Malindan word for the life-giving rains, was also the Malindan term for 'Greetings'. The girl was obviously looking for someone to talk to.

'Pula!' Toomi said as the girl reached her.

The girl stopped and pointed at herself. 'Cuburu,' she said. 'You?'

'Toomi.'

Toomi looked at her.

The girl was about fourteen. Her head was slumped to one side, her tongue hung out from her mouth, and saliva was dribbling down her chin. Cuburu, Toomi guessed, had the mind of a small child.

'I'm going to see the king,' Cuburu began to chant. 'I'm going to see the king.'

When she stopped, Toomi asked, 'The king of where?'

The girl sucked her thumb and gazed at the ground. She pivoted awkwardly in a circle on her heel. Then she began chanting again.

'I'm going to Galla! I'm going to Galla!'

At the first mention of Galla, Toomi felt a chill sweep over her.

In common with Abyssinia's other kingdoms, the country of the Galla took its name from its people's principal settlement. The mountain town of Galla was the home of the terrible king, Culembra. Like all Malindan children the twins had been scolded with stories of what King Culembra would do to them if they misbehaved.

Culembra was a demon, a cannibal, an ogre in the night. He ate small children alive and slept on a bed of their skulls.

'Am I going to Galla too?' Toomi managed to ask.

Cuburu, frowning and gnawing at her thumb, struggled to understand the question.

'We all go to Galla,' she mumbled.

Cuburu paused. Then she jabbed out her hand towards Toomi and added, 'You go to the war women.'

She turned and wandered away. Toomi hurried after her but there was nothing more she could get out of the girl. Toomi watched her muttering incomprehensibly to herself, as Cuburu squatted by the fire.

Toomi knelt down on the other side and gazed at the

flames. Sparks landed on her skin and burned her. Toomi didn't even notice. She was frozen with terror.

The war women. They were Culembra's most feared and hated soldiers. If anything they were even more frightening than the king, evil old hags with razor-sharp swords who carried out his cruel bidding and drank the blood of their victims. They were the worst of all the monsters who inhabited the nightmare lands of the Galla.

If the dull-witted Cuburu was right, Toomi was going to be given to them.

The fire died down. The night wind keened over the mountain ridges. Toomi never moved. She was still kneeling by the embers when day broke. At Maigri's shouted order she stood up vacantly and took her place in the column for the day's march. It was to be the last day of the journey. At midday they arrived at Galla.

An hour later Toomi was handed over to her monster.

—— 28 ——

'Greetings,' Maigri said. 'I bring gifts from the king.'

She inclined her head politely.

On the ground at the back of the tent the woman, who had been lying sprawled on cushions stuffed with horse-hair, propped herself up on one elbow and grunted. She was smoking a blackened corn-cob pipe.

The woman removed the pipe from her mouth. 'What gifts?' she demanded.

Her eyes, narrow and shrewd in her dark heavily wrinkled face, stared greedily at Maigri.

'They are outside,' Maigri answered. 'They await your inspection.'

Maigri waited as the woman struggled to her feet – she had, Maigri guessed, been drinking palm wine. Then Maigri accompanied her into the afternoon sunlight.

The woman's name was Tamule. At forty-two – although from her scarred and withered features and the grey hair at her armpits she might have been twenty years older – Tamule was one of the six colonels of Culembra's regiments of female soldiers. She was not the most senior of the six, nor was she the most intelligent. But as Maigri knew, Tamule was the king's favourite.

Culembra had never known any soldier, male or female, as ferocious and pitiless in battle.

Like almost all of Culembra's women warriors, Tamule had become a soldier as a result of her misdeeds. Tamule's offence had been adultery. In her husband's absence she had slept with three of his brothers. For centuries serious transgressions by women of Galla tribal law – which covered everything from murder to sexual

206

conduct, soil abuse and theft – had been punished by death. Then one of Culembra's ancestors had decided the system was wasteful of the tribe's human resources.

Instead, the long-ago monarch decreed, guilty women should be removed from their families to serve for life in the royal army.

From the beginnings of human conflict women had fought beside men in war. On the field of Waterloo the undertakers, stripping the uniforms from the dead on both sides, had found one in every twelve bodies was a woman's. The proportion in the Galla's endless battles was higher. The chief difference was that the Galla's women soldiers never fought disguised as men.

The Lendama, as they were known, lived together, trained together, and went to war as themselves.

Tamule was convicted before she was twenty. Starting as a humble foot soldier she had risen from the ranks over more than two decades of campaigns, distinguishing herself in every one by her courage and ferocity, to the position she held now.

'What has the king got for me?' she asked Maigri as they stepped on to the beaten earth.

Culembra's autumn gifts were always meant to be a surprise, and he took a childish delight in trying to make them so. Some years it was impossible. A distribution of hill cattle involved bringing the beasts into the stockades, and inevitably the round-up became public knowledge. Slaves were different – particularly if, as this year, they arrived on the gift-day itself.

'Look, Tamule,' Maigri said.

As usual several of the slaves Maigri had bought had died on the journey home. She had finally returned with sixty. Maigri had split them into groups of ten and distributed them on Culembra's behalf to the women colonels.

Tamule was the last to receive her gift.

For Tamule she had kept back the ten best. A big Yoruba, the only remaining male and the brother of the man killed by the lioness, who would be put to work in the stables. Eight well-fleshed young women. And Toomi. Alone among them Toomi was a gamble. The six colonels would compare their presents. Either Tamule would resent the child as the minnow of the group. Or she would see the girl as Maigri saw her – a lean long-boned plaything who would mature into a warrior.

It mattered greatly that Maigri had gambled correctly.

The king, although Tamule was unaware of it, was watching the presentation hidden behind a screen. If Maigri's choice displeased Tamule, the blame would be hers. Maigri might be a royal chamberlain – but Tamule fought alongside Culembra in battle.

'So.' Tamule chewed on her pipe, frowning as she surveyed the group in front of her. 'Let me take a closer look.'

She strode forward. Maigri followed her.

For Tamule the slaves were not so much a gift as a rightful payment for her services to the king. She squeezed the Yoruba's biceps and scratched in turn his lifted feet, testing his reactions in the same way as she would have scraped the teeth of a bullock. Then she scrutinized the young women. She grunted in approval.

Finally she came to Toomi.

'What's this scrap?' she demanded.

'The best of them all,' Maigri answered confidently. 'I saved her specially for you. She's bright and strong and she speaks Malindan. Use your imagination, Tamule. In a couple of years she will be a jewel.'

Maigri held her breath as Tamule stared at the child.

For quite different reasons Toomi was also holding her breath. Hidden at the back, she hadn't been able to see Tamule until then. Now in the sunlight she was suddenly face to face with the monster from her childhood nightmares.

Her mouth dry with terror, Toomi gazed up at Tamule.

At first sight all Toomi's worst fears were confirmed. What Toomi saw was a tall muscular woman with matt black skin, the blackest she had ever seen, and a gleaming scalp shaven bare apart from a single lock of filthy greying hair twisted through a silver bangle. On a chain round her neck hung another piece of silver, a crudely hammered fleur-de-lys. She was wearing a faded pink and white shirt with a soiled collar, and a long blue-striped waist cloth. The waist cloth was held up by a black leather cartridge belt from which hung a bulky ammunition bag.

In one hand she was carrying a short musket hung with charms, in the other she grasped her pipe.

Smoke from the burning tobacco billowed into Toomi's nostrils. The fleur-de-lys dazzled like an evil totem. The sun haloed the scar-hatched darkness of the woman's face with an aureole of menace. Every nerve in Toomi's body called out for her to scream and run. Somehow – instinctively – she knew it would be the worst thing she could do. Toomi willed herself to stand her ground.

'You could be right, Maigri,' Tamule said at last. 'She might plump out into a tasty meal. And I'll get a lot of fun and exercise out of her on the way.'

Tamule bent down and pinched Toomi's cheek hard. Involuntarily Toomi winced. Tamule burst into laughter.

Maigri let her breath out and smiled in relief. Across the yard Culembra ordered his servants to drop the leather screen that had concealed him. Chuckling with pleasure, he advanced on the group.

'Are you pleased, Tamule?' he demanded.

'Well pleased, my lord,' Tamule answered, bending stiffly on one knee.

'Just remember that when she ripens the first bite is mine,' Culembra teased her.

'Not this one, Culembra,' Tamule replied. 'You can harvest from the rest of the basket, but this fruit has been given to me.'

Culembra shook with laughter. As the joking between the king and his favourite went on, Maigri gestured for the slaves to be removed.

Toomi choked down the bile rising in her throat and shuffled away behind the others.

*

'Come here, child!'

Tamule patted the kaross that covered the moss-filled mattress on her wooden bed.

Toomi lifted her head from the straw pallet where she was lying by the doorway. Eyes wide open with fear, she gazed across the floor of the tent.

It was several hours later and night had fallen. The kaross on which Tamule was sprawling was made out of silver-backed jackal and striped genet pelts, the skins stitched together in alternating rows with rush fibre. The glossy fur rippled and gleamed like mountain water in the wavering light of the fire's embers.

The old woman – to Toomi her plume of grey hair meant she could only be old – beckoned for her again.

'Here!'

Tamule had drunk a great deal more palm wine since the morning. It had left her feeling drowsy and warm. She creased her face into what was meant to be an encouraging smile.

What Toomi saw was a chilling gap-toothed leer.

Trembling, Toomi stood up and approached the bed. Tamule inspected her through blurred eyes. She scratched herself and drew on her pipe.

'Take off your shift, child,' she instructed.

Toomi plucked off the cotton wrap that she, like the other female slaves, had been given when they entered the compound. She stood naked beside the bed. Tamule studied her again. Then Tamule blew out a last mouthful of smoke and tossed her pipe away.

'Clean and firm,' she murmured, coughing as the tobacco fumes drifted away. 'Clean and firm was what Maigri said. Well, at least you look like it. Let me feel you to see if it's true.'

Tamule reached out and caught Toomi by the waist.

Tamule swung the child round, and pulled her down on to her lap. Whispering to herself, Tamule nuzzled Toomi's neck with her lips. Then she began to explore Toomi's body with her stubby fingers.

Perched helplessly on the war woman's thighs, Toomi sat frozen and terrified.

Tamule's hands ran down Toomi's flanks. They travelled across the hollows at the back of her knees. They caressed her calves. They slid under her feet and curled round her toes, feeling for each one by one. Then her hands returned to Toomi's waist.

They fondled her ribs and dipped down to her groin. Toomi felt the woman probing between the cleft at the top of her legs. She stiffened. Her body seemed to dry and she quivered like a trapped bird.

'Be patient, little one, be patient,' Tamule said. 'You must learn.'

Tamule's hands moved upwards.

She encased Toomi's flat childish breasts between her fingers and began to massage Toomi's nipples. Tamule plucked at them gently, almost teasingly, drawing them out with the slow rhythmic pressure of her finger-pads and knuckles.

In spite of herself Toomi, still awed and terrorized, started to respond. She had no idea what was happening. All she knew was that her nipples were hardening and that strange unfamiliar sensations – hot and dizzying – were flooding her body. Nothing like it had ever happened to her before. She trembled again.

The circling movement of Tamule's hands grew fiercer and more insistent. Toomi began to pant. Her skin flushed. Her cheeks were on fire and her knees seemed to fill with water. If she had tried to stand Toomi knew she would have fallen over. She swayed giddily on Tamule's knees, heaving for breath as the strange pricking sensations arrowed through her.

Suddenly Tamule let go of her breasts.

Tamule was breathing heavily herself. For an instant she thrust Toomi away. Then she gripped Toomi by the head with both hands. She buried her hands in Toomi's hair and clenched at her scalp.

Toomi moaned as the old woman's nails dug into her skin. Then she felt her head being forced down between

Tamule's parted legs and her mouth was pressed against Tamule's groin.

'Your tongue, child, use your tongue!' Tamule urged.

On either side of Toomi's face, walls of muscled blackness stretched away behind. The walls seemed to form a valley with a river at its head. Blindly and in utter dizzying confusion – her own body was still resounding with chimes of incomprehensible sensuality like a wildly struck bell – Toomi licked up the waters at their source.

Hours later still Toomi crept back to her pallet on the far side of the tent. Tamule, sated, had lapsed into sleep. She lay on her back snoring and occasionally twitching. The coals of the fire had almost died, but each time Tamule moved the last light from the ashes caught the silver fleur-de-lys round her neck.

Toomi, exhausted but still awake, cringed and huddled deep inside her own rough blanket whenever the fire's gleam flared off the amulet.

She had been delivered into the keeping of a creature more fearsome and savage than Toomi had believed existed. Yet the monster was not going to change or dismay her.

For Mamkinga she was going to survive and escape.

—— 29 ——

A month after Toomi's arrival the Galla's western border was crossed by a roving Sudanese war party.

The Sudanese began raiding Galla settlements in the foothills. The trouble was not serious enough to warrant Culembra's personal attention, but he sent out a force from Galla to deal with it. The force included Tamule's regiment of Lendama. As a member of Tamule's household, Toomi went with them.

The experience was a grim confirmation of some of Toomi's worst fears about her new mistress.

The Galla expedition found the Sudanese camp. They attacked it in a dawn raid, and routed the invaders. In the course of the battle a number of the enemy were captured. Several were slaughtered but most were either kept to become slaves or released, after their ears had been cut off, and chased away. Not so those taken by Tamule's warriors.

They had captured about thirty prisoners. Five were tied. The rest at Tamule's orders and as Toomi watched — she had come up to the battlefield from the Galla camp with the other slaves after the fight was over — were staked out vertically on a steep slope with their heads below their feet.

Tamule lit her pipe. Her tunic was still damp with blood in the cool morning air. She called for palm wine.

'Drink!' she shouted, and her troops cheered.

For the next hour as the sun rose the women celebrated. Toomi had to run faster and faster among them, refilling their horn mugs. From time to time one of the women would try to slip away to relieve herself. Each time Tamule's sharp eye spotted her and she was called back.

'Wait until I give permission,' she ordered.

Soon the women's bladders were filled. The prisoners, lying pinioned in the growing heat, were sweating and their mouths were parched. Tamule drank a final toast and bellowed for silence.

She strode over to the nearest of the staked-out captives. Tamule dragged his mouth open, and forced in a stick to keep his jaws apart. Then she hitched up her waist cloth. She squatted over his face, and urinated. Unable to swallow, the man started to heave and choke. Within a few minutes, as Tamule stood watching, he shuddered and died, drowned by the urine blocking the passage to his lungs.

Tamule looked up, chuckling, and lit her pipe. 'Now!' she called out.

The women raced towards the captives, cheering and shouting. Soon all the men who had been lashed to the ground were dead. Tamule went across to the five who had been bound and who had witnessed the slaughter, terrified, from a mound above the slope.

'Go back where you came from,' Tamule said. 'Tell your people what you have seen. Say this will be the fate of any who dares to cross into the Galla's lands again.'

She pulled a dagger from her belt. She cut the thongs that tied them and jabbed them away with the dagger's point. Whimpering with fear and pain, the men stumbled down the hill and vanished in the bush below. Tamule wiped the blood from the dagger and slotted it back in its sheath.

'More wine!' she bellowed. 'Toomi, where are the flasks?'

As the women cheered again, Toomi hurried forward with the leather jugs of wine.

Tamule's treatment of the captured Sudanese showed her at her most brutal.

Yet, although it was long before Toomi began to

realize it, in falling into Tamule's hands she had fared better as a child-slave than she might have done. Tamule had become a soldier because she had no choice. In battle she was merciless. She killed the enemy with as little compunction as if she were slaughtering chickens for the pot.

But away from the battlefield Tamule reverted to what she had been before she joined the royal army – a coarse and simple but not unkindly peasant woman.

She and the women under her command lived in a compound segregated from the rest of the village. It was there Toomi found herself living too, housed in a shed at the back of Tamule's living quarters with her four other personal slaves. Even for a slave of a warrior nation, life in the all-female community was relatively tranquil and undemanding. As Culembra's favourite soldiers the regiment was kept well supplied with food, and absolved from work in the mountain pastures.

Instinctively all the women, soldiers and slaves alike, shared the tasks of daily life that in ordinary Galla households were carried out by the slaves alone. Quarrels were few and swiftly settled by Tamule. In the compound her word was almost as powerful as the king's. Men were strictly barred. For a female slave to grow up in mid-nineteenth-century Africa without bearing a child, let alone remaining a virgin, was almost unknown.

Toomi did both. The compound was her main protection. Her relationship with Tamule was almost as important.

One evening a few months after her arrival Toomi went down to the stream which flowed beneath the Lendama's compound to fetch water. She had often done it before, but until then there had never been anyone else there. That day one of the women soldiers was also collecting water further along the bank. Toomi bent down and dipped the jug in the stream.

As she did there was a sudden violent shout of 'No!'

Toomi looked up, startled and alarmed. The woman had dropped her own jug and was running towards her.

As the woman reached her Toomi saw that her face was hard with anger.

'You thought I could not see!' the woman screamed at Toomi accusingly. 'You were wrong. I saw it all. You will answer to Tamule!'

The woman seized her roughly by the arm and started to drag her back towards the compound. Bewildered and even more frightened, Toomi stumbled behind her.

Inside the compound the woman took her straight to Tamule's tent. Tamule was lying on her bed, smoking. The woman stopped in front of her and hurled Toomi forward. Toomi fell to her knees on the ground.

'I caught her trying to draw foul water,' the woman said.

Tamule took her pipe from her mouth and frowned.

'She did not throw grass,' the woman went on. 'It was deliberate. She thought I could not see.'

Tamule glanced down at Toomi. 'Is this true?' she demanded.

Her voice was harsh and her gaze terrifying.

Toomi shook her head in despair. 'I do not know what I have done. I intended nothing. I swear it by the spirits.'

There was a long silence. Toomi had no idea what she was accused of. All she knew was that if it was serious enough for her to be dragged before Tamule, it would result in a terrible beating.

Eventually Tamule turned back to the woman. 'I will deal with her,' she said. 'You may go.'

The woman left the tent and Tamule patted the bed beside her.

'Come and sit by me,' she ordered.

Although her voice was more kindly now, Toomi was still trembling as she climbed on to the bed. She sat stiffly beside the old woman.

'You truly do not know what it means to throw grass?' Tamule asked.

Numbly Toomi shook her head again.

'I believe you, child,' Tamule said. 'But if you are to

be a good servant of the Galla, you must learn the Galla ways. Listen to me – '

She began to explain. 'The water belongs to the spirits. It is where they dwell and they guard it well. It can only be taken after respect has been paid to them. That is done by throwing a handful of grass on the stream. If the grass is not thrown, they may poison the water. Then anyone who drinks it will become sick and perhaps die. Do you understand now?'

Toomi nodded.

'So never again draw water before throwing a handful of grass to the spirits first.' Tamule paused. 'Come closer to me, child.'

She smiled and drew Toomi against her. Then she lay back.

'Give me your mouth,' she said.

Tamule lifted her withered breasts in her cupped hands and held them out to Toomi.

Toomi took the dugs between her lips. She stroked them in turn with her tongue until they hardened and Tamule was panting. Suddenly Tamule's legs stiffened and she shuddered.

Afterwards she gathered Toomi in her arms and held the child close to her. A soft rhythmic chanting filled the tent. Toomi listened. She realized the war woman was singing. The song was long familiar to Toomi. It was an old cradle song that was sung to small children all over Abyssinia. She remembered it being sung to her and Mamkinga in their earliest childhood.

Toomi lay in the old woman's arms and thought of her brother.

Toomi's visits to Tamule's bed soon lost their terrors.

The child quickly realized that to the old woman she was physically no more than an animal plaything, a household pet like one of the hunting hounds her father, the embrenche, kept in his night house. Sex alone had never held out any terrors for Toomi. When she discovered that all Tamule wanted was to be pleasured –

and that the commands to join the old woman on the kaross were not a prelude to some fearsome ritual of torture and cannibalism – Toomi climbed up beside her without hesitation.

'Gently child,' Tamule would say. 'Do it here and there and there – '

Tamule pointed with a rough but gentle finger between Toomi's own smooth young thighs.

'You learn well, little daughter,' the old woman would mutter later, as she sank back with a sigh of contentment. 'You are as skilful as a little cane rat burrowing in a grain store. You will never give such pleasure to a man. They are good for nothing but planting the seed. Breed from them one day if you must. Then discard them as fast as you can and come back to me!'

Tamule gave her deep rumbling laugh, her throat hoarse from the long years of the bitter foul-smelling tobacco smoke.

At other times, her eyes half-closed, the war woman would make Toomi lie on her back with one leg arched.

Tamule straddled the girl's thigh. She rocked backwards and forwards until she had rubbed herself to orgasm. Afterwards, spent, she toppled forward and lay embracing Toomi – her hands slowly combing Toomi's hair and her scarred wrinkled face brushing the sweat from Toomi's skin.

Once, after Tamule had fallen asleep on top of her, Toomi reached down and drew her finger through the moisture left on her thigh. She lifted her finger to her mouth. It tasted cool and sharp like the water of the fern-ringed mountain pools she and Mamkinga drank from when they woke at dawn on hunting trips with their father.

Toomi gazed at the roof of the tent as the prickings of cramp filled her limbs under Tamule's weight, and the old woman snored beside her.

From the start sex was a major factor in the relationship between the two. It remained so until the end. Yet as first the months and then the years went by, its role became less and less important. Increasingly Tamule wanted Toomi in her bed not for physical pleasure, but as a companion.

Tamule liked to hold and caress the child. She liked the warmth of Toomi's presence beside her. She liked falling asleep with Toomi's head resting against her chest, and waking to see Toomi, clear-eyed and fresh-smelling, gazing up at her in the early morning light.

In the early days Tamule's summons of the child to the jackal- and genet-skin kaross coincided with her heavier bouts of drinking palm wine. Soon Tamule would call for her whether she had been drinking or not.

Within a year Toomi didn't even need to be called for. She no longer slept with the other slaves in the hut behind the tent. Her place in the hours of darkness was beside her mistress.

Like a small animal Toomi accepted it without question.

Toomi remained at Galla for ten years.

On a dozen occasions during those years Culembra called Tamule's regiment out on campaigns that lasted from a few weeks to several months. Each time Toomi accompanied Tamule. The slaves who marched out with the Lendama were taught to ride on horseback but they were not allowed to carry weapons, for fear they might use them against their captors.

Instead they were taught to use slings so they could kill small game for the soldiers.

Toomi had quick reflexes and a superb eye. Soon she became an expert with the leather thong and the small iron balls that were used for ammunition. She could stun a tiny dik-dik antelope or fell a roosting bustard from a branch at thirty paces.

During one campaign Tamule went down to a nearby river to bathe. Toomi was away from the Lendama's camp, hunting. As she returned, a suckling wart hog draped across her shoulders, she heard the old woman calling for her. Toomi put the wart hog down by the fire.

Then, the sling still in her hand, she ran towards Tamule's voice.

On the bank above the river Toomi stopped and froze.

Tamule was kneeling on the edge of the water with her back to the shore. Unwittingly she had entered the river in front of a deadly green mamba's nest. The snake must have had young. Disturbed by the sound of Tamule washing, it had slid out of the nest. As Toomi watched, its hood flared and it reared up to strike the old woman from behind.

Toomi slipped a ball into the sling. She whirled the leather thong round her head, and unleashed it. The ball smashed into the mamba's head, breaking its jaw and fangs.

Tamule heard the whistle of the ball and swung round. The snake was slithering away, trailing venom from its shattered mouth. Tamule's glance travelled from the mamba up to Toomi on the bank above, with the sling hanging by her side.

Tamule walked slowly up to her and touched her cheek.

'I shall not forget that ever, child,' Tamule said. 'One day it will be repaid.'

Naked and still dripping, the war woman walked back through the thorn bush to camp. Toomi trudged behind her.

A year and a half after Toomi arrived at Galla she learnt to her horror that the Lendama were being sent out to raid Malinda. Sick at heart she rode out with the column early next morning. They travelled for three weeks until they crossed into Malinda. Their target was an upland cattle village close to the border of the Galla's lands.

Because of its position the village was well fortified. Its defences were no match for the Lendama. As dawn broke the regiments of women soldiers surged forward in screaming waves. There was a brief bloody battle round the village gates. Then the Lendama broke through. Waiting by the column's waggons, Toomi listened in anguish to the moans of the dying, and the screams of the Malindan women as their children were torn from them to be herded away into slavery.

It was even worse when the Lendama returned driving the slaves before them.

The captives had all been hobbled by then and they stumbled past her wailing in Malindan. It was the first time since her own capture by the Oye-Eboe that Toomi had heard her native tongue. Toomi had to clench her teeth to stop herself from weeping.

When the children appeared and a girl only a few years younger than Toomi reached out her arms calling 'Help me! Help me!' Toomi could control herself no longer.

Tears streaming down her face, she put her hands to her ears and buried her head in the waggon's hide covering.

The column left immediately to head back for Galla with the slaves and the plundered cattle. That night Toomi lay down beside Tamule among the soldiers, wrapped in her cape on a pile of dry grass on the open hillside. Refusing to say why, Toomi sobbed herself to sleep. She tossed restlessly as the wind keened down from the Mountains of the Moon and the stars shone chill and bright overhead.

In the middle of the night Toomi fell still.

She started to dream. She was no longer lying out in the icy windswept uplands. She was a bird in flight, a hunting owl. It was night but the darkness now was warm and still. She swooped silently from the sky and plucked a small animal from the ground in her talons. She carried it to a hollow tree and dropped it inside to feed her young in a nest she had built there.

Then she perched on a branch to watch the nestlings eat.

They lifted their heads towards the food and the heads became one and it was Mamkinga's. Mamkinga was caught in a trap. He was tired and hungry and thin. Toomi stared at him sorrowfully. Her brother was asking for more food, so she flew away and hunted again. Toomi hunted for him all night long – and then suddenly it was dawn.

She woke to find the dew cold and heavy on her face.

Propped on one elbow, Tamule was staring down at her in the thin early light. Scavenging jackals were barking and the chill air churred with the flight of morning birds. She could hear the impatient calls of crimson-breasted shrikes, and the tumbling liquid song of the mountain larks.

'What did you dream of?' Tamule asked her. 'I woke once and your eyes were wide and unblinking like an owl's. Yet when I spoke to you, you were asleep. Where did you fly, little bird?'

Toomi, the dark-eyed growing child, stood up without answering. She walked away to prepare the morning meal. Like all the slaves on campaign she was wearing heavy chains.

The chains dragged behind her, leaving a dark smear on the wet grass like the track of a snail.

The girl wishes to keep her peace, Tamule thought. The old woman frowned. Then she decided not to press her little slave.

A child who could slay a striking mamba was entitled to her silence.

'The forceps,' Dr Cameron said. 'The big pair. I mind I packed them on the right.'

Jamie searched through the mahogany box of instruments.

He found the pair Cameron wanted, and passed them across. Jamie waited while the doctor pulled the sides of the wound together with his fingers, and clamped the forceps over the centre of the wound's mouth.

The man moaned as the metal tongues bit into his flesh.

It was almost dusk in late August. The patient lying between them on a bed of straw in the wooden byre was a lanky Galloway farmer. The farmer had tripped over his scythe and slashed himself open from his buttock to his knee. Dr Cameron called for the smaller pair of forceps. He closed the wound along its length and stitched it up with a needle and cat gut, removing the clamps one by one as he worked. At each incision of the needle the farmer arched his back and writhed.

Finally Cameron bound the leg with a heavy linen bandage.

'Get your wife to change the wrap night and morning,' Cameron said as he got to his feet. 'Stay indoors for the next week and don't move about overmuch. I'll be back the week after to take the stitches out.'

'And who's to cut the harvest?' the farmer complained.

'I'm a doctor, no an agricultural adviser,' Cameron answered. 'But I reckon ye could hire someone — '

He turned to Jamie. 'Have ye made out the account?'

'Aye.'

Jamie handed the farmer a sheet of paper. Still

grumbling, the man said, 'I dinna have the bawbies to hand.'

'Then ye can pay me next time,' Cameron replied. 'But mind ye do, or the stitches stay in.'

Cameron walked out of the byre with Jamie carrying the box of instruments at his side.

'It isna right a doctor should have to make threats like that,' Cameron said, shaking his head. 'But I tell ye, Jamie, if I didn't I'd have been bankrupt long syne. Those without money can't pay. Those with it, like our friend back there, won't pay – at least if ye give them half a chance. Ye have to be firm.'

'Ye could have been a deal firmer,' Jamie observed. 'Ye could have made him settle now. He'll have money in the house.'

Cameron smiled. It was a rebuke for his well-known reluctance to pursue any patient for money, whether they were rich or poor.

'You're like all the young, Jamie,' he said. 'You're unforgiving. Well, right or wrong, ye must let an old fogie like me do things in his own fashion. Your turn will come and it's no that far off – '

He paused. 'Go ahead and fetch me the trap, will ye, laddie? It's been a whole jug of a day and I've done with tramping.'

Cameron stopped.

He watched Jamie run forward, the heavy box swinging easily from his arm, to where they had left the pony and trap a hundred yards away by the farm gate.

Jamie had grown up into a fine young man, Cameron reflected. How long had it been? Eleven years. Eleven years and a few months since he'd stumbled over what he thought was a dropped sack on the Oban pier. Jamie had been tall for his age then. He'd reached his full height, the height he carried now, four years later – well over six feet according to the measuring rod in Cameron's surgery.

Afterwards Jamie's bony adolescent frame had started to fill out.

At twenty the young man was still lean. There wasn't a

spare ounce of flesh on him. But his shoulders were as broad as a border ox's, his neck was thick and strong, and the muscles in his arms and legs stood out like lengths of mooring cable beneath his summer-tanned skin. He had the body of a true Highlander, Cameron thought, lithe and powerful and long-striding. Many generations of hard mountain men must have gone into his making. Yet Jamie's towering physical presence wasn't only a matter of his height and build.

Jamie's face was memorable too.

He still had the red hair and quick blue eyes of his childhood. But with the years the hair had become thicker and glossier, and the eyes, it seemed, darker. They were no longer a clear periwinkle blue but the colour of the Hebridean sea in winter, deep and flecked with grey. Gazing steadily out from his flat high-cheekboned face, they gave him an almost catlike look, wary and inscrutable.

It was a face, Cameron decided, which would break more than one heart before the boy was through, although all the time it would tell the world to keep its distance.

The man who carried Jamie's rugged countenance and fearsome muscles would be a perilous man to cross.

'Here ye are, doctor.' Jamie reappeared leading the pony by the bridle.

He helped Cameron into the passenger seat, then swung himself up beside the doctor, and picked up the reins.

As Jamie urged the pony forward on the road home, Cameron glanced at him thoughtfully again.

Dr Cameron had kept his promise to Mary Livingstone. Over the years Cameron had done his best for the lad. No one could accuse him of failing in that. From the start it had seldom been easy. To his wife's fury, and overruling her bitter protests, Cameron had insisted that Jamie remained with them after he learned of the sinking of the *Hercules*. He'd paid for Jamie to attend Blantyre Academy, and made sure the child had a decent education.

Jamie hadn't let him down.

The boy was an excellent pupil. His teachers' annual reports were always outstanding. Predictably they made no difference to Mrs Cameron. She resented Jamie's presence in her house. She begrudged every penny spent on him. She took every possible opportunity to abuse and humiliate him. To her frustration the opportunities were few. With a child's razor-sharp intuition Jamie had grasped his position in the household on the day he first met her.

Afterwards his behaviour was as exemplary and self-effacing as it was at the academy.

When Jamie reached the age of sixteen, the situation improved. Like every Highland doctor, Cameron employed a young assistant to drive his trap, carry his instruments, write out his accounts, and generally help him in his practice. Soon after Jamie's sixteenth birthday Cameron's former assistant left.

Cameron appointed Jamie to take his place.

'I willna be paying him of course, my dear,' he told his wife when he announced the decision. 'So there's money to be saved. It'll give the lad a chance to put something back into the household. I know he'll welcome that. At the same time mebbe a little medicine will rub off on him.'

As always when anything connected with Jamie came up, Mrs Cameron's eyes narrowed and her mouth tightened.

'You will no doubt do as you choose, Charles,' she said. 'Please don't blame me if your so-called "savings" prove a fanciful illusion. I would no more trust the smallest part of my affairs to that boy than I would to a passing tramp.'

Mrs Cameron left the room before he could remonstrate.

Well, Cameron thought, four years later Jamie had proved his wife wrong. Jamie had been a diligent and trustworthy assistant. He had kept the surgery's accounts scrupulously. He had driven the trap, he had carried the box, he had helped with the patients the length of the

Clyde estuary. The job was often tedious and demanding. Jamie had never complained once. And, to Cameron's immense satisfaction, Jamie had learnt eagerly.

Jamie had made himself little short of an expert on the countryside herbs which were a staple of Cameron's practice.

He could prescribe and prepare medicaments for a wide range of illnesses and disorders. He could even, if necessary, carry out a little simple surgery on his own. In another year he would be ready to go to Glasgow medical academy. That, Cameron knew, would involve another battle with his wife. It was one he was prepared to face and win.

Cameron might have done well by the crofter's child – but the child had done even better by him.

Yet proud as Cameron was of the boy, Jamie was still an enigma to him. From the start he had been the most private and self-contained child Cameron had ever encountered. Jamie gave away nothing. He seemed to lack any emotion at all, showing neither fear nor anger, misery nor happiness, affection nor dislike. At first Cameron put it down to the shocks Jamie had experienced in the months before he found him. Somehow they seemed to have numbed the boy, to have sealed him away from the rest of the world.

As Jamie grew up, Cameron believed, their effect would pass and he would begin to open out.

Jamie did not.

If anything he became more remote and inaccessible. Sometimes Cameron found his detachment almost frightening. Jamie appeared insulated from any normal human response. It wasn't because he existed in a vacuum, Cameron was certain of that. On the contrary. Under Jamie's imperturbable exterior, Cameron sensed, a cauldron of ideas and feelings and passions was simmering.

For whatever reason Jamie had learned to keep them locked away deep inside himself. If they ever forced their way to the surface, Cameron knew they would erupt in a volcanic explosion.

The trap drew up by the front door of the Camerons' Blantyre house. Jamie jumped down and helped the doctor out.

'Will ye join me in the study for a wee dram?' Cameron asked as they stood in the darkness by the pony's head.

Jamie shook his head. 'Thank ye, doctor, but I'll put the beast in the byre and be away to my bed. It's an early start I'm after tomorrow.'

Apart from Sundays Jamie was allowed one free day a month. Indulgently Cameron allowed him to select the day himself. For August Jamie had chosen the following day, a Saturday.

Cameron rubbed his chin thoughtfully.

'Isna this the week of the fair at Hamilton?' he asked.

'Aye, mebbe it is,' Jamie answered cautiously.

'Well, if it is and if ye go,' Cameron said, 'try not to damage too many gateposts with your heid on your way back.'

'I'll be verra careful, doctor,' Jamie replied.

It was as close to a joke as existed between them.

Jamie, or so Cameron strongly suspected, tried his luck in the boxing booths of the fairs that travelled Scotland during the spring and summer. The first time Jamie came back with a blackened eye and a cut mouth, he told Dr Cameron he had walked into a gatepost in the dark. Cameron had never queried the explanation, but he'd teased Jamie with it ever since.

As Jamie led the pony away, Cameron smiled.

Although his wife would have disapproved violently had she known, in Cameron's view it was a harmless enough pursuit for a strapping young man. If it put a few pennies in his pocket, so much the better. They would at least add to the pittance which Cameron, in spite of his protestations to his wife, had paid Jamie from the day he made him his assistant.

Cameron went indoors.

— 31 —

Jamie rose just before dawn the following morning.

He dressed in the little attic bedroom on the servants' floor where he'd slept ever since his recovery. Then he walked quietly downstairs and let himself out of the house. Hamilton was sixteen miles away. At a brisk walk he'd cover the distance in four hours. It would be another four hours back on foot that evening, but he'd been promised the double journey would be well worth the effort.

In the pale but already clear light of a summer morning, Jamie set off down the road.

Dr Cameron was right. Jamie had taken to boxing in the fairground booths. What Cameron didn't know was quite how successful Jamie had become. He'd started four years before when he was sixteen. Jamie saw a poster advertising the Blantyre fair. Among its attractions it offered five shillings to any young man who could last three rounds on his feet with the 'Champion of the Clyde – Battling Jim Macallan'.

To Jamie five shillings, a labourer's wages for a week, was a fortune.

The entry fee to the booth was sixpence. That was a substantial sum in itself, but Jamie decided it was worth risking some of his precious savings. The Blantyre Academy had adopted the fashionable southern practice of including lessons in pugilism in its curriculum. To Jamie, with his beating at the hands of the cattle-boy on the Oban pier still a vivid scar on his memory, it was a God-given opportunity to make sure the humiliation never happened again.

He threw himself into the lessons with the same passionate commitment he gave to everything else. Strong and athletic with cat-like reflexes and a total defiance of physical pain, Jamie proved a brilliant pupil. Very soon, after beating boys several years older and much more experienced than himself, he was school champion.

Jamie didn't win the five shillings on offer at the Blantyre fair.

To his fury the booth fighter, after sparring with him for the first two rounds, caught him in the pit of his stomach in the third and dropped him gasping to his knees. To good-natured jeers from the watching crowd Jamie crawled out of the ring, clutching his belly and sixpence the poorer. He recovered his breath and hauled himself up. Then instead of returning home he joined the spectators. Jamie began to watch intently.

When the booth closed for the night Jamie was still there.

What Jamie discovered that night was that strength, courage and rudimentary skills weren't enough. He might be a champion among boys, but in a world of men he was still a child. Fighting was a craft. Only with application, knowledge and experience would he ever complete his apprenticeship and master it. As eagerly as he studied medicine with Dr Cameron, Jamie set about learning.

He visited every fair that passed within a twenty-mile radius of Blantyre. He watched every move made by the professionals. He analysed the mistakes of their challengers. He went home and practised the lessons he'd learned, bobbing and weaving and ducking in the early morning for hour after hour before the hall mirror.

Six months later when the fair returned in the spring, Jamie paid his challenge money again. This time the outcome was very different. Jamie didn't only last the three rounds. By the end of them it was the booth fighter who was in trouble – if the bell hadn't sounded he might well have gone down himself.

Jamie collected his prize and again settled down to watch the other challengers. He was the only one of them to win all evening.

Jamie had never failed to win a prize since.

Winning in the booths was important to Jamie. Yet it wasn't the real reason he continued day after day over the years that followed, winter and summer alike, to put himself through a training routine that often left him dizzy with exhaustion. He had another much more compelling motive. He needed the money the fairs offered. Contrary to what Dr Cameron believed – and Jamie had never tried to disabuse him – Jamie had no intention of going to the Glasgow medical academy and becoming a doctor himself.

Jamie had other plans.

They were not so much plans as a burning obsessive determination. Jamie was going to Africa. He would find the source of the Nile, the river of life. He would also find a queen there. He would build the memorial to his sisters he had vowed to create when he buried the little girls alongside their grandmother in the graveyard of the Scottish kings. His entire life was dedicated to nothing else. The prize-money from the bouts was simply a weapon he needed to achieve it.

When he left Blantyre that early August morning on the road to Hamilton, Jamie believed he was about to record his biggest – and richest – win in the fairground boxing booths.

As word of his success in the booths spread out along the Clyde estuary, Jamie was approached with offers to take part in true challenge matches – matches where it wasn't a question of lasting three rounds with the fairground professional, but of beating him. The offers came from local landowners with a taste for gambling who were prepared to wager large sums on the outcome of a bout.

Jamie had no hesitation in accepting.

The fights were little different, but the rewards if he won were far greater. As opposed to ten shillings or even a guinea, he could earn himself as much as ten pounds. That day at Hamilton he had been offered his biggest prize yet. If he put away the Bull of the North, as the fair's champion was known, he would receive twenty pounds. Jamie was certain the money was as good as his. He had never lost a challenge match. He was gaining in strength and experience with every month. And he had a passionate hunger for the money.

Three hours after he left Blantyre Jamie reached the village of Auldhouse.

The match was scheduled for midday. He had arranged to meet his backers at the Auldhouse Inn for a hearty pre-fight breakfast to discuss his tactics during the bout. Jamie entered the inn's dining room. To his surprise none of the men he'd expected to find was there.

'Will ye be Jamie Oran?' a voice said from behind the counter.

Jamie nodded. The voice belonged to a small pot-bellied man who was clearly the innkeeper.

'Well, I've some sore news for ye, young man,' the innkeeper went on. 'Ye ken the Farquarson of Inver-gordon and his cousin from Kilvey?'

'Aye.' Jamie nodded again.

They were his backers. Or more precisely the Far-quarson was. His cousin was no more than Farquarson's drinking companion, whose only role had been to introduce Jamie to Farquarson. Farquarson, an amiable freckle-faced young man with sandy hair, was a kelp laird who had put up the prize-money for the bout – and wagered heavily in Jamie's favour on its outcome.

Jamie had met him only once. By all accounts Farquarson was an inveterate dissolute and gambler who had lost several fortunes in the south. It was of no concern to Jamie – although he had rather liked the cheerful roguish cast to Farquarson's face. If Far-quarson's money was good enough to stage the match, then it was good enough for Jamie.

'The Bull of the North willna meet ye,' the innkeeper continued. 'The word's out the baillies have distrained on the Farquarson's lands again. His cousin canna find the purse, and the Bull willna fight without the siller on the table.'

'So the match is off?' Jamie said.

The innkeeper nodded. 'Aye. It's sorry I am too. I'll tell ye this for nothing. I had a few bawbies of my own on ye, laddie. So tak a ladle of my haggis for the journey hame. Ye can repay it when yon Farquarson digs his siller from out under the baillies, and ye come back and crack the Bull. I'll wager ye'll do it still.'

Jamie ate the plate of haggis.

Then he headed home. He was disappointed, but he wasn't discouraged. The bout would be rearranged. There were other rich and feckless sportsmen who would back him. Jamie didn't have the slightest doubt he would win. And when he did the twenty pounds would still be his.

He reached Blantyre at mid morning. It was the third Saturday in the month and the servants' day off. When the servants were away, Mrs Cameron always travelled to Glasgow to visit her aunt. Dr Cameron would have taken the pony and trap on his rounds alone. For once Jamie had the house to himself. He let himself in and climbed the stairs. He would change out of the clothes he had put on for the fair. Afterwards he would spend the day reading in the doctor's study.

Jamie opened the door of his room and stepped forward. Then he stopped in mid stride.

For some reason Mrs Cameron hadn't gone to Glasgow. She was standing beside the little pine chest by his bed. The drawers in the chest were open and his few possessions were scattered over the floor at her feet. As he entered she swung round. For an instant she stared at him, startled. Then she recovered and her face hardened.

'So you've come back early,' Mrs Cameron said. 'Well, maybe it's just as well. With the explaining you've got to do, you're going to need every hour in the day – and then more.'

Jamie gazed at her in bewilderment. All he could take

in was that Mrs Cameron had been searching his room.

'I dinna understand, ma'am,' he said.

'I think you understand very well,' Mrs Cameron snapped. 'Perhaps you'd like to start your explanation by accounting for this!'

She held up something.

Jamie peered forward. It was his sporran, the old and now worn leather wallet he'd been wearing at his waist the day Dr Cameron found him on the Oban pier.

For as long as Jamie had owned it the sporran had barely ever been out of his sight. After he came to live with the Camerons he kept it hidden under the little table by his bed. Jamie used it to store the few possessions he valued which he had collected over the years.

As he watched Mrs Cameron reached into the sporran and pulled out a handful of the money he had won at the fairs.

'There's almost fifty guineas here,' she went on. 'Where did it come from?'

'But that's mine,' Jamie protested. 'I earned it all.'

'Earned it?' Mrs Cameron sneered. 'How?'

Jamie was silent. He couldn't tell her the truth. If Mrs Cameron knew what he'd been doing, she would have him thrown out of the house.

'I earned it honestly,' he said stubbornly.

'You didn't earn it – you stole it!'

'No, ma'am!' Jamie shouted.

'Yes, you did. And I know who you stole it from too. You stole it from the doctor.' Her voice lashed him.

As Jamie stood appalled, Mrs Cameron rummaged in the sporran again. She drew out the letter Mary Livingstone had given him as a child eleven years before.

' "For the personal attention of the President of the Royal Geographical Society",' she read from the envelope. 'Stolen too, I imagine. I think I should see what it says.'

'No!'

As she made to open the envelope, something inside Jamie snapped.

Although Dr Cameron had always tried to shield Jamie from his wife, Jamie had known for years what Mrs Cameron felt about him. She hated, despised, and resented him. Out of his respect and affection for the doctor, until then Jamie had always managed to accept her insults and sneers in silence.

No longer. The letter was his most precious possession in the world. It was his passport to a still confused and uncertain future, but one where he knew he would redeem all the most sacred promises of his childhood.

Like a thief in the night, Mrs Cameron was trying to steal it from him.

Jamie sprang across the room and seized the letter from her hand. He scooped up the money and thrust everything back into the sporran. For an instant he stood towering above her. Then he stepped back. The tendons in his wrists were quivering with shock and anger.

'You attacked me!' Mrs Cameron's voice was a venomous whisper and her face was white. 'You physically attacked me!'

'I didna so, ma'am – '

Jamie's voice was as cold as hers. Something had changed for ever between them.

'It's all mine, even yon letter, and it's all honest come by. Whoever says other, speaks in falsehood.'

Mrs Cameron ignored him.

'You stole under the roof of those who took you in,' she continued, her eyes narrow with hatred. 'You abused their kindness and betrayed their trust. And when you were away from here you stole from others too. You are a liar and a common thief. When the doctor returns I shall tell him to send for the sheriff immediately.'

She swept out of the room, slamming the door behind her.

Jamie sat down on the bed.

He remained there for a long time. His face was grim and his stomach felt icy. For eleven years the house in Blantyre had been his home. Now in a few bewildering moments it had been snatched away from him. Privately

Dr Cameron might believe him about the money. Dr Cameron might even believe that Jamie hadn't attacked Mrs Cameron. But Jamie knew the doctor wasn't a strong enough man to stand up to his wife.

Mrs Cameron, Jamie realized at last, was close to madness. With the cunning and the obsessive malignancy of the near-mad, she would go on at her husband until the sheriff was summoned. And then –

Jamie clenched his fists in fury and frustration.

Then he pulled himself together. He forced himself to think. It was close to midday. Dr Cameron wouldn't be back until the evening. Jamie could wait until then and try to explain. It would make no difference. At best he would gain one more night, but the outcome would be the same – whether the sheriff was called or not, Jamie would be out of the house the following morning.

He was better off leaving now. Jamie stood up.

When he became Cameron's assistant the doctor had given him a stout leather satchel for his use on their journeys. Jamie packed everything he owned into the satchel now. It wasn't much – some clothes, a heavy clasp knife with a stag's horn handle, the books Mary Livingstone had left with him, his second pair of boots and a few other cherished oddments. He slung the sporran round his waist on a length of cord.

Then he hesitated.

Jamie drew the chair up to the table. He sat down, found a piece of paper, and began to write with a quill pen in a neat flowing script.

'Esteemed Dr Cameron,' Jamie wrote. 'I pen these words with a heavy heart. Mrs Cameron will have told ye the circumstances of our encounter today. I wish not to question the interpretation of your good lady. She has, as always, my profound respect. But before God I tell ye this, sir. The money was mine own, hard won but honestly won. Not a penny was of yours. If I lie, may the Almighty strike me down now as I write. The letter too was mine and given openly to my hand by your cousin. Believe me, sir – '

Jamie paused reflectively. Then he continued.

'I am away south. The sheriff may find me on the road if ye direct. I will neither hasten nor tarry. I will stand on my word against all the world and the world above. Let the sheriff ride after me. He will see my face and not my back.

'South is my course, but my destination is far. I am for Africa, sir. I know not how I will reach the distant continent, but I am steadfast in my resolve. For many a year I have known my destiny is there. I trust to the Lord to guide my steps.'

Jamie took a deep breath. Then he finished:

'With my profound gratitude for your unfailing kindness, your patience, your sustenance, and the share of your learning so freely given across the years, I leave your hearth and your company as your servant to the grave: James Oran.

'P.S. On my heart crossed with the Lord's sign, I say to ye again, sir. I didna take the money.'

Jamie sealed the letter with wax. He propped it up against the pewter candlestick on the table, with Dr Cameron's name inscribed on the front. Then he picked up the leather bag and went downstairs.

Mrs Cameron, Jamie guessed, was in the parlour.

The door was firmly closed and he could hear a murmur of voices inside. She was probably entertaining some of the other stalwarts of the Blantyre kirk to coffee, and no doubt telling the worthy ladies what had happened an hour earlier. Jamie crossed the hall silently. He stepped into the street, and turned left towards the Blantyre Inn from where the coach left for the south.

He was on his way to London. His childhood and his youth, Jamie realized suddenly as he walked down the street, were over.

He was a man now with promises to keep.

— 32 —

The caravan of slaves into which Mamkinga was sold, after his escape from the Widow Okuma's house and his capture by the Waziri nomads, left for the Atlantic coast the morning after he joined it.

In all there were over eighty slaves divided into manacled bands of a dozen each. The Arab, Ben-Alu, led the procession himself, riding on a handsome bay horse. Behind him were two other horses ridden by two of his servants, and an ox-drawn waggon containing his belongings. After the waggon came the slaves. They were escorted by six of Ben-Alu's trusted slaves who patrolled the column unshackled on foot.

The trusted slaves carried long cane staffs. If anyone stumbled or slowed they were beaten until they were moving again. Right at the back was a second waggon carrying sacks of ground maize which supplied the slaves with their single daily meal.

The group of women to whom Mamkinga had been shackled travelled at the end of the procession. There were penalties in being at the rear. It was the dry season and they were moving along well-trodden tracks. Great clouds of choking dust billowed back, making their eyes water and their chests heave. On the other hand the trusted slaves were less interested in the end of the column than its head. If a man fell, everyone in his group was liable to be beaten indiscriminately too.

At the rear there seemed to be less urgency and consequently less violence.

The women, too, Mamkinga discovered, were hardier than the men. They might walk more slowly but fewer of them buckled and fell. On the rare occasion one did, she was quickly surrounded by the others and even the most brutal of the trusted slaves hesitated before using his staff to lash her back on to her feet. In spite of the dust, Mamkinga soon realized, he was lucky to have been put where he was.

It wasn't an unqualified privilege. One of the prerogatives of the trusted slaves was the right to copulate with any woman there. The quiet well-fleshed girl immediately in front of Mamkinga in the chained line – she was named Zia, he found out – was the youngest and prettiest in the caravan.

Inevitably Zia became their favourite prey.

Again and again, generally at night but sometimes during the caravan's day-halts too, Mamkinga would feel a painful tug on the chain that linked them. His head would be plucked round and he would see one of the slaves lowering himself hungrily on top of Zia. The chain jerked backwards and forwards as the man heaved until he spent himself. Then he climbed to his feet, casually wiped the wetness from his groin, and moved away, often to be replaced by one of his companions.

Sometimes Zia screamed and fought against the assaults, and the other women would come to her help.

Occasionally then the men backed away, either ashamed or frightened by the ferocity of the women's reaction. More often Zia, exhausted from the day's march, lay back limply and received the discharge of the semen without protest, brushing her body when the man left and waiting inertly for her next assailant.

To Mamkinga, as a child, the repeated assaults on Zia were incomprehensible. He knew they were uninvited and somehow degrading – although he couldn't work out why. Zia was obviously distressed, yet the couplings left no mark on her, unlike the beatings from the trusted slaves' staffs. The following day she seemed to have no memory of what had taken place during the night.

Drifting into sleep, as his neck chain jangled while yet another of the men plunged down on her, Mamkinga would cup his hands to his ears and try to shut out the sound of Zia's moans.

For Mamkinga the journey lasted three full moons.

Day succeeded day identical to the one before. The caravan's route followed the course of the streams and rivers flowing westwards. Early every morning the slaves were given a gourd of water each. Then the column set out. If the heat was unusually fierce there were brief halts at midday and in the afternoon, when more water would be issued – providing the caravan was close to a river at the time.

If not, the slaves lay gasping in whatever shade they could find until they were forced on.

In the early stages the landscape was flat and monotonous. There were great undulating dunes of grey sand interspersed with areas of sluggish marsh. On the dune crests silver-backed jackals trotted like wraiths against the wavering haze of the skyline. In the marshes mosquitos hung in curtains sixty feet high, so dark and thick they dulled the glare of the morning sun.

Often at the end of a day's march through the watery basins, the slaves' eyelids were so swollen with insect bites they could only stumble blindly through the evening's camp, groping to carry out the tasks Ben-Alu had assigned to them.

Dehydration, exhaustion, the skin-rending attacks of sand storms and the tormenting assaults of insects, were all constant hazards of the journey. But there were others too. Both the dunes and the swamps harboured colonies of scorpions and snakes. Seeking warmth, the scorpions would gather round the slaves' bodies as they slept at night. When the slaves woke and stretched in the morning, the scorpions would arch their poisoned spines and strike at them.

The wounds were seldom fatal but the injected poison left open sores that festered for days.

The snakes were more deadly. Most African snakes registered the vibrations of a human foot and slithered away before an intruder's approach. The puff adders were different. Slow and somnolent, they lay lethargically half-buried in the dust. If a foot touched them, they reared up and struck like a flare of lightning. The venom they expelled was lethal. Three of Ben-Alu's captives died because of them.

Worst of all were the spitting cobra.

With unerring accuracy they could hurl their poison from a distance of five paces straight into the eyes of what they took to be a prey or an attacker. Twice Mamkinga, trudging through the sand, spotted them just before they lifted their hoods and struck. He managed to raise his hands in time to shield his face and took the venom on his skin.

The poison still left blisters which, like the scorpion bites, suppurated for days.

After the dunes and the marshes the caravan entered the forest. The huge shimmering spaces of the open lands were replaced by dense and dripping walls of vegetation. The air enclosed beneath the tree canopy was so humid the slaves' bodies glistened silver with moisture from dawn until dusk. They stumbled along the narrow paths like a procession of ghosts, the rattling of their chains the only sound in the oppressive silence.

The flickering green twilight of the forest glittered with reflections from the endless streams that threaded the trees.

Each time the caravan crossed one, leeches would rise from the water and attach themselves to the splashing legs, crawling upwards to gorge on the surface blood cells round the slaves' groins. When they halted in the evening Mamkinga would find as many as fifty clinging to his skin, hanging like a grey and swollen growth around his testicles.

At the start Mamkinga tore them off in disgust as quickly as he could. The young woman Zia, whose homeland lay in the forest, taught him not to.

'If you pull them away,' she explained, 'you will break the body and leave the head behind. The head has poison and the wound where it remains will rot.'

Zia was right, Mamkinga discovered.

Wherever the leeches' heads were left on his body, the skin became discoloured and swollen. Instead Zia showed Mamkinga how to take a glowing twig from the fire and touch it to the leech's back. The slug then released the grip of its jaws, and the whole creature dropped away.

From then on Mamkinga cleaned himself by the fire every evening.

As the leeches fell to the ground he stamped on them vengefully with his heel, watching the blood – his own blood – spurt out and stain the earth.

The day's single meal came at dusk when the column stopped for the night. Ben-Alu's tent was pitched at a distance from the general campsite and his food was prepared separately. The rest ate from basins of gruel crudely cooked by the trusted slaves over a ring of open fires. There was never enough to satisfy anyone's hunger, and among the men there were constant fights as they plundered each other's bowls.

Once again Mamkinga realized he was fortunate to be with the women.

The women were far more generous than the men in distributing what was given them. If one of the group had sickened during the day, the others always spooned a little of their own ration into her bowl. In Mamkinga's case, as the only child in the column, his gourd was invariably filled until it overflowed.

In spite of that he was almost always hungry. The occasional brief satiety in the evening was followed by the long hours when he, like everyone else, had nothing. During Mamkinga's three months with the caravan over a quarter of the slaves died. The main cause was malaria, but the ravaging effects of the sickness were compounded by malnutrition. The slaves' bodies were too weak to fight back against the fever.

The smith, Etoshi, who had welded on Mamkinga's chains, travelled with the column. Most of the deaths took place at night. Whenever a slave died, the rest would wake to the sound of Etoshi's hammer and chisel cutting through the chains round the corpse. Then his tools hissed in the fire as he made ready to weld the empty bonds to the dead man's nearest neighbour.

Occasionally a slave collapsed and died during the day's march.

The procession came to a halt and Ben-Alu rode back from the head of the caravan. He irritably inspected the body from his horse and issued curt instructions. The smith ran forward. Drawing an axe from his satchel of tools, he chopped off the slave's hands and feet and pulled his carcass clear from the manacles. Then he looped the chain over the shoulder of the man in front, and the journey continued.

The dismembered body was left lying by the narrow track in the bush with its severed hands and feet scattered round it.

Looking back, Mamkinga would remember for the rest of his life the circling shadows of the vultures which gathered even before the dust of the passing column had settled.

Three months after they set out the caravan reached the town of Melfi in Chad. They had passed through many towns and villages during the journey, but Melfi was the largest. It was a market town and the centre of the Chad goldsmithing industry.

Ben-Alu ordered the trusted slaves to make camp and prepare for a stay of several days. Then he rode into the town. He visited Melfi twice a year and he had several matters to attend to there, including taking delivery of a new consignment of slaves to replace those who had died on the march. The evening he arrived he met an old acquaintance of his, a forty-year-old Turgana named Ndele.

Ndele was one of the town's leading goldsmiths. He urgently wanted to acquire a young slave for his workshop.

Ben-Alu seldom sold slaves to Africans. They were

worth much more delivered to the coast for sale to the European dealers as plantation labour on the other side of the Atlantic. However Ndele was in a hurry to buy and was prepared to pay a reasonable price. Furthermore the worst part of the journey, through the malarial rain forests, lay ahead. On his last few trips Ben-Alu had lost most of the children in the caravan through fever – and there was no profit in dead children.

Ben-Alu decided to offer Ndele the only boy he had with him.

It was Mamkinga. Ndele visited the camp next morning and inspected the child. He pronounced himself satisfied. The two bargained over the sale and finally the smith was called for.

'What's happening?' Mamkinga asked, bewildered, as Etoshi hammered through the chains that linked him to the plump Zia.

'You've been sold,' the man answered. 'With what we've got in front of us, you're lucky too.'

Mamkinga was led away.

As he went he glanced back over his shoulder. The women were all gazing gaunt and hollow-eyed after him. For the past three months they had been his companions every minute of the day and night. The experiences in which they'd been yoked together, the heat and cold, the hunger, exhaustion and pain, seemed to have welded them into a single being whose fragile existence depended on their unity.

Now Mamkinga was being ripped away from them.

Mamkinga opened his mouth to shout something back to Zia and the others. A call of gratitude, of grief, of hope. The child did not know. It didn't matter. Before Mamkinga could call out he was pitched into a cart. A whip cracked, and wheels rumbled beneath him.

Lying with his face bumping on the floor, Mamkinga was aware that once more something had ended – and something new had begun.

33

Ndele the goldsmith was a sour and taciturn man, famed equally for his skill, his temper, and the tight hold he kept on his purse strings.

Tall, bald and round-shouldered, with a protruding head he carried bobbing in front of him, and a heron's long stiff-legged gait, he lived in a cluttered house in a compound just outside the town. Unusually for a man of his wealth Ndele had taken only one wife.

In complete contrast to her husband she was a small, plump and smiling woman, named Bajmira.

The house formed one side of the compound. On the other, across a dirty yard filled with scratching chickens and emaciated dogs, was the workshop with the slaves' quarters behind. The workshop was considerably larger than the house, a dark sooty brick building with a constantly burning fire against one wall and a floor littered with benches, tables and stools.

The quarters of Ndele's slaves were a low-roofed shed containing some straw-filled cotton mattresses and a few lengths of tree trunks as seats.

Ndele's wealth had enabled him to buy several other properties in the town, and the slaves to look after them. Most of his slaves were rotated according to the requirements of the season. But the gold workshop remained his principal business, and the compound housed four permanent slaves. One took care of the house. The second was what Ndele called the 'donkey', a simple slow-moving man whose job was to gather and chop wood and stoke the fire. The third was a much older man with failing sight who was Ndele's assistant.

Mamkinga was the fourth.

Ndele had bought him with the intention of training Mamkinga up and using him to replace the old man when he eventually went blind. Ndele had already acquired two youths for the task. The first had died soon after he arrived. His death had infuriated the goldsmith who was convinced the boy had been infected with fever when Ndele bought him. The second, to Ndele's even greater rage, had run away.

It was little consolation to the goldsmith when he was found drowned in the nearby river, his hands still chained, a week later. Ndele remained convinced he'd been cheated again.

The experiences had made him even more than usually suspicious of his latest acquisition, Mamkinga, and even harsher in his treatment of the boy.

'You will learn the bellows first,' Ndele instructed him the morning after Mamkinga's arrival. 'Whether I am here or not, you'll keep pumping until I tell you to stop.'

The bellows fanned the heat of the flames over which Ndele melted the gold before it could be cast. A pair of large leather bags mounted on a wooden frame, they were worked by a mahogany pole.

'Any slackening,' Ndele finished, 'and I'll whip your hide until you roar like a buffalo.'

Ndele meant exactly what he said.

Mamkinga worked the bellows conscientiously all that first morning. Then at midday Ndele went out. There had been no conversation in the workshop until then. But on Ndele's departure Akiri, the goldsmith's old assistant, started to talk to Mamkinga. Absorbed in listening to him, Mamkinga slowed the rhythmic movement of the pole and the flames began to dip.

A moment later Ndele hurled the door open. He rushed back in and pulled the pole from its mount.

'I knew it, I knew it!' he shouted in fury. 'I've been cheated again. You're worse than the others. At least they worked while they were here. You're not even doing that. See if this encourages you, you lazy little mountain savage!'

Ndele lifted the pole in the air and began to beat Mamkinga across the back and shoulders.

The mahogany pole was heavy and Ndele's rage gave a frenzied energy to his attack. Mamkinga clasped his arms round his ears to protect his head. He scrambled away, trying to hide between the tables. It was useless. Ndele tore the workshop furniture aside and rained blows down on the boy.

'Ignorant idle devil!' Ndele bellowed. 'The spirits cursed me the day they let me see you. May you feel my curses on your bones in return!'

Finally, panting and exhausted, the goldsmith stopped.

Mamkinga, his body throbbing with pain, lay on the floor. Every inch of his flesh ached with the punishment. Still muttering in anger, Ndele stormed out of the workshop. Gingerly Mamkinga flexed his fingers to see if any of the joints were broken. Then he clambered to his feet and started working the bellows again.

The lesson certainly achieved Ndele's intention. From that morning on, whatever the distractions in the workshop, Mamkinga never once ceased his steady pumping nor allowed the glowing fire to cool.

Compared to the Widow Okuma's household, life as a slave in the smithy was bleak and monotonous.

There were no locks on the shed – it did not even have a door. Instead, more humiliating and much more effective as a barrier to escape, Mamkinga was permanently shackled by chains. They were loose enough to allow him to work but they were also too heavy, too clamorous and restricting, to give him any chance of running away.

Mamkinga woke each morning with the light.

He pumped the bellows all day. At evening he left the workshop and walked the few paces back to the slaves' quarters. He ate a meal of maize gruel with his companions. He listened as they talked and quickly learned the language they used, but he almost never spoke himself. Then as the sun set and the compound darkened, he fell back on his bed of dried grass and drifted into a troubled unhappy sleep.

Occasionally Mamkinga heard the owls calling as they hunted the grasslands beyond the village.

On those nights he would see in the darkness Toomi's face, framed by the pearl-spotted wings of the owl which had brought him food in the Widow's house at Nasir. Mamkinga would pretend she was with him again and they were lying together as they did when they were children, their arms curled round each other. Then he would sleep peacefully.

All too soon dawn would come. Mamkinga would wake to find he was alone, and the monotonous grinding work of another day would begin.

In spite of its harshness, life in Ndele's workshop had one unexpected compensation. Bajmira, the goldsmith's wife, took a liking to the tall silent boy. Sometimes she would give him the leftovers from her husband's dinner – a joint of cold roasted meat from a spring hare, or a bowl of broth made with marrow bones from a gazelle the village's huntsmen had trapped. Fearful of Ndele's anger if he were caught eating the goldsmith's food, Mamkinga would snatch whatever Bajmira gave him. He devoured it swiftly and ran back in silence to the workshop.

Bajmira would watch him race away. With his wary hunted eyes, the boy reminded her of a wounded forest animal. She would sigh and return to her fire and her cooking pots.

As a goldsmith the sour gangling Ndele – for long the shadow of his body on the floor whenever he entered the workshop made Mamkinga shiver – was a consummately skilled craftsman. People came from all over the surrounding countryside to bargain for his services. Many of them were women. They would bring a leather pouch of gold dust, sieved from the rivers, and ask him to create something out of it.

Often they had no idea what they wanted. They were, too, nervous of approaching such a famed artist. So they hired asamas to come with them. The asamas were a combination of troubadour, advocate and adviser. Singing and chanting, they extolled the virtues of their client. Even more fulsomely they praised Ndele's art. Finally, still in song, they made suggestions about what Ndele might fashion out of the raw metal the women had brought with them.

Mamkinga loved the asamas.

Their ballads were bold and joyous, with haunting refrains in which they sang of birds and mountains, sunset and wind, colours and water and laughter: a kaleidoscope of images which brought back to him – so vividly that he ached as he listened – the texture and feel of his lost home, Malinda.

The asamas accompanied themselves on instruments. Whenever one entered the goldsmith's courtyard, dragging his often shy and blushing employer behind him, the sound of pipes or the plaintive water-like ripples of the hardwood lutes of the river villages rose into the air. The passers-by on the street would forget their business and crowd in to listen too.

Then, as the music lifted and the applause of rhythmically clapping hands flowed through it, the dark grimy shed would be turned into a place of carnival.

Ndele, for all his fretful and often cruel behaviour, fully deserved their praise, Mamkinga decided. As an artist, a craftsman, a designer of rings and brooches and ornaments, he was peerless.

'How do you see it – ?' Ndele would demand of some woman who had come in bearing a pouch of gold dust that represented perhaps five years' panning of her local river shallows. 'As a little gazelle, a gerenuk maybe? Well, that's what your asama is telling me. But, no, I don't agree. It's wrong, entirely wrong – '

The master goldsmith shook his head. Ndele puffed out his cheeks, and expelled his breath with a long sigh. Then, swaying like a pendulum, he bent over the pouch.

'No, lady, this is not a gerenuk.' He cupped the gold dust in his hand as if he could see the hidden shape inside. 'This is a slender crocodile, a young one just slipped from the egg. Or maybe a fish eagle. Yes, I think I see the feathers stirring. But we must wait for the fire – '

Ndele tipped the dust into a little iron pot with a long handle, and held it over the flames.

The gold dust coalesced and liquefied. Ndele studied the molten globule intently. Then he pronounced.

'No,' he said with absolute assurance. 'Neither a crocodile nor an eagle. The gold has spoken to me and I, Ndele, know how it wishes to be born. Caged here, waiting to be freed, is a swallow.'

Ndele gave one of his rare smiles.

Everyone clapped in acclaim. The asama launched into a new song, explaining that the gold all along had been waiting to take shape as a white-throated fork-tailed bird.

Mamkinga listened then, his fingers tense with desire to handle the precious metal himself, to pattern the coat of the golden hunting leopard or fashion the tail of a leaping river fish. Sometimes he became so absorbed he almost allowed the fire to die – but never quite.

The lesson of his first morning was seared indelibly into Mamkinga's memory.

As the glow began to fade Mamkinga pumped the bellows harder and the flames leapt upwards, as clear and warm and shining as the asama's song.

A year after his arrival Mamkinga was unexpectedly promoted.

Akiri, the old slave with the failing eyesight, was sent out one morning into the countryside on an errand. On the way home he was bitten by a jackal. Rolling and staggering, Akiri made his way back to the compound. By nightfall he was in a coma.

Before the sun rose Akiri was dead.

Twenty-four hours later Ndele told Mamkinga that he was to take over the old man's job. A youth was hired from a neighbouring compound to operate the bellows, and Mamkinga found himself working as the goldsmith's assistant.

Mamkinga remained Ndele's assistant for the next seven years.

There was no obvious change in his circumstances. He remained shackled and he continued to live in the shed behind the workshop. But Mamkinga's life now was infinitely more interesting and varied. Instead of squatting for hour after hour behind the bellows, he followed Ndele wherever the goldsmith went. He scoured the melting pots and held them over the flames as their precious contents were reduced. He cleaned out the moulds that formed the most popular ornaments. He polished the rings and brooches and figures which emerged after the casting.

Only one task was unchanged. When the day's work was over Mamkinga had to sweep the workshop's packed-earth floor.

Bajmira had given him a length of old cloth to wrap round himself at night. Every evening Mamkinga tipped the pile of sweepings into the cloth and carried them down to the river. There he washed them carefully. Quite often when all the dirt had floated away one or two bright grains of gold would remain embedded in the weave.

Mamkinga gathered the golden grains and stored them carefully in a porcupine quill which he hid in a crack in the hut's wall. One day, he knew, they might provide his means of escape.

One morning, when Ndele had gone downriver to deliver a commission to a caravan of merchants, Bajmira came to find Mamkinga as he ate his gruel by the fire. As always he was sitting apart from the other slaves. Bajmira's face was alight with happiness.

'The wise woman has told me what I knew already,' she said, smiling. 'After all these years I am finally with child. There will be six months of the moon before the little one is born. Then you will be able to rock him for me at night when he cries.'

She patted her belly and laughed. 'I have brought something special for you, Mamkinga. Sweet things to celebrate sweet news!'

From the folds of her robe Bajmira produced a length of smooth-skinned pale yellow cane.

'It is chewed and eaten thus,' Bajmira explained.

She showed Mamkinga how to extract the sugar from the cane. Then Bajmira gave it to him. Mamkinga licked the cane experimentally. The bristly white fibres seemed to be soaked in juice as sweet as the combs of honey he and Toomi used to rob from the nests of the wild bees.

Mamkinga looked up at her. He thanked Bajmira. For the first time he smiled.

One afternoon, six months after Mamkinga was given his new job, the workshop was unusually busy. Ndele was engaged in applying the final embellishments to several commissions, when a group of new customers and their asamas appeared at the door. The goldsmith broke off to usher them in. Then he turned and gruffly called for Mamkinga.

Mamkinga, his chains rattling behind him, hurried across the floor.

'I must see what lies in their gold,' Ndele said, 'but this has to be finished by nightfall – '

He held up a tiny figure of a woman he had cast earlier in the day.

'She lacks only her nipples,' Ndele went on. 'Can I trust your clumsy fingers to add them?'

Mamkinga looked at the figure. He thought for a moment. Then he nodded.

The goldsmith glanced at the doorway. The new customers were clamouring for his attention. Ndele looked back and grunted suspiciously.

'For your sake I hope you are right,' he said. 'The pole has made you bellow often enough. But I tell you this. If you harm my work here, I will beat you until only the jackals are doing the howling.'

Ndele handed Mamkinga the figure. The goldsmith turned and bobbed away.

Mamkinga examined the little statuette. The woman, simply but gracefully shaped, was bare to the waist. Below the waist Ndele had draped her in a wrap, its hanging pleats skilfully sculpted out of the gold. Above, her breasts stood out firm and strong, lacking only the minute nipples needed to finish them. Even in its un-finished state it was, Mamkinga knew, a superb example of the goldsmith's art. Completed, it would be one of Ndele's masterpieces.

Mamkinga carried the figure over to a bench at the far end of the workshop.

Mamkinga's mouth was dry and he could feel nervous flutters in his stomach. He had never been allowed to attempt anything like this before, but he had watched Ndele so often he was certain he could do it. Mamkinga took a deep breath, steadied himself and set to work.

Figures of women were often asked for and there was a pre-made mould for their nipples. Mamkinga melted the last of the gold and cast two little rounded pyramids. When they had set firm, he tapped them out on to the bench. Now it was only a matter of soldering them in place on the woman's body.

Mamkinga picked up the slender soldering iron. He heated its point in the fire, and applied it gingerly to one of the breasts.

The gold softened under the heat. Mamkinga pressed a nipple against the mound. He was either too slow or he hadn't heated the gold enough. The nipple refused to weld and dropped on to the bench. He tried again and then again, and then for a fourth time. Each time the result was the same. The tiny moulded pyramid would not bond to the breast.

By now Mamkinga was sweating, partly from the heat of the fire, but mostly in anxiety and frustration.

Mamkinga paused. He had watched Ndele carry out the operation countless times. Always it had worked flawlessly. All Mamkinga could think was that he hadn't heated the soldering iron enough.

Mamkinga wiped the sweat from his face and tried again.

He put the point back into the fire. He heated it until it was glowing. Then he touched it to the figure's breast once more. Mamkinga had no idea what happened next. Perhaps he had overheated the iron, perhaps he was clumsy and pushed too hard. All he knew, as he watched in horror, was that the point had sizzled through the delicate sculpture and that Ndele's exquisite creation had dissolved in an ugly puddle of hissing metal.

'You savage – !'

Somehow over the clamour of his thronging customers and the competing songs of their asamas, Ndele had registered the catastrophe.

The goldsmith threw the crowd around him aside and plunged back across the workshop. Anguished, he gazed down at the wreckage of his creation. He looked up and saw Mamkinga staring back at him. Mamkinga's face was desolate but defiant.

Ndele seized the bellows pole from its mount and gave Mamkinga a terrible blow across the shoulders.

Mamkinga rocked back as the pain flooded through him. He was ready for the chastisement. He had expected it. He expected more and he was ready for that too. What Mamkinga was not ready for was what happened next.

Ndele swung round and drove the throng out of his workshop.

'Tomorrow!' he cried as he pushed them furiously into the yard. 'Today I shall see nothing more in the gold. Tomorrow there will be eagles and flowers and spirits. But for today it is over!'

As the people streamed out Ndele closed the door and turned back. He picked up the now grotesquely misshapen lump of gold and studied it.

His back against the wall where Ndele's first blow had sent him sprawling, Mamkinga waited for the goldsmith to lift the pole and strike him again. Ndele did not. He let the pole drop to the ground and gazed down at his apprentice. Ndele's head swayed on his long bird-like neck and his eyes stared into Mamkinga's.

'You heated the iron first too little and then too much, was that not so?' Ndele demanded.

Miserably Mamkinga nodded.

Ndele glanced at the workshop window. Outside the sun was lowering, but it was still a full hour before dusk.

'There is still time,' Ndele said. 'Before darkness falls we shall fashion her again. Build the fire!'

Within the hour the lump of gold had been melted, re-cast in the mould, and returned to its original form. When the figure had set and cooled, Mamkinga lifted it out of the mould and gently handed it to Ndele. At any moment the customer would appear to reclaim it. All that was needed, as before, was for the nipples to be added.

'Very good,' Ndele said. He paused. 'Now finish it.'

Mamkinga stared at him, astounded. 'But the customer – '

'There was a message,' Ndele cut him off abruptly. 'He does not come until morning. Your eyes are sharp and you have the lamp. If you blunder again, then you must melt and cast again. You have the whole night before you.'

Mamkinga was silent. He shook his head in bewilderment and apprehension.

'Listen to me,' the master goldsmith said. 'To be a craftsman is rare. You are young and idle and clumsy, but deep within you the gift is buried. I know such things. To bring the gift to life you must change. Now you lack patience. You are proud but irresolute. Your mind cannot find its path. When things go wrong, as today, darkness numbs your spirit. You are without courage or conviction – '

Ndele shook his finger at Mamkinga.

He was speaking with an intensity Mamkinga had never heard before. Wide-eyed, Mamkinga stared at him. For once the goldsmith's voice was not angry but thoughtful.

'A craftsman is bold and patient and sure and strong. I can teach you so much, but that you must learn for yourself. Start now. I shall return with the light. Be sure the work is done and the making is good.'

With his angular rocking stride, Ndele paced out of the workshop.

For a long time after the goldsmith left, Mamkinga gazed at the doorway. He was trembling and his mind was in a tumult. He forced himself to breathe slowly and deeply until the trembling passed. Then he set to work.

It was infinitely harder than he had imagined when Ndele first entrusted him with the job. Three times the soldering iron slipped as before. Three times he had to re-cast the entire figure. Then on the fourth casting everything suddenly changed.

It was midnight by then and the full moon was at its height.

Mamkinga was tired and working more slowly. He touched the iron twice in quick succession to the figure's tiny body and immediately set the nipples in place. It was what he had seen Ndele do but had never dared to do himself. Even to apply them one at a time had so far been beyond him. Yet now the nipples bonded swiftly and perfectly to the figure's breasts.

Hardly daring to believe he had finally succeeded, Mamkinga picked up the figure and examined it closely under the lamp.

It was flawless. He polished it gently for a while with water and fine white river sand. Then he put it down. It was finished. Ndele himself, Mamkinga knew, could do no better.

Mamkinga turned to extinguish the lamp. He paused. The figure was not finished. Something was missing. Mamkinga knew instantly what it was. He went outside and crossed the silent yard to the slaves' quarters. He found the porcupine quill of gold he had hidden and returned to the workshop.

As he opened the workshop door again Mamkinga checked briefly. The owls were calling. He smiled and stepped back inside.

Mamkinga worked throughout the remaining hours of darkness. As the first rim of light lifted over the river and touched the roof of Ndele's house, he put down his tools and gazed down at the bench. Lying in front of him was a tiny garland of golden flowers, each miniature blossom and leaf sculpted so delicately they might have been carved out of the frost that every winter morning crisped the pastures of the Mountains of the Moon.

Mamkinga picked up the garland. He settled it round the little figure and with the barest touch of the iron fixed it to her neck. Then he stepped back. Now it truly was finished.

'Is the work done – ?'

The voice behind him was Ndele's. Mamkinga hadn't heard him entering the workshop, but he turned to find the goldsmith standing at his shoulder.

Ndele picked up the figure and examined it critically for several minutes in silence.

'I do not know these flowers,' Ndele said. 'They are not from here. Where do they come from?'

Mamkinga swallowed. 'They came to me in the night.'

Ndele looked at him sharply. Then for an instant his face softened. 'May you have more such nights,' he said. 'The work will serve – '

Ndele broke off.

He turned and clapped his hands irritably. 'Why is the fire not burning? We cannot be standing idly all day. To business, everyone, to business!'

That night, as Mamkinga swept the floor, he noticed the figure had still not been collected by the customer who had commissioned it. Ndele had placed it on a shelf by the door where it would be seen first by everyone who came into the workshop.

As Ndele went out he saw Mamkinga looking at it.

'I decided not to sell it,' the goldsmith said shortly. 'I will make the customer something else with gold of my own.'

Ndele stalked away.

Before he left the workshop to go back to the slaves' quarters to eat, Mamkinga stopped before the figure. He touched the tiny face and then the garland round her neck. The face was not Toomi's – but the flowers were. He and Toomi had gathered them every spring on the banks of the river that ran below Malinda. It would be spring, Mamkinga knew, in Malinda now.

He dragged his chains behind him across the dusty yard.

From that day on Ndele entrusted Mamkinga with adding embellishments to every sculpture the goldsmith made. Mamkinga would put a hand-moulded beak to an eagle, a fin to a fish, a set of fangs to a miniature attacking lion. The idea for each piece, its form and line and dimensions, remained the goldsmith's – but more and more the details were Mamkinga's.

'A clumsier sow's offspring I've never met,' Ndele would say angrily on the rare occasions when something Mamkinga had done went wrong. 'You will ruin my business yet. Do it again and get it right – or before the sun sets I will whip you round the village faster than a cheetah may gallop!'

Ndele's threats were empty now.

Mamkinga was the best assistant the goldsmith had ever had. He was quick, imaginative, and utterly dependable. Mamkinga was aware of his value too. He knew the days of his beatings were over.

He was almost as good a goldsmith as his master and to Ndele he was irreplaceable.

34

Mamkinga remained with Ndele until he was nineteen. By then he was fully grown.

In spite of his moroseness Ndele was a fair master who believed in seeing his slaves were adequately fed – not least because he knew a fit and healthy slave was a better worker. In that respect Mamkinga fared better than many free Africans in the surrounding countryside. The combination of regular food and hard exercise, coupled with a naturally strong physique, turned him into a striking and exceptionally powerful young man.

Well over six feet in height, Mamkinga had a massive chest, thickly muscled arms, and broad sinewy thighs.

Unusually for someone of his size he was also extraordinarily well coordinated. His reflexes were like quicksilver. Sometimes in the workshop he would notice something toppling off a table. The object might be halfway across the room and Mamkinga was always burdened with his chains. Invariably he managed to spring across the floor and pluck the object out of the air before it hit the ground.

'If the spirits send you back,' the gangling grey-haired Ndele would say with reluctant gratitude, 'it will certainly be as a leopard. In which case I hope you'll have learned enough to stay away from my goats.'

It was the only joke Ndele ever made.

Sometimes Mamkinga smiled. His smiles were as rare as the goldsmith's humour.

Mamkinga had shelter, food, and, for a slave, varied and interesting employment. None of it counted for anything. The misery, the aching feeling of loss, the sense of pain and darkness shadowing his mind, never once deserted him. They grew stronger as the years passed. Day after day, week after week, month after month, he thought of nothing but Toomi and Malinda and his home.

Often Mamkinga came close to despair. He would never see them again, he thought. They were gone irrevocably and the world had been emptied of its meaning. Then, in a frenzy of grief, he would decide to find a way to kill himself. The desolation remained but the mood of suicidal grief always passed. One day Toomi might need him.

Mamkinga had to go on. For his sister alone he had to survive.

He did more than survive. Mamkinga prepared himself for the remote moment when he would join Toomi again. He had no doubts about his body. That was an instrument, a weapon, in his care and under his control. He honed it deliberately. Ndele, seeing him jump to catch a falling bowl, saw only a swift and athletic young giant behaving as any conscientious slave should. For Mamkinga the sudden leap had a different purpose.

Like a cat jumping for a fly, he was testing and sharpening his reactions.

Just as important was his mind. Again Mamkinga had been lucky. He might have been sold to the owner of a remote farmstead, isolated from the affairs of nineteenth-century Africa. As it was he found himself in a trading town, a major crossroads on the dusty highways which snaked across the central belt of the continent. Even more important was Ndele's business and his reputation as a craftsman.

People of every sort flowed in and out of the workshop. They came not just from the surrounding region but from thousands of miles away. There were local landowners, farmers, Arab slave traders like Ben-Alu, Berber merchants from the north, ranchers moving cattle, dark-skinned Watusi, lofty and elegant Masai, pug-nosed Comeri, sallow Sudanese, blue-painted Touregs, and many, many more.

Nor were they all African. European interest in the dark continent – and Europe's presence there – was growing every year. Slavers, traders and explorers, Portuguese, British and French – particularly the Portuguese and the British – became more and more frequent visitors as the years passed.

They came to the workshop. They stayed to talk, argue and gossip. And Mamkinga, the master-goldsmith's ever-present assistant, listened intently to every word they said.

By the age of nineteen he knew almost as much about what was happening in the part of Africa which concerned him as anyone else. The little Scottish trader, Butter, had taught him English. Now Mamkinga could speak in six other languages and understand what was being said in as many more. He learned of the famines and gluts and wars and the ever-changing boundaries of the many African kingdoms, of the shifts in the gold and slave and ivory markets, of the increasing European pressure on the continent and the presence of ever-growing numbers of foreign ships off the Atlantic coast.

What Mamkinga failed to discover anything about was the Abyssinian kingdom of Malinda. It was too remote, too forbidding, too walled in by the daunting Mountains of the Moon, for news of its events to have reached the travellers who passed through Ndele's workshop.

Every evening as the sun set Mamkinga looked first at the lowering red ball on the western horizon. Then he turned and stood gazing east until the last rays of light faded and the stars appeared in the night sky. East was where Malinda lay.

If he ever escaped from Melfi, Mamkinga vowed each night, that was where freedom would take him.

He repeated the vow with particular fervour on the first day of his birthday month of June when he reached the age of nineteen. Six weeks later, although he had no idea as he silently spoke the words, his time at Melfi was to come to an end. But when Mamkinga left it was not as a free man – and not on the road to the east.

Six years earlier Bajmira had given birth to the long-awaited child. The baby was a girl whom the goldsmith and his wife named Mara.

Ndele doted on his little daughter.

She became the focus of his entire life. He no longer spent even one night a week at his house across the compound from the workshop. Every evening he left early so he could sleep at Bajmira's house, simply to be close to his child. As Mara grew up the routine in the smithy was changed to accommodate her. In the past the fire had always been stoked at dawn and Ndele would appear thirty minutes later to begin work.

Now the time for the raising of the flames was put back an hour to allow the child to finish her sleep and let Ndele bring her with him to the workshop.

The workshop became the little girl's playroom. There was the clay for the moulds which could be dampened down to be fashioned into clumsy little birds and beasts. Mamkinga would sometimes break off from his work to put an eye in a doll's face, or fashion a tiny animal for her to play with. In return Mara would fetch little sticks to start Mamkinga's fire. She collected water from the stream to wash the golden grains, and pounded up the red chalk for the paste which Mamkinga used to polish up the rings and bangles.

Sometimes she would sit quietly watching the dancing flames while Ndele sang songs to her – stories of cunning jackal gods and the elephant who held up the sky. Best of all she liked to hold the little golden figure which Mamkinga had garlanded.

The little girl would squat for hour after hour, tracing the shapes of the flowers with her fingers while Mamkinga patiently named each one for her.

In Mamkinga's birth month Mara decided to make him a special present – a little basket specially woven to hold the miniature goldsmith's hammer and chisel which

Mamkinga used. For days she sat out on the stone which flanked the door, her small fingers working busily as the basket took shape.

From her vantage point on the stoop Mara could see the village and all the traffic which passed through. One day as she was putting the finishing touches to the basket's looped handle, a caravan of packhorses came into view.

The men driving the packhorses were heavy-limbed and sunken-eyed. Swarms of dark flies clouded their faces, and sickness hung heavy about them.

Everyone in the village knew what the signs meant. The men had been stricken by one of the many plagues and fevers that ravaged African caravans. Whenever an infected caravan passed by Melfi, the villagers barriered the gates in the fences and kept the children inside the huts. Only the good-hearted Bajmira, her round face serious and concerned, would dare visit the dangerous travellers, taking them a dish of boiled corn and gourds of fresh water. Ndele had beaten her more than once when he caught her doing it, but Bajmira refused to be deterred.

Mara glanced up from her work. As she stared at the caravan, Mara's eyes narrowed thoughtfully.

She needed only one thing to finish the basket, and one of the packhorses was laden with exactly what she wanted – a bale of bright blue glass beads. Strings of them were dangling down from the calico wrapping. A dozen beads would decorate the loop perfectly. Mara saw that her mother Bajmira was already approaching the leading drover with a gourd of water in her hand.

Forgetting all the warnings she had been given, Mara jumped up and trotted happily across to join her mother.

Before Bajmira was even aware she was there, Mara had taken the drover's hand and was pulling him round towards the bale to show him what she wanted.

'Don't touch him, Mara!' Bajmira screamed.

She seized the bewildered child away and hurried her back to the house.

Two days later Mara could not swallow her supper.

Her small body shook with heat and sweat. The fever raged for six days. Ndele the goldsmith never left the crumpled bed of sweet hay on which his daughter tossed. As dawn broke on the seventh day Mara lay still.

Ndele crooned to her cold stiff body for two nights and days. Bajmira could do nothing with him. In Ndele's tormented grief-stricken mind both she and Mamkinga were to blame equally for the tragedy – the one for carelessness, the other for having been born at all.

In despair Bajmira summoned the village elders.

When the elders came to reason with him Ndele left the house abruptly and without speaking. He abandoned the smithy, retreated to the chicken hut at the corner of his thorn-hedged enclosure, and barricaded himself in. There, crazed with grief, he lay tossing and howling like a wounded animal.

The moon revolved through a full cycle.

Maddened and stricken by the spears of malevolent spirits, his body streaked with dirt, Ndele haunted the village by night, standing silently outside Bajmira's house as he stared at the sleeping form of his wife within. Then on the night of the full moon the village was woken by a single scream as loud and as desolate as the howl of a pack of jackals. The following morning Bajmira's body was found. Her throat had been slashed from ear to ear with the goldsmith's chisel. Ndele himself dangled from a beam in his workshop, his anvil split and his tools hurled quivering into the wooden walls.

On the floor lay the battered and twisted wreckage of the little golden figure with the garland of flowers.

Mamkinga was ordered to clean the bodies and sew them into their shrouds. Perplexed and sorrowful – little Mara's death had grieved him deeply – Mamkinga carried out the task slowly and with care, according to Melfi custom. He scented the cold skins with myrrh and musk. He gave them food and palm wine for the long journey into darkness. He placed the tools of the goldsmith's trade in Ndele's hands, and the broken figure in Bajmira's.

Before he closed the shrouds for the last time, Mamkinga looked down at the two faces.

Ndele had been a hard and often cruel master but he had taught Mamkinga much – and more than the craft of the goldsmith alone. Mamkinga had entered the workshop as a sullen and indecisive child. His way-wardness, his vacillations, his dark and sudden changes of mood, would always be a part of him. But now at nineteen he was not only physically mature. He was patient and confident and resolute.

He owed the goldsmith much, Mamkinga knew, for that.

Mamkinga's eyes turned to Bajmira's face. For the kindly Bajmira he had felt nothing but affection from the start, however frightened he'd been of her and what he believed were her husband's stolen dinners then. In life Bajmira's features had been plump and unremark-able. In death they had changed. They were finer, more delicate, almost beautiful. For an instant he might almost have been looking at a shadow of Toomi's face.

Mamkinga started and his stomach contracted. He shook his head and quickly set about the final stitching of the shrouds.

That night no owls called over Melfi.

The council of the village elders met and conferred again. Ndele had no heirs. As by tribal custom they had the right, the elders took over management of every-thing Ndele owned on behalf of the community.

They put the compound, the house and the workshop up for sale. They also placed his slaves on the market. The property took several months to dispose of, but the slaves went quickly. One of the many caravans heading for the coast was passing through Melfi when the elders reached their decision.

The tall and majestically built young man, as Mamkinga was by then, was promptly bought by another Arab slave dealer. Manacled to a different group – as a grown man now there was no question of putting the huge slave with the women – he set off again. As before, Mamkinga's destination was the Atlantic shoreline.

As he set out, bowed down with his shackles, Mamkinga knew with rage and despair that he was once more heading not east but west.

The year was 1853.

On the same day of the same year another young man, also fully grown now and as tall and powerful as Mamkinga, had just left the little Scottish town of Blantyre and set out for London on a journey that would change his life too.

— 35 —

It was almost ten years to the day when Salama returned
to Abyssinia from exile.

He had bided his time, suffering the weary years in
North Africa, until his spies – and his own feeling for the
right moment – told him that it was time to strike.

The Acab Saat was returning to Gondar, and he would
arrive as its conqueror.

He slowed his horse and coiled the reins over the
carved wooden pommel of the saddle.

Behind him his escort of thirty men came to a halt and
waited too. The horses' bits jangled in the still, sultry air.
The day was bakingly hot. Salama shook the sweat from
his face and kicked away the stirrups to stretch his legs.

Leaning on the pommel, he gazed forward.

He had stopped on the crest of a ridge on Malinda's
western border. Gondar was to the south, the lands of the
Galla to the north. Ahead for almost as far as he could see
the plain sloped away from him up towards the hills – so
distant they looked like a ripple of cloud on the horizon.
The plain was similar to the one beneath Gondar but here
in Malinda, without the rain-creating wall of the
mountains behind, the land was more arid. Dust devils
snaked and jumped across the ground. The air was hazy
with blown particles of summer-dry soil. The watercourses of the few rivers were barren and white under the
sun.

In mid August it was a harsh, forbidding landscape to
stare down on.

Salama turned in the saddle and beckoned to Murabit
– it was too hot and the air too parched to use

unnecessary words. Murabit spurred his horse and rode up to him.

'How many days' riding to Malinda itself?' Salama asked.

Murabit rubbed his heavy black moustache, and studied the view in front of them.

A short stocky man with immensely long arms and strutting bow-shaped legs, Murabit came from high up in the Mountains of the Moon. On foot he looked clumsy and inept. In the saddle he seemed to be part of his mount, no longer a man but the upper half of a centaur. He had joined Salama many years before when the Acab Saat, then an ambitious young priest, was riding towards Gondar in the wake of Ras Michael's victorious army.

Salama, a superb horseman himself, had recognized the finest rider he had ever seen. He made Murabit a member of his bodyguard. The squat mountain man rode at his side when Salama followed Ras Michael into Gondar after the city fell, and the line of Sheba and the river's child were restored to the throne. Since then Murabit had risen through the ranks of Salama's entourage until he became its captain.

Throughout the Acab Saat's exile Murabit – uncouth and illiterate, but fearless, ruthless and cunning – had remained loyal to the bishop. He had also kept together the thirty-man bodyguard who now rode at their backs. For the Acab Saat he was the ideal lieutenant.

'It depends where we can find water for the horses, Acab,' Murabit said eventually. 'Maybe eight days.'

'And the country along the way?'

'Apart from the heat and the flies, fast riding, Acab.'

Salama nodded. He spurred his horse and rode on. The escort followed jangling behind.

The relationships between Abyssinia's three great kingdoms had always been wary and delicate. Over the centuries first one and then another had gained the ascendancy, pushing back the frontiers of the others and sometimes even reducing them to vassal states. But for years now, and particularly since the victorious emergence of Ras Michael, Gondar had been the strongest, and a rough balance had come into being as a result of the Ras's rule.

Gondar reserved for itself most of Abyssinia's lucrative trade with the outside world. Malinda was allowed to be the region's granary and food producer. And the Galla, well, the Galla, in Ras Michael's view, had to survive as best they could in the vast inhospitable ranges of their uplands as the mountain thieves and bandits had always done. As far as Ras Michael was concerned they could continue to harry Malinda –providing they did so within the traditional limits.

If the Galla ever attempted to invade and take permanent possession of Malinda, let alone begin to plunder Gondar, then the full might of the ancient kingdom would be thrown against them and Culembra's nation would be crushed.

The balance had worked well for decades now.

Gondar consolidated its strength and thrived. Malinda's crops were good and its people content. The Galla harried and raided but never to excess, never to the extent of provoking retaliation from their neighbours – certainly not from their old foe, Gondar. Yet like any measure hanging level in the scales, Abyssinia's peace was precarious and vulnerable.

As his horse picked its way down a stony winding path on that torrid summer morning, Salama's mind was relentlessly sifting through its points of weakness, the little additional weights which, added on one side or the other, could throw the whole scales out of balance.

Two hundred years earlier the three kingdoms – Gondar, Malinda and the lands of the Galla – had been united under a single ruler, the queen Shinga. Shinga was an ancestor of Esther and, through the bizarre circumstances of his accession, of the Galla's present king, the feared Culembra.

In Malinda, Salama sensed, he would find what he needed to upset Abyssinia's equilibrium.

All Salama could count on to help him were the thirty

men in the saddles behind, and his own driving personality.

It was enough. Other men had built empires on less, and Salama was not like other men. One mounted soldier to guard his back would have been sufficient, let alone thirty. And if there had not been even one, he would still have gone on, relying on his own sword to defend him.

The tormenting flies swarmed round him. The heat hammered down from the baked white sky. Vultures coiled slowly in the midday air. By night lions roared within feet of the scoops in the earth that formed their beds.

Salama narrowed his eyes against the dust clouds and rode steadfastly on.

They reached the town of Malinda eight days later.

Well before then, they had learned that the embrenche of the isolated kingdom had suffered a personal tragedy ten years earlier. One day when most of the village was out harvesting the common, the embrenche's twin children had vanished. Nothing had been heard of them since. Although no one knew for sure, it seemed almost certain that the children had been seized by slavers. The embrenche was reported to be distraught with grief.

The morning after his arrival Salama rode into the village from where he'd made camp outside.

The Acab Saat presented himself at the chief's compound, and asked for an audience with the embrenche. Half an hour later he was shown into the chief's day house. The embrenche, a tall grey-haired man wearing an embroidered cap and a long black gown, rose to greet him.

'Welcome to Malinda,' he said. 'I trust the spirits watched over your travels and your journey was peaceful.'

Salama inclined his head in a small bow that conveyed respect without diminishing his own position as an equal.

'God and the spirits favoured me,' the Acab answered. 'I travelled well and I am honoured to be here.'

They formally embraced each other. Then they sat down.

The next few minutes were tense. Malinda's relations with Gondar were excellent. The embrenche knew well that the Acab Saat had been exiled from Gondar, and he was wary of any dealings with the bishop that could bring on him the wrath of Ras Michael.

Salama dealt with the problem immediately and uncompromisingly. His long-ago dispute with Ras Michael, he said bluntly, had been a disaster for his church, his country, and himself. The fault in part had been his. He had sued for peace with Esther, the queen-empress, and her consort Georgis, and they were now prepared to receive him back – the kingdom needed him.

The embrenche, knowing that Ras Michael had sworn never to allow the Acab Saat to return to Gondar, responded to Salama's tale with nods and sympathetic murmurs, but his gaze was doubtful.

'Ras Michael is reluctant to agree,' Salama admitted. 'However, a serious dispute has arisen within the church, and I am being called for by my fellow bishops. Delicate and secret negotiations are under way. It is possible that Ras Michael will relent and allow me to return.'

In his younger days the embrenche might have continued to doubt Salama's tale. But the old man accepted it, and agreed to allow the Acab Saat to remain at Malinda whilst negotiations continued.

Then as the Malindan chief leant back on his seat Salama said, 'I am saddened to hear you have also experienced sorrows.'

Salama paused.

Before he could say anything else the embrenche sat bolt upright again. An expression of pain crossed his harrowed face and he began to speak compulsively. He had entirely forgotten any possible problems with Gondar created by Salama's arrival. All he was concerned about was the disappearance of Toomi and Mamkinga.

'The loveliest children any father could ever hope for,'

he said. 'Not just one, no, but a pair. Any father can sire one. The spirits blessed me with two. Perfectly matched. A boy and a girl. Separate from each other but the same. Two plants with a single root – '

The embrenche plucked obsessively at the sleeves of his gown as he spoke.

'I left in the morning for the common. They were here. I returned in the evening. They were gone. What happened? We do not know. They could not have been taken from the compound – no one would dare venture here. Maybe they wandered into the streets. It does not matter. They were seized and my life was seized with them. For years now I have been sending out parties to search throughout the countryside. Day after day, month after month, and still they have found nothing. Yet I will continue – '

Tears welled out of the embrenche's eyes and streamed down his cheeks. As he rambled on Salama sat patiently listening.

The reports by the Malindan villagers of the chief's distress had not been exaggerated. The embrenche's cheeks were hollow and sunken. His hands, gesturing vaguely in the air, trembled. Saliva trickled from his mouth and periodically his head drooped wearily on his chest. The man's mind, Salama realized, had been virtually unhinged by the children's disappearance. They had been not only his pride and delight, but the joint heirs to the kingdom of Malinda.

Now they were gone the embrenche had lost his reason for living.

'My condolences, my deep condolences,' Salama said when the chief eventually broke off. 'If there is anything I can do to secure their return, my entire services are at your disposal. Meanwhile, I trust I and my small escort may be permitted to remain at Malinda.'

'As long as you wish,' the embrenche answered distractedly. 'But if you had known the two. So bright, so strong, so full of promise. I remember once – '

As he embarked on another story, Salama got to his

feet and quietly left the day house. Muttering to himself, tears streaming down his face once more, the embrenche failed to notice his departure.

Murabit was waiting for Salama with the horses and half a dozen men at the compound gate.

'How did it go, Acab?' Murabit asked as Salama swung himself into the saddle.

'Well, Murabit,' Salama answered, smiling. 'Very well, indeed. We are invited to stay here for as long as we want. I think a few months will be enough. Malinda's chief has lost his wits. And a land with a witless leader is ripe for the picking.'

The two men laughed.

Then with the escort riding behind them, they set off through the hot dusty streets for their camp outside the village.

Salama stayed at Malinda for seven months.

It was high summer when he arrived. By late autumn he had learned all he needed, but the first rains had already started to fall. The road to the country of the Galla led upward into the hills. It was no easy journey at the best of times, and certainly not one to be embarked on in the wet.

Frustrated and impatient but knowing he had no other choice, Salama sat out the rains in a compound provided by the embrenche.

Murabit and a small escort were sent out during the rains and told to keep well away until early spring. When they returned, Salama joyfully announced to the embrenche that they had brought his pardon from Ras Michael. The Acab Saat was to return to Gondar at once.

He bade farewell to his grief-stricken host – the hair of the distraught embrenche was white now and his words were almost incoherent – and Salama set off. As a parting gift the embrenche presented him with a dozen slaves.

Watching the slaves trudge through the mud behind the horses as they rode away Salama remarked, chuckling, to Murabit, 'Little does the old madman know, but that's just to give us a taste. There will be plenty more where those came from – and they will not need paying for either.'

They moved for a day in the direction of Gondar. Then they swung about and headed for the lands of the Galla. The journey took a month and a half.

For the first two weeks they rode across the plain. Then they began to climb into the hills. It was early spring and the Abyssinian highlands, in their brief annual flowering, were at their loveliest. The air was crisp. The days were warm and sun-filled but without the searing heat of summer. The nights were cool and bright with stars. Deep mountain water poured in torrents down the streambeds and there was thick pasture for the horses everywhere. Game, from antelope to birds to fish, abounded. Every evening the column gorged itself on whatever had been caught during the day.

One evening as they wound up the misty blue ridges into the hills, Murabit came to Salama's tent. He bowed as he entered. Then he stood stroking his heavy black moustache.

'The men found elephant spoor today, Acab,' he said. 'There is a herd of maybe thirty beasts somewhere close to us. They ask your permission to hunt tomorrow. It will be the last chance they get before we climb higher.'

Salama thought for a moment.

The men he had chosen as his escort were all experienced horsemen. They prided themselves on their skill in the ancient Abyssinian technique of hunting elephants on horseback. They had been patient and loyal during the long, often frustrating months since they had ridden out of Gondar. They deserved a reward, and the meat might be useful as they travelled up into the desolate mountainous lands of the Galla.

Salama nodded. 'They may hunt. I will hunt with them.'

With Salama riding at their head the hunting party left the camp at dawn.

Hours earlier while it was still dark one of the men had ridden out on reconnaissance. To find and hunt elephant on horseback, it was necessary first to find where the herd was drinking. The man had traced the elephants to a large pool in one of the rivers that flowed westwards beneath the camp. By daylight the huge animals had long since scattered to feed, but the imprint of their tracks was still clear in the crushed dew-laden grass.

The guide led them to the pool.

There Salama divided the party into groups of five. He kept Murabit and three other men with him. The rest he sent off in different directions, each following a separate spoor.

The tracks Salama followed belonged to the herd's dominant male. The stocky Murabit, a brilliant interpreter of elephant spoor and casts, had chosen the animal for his master. It was a mature bull in its prime, with huge sweeping tusks.

'Look, Acab, where it has browsed.' Murabit pointed at the trunk of a sapling acacia where the bark had been gouged away almost at ground level. 'The ivory reaches close to the earth. The sap is still running. The beast is not far off.'

Murabit was right.

Ten minutes later the riders came out of the dense riverside forest on to a stretch of plain. The great bull elephant Murabit had been tracking was swaying through the grass less than half a mile in front of them.

Salama grunted in satisfaction as he watched it. It was a truly magnificent animal with the curving tusks that Murabit had predicted. Salama turned and glanced back at the three men behind him.

'Who will ride first?' Salama asked.

One of the men rose in his stirrups and leant forward.

'Let me take him, Acab,' the man answered, his dark face lit by an excited grin.

Salama waved him on. The man spurred his horse and galloped away across the plain.

The elephant registered the vibration of the drumming hoofs almost immediately. It whirled round. Too large and strong to be vulnerable to attack by any natural predator, it was none the less intensely jealous of the territory that surrounded it. Even a small antelope incautiously venturing too close was liable to be driven off by an angry charge.

The elephant raised its ears and its trunk, scanning the air for the intruder's scent.

As the horseman galloped closer it trumpeted warningly. The rider and his mount entered the elephant's range of vision. What the elephant saw was a strange and hostile shape that seemed to be challenging for the space of grass off which it was feeding. The bull tossed its tusks. It trumpeted again and launched itself at the interloper. The provocative silhouette vanished before it, but the alien scent still hung heavily in the air and the tremors from the horse's feet continued to trouble the earth.

Screaming with rage and disquiet, the bull wheeled away.

For the next few minutes the two, the horseman and the elephant, cut backwards and forwards across each other. The horse moved in short explosive bursts of gallop, the elephant at a stiff-legged canter which occasionally became so fast it seemed to be travelling like a wind-driven grey cloud through the grass. The bull would head for a clump of trees and the rider would cut it off. The horseman would try to turn it back towards Salama, and the elephant would round on him in a murderous charge, forcing the rider to veer frantically aside.

Finally the bull came to a halt. Its flanks heaving, it lifted its tusks and screamed in a frenzy of fury and defiance. Then it raised its trunk once more. It stood knee-deep in the rippling grasses, the dark distended tulip of its nostrils menacingly beginning to search the wind.

The horseman rode back to the others.

'It is ready, Acab,' he said to Salama. 'The beast will run no longer. Now it stands and fights.'

'Do you wish me to turn it, Acab?' Murabit asked.

Salama shook his head.

Turning an elephant so that it could be cut down was the most difficult and perilous part of the hunt. By now the animal's natural fear of the unknown had been run out of it. It had given up trying to defend its territory or to escape. Instead it had taken up a position where it could strike back at its persecutors.

Vast, intelligent, lethally dangerous, and armoured with its slashing tusks, a cornered bull elephant was the most deadly animal on earth.

'You may make the cut, Murabit,' Salama said. 'I will make the beast dance.'

He rode out on to the plain.

Murabit and one other of Salama's companions followed him. Murabit's normally impassive face was taut as he watched the Acab ride ahead. Better than anyone else he knew how destructive a solitary trapped bull could be. The animal in front of them was an engine of death.

The little mountain man's hands plucked warily at his reins as he kept his horse only feet from the haunches of Salama's.

Fifty paces away from the elephant Salama suddenly kicked his mount into a gallop. He rode head-on at the lowered tusks. Within feet of the ivory spears he wrenched the horse's head aside. The elephant screamed and lunged forward viciously. The shadowy target in front of it had gone and the tusks sliced through the empty air. The great bull steadied itself. With its trunk uplifted, it probed the wind again for the wraith that was tormenting it.

Salama laughed aloud.

He lashed his horse with his whip and galloped back across the tusks. There was another savage lunge, another frustrated scream, another furious stamping of the huge feet. The elephant retreated. Then it surged forward at the blurred and taunting silhouette again.

'Now, Murabit, now!' Salama shouted.

Hypnotized by the Acab Saat's riding – Salama was dancing his horse between the elephant's tusks as the bull lunged at him – the mountain man had almost forgotten his own role in the hunt.

As Salama shouted he came to life.

Murabit called in an urgent whisper to the other horseman who had ridden out with him. Together they circled forward until they were immediately behind the elephant's haunches.

'One last pass!' Salama shouted at them. 'Then make the cut!'

Salama rode in at the animal again.

This time he was closer than ever before. As the

elephant slashed out, one of its tusks caught the girth of Salama's saddle. It cut through the heavy leather as if it had been silk. Sickeningly, Salama found himself slipping. He gripped the horse's mane and desperately tried to retain his seat.

Freed of the girth's constriction, the horse checked and whinnied. It had come to a halt directly below the elephant's upraised tusks. The horse tossed its head in bewilderment. Above it the tusks started to smash down.

Salama let go of the bridle. Raising his arms in a desperate attempt to shield his head, he flung himself backwards. As he did the elephant gave another scream. This time it was a scream of agony.

Behind the bull Murabit had vaulted down from his mount. In his hands was an axe, its blade honed to the sharpness of a razor. He raised the axe and sliced it down on the elephant's hind leg, severing the tendon. As the elephant lurched in pain and confusion, Murabit hacked at the other tendon. The elephant sank down on its hindquarters. Blood from its arteries spouted out over the grass in crimson fountains that soared and glittered in the sun.

Immobilized and in agony, the bull screamed and stabbed wildly at the air. Then slowly its mighty head sank. Its tusks drove deep into the ground, and the great animal toppled to one side.

'You must take me hunting more often, Murabit,' Salama said as he struggled out between the splayed crescents of ivory, each as thick as a man's thigh. 'We are growing soft as we ride. We need the chase to bring our spirits back to the cutting point!'

Salama laughed and clapped Murabit boisterously round the shoulder.

The mountain man looked up at him. Salama's skin was coated with sweat and the hide of his trembling horse was ridged with foam. Yet for the first time in months the Acab's lined hawk-like face was alive and his eyes were bright.

Murabit stroked his moustache and smiled.

'Next time let me make the turn, Acab, and you take care of the cut. I gather grey hairs when it is the other way.'

As Salama chuckled, Murabit applied himself to the butchering of the elephant's carcass. All of the other hunting teams, Murabit had no doubt, would have killed too.

They would have meat to feed an army.

Salama ate hungrily and slept well in the high thin air.

Otherwise he was barely aware of his surroundings. Trapped in Malinda, he had chafed and cursed as the rain drummed down, turning the streets into channels of mud and filling the nearby rivers with cataracts of foam. To be on the move again should have eased his restlessness. It did not. If anything the urgency increased.

Soon it would be ten years since the start of his exile from Gondar. Each night as he lay on his bed – an armful of branches draped with a hide cover – vivid images of the town tumbled across his mind – its colours and smells, its shapes and sounds, above all its people. With all his passion for horses, hunting and Abyssinia's immense open landscape, Salama at heart was an urban creature.

The Acab Saat lived off the meat of action and intrigue among men.

Here in the wilderness he was starved. Ten years away from Gondar was too long, far too long. Everything in him, his pride, his ambition, but most of all his remorseless inexhaustible appetite for living, demanded he should be back there.

His journey to the Galla was a dangerous but vital gamble. Salama knew he would only return to Gondar by force of arms. For that he needed an ally. The king of the Galla was reputed to be a bloodthirsty savage, coarse, brutal and treacherous. But he led a fierce warrior nation and he had the command of a powerful army – and an army was what Salama wanted.

Salama's little group arrived at Galla, the country's

capital, early on a June morning at the start of the Abyssinian summer.

During the journey through the hills they had passed by a number of Galla settlements. They had carefully circled the settlements, and Salama had posted double guards when they camped at night. Except when threatened the Malindans were peaceful. The Galla, in contrast, were always volatile and predatory. No traveller was ever safe in their country. Now Salama was about to meet them face to face for the first time.

He studied the village carefully from his horse as the column paused on the crest above it.

Galla was built on a series of terraces at the head of a steeply-sloping valley. The site was a natural fortress. From above it was protected by the precipitous flanks of the surrounding mountains. From below an attacker would have to struggle up the almost sheer gradients of the valley's walls. On every side the landscape was covered in dense forest.

Murabit, seated on his horse beside Salama, whistled softly as he gazed down.

'They may be savages but they are not fools, Acab,' he said. 'This place could hold out against a dozen armies.'

Salama nodded.

The Acab Saat stared at the village for a moment longer. Then he spurred his horse down the slope.

Galla was very different from any of the other villages they'd seen since leaving Gondar. For a start it lacked any obvious fortifications – its natural defences were enough. Then the village had no plan or pattern to it. The houses were scattered at random across the terraces. They were poor shabby buildings too, patched with hide and linked by narrow lanes littered with garbage. The air smelt foul and in spite of the altitude clouds of flies swarmed everywhere.

It was a typical nomadic encampment, Salama thought, filthy and impermanent and no doubt riddled with disease.

The entrance to the village was marked by a simple

open arch. As the column approached it – on Salama's orders they were riding tightly grouped behind him – a number of women rushed out and barred their way. The women were middle-aged and heavily built. They wore striped blue waist cloths, but from the waist up they were naked. Their heads were shaved and each one was carrying a short broad-bladed spear.

They gazed fearlessly up at the column and raised their spears menacingly.

'We come in peace,' Salama said. 'I am the Acab Saat of Gondar. I wish to speak with your king.'

The leader of the women inspected him warily.

She had a gap-toothed mouth and shrivelled breasts that hung down over her chest like empty leather pouches. Behind her Salama's eye was briefly caught by a much younger woman, tall and slender and attractive, who seemed to be her servant. Then the old woman spoke.

'Why?' she demanded, scowling.

'I have news that will please and interest him,' Salama replied.

'Stay here!'

She spoke to the other women in a country patois. Then, as the women formed themselves in a line across the entrance, she disappeared into the village.

'Lendama,' Murabit said quietly to Salama as they waited. 'Women warriors. They are the heart of the king's army. Dangerous people, Acab.'

Salama nodded.

He had heard stories of the king of the Galla's terrible Lendama. They were a legacy of the rule of the great Queen Shinga. If everything went as he planned, Salama knew he would see more of them.

The king kept them waiting outside the arch for six hours.

As the sun climbed to its zenith and the heat grew, Salama became increasingly angry. Several times, he guessed, when there was a flurry behind the arch, the king came forward to examine his visitors. Each time he retired unseen, leaving the column to sweat in the open. Salama controlled himself. It was both a test of nerves and, on the king's side, a demonstration of Culembra's power. It was a demonstration that, Salama knew, he had to match. No one, Salama ordered, was to dismount.

The day passed.

The horses tossed their heads, skittering from time to time at the attacks of the flies, and evacuating themselves on the earth. On their backs the men shifted wearily. They relieved themselves too, allowing the urine to run down the horses' flanks. Stubbornly, as the Acab Saat had instructed, they kept their seats.

Then as dusk approached there was another flurry behind the arch.

A dozen men carrying bundles of logs ran forward. They built a fire on an open space behind the mounted column. A bullock was led out. The animal was slaughtered, butchered and put to roast above the flames.

Finally as the smells of the roasting meat lifted into the darkening air the king, Culembra himself, appeared.

— 37 —

'I greet you in peace,' Culembra said to Salama. 'I regret I was not here at your arrival. I have been away hunting all day. I invite you and your companions to join me to eat.'

'We accept your invitation with pleasure,' Salama replied. 'For my men it will be a strange experience. They are used to spending twenty-four hours in the saddle. To dismount and eat now after only six is rare. Forgive them if they do not do your meal justice.'

The king stared at him thoughtfully. Then he turned towards the fire.

Salama gave the order to dismount and the men climbed wearily down.

The practice of using chairs and tables at meals, introduced by Portuguese traders, had been adopted throughout Abyssinia. Salama sat down at the chair prepared for him and studied the king.

Culembra, King of the Galla, was a tall broad-shouldered man in his late thirties. He had copper-coloured skin, much lighter than that of the warriors clustered round him, a heavily jowled face ridged with scars, and deep-set eyes which the pipe he constantly smoked had left permanently bloodshot. He was wearing a short cylindrical straw hat bound with a ribbon of purple velvet, a waist-length white tunic, violet silk shorts, and a pair of gold-embroidered Moroccan slippers.

Welded at evenly spaced intervals around his arms and legs were iron bands to protect him from sword cuts in battle. Culembra, as Salama had known for years, had a fearsome reputation as a fighter. Seeing him now for the first time in his grotesquely opulent costume, Salama sensed he was self-indulgent but shrewd and dangerous.

A servant placed a slice of meat on the table.

Culembra speared it with his dagger and began to eat. It was the signal for everyone else to eat too. There was little conversation during the meal. Watching the blood from the meat run down the king's chin as he methodically chewed away in silence, Salama remembered how Culembra had come to power fifteen years earlier.

Murabit, Salama's aide, was a mountain man and he knew the story well. He had told it to Salama as they rode towards the village. It was a strange and gruesome tale.

As a young man Culembra had been a foot soldier in the bodyguard of the Galla's most famous and feared leader, the psychopathic woman warrior Mussassa, known as the 'blood-mother'. Like all the Abyssinian peoples the Galla had a long tradition of women leaders. It started with the Queen of Sheba and included Esther's ancestor Shinga, who had united the three kingdoms two hundred years before.

Mussassa was the most bizarre of all.

Recklessly brave and a brilliant strategist, she had a string of victories in battle as a young woman which gave her enough power to turn on and murder her mother – then the Galla's queen. Afterwards she directed her tormented mind against men. Her obsession was double edged. She had an insatiable appetite for men as sexual implements. But as soon as she was sated by them, she had them put to death – torturing them before they died.

Finally Mussassa's mind collapsed. She decided to turn the world into a wilderness, killing every living creature and burning the earth's green mantle, its forests, bushes and grasses, which supported them. Her subjects' only food would be the flesh of male humans and their only drink human blood.

In every quarter of the Galla's lands smoke rose into the sky as Mussassa's dazed, cowed and deeply superstitious people fired their meagre vegetation on their queen's orders.

For Mussassa it still wasn't enough. She had given birth to a male child, then only a few days old. In a frenzy she seized the child from his nurse, flung him into a mortar, and pounded him to death. She threw the child's remains into a large earthenware pot and added leaves, oils and powdered roots. Mussassa stirred the mixture into a paste and rubbed it over herself, proclaiming in a scream that it was an armour which had made her invulnerable and would do the same for everyone else.

Culembra, a tall well-made young man, was the nearest member of her bodyguard in the terrorized throng.

She slashed his chest with a knife, and smeared the ointment over the cut. One of the herbs she had thrown into the paste contained a powerful coagulant. The bleeding from Culembra's wound stopped instantly. As the crowd cheered hysterically, Mussassa pulled him triumphantly into her tent. Culembra had a brief moment of pleasure from the coupling that followed. But, young as he was, he had not the slightest doubt what it presaged.

Even as he spent himself he knew he was as expendable as any other young man on whom Mussassa's gaze had alighted. As she lay back satisfied and smiling, her hair lank with sweat – and grey now, and her cheeks withering – some instinct of self-preservation made Culembra put his hands round her neck and strangle her.

Culembra had no thought about the throne. He was simply protecting his own life at the expense of a monster who would otherwise have slaughtered him. Culembra went outside. The crowd greeted him rapturously. The ogre-queen was dead – it did not matter how or why – and Culembra, the bodyguard and foot soldier, was alive.

A new reign had begun and it was Culembra's.

'That is how the story is told,' Murabit finished. 'Some whisper there's more to it than that. They say a group of Mussassa's old warriors knew she had gone mad and thought she would lead all the people into suicide. They murdered her themselves and Culembra was to be the scapegoat if the people demanded blood. But the Galla did not. They were sick to their gullets with the slaughter and wanted an end – '

Murabit shrugged. 'However it happened, Culembra became their leader. He was bold and strong. He took the chance. Since then he has made himself a true king of the Galla in his own right.'

Murabit smiled grimly. 'He was not the blood-mother's lover for nothing.'

Salama stared at Culembra as he finished eating.

The king wiped the trickling blood from his chin, and flicked it at the ground. Then he waved his men back. Salama did the same and the two leant forward to talk.

'The captain of the gate told me you had interesting news,' Culembra said. 'I am sure it is interesting. But first, and for me more interesting still, is why the Acab Saat of Gondar comes here unannounced with only thirty men.'

'The news and my arrival are part of the same,' Salama answered. 'I will explain.'

Salama repeated the story he had told the embrenche about his dispute with Ras Michael. Then Salama moved on to talk about Malinda.

'The embrenche's children have been taken by slavers,' he said. 'The old man is distraught, more and more so with each year that passes. The country is already ill led and weakened. Soon, perhaps even now, it will be ready to fall.'

Culembra laughed.

'You must truly take us for ignorant savages, Acab, if you believe that is news to us. Of course we have heard of the missing children and the embrenche's despair. The word of his loss has been stale for many seasons now. We have made our plans. When we judge the time is ripe we will move. We, the Galla, have many thousands of men. We do not need an extra thirty to march with us – '

He paused. 'Even if those thirty can remain in their saddles for twenty-four hours without dismounting.'

'Malinda's barns are built for dwarfs,' Salama answered him imperturbably. 'Gondar, on the other hand, is a granary for giants.'

Culembra's head swung round. He looked sharply at Salama.

'What do you mean?' he demanded.

'Malinda is only a stepping stone,' the Acab Saat answered. 'On the other side lies Gondar. And Gondar would be a real prize.'

'Gondar is rich and strong.' Culembra was watching Salama warily now. 'Ras Michael is a great warrior. Under him Gondar's army, they say, could march to the sea and none could stand against it. Even to move on Malinda would be greatly hazardous. Why do you think we have waited so long? But to attack Gondar –'

Culembra checked and his face flushed with anger. 'Are you trying to lead me into a trap?' he shouted.

Before Salama could reply Culembra leapt to his feet. His warriors surged forward. As they did Salama's own escort closed round him and raised their guns.

Salama sat immovable.

He gestured at his men to fall back. Then the Acab Saat spread out his arms on the table, his open palms upwards.

'There is no trap,' he said calmly. 'I conceal nothing. But I tell you Gondar can be taken too. Sit down in peace and talk.'

For several minutes Culembra remained where he was, his hand on his dagger and the light from the flames flickering over his face. In the end greed, curiosity, and his confidence in the overwhelming superiority of his strength, overcame his suspicions.

Culembra came forward and sat down again.

'Tell me,' he said bluntly.

'Gondar is not a kingdom,' Salama said. 'It is a coalition of groups and interests and factions held together by one strong man. The Ras Michael. The queen-empress is no more than a well-fleshed child. Georgis, her consort, is a vain and empty headed pervert. He can no more lift a sword or give an order than penetrate an old whore even if a whole army has been through her first. Without the Ras, Gondar is nothing. The country would fall apart and become as weak as Malinda.'

Culembra considered for a moment.

'But Ras Michael is alive and vigorous,' he remarked.

'Alive, yes, but vigorous?' Salama laughed scornfully and shook his head. 'You may have the frame and spirit of a young man, Culembra, but your intelligence has a grey beard. It is as old as Ras Michael and belongs, like him, to the past. You talk of him as he was, not as he is now. The Ras is fast filling the horn of his years. His hair is white, he cannot mount his horse unaided, his memory fails. He is like a dry plant ready for the scythe.'

'The blade may miss him for a while yet.'

'Not if a sure hand guides it – '

Salama paused.

'The Ras can be cut down,' he went on. 'He is no longer fit to lead Gondar in battle. He knows it. When the army rides out now, he delegates command, and a deputy rides for him. All that remain are his passion and his pride. They are enough to trap him.'

Culembra looked at him suspiciously through narrowed eyes. 'How?'

'Ras Michael's passion is one of hatred,' Salama said. 'What he hates with all his heart and soul is seated here before you – myself. And his pride is lodged in the same, that he can defeat and destroy me. If he heard that I rode against him, against Gondar, no power on earth would prevent him from riding out to stop me – '

Salama stretched out his arm and gestured in the darkness.

'All his wits and skills, all the cautious restraints of age, would abandon him. He would become as frenzy-struck as once, I am told, the queen Mussassa was here. She was felled by a bold and brave man who went on to greatness. Such a man could go on to a much larger greatness by striking down the Ras. Once the ailing whitebeard was felled, the road to Gondar would be open.'

The Acab Saat was silent.

Culembra sat in thought. Salama sprawled back

casually in his chair. His eyes apparently on the night sky above them, he was watching the king closely.

Culembra glanced at the circle of Galla warriors behind Salama. There was nothing to be learnt from their blank faces. Culembra's gaze returned to the fire. The king, Salama knew, was intrigued. More than intrigued he was almost seduced – seduced by greed. Malinda, as Culembra had admitted, was a prey the Galla had long been considering.

The fabled kingdom of Gondar, the rich and fertile lands of Sheba and the river's child, was booty that had never entered Culembra's dreams.

Malinda, in Salama's own phrase, contained barns for dwarfs. Gondar was a granary for giants – and Culembra saw himself as a giant. Suddenly Salama had offered what to the Galla bandit warlord had before been unbelievable: a key to the riches of Abyssinia's treasure chest.

'Even if all this were so' – Culembra frowned at the Acab Saat, greed and suspicion moving like dark alternating clouds across his face –'there would still remain the queen and her consort. What of them?'

'Georgis, as I have said, is beneath contempt,' Salama replied. 'A jackal cub would not find meat on him to break the night's fast. The queen may be an infant in knowledge, but in years she is a woman and a very beautiful one – '

He looked keenly at Culembra. 'She would make an appetizing wife for any king of Gondar.'

Culembra pondered. 'She has a child,' he objected. 'The river's child.'

'As a focus of discontent? The queen's daughter, the so-named river's child, has not even bled yet. When have horses flown or children ruled countries?'

Culembra was silent in thought again.

'I say once more,' he replied eventually. 'Even if all you claim is true, how could you and the thirty men you command assist an invader of Gondar? Your presence at an army's head, you believe, will bring Ras Michael to horse and goad him out. Maybe so. But the army will still be mine, and Ras Michael's the greater. Thirty men, however sharp their swords, will not change the outcome in a meeting of thousands.'

It was the moment Salama had been waiting for, the moment of his strength.

The Acab Saat lifted his head. A smile spread over his broad fleshy face. His dark eyes glittered and the thrusting curve of his nose arched forward like the beak of a falcon in the firelight.

'I do not command thirty men,' Salama answered. 'I command thirty souls. On that difference the fate of nations depends. I am the Acab Saat, the bishop royal but, more important, a bishop of Gondar's church. All Gondar is my congregation. Within Gondar *all* the people are my army. Together they are more than any attacker or defender can raise – you or Ras Michael alike. Who rides with me rides with Gondar. They ride to victory.'

There was another silence, longer than any that had gone before.

Moths and insects swirled around the heavy tallow candles on the table. Owls and nightingales filled the crisp night air with their calls. Roaming hyenas, plundering Galla for its garbage, howled and laughed. Culembra's soldiers plucked restlessly at their daggers, the blades flashing blue-green like the mountain streams in the moonlight.

Then the king leant forward. He crossed his arms, matted with black sweat-drenched hair, over the table. For the first time Culembra laughed.

'Yes,' he said. 'We should talk carefully, Acab, you and I. Together we have much to do.'

The young woman Salama had noticed standing behind the Lendama at the gate when he arrived at Galla was Toomi.

Ten years had passed since her capture by the Oye-Eboe. The little brown-skinned creature who had stared up at Tamule when she arrived as a child slave, her stomach churning with fright, had become a tall and striking woman. Fine-boned, with a supple full-breasted figure, dark shining hair and clear confident eyes, Toomi turned the head of every man in Galla who saw her.

Throughout the ten years Toomi had tended the fires in the women's compound. She had slept at night in Tamule's bed, and ridden behind the war woman when Culembra called out the Galla raiding parties. Her mistress was ageing swiftly now. Tamule's single lock of hair had turned white, and the damp and cold had aggravated the racking arthritis in her back and shoulders.

More than once, as Toomi lay beside the old woman listening to her wheeze and toss painfully, she wondered whether Tamule would ever be able to march out again. But when spring and the sun returned, somehow Tamule struggled back to health and was ready each time Culembra called for her.

As she grew up Toomi remained outwardly as impassive and reserved as the day she entered Tamule's service. Sometimes the old woman teased her about it.

'Are you practising to join the Qasiri?' she would say. 'Well, if you do you won't need to carve your mask – you have one already, child.'

The Qasiri were a fabled tribe of forest-dwelling pygmies far to the west, who wore blank masks to conceal their identities at their spring bacchanals.

Toomi would give a brief smile and turn the talk aside.

Behind her inscrutable façade Toomi was tormented. She was able to endure because of a natural capacity for self-discipline and a certain fatalism – the fatalism of all who have always lived with the constant presence of hazard, change and death. At a deeper level Toomi remained restless and wounded.

The wound would not heal. It had been hacked deep into her by a sword of loss. Her family, her home, her country, all had been taken from her. Worst of all she had lost her brother, Mamkinga. In time she might come to terms with her severance from the rest. From Mamkinga, never.

Without him she was a ghost, bloodless and empty.

Toomi yearned, with a longing that made her physically dizzy, to put her arms around him and hold him again. She wanted to lick his skin, explore his mouth with her fingers, feel his muscles and the bones beneath them. She wanted to thread her fingers through his and run with him, hand in hand, through the bush. She wanted to say half of something and wait for him to complete it. She wanted to see his eyes and talk to him with hers, each part of a whole that would never be fully alive without the other.

Sometimes at night Toomi would wake to a sudden stab of pain as if someone had hit her. Sleepy and puzzled, she would search the darkness. Then she would realize that the blow had not been delivered to her, but to Mamkinga. Someone somewhere had kicked him brutally in the thigh or struck him violently in the face.

Toomi would lie back, weeping for the shared hurt. Over the years she wept often.

Then one summer morning she was sitting with Tamule when a messenger came from the king. It was a month after the arrival at Galla of the thirty horsemen. The king was on his way to visit Tamule. Toomi barely had time to prepare Tamule's house to receive him when Culembra arrived.

'How are you, best of my colonels?' Culembra asked as he walked in.

The old woman drew herself up proudly, clenching her teeth as the arthritic pains ran through her.

'Ready for whatever the king commands,' she answered.

'I am glad,' Culembra said. 'We march tomorrow for Malinda. This time not to raid, but to take Malinda itself. We will not stop there. We are going further – '

Culembra paused. An avaricious smile crossed his dark and scarred face, and his red-veined eyes gleamed.

'We have a powerful ally and our goal is Gondar. We go to take Sheba's city and kingdom.'

Culembra sat down. He spread out his bulging thighs and began to talk excitedly to his favourite warrior. Tamule drew on her pipe and listened.

At dawn next day an ox-waggon carrying Toomi rumbled out of Galla. She was seated in the back and Tamule's women soldiers were tramping on either side. The battle column was larger and longer than Toomi had ever seen before. The entire Galla people seemed to be on the march.

The Lendama always travelled close to the king near the head of the column. As they wound down from the mountains, Toomi saw a band of horsemen riding immediately behind Culembra. From time to time their leader would spur his mount forward and draw level with the king, talking to him as if to an equal.

Once the man reined in his horse.

He turned and gazed back at the seemingly endless line of soldiers circling down the mountain path behind him. He was wearing a white cloak, and a gold cross glittered on his chest. For an instant the sunlight caught his face. Toomi glimpsed a powerful jaw, a hawk-like beak of a nose, and two staring eyes. Narrow, fanatical and filled with hate, they were the most frightening eyes she had ever seen.

The horseman whirled his mount round. His white cloak flared out, and he rode on. Then he disappeared round a bend in the track. Toomi shuddered as the waggon jolted forward.

Somewhere ahead of them were Gondar and Malinda. Toomi had no idea what this sudden strange migration of what appeared to be the entire Galla nation heralded. Even old Tamule, coughing and wheezing over her pipe, seemed to be confused.

'We ride to take Sheba's lands,' Tamule had said to her. 'That, at least, is what Culembra tells me. But the mountains belong to the river's child. Whoever marches against those slopes risks the vengeance of the great queen herself. I am not happy, little bird.'

Tamule shook her head grimly.

Now Toomi's face was set and puzzled. She could not rid her mind of the horseman at the column's head.

Culembra was evil but his new ally, the rider in the white cloak, was mad. Now both evil and madness were travelling with them.

— 39 —

'Five minutes gentlemen, please.'

In the silence of the British Museum reading room the voice of the junior librarian sounded as raucous as the call of a street tinker.

The young man sitting at the desk in the far corner glanced up in irritated surprise. Absorbed in a thick ledger bound in plain blue cloth, he had lost all track of time. He pulled out his silver fob-watch. The librarian was right. It was almost seven and only a few minutes before the museum closed.

The young man opened a bright yellow pamphlet lying beside his elbow. The title page, decorated with a lacy pattern round the edges, read: *Manifest der Kommunischen Partei*, Februar 1848, London. He scrawled the number of the ledger page below the pamphlet's title, to remind himself where to start again the next day. Then he slipped the pamphlet and his notebooks into a large oilskin wallet. He gathered together the books he'd taken from the shelves, returned them to the desk in the centre of the reading room, and headed for the glass-paned doors that led to the hall.

'Don't forget your coat, sir,' the porter called as he hurried through. 'It may only be September but there's a fair bite in the air and the makings of a nasty fog tonight.'

The young man turned back. He picked a worn black coat from the rack and slipped it on over an even more threadbare suit of grey tweed. Then he smiled gratefully at the porter.

'Thank you, Jack,' he said in a thick German accent. 'Without you I'd be down with the pneumonia long since.'

'If I didn't look after my regulars I wouldn't have a job, would I, sir?' The porter chuckled. 'Goodnight, Mr Marx.'

The young man went out.

He shivered at the sudden chill on the street. Pausing to light a cheap cigar, he hunched his shoulders and stepped out briskly through the dusk in the direction of Soho.

At thirty-four Karl Marx was stocky and strongly built, with dark skin, an untidy shock of already greying hair, and a thick black beard. His face was square and pugnacious, and his eyes large, bright and piercing – almost sinister in their intensity. His clothes invariably reeked of tobacco and his breath almost as often stank of alcohol. Marx's drinking bouts had become legendary among his family and friends. He would stay up through the night, until he collapsed in a stupor towards dawn. Then he would sleep through the day until evening came, when he would start again.

'I am married to a drunken gypsy,' his wife, the affectionate and long-suffering Jenny, used to complain.

'But a gypsy with a dream,' Marx would chide her, laughing. 'Dreams need fuelling. Bring me a glass!'

Marx crossed Oxford Street and walked down the narrow passageway that led to Soho Square.

The fog had thickened since he'd left the British Museum. It swirled in soft grey streamers round the pools of light given out by the gaslamps and eddied over the cobblestones, rising to choke his throat as he breathed. The air smelt foul. Mixed with the fog's own bitter stench of coal fumes and sulphur were the smells of rotting garbage, horse manure, human urine and excrement, decaying vegetables and decomposing meat.

The evening streets rang with noise. In spite of the lateness of the hour hawkers were still calling their wares. A crippled old woman at the corner wheezed out the virtues of her flowers. A wandering muffin-seller shouted his goods. A man hunched over a brazier bellowed that he had the first roast chestnuts of the year. Carriages, cabs and traps rattled past. Squealing urchins skipped in and out between their wheels. Gypsy women ran forward, offering single wilting carnations and sprigs of lucky heather. Prostitutes, many of them no more than children, patrolled the gutters, their constantly smiling faces heavy with powder, rouge and fennel.

Marx shouldered his way good-naturedly through the throng, laughing and joking as he went.

Life on the streets of Victorian London was clamorous, boisterous, bawdy and foul-smelling. Above all it was decadent. Marx had no doubt about that. He was watching a society in its death throes. Once the people grasped that they and their labour were being cynically exploited by a handful of their fellow citizens, they would throw off the brutal yoke of capitalism and take their affairs into their own hands. When that happened everything would change. There would be no need any longer for prostitutes, flower-sellers, or even muffin-vendors. They would all vanish overnight with the revolution.

Marx brushed off a beggar and pushed on.

All Britain needed, all every country in Europe needed, was an awakening to the fundamental evils of the system men had unwittingly created to govern their societies. Once they threw off the manacles of the past, people everywhere would be able to live in peace and justice. He, Marx, was the man who would open their eyes. He had unravelled the chains which bound them, the chains of slavery gathered in the hands of those who controlled the means of production and distribution. He had traced the chains to their beginnings and reached an irrefutable conclusion.

Sever the bonds and the people would be free. It was as simple as that.

Marx turned into Soho Square. In front of him a tall well-dressed woman was crossing the little garden at the square's centre. As Marx watched, a man appeared through the fog and approached her. The man was wearing a top hat, plaid trousers and a foppish green velvet topcoat with silver buttons. He pirouetted round the woman, stopped in front of her, swept off his hat, and gave an extravagant bow. The woman smiled at him. Then she continued on her way across the garden.

Marx ran forward and caught up with her.

'Jenny,' he said anxiously to his wife. 'How many times must I tell you it's dangerous to walk through Soho after dark? God knows what might happen to you.'

Jenny gave him an amused smile as he took her arm.

A patient, resourceful and cultured woman, the sister of the Prussian Minister for the State of Westphalen, she had long since accustomed herself to her husband's Bohemian way of life and the unusual neighbourhoods in which it led to the family living. They frightened her not at all.

'As God, according to you, my dear, doesn't exist,' she said, 'He's the one person who certainly won't know what's going to happen to me. In any event there was nothing very threatening about that young man. In fact I encounter him quite often. He has an engaging manner and we are almost on speaking terms. True, he was a little the worse for wear from drink tonight – but that's not a problem I'm unfamiliar with.'

Marx scowled. 'I'd much sooner you weren't abroad at this hour.'

'When the revolution comes, Karl, I shall be happy to stay at home and have the children's food brought to the house,' Jenny replied. 'Until then I must go out and fetch it back myself. Except, of course, when the revolution does come, I shall be perfectly safe to go wherever I want, won't I?'

She smiled innocently again.

For a moment Marx continued to scowl. Then his face relaxed, he shook his head, and burst into laughter.

He could never be angry with Jenny for long. He adored her – not, of course, that that inhibited him from taking to bed any other attractive young woman who passed through the house. But Jenny was different. Funny, fearless and wise, a loving mother to their three children and a loyal companion on his often harassed and uncomfortable wanderings, she was unlike anyone else he had known.

Marx removed the cigar from his mouth. He threw his arms round her, and embraced her exuberantly.

'Do as you wish, my dear Jenny,' he said, 'before and after the people's triumph. Just make sure no harm comes to you. Without you I doubt whether I could survive.'

Arm in arm, and both of them laughing now, they made their way across the square into Dean Street, and along the muddied pavement towards the lodgings Marx had rented at number 28.

Fifty yards behind them the man in the plaid trousers and the green velvet topcoat caught hold of a lamppost.

He swung himself drunkenly round it, and then swayed into Dean Street too. In his hand was an ebony-handled cane. It was 8.00 p.m. Night had fallen and the fog was growing denser by the minute as the temperature dropped with the onset of darkness. The man lifted his cane and thrashed it through the air, as if it would clear the greyness and allow him to make out the numbers on the houses.

He rocked on his heels, and peered forward. He was standing before a large Georgian house near the street's entrance. Beside the imposing mahogany door was a porcelain plaque bearing the number 4. He smiled. Still swaying, he lifted the cane and jabbed it against the brass bell-button. The door opened and a funnel of light spilled out on to the pavement.

'May the Blessed Virgin have mercy!' a woman's voice exclaimed in a broad Irish accent. 'It's my lord of the seaweed himself. There are miracles yet! Is it come to pay your debts you have, sir?'

'We are rich again, Madame Belle,' the man answered. 'Since last week we no longer harvest sea-weed but the Cheviot. A most noble animal it is, too. Feel the texture of its fleece!'

He reached inside his coat. Pulling out a pair of sovereigns, he chimed them together in his hand. Then he leant forward laughing and dropped them down the woman's décolletage.

'There are details to be arranged before the craft bearing the golden fleece returns to harbour,' he went on. 'I crave a week's indulgence as we await the following wind. Meanwhile, may a veritable sheep beg entry?'

He doffed his hat and bowed.

The woman, Madame Belle – or Mrs Rourke as the girls of the house knew her – made a rapid calculation. She had never heard of a crop called Cheviot and the reference to sheep meant nothing to her. But the seaweed lord was an excellent client – at least when he paid. The two sovereigns would cover most of his outstanding account. It was worth taking a chance on the balance and whatever he ran up tonight.

'Welcome, my lord,' she said. 'No doubt you'll be wanting fresh blossoms from the hedgerow. As it happens I have the very thing. Three sweet virgins from the Highlands of your own native land and all newly taken before they reached the wicked city. Come in and take a glass while I ready them for your inspection, sir.'

She stepped back to let him through.

The man entered. Mrs Rourke, a stout middle-aged woman with an immense bosom swelling forward over stays laced almost to bursting point, led him upstairs to a private room on the first floor.

'The best claret in the house,' she said, handing him a glass, 'and your patience for a few moments.'

As she went out the man dropped into a gilt-framed armchair to wait. Madame Belle ran the best brothel in London. The reputation of her new girls was unrivalled.

Gulping the wine, he scratched his groin happily.

The young man was named Aldred Farquarson of Invergordon.

At twenty-eight he was short and slight. Beneath his already receding sandy hair he had a round high-coloured face, plump freckled cheeks, and small grey eyes fringed with lashes so pale they were almost invisible. As Jenny Marx had noticed when he pirouetted round her, he had a pleasant, even attractive appearance, youthful and slightly mischievous, with an easy boyish smile. What she'd failed to see in the dusk and fog were his heavily bloodshot eyeballs, the deep shadows beneath them, and the livid blotches that darkened his ruddy skin.

Since the age of eighteen Farquarson had led the life of a dedicated rake.

The Farquarsons owned large estates on the west coast of Scotland near the mouth of the Invergordon river, from whose name the family took their designation. Aldred, an only child, was six when his father died. For the next twelve years the lands he'd inherited were administered for him in trust. When he reached eighteen they passed into his control. For nearly half a century the Invergordon estates had been farmed for kelp. The revenues they generated were vast and had been spent recklessly by the three preceding lairds.

Aldred Farquarson was no exception to the family tradition.

Like many other Highland landowners he abandoned Scotland and established himself in London. There he set about disposing of his fortune as prodigally as his ancestors had done. He bought himself a large mansion in Mayfair. He acquired horses, carriages and an army of servants. He drank, he whored, he gave lavish entertainment to a throng of friends and hangers-on. He backed madcap mercantile adventures. Most of all he gambled. He wagered on horses, prize-fighters, cards, dice, on anything on which it was possible to lay a bet. And, like his forays into commerce, he always lost.

By the time he was twenty-six Aldred Farquarson was heavily in debt.

He had embarked on London life not only with the underpinning of his annual income from the kelp, but with a huge financial cushion in the form of the estates' accumulated earnings during his years as a minor. Those had been spent or gambled away. Much worse, the income from the seaweed had tumbled disastrously. Two years later his circumstances were, by Farquarson's standards, desperate. The Mayfair house had been sold, his possessions auctioned, his servants dismissed. Even then he still had dozens of claims by his creditors outstanding in the courts.

Farquarson was saved from bankruptcy by his factor, a grim-faced man named Hugo McNeil.

McNeil had watched the success of the Cheviot flocks as they spread across the Highlands. He wrote asking his laird to come north and discuss a change in the land's use. Farquarson went back to Scotland for the first time since he came into his inheritance. He made his stay as short as he could – the only pleasure he got from it was to pledge the stake money for a bout involving a promising young prize-fighter, who was brought to his notice by his cousin from Kilvey.

Farquarson had no interest in the estates. His only concerns were whether sheep would rescue his income, and if in the meantime their introduction would stave off his creditors by allowing him to borrow from the Edinburgh moneylenders.

Farquarson still didn't know the answer to the first question. It would take several years, his factor told him cautiously, to find out how the Cheviot fared at Invergordon. But the answer to the second was, yes. The moneylenders were more optimistic about sheep than McNeil was – or rather they had land as collateral to fall back on if they were proved wrong.

Farquarson returned south with enough money to pay off the most pressing of the claims against him.

Mrs Rourke was the least among his creditors. His visit to her house that night was a celebration. Farquarson hadn't the slightest idea what would happen in the future or how long the loans he had raised would last him. Cheerful, feckless and improvident, all he knew was that for the first time in months he could venture out of his lodgings without being dunned at the door. That alone deserved to be marked by a triumphal visit to the famous Dean Street brothel.

'The goods are ready for examination, my lord,' Mrs Rourke said as she reappeared.

'Lead on, Madame Belle, lead on!'

Farquarson struggled to his feet. They climbed to the second floor and stopped in front of a door with a gauze-covered spy hole cut in the central panel. Farquarson peered through.

On the other side was a tiled bathroom wreathed in steam. Several white-enamelled iron tubs were set into the bathroom's floor. Three of the tubs were filled with water and occupied by the newest recruits to the brothel. None of the three girls was more than fourteen and all were naked. Each was being bathed and scrubbed by an older member of Mrs Rourke's staff. Apart from frilled caps and lace aprons the girls outside the baths were naked too.

As Farquarson watched, the older girls made the younger ones stand up in the water and revolve slowly, teasing them and flicking at their breasts and buttocks with soap-sudded sponges. Giggling and unaware that they were being observed, the new arrivals did as they were told.

Farquarson caught his breath. Even by Mrs Rourke's standards all three were exceptional. But the one on the left, the little dark one with the cheekily upturned nose, the provocatively rounded bottom, and the wisp of black hair between her legs, was irresistible.

'Her!' His voice thickened as he pointed.

Mrs Rourke squinted through the spy hole. 'Little pretty Nelly,' she said. 'And how would you like her, sir?'

Farquarson thought for a moment. He chuckled. 'Why not *en bergère*, in homage to my new paymasters?'

'To be served as you wish – '

Mrs Rourke gave him a mock curtsey. She led him down the corridor and opened another door.

'Make yourself comfortable in the dairy,' she said. 'Your shepherdess will be dried, powdered and delivered to you instantly.'

She went out.

Farquarson glanced round and grinned. The 'dairy' was one of his favourite rooms in the house. Farm implements lined the walls, straw bales were scattered across the floor, a flight of wooden steps led up to a mock hayloft. In one corner was a soft down-frilled mattress, covered in linen dyed to resemble agricultural hessian. In another was a milkmaid's stool and a brass-mounted oaken butter churn.

He stripped off his velvet topcoat and tossed it aside. Then he went over to the churn. Reaching inside, Farquarson found the expected bottle of claret. He drew the loosened cork with his teeth and sniffed at the neck. Madame Belle hadn't cheated him. It was the best in the house – and the perfect accompaniment to a meal of prime young Highland flesh.

Still chuckling, Farquarson rolled back on the mattress and put the bottle to his lips.

A few moments later the door opened again. Into the room came the dark-haired girl he'd watched being scrubbed in the bath. She was no longer naked. Now she was dressed as a shepherdess with flowered ribbons in her hair and a low-cut embroidered smock whose skirt had been pinned at the front up to her waist to reveal the split pantaloons beneath. In her hand was a posy of fresh flowers. Her skin was heavily powdered and she brought with her waves of the cloying scent of bergamot.

Farquarson licked his lips and leered at her. He started to struggle to his feet. Suddenly his eyes glazed over and he fell back. His head lolled to one side, and the bottle dropped from his hand. An instant later he was asleep.

The girl looked down at him, bewildered. Before she had time to turn, the door behind her swung open and Mrs Rourke appeared.

'Can't hold it, but then he never could,' Mrs Rourke said crisply. 'Don't worry, child. This isn't any fault of yours. We'll just see how he's stacked – '

She reached for the coat beside Farquarson and counted out the coins from the inside pocket.

'Not as much as he's pretending but enough to buy him credit for a few days yet – at least if we take it in advance.'

She slipped some of the coins down the neck of her dress and returned the rest to the coat.

'Back with you downstairs, my dear. Keep your playthings on. This one may buckle to and want his cherry's bite yet. If he doesn't, I'll spin another for you.'

'Yes, ma'am.' The girl backed away and hurried from the room.

For several moments after the girl left, Mrs Rourke continued to stare down at Farquarson.

Mrs Rourke had run her Dean Street house for fifteen years. In that time she had seen many young men like Aldred Farquarson come and go. She addressed them all as 'sir' or 'my lord', although most of them barely warranted an esquire after their names. She played the games they wanted to play. She indulged their fantasies. She provided them with her best girls. And she took their money. She was after all a businesswoman. But Mrs Rourke was also, at least in her own estimation, a businesswoman with a heart.

Among the young men money came and went. In her experience it tended to be drawn back as if by a magnet to its fount. The young blades sometimes needed a little support in the lean periods between. Aldred Farquarson wasn't rich again yet. But perhaps he was on the way back.

He'd said he needed lodgings until his new arrangements were completed. Well, he could have one of the garret rooms and the run of the house for a week. But not a day more. If at the week's end he hadn't settled all his bills and put down a handsome advance on his future entertainment, then he'd be out on his ear.

Mrs Rourke tossed a sheepskin over him. Dismissing Farquarson from her mind, she left the room.

The new little girl looked very fetching in her shepherdess's costume. It would be a pity to waste all the effort that had gone into dressing her up. She was a real virgin too. Mrs Rourke would have to see if she couldn't titillate one of the regular Friday-night private clients in the salon below.

She headed determinedly downstairs.

— 41 —

Ozoro Esther's daughter Rachel was five when Salama, the Acab Saat of Gondar, was exiled from the kingdom.

As the child of the river, and so one day destined to become Gondar's queen-empress, she would normally have had her religious education from Salama. Ras Michael, deeply suspicious of the ambitious bishop, had been determined to keep her away from Salama's influence. Breaking with tradition, the Ras directed she should be tutored by another dignitary of the church, the white-haired and ailing Welorin.

Welorin ranked almost equally with the Acab Saat, but Ras Michael knew the old man could be counted on not to manipulate the child's mind for his own ends.

As a result Rachel had little contact with Salama. His disappearance from court meant nothing to her. Rachel's religious studies, in any event, occupied a very small part of her time. Most of her life was taken up with other and more practical aspects of her preparation for the throne. Ras Michael laid down the general lines of Rachel's education and kept a keen eye on her progress, but he was happy to leave the organization of her day-to-day activities to the dwarf, Doho.

Like his master Doho was at heart a soldier. Doho knew Gondar's ruler had to be prepared to lead the country in war. It didn't matter whether the ruler was a king or queen. Rachel needed exactly the same talents as a boy. The first was to become a skilful rider.

'Isn't he beautiful?' Doho said when he took Rachel out to see her first mount, a sleek little pony with a shining bay coat.

'He's called Armit, the firefly. Every time you see him you must speak to him by his name, give him something to eat, and rub his nose. Here, I'll show you.'

Doho lifted the child on to his shoulders. He produced a waxy lump of dried honeycomb from a pocket in his tunic, gave it to the pony on the palm of his hand, and caressed the animal's head. The pony snorted content-edly and nuzzled Doho for more.

Rachel watched entranced. In all her six years she had never seen anything so beautiful.

'Right.' Doho lowered her to the ground. 'Now you're going to get on Armit's back. First, take off your boots.'

The pony was harnessed with a leather bridle, leather reins and, because it was to be ridden by a future queen, a solid silver bit. On its back was a light wooden saddle from which hung adjustable straps, with two silver rings in place of stirrups.

'Why can't I wear my boots?' Rachel demanded as she sat down and began to unlace them.

'Because they might trap you if you had a fall,' Doho told her. 'More important, because you'll ride Armit better if both of you have bare feet. There'll be nothing between your skin and his. You'll understand each other. It's the way the people of Gondar have always ridden horses. We're the best riders in the whole wide world – and you're going to be the best of all of them.'

Doho helped her up into the saddle.

He scrambled on to the pony which had been led out for him. Then with four mounted grooms in attendance they set off across the park. The hunchbacked Doho crouched expertly in his saddle. Rachel laughed delight-edly as she rocked uncertainly in hers.

To Doho's pleasure the child proved not only to be fearless on horseback. She had an extraordinarily natural aptitude as a rider. Within a few years she had exhausted the plump little pony's capacities. Armit had to be replaced with a larger and more demanding animal.

Rachel's new mount was a pure-bred Arabian mare, a swift and beautiful but highly strung grey. It took her only months to achieve the same devoted domination over the Arabian as she had over the pony.

'Look at her, Ras,' Doho said proudly to Ras Michael one day as they watched Rachel, still not ten years old, guide the horse in full gallop on a weaving course between the trees in the park.

'The old woman lied to us. The child wasn't delivered beneath a roof. She was born out there in the saddle. Even the grooms can't keep up with her.'

Ras Michael chuckled contentedly.

Doho was right. The grooms, who escorted Rachel whenever she rode, were labouring far behind the child as she bent the Arabian from side to side between the trunks.

'The girl's arse fits a horse's back,' Ras Michael said. 'But she'll need more than that to rule Gondar. I want a queen, Doho, not a stable-girl. Make sure she's as good at everything else.'

The old warlord walked back into the palace.

Doho didn't neglect the many other aspects of Rachel's education. To ride well, he knew, was useless if she didn't also know how to fight on horseback. She had to learn how to defend herself with a shield, how to throw a spear, how to wield the short Abyssinian sword at close quarters in battle. Using his own specially made scaled-down weapons – by the time she was eight Rachel was the same height as the dwarf – Doho taught her the rudiments himself.

Soon, as the child outgrew him, she needed other tutors.

Veteran soldiers from Ras Michael's troops were brought in from their camps outside Gondar and lodged at the palace.

Day after day, as Doho intently supervised the lessons from the shade of a tree, they passed on their skills to Rachel. Uncomplaining, the girl listened, observed and practised. The arts of war were neither as interesting as riding, nor as suited to a child's abilities, but within the limitations of her age and strength Rachel became almost as proficient in them as she was on horseback.

Much of the training took the form of games that had been devised long ago to hone the warriors' skills on and off their horses. Rachel's favourite was known as the bead game. The acknowledged champion at the game in Ras Michael's forces was a tall blue-black Sudanese mercenary named Golan, who rode bareback as well as barefooted.

The contestants lined up on their mounts at one end of the training field. At the other end was a narrow-necked earthenware jar. On the ground midway between them was a line of coloured glass beads, one less in number than the riders.

Doho dipped a scarlet-tasselled spear and the race was on. Each horseman had to reach the beads and dismount at full gallop to pick one up. Remounting, he then had to race with the bead to the jar and place the bead inside. The jar's neck was so narrow that only the most skilful could hurl it accurately into the tiny funnel without dismounting again.

The horseman who failed to retrieve a bead was eliminated, as was the last to return his bead to the jar. The game continued until only one rider was left.

Rachel was small and agile, and the Arabian mare was more than a match for any of the men's horses in nimbleness. She had no difficulty in learning how to throw herself off and then back into the saddle, seizing one of the precious beads in between. The trouble came when Rachel tried to put the bead in the jar.

Time and again her throw fell short, or the bead would go wide and bounce away in the dust.

Angry and frustrated, she would wait while Doho scuttled up to retrieve the bead so that she could try again. Golan meanwhile would be casually practising. Rachel would watch enviously as the tall Sudanese flicked the bead unerringly into its target.

One parched night in Gondar's dry season, after Rachel had been eliminated in the first round of the game three times in succession that day, she woke suddenly. The palace was as quiet as a cave in the mountains. Even the nightingales had fallen silent. Through the unglazed window the light of a full moon bathed the park and the flat dusty surface of the soldiers' training ground at the northern corner of the walls.

Rachel clenched her fists, feeling the nails bite into her palms.

She had been playing the bead game for a month now and she felt humiliated that she was still always the first to go out. It made no difference that she was competing against grown men who had trained for years.

'You are the river's child,' Doho had said dejectedly as they rode back to the palace. 'You are not judged as others are. You are different. But maybe this is too much for you. I shall consider again tomorrow.'

The disappointment in his voice was something Rachel had never heard before. Her cheeks burned with shame as she remembered the dwarf's puzzled face lowered beside her.

Rachel quietly got out of bed and wrapped her indigo robe round her slim body. Doho was lying outside in the passage at the door to her room. He grunted and stirred as she stepped carefully over him, but he didn't wake. She went downstairs and walked silently through the palace.

At the door of the soldiers' dining hall she paused, startled, as a rat rustled in the sweet herbs and rushes which carpeted the stone floor. Then she went on. Most of the soldiers were asleep on the floor or lying over the tables. Rachel stepped carefully over or round them. She was looking for Golan and she found him at the far end.

The tall Sudanese was sleeping upright against a pillar, one leg carrying his weight and the other tucked up beneath him with his bare foot braced against the stone. Rachel could not remember him ever reclining to eat or rest. Golan's eyelids flickered open long before Rachel reached his side.

'Come with me, Golan,' she whispered.

Together the two, the tall ebony-skinned warrior and the apricot-pale child, slipped out through the doorway into the park. The horses were penned in a corral a few yards away.

Golan slipped into the corral and came back leading the pony and his own mount. Rachel turned to fetch the Arabian's saddle but Golan shook his head.

'When we ride to battle, we ride bareback,' he said. 'That is the way you must learn, princess.'

They mounted and rode through the moonlight to the training ground. Golan swung himself off his horse and searched among the pile of equipment that had been left behind from the previous day. He found a jar with an even narrower neck than the one they had been using before.

'If you cannot achieve the task when it is easy,' Golan said, 'you must make it harder for yourself.'

He placed the jar on the ground and picked up a bead.

'Watch me, princess,' Golan went on. 'Hold the bead between your thumb and your first finger as I do. When you throw it, the secret is in the movement of the wrist. Flick it gently and it will fly straight as the honey-guide to the wild hive.'

Golan gave Rachel a demonstration. Then he handed her the bead.

He made her practise on foot for two hours. By then Rachel could barely lift her arm to her shoulder, but at the end the bead was rattling into the jar almost as often as when Golan threw it. Only then did Golan allow her to mount her pony.

Rachel cantered away. She turned, galloped back and threw the bead downwards. The bead missed its target but at least – for the first time – it struck the jar.

Golan watched expressionlessly.

'The eye, princess,' he said as she paused. 'Your arm must be extended and your fingers relaxed, but above all your eye must never wander. Think of the jar as the most precious object in Gondar. Think that this is the last time you will ever see it. Let your eye know it so well you could fashion it yourself from clay, blindfolded in darkness.'

Rachel rode off and tried again.

Three hours later still, when the stars paled and the walls of the palace began to turn golden in the dawn light, Rachel was throwing the bead into the jar's narrow mouth every time.

She played the game with the soldiers all that morning. Rachel wasn't strong enough yet for her to win. But in every game she was among the last few horsemen to be eliminated. Riding home again in the evening, she was dropping with exhaustion in her saddle.

Doho barely noticed. The dwarf's misshapen face was glowing with pleasure and pride.

Rachel had other lessons to learn too.

Gondar was a mercantile crossroads. Merchants visited the capital from all over eastern Africa and far beyond. As well as Africans, Arabs, Portuguese, Britons, Turks, Indians and Greeks all came to trade, negotiate concessions and treaties, and conduct every manner of business with Gondar's rulers. For a future queen it was important to be able to speak to them in their own languages.

Other tutors were brought to the palace, not Ras Michael's scarred and taciturn warriors but studious articulate men, often in foreign dress, who coached Rachel in the tongues and dialects and customs of many different nations.

To Doho, who spoke only Abyssinian and a few phrases of kitchen Arabic, they were as remote and incomprehensible as visitors from the stars. Rachel, on the other hand, proved as natural and fluent a linguist as she was a horsewoman. The dwarf would squat nodding happily as Rachel with increasing confidence babbled away in languages whose names he barely knew.

She learnt Portuguese from the traders in gold; English and German from the stern-browed Jesuit missionaries who passed through Christian Ethiopia on their way to the dark interior; Arabic from the slave merchants who trekked the salt routes of the desert; Farsee from the little

Indian spice traders; a variety of Malindan and west African dialects; and once, from a group of splendidly dressed emissaries from Constantinople, some phrases of Greek and Turkish.

Sometimes at the end of a day's lessons Rachel turned to Doho and teased him.

'Salaam aleikem!' she said. 'Adieu! Benelet! Goodbye!'

As Doho looked at her bewildered, she would throw her arms round the dwarf's neck and kiss him.

'I'm only saying goodnight,' she explained, laughing.

Doho wasn't present at all of her lessons.

There were some things Rachel had to learn, the feminine arts, which she was taught by the women of the palace. When she was tutored in those, and they took up more and more of her time as Rachel grew older, the dwarf was excluded. Rachel's principal teacher was her mother's old nurse, Kalima.

From Kalima she learned how to ferment a group of plants in the wild pea family and extract a dye. When the dye was oxidized it turned cloth the deep blue-bronze indigo colour of the royal gowns. Kalima taught her how to make medicines and sleeping draughts from herbs and the bodies of insects, how to use oils and incenses, and how to prepare aphrodisiacs.

Increasingly as the years went by the few playmates Rachel had had of her own age as a child fell away. Her interests and preoccupations were so different from theirs that they ended up with nothing in common. Worried that she might become lonely, Doho decided to give her a pet animal. Out hunting one day he found a baby gazelle whose mother had been killed in the chase.

Doho wrapped the gazelle in his saddle blanket and took it back to his young mistress.

Rachel adored the little creature. For the first week she sat up all night with it, persuading it to take milk from her finger. Then, fed on a diet of young leaves from the palace gardens, the young faun began to thrive. Afterwards the graceful animal, its first horns budding on its russet-curled forehead, trotted behind Rachel everywhere, its feet clicking on the palace's stone and baked-clay floors.

As Rachel grew, Kalima's lessons occupied most of her evenings. When the light began to fade the old woman, the young girl and the faun would go out to the nightingale garden to take advantage of the cool of the evening. The gazelle would browse, its coat shining in the lowering sun, while Kalima instructed Rachel.

'Today,' Kalima said one evening as they settled down as usual, 'we shall learn about a herb used to shrink the vagina and create the impression of virginity –

'Not, I trust, that you'll ever need it, child,' old Kalima added sternly. 'But better to be safe than sorry, I always say. So if an accident happened, this is what is done.'

She picked up a stoppered pottery flask. Rachel, frowning in concentration, leant forward to listen as Kalima explained.

Neither of them noticed the gazelle pushing its way through the hedge of lavender bushes at the end of the garden. Nor, a moment later, did they hear the velvet wings of the huge eagle owl swooping out of the sky, its feathered talons, broad as a warrior's fist, extended as it dropped on to the prey it had spotted on the edge of the terrace.

The gazelle gave a startled cry of pain as the talons struck into its back. Rachel's head jerked up. To her horror she saw the faun dangling helplessly in the eagle owl's grasp as the bird lifted heavily into the air.

Clenching her fists and screaming, Rachel hurled herself through the bushes.

The eagle owl's nest was in a rocky crag that ran down to the outer parapet of the park a hundred paces north of the garden. Inside the nest were three hungry and almost fully-grown owlets. The gazelle was a larger prey than the owl normally took, and the great bird was forced to pause several times on the parapet as it made its way round towards the crag.

Rachel pursued it furiously along the wall. Each time

she caught up with the bird, the owl would heave itself into the air and carry the faun a stage further. Finally it reached the base of the crag and began to flap upwards, dragging its prey from ledge to ledge behind it. Unhesitatingly Rachel scrambled on top of the wall and climbed the crag after it.

Below her Kalima was screaming in terror.

Rachel didn't even hear her. Her face tense with rage, her eyes fixed on the faun, her muscles straining, she pulled herself up the jagged crevices. Once her fingers even touched the faun's leg and its liquid brown eyes gazed beseechingly back at her. Then the owl snapped its bill and tugged it on again.

The face of the crag grew steeper and more treacherous. First one of Rachel's feet slipped, then her hand grasped a spur of limestone that crumbled between her fingers. She almost fell but she recovered her grip and pressed blindly, obsessively on. Suddenly she saw above her a short steep wall of smooth rock. Protruding over its lip was an untidy bundle of twigs. It was the eagle owl's nest.

The owl dug its talons deeper into the faun's back and launched itself into the air, trying to circle upwards and deposit its prey in the nest. The faun's weight was too great. The gazelle broke from the talons and plummeted downwards. Rachel gave a cry of anguish. She turned her head as the wretched creature fell past her and vanished. Then she froze.

In the frenzy of her concern about the gazelle she had been unaware of what she was doing. Now she saw. The crag angled away from the park over the plain. She had climbed to a point where the cliff fell sheer beneath her for more than a thousand feet. There was nothing below but a sickening dizzying emptiness.

Her limbs paralysed, her palms icy and sweating, her head spinning and her stomach hollow, Rachel shrank back against the crag. She closed her eyes, opened her mouth and screamed. Her screams blended with the now-distant wails of the fearful Kalima far below.

It was inevitably Doho who rescued her.

He had heard Kalima's shouts from the palace. Racing across the park to the nightingale garden, he had seen the slender figure inching up the crag. Instantly Doho had set off behind her. On the rock face the dwarf was transformed. No longer the shuffling lopsided figure he presented on the ground, Doho moved as swiftly, surely and fearlessly as one of the graceful vervet monkeys which thronged the trees round the palace walls.

Fear for Rachel's safety made him climb faster than he had ever climbed before. Yet it took Doho an hour to reach her, and the stars were bright in the night sky when he eventually pulled himself on to the ledge where Rachel was huddled. Her face was streaked with tears and she sobbed as he put his arm round her.

'Calm yourself, little princess, calm yourself,' Doho said soothingly. 'I am here with you. Now you are safe.'

'I let her die, Doho,' Rachel murmured between her sobs. 'I could have saved her but I was afraid and I let the owl take her. It is all my fault and my weakness.'

'Owls must do their business and animals must die,' Doho answered crisply. 'There is neither fault nor weakness in you, princess, except for being foolhardy in going where you could not return. Learn from that – and leave the owls and their prey to the mountain wind.'

Doho buckled Rachel to him with leather thongs. With Rachel pressed against his back, he began the long slow descent to the palace wall.

For the first time in her young life, the dwarf reflected as he climbed down, Rachel had had to acknowledge defeat and death. It was no bad lesson for the young woman to learn. She might be the river's child, she might be the finest and loveliest issue the river had ever sired, but there were matters even Rachel could not control and places even she could not go.

The moon had risen when they finally set foot in the park. Doho untied the thongs and let Rachel stand. She swayed and began to fall. Doho gathered her in his arms and carried her back to the palace.

Rachel slept all the way.

— 42 —

'The river's sired many a king and queen, Ras,' Doho said, 'but there's never been one like her. That's the royalest that ever walked.'

The dwarf and Ras Michael were standing side by side on one of the palace balconies overlooking the park.

It was approaching dusk on a warm and clear evening. The sun was setting over the hills and a crescent moon was already climbing the sky above the plain. Below them Rachel, the day's lessons finished, had just emerged from her room for her evening ride. A groom was waiting with the Arab mare in the forecourt.

Ras Michael watched as she walked forward and swung herself up into the saddle. Rachel gripped the reins, gently kicked the horse into a canter, and rode away towards the trees. The Ras glanced at Doho and smiled indulgently. The old warlord was far from being a sentimental man, but it was difficult not to be touched by the adoration in Doho's voice. The dwarf worshipped his charge.

Well, he had good enough reason, Ras Michael thought. Even by Ras Michael's own daunting standards the slender figure, distantly outlined now against the first stars in the darkening sky, had become a very remarkable young woman. Most of it was due to her own qualities, but there was no denying the part Doho had played in encouraging and bringing them out.

Ras Michael reached down and ruffled the dwarf's hair.

'You've done well, Doho,' he said. 'Now let's finish the job. I want her baptized, married, and brought into court as an adult. I want to get her ready to take over – '

He paused. 'So when the hell is she going to bleed so we can get on with it? God knows, she's late enough. You've looked after everything else. What are you going to do about that?'

'You know there's nothing I can do, Ras,' Doho answered defensively. 'That's up to the river that made her. But she'll bleed soon, she must do.'

Ras Michael chuckled.

He'd been teasing the dwarf. Of course there was nothing Doho could do to bring on the arrival of Rachel's puberty – the moment when she officially changed from a girl into a woman. Rachel was older than any girl the Ras had ever heard of in reaching it. But Doho was right. It must happen soon now.

The two men gazed across the park where, in the twilight, the hoofs of the Arab mare were sending spirals of dust into the evening air.

On the horse's back Rachel was unaware that she was being watched.

Her feet were bare in the silver hoops of the stirrups. She guided the mare in a controlled canter through the trees until she came to the park's parapet wall. There she reined in the Arab and stared down over the plain. Clusters of lights from cooking fires were beginning to glow in the villages below and the scent of charcoal smoke, carried upwards by the wind, reached her nostrils.

Rachel breathed in and leant back in her saddle.

At fifteen and almost fully grown, Rachel had fulfilled all the physical promise of her childhood. Esther, her mother, was counted a famous beauty, but all Gondar knew that Rachel surpassed her. She had her mother's dark eyes, her shining black hair and flawless skin, but Rachel was taller, her features were finer, her long-legged body more supple and graceful. Although Esther was not yet thirty and had given birth to only one child, her face was already becoming plump and her figure beginning to thicken. There seemed no chance that either would ever happen to her daughter.

She appeared, as Doho remarked when she was born, to be fashioned from the austere north wind that swept down from the Mountains of the Moon in winter.

Looking across the plain beneath the mountains' shadows Rachel was as unconscious of her appearance as she was of Ras Michael and Doho in the palace behind. Although she had nothing to compare them with, the years of her childhood in Gondar had been totally unlike the childhood of any of her contemporaries. She was of course the heiress to the throne. Rachel had become aware of that very early. She knew that it somehow set her apart from the other children in Gondar. But there were other differences between them and her.

She had grown up without a family. Her mother lived apart from her father, and she had seen little of either during her life. Georgis was uninterested in a small girl, who in any event wasn't even his daughter, while Esther, partly at Ras Michael's insistence and partly because of her own indolence, had played no part in Rachel's upbringing. Rachel had no brothers or sisters. From the start her only intimate companions had been adults who, paradoxically for a princess, came from a much humbler background – she was far closer to Doho and the illiterate old Kalima than to anyone else at court.

Equally unusual was the education Ras Michael had ordered for her.

Very occasionally an Abyssinian nobleman might teach a favourite daughter how to ride. Once in a generation perhaps she would be shown how to carry a shield. But never before had a girl been made an expert horsewoman, schooled for day after day in the use of arms, tutored in foreign languages and customs, taught the arts of generalship and diplomacy until she could discuss them for hours on end with men four times her age. Inevitably it set Rachel apart from her contemporaries as much as her position as heiress to Gondar's throne.

Distanced from her parents, wary of the circles of the court, lacking other children as friends, Rachel was happiest in the company of the gruff blunt-speaking dwarf or the fussy and wise old Kalima as she moved about the dusky palace kitchens.

In the gathering darkness the young queen-to-be looked out over her kingdom.

She loved Doho and Kalima dearly. She would love them for ever, as she knew they loved her. But as she thought about them, it occurred to Rachel for the first time that even they were part of Gondar – of the vast all-enveloping tapestry of land and people and history that the accident of her birth had wrapped about her. They were no longer enough for her.

With an acute and bewildering yearning she wanted something of her own, something private that was hers alone. She didn't believe she would ever find it. The presence of Gondar was so immense, so suffocating, it controlled and dominated every facet of her life. But if she ever did find it, Rachel thought, it would come in the form of a person – a person who loved and belonged to her freely as she freely loved and belonged to him.

Him. In her mind she had used the word quite unconsciously. As soon as she'd done so Rachel knew he was a man. She knew instantly too he could never come from Gondar. And because Gondar was all she would ever know, it meant she would never find him.

Rachel swung the horse's head round sharply in frustration and set off at a gallop back for the palace. As she rode she found to her surprise that her eyes were clouded.

— 43 —

'There, child, it's done,' Kalima said. 'Now, stand up and let's have a look at you.'

Kalima moved back. There were a dozen other women in the bedchamber. As Rachel turned, gasps of delight and admiration lifted from their throats.

Rachel had finally come to womanhood the week before. Now at last she could be baptized in the river. Kalima had woken her long before dawn. The day began with Kalima dressing her quickly in a simple white shift and leading her downstairs to the courtyard.

Outside in the darkness Bishop Welorin was waiting for her with a group of priests and a detachment of the royal guard. Escorted by the torch-bearing soldiers she had followed the old man through the palace grounds to the tunnel down to the caverns of the river's source.

The soldiers left them at the tunnel's entrance, and Rachel continued with the bishop and the priests. A quarter of a mile later the priests also stood back, leaving Rachel and the bishop, who was carrying a single wavering candle, to go on alone. Ten minutes afterwards they came to the first pool in the river's source, a little waist-deep saucer of warm clear water high above the cavern from where the main spring burst.

On the bishop's instructions Rachel disrobed. Then, as the old man muttered prayers and incantations, she slipped naked into the pool and bathed.

'To Thee, O Lord,' he said, 'I commend this child. She is the river's daughter and Yours. May You bless her, keep her, endow her with grace, and bring her to reign in peace over Gondar.'

He beckoned her forward. Rachel stood up and waded towards him. The bishop dipped his hand in the water and raised it to her face.

'Child of the river,' he said, tracing the mark of the cross on her forehead. 'I baptize you as a woman now in the name of Rachel.'

They stood for a moment, the naked young girl and the rheumy-eyed old man in his long purple robes, in the silence of the rock chamber with the candle's flame gleaming on the surface of the pool.

Then the bishop turned and shuffled away. Rachel dressed and followed him.

That was almost six hours ago. Now it was mid morning. Most of the intervening time had been spent in preparing Rachel for the baptismal feast. First she had bathed again, this time in warm and heavily scented water. Then Kalima set about the laborious business of dressing her hair. Every few strands were coiled together and threaded through with tiny polished cowrie shells, until hours later Rachel's head looked as if it were covered by a gleaming helmet.

Afterwards she put on her ceremonial robes, six shifts of sheer silk layered one over the other and all dyed the royal colour of deep indigo. Next came her jewellery – gold bracelets on her wrists, a gold filigree choker round her neck, heavy pendant gold earrings carved with lions' heads. On her feet were light leather slippers, the leather dyed indigo like her robes and embroidered with gold thread. Finally, covering all her elaborate work with the cowrie shells, Kalima had placed on Rachel's head a white silk turban with a plume of eagle feathers pinned to its side.

As the cries of delight filled the room Rachel walked over and stood for a moment in front of the ebony-framed mirror on the wall, peering at her reflection.

The gold dazzled back at her. The rich layers of silk rippled and shone like cascading water. The eagle feathers flared up proud and erect, with the sunlight from the windows burnishing the quills. She blinked uncertainly. She felt as if a sumptuous jewelled tent had been pitched round her. Hidden somewhere inside the magnificence was herself. She wriggled and pressed her bare skin against the silk. The contact suddenly seemed to bring her face into focus – pale and tense but unmistakably there in front of her in the glass.

Rachel closed her eyes in relief.

For a moment she'd almost thought Kalima had somehow managed to make her invisible. From the day when Doho had introduced her to her first pony and she'd been dressed to ride in a miniature version of male Abyssinian clothing – a cotton tunic and pants with leather chaps over them – she'd worn almost nothing else. The elaborate shifts and dresses worn by Gondar's women were alien and unfamiliar to her. She knew she was a girl, she knew and accepted that on certain rare occasions – today was one – there were conventions of dress and behaviour she had to obey.

Yet for most of her life Rachel had been brought up as a boy destined for manhood in a man's world. She had always been happiest there. Happiest on horseback, happiest with her fierce and beloved little Doho, with the warriors who came in from the camps to school her, with the bearded teachers who taught her languages, with Ras Michael's white-haired generals with whom she discussed the arts of war.

As she stared at herself now Rachel felt something different. She stretched up her neck, turned her head to the side, and lifted her hand to adjust the turban.

For the first time in her life Rachel was aware of herself as a woman.

It was a strange, almost intoxicating feeling. She could sense the outline of her body beneath the robes, and feel the roundness of her breasts. Her skin seemed to be glowing and her eyes were shining in a way they had never done before. She drew herself up tall and proud, presenting herself not to the mirror or the other women in the room but to someone else, someone who wasn't there – someone she had never met.

Watching her somewhere from far beyond the mirror was a stranger. The stranger was the young man who had come to her mind as she sat on her horse looking out over Gondar in the dusk. She had become a woman not for herself, not for her family, not even for Gondar, but for her distant unknown watcher. She had dressed herself for him. Her body and its adornments were a gift she wanted to give him. In return he would give himself to her.

Rachel stared into the mirror, searching for his face.

'Come, young lady,' Kalima's voice interrupted her. 'It's time we left.'

Rachel turned and the sensation vanished. She shook her head, not certain for a moment where she was. Then she remembered.

Someone was knocking at the door again. The knocking had grown more and more urgent over the past hour. The other women formed up in procession round her, four in front, Kalima immediately behind, and the other eight at the rear. They crossed the chamber and went out into the corridor.

Doho was waiting outside.

As the door opened the dwarf darted forward. An instant later when he saw Rachel he stopped and the excited anticipation on his face was replaced with a look of awe. He gazed at her. Then he dropped to his knees.

'Your majesty's servant,' he mumbled.

The shock was so unexpected that Doho could barely speak. The slim child in boy's clothes he had known and adored all her life had been transformed. In a matter of hours she had become not only a woman, but a queen. He reached out blindly for Rachel's hand, and kissed her fingers. Then he lowered his head as tears began to stream down his face.

Rachel laughed. 'It's still me, Doho,' she said. 'I want you to walk right behind me alongside Kalima. Now stand up and don't be so stupid.'

She pulled Doho to his feet. The still-bewildered dwarf took his place beside the old woman, and the procession moved forward again.

Rachel had been aware of the noise in the bedchamber, but the room faced away from the town over the royal park. Now, as they descended the stairs and came out into the courtyard, the sound reached them in great clamorous waves. For days, people from the surrounding countryside had been streaming into Gondar to celebrate the occasion. With them they had brought their waggons, children, horses, tents, musical instruments, and herds of cattle to be slaughtered for the feast.

By dusk on the previous evening the streets of the town had become impassable. There were encampments, cooking fires, makeshift byres and stables everywhere. Bellowing cows and bulls roamed through the crowds. Jugglers, acrobats, snake-charmers and conjurors, all shouting the attractions of their acts, performed to cramped and constantly changing audiences.

Children squealed and fought and played in the dust. Packs of half-wild dogs scavenged the alleyways. Columns of smoke lifted above the roofs. Smells of herbs, roasting meat, urine, sweat, oiled leather, incense and baked mud swirled together in the hot summer air. Flutes, drums and deep throbbing string instruments shrilled and pulsed from dawn until far into the night – when tumbling rainbows of fireworks filled the sky.

The royal banqueting hall was near the main gates of the palace.

As the procession approached it the sounds of the celebrations beyond the walls grew louder and louder, and the tangled smells stronger and more pungent. By the time they stopped in front of the doors the noise was almost deafening.

The officer in command of the escort hammered three times with the hilt of his sword on the wooden panels. The doors swung open. The ladies-in-waiting ahead of Rachel stepped back, and she walked forward alone.

44

The hall was a huge vaulted room with five widely spaced lines of tables running its length.

At the far end, set cross-wise to the room and raised on a low platform, was a separate table for Ras Michael and the royal family. Standing behind the tables below were the guests who had been summoned to the baptismal feast. As well as the courtiers and the leaders of Gondar's church and army, there were three hundred members of the country's most important families.

As Rachel appeared they all lifted their cupped hands and clapped them sharply once. Ras Michael walked through the hall to greet her. He was wearing a cloak and his great war-sword was buckled at his waist.

'Welcome, young lady,' he said. 'You have come here to take meat for the first time as an adult in your mother's house and with your mother's subjects. May you eat well.'

Ras Michael led her through the hall to the royal table.

Rachel's place was at its centre. On one side of her was her mother, on the other Georgis. Esther was plump, proud and beaming. Her consort was fretful and bored. He gave Rachel a cursory nod. Then he plucked impatiently at the sleeves of his tunic.

Rachel stood behind her chair waiting.

The hall's doors, which had been closed after her entrance, were swung open again. Outside in the stone-flagged courtyard was an immense bull held by a chain through its nose by two of the royal butchers. The men led the animal forward until it was immediately beneath the archway into the room. One of them lashed its feet together with leather thongs. The other tugged on the chain until the bull toppled over. The first butcher drew out a knife. He knelt by the bull's head, and made a tiny incision in its dewlap. A few drops of blood fell on to the stone and the helpless animal bellowed.

At the sound the company in the hall sat down on the benches ranged on either side of the tables. Rachel sat down too. She knew what was coming and although she detested it — animals of every sort had always been a major part of her life and she hated seeing them suffer — she accepted it was an important ritual in Gondar's world.

She watched impassively as the butchers skinned the bull alive.

Starting at the neck and carefully avoiding the arteries, they rolled back and cut away the hide, until the animal's flesh was bare to its haunches and halfway down its ribs. Then they began to remove the meat, carving it out in large square lumps. All the while the bull bellowed in agony and struggled helplessly on the stone floor. Only when all the best meat had been sliced off were the bull's arteries cut and the animal allowed to die.

From the doorway servants carried the meat in their bare hands to the tables.

The first and best cut was taken to the royal table and placed in front of Georgis. Like all the other men in the hall Georgis had a curved dagger in his belt. He pulled it out and carved off two long thin strips. He pushed one towards Esther and the other towards Rachel. Rachel knew exactly what was expected of her. No Abyssinian male of any standing ever fed himself. Even among royalty it was a woman's duty to prepare the man's meat.

Rachel also had a knife, a small simple clasp knife. She chopped up the strip of meat. In front of every guest was a pile of flat circles of unleavened bread. Those at the bottom of the pile were coarse and thick and dark. They served as plates and napkins, and were eaten by the servants when the feast was over. The upper loaves were thin and pale and powdered with rock salt and black pepper.

When Rachel had cut the beef into little dice-sized cubes she piled them on the topmost loaf. She wrapped the soft white bread round the meat, and held it up to Ras Michael.

'Eat, Ras,' she said.

Ras Michael placed his hands on his knees. He lowered his head towards the cartridge of meat and bread, opened his mouth, and took an immense bite.

On Rachel's other side Georgis, served in the same way by Esther, was doing the same. Both men chewed and swallowed with grunts and belches. The more food they crammed into their mouths and the greater the noise they made in eating it, the higher their position was considered to be. Rachel waited until Ras Michael had finished his mouthful. Then she raised the cartridge again. Ras Michael shook his head.

'I'm an old man,' he said. 'What would be hard commons for the young is a feast to those of my years. Besides, it's a ridiculous convention. I have honoured it – but I've honoured it enough. Now it's your turn, young lady. Like all the young, you're probably starving.'

He took the rest of the roll from her, chopped it in segments with his dagger, and speared one on the dagger's point.

Rachel smiled at him gratefully. She had had nothing since Kalima woke her, and she was famished. She lowered her head and bit hungrily into the roll as Ras Michael held it out to her.

Until the skinning of the bull the atmosphere in the hall had been formal and constrained. As soon as the meat was distributed and the company began to eat, the mood changed. The guests started to talk and joke and laugh. When they had filled themselves the men drank mead from horn mugs. Then they fed the women who sat alternately among them. Afterwards the women drank too. Groups of musicians came in and the throng continued to drink as the instruments played and songs lifted towards the raftered roof.

As the atmosphere grew more relaxed still, couples

began to slip from the benches and entwine themselves on the bull-hide rugs beneath the tables. Whenever it happened the two on either side would rise and decorously hold out their tunics to screen the vigorous and often noisy coupling on the floor below. Then, when the sated pair reappeared, they would sit down again and continue their conversation.

From the table on the dais Rachel watched unconcerned.

While she had no experience of sex, like every other Abyssinian child she had grown up to regard it without fear. Sex was no mystery. It was an activity as natural and apparently as pleasurable as eating or drinking. In due course she would discover its pleasures for herself. Now that she had at last achieved womanhood, the time would not be long in coming. Meanwhile the moaning and tossing and panting of the couples on the bull-hides was as familiar as the grunts and belches which had followed the eating of the raw beef.

Occasionally Ras Michael inclined his head and spoke to her, raising his voice to make himself heard above the clamour. From time to time Rachel's mother leant across, tugged at her wrist, and said something, struggling too against the uproar. Once Georgis impaled a tiny choice piece of meat on his dagger and fastidiously offered it to her. Guests came to the table and greeted her, most of them unsteady and incoherent from the effects of the mead.

Smiling, Rachel responded politely to them all. The feast was in her honour, she was Gondar's future queen, it was her duty to be courteous and attentive to everyone.

But for most of the time she sat silent and alone. In spite of the fixed smile on her face, she was remote from the increasingly raucous gathering. This was not her world. She felt herself lost, a stranger among the intrigues of the court, the elaborate rituals of the banquet, the constant to-ing and fro-ing of the intoxicated aristocracy of Gondar. She longed for the company of Doho and old Kalima. They represented things old and familiar and safe, things she knew and understood, but they had been separated from her when she entered the hall.

'Young lady – '

A hand was tapping her arm. Rachel blinked and shook her head. For a moment her thoughts had been far away. She turned and saw that Ras Michael was attracting her attention.

'The jongleurs are approaching,' he went on. 'When they reach the table, stand and bow to them. Then sit until they've finished. Afterwards get up and bow again.'

Rachel nodded obediently. By tradition at the baptismal feast the jongleurs, the court musicians and storytellers, composed and delivered elaborate songs of praise in honour of the future queen.

Inwardly Rachel's heart sank.

The jongleurs' tributes were likely to last for at least two hours. Afterwards there would be speeches by Ras Michael, Georgis, the royal confessor, the chief ministers, and any of Gondar's noblemen who decided to take the opportunity of addressing the gathering under the guise of honouring her.

Darkness might well have fallen before they had finished and she was free to go. Meanwhile she would have to sit there serenely among the fumes and stench and clamour as the voices droned on, while her back began to ache, her head became dizzy, and her mind numb.

Fighting back an almost irresistible impulse to plead faintness and beg to be allowed to leave, Rachel turned to face the gathering again. Her smile was glazed now and her face beginning to pale with tiredness. Otherwise she gave no sign of what she was feeling. She watched the jongleurs, three grinning gap-toothed old men accompanied by two younger men carrying string instruments, push their way towards the dais.

As they stopped and bunched themselves in front of the table, a cheer went up from the audience. Rachel got to her feet. She forced another smile and bowed. The men bowed low in return. The oldest straightened up, lifted his arm, and opened his mouth to sing.

Suddenly, and before any sound emerged, a frantic shout rang out from the courtyard.

'Ras! Ras!'

The jongleur froze with his mouth distended. The background swell of laughter and talk died away. On the dais everyone stiffened. The entire company swung round to face the door.

By then the space on the flagstones outside was piled with the bones, hides and stripped carcasses of the bulls slaughtered for the feast. The blood-soaked detritus made a waist-high barrier across the entrance to the hall. Clambering over it, tossing the bones and discarded entrails aside and hurling back the court butchers trying to restrain him, was a man. He was bare-headed and his clothes were in sodden scarlet tatters.

Gazing at him in the first few seconds of confusion, Rachel's immediate thought was that he was a madman, perhaps one of Gondar's deranged beggars, who'd scaled the palace walls and was attempting to burst in on the feast. Then she realized that the dangling strips of cloth hung from a suit of padded body armour, and most of the blood didn't come from the bulls' bodies – the stains were brown and caked and dry.

The man was a wounded soldier and there was nothing insane in the determination on his face as he struggled towards the entrance.

'Let him through!'

Ras Michael's voice cut through the clamour. The throng parted and the man limped painfully up to the dais.

'Who are you?' Ras Michael demanded.

'Fasil, lord,' the man answered. 'I serve with the fifth border guards.'

'So you come from Peralat on the Malinda border.' Ras Michael nodded. He was old but he knew unerringly where every one of his army's units was stationed.

'What brings you here?'

'The Galla, my lord,' the man answered. 'They are invading.'

'Invading?' Ras Michael looked at him, frowning. 'The Galla haven't come down from the mountains for eight seasons. They haven't even raided Malinda since the rains set in. They've no need to. They can pasture their herds in the highest uplands. What do you mean, invading – ?'

In a sudden fury Ras Michael leant forward. He gripped the man by the front of his tunic, and pulled him over the table.

'There was a little border raid and you ran away. Isn't that it? I'll have you pegged with iron against the door, hands, knees and ankles. Guards!'

'It is the truth, Ras,' the man choked. 'It was no raid. There are thousands of them. They have come by way of Malinda. They have killed the embrenche and all his family, and taken the country. Now they have crossed into Gondar. The Acab Saat is with them.'

Ras Michael held the man for a moment longer. Then he released him.

'The Acab Saat is marching with the Galla?'

'Yes, my lord. He rides with King Culembra. I was captured and brought before them. They gave me their terms to bring to you.'

'Terms? What terms?' Ras Michael demanded.

'Their terms for peace, Ras. They want all of Gondar west of the river. Also a thousand slaves, and the queen and the princess to be delivered to their camp within a week. If not they will march on Gondar itself.'

Ras Michael stared at him in disbelief. Then his face darkened with fury.

'That treacherous thieving priest!' he said. 'Half the kingdom, slaves, the queen, the princess – he has gone mad! Not even his cloth will save him now.'

He broke off.

'From this moment Gondar is at war,' Ras Michael shouted. 'It will not see peace again until Salama is dead. I myself will lead the army.'

Ras Michael strode from the hall. The gathering started to break up in clamour and confusion. Rachel sat very still.

Her childhood was over with the feast. With a chilling certainty she sensed that its end marked the start of something terrible for Gondar.

45

Jamie Oran waited for a gap in the seemingly endless stream of carriages swirling round Piccadilly Circus.

He darted across the road and found an unoccupied space on the low wall round the fountain. Wearily he sat down. On either side was a throng of tramps, urchins and drunks, all like him using the island as a haven in the midst of the clattering horse-drawn traffic. Jamie cupped his hands, reached into the water, and drank. Then he unlaced his boots and rubbed his feet.

Jamie was exhausted.

It was approaching dusk and he'd been walking since dawn. On the springy turf and heather of the Scottish hills he'd often walked all day and finished as fresh as he'd started. London, he'd just discovered, was different. The cobbles and stone-flagged pavements jarred his legs, the stench and fumes clogged his nostrils, the noise battered at his ears and made his head ache. He replaced his boots and lowered his head. Then he sat for a moment dispiritedly staring at the ground.

It was exactly two weeks since he'd left Blantyre.

When he slipped quietly out of the house that day Jamie was aware that something momentous had happened. His childhood and his youth were over. Eleven years of shelter and support had suddenly come to an end. Finished just as abruptly, too, was the future Dr Cameron had envisaged for him as a doctor who would follow in Cameron's own steps, take on his practice, and maybe eventually inherit his house. After his encounter with Mrs Cameron in his attic bedroom, Jamie knew he could never return to the place which, as far as he had one, he had come to regard as his home.

Jamie was on his own.

In his mind there was only one thought: to reach London and hand Mrs Livingstone's letter to the President of the Royal Geographical Society. Afterwards, he believed, everything would somehow resolve itself. He would be launched on his way to Africa. He would set out in search of the Nile's source. And –

There even Jamie's youthful and buoyant imagination failed him. He did not know what the outcome would be. The perils and problems were immense. Africa was still only a name, the Nile no more than an image from a steel engraving made by an artist who had never seen the river. Jamie could still not properly separate it from his memories of Iona's tumbling burns. It wasn't important. All that mattered was to be on his way.

Jamie's first steps on the road were not encouraging.

He went from the Camerons' house to the coach halt at the Blantyre Arms. There was indeed a coach south that evening. The journey took only fifty hours, but the price of a seat was a fearsome four guineas – almost one tenth of Jamie's entire savings.

It had taken Jamie four years to accumulate his capital. There was no question of a large part of it being wasted on the journey to London. He would have to walk. Jamie set out. With the help of an occasional ride in a waggon and after sleeping out nightly in the woods along the way, he reached Richmond on the outskirts of the capital. It was almost dark. He spent the final night of the trip in the royal deer park. At first light the following morning he headed into the centre of the city.

The Royal Geographical Society, Jamie discovered, was in South Kensington. He arrived at the society's headquarters, an imposing red-brick building facing Hyde Park, in the late afternoon. Presenting himself with his letter at the door, he learned to his dismay that the society's president, a certain Sir Roderick Murchison, was away. He would not be back for three weeks. The porter offered to take the letter and deliver it to Sir Roderick when he returned.

Jamie thought for a moment. Then he shook his head.

Over the years the letter had become his talisman. It was far too precious to be entrusted to a third party who, for all Jamie knew, might lose it in the interval. He had to deliver it to the president himself.

Putting the envelope back in his jacket, Jamie asked, 'Can ye recommend anywhere I might find lodgings until the president gets back?'

The porter stared at him.

The tall young man was a puzzle. His clothes were poor, he was clearly travel-stained, and he spoke with a Scots accent. On the other hand his voice was educated and there was no mistaking the authority of the writing on the envelope. The youth said it had been given to him by Mrs Livingstone. The porter had twice seen the great explorer's wife when Dr Livingstone came to speak to the society. He had little doubt that the young man was telling the truth.

'Try Soho,' the porter suggested. 'You'll find a fair number of lodging houses up there.'

Jamie thanked him and left.

That was two hours ago. He bought himself a glass of ale and an eel pie, the first food he'd eaten all day, in a tavern. Then, following the porter's directions, he'd headed for Piccadilly.

'Ask again when you get to the Circus,' the porter had advised.

Jamie glanced up at the sky.

The light was fading and there was an edge of cold in the September air. If he were to find lodging before darkness fell he would have to hurry. He didn't mind sleeping out in the countryside but a night on the foul-smelling streets of London was another matter altogether.

Jamie picked up his bag and got to his feet. One of the urchins pointed towards Soho, and he set off.

Two hours later, chill and dispirited, Jamie was

standing at the entrance to a narrow street leading off a little square. He was somewhere in Soho, although he had no idea where. Soho proved to be a warren of dirty lanes and alleyways, filled with small shops and grimy taverns. The porter seemed to have been mistaken about the area's lodging houses. In the two hours Jamie had found only three. All of them were full. In the last he'd been offered a pallet in a courtyard next to the privy. The yard was already littered with sleeping drunks and the stench from the privy was so strong Jamie recoiled in disgust.

Jamie had reconciled himself to sleeping in the open after all.

He hesitated, trying to decide between the square or the larger and quieter space of St James's Park. As he stood there, Jamie became aware of a man weaving his way up the street. It was too dark to make out the man's face but as he passed beneath one of the few lamps, Jamie saw he was wearing tartan trews. A few yards away he stopped. The man rang a doorbell and vanished into a house.

Jamie walked forward. From his trews the man was a fellow Scot. It was the only encouraging sign Jamie had had since he left the Royal Geographical Society. He tugged at the bell pull. A young woman in a low-cut dress opened the door and smiled at him.

'I'm looking for a bed,' Jamie said.

'And no doubt something to warm it,' the young woman replied, laughing. 'Well, come in, sir, and view.'

Jamie stepped through the door.

He found himself in a large room draped in red velvet and lit by two ornate gilt chandeliers. Wax was dripping from the candles into tin plates on the embroidered rugs which covered the floor. The air was warm. It reeked of gin and, even more overpoweringly, of scent. Round the walls a number of men, from their uniforms mainly soldiers, were lounging on brocaded couches with glasses in their hands. Several girls in loose half-transparent shifts wandered in and out. In one corner a tall negress, dressed in a leopardskin tunic and holding a long whip in her hand, was standing immobile like a statue.

As Jamie stared round in bewilderment, a buxom woman descended the stairs at the far end of the room.

'Welcome, my lord,' she said. 'A first visit, I think. Always a cause for celebration. Victoria – the house has a new guest!'

The woman clapped her hands. One of the scantily clad girls ran forward. She curtsied and handed Jamie a glass.

'Remember your manners, my dear,' the woman went on. 'His lordship is interested in landscape as well as refreshment.'

The girl simpered and curtsied again. She caught the hem of her shift and pulled it up to her neck. Jamie gazed at her in disbelief. Underneath she was naked. He had a glimpse of upwardly tilted breasts, a flat young stomach, and a pair of plump thighs. Then he dipped his head towards the glass and swung away in confusion.

'A little hors d'oeuvre, as the French have it,' he heard the older woman saying. 'But you must examine the full menu, sir.'

'Ma'am, I think there's a wee misunderstanding.' The gin had made Jamie choke and he looked up at her, spluttering. 'It's no more than a bed for the night that I'm after. Would ye be having that?'

The woman's smile vanished. Her face hardened and for an instant she stared at him icily.

'You want lodging – is that all?'

'Aye,' Jamie nodded. 'I saw a wee loon in trews come into the house and I thought ye might be able to help – '

'Get out!' the woman shouted. 'You, whatever your goddamn names are, get this creature out of here!'

Jamie had little idea what happened next.

He was dimly aware of the men lying on the couches putting down their glasses, jumping up and surging round him. A fist slammed into his mouth, arms seized him, and his feet left the floor. A moment later he found himself sprawling in the gutter outside. His bag was pitched on to his chest and the door slammed.

Jamie had hardly climbed to his feet before the door opened again and another figure was pitched out into the street. As he tumbled past, Jamie saw it was the man in the tartan trews he had followed there. A window opened above and a top hat came floating down through the darkness.

'Have charity, Madame Belle,' the man called up from his knees. 'Charity for a poor innocent defrauded by his friends.'

'Defrauded, my arse!' the woman bellowed down. She was the same buxom lady who had just evicted Jamie. 'You're the only fraud around here. You've had charity by the bucketful. One week, you asked for, and one week it is. I don't want another sight of your face until every last penny's paid.'

The window slammed down.

'Heartless strumpet!'

Unconcerned, the man stood up and dusted off his hat. Then he noticed Jamie.

'Do I see a victim of the same injustice, sir?' he asked amiably.

'I was under a misapprehension,' Jamie answered. 'I thought yon was a lodging house.'

'Madame Belle's harlot parlour a lodging house? Oh, rich, sir, rich!' The man chuckled with pleasure.

'Aye,' Jamie added irritably. 'And it was yourself who led me there.'

He told the man what had happened. By the time he finished the stranger was almost helpless with laughter.

'My apologies.' The man finally managed to control himself. 'But the irony is a delight. Let me introduce myself, sir. Aldred Farquarson is the name.'

As he spoke the moon appeared. Jamie stared at him in its light. He had a glimpse of fair thinning hair, a round red face, and a pair of unfocused eyes.

'Aldred Farquarson?' Jamie repeated. 'Would that be the Farquarson of Invergordon?'

'At your service, sir. You have the advantage of me. But

to judge from your voice, you are a native of my own land too. Am I right?'

'Do ye no ken me?' Jamie asked. 'Jamie Oran from Blantyre, it is, as ye'd backed in the Hamilton fair against the Bull of the North – until, so they told me, the baillies came in and ye cut and run.'

'Good God!' Farquarson stared back at him in delight. 'Heaven help me if it's not the gamecock from the doctor's house no less – the one my cousin of Kilvey found. I stood to win five hundred sovereigns on you, sir.'

'I'd have settled for twenty,' Jamie said bleakly, 'if your money had been as bonny as your mouth.'

'Let us not dwell on that now,' Farquarson replied. 'Bailiffs pass like summer clouds. You will come to the mark with that brute yet, and we will both be rich. Meanwhile to immediacies. Two fellow countrymen in the same boat. Thrown out of a bawdy house and lacking accommodation for the night. We must stick together, Mr Oran. Let me think.'

He rubbed his chin, frowning. Then he snapped his fingers.

'Of course! We shall try the lady with the parasol. We know each other by sight, we exchange greetings, and she has a comradely smile. Follow me.'

Farquarson set off along the street.

For an instant Jamie hesitated. The laird of Invergordon was clearly drunk. He was also, as Jamie knew from hard experience, a man on whose word and purse no reliance whatsoever could be placed. On the other hand he had a friendly face, he seemed confident that he knew what he was doing, and by then Jamie was as cold and tired as he'd ever felt.

Jamie picked up his bag and hurried after him.

46

Farquarson, it became apparent, was a compulsive talker.

As they walked Jamie learned how he'd come to be thrown into the Dean Street gutter. The matter of the prize-fight, the Hamilton fair and the bailiffs had been a passing trifle. Having turned his estates over to the Cheviot and raised some loans in Edinburgh to settle his most pressing debts, Farquarson had returned south confident that his problems were at an end. He was still the owner of vast lands. The sheep would soon be in profit. He could raise further loans from the London bankers on the strength of his assets meanwhile.

Farquarson had engaged a broker to negotiate with the banks on his behalf. Then he had gone to ground in Mrs Rourke's brothel until the money was advanced to him.

'But do you know what those bastards, my creditors, have just done?' Farquarson exclaimed bitterly. 'They went to the courts. They obtained an injunction today, and had an administrator appointed.'

Jamie frowned. 'What does that mean?'

'It means, my dear Oran, that in effect I no longer own my own lands. Until the claims are settled, every penny of my revenues must be paid to this monstrous creature.'

'Which Madame Belle discovered?'

'There's no health in this city any longer.' Farquarson shook his head in despair. 'There are mischievous eyes, ears and tongues everywhere. The whore had the news this evening even before I knew myself.'

'So she threw you out and now you're as broke as a sandsnake's back under a hillman's boot?'

Farquarson looked at Jamie, pained.

'Oran, you have a most uncouth turn of phrase. But, yes, I fear in a sense you are right. Money and I will not be seen in company for a while yet – '

He glanced at Jamie thoughtfully. 'Unless, of course, you are in a position to make a modest advance in the meantime.'

'No, sir,' Jamie said bluntly. 'I have my wee capital. It was hard earned and it has work to do. I regret I cannot aid ye, Mr Farquarson.'

Farquarson shrugged philosophically. Then he brightened. 'We are both men of mettle, Oran. Temporary reverses discourage such as us not at all. Indeed, we make a virtue of misfortune. Let us see how we fare with the lady of the parasol.'

He stopped in front of a door. There were several cards pinned to a panel on one side, each with a bell pull below it. Farquarson scrutinized the names on the cards.

'I don't know what the good lady is called,' he said, 'but we have exchanged words and her accent is foreign. It would seem to make sense to start with the one foreign name here.'

He tugged at one of the knobs. A bell sounded distantly on an upper floor. Several minutes passed. Then the door opened a crack and a small girl poked her head round it.

'Miss Marx?' Farquarson inquired.

The child wrinkled her face uncertainly. 'Well, I'm Tussie,' she said. 'Dad says if it's about the rent, he's going to do it all on Monday.'

'No, no, it's not about the rent. Tell me, Tussie, does your mother have a red parasol?'

The girl nodded.

'Excellent.' Farquarson beamed. 'This gentleman and I are old friends of hers. Will you take us up to her, please?'

Tussie examined them. Her eyes were large and dark and solemn. Then she nodded again. She stood back and opened the door wider. They went in and followed her up three flights of stairs. At the top of the house another door was standing ajar. From inside came a clamour of voices. The air drifting out was thick with tobacco smoke.

'Leave it all to me,' Farquarson whispered to Jamie.

He straightened his coat and strode confidently into the room.

The smoke inside was so heavy that for a moment Jamie could barely see. He blinked and rubbed his watering eyes. Gradually he made out that he was standing in what must be the Marx's living room. It was small, crowded and so shabby it was almost squalid. The walls were discoloured dark brown with grime. Horse-hair stuffing leaked from torn upholstery on the chairs. The carpet was threadbare and the patched boards were stained with spilt wine. Empty bottles, discarded plates of food, old newspapers and mounds of books littered the floor, and the glass in the two uncurtained windows was coated with grease.

What redeemed the room from squalor was its atmosphere. There were eight or nine adults and several children packed into the tiny space. Two of the adults were hunched in concentration over a game of chess on a rickety table. Everyone else was talking or laughing, drinking or telling jokes, arguing good-humouredly or playing with the children. The mood was boisterous, relaxed and happy.

'Mrs Marx?'

Farquarson had spotted Jenny, the lady with the red parasol. He threaded his way through the throng towards her.

Jenny looked up. 'Indeed,' she answered. 'What may I do for you — ?'

She broke off, frowning.

The sudden appearance of strangers in the Marx household was something she'd long grown used to, but she felt there was something familiar about this one. Then she remembered. He was the tipsy but amiable-looking young man with whom she'd exchanged smiles in Soho Square over the past few weeks.

'Of course,' Jenny laughed. 'My companion from the square.'

'From now on, if I may be so bold, to be known by the name of Farquarson, Aldred Farquarson of Invergordon,' Farquarson replied.

'Invergordon – ?'

Marx, who was sprawled in a chair near his wife, sat up with interest.

'There is what the Scots call a "laird" of Invergordon, a local chief and large landowner. I have been studying the economic consequences for his workforce of the exploitation of the seaweed crop. Maybe you know of him?'

'For better or worse I have to declare I *am* him,' Farquarson said.

'You are?' Marx stared at him with astonishment which swiftly turned to delight. 'What a stroke of fortune! I have tried without success to find you for months now. There are so many questions I wish to ask. But your servants have put me off at every turn.'

'They guard my privacy well, sir,' Farquarson said. 'Now I am happy to make you a gift of it myself. What can I tell you?'

'Give him a glass of wine, Jenny. Sit down, sit down!' Marx excitedly swept a pile of newspapers to the floor and cleared a chair for Farquarson to sit on. 'Let me explain first what I am doing – '

Marx began to talk. Five minutes later Farquarson raised his hand to interrupt him.

'I am no student of what you term economics,' Farquarson said. 'But if I follow your drift you are inquiring into the relationship between capital, which to my simple mind is honestly inherited property, and labour, that is uneducated folk fortunate enough to work it.'

'If those are your definitions, then, yes,' Marx answered.

'And in me you have an owner of property?'

Marx nodded.

'So what would you say if I could also furnish you with

347

a representative from the other side of the divide?' Farquarson asked. 'A living breathing member of the labouring masses?'

Before Marx could reply Farquarson jumped to his feet and dramatically beckoned Jamie across the room.

Until then Jamie had remained standing just inside the door. Little Tussie Marx had given him a glass of wine but apart from her no one else had paid any attention to him. Now he came forward.

'Let me present my childhood friend, Mr James Oran,' Farquarson said with a flourish. 'Oran's life has been spent harvesting the kelp on my foreshores. What I cannot tell you, he can. Between us you have a mine of information that will provide you with rich ore for weeks.'

Jamie glanced bemused between Marx and Farquarson.

'But I've never – ' Jamie began.

'He's travelled far and he is tired,' Farquarson interrupted. 'If I may, another glass of wine will restore his spirits.'

Farquarson seized the glass from Jamie's hand. He put an arm round Jamie's shoulder, and swung him towards the bottle which was standing on a nearby table.

'Just do exactly what I say,' Farquarson hissed in a whisper as he filled Jamie's glass. 'You're a kelper. Be one. Answer the foreigner's questions, however daft they are. Do that and between us we've got a warm bed for as long as we need one.'

'But what can I say if he asks me about Invergordon?' Jamie protested.

'Improvise, man, improvise,' Farquarson whispered back.

Jamie shook his head. 'I canna do it – '

'Where do you want to sleep, Oran?' Farquarson interrupted him acidly. 'Here under blankets in the warmth, or out in the gutter with the drunks?'

Jamie hesitated a moment longer. He glanced at the window. Rain had started to fall and chill dark drops were drumming against the panes. Silently cursing Farquarson, he gave a helpless shrug. The two turned back towards Marx.

'So you've been in your friend's employ gathering kelp from your first years?' Marx asked Jamie eagerly.

Jamie spluttered as he raised the glass to his lips. 'Aye, in a sense I suppose ye could say that,' he answered.

'This is very interesting. I must find my notebook.'

Marx rummaged under his chair and found a leather-bound book. He spread it open on his knee and poised himself to write.

'Before the two of you begin,' Farquarson interjected. 'I fancy this could take some time. Without intruding on your hospitality, it might be more convenient for every-one if we remained overnight. In which case a modest pallet – I'd be happy to share one with my companion as we've done so often in the past – would perhaps suit us all.'

'Of course. Jenny!' Marx called impatiently to his wife. 'Please find our two friends a bed. It cannot be difficult. Surely you can move the children – '

He waved his hand vaguely. Then he placed his pen back on the paper and gazed intently at Jamie, his strong square face alert and wrinkled in concentration.

'Now, please describe to me,' Marx said, 'in the Scottish economic context what exactly is the relation-ship between a working child and his landowning master?'

Jamie closed his eyes.

He was aware of Farquarson standing expectantly beside him. He was also aware that he was very tired, it was warm inside the Marx's apartment, and Jenny Marx was bustling about in the background with pillows and blankets.

Jamie took a deep breath and tried to answer.

47

Jamie and Farquarson stayed in the Marx's Dean Street apartment in Soho for three weeks.

The first night they slept on the living-room floor. Afterwards they were given what had been the maid's bedroom. The Marx's fortunes that year were at a low ebb, and a maid was a luxury they could not really afford. The maid, Anna, a pleasant simple girl, would have been happy to remain in the household without wages. But Jenny, finding Karl more and more frequently absent from their bed at night and knowing full well where he was sleeping instead, decided there were other good reasons for getting rid of Anna.

Jenny could tolerate Karl's occasional, or even frequent, transgressions. But when they settled into a constant pattern, particularly one which left her alone and cold at night, it was time to object. Anna was dismissed. It happened the day of Jamie's and Farquarson's arrival. After the sobbing Anna left next morning, Jenny was able to offer them her room.

Once they'd adapted to its somewhat eccentric rhythms, life in the household for the two young men was both invigorating and undemanding.

Marx was in the midst of one of his intense bouts of research. He left early each morning for the British Museum and didn't leave it until the reading room closed. As he had to rise at dawn, the all-night drinking and debating sessions with his friends for which Marx was famous were temporarily in abeyance.

People did gather in the apartment every evening – and to Jamie a bizarre and dazzling group the constantly changing guests were – but generally by midnight Jenny had chased most of them away. She led her husband to her own bed, and peace fell on the household.

The days were much quieter. The Marx children attended the local Church of England school alongside St Anne's church in Frith Street. Jenny, always the still centre at the heart of whatever storm was raging round Karl, did her best while they were out to clear up the detritus of the previous night, and see the family's domestic arrangements were kept at least moderately orderly.

Jamie's and Farquarson's contributions to the household were the occasional case of wine, a daily market bag of groceries – Jamie enjoyed shopping in the open-air Brewer Street market and had an even shrewder eye than Jenny for the day's best buys – and their nightly question-and-answer sessions with Marx about the kelping industry, the advent of the Cheviot, and the Scottish economy.

'As a way of paying rent for a fire, shelter, square meals and a warm bed,' Farquarson remarked one night as they retired to their room, 'does it not beat into a cocked hat the shelling out of gold sovereigns to some hatchet-faced old harridan? Jenny has a sweet smile, the wine – at least when I direct its purchase – is excellent, and who could complain of the conversation? Am I not, in my own modest way, a genius, Jamie?'

'You're right canny with your siller, I can tell ye that for nothing,' Jamie answered shortly. 'It's a week at least since the groceries felt the colour of your money. And the wine's been my offering from the start.'

'But without me, lad, consider where you'd be.' Farquarson gripped his arm. 'As it is here are the two of us, snug as fleas on a sleeping porker – and all for the price of a tinker's tune. Rejoice, Jamie, rejoice in the fortune that bound us together!'

Jamie gave a reluctant smile.

It was almost impossible, he'd discovered, to be irritated, let alone angry, with Farquarson for long. The little Scottish laird with his round freckled face, thinning sandy hair and short-sighted eyes, blinking like a worried owl, might be a rogue. But at least he was a rogue with a generous heart, an inventive mind, and a wonderfully exhilarating flair for living.

In trouble, Jamie had no doubt, the laird of Invergordon would prove a staunch and brave friend.

In fact, apart from sharing the maid's tiny room, Jamie saw little of Farquarson during their stay in Dean Street. At the nightly gatherings the gregarious Farquarson was always at the centre of a group of Marx's friends, drinking, laughing or disputing with the most vociferous street-corner revolutionary. Jamie, in contrast, was shy and reserved. He liked talking to the good-hearted Jenny but except with her and at his regular sessions with Karl, he spoke little. He felt remote from the others and somehow trapped by a past that was wholly different from theirs.

What Jamie liked doing best when the company assembled was playing chess, which he was taught by one of the regular evening visitors – a tall man with a shock of prematurely greying air whose name Jamie never learned.

By day it was Farquarson who was trapped – and in a much more literal sense than Jamie. The morning after their arrival Farquarson strode out to buy a newspaper. Minutes later he was back, panting for breath and his freckled face pale. In his hand he was clutching a document stamped with a large scarlet seal.

'Is there no justice?' He collapsed into a chair and rolled his eyes upwards in anguish.

'What's the matter, man?' Jamie asked, alarmed.

'They're out for the shirt from my back and the trews from my legs, that's what,' Farquarson shrieked. 'No doubt those swine have told them they can take the food from my mouth too. I will starve, Jamie, starve!'

Farquarson writhed and groaned.

In alarm Jamie took the document from him. He tried to read it but the legal jargon was impenetrable. Jamie cast it aside. Gradually he managed to extract the story from Farquarson.

On his way to buy his morning news-sheet Farquarson had made a sentimental detour past the doors of Madame Belle's brothel. Outside he spotted a clerk from the lawyers who handled his affairs. Farquarson greeted him. The clerk was there, he discovered, because the brothel was Farquarson's last known address. That morning his lawyers had been served with a writ of attainder on behalf of his creditors on his personal property. The clerk had been sent to find Farquarson and warn him.

'He gave me the damn document,' Farquarson finished. 'Before I could even glance at it, a pair of the scoundrels executing it appeared at the end of the street. They had Madame Belle's address too.'

'So you ran?' Jamie said.

'What the hell do you think I did?' Farquarson replied. 'The clerk was screaming at me, the bailiffs were giving tongue, I took off like a hare before the slip. Mercifully I had the legs of them. I'm back and they've lost me.'

'But what does it actually mean?'

'Mean?' Farquarson howled. 'It means, you ignorant peasant, that whereas before they could plunder my revenues and still can, now they may also remove the boots from my feet – '

He shuddered. 'God knows, they may well be able to attain and auction you for being conversant with my name.'

Jamie thought for a moment.

In spite of the hysteria, as far as Jamie could judge this new writ of attainder on Farquarson's goods meant little more than that it would be prudent for the laird of Invergordon to absent himself for a while from the streets where the bailiffs were prowling.

'Well, I'm away to the Royal Geographical Society,' he said. 'I'm told they've an excellent library there. I'll see if I can't borrow a few wee books to lend ye to read.

It's a fine opportunity you've been given to bide indoors for a while and improve your mind.'

Jamie grinned at Farquarson and went out.

Over the next weeks while Farquarson remained imprisoned in the Dean Street apartment, Jamie spent most of the daylight hours in the Royal Geographical Society's building in Kensington. As he'd promised he periodically borrowed books from the society's library for Farquarson to read. Whether the cooped and fretful laird of Invergordon ever glanced at them, Jamie had no idea.

Jamie was not a Fellow of the Society but Mrs Livingstone's name was enough to accord him most of the privileges he would have enjoyed had he been one. To make a favourable impression on the head porter was all Jamie needed to acquire the rest.

Like Jamie the head porter, Maitland, was a Scot. Maitland had liked the bold young man with the level blue eyes and the high-cheekboned face as soon as he set eyes on him. When Jamie returned, Maitland went out of his way to be helpful. He called down the librarian. He introduced Jamie. And he suggested that as a protégé of the great Dr Livingstone's wife, Jamie should be given every assistance in finding his way round the society's shelves.

From then on nothing was too much trouble. From the map room to the geological stacks, from biography to the latest volumes on zoology and natural history, Jamie found, almost to his embarrassment, that every door was opened before him.

Jamie spent three of the happiest weeks of his life.

Much of what he read was familiar. In the mid nineteenth century the literature on Africa was still sparse. Blantyre had a good library and nearby Glasgow an even better one. As he grew up Jamie had managed to keep up with most of what was published by travellers to the dark continent. But reading their books again in the dust-moted silence of the society's library was an entirely different experience.

Many of the expeditions they chronicled had been planned in that very room. The books themselves were signed by the authors – some had even been written at the long tables down the library's centre. One chair, used by Mungo Park on his visits to the society, bore a brass plaque commemorating the great explorer. Another, lovingly polished twice a week by the junior porter, carried no plaque because its most famous user was still alive.

'That's where Dr Livingstone sits when he comes to see us,' the librarian told Jamie on the day he showed him round. 'He's been away many a year now in the eastern forests, so they say. But he'll be back to claim his seat when he's ready.'

For days afterwards Jamie sat on the other side of the room. Each time he lifted his eyes he would see the chair and gaze at it with awe. It might almost have been the high altar in a cathedral.

One morning Jamie got to his feet.

He glanced left and right. For once there was no one else in the library. He tiptoed across the floor and checked again that the room was empty. Then, his heart hammering, Jamie pulled the chair round and cautiously sat down. He held his breath, but nothing happened. Still hardly daring to breathe, Jamie opened his book and began to read.

The book in his hands was the great doctor's own account of his searches for the Nile's source. It had been published that summer. The year was 1853. Livingstone had come tantalizingly close to finding where the great river rose – but like every other African explorer he had ultimately failed. The springs of the river of life still eluded him.

They would not elude Jamie, the young man with the implacable eyes – eyes the colour of the blue-grey Hebridean waters. Jamie turned the pages hungrily.

He was reading not about Livingstone's evasive goal. He was reading about a distant kingdom of his own.

48

The bile rose in Rafael Perez y Latera's throat, filling his mouth with the taste of vomit.

Perez got hurriedly to his feet. He ducked out of the rush-built cabin between the masts, hurried along the deck, and threw up over the stern. Then he leant sweating and shaking against the mahogany rail above the sea. On the rare occasions when a breeze blew by day it always seemed freshest there. Today there was no movement in the suffocating air. The sun blazed down out of a sky that pulsed like the lining of a furnace, and the seaward horizon shimmered in bands of haze.

The heat was ferocious and implacable – but the stench was worse.

Perez gripped his nostrils and tried to breathe through his lips. It made no difference. The foul reek, compounded of sweat, disease, excrement and rotting flesh, enveloped the ship like a poisonous cloud. It gorged his mouth and seemed to lift in fumes to his brain. There was no escaping it anywhere on board. Even at a distance it was horrific. The sailors claimed a slaver could be smelled a mile away on the high seas. The *San Cristobal* had been taking on its cargo for a week. Now the ship was almost fully laden.

Perez gave up the attempt to shut out the smell. He lowered his hand and gulped as the cauldron of noisome odours assaulted him again. Then he made his way unsteadily back to the rush cabin.

Bartolomeo Gomez, the *San Cristobal*'s bald-headed mate, glanced up from the table as he came in.

'You'll notice it less when we're under canvas, Don Rafael,' he said. 'The first run's always the worst.'

Gomez was an old hand in the slave cargo business. He'd made the Africa–Rio crossing fifteen times in the past ten years. Perez, a nephew of the *San Cristobal*'s owner, had only just joined the ship as its new captain.

'Holy Mother of God!' Perez slumped down into his chair. 'For me it'll be the first and the last. Never again! It's like trying to breathe through a shower of whore's vomit.'

He shuddered.

Gomez grinned to himself. The young man would forget the smell quickly enough when they docked at Rio and he received his share of the proceeds from the trip from his uncle, old Don Ricardo. The rewards of slave freighting made any other cargo seem like so much ballast. Even as a comparatively low-paid mate Gomez had already become a wealthy man. As captain, little Don Rafael – Gomez used the courtesy title although, as he knew well, he himself would be the real skipper during the voyage – would soon discover that he could earn a fortune.

A slave cargo had other attractions too.

Gomez had already made his initial choice, but he'd sample all the wares on board before the journey was over. He scratched his groin reflectively. Then he stood up. He walked to the entrance and peered at the shore. A crowded open boat had just pulled away from the little wooden jetty and was making its way at a snail's pace towards them across the leaden sea.

'The last consignment's on its way,' Gomez said. 'As soon as they're logged and stowed, we can set to take the tide.'

Perez, a small dapper man with a goatee beard, wiped the sweat from his face.

'Holy Mother of God, let them be quick!' he said plaintively.

Gomez smiled again. He returned to the table and opened the ledger in front of him. The two men sat waiting in the clammy air.

The *San Cristobal* was lying at anchor half a mile out in

the Atlantic off the west African coast of Guinea. A three-masted schooner out of Rio de Janeiro she was, like her captain, mate and crew, Brazilian – although both the ship and her complement were always referred to as 'Portuguese' after the language they spoke and their homeland of Portugal, the colonial power which had settled Brazil.

The *San Cristobal*'s task was to ferry slave labour from Africa to South America to work in the Portuguese coffee and sugar cane plantations.

The slave trade was concentrated, on one side, in the hands of men like Perez's uncle, a rich Rio de Janeiro merchant who chartered, crewed and financed vessels like the *San Cristobal* to transport the human cargos for which he paid cash at the African point of loading. In Africa the trade belonged to agents and entrepreneurs – Arab, African, European or half-caste – who acquired the raw materials of the commerce and brought the slaves down to the coast for shipment.

The rush cabin between the masts on the *San Cristobal*'s main deck was a temporary structure, built as shelter against the sun whilst the captain and mate logged in the slaves during the often-lengthy period of loading. As soon as the holds were full – the *San Cristobal* could carry over four hundred slaves – the ship would set out on the long voyage back to Brazil.

Gomez raised his bald head as the open ferry bumped alongside. A chorus of shouts and curses lifted from the gunwhale. A few minutes later a sallow-skinned man with an immense pot belly bulging out from a tattered open shirt appeared in the cabin doorway. He had thick arms covered in curling black hair and a jowled face with dark bruised patches beneath his eyes.

'You'll like this bunch,' the man said. 'I've saved the best for the last.'

The man was a Portuguese half-caste named de Souza. The most brutal and notorious slave dealer on the Guinea coast, he had supplied most of the *San Cristobal*'s cargo for the voyage.

'They'd better be an improvement on the winter consignment,' Gomez answered. 'We lost damn near a quarter of them before we were even halfway back.'

'You starve the bastards of air, man.' De Souza spat on the deck. 'I've told you before and I'll tell you again. Give them a whiff of the wind once a day and they'll keep as fresh as pickled herrings.'

'For Christ's sake!' Perez interrupted. 'Let's get them up.'

De Souza bellowed an order. Iron manacles clanked outside and a line of men, prodded by two black overseers with sharpened staves, shuffled into the cabin. The delivery consisted of sixteen slaves. All were naked apart from loin cloths, and each was chained by the neck and ankles to the man in front.

'Sbeli na kama!' de Souza shouted in Bantu, kicking the first one forward to the table. 'Tell the bwana your name, your tribe, and your age!'

As the man mumbled the answers de Souza spelt them out in Portuguese for the mate to write down in the ledger. Then the burly half-caste clubbed the slave away and the next was jerked forward.

The two, the mate and the dealer, worked through the group until they came to the last in the line. De Souza studied the man for a moment. Younger, much taller and more powerfully built than any of the others, he was a magnificent specimen, as fine a slave as even de Souza with twenty years' experience of the trade had ever seen.

'Didn't I say you'd like this lot? Put this one up for auction and he'll set the record – '

De Souza chuckled. He reached out, grabbed the slave by his hair, and wrenched his head downwards.

'What's your name, boy?' he demanded. 'Where are you from?'

The man was Mamkinga.

His legs, arms and neck chained, and his face twisted painfully at an angle by de Souza's grasp on his hair, Mamkinga stared unblinking into the half-caste's bloodshot eyes. There was a moment's silence. Then, in a voice acid with hatred and contempt, Mamkinga answered.

'My name and my people's name are my own to give,' he said. 'I would sooner offer them to the jackals than to a creature even they would reject as carrion.'

Mamkinga rolled his tongue round his cheeks and hurled a mouthful of spittle in de Souza's face.

Half-blinded, de Souza let go of Mamkinga's hair and recoiled, spluttering and swearing. He brushed the spray from his skin and blinked. Then he grabbed a stave from one of the overseers. He raised it above his head and advanced murderously on Mamkinga again.

'No!'

Gomez pushed back his chair and stood up.

The mate hadn't understood what Mamkinga had said but the meaning behind the words and the gesture that followed them was all too clear. The massively built young slave was a troublemaker. In Gomez's experience there was one in almost every cargo and they had to be disciplined right from the start – not by the dealers who supplied them but by their new owners.

'Caraval! Medina!' he shouted and two of the crew ran into the cabin. 'Unclip this one and take him out. Put him across the windlass – and see that the others watch!'

The two sailors unshackled Mamkinga from the line.

With his wrists and ankles still chained, they hauled him on to the deck and splayed him face down over one of the bollards that anchored the running sheets to the mainsails. Afterwards, cuffing and kicking, they arranged the other slaves in a circle round him. Then they each seized a length of heavy tarred rope.

'Right,' said Gomez, who had led Perez and de Souza out behind them. 'Now educate the animal!'

They started to beat Mamkinga, lashing him in turn, the ropes rising and falling rhythmically as one worked downwards from his shoulders to his kidneys and the other upwards from his thighs to his buttocks.

Mamkinga opened his mouth to scream but somehow swallowed the cry in his throat.

He clenched his teeth, arched his back, and began to jerk convulsively. The pain was unlike anything he had ever felt, had ever imagined. It came in three repeated waves of agony. First the searing burn on his skin as the rope whipped down. Then the shock to his flesh and muscles as the blow cut into him. Afterwards the terrible sickening sensation as the impact rippled through his body.

The beating went on and on.

Mamkinga had no idea how long it lasted. Eventually, limp, dizzy and gasping for breath, he slid off the windlass and crumpled on the deck. For a moment he was aware that the planks round him were spattered with blood. As he lay supine a final blow struck the back of his head and he lost consciousness.

'Get him and the rest of them below,' Perez ordered as the two sweating sailors let the lengths of rope drop by their sides.

The sailors pushed the other slaves towards the entrance to the hold. Then they seized Mamkinga by the feet and dragged him after them. As Mamkinga passed, de Souza kicked him viciously in the ribs.

'Give the animal the same treatment every day for a week,' he said, 'and you won't have any more trouble from him.'

Perez glanced at the deck. The blood round the windlass was already dry and lifting in blisters from the planks. He could hear the sound of wailing from below. The pervading stench seemed even more noisome than before.

Choking as the bile rose in his throat again, Perez headed for his own cabin. Gomez could take over until they were well out to sea. It was, Perez vowed to himself once more, the first and last voyage he'd ever make as master of a slaver.

49

Mamkinga stirred.

He opened his eyes and stared upwards. He tried to find something to focus on, but there was nothing in front of him except blackness —blackness and a smell so foul and rancid it seemed to cover him like a layer of soot.

Instinctively he attempted to lift his hands and brush it away. His arms refused to move. He struggled weakly but they remained where they were, spread out on either side of him. Then he realized why. They had been chained down. Cautiously he tested his legs. The result was the same – they had been manacled too.

Mamkinga gave up the attempt and lay still.

The entire length of his back, from his ankles to his shoulders, throbbed as if it were on fire. For several moments he could think of nothing except the pain and the stench. Then as his mind adjusted to the pain he began to take stock. He was bound by the wrists. It meant he should at least be able to sit partially upright. He started to raise the upper half of his body. An instant later his head bumped against something above him.

Mamkinga dropped back. He turned his face to one side and peered into the darkness. Gradually he began to make out his surroundings.

He was in one of the ship's holds, tied down on a bare wooden shelf. There was another shelf above him – that was what his head had struck – and a third below, each forming the base of flat narrow boxes barely two feet in height, like open-sided quail coops. Further stacks of the wooden boxes stretched away on either side and a second line of them faced him across a passage of decking. Every box was occupied by a slave. Some, like Mamkinga, were manacled inside them. Others, mainly women and children, seemed to be at liberty to move about.

Until then, his body aching from the beating and his nostrils clogged with the stench, Mamkinga had barely been aware of the noise in the hold. Now it flooded over him. Children were screaming, women keening and weeping, men moaning and coughing and shouting out to each other in a babble of languages. Chains rattled and grated, ripples of filthy water splashed up and down the decking as the ship rocked, the beams heaved and ground against each other.

Suddenly most of the cacophony died away.

Mamkinga shifted his head. A lantern had appeared at the far end of the hold. As the pool of light came closer Mamkinga saw that the lamp was being carried by one of the Portuguese sailors. The man was short and stocky. From his scarlet sweating face and unsteady gait he had obviously been drinking. He began to search through the wooden cubicles, holding up the lantern and shining its beam into them one by one. He was immediately opposite Mamkinga when he stopped.

'You!' he shouted, beckoning. 'Get down here!'

The cubicle was occupied by a girl of about thirteen. Wide-eyed and terrified she climbed down to the deck.

'Let's have a closer look at you,' the sailor went on.

The girl was wearing a cotton wrap that reached from her waist to her ankles. The man snatched it away and inspected her as she stood naked and trembling in front of him.

'I like them with a little more flesh, but you'll do,' he chuckled. 'Down on your knees with your arse up!'

During his years with the goldsmith Mamkinga had picked up enough Portuguese from passing traders to understand what the man had said. The girl had no idea.

She stared, bewildered, as the sailor shouted again.

The sailor lost his temper. He knocked her to the deck and kicked her until she was crouching with her buttocks in the air and her elbows on the boards like a kneeling dog. The sailor grinned. He unclipped something from his waist and raised his arm. In the flickering light Mamkinga saw that the man was holding a short hide whip. He slashed it down and the girl screamed.

The sailor bellowed with laughter. He lurched after her as she scrabbled frantically away in front of him.

'Enjoy that, you little slut?' he shouted. 'That's good – here's another!'

He whipped the back of her knees. The girl howled again and tried to escape by jack-knifing into one of the floor-level cubicles. The sailor dragged her out by the hair, and began to beat her up and down the passageway.

Mamkinga watched, sickened and helpless, as the whip rose and fell sadistically. Lines of blood appeared on the girl's skin and her screams became shriller and shriller. None of the other slaves moved or made a sound. As the beating went on the sailor became increasingly aroused. His eyes narrowed, he started to pant, and his breeches bulged out at the groin.

Finally he drove the girl forward until her head was wedged inside the cubicle where she'd tried to escape before. The man placed himself behind her and fumbled at the clasp of his belt. He gave her a last slash with the whip and put down the lantern. Then he pushed his breeches down his thighs. He gripped his swollen penis in his hands and thrust it violently into her from the rear.

Blood-smeared, trapped and exhausted, the girl struggled feebly for a moment.

Then she dropped her head on to the wooden shelf and waited, shuddering, her buttocks still raised grotesquely, as the sailor rocked himself to orgasm inside her. The discharge came. Sweat sprayed off him, he gasped, and his mouth slackened. An instant later he withdrew from the girl as roughly as he'd entered her. He pulled up his breeches, fastened the buckle, and picked up the lantern.

'That's the first lesson,' he said. 'There'll be plenty more – and next time see you show a little obedience.'

He didn't bother to use the whip again. Instead he kicked her. Afterwards he reeled away and the light vanished. As the darkness returned the only sounds were the slap of water, the heaving of the ship's timbers, and the girl's long-drawn-out sobbing.

Mamkinga lay quite still, staring into the blackness, as the stench invaded his nostrils again.

50

'Pula!'

The word – 'greetings' in the group of tongues of which Mamkinga's native Malindan was one – had been spoken softly close to his ear.

Mamkinga turned his head. 'Pula!' he replied.

It was the first time anyone in the hold had spoken in a language he could understand. The voice belonged to a girl. He gazed into the darkness, trying to see her.

'I am Aldoa,' the girl said.

'I am Mamkinga,' he answered.

Mamkinga could just make her out now. She was bending down and looking into the cubicle.

'The men who were brought in last said how you had stood against the Portuguese,' the girl went on. 'That was brave. De Souza is the most evil trader on the coast. They also said the sailors had beaten you afterwards. How are you now?'

Mamkinga shifted slightly on the board and winced. 'It will go,' he answered.

'This will help. Sit up as far as you can.'

Mamkinga did as he was told. He felt Aldoa rub something gently on his back. Then she made him twist on to his side and did the same to his legs.

'It's butter,' she said. 'I will try to bring some more later.'

Mamkinga lay back. The butter was cool and soothing. Even after a few seconds the rope burns on his skin felt less painful.

'Where did you get it from?' he asked.

'His cabin.'

Mamkinga frowned. 'Whose cabin?'

'I do not know his name. He's the second on the ship to the small one, the captain. He chose me when I came here a week ago – '

She lifted her hand to her breast and something glinted in the darkness. Mamkinga peered upwards. A small brass button was hanging from her neck on a leather thong.

'It means I am his,' Aldoa continued. 'All the sailors do the same. No one else can touch me. He has other girls too for the nights when he wants them, but I wash his clothes and clean the cabin. That is why I can get the butter.'

She was about to go on when the glow of another lantern appeared at the hold's entrance.

Aldoa glanced round and whispered hurriedly, 'After what you did they will be watching you. They must not see me talking to you. I will come back when I can.'

She vanished into the darkness.

Mamkinga watched the pool of light advance along the passageway between the rows of cubicles. The lantern was being carried by a different sailor, but he was clearly there for the same reason as the first. He examined the female slaves until he found one who appealed to him. He dragged the girl cowering out of the cramped box where she was lying. He ripped off her wrap, held the light up to her groin, and inspected her for any signs of venereal pox.

'Get up top,' he said, apparently satisfied.

He slapped her hard across the buttocks and propelled her towards the flight of steps to the deck. Unlike the first man, he must have decided to rape her in his quarters.

With his head raised Mamkinga followed the lamp as it wavered away and the pair disappeared, the sailor kicking the girl in front of him. Then, spread out like a starfish, Mamkinga settled on his back again.

Aldoa returned several hours after dark. Mamkinga knew night had fallen because by then he'd realized that the filigree of light above the passageway was created by the sun filtering down through cracks in the decking.

Long before she came back the light had vanished and the darkness had become impenetrable. Strangely, the onset of night only seemed to intensify the heat and the appalling smell in the hold.

This time Aldoa was carrying a candle. She smeared more butter on Mamkinga's back and legs. Then she knelt down by the cubicle.

'He has taken two other girls from the forward hold,' she said. 'He was drinking and he has spent himself in one of them. They are all sleeping together now. I am meant to be sleeping too on the pallet by the bed, but I came away. He will not notice.'

She smiled.

Studying her in the light from the candle's flame, Mamkinga saw why the mate had picked her as his personal property for the voyage. Aldoa was about fifteen. Like most of the other female slaves on board she was wearing a cotton wrap that reached from her waist to her ankles. She had a delicate heart-shaped face, bright intelligent eyes, and a trim long-legged body. She looked young and vulnerable, and at the same time confident and experienced.

'Where are you from?' Mamkinga asked her.

Aldoa told him.

She came not, as Mamkinga had hoped, from Malinda itself but from the land to the west. Aldoa had no idea how far to the west. All she knew was that she had heard as a child of Malinda's mountain kingdom and she had grown up in a village somewhere not far from its borders. At the age of ten she, her family and most of the villagers had been captured and marched to the coast by a slaving party led by one of de Souza's agents.

Aldoa's father had died on the journey. Her mother and her two brothers had been shipped out soon after they arrived, but de Souza had kept Aldoa back to work in his house a mile inland from the shore. She had been there for almost three years. She would be there still if a consignment of slaves due for shipment on the *San Cristobal* hadn't failed to arrive from the interior. Having contracted to deliver them, de Souza had made up the missing numbers from members of his own household.

'Do you know when the ship sails?' Mamkinga asked as she finished.

Aldoa nodded. Like Mamkinga she had learned some Portuguese during her years in de Souza's household.

'With the early tide,' she answered. 'I heard the man telling one of the sailors to wake him.'

'Where are they taking us?'

'To the white man's land,' Aldoa said. 'There is an old man, a Kanu, who works in the sailors' kitchen. He has made many voyages and he told me. We go across the sea for many weeks until we come to a new land, where the white man has a big village at the mouth of a river. There we are sold to work in his fields.'

The big village, although Aldoa didn't know its name, was Rio de Janeiro – the January River as the Portuguese explorer Magellan had christened both the waterway and the human settlement on its banks three centuries earlier.

Mamkinga was considering what Aldoa had told him when something thumped on the deck above. Several minutes earlier the ship had started to rock. Now voices were calling out in Portuguese. Aldoa glanced up anxiously.

'A breeze has lifted,' she whispered. 'They will want to take advantage of it and leave before the tide. I must go before they wake the man.'

She raised the candle and smiled down at Mamkinga again. 'I will bring you more butter. Pula!'

'Pula!' Mamkinga whispered back.

Aldoa blew out the flame. Then she disappeared again.

Half an hour later Mamkinga felt the board tilt slightly beneath him. At the same instant there was a distant whistling sound somewhere high above. He frowned. Then he realized what was happening. The anchor had been hauled up. The sails had filled, and the ship was nudging out into the ocean.

The *San Cristobal* was under way.

51

'Just stand up straight, sir – '

Maitland, the Royal Geographical Society's head porter, gripped Jamie by the arm.

'Sir Roderick's a hard man but fair. Look him square in the eye and you'll have nothing to fear.'

With a final encouraging squeeze he propelled Jamie towards the stairs that led up to the president's office. Jamie pulled down the skirts of his worsted jacket, squared his shoulders, and strode resolutely upwards.

It was exactly three weeks since Jamie's arrival in London.

Sir Roderick Murchison, president of the society, had returned from his holiday that morning. Most of his first day back at work had been taken up in dealing with matters that had accumulated during his absence. Now in the late afternoon he had found time to see a visitor sent to him, or so it appeared – the letter of introduction was worn and crumpled – by Mrs Mary Livingstone.

There was a knock on the door and Sir Roderick called, 'Come in!'

As Jamie entered he glanced quickly round.

The president's office was a large high-ceilinged room with windows overlooking the society's gardens at the back. The walls were lined with bookshelves, and two ancient astrolabes, their globes faded and yellowing, stood in the centre of the floor. On the other side of them was an ornate oak desk, its surface piled with papers and scientific instruments. Sir Roderick was seated behind the desk.

'Mr Oran?' he asked.

Jamie nodded. 'Yes, sir.'

'Please come over here.'

Jamie walked forward.

Sir Roderick Murchison was a tall stern-looking man with a balding head, bushy eyebrows, and grey mutton-chop whiskers. His eyes were dark and forbidding but his voice had a marked Edinburgh lilt. At least, Jamie thought with relief, like the porter he was a fellow Scot.

Murchison read the letter again. 'So you're a friend of Mrs Livingstone,' he said.

'I would not presume to call the good lady a friend,' Jamie answered. 'Mrs Livingstone was kindness itself to me some time ago. I am deeply grateful to her.'

'Well, she seems to think highly of you – '

Murchison broke off. He sat for a moment, frowning. Then he looked up again.

'How did you come by this letter, Mr Oran?' he asked. 'Mrs Livingstone writes from Blantyre, but it's just occurred to me that she's been travelling in Africa with her husband for several years now. When was this written?'

Jamie swallowed. 'I think it's dated at the top, sir.'

Murchison hadn't looked at the date until then. He did so now and drew in his breath sharply in astonishment.

'Good God, man, Mrs Livingstone wrote this in 1842,' he said. 'That's eleven years ago. How old are you now?'

'Twenty, sir,' Jamie replied.

'Which means you were nine then, no more than a child. Is that right?'

'Yes, sir,' Jamie answered.

'And you come to me now with a letter written on behalf of a child,' Murchison paused. 'I think you'd better explain yourself, young man,' he went on ominously.

Jamie clenched his jaw in determination. He took a deep breath and started.

'So,' Murchison said five minutes later when Jamie had finished, 'if I understand the story correctly, it is this. When you were a small child Mrs Livingstone read to you about Africa. The idea of Africa took root in your mind. You told her that one day you wanted to go there. You impressed her sufficiently for her to write this letter to help you. You have kept the letter ever since. Now, eleven years later as a man, you bring it to me – '

Murchison paused. 'It is a very strange tale, Oran, is it not?'

'It's the truth, I promise ye,' Jamie said stubbornly.

'And what do you hope to achieve in Africa?'

'I wish to find the Nile's source.'

For the first time Murchison allowed himself to smile. 'If I may say so, young man, you are not exactly modest in your ambitions.'

'I have my reasons, sir, good reasons.'

'May I ask what they are?'

Jamie was silent.

In spite of Murchison's forbidding presence and awesome authority – in the field of African exploration the society's president was the most powerful man in the world – Jamie had begun to sense that he wasn't wholly unsympathetic. He was also, Jamie felt, a man to be trusted. Yet there were certain matters too deep and heartfelt, too raw and tangled for words to express. Jamie could entrust them to no one. They touched on queens and childhood vows, on the dead bodies of his sisters lying cradled in their grandmother's arms, on Iona's white sands and the royal graveyard and the whole kingdom of the Highland past which his mother's blood threaded through.

A terrible hurt had been done to Jamie and those he loved best. It was long years old but the wound was still sore and open. It needed healing. Only Africa and the river of life could do that.

'I have made promises,' Jamie said quietly at last. 'They are promises I must keep. I trust ye will accept that, sir. I can say no more.'

For a long time Murchison was silent too.

He got up from his chair and walked to the window.

There he stood with his back to the room, looking down over the garden.

It was not only a strange story, it was the strangest story Murchison had ever heard. Mrs Livingstone was something of an eccentric, but more than eccentricity was needed to explain her letter. Mary Livingstone was also a mature, experienced and widely travelled woman. She had briefly known Jamie Oran as a child. Yet even at the age of nine he had made such a vivid impression on her that she had felt impelled to write on his behalf, knowing years would pass before he could use her recommendation.

She had trusted him and Oran hadn't let her down.

The years had passed. He had grown into a tall and muscular young man with vivid red hair, a striking face – hard and angular and high-cheekboned – and penetrating blue eyes. Throughout his childhood and adolescence he had kept Mrs Livingstone's letter. The letter, Murchison guessed, had become a talisman. For some reason Africa was Oran's lodestar and Mrs Livingstone's letter his passport to reaching it.

Murchison had no idea what his reasons were. Oran said they were private. It did not matter. Whatever they were, Oran's aim, to find the Nile's source, was madness. Since the beginnings of recorded time men had been trying to discover where the great river rose. No one had succeeded. Many – older, wiser and infinitely more experienced than the young Scotsman – had died in the attempt.

In Oran's case it was a youthful craze, a young man's reckless dream. Mrs Livingstone – an admirable but impetuous woman – had written the letter on a whim. Now, years later, she must certainly have forgotten the child whom in a moment of aberration she had misguidedly sought to encourage. Oran – poor lad, for it was no fault of his – had cherished a fantasy. He had come to claim an inheritance that did not and had never existed. The young man should be told to forget about Africa. He should return home, and get on with his life.

Murchison shook his head. He turned to tell Jamie bluntly what he had decided. As he opened his mouth to speak, he stopped.

Jamie was still gazing at him.

His eyes, slanted downwards, were the bluest Murchison had ever seen. Blue and uncompromising and frighteningly, almost mesmerizingly, direct, they stared at Murchison with an intensity that seemed to penetrate to the farthest reaches of Murchison's brain. The older man almost recoiled as he looked back at them.

Murchison steadied himself and considered again.

Oran's gaze was terrifying. Murchison could have dealt with that. He knew explorers, those strange and haunted and hag-ridden men. He had a lifetime's experience of them and he could handle them all. This young man was of their company but there was a difference. The others were old and Oran was young – and it was his youth which caught in Murchison's throat. Behind the ferocity in his blue eyes there was a yearning, an optimism, a wild buoyant hope and trust that none of the others had – not even the great Dr Livingstone who had stood so often where Oran was standing now.

Murchison recognized it.

He recognized it because he too had once been young and vigorous and full of hope. He also had dreamed of going to Africa and searching for the Nile's source. His dreams had been frustrated. He had never even crossed the Channel. Instead, with his formidable gifts for scholarship and administration, he had slowly climbed the ladders of bureaucracy to reach the position he held now.

The presidency of the august Royal Geographical Society was a great and glittering prize. Looking at Oran, Murchison realized, with an aching sense of regret, that he would happily have traded it for a single week on foot in the forests of the dark continent. That was what Oran was asking of him, the chance only to travel where he himself had never gone.

Murchison knew it was something he could not deny him.

'Are you funded, young man?' he asked eventually.

'I have modest means,' Jamie replied. 'I have been prudent, I trust, with my savings. They are enough for my passage and my expenses ashore for a while.'

Murchison consulted a paper on his desk.

'The frigate *Forerunner* sails the day after tomorrow from Plymouth,' he said. 'Its destination is the port of Lagos on the Bight of Benin. Six weeks' march inland is the trading town of Garoua. Six months ago Mr Walter Baimbridge, with the society's sponsorship, assembled an expedition there and led it westwards. His goal is to trace the source of the river Nile. He believes it rises somewhere in the lands of the ancient Abyssinians. Where Mr Baimbridge and his party are now I have no idea – '

Murchison looked up.

'I shall give you a letter, young man, introducing you to Mr Baimbridge and authorizing you on the society's behalf to join his expedition. You will pay your own way. How you find him is up to your own devices. No doubt you will receive advice once you have made your way to Garoua. The British consul there will have much more recent intelligence of his plans than I. The rest is for your own initiative.'

Murchison sat down at his desk and began to write on a sheet of the society's notepaper. Jamie looked down at him.

'Am I to take it ye are sending me to Africa, sir?' Jamie asked.

'No, young man.' Murchison glanced up. 'You have hoisted and set your own sails. *They* are taking you to Africa. I am merely the first puff of wind to launch you on your journey.'

Jamie shook his head, bewildered. 'And I owe all of this to Mrs Livingstone's letter?'

'You owe much to that remarkable lady,' Murchison answered. 'But not all. In spirit, I take it from what you have shown me, she will accompany you on your journey.

A finer, doughtier companion no traveller could wish for. But you will also bear the hopes and dreams and aspirations of others – '

Murchison had finished his letter. He folded it, tucked it into an envelope, and sealed it in wax with the society's heavy gold seal. He handed the envelope to Jamie. Then he stood up.

'I wish you fortune, young man, and a fair following wind.' He held out his hand. 'Would to God I was travelling with you. The Almighty in His wisdom has assigned me other tasks. But when you keep those promises of yours, keep one for me too – travel boldly and find the river's source.'

'Yes, sir.'

In a daze Jamie shook Murchison's hand. As he turned to walk out of the room the sunlight flaring off the astrolabes made Jamie's eyes water until he could hardly see.

Jamie barely noticed.

All he knew was that with the blessing of the President of the Royal Geographical Society he was on his way to Africa.

52

Outside the society's headquarters Jamie leapt in the air in exhilaration.

Then, still hardly daring to believe what had happened, he set off at a run for Soho. The news was so momentous that he had to share it. Farquarson of course was aware of his plans by then. So were Karl Marx and the good-hearted Jenny. Jamie knew that all three would be delighted. He could barely wait to tell them. Laughing as he ran, to the bewilderment of the passers-by, Jamie raced across Hyde Park Corner and headed up Piccadilly.

He was only fifty yards from Piccadilly Circus when he had to check his pace. A crowd had spilled out across the road, halting the flow of carriages and traps. Horses were stamping and whinnying, people were clustered together talking and pointing, whistles were shrilling, somewhere an urgent voice was shouting instructions.

Jamie came to a halt. As he stopped, a constable in a grey cloak and rounded helmet, one of Sir Robert Peel's recently created metropolitan police force, burst through the crowd.

He paused for a moment, panting, beside Jamie.

'What's afoot?' Jamie asked.

The constable glanced at him. He took in Jamie's jacket, dark trousers, confident face and imposing height. Jamie was young but clearly a gentleman. He could be told the truth, the constable decided.

'A hue and cry, sir,' the constable said. 'It's some foreign villain. The Grey Wolf, he's called, a real troublemaker so they say. He slipped in through one of the Channel ports. We've been after him for weeks. Some bright spark spotted him near the Circus an hour ago. He took off like a greased pig, but we've got the whole area cordoned now. Don't you worry, sir, he won't get far. If we don't get him in the streets we'll go through the houses until we do.'

The whistle sounded again and the constable disappeared.

The crowd had brought Jamie to a halt beside an alley that angled north-east from Piccadilly into Regent Street. It provided a short cut to Soho but one that Jamie, after trying it once, had chosen to avoid. The alley was narrow, dark and foul-smelling. Jamie much preferred the sunlight and bustle of Piccadilly itself. Now, anxious to get back to the apartment but with the throng barring his way ahead, he reluctantly turned into it.

There were no gas lamps and the alley was in deep shadow in the gathering dusk. Jamie had walked only a few steps when he thought he heard a hoarse whisper.

'Jamie!'

Jamie paused and glanced round. The light was so dim it was difficult to see anything. As far as he could tell there was no one else there. He must have been mistaken. Jamie walked on.

'Jamie! Jamie!'

There was no doubt about it this time. Someone was calling to him. Jamie stopped again. A movement caught the corner of his eye, a raised hand waving from a well of darkness inside a doorway.

Jamie stepped over and peered into the shadows.

Beneath the lintel a man was standing balanced tensely on the balls of his feet, ready for flight. Jamie stared at his face. As his eyes adjusted to the dusk Jamie recognized him. The man was a fervent disciple of Karl Marx and a regular nightly visitor to the Marx's apartment. It was he who had taught Jamie to play chess.

Jamie still didn't know his name, but as far as Jamie remembered the man was a journalist and came from Austria.

'What on earth are ye doing?' Jamie asked.

'For God's sake, man, lower your voice – '

The man glanced at the square of autumn sunlight where the alley opened on to Piccadilly. People were still surging excitedly backwards and forwards on the roadway beyond, and the scurrying silhouettes of uniformed constables kept appearing and reappearing.

'They're hunting me, Jamie, they're all over the place.'

'Rubbish, man,' Jamie answered. 'They're not looking for you. They're after some foreign criminal – '

Jamie broke off with his mouth still open. He gazed at the man's shock of grey hair. Before Jamie could continue the man nodded grimly in reply to the unspoken question.

'Ferdinand Wolf,' he said. 'The Grey Wolf. It's me they're after, Jamie. For God's sake help me, man. If they catch me it's the Tower and the muskets against the wall.'

'But why – ?'

Jamie stopped again.

For now the whys and the wherefores didn't matter. Karl and Jenny Marx had proved staunch and generous friends. Ferdinand Wolf was a friend of theirs. On their behalf alone Wolf deserved any help Jamie could give him.

Jamie turned.

The police had cordoned the area. They would be searching the principal highways first – Piccadilly, Regent Street and the Haymarket. But any minute now, Jamie guessed, they'd be spreading the search into the warren of side streets that ran off them.

Jamie's gaze swept the alley.

Immediately opposite was a garment workshop. In its window were samples of its products, long dark skirts and dresses in black and grey serge tailored for the huge labour market of domestic servants. The workshop had closed only moments earlier. Jamie had noticed an elderly man lock the door and walk away.

'Is Karl's place safe?' Jamie whispered.

'I think so.'

'Wait here!'

Jamie crossed the narrow band of cobblestones. The garment workshop door was secured by a simple padlock. The goods inside, it seemed, were thought unlikely to attract the attention of thieves. Jamie put his shoulder against the frame and gave it a violent jolt. The wood splintered and caved inwards. Jamie stepped through.

Hanging from an iron display stand was a complete parlourmaid's uniform – floor-length skirt, high-necked lace blouse, bonnet headdress and black jacket. Jamie scooped the clothes off the stand. He crossed the alley again and thrust the bundle at Wolf.

'Strip and get dressed in these,' he instructed. 'Hurry, man, hurry!'

Jamie looked left and right. The crowds were still rippling up and down Piccadilly but no one had come into the alley.

Wolf tore off his corduroy suit. He dropped the skirt over his head, and put on the blouse. He tried to do up its buttons but his chest was too broad.

'Never mind,' Jamie hissed. 'Throw this over your shoulders and put on the cap.'

He handed Wolf the jacket. Wolf pulled it round him and placed the bonnet on his head. Jamie examined him critically.

'You'll do,' he said. 'Take my arm and keep your head down.'

He linked his arm through Wolf's. Then they set off up the alley towards Regent Street.

The journey proved easier than Jamie had dared hope. With his head lowered on to his chest Wolf could easily have been any tall and gawky serving maid on her way home with her master. Regent Street was cordoned by police constables. As they reached it Jamie waved his hand imperiously and the constables stepped aside.

They were looking for a dangerous foreign anarchist, not a shuffling servant returning home with her employer.

Arm in arm Jamie and Wolf hurried up the length of

the Brewer Street market, across Frith Street and into Dean Street. Halfway up, at the entrance to the building which housed the Marx's apartment, they halted. Jamie put his key into the lock and strode in ahead of the servant woman.

Inside the cramped hall Wolf removed the bonnet from his head. For an instant they both stood in the hallway, their chests heaving with relief. Then they climbed the stairs.

'May the Lord send fire over Edinburgh – !' Farquarson greeted them in astonishment. He surveyed Wolf in disbelief.

Almost as tall as Jamie, Wolf had a craggy pockmarked face with a curving beak-like nose, bold walnut-coloured eyes, and the mane of prematurely grey hair that tumbled haphazardly over his high forehead and made him so unmistakable.

With the black skirt swirling round his ankles and the white lace blouse bursting across his chest, Wolf looked like a grotesque travesty of the male transvestites who haunted the murkier Soho taverns.

'Could someone explain what's going on?' Farquarson added, bewildered.

Jamie ignored him.

As Wolf struggled out of the skirt Jamie went over to the window and looked out. It could have been only a few minutes since they entered the building, but the police had already spilled out from Regent Street and were working along the roadway below, peering into every window and doorway. Wolf was safe enough for the moment but if the constable was right, they'd soon turn their attention to the houses.

When they began a house-to-house search it wasn't only Wolf who would be at risk. So would anyone found with him. If that included Jamie it would mean the end of his voyage to Africa.

Jamie turned and looked at Wolf. 'I have a feeling it's ye that should be doing the explaining,' he said bleakly. 'What the hell's happening?'

Wolf finished changing and sat down.

'I've kept nothing from Karl and Jenny,' he said. 'Now I'm so deeply in your debt, I can keep nothing from you too.'

He began to talk.

Jamie was right in his recollection. Wolf was originally an Austrian journalist. He'd been forced to leave his native Vienna after the Austro-Hungarian authorities declared his writings subversive, and issued a warrant for his arrest. From Vienna he travelled to Paris. In Paris he came across the first writings of the youthful Karl Marx. What Marx had written confirmed everything Wolf felt about the decay and rottenness of the Austro-Hungarian empire – the very views which had forced him to flee his homeland.

Wolf wrote to Marx, who had settled with Jenny in Britain. A correspondence started between them. At the same time Wolf joined forces in Paris with a like-minded French group of 'radical subversives' – the ruling French authorities viewed them exactly as their Austrian counterparts did. The group assassinated a judge and planted a bomb in the carriage of one of the great Parisian property owners.

The bomb failed to detonate but Wolf was spotted running from the scene. The French, helped by intelligence from Vienna, also issued a warrant for his arrest. Once again Wolf had to flee. This time he escaped to England and the Marx household in London. Now the British police, no doubt with help from Vienna and Paris, were on his trail.

'So here I am,' Wolf finished. 'A man with the modest desire to change the world in favour of the vast majority of its ordinary folk. What ambition could be more harmless than that?'

'What's nae so harmless,' Jamie said, 'is that ye seem to have three of Europe's police forces chasing after ye as you're about it.'

'It's no worse than having the bailiffs combing the streets for one's last goods and chattels,' Farquarson, who had also listened to Wolf's story, observed.

'That's as may be,' Jamie answered. 'As far as I'm concerned the two of ye can stew in the porridge ye've each put on the fire. I want no part of the scalding. I'm away for Africa.'

'For Africa?' Farquarson leapt to his feet. 'You were successful, then? Good God, man, that's wonderful!'

'Aye –'

Jamie grinned. In his delight at what had happened that afternoon, he temporarily forgot about Wolf's troubles.

'I'm to join Mr Walter Baimbridge's expedition,' he went on. 'Sir Roderick has given me a letter of accreditation from the society.'

Farquarson was as thrilled on Jamie's behalf as Jamie had expected. He gripped Jamie's hand, pumped it up and down, and danced round him with pleasure. Jamie chuckled and beamed.

'When do you leave?' Farquarson demanded.

'I sail the day after tomorrow from Plymouth,' Jamie said.

'As soon as that? And what will we, the friends and companions of your childhood, do when you're gone?'

'For pity's sake, man!' Jamie laughed. 'You're not conning a bed out of Karl and Jenny now. You'll both be about your business without needing any help from me. You'll be tucked away here hiding from your creditors. And Ferdinand, he'll be here too hiding from the police –'

Jamie stopped.

Wolf had joined in the pleasure that greeted Jamie's announcement. Now his face was suddenly pensive and Farquarson had gone silent too. Jamie glanced from one to the other. They were looking at each other thoughtfully. The same idea, Jamie realized, had crossed both their minds as he spoke.

'No –' Jamie began, appalled, but Farquarson interrupted him.

'Why not?' Farquarson said. 'You have a hazardous journey ahead. You will need companions. There is nothing to keep either of us here – indeed the very reverse, is that not so, Ferdinand?'

Wolf nodded. 'I doubt the British police will put any obstacle in the way of my leaving their shores.'

'Exactly,' Farquarson went on. 'And as for me, the Cheviot, like a good wine, needs time to mature. The flocks will ripen in my absence. When I return I will tread a carpet of fleeces to Madame Belle's door. The old harlot-farmer will be pissing with greed as she walks backwards to let me in – '

Farquarson clasped an arm round Jamie's shoulder. 'When the good Lord sent me to be your shepherd, Oran, He was thinking ahead to just this eventuality. He is sending you to Africa, but He wishes you to travel in safe hands.'

Wolf nodded in assent. 'We'll keep an eye on you. And for myself it will be interesting to see how those primitive societies respond to the ideas Karl and I have been developing.'

'Then we are agreed?' Farquarson spread out his hands. 'Let us consider ourselves three standard-bearers. We carry the banners of wealth, labour and inquiry. Wealth and inquiry will travel, as always, behind labour. Oran, lead on!'

Jamie looked at both of them again.

He tried to visualize them in the African forests. The little laird of Invergordon with his inquisitive face, his sandy hair, and his owlishly blinking eyes. The Austrian journalist with his gaunt features, his passion for chess, and his dedication to the ideas of Karl Marx.

On the face of it it was absurd. Yet Jamie knew that beneath their incongruous exteriors they were both men of resolve and initiative, with quick inventive minds and abundant energy. If he had to have companions thrust on him, he might have fared much worse.

Jamie shook his head ruefully. Then he laughed.

'We take the stage for Plymouth at dawn,' he said. 'And make no mistake about it, ye'll be paying your own passages.'

Two days later Jamie, accompanied by Farquarson and Wolf, boarded the packet *Forerunner* in Plymouth harbour. The same evening the *Forerunner*, under the command of its skipper, Captain Culglass, slipped out into the Channel and headed south.

Its destination was the port of Lagos in the infamous Bight of Benin. To old African hands the Bight of Benin had long been better known as the slave coast.

— 53 —

The two weeks that followed the sailing of the *San Cristobal* were the worst of Mamkinga's life.

The light breeze which took the ship away from the Guinea coast died out within hours, leaving it wallowing still almost within sight of the African shore. The flat calm continued for day after day. Each time the Atlantic tide ebbed, the ship would be pushed a little way into the ocean. Then the tide would turn and it would be washed back to its starting point.

Gomez, the mate, had never encountered conditions like it in the ten years he had spent ferrying slaves between Guinea and Brazil.

'The wind will rise tonight, Don Rafael,' he said to the captain in the wheelhouse at the end of the first week. 'It is bound to. This cannot last – it is not natural.'

'For Christ's sake, just find the air!' Perez snapped back. 'There's a fifth of my share for you if you can get me home before the stench kills me.'

He pulled out his handkerchief and retched into the square of calico.

There was no wind that night. The smell in the wheelhouse and on the upper decks was horrifying. In the holds which housed the slaves it was worse.

The heat and the humidity increased. The slaves were fed and watered once a day but there was not enough of either – least of all water. As dehydration set in they began to fall sick and fevers swept through the cubicles.

The first death occurred when the ship was only three days out.

By the end of the week several slaves were dying daily,

sometimes even hourly. Each evening at feeding time – a ladleful of maize gruel slopped into a rusting bowl – the bodies were dragged out and piled in the passageways. Then the women slaves who were still strong enough to work carried the corpses up on deck and pitched them over the sides.

Gomez, following de Souza's advice, tried to check the spread of infection by 'airing' the human cargo. Every day part of the shipment would be driven up on deck and made to lie, still manacled, for two hours beneath the rigging. The sun blazed down, there was no shade in the stagnant air below the limp empty sails, and the result was even worse than if they had been left below. Sweat poured off the slaves and they stumbled back into their quarters weaker and more dehydrated than before.

As the days passed the conditions in the holds deteriorated even further.

The sanitary arrangements consisted simply of great open tubs placed at intervals along the stacks of cubicles. The tubs were meant to be emptied each morning, but they were too heavy for the women to move and the sailors refused to unshackle the men to do it. The tubs filled up until their contents were slopping over the brims and oozing along the floor. Several times small children attempting to use them fell inside and drowned. The air in the permanent darkness became so rank and foetid that the candle flames in the lanterns carried by the sailors on their tours of inspection guttered out from lack of oxygen.

All the while the pattern of sadism and sexual degradation accelerated in brutality.

Trying to combat the mood of torpor and sullenness induced in the crew by the heat and the monotony, Gomez authorized a trebling of the daily cane spirit ration. The effect on the men was predictable. Every night groups of drunken and inflamed sailors would descend on the holds and hurl themselves on the women. Some were beaten and raped in the passageways. Others – the prettiest – were dragged up on deck and assaulted by half a dozen men in succession.

Sometimes for amusement the sailors would make the slaves couple among themselves. They would haul out a girl and two men, force the girl to arouse the men with her hands and her mouth, and then make the men penetrate her simultaneously – one from the rear and one from the front, beating them if they tried to back away. Afterwards, goaded into lust by the exhibition, they would mount the girl themselves as she lay heaving and panting in the swill of water and excrement.

Mamkinga, pinioned in his cubicle, listened to and watched it all with a grim black face.

On the third day a pair of sailors unlocked his leg manacles and hauled him out. Both were carrying the inevitable rope lashes. Mamkinga had no doubt he was about to be beaten again, but at that moment Gomez appeared. The mate was making one of his rare inspections of the holds.

Gomez held up his lantern and peered at Mamkinga. Then he shook his head.

'He may be a troublemaker,' he said, 'but with those muscles he's going to fetch a barrelful of cruzeiros at market. See he's well tied up, but lay off him. I want the animal landed undamaged.'

The sailors pitched Mamkinga back on to the bare wooden shelf and shackled his arms and legs again. Afterwards he was left alone.

Although his expression revealed nothing, Mamkinga seethed with murderous anger. He had never accepted being a slave himself, but until then he had always considered slavery as a normal condition of life – there had, after all, been slaves working happily in the embrenche's household from his earliest childhood. Even his own experiences during his years of captivity hadn't altered Mamkinga's basic conviction. Only ill fortune had reduced him to slavehood. One day he would escape, return home, and himself be served by slaves again.

Now everything changed. The treatment meted out by

the white men was so horrific that no human being could tolerate it, whether for himself or anyone else. To Mamkinga slavery wasn't a condition of living any longer. It was an obscene denial of life, which had to be challenged and defeated.

On board the *San Cristobal* there was only one way to do that – to overwhelm the crew and take over the ship.

The idea took hold in Mamkinga's mind and filled it every waking hour. For ten days, as the ship wallowed in the heat of the calm, it also seemed a fantasy. Although the crew were few in numbers compared to the slaves, they were well fed, armed and in complete control of the ship. The slave-children and some of the women were at liberty to move around, but against the sailors they were helpless. The male slaves were constantly chained.

The chance of freedom, the possibility of seizing the *San Cristobal* and liberating both himself and his companions in irons, was as tiny, elusive and fragile as the glow-worms that had lit the night streets of Malinda in his childhood. Mamkinga had often tried to capture the darting little specks of light. Always he had failed. Their gleams had shone on unshackled in the darkness – and so now, in spite of everything, did Mamkinga's spirit.

Then late one night Aldoa appeared at Mamkinga's cubicle. She had visited him whenever she could since they sailed, first with butter for his wounds and later, when they healed, with occasional scraps of food she stole from the mate's cabin. That night her eyes were shining excitedly.

'Sit up,' she whispered.

Mamkinga raised himself on one elbow. There was a jangle. To his astonishment he felt his arms were free. A moment later the same happened to his legs. He climbed stiffly out of the cubicle and stood up.

'How did you do it?' he asked, bewildered.

Aldoa held up a bunch of keys.

'The man wears them on his belt,' she explained. 'At night he locks them away in a chest with another key he keeps on a chain round his neck. When I was cleaning the cabin today I moved the chest and a panel fell out at the side. The wood had rotted away. I wedged the panel back. Then tonight when he'd gone to sleep, I removed it again and took the keys out.'

She smiled, her teeth flashing white in the darkness. Mamkinga stared at her, awed by the girl's courage. In stealing the scraps of food Aldoa had risked at the least a terrible beating. If she were discovered with the keys, she would certainly be killed.

'Salama!' Mamkinga said and touched her gratefully on the forehead.

He took the keys from her and examined them. There were about a dozen. Most were small and clearly fitted locks on doors and cupboards in other parts of the ship. The remaining three were much larger. Aldoa had used one of them to release him.

Mamkinga found which key it was. Then with mounting excitement he walked quickly along the passageway, holding the other two large keys apart from the rest.

A handful of slaves, the ones like Mamkinga who were thought to be troublemakers, were manacled individually by their wrists and ankles. The remainder, for convenience in moving them, were secured to chains that ran the length of each group of cubicles. The chains passed through holes in the wooden partitions and were fastened at either end by heavy padlocks. By unlocking a padlock and pulling the chain through the holes, the sailors could release fifteen slaves at a time.

Mamkinga inserted one of the keys into a padlock and turned it. The spring clicked back. The lock opened and the chain dropped free. His spirits soaring, he tried the third key in the padlock above. It refused to turn. Mamkinga replaced it with the original key and the lock sprang open.

Mamkinga thought for a moment.

The first key opened the individual locks. The second key released the chain locks in the hold where he was imprisoned. The third key had to open the chain locks in the other hold. With the three keys he could free every slave on the ship.

Mamkinga swung round triumphantly towards Aldoa.

As he opened his mouth to speak Aldoa put her hand over his lips and pressed him back against the bulwark. Over her shoulder a light was wavering in the stairwell to the deck. Mamkinga froze. The glow grew brighter. The night crew patrol was on its way down to the hold.

For an instant Mamkinga hesitated, his mind churning. The chance might never come again but the slaves were still chained and asleep. The patrol would have guns, and there was nowhere for him to hide. It was hopeless. Unarmed and alone, he was as helpless against the sailors as the women. With a crushing sense of defeat he made up his mind. Quickly he refastened the one padlock he'd opened.

'Back!' he whispered urgently to Aldoa.

With Aldoa behind him Mamkinga padded silently along the passageway. He threw himself into the cubicle and spread out his arms and legs. Aldoa snapped the locks shut.

'Go!' he said.

There was no time even for Mamkinga to tell her to try to come back the following night. The pool of light was advancing towards them. Aldoa glanced at it fearfully and vanished.

A moment later three sailors led by an officer carrying a lantern came into sight. They paused when they reached the cubicle and the officer checked Mamkinga's manacles. Then they tramped on.

Mamkinga lay in the darkness, his chest heaving and sweat pooling on his skin.

It was as chokingly hot as ever and the stench in the clammy air lay like a poisonous mask over his face. But he didn't notice. Mamkinga was praying and the intensity of his prayers, a litany repeated in silence again and again, drove every other thought from his mind.

He was praying to the old gods of Malinda, the spirits of wind and sun, rain and stars, earth and trees, animals and rocks. Their spirits were the unseen presences who determined all that happened to man and decided what man himself could do. Mamkinga had prayed to them since childhood, but never so fervently as now.

He begged them to bring Aldoa back when night fell again.

— 54 —

Aldoa did not return the next night. Nor the one that followed. Nor the one after that.

Spreadeagled in the cubicle for hour after endless hour – in the hold only the tiny cracks in the decking overhead recorded the periodic changes between light and darkness – Mamkinga began to despair. He cursed himself savagely for not having tried to do something in the few moments he had been free. He raged against Aldoa for her cowardice in not coming back, aware even as he did so of the stupidity and injustice in his anger. She had been brave, brave beyond imagining, in what she had done already. Fear was not keeping her away now. It was something else.

What was it?

His mind turned endlessly over the possible answers. Maybe on her way back to the mate's cabin she had been found with the keys. If so she would have been murdered immediately. Her body would have been pitched over the side, and he would never know. Maybe she had got back safely, but the mate had discovered the rotten panel in the chest and taken to storing the keys at night elsewhere. Maybe there was some other explanation.

Mamkinga did not know.

Bitter and frustrated, he tossed and twisted under the confining chains. The heat continued, monotonous and deadening. The air in the hold thickened and darkened. The smell grew fouler and fouler. The level of the water and excrement rose until the liquid was lapping against the bottom rung of the cubicles. The emaciated women and children hauled themselves torpidly along the passageway. On the wooden shelves the men panted and choked and died.

And then on the fourth night after she vanished Aldoa reappeared.

It was very late and Mamkinga was dozing when he heard her voice. For several moments he thought she was speaking to him in a dream. A hand seemed to be shaking his shoulder and he rolled his head away, muttering to himself. The shaking became harder and the voice more urgent.

'Mamkinga, wake up!'

He opened his eyes and suddenly jerked up, hitting his head against the shelf above.

'Where have you been, Aldoa? Why didn't you come back? Have you got the keys?'

Aldoa placed her hand against his mouth.

'Be quiet and listen to me,' she said. 'I have the keys. The man made me sleep in his bed. I could not get away until now. Then tonight one of the sailors woke him. The weather is changing. They think wind is coming – '

As Aldoa spoke she was quickly opening the locks on Mamkinga's chains.

'The man has gone up to the wheelhouse,' she went on. 'All the sailors are on deck getting the ship ready. When they have finished they will come down to check the holds. For the moment we are safe, but there is little time.'

Mamkinga levered himself on to the boards. He stood up stiffly and massaged himself as the water slopped round his ankles. Aldoa began to knead his muscles too. As her hands moved up and down his thighs Mamkinga struggled to gather his thoughts.

The crew were preparing the *San Cristobal* for the approaching wind. When the decks and sheets were trim, patrols would descend to inspect the slaves' quarters. Lying sweating in the cubicle as he'd waited for Aldoa to come back, Mamkinga had thought he would have two or three hours to release and organize his fellow captives.

Now he realized he had ten or fifteen minutes at most. There was no time to gather, explain and plan. All he could do was free as many men as he could and launch a wild attack.

'Give me the keys!' he said.

Aldoa handed them to him. Mamkinga bit through the leather thong with his teeth, and gave her back the key to the chains in the other hold.

'Go through and free everyone you can,' he ordered. 'Say I'm doing the same here. Tell them to arm themselves with anything they can find and gather by the stairs. As soon as they hear me shout, they must run up to the deck and attack.'

Aldoa vanished.

Mamkinga raced to the end of the line of cubicles and unlocked the three sets of padlocks. He crossed the passageway and did the same with the other sets. Then he began to hurry between the cubicles pulling the chains free on alternate sides.

'Quick, get out! We're going to take over the ship. Find something to fight with and wait by the stairs!'

Mamkinga repeated the words again and again.

He was aware of faces staring at him, bemused, in the darkness. Several of the slaves didn't move from the cubicles after he released them. Some didn't understand what he was saying. Others were too cowed or too weak to respond. But the majority tumbled down on to the boards, staggering and swaying as they stood upright, and a murmur of voices built up behind him.

Mamkinga reached the end of the first two rows of cubicles and unlocked the next sets of padlocks. As he continued along the passageway a hand caught his elbow.

'Give me the key,' a voice said. 'I will go on and open the next ones. We can do it twice as fast.'

Mamkinga glanced back. A short sunken-cheeked man with grey hair and a resolute face was gazing up at him. Mamkinga nodded gratefully and handed him the key. The man pushed past him and headed forward.

Cursing himself for not thinking of it earlier, Mamkinga frantically went on pulling out the chains.

When he reached the foot of the stairs he brushed the sweat from his face and looked round. All the cubicles had been unlocked and a throng of perhaps eighty men had gathered at his back. Someone had wrenched the iron hoops off a couple of sanitation barrels and split the staves apart. About half the slaves were gripping curved lengths of heavy mahogany. The rest, including Mamkinga, were empty-handed.

For an instant Mamkinga calculated.

If Aldoa had worked as quickly as he had, there would be as many men again free in the other hold. Between them they outnumbered the crew four or five to one. The slaves had surprise and the darkness on their side, but the crew were disciplined, and they knew the ship. Above all they had guns. The effect of gunfire on the sick and emaciated rabble behind him would be devastating.

Mamkinga shook his head in anguish. Then he stiffened.

A light had appeared at the top of the cone of darkness above the stairs. The sailors must have finished readying the ship. Someone was coming down.

Towering above the others, Mamkinga raised his arm and hissed between his teeth for silence. Its brightness growing, the light came closer. Mamkinga waited until the glow filled the stair landing. Then he seized the wooden guide-rail and tore it away from the wall. Whoever was on the stairs must have heard the sound of splintering wood. The footsteps stopped and a voice called out in Portuguese.

Mamkinga didn't hesitate.

'Now!' he shouted in a roar which seemed to fill the hold. He hurled himself upwards.

There was only one sailor on the landing. When Mamkinga came into sight the man was struggling to pull his long-handled pistol from his belt. Mamkinga swung the rail up from beneath and scythed the sailor's legs from under him. He gripped the man by the hair as the sailor tumbled forward, battered his head against the step, and threw him aside. Then he raced on.

Moments afterwards, with the slaves streaming up behind him, Mamkinga reached the deck. A crescent moon was shining through the streamers of cloud that had accompanied the wind's arrival. In its thin and fitful light Mamkinga gazed round.

Seconds earlier when Mamkinga's shout lifted from the hold, Perez and Gomez had been standing in the wheelhouse. The inexperienced Perez had no idea what the shout might have meant but Gomez, veteran of many slaving voyages, guessed instantly.

The nightmare every slaver dreaded had happened – the slaves had broken free.

'Guns!' Gomez bellowed. 'Get the guns on them! Cover the hatches to the holds and shoot the rats as they come out!'

Ras Michael gazed down, grim-faced, over the plain of
Gondar.

It was soon before dawn a week after Rachel's
baptismal feast had broken up in fear and confusion at
the news of the Galla invasion. The Ras had immediately
assembled the soldiers who were garrisoning Gondar
itself. They included the palace guards and the Ras's
personal regiment of bodyguards. All of them were
seasoned warriors, well mounted and well equipped, but
they numbered barely five hundred in all.

The rest of Gondar's forces, the vast majority, were
scattered throughout the kingdom and along its borders.
The Ras had dispatched messengers to call them back to
the capital. The outlying garrisons were well disciplined
and the messengers were furnished with gold and
promises of access to the palace grain stores. The far-
flung regiments would arrive as soon as time and distance
allowed.

The problem was that there was no time.

The preparations for battle had taken six days. The
night before, Ras Michael himself had led all the troops
he had been able to gather out of Gondar and down on to
the plain. They had ridden almost until dawn, but they
had left late. Now in the early hours they were still within
sight of the city. The Ras had counted on several days'
riding before they encountered the enemy.

It was not to be. As his weary eyes quartered the
shadowy plain in front of him, Ras Michael knew he had
been outmanoeuvred by a swift and bold opponent.

The Galla were before him, a vast army as silent as a

hunting pride of lions in the silver moonlight. Their fires dotted the plain like constellations of fallen stars. They hadn't waited for a reply to their mad and provocative demands. Salama, the Ras realized, had never intended them to. The terms carried to the palace by the wounded captain were simply a trick, a device to goad and enrage him. As soon as the captain had been sent on his way, the Galla had struck camp and marched for Gondar itself.

The trick had worked, Ras Michael reflected bitterly.

He had been lured out of Gondar, and the Galla were within sight of the city too. Motionless on his red-caparisoned black charger, its silver bridle glittering in the moonlight, Ras Michael studied the shadowy Galla force again.

It was the largest army of mountain men he had seen in thirty years' campaigning. There must be five thousand men in front of him. They were not in the usual Galla battle formation of random village bands each under its own commander. Instead the Galla soldiers had been drawn up in a tight and disciplined crescent with the horsemen on the flanks. Someone had been giving Culembra lessons in warfare. The Ras knew well enough who it was.

As the moon came out from behind a cloud a shaft of light caught a flash of the Acab Saat's familiar white cloak near the Galla king's tent.

Ras Michael's face hardened with anger. Ten to one were not the odds he would have chosen, however much of a stick-wielding rabble confronted him, but they were the odds he faced. The Ras straightened in his saddle and turned back towards his own small army. Dozing in their heavy saddles, the men of Gondar were snatching what sleep they could without dismounting.

Ras Michael searched the ranks with narrowed eyes, looking for the little misshapen figure who would be somewhere close behind him.

'Doho!' the Ras called softly.

The Galla had eaten sparingly after the long forced march

from the border with Malinda, and the night had been spent in preparations for the morning's battle.

On the Acab Saat's instructions every warrior, man and woman, had greased themselves heavily. Among the Galla grease and pomade, the more of both the better, were considered to enhance the natural beauty of the wearer. Those who had suffered at their hands swore they could smell them half a mile away, so rancid was the scent. Grease was normally applied for celebrations, including victories. Today Salama had ordered it to be put on before the battle began.

The sight of the festive preparations had put Culembra in such high spirits he insisted on the Acab Saat drinking from his personal vessel.

'It is good palm liquor,' he bellowed at the white-robed priest. 'Drink deep of the blood of my enemies.'

The Acab Saat's jaw tightened with distaste as he forced the liquor down his throat.

The liquid itself was fiery and sour, nothing like the fine clear nectar he had enjoyed in Gondar's halls and would soon enjoy again. Salama could have put up with that. It was the vessel which disgusted him. Culembra's favourite drinking goblets were the scrubbed bleached skulls of his most dangerous enemies.

Today the skull was that of Culembra's own nephew, whom he had murdered after an unsuccessful uprising. As Salama drank, the young molars embedded in the jawbone clicked unnervingly against his own teeth. He wiped his mouth with the edge of his robe and wrinkled his face.

The Lendama, the most feared of Culembra's soldiers, were drawn up inside the right-hand wing of the cavalry to act as bodyguard to the king himself. To the women the Acab Saat had given a particular task. They were ordered to collect all the polished metal in the Galla waggons, and scour it until every surface was mirror bright.

Culembra had rocked with laughter when he saw what the women were doing.

'Is this what you really want, Acab?' he shouted. 'Don't you know my warrior women are so ugly that if they see their faces in your mirrors they will run for the hills?'

Salama smiled sourly.

It was on the slaves that the full weight of the task fell.

Toomi's arms ached with exhaustion as she worked. Each time she finished a piece of metal she glanced in the shining surface to see her own face reflected back at her. Once by some trick of the moonlight it was not her but Mamkinga who gazed back. Toomi's spirit leapt. For an instant his presence in the burnished metal was so vivid she touched her lips to it, almost feeling the warmth of his skin beneath hers.

Then a cloud crossed the moon. The image vanished and she wearily returned to work.

Towards dawn the moon sank and darkness closed in over the plain. The Galla began their final preparations for the battle. Each of the Lendama warriors was given a shining metal disk. Then they listened silently as the Acab Saat told them what they were to do.

Proud and martial in his rhinoceros-hide jerkin, Doho rode up to join Ras Michael when he heard his master call his name.

The Ras had stopped his horse on an outcrop of rock which afforded a view of the Galla army. The old warlord was silent for a moment.

Then he said, 'I want you to return to Gondar, Doho.'

'When we ride against this mountain scum?' the dwarf protested in outrage. 'You have never ever gone into battle without me to guard your back, Ras.'

Ras Michael rubbed his face and shook his head tiredly.

'We have fought many battles back to back, Doho,' he answered. 'This one is different. I fear for Gondar. The Galla are scum indeed, but the hyenas outnumber us ten to one. We have faced worse odds and triumphed. Yet for once the Galla have a leader well trained in the arts of war. He should be. He has had me to watch and learn from for long enough – '

The Ras paused. 'The Acab Saat knows my mind and my ways in battle. I would not wager on the outcome today.'

Doho stared at him.

Suddenly he felt cold and the hairs on the back of his neck bristled with anxiety. He had always believed the Ras to be invincible. For the first time, it seemed, Ras Michael was uncertain of victory.

'What do I do in Gondar, Ras?' Doho asked quietly.

'Go to the palace,' Ras Michael said. 'Find Ozoro Rachel. However much she protests, keep her close to you. From the walls you will see what happens here. If the Galla and that murdering baboon of a priest break through, get her away from Gondar – '

The Ras swung round in the saddle.

'Unless he can take Rachel, Salama will never be safe. She is Gondar. While she lives, so does the kingdom. Guard her with your life, Doho. If the worst befalls, on you will the princess's head and Sheba's lands depend.'

'I bear your trust.' Doho turned his horse at last. 'I will carry it unbroken to the grave.'

As he rode towards Gondar Doho's heart was heavy with foreboding.

He sensed he had seen the face of the old warlord, his master and idol for so many years, for the last time. Momentarily tears filmed his eyes. Doho blinked and shook them away. Into his care had been given the safety of the young woman who, together with Ras Michael, he loved more than all the world.

It was a sacred trust and one he would never betray, Doho thought, as he rode through the gates of Gondar.

As he felt the first warmth of the sun's rays on his neck, Ras Michael swung round in the saddle.

The men behind him might be few in number, but their backs were against Gondar and they had wives and children within the walls. The city would not be lightly lost. Close to the Ras in Doho's accustomed place was Golan, the Sudanese mercenary. As always Golan rode bareback and barefooted, but he was wearing the scarlet cloak of the royal soldiers and carrying a scarlet pennant tipped with a golden hunting leopard which was the Ras's personal battle emblem.

On either side of Ras Michael the horses of Gondar's cavalry snorted and shifted their heavy feet restlessly as they scented the coming battle. All of the Ras's forces were mounted. There had been no time to assemble foot soldiers. Those were drawn from the young men in the outlying villages. There the harvest was already in progress. Ras Michael would have needed days more to raise an effective body of infantry.

The old warlord turned back towards the massed ranks of the Galla.

Among them, unmistakably, moved the white cloak of the Acab Saat. The Ras had ordered his battle line as he always did. His warriors were tightly grouped on the higher ground with their backs to the east and the gathering dawn. When the sun rose they would be ready to surge forward in attack as the dazzling light of the African morning blinded their enemies in front.

As the Ras gave the signal to advance it occurred to him that it was also a lesson the Acab must have learned. He dismissed the thought and rode down towards the plain.

From where he sat on his horse behind Tamule's Lendama, Salama watched with grim satisfaction as the red cloaks of Gondar advanced.

The old leopard had not changed his hunting habits, and it was to be his undoing, Salama thought. He glanced down the ranks of the women warriors, their bodies greased for battle and their bare breasts jangling with a motley collection of weapons. Even to the priest's greedy eye, they were a repulsive lot.

All except for one – the young slave girl they addressed as Toomi. Salama ran his tongue round his lips. She was a tantalizingly attractive morsel. Had it not been for the old hag Tamule keeping her closer than a merchant's money-bag, Toomi would have had a taste of more than the weapons of war last evening.

The Acab rubbed his sword hilt reflectively. By the time night fell again everything would be changed – and not even Culembra's favourite colonel could deny him the spoils of victory.

Two hundred paces in front of Salama, Ras Michael felt the muscles of his thighs strain as he squeezed the flanks of his horse to try to calm it. The horse was unsettled. It whinnied, side-stepped, and tried to rear. Like all the Gondar cavalry it was close enough to the Galla army to smell the grease and pomade on the soldiers. The Ras patted the horse's neck and brought it back under control.

The old warlord rode on. As he did he knew something was wrong.

In battle the Galla's practice was to rush blindly at the enemy, counting on their fearsome appearance and blood-curdling screams to gain them the advantage. Today they were holding their line. In the centre even the Lendama, always the first into the fray, were leaning on their spears.

Ras Michael did not know what it meant, but suspicions crackled across his mind like summer flares of lightning.

Ahead of him the Acab Saat narrowed his eyes. The sun had just lifted over the horizon. Light began to ripple like a tide across the plain.

Now.

Salama signalled to Culembra. The king raised his hand and shouted. Behind Culembra a horn echoed out his order to the Galla forces. As it did the Galla swept forward.

Salama watched as Culembra's soldiers raced past him. Every warrior in the Lendama was holding a brightly polished sheet of metal. The women raised the metal sheets to the sun and a thousand burnished surfaces caught its rays. Reflected back from the mirrors, the gathering light dazzled in the eyes of Gondar's advancing cavalry.

Blinded, the horses reared up and wrenched their heads away.

In an instant the Galla foot soldiers were upon them, hacking at the horses' tendons with their axes. Hamstrung and crippled, the horses began to fall. As they toppled, their riders reached down to grapple with the attackers. The bodies of the Galla were so slippery with grease, the horsemen could get no grip on them. Rider after rider was wrenched from the saddle and chopped to pieces by Tamule's warriors as he fell.

Wheeling his horse away from the carnage and cursing the lack of infantry, the Ras shouted the order to dismount. There was nothing else to be done. In the crush of hand-to-hand combat every advantage lay with those on foot.

All the Gondar forces could do was fight it out face to face on the ground.

Heavily outnumbered and hampered by the weight of their body armour, the royal soldiers began to give way. As they retreated the Galla swarmed forward. Careless of the still bravely flashing swords and the rising mounds of bodies, all Culembra's warriors could think of were the fabled riches of Gondar that lay before them.

Ras Michael himself tried to stem the retreat. With his Sudanese standard bearer, Golan, and three of his closest bodyguards, the Ras alone was still mounted. He called the four of them to his shoulder as the tumult eddied round him.

'Forward!' he shouted. 'See where Culembra rides! Strike through the rabble and cut him down!'

The four gathered behind the Ras. With the old warlord at their head they charged into the heaving throng.

For an instant the galloping horsemen unnerved the Galla waves. Culembra's soldiers checked and parted in terror as the pounding hoofs bore down on them. Ras Michael, his white beard plucked back around his neck and his face set tight with rage, cut through the ranks and spurred on towards the king, slashing to left and right as he rode.

He was almost on Culembra when an old woman leapt up in front of him.

The old woman was Tamule. In her hand was a short broad sword, its blades as sharp as the mountains' winter frost. She slashed the sword across the neck of Ras Michael's horse, severing the animal almost to its spinal column.

As the horse crumpled, blood pumping into the air from its arteries, the Ras pitched over the animal's head. Tamule whirled the sword above her and plunged it down. The sword's point entered Ras Michael's back, and drove through to his heart.

Golan, carrying the Ras's pennant in one hand and an axe in the other, was immediately behind Ras Michael as he fell. He spurred his horse forward and struck at Tamule with the axe, cleaving her open from the shoulder to the stomach. Tamule shuddered and crumpled to the ground. Golan turned on Culembra, but the Lendama enveloped him.

His horse was cut away under him and he disappeared beneath a ring of stabbing swords. Moments later the Ras's other three bodyguards were cut down too.

From a watchtower high on Gondar's walls Doho surveyed the battle for as long as he dared, his knuckles white with anxiety and frustration round the hilt of his sheathed sword. Only when he saw the golden leopard of Ras's pennant vanish in the hordes of the advancing Galla, did he turn away. As he turned the Ras's scarlet cloak, ripped and sodden now with blood, was hurled into the air, and a great cry of victory lifted from the Galla forces.

Doho ran down the steps of the watchtower and headed for the palace. There was not a moment to be lost. Ozoro Rachel, child of the river, was now the last hope of Gondar.

*

By nightfall Doho's vantage point on the battlements had been taken over by the Acab Saat.

Below him the victorious Galla streamed through the gates behind their leader Culembra. The Acab frowned grimly as he watched the bloodsoaked rabble pour into the streets. The people of Gondar would not have an easy dawn. He himself had been first into the city, hurrying to the palace in search of the young Rachel. The Child of the River was nowhere to be found. His own men, led by Murabit, were out now, quartering the hills in search of fugitives.

She would not run far before they found her.

Meanwhile his own appetites had been stirred by the battle – and the young Lendama slave girl would do well enough for the present. The old woman, Tamule, had been first into battle, and Salama had already had word that she had been wounded. The girl Toomi would surely be attending her. The Acab smiled with anticipation. Then he wrinkled his nostrils at the stink of the Galla hordes blocking the gateway.

The priest descended the steps carefully – they were slippery with the blood and viscera of battle. He made his way back across the plain towards the Galla encampment. The bodies of the defeated Gondar horsemen were already naked, stripped clean by the victors.

It would make the job of the vultures, which were already gathering overhead in great sweeping circles, all the easier, Salama thought as he walked.

The blow Golan had given Tamule with his axe was a mortal one.

Moments after she fell the old woman was picked up by the Lendama and carried back to her tent. The Lendama laid her down on a pile of cushions hurriedly prepared by Toomi. Then they gathered weeping round their leader.

Toomi pushed her way through to kneel beside the old woman.

The axe had slashed off Tamule's left breast, shattered

her ribs, and cut deep into her stomach. The flow of blood from a dozen severed veins and arteries had slowed, but the trauma of the immense wound was too great for her body to bear. The old woman was dying.

'Stand back,' Toomi pleaded.

Reluctantly the women gave way. They were soldiers and Toomi was only a slave, but she was Tamule's personal servant. At that moment of their colonel's approaching death Toomi took precedence over them. As they retreated Toomi began to do what she could for Tamule.

It was not much. She smeared a herbal paste over the exposed tissue to staunch the bleeding, and used camel thorns to bind the edges of the wounds together. Then she sat bathing Tamule's face with rosewater.

The old woman survived for three hours. Most of the time she lay still, her chest barely moving as her breathing slowed and her face became greyer and more waxen. Once towards the end she recovered consciousness. Her eyes opened and she peered uncertainly up at Toomi. Then Tamule recognized the face above her.

'You are a good child, little honey badger,' she whispered in a voice so frail that Toomi had to bend down to hear. 'I count on you to keep the garden well.'

Toomi smiled. She gently touched Tamule's forehead.

For ten years Tamule had been her mistress and captor, the ever-present symbol of the misery that had never lessened from the moment she was parted from Mamkinga. The old woman was greedy and demanding. Yet towards Toomi she had in her own fashion been generous and kindly. In spite of everything a bond had developed between them. Now, as death approached, Toomi felt something that was close to affection for her.

'Speed me to my ancestors,' Tamule continued. 'One day you will join me there. Until then I have a gift for you to remember me by.'

Tamule gestured weakly at her neck. Hanging round it on a chain was a silver key. It was the key to the padlocks which fettered Tamule's slaves.

'Take it,' Tamule said. 'When the battle is over bear it to the king. Only he can give you your freedom, but when he sees it he will know it is my desire. He will not refuse me. My Lendama here will be the witnesses that you did not steal it from me.'

The women murmured in assent.

Toomi removed the key from Tamule's neck. 'You will go well prepared to the spirits,' Toomi said. 'It is my promise.'

Tamule smiled.

A few minutes later the old woman gave a thin cough. A ripple ran over her body, the tremors faded into stillness, and her jaw sagged. Toomi felt the pulse-vein in her temple. There was no movement. She looked round at the women and lowered her eyes. For several minutes there was a pandemonium of tears and wailing as the women threw themselves on Tamule's body.

Then Toomi reasserted her authority as Tamule's servant.

'I must make her ready,' she said.

Still weeping, the women withdrew. According to the Galla's funeral customs Tamule's body had to be bathed and dressed before it could be taken to the rocks for the vultures to clean. On the field of battle the task belonged to the dead warrior's servant.

Toomi laced tight the cords at the tent's entrance after the women left. She glanced down at Tamule. The old woman was lying where she died, with her head slumped on her chest. The key that had hung round her neck was now in the pouch at Toomi's waist.

Toomi had no intention of taking it to Culembra.

The king might grant her freedom from slavery but there was no guarantee that would mean she was free to leave the Galla. What Toomi wanted was to escape from the mountain people altogether. Her best chance would come, Toomi guessed, over the next few hours in the confused aftermath of the great battle. When it did, she at last had the means of unshackling her fetters.

Meanwhile she had time to keep her promise to the old

woman. Toomi knelt down and set about preparing Tamule to meet the birds of death.

— 56 —

'Wait!' Culembra shouted.

He was standing on the steps in the main courtyard of the palace of Gondar. The last eddies and surges of the battle had ended and the victorious Galla army was swarming through the city.

Culembra had ridden in at the army's head shortly after the Acab Saat. He had gone straight to the palace. While Salama disappeared in search of the queen-empress and her daughter Rachel, Culembra began to distribute the spoils of victory.

From the moment of his entry into Gondar his soldiers had been rounding up groups of prisoners and shepherding them before him to be allocated to one or other of his commanders. In the torchlight Culembra saw that the group in front of him now consisted of young women. They had been taken in the palace itself and they were presumably some of the royal servants.

Culembra had been about to give them to a warrior named Ishkadi, who had commanded the left flank of his army and was at his side, eyeing the women hungrily. Then he thought of Tamule. He had seen the old woman cut down. Culembra didn't yet know she was dead, but he remembered her valour in the fight.

More than anyone she and her soldiers deserved recognition.

'Take these to Tamule,' he called out. 'Tell her from me there will be more to follow.'

Culembra waved the group away. The soldiers cheered. All the Galla knew how valiantly Tamule and her warriors had fought.

At swordpoint the young women were driven out of the courtyard and down along the path from the palace gardens towards Tamule's encampment on the plain below.

At their centre, her face hidden by a muddy servant's cowl, was Rachel.

Doho had kept his promise to Ras Michael well.

Taking Rachel with him, he searched for Kalima. He told the old woman to dress the princess in the clothes of a serving maid and hide her with the other girls in the vaults beneath the palace kitchens.

'As soon as the Acab reaches the palace,' Doho told Rachel when he left her there, 'he will search for you. When he can't find you, he will look for me. He will guess that I know where you are. He will find me without too much difficulty – I will make sure of that. I will let him beat me for a while – '

The dwarf managed to smile briefly.

'Do not worry about that. I've been beaten by better men than Salama and I live still. But when he's convinced, when he thinks he's forced the truth out of me, I'll tell him you escaped from Gondar before the battle finished. Then he will have to think again. You must stay with these girls, princess. Keep your mouth shut. Admit nothing. You may be sold or given away. It doesn't matter – '

The first wave of the Galla soldiers was pouring into the city. The screams and uproar that accompanied their arrival could be heard even in the vaults below the palace kitchens.

Doho dropped to his knees.

'You are my queen,' he said, tears glistening on his face. 'Stay alive, stay free for all of us, for Gondar.'

Doho kissed Rachel's hand.

Then he leapt to his feet and scuttled up the stairs that led to the kitchens. He slammed down the hatch over the steps to the vaults and ran on to the royal apartments. He squatted in his usual place before the door to Ras Michael's chamber.

The dwarf was still there an hour later when Salama burst into the passage, his sword in his hand. It took a further hour for Salama's men to search the palace and find the kitchenmaids in the vaults. They drove the slovenly and smoke-smeared group of girls upstairs and handed them over to Culembra.

The girls were delivered to Tamule's tent at midnight, just as the old woman's body was being carried out on a wooden bier.

After Tamule's death Sevoro, Tamule's deputy, had taken command of the regiment. Sevoro had also been wounded in the battle. As Sevoro limped away behind the cortege, she ordered Toomi to keep guard on Culembra's gift of the new slaves until morning.

Toomi acknowledged the instructions with a bow of her head. The young women were driven into the tent and the funeral procession disappeared into the darkness.

As the new slaves thronged round her, Toomi stood thinking.

Beyond the hide walls the night air rang with the beat of horses' hoofs, the clamour of drunken shouts, the bellowing of cattle being slaughtered and the intermittent screams of terrified women. The Galla were celebrating their victory with wine, feasting and rape. For hours yet it would be suicidal to venture out. Only when the soldiers, intoxicated with triumph and drink, had sated themselves could she think of trying to slip away.

Meanwhile she desperately needed sleep. The cushions on which Tamule had died were still piled at the other end of the tent. Toomi pushed her way through the young women, clustered terrified at the tent's centre, and lay down. She closed her eyes and prepared herself to rest until the uproar outside died down.

'Pula!'

Toomi blinked and looked up. One of the girl slaves driven in by Culembra's soldiers was kneeling beside her.

'Pula!' Toomi returned the greeting. 'What do you want?'

The girl hesitated.

Her face was mantled by a dirty servant's cowl. After a moment's indecision the girl pulled the cowl back.

The girl's face was coated in grime. Beneath the dirt Toomi saw large dark eyes, finely cut features, and a tousled mane of black hair. The young woman was, by any standards, remarkably beautiful. Yet what struck Toomi most was her extraordinary resemblance to herself. Toomi might almost have been staring into a mirror.

Toomi raised herself on her elbow and looked at her, bewildered.

'Who are you?' she asked.

The young woman was Rachel. For several moments she didn't answer.

A combination of instinct and despair had made her approach Toomi. She knew from Toomi's shackles that she was a slave. Yet Rachel had sensed there was something different about her. Her face was sensitive, intelligent, even compassionate. She could be trusted, Rachel had decided.

It didn't matter if she was wrong. Gondar's future queen had no choice except to trust someone. She had escaped from the palace with the kitchen servants but the Acab Saat wouldn't rest until he found her. He would already be searching the town. Doho might delay him for a while, but at first light Salama would turn to the Galla encampment and the captives Culembra had distributed among them.

No one would be allowed to move until she was traced and caught.

'I must get away,' Rachel said. 'I can't explain why but I must escape before morning. Please help me. I have some gold I can pay you with.'

'Gold?'

Rachel nodded.

She glanced over her shoulder at the other girls. They were speaking fearfully in whispers to each other. Rachel reached under her tunic and produced a leather pouch tied to a girdle round her waist. She moved closer to

Toomi and opened it. Inside Toomi saw the glitter of gold and jewels.

'Just take me outside and let me go,' Rachel pleaded. 'I will give you half of it all.'

Toomi stared transfixed at the dazzling coins and jewels. She hurriedly pushed the pouch back under Rachel's tunic.

'Who are you?' Toomi asked.

Rachel looked at her in anguish.

In showing the slave-girl the gold she had virtually given herself away. Rachel knew she had to trust her further. She told Toomi the truth.

Toomi listened in astonishment.

Even as a child in Malinda she had heard about the daughter of Gondar's emperor. Later in captivity Rachel's name had often come up in conversations among Tamule's women warriors in their compound at Galla. Gondar, its wealth and its ruling family were an unending source of fascination.

Now the young woman, Gondar's future queen-empress, was standing in front of Toomi in the clothes of a kitchenmaid.

'If you go now,' Toomi said, 'you will be dead or captured within minutes. Listen to the Galla. They're everywhere outside.'

'I will take that chance,' Rachel insisted. 'I can lose nothing. If I stay here I will be found and I will die anyway.'

Toomi shook her head. 'It's hopeless.'

'So you will not help me?' Rachel gazed at her despairingly. 'Are you going to tell them who I am?'

'No,' Toomi answered. 'I'm going to escape with you. But we're going to wait until we have a chance to truly get away.'

Toomi began to explain.

57

'Walk beside me,' Toomi whispered. 'Look confident, and do not hurry.'

Rachel nodded.

It was shortly before dawn and the captured palace servants were all asleep on the ground. The two young women stepped over the recumbent bodies and out of the tent into the darkness. Toomi paused for a moment. Orientating herself by the stars, she headed towards the north.

Fires still guttered all over the plain and the late night air was thick with wood smoke and the smell of charred meat.

Each time they passed a ring of flame they saw groups of Galla soldiers sprawled round it in a drunken stupor. From time to time they stumbled over a body and occasionally a terrified animal, a riderless horse or a cow, careered by. Twice they were stopped and challenged by reeling sentries, almost as drunk as those they were supposed to be guarding.

Each time Toomi held up in the wavering torchlight a medallion she had also taken from Tamule.

'We are from Tamule's regiment,' she said boldly. 'We have been sent to check her waggons. Let us pass.'

On both occasions the men peered at the silver amulet, and waved them on.

Half an hour later the fires on the battlefield were behind them. Toomi paused again and peered ahead. In front were more fires. Unlike those scattered at random across the plain, the new fires were in orderly lines.

'From now on,' she whispered to Rachel, 'do not make a sound.'

They set off again. Ten minutes afterwards a low untidy mound rose in front of them. Toomi stopped. There was silence ahead. Toomi licked her finger and raised it to the air. A tiny night breeze was blowing from the west.

Moving with immense care Toomi circled round the mound until the breeze was in their faces. She lowered herself to the ground. Rachel did the same. Toomi pulled out a bag from beneath her cloak and started tossing a number of little objects forward into the darkness. The objects landed almost soundlessly on the dry grass.

When the bag was empty Toomi sucked in her breath and whistled. Then she snorted through her teeth. At the base of the mound a dog gave a short uncertain yelp. A few seconds later half a dozen dogs were rustling towards them through the grass. The dogs stopped and began to eat.

Toomi raised her finger to her lips.

The idea had come to Toomi as soon as she saw the gold and jewels in Rachel's pouch. Behind every Galla expedition there travelled groups of Arab merchants. If the expedition was successful, the merchants bought the plunder and transported it in caravans for sale in the central African markets.

After a major battle like the one on the Gondar plain, the trading could go on for days. It started even while the fighting was in progress and the first spoils began to come in. The first caravans had left before darkness. The remainder were encamped in front of Toomi and Rachel now. The mound consisted of looted goods ready for transportation next day. It was guarded by a pack of the merchants' dogs.

Toomi had learnt how to deal with them from the Galla, who often used the trick when they raided villages. Small pieces of meat were cut open and filled with the same laudanum paste she had used to anaesthetize Tamule's wound. Then the dogs' attention was attracted with an imitation of a camel or a cow. They came forward to investigate and found the meat.

The laudanum acted swiftly. Within minutes Toomi heard the dogs begin to lurch and topple over. Soon there was silence in front of them. Cautiously Toomi stood up.

'We need a dozen bales,' she whispered.

They crept forward.

The mound contained everything from hides and furs to gourds and sacks of spices. At one end there was a pile of bolts of cloth, pillaged from the city. The two young women dragged down twelve of the bolts and carried them back to where they'd lain waiting for the laudanum to take effect.

'Wait for me here,' Toomi said. She set off again.

The Arab encampment was laid out in a series of parallel lines. Each merchant had his fire, his personal waggon, a stock of the goods he'd bought from the soldiers – often consignments of slaves – and space for his servants, horses and camels. At the end of the lines was another untidier area. Here the poorer traders who travelled with the Galla army had made camp. Among them were men who rented out pack animals to merchants who had bought too much for their own camels to carry.

Skirting the Arab fires, Toomi made her way to the second camp.

In the darkness it seemed to consist almost entirely of beasts. Broken-down horses neighed, donkeys brayed, camels whistled and belched, goats tugged restlessly against their tethers, wide-horned cattle stamped and bellowed. In spite of the noise all the men were asleep.

Toomi crept forward.

It took her only a few minutes to find what she was looking for. A mature female camel was resting on the ground beside a group of restless, head-tossing companions. Their owner was sleeping beside a fire a few yards away. The camel was saddled with panniers and harness, ready to be hired out if needed as soon as dawn came. In the flickering firelight the animal looked placid and healthy.

Toomi untied the camel's halter. She jabbed her knuckles into the skin below its jaw to force it to stand up. Then she led it away. Behind her the other camels snorted suspiciously, but the man didn't stir.

'We will travel for an hour,' Toomi said. 'By then it will be almost dawn – '

She had found Rachel again, the camel's panniers had been loaded with the bolts of cloth, and they were ready to move.

'When it's light we'll stop for a while,' she continued. 'Then we must head on. We have to catch up with one of the caravans as soon as possible.'

Toomi gripped the camel's halter and set off.

Half a mile from the Arab camp she began to cast around. She had plotted their general direction by the stars. Now she needed something more precise, the very route the first caravans had taken. The sky was already beginning to pale and she soon found it – the print of other camels' tracks in the soil.

With Rachel beside her and the camel plodding behind, Toomi followed the spoor westwards.

'Turn your head to the right,' Rachel said.

Seated on the rock below her, Toomi turned her head. Rachel lifted a lock of Toomi's hair and drew it out between her fingers. She picked up the knife and carefully cut the hair a few inches from Toomi's head.

It was three hours later and already full daylight.

They had halted in a little gully beside the tracks they were following. During the darkness they had travelled over ten miles. The battlefield was well behind them, although on the horizon they could still see smudges of smoke rising from the still-burning fires.

'Right,' Rachel said, 'now the other way.'

Rachel started on the other side of Toomi's head.

Rachel's hair had already been cropped and they had both changed into Arab clothes. The outline of the plan had been in Toomi's mind from the moment the dying

Tamule gave her the key. It was only when Rachel produced the gold that Toomi saw how it could be done.

Toomi had only one idea – to find her brother. She had last seen Mamkinga ten years before, in the marketplace of the village whose name she still didn't know. Over the years she had discovered that the three great central African trading centres were the towns of Kano, Timbucktoom and Garoua. An old slave in Galla had told Toomi that her brother might well have been sold in the slave market of one of them at some stage.

For anyone searching for a long-missing slave, one of the three towns was the best place to start. The slave markets were run by Arabs, and their scribes kept written records of the transactions that took place. Kano, three months' march away, was the nearest of the three to Gondar.

To get there Toomi knew they would have to travel under the protection of one of the caravans bound there too. After the battle there would be many of them, but the caravan master had to be paid. The answer was Rachel's gold.

Toomi had explained the plan to Rachel as they talked together in Tamule's tent. Rachel agreed immediately. She was still in a state of shock after Gondar's defeat and the death of Ras Michael, and her only concern was to get as far away from the Acab Saat as possible.

'It is finished.' Rachel put down the knife. 'Let us see how we look now.'

Toomi stood up and the two young women put on the Arab headdresses. They stared at each other.

In the sunlight they were no longer two young Abyssinian women. They were Arab youths, tall and slender, with the beardless faces of the desert Arabs and the traditional curved daggers at their waists. Toomi's skin was slightly darker than Rachel's, but from their identical height and the extraordinary similarity of their faces, anyone would have taken them for brothers.

'Which from now on is what we are,' Toomi said, voicing the thought that had occurred to them both.

She smiled. Spontaneously they reached out and quietly embraced each other. Then they set off again.

They caught up with the caravan in the early afternoon. The caravan master had chosen to stop for the midday halt at a river ford. When Toomi and Rachel appeared, the caravan was about to move on. It consisted of some sixty laden camels, a dozen mules, some pack and riding horses, three waggons, manacled groups of slaves and sixty men.

Speaking in Arabic, Toomi asked one of the men at the rear where his master was. The man took her forward.

'Allah be praised!' Toomi said. 'We ask permission to travel with you.'

The caravan master, a stocky Aden merchant, looked down from his horse. Below him he saw two youths in jellabahs and Arab headdress with a laden camel behind them.

'Where have you come from?' he asked.

'Gondar,' Toomi replied promptly. 'Our father is Ibn Matutua, a merchant trading out of Massawa. He heard the Galla were going to war, and he sent my brother and me to see what we could buy – '

Toomi gestured towards the camel.

'We picked up some good cloth. It is the first time we have bought without him, but I think he will be pleased. Now we are heading for Kano to meet his agent there. We were travelling with another caravan but their horses were lame and there were quarrels with the other traders. We decided to leave them and ride on in the hope of finding someone such as you.'

The caravan master wrinkled his face suspiciously. 'The two of you rode alone?'

'Your tracks were clear and fresh,' Toomi said. 'Allah looks after those who ride boldly.'

Toomi smiled up at him brightly. Inwardly she was holding her breath.

On his horse the caravan master frowned in silence. Then he grudgingly nodded.

'You may join us,' he said. 'On one condition – that

you pay now. I do not know your father and I will not take your token of hand. You will pay me in coin or gold, or you travel alone. And I'll put my men on you to see you do.'

Toomi breathed out in relief.

'We have a little gold,' she said.

Fifteen minutes later Toomi, Rachel and their camel had become part of the caravan. They splashed across the ford and headed west again.

58

The young women travelled with the caravan for three months.

The daily routine changed little as they moved west. Mohamet Asa, as the caravan master was named, had traded with the Abyssinians for years and knew the route between the mountain kingdom and Kano well. Each evening he would stop at a campsite, usually beside a river, which he had used many times in the past.

The animals would be hobbled and turned loose to graze, and Asa's working slaves would make fires for the evening meal. When night fell the slaves were sent out to watch over the animals, and the guards took up their positions. Between them, Asa and the other eight merchants with the caravan had fifty servants. All were armed. During the journey the caravan lost two camels and a mule to leopards, but no war party came near them.

For Toomi the days passed with frustrating slowness. She was free. She was her own person again. She watched other slaves perform the tasks she had carried out for Tamule for so long. None of it gave her any pleasure. All that mattered was Mamkinga. Each evening when the shadows began to lengthen she would start to pray under her breath that tonight Asa wouldn't halt the caravan before dark, and instead would continue into the night. All she wanted to do was press on.

Every mile brought her closer to Kano. Toomi ached to reach it. She knew the chances of finding Mamkinga there were remote, but at least she could do something —

at least she could start searching. Until she got there Toomi's frustration was almost as great as she'd felt in Tamule's compound.

For Rachel every day's journey had the opposite effect. Every day took her further from Gondar.

For the first few weeks it didn't matter. Her only goal was to get away. Then one day another caravan bound for Kano caught up with them. It had left Gondar well after them but it was much smaller and travelling faster. The new caravan camped beside them that night. The caravan master had more recent news from Gondar.

Over the evening fire Rachel learned that Salama had killed Georgis, her mother's husband, and given her mother Esther as a wife to Culembra.

'The Galla are taking over the whole country,' the man went on. 'Culembra is the new king, but it is in name only. The power over the people lies with the Acab Saat. He wields it mercilessly. Many die every day. Gondar has been made a nation of slaves. They say the princess, the river's child, escaped. The Acab denies it. He claims the river's line is ended. But it is known he has sent out search parties everywhere and thinks of nothing else.'

Rachel listened in silence. That night after she and Toomi returned to their tent she lay awake for hours.

The news about Georgis's death shocked but didn't grieve her. Georgis had never been more than a distant and petulant presence at the edges of her life. To learn that her mother had become the wife of Culembra was different. Remote as Esther had also been from her daughter, the queen-empress was Rachel's mother and in a way Rachel loved her. To think of her living with the barbarian mountain bandit was horrifying.

Yet Rachel had grown up among the realities of Abyssinian dynastic life and politics and warfare, and that too she could understand. What kept her awake was the Acab Saat and his newly established power over Gondar.

It was ten years since Salama's exile. In that time Rachel had crossed the bridge from childhood into maturity. Over the bridge she carried with her vivid images of the priest from her first years – images of a brutal, ruthless and vindictive man. Salama was evil. Now he ruled Gondar and all of Gondar's people.

Suddenly Rachel's fear of him had gone. Even the news that he was sending out search parties didn't frighten her. In place of fear Rachel felt a new and troubling sense of herself as Gondar's future queen.

By nature passionate, intelligent and strong-willed, Rachel had been brought up to believe it would be her duty and her right to rule Gondar. The kingdom had been seized from her and she had lost everything. She cared nothing for material possessions. She was trained as a warrior and she knew all a warrior needed was a horse, a sword and a bowl of gruel.

What she had lost was far more valuable than the palace and its splendours. The high clear air of the mountains – here on the plain it was thick and humid. The great sweeping vistas from the ridge. The smells lifting from the plains at evening, wood smoke and drying hay and the flowers after the spring rains. The flanks of her horse shining as they galloped through the park, the laughter of the soldiers she knew so well, the companionship of Doho and old Kalima.

She had known and loved them all her life. They had gone and she missed them bitterly. But Rachel at least was free. Her people were not. The best were being slaughtered. The ordinary people, the people Doho had taught her to know and respect, were enslaved. The Acab Saat had unleashed a reign of terror on the land.

'You are my queen,' the dwarf had said in tears when he left her. 'Stay alive, stay free, for all of us, for Gondar.'

Rachel was alive and free. But with each mile she travelled further from Gondar, she felt a mounting sense of betrayal towards her kingdom and her people. If it hadn't been for Toomi she would have despaired.

Locked together but plucked now in opposite directions, the two young women might have found tensions growing up between them. They did not. Instead each made the other's fears and frustrations bearable. They had certain common bonds. They both came from royal families. They were close in age. They spoke almost the same language and they were both in danger.

There was something more, something deeper even than their astonishing physical resemblance. At times it seemed they might almost have been brought up together.

One night, early in the journey and while they were still in the highlands, Rachel woke. The ground was sparkling with frost and the air was icy. On the other side of the fire Toomi, wrapped in an identical thin blanket, was asleep. After her expeditions with Tamule, Toomi was used to sleeping out in the mountains.

As Rachel lay there shivering she saw Toomi drowsily stand up. Without a word Toomi walked round the fire. She slipped in under Rachel's blanket, and put her arms round her. As the warmth of Toomi's body invaded her, Rachel thanked her. Toomi didn't answer. Soon Rachel fell asleep.

In the morning Toomi woke and sat up startled. 'Where am I?' she asked.

'You came over in the night when I was cold and could not sleep,' Rachel answered. 'Do you not remember?'

Toomi shook her head. 'I don't remember anything.'

The two gazed at each other. Then slowly, shyly, they both began to laugh.

Rachel had never had a brother or sister. Her relationship with Toomi, the silent communication, the shared awareness, the trust and support and laughter, were startling and new. For Toomi it was even stranger.

It was almost as if Mamkinga had returned to her in the form of a sister.

Toomi knew it could not be so and she remained just as achingly aware as she had ever been that Mamkinga existed somewhere remote and apart. Rachel was a separate being. Yet Rachel somehow mirrored and complemented Toomi as if she had always been a part of Toomi's life.

Toomi was bewildered. An incident one day summed up everything in the unknown hidden world they both seemed to have inhabited.

The young women took turns in riding the camel, one seated on the panniers while the other walked ahead holding the bridle, and then changing places. Towards the end of the fourth week of the journey Toomi was leading the camel through a thicket of acacia thorn when she felt a sharp pain on her thigh.

Involuntarily Toomi called out and glanced down. Surprised, she saw that nothing had touched her, but when she looked up she saw that Rachel was clutching her leg. A branch had whipped across the track and the thorns had torn her skin.

As Toomi helped her to bandage the wound, Rachel asked, 'What about you?'

'Me?'

'You cried out too. Were you not cut as well?'

Toomi frowned. Her own cry had slipped from her mind. Now she remembered. She thought for a moment. It hadn't occurred to her but it was exactly what had happened time and again when Mamkinga hurt himself.

'I was hurt only because you were hurt,' she said. 'The spirits made me feel your pain.'

Toomi smiled. Then she embraced Rachel.

'I have found a true sister,' she said simply. 'Welcome.'

Rachel put her arms round Toomi and they held each other wonderingly in silence.

— 59 —

When the slaves broke out of the *San Cristobal*'s holds, Gomez threw himself down the steps towards the deck, leaving the captain behind in the wheelhouse.

Gun in hand Gomez reached the deck at the same moment as the silhouette of Mamkinga appeared thirty feet away above the hatch. Gomez levelled his pistol and fired. Then he raced for the mainmast.

Mamkinga saw a flash and something scorched his armpit. The bullet had passed between his arm and his chest, cutting a trench in his side. Unaware of any pain, Mamkinga leapt in the direction of the shot. A capstan reared in front of him. He swerved round it and cannoned into a sailor racing in the opposite direction. As the sailor fell Mamkinga raised the rail like a club and crashed it down across the man's face.

Mamkinga ran on.

Behind him the slaves poured out from the hold and streamed across the deck. Those who were still unarmed picked up anything they could find, from barrels to marlin-spikes. Then they began to advance towards the middle of the ship. As they moved a volley of gunfire rang out from a group of sailors gathered by the mainmast. Three of the slaves screamed and fell. The rest hesitated. Then a clamour of shouts rose from the stern. The slaves from the rear hold were streaming on to the deck too.

The sailors turned their guns in the opposite direction. The first group of slaves ran forward again.

At their head Mamkinga dropped to his knees. He peered into the darkness. The space beneath the wheelhouse steps, where he'd seen the bullet's flash, was empty.

The man who'd fired at him had vanished, but a lantern was still burning in the wheelhouse above. Mamkinga put down the rail and crawled up the steps until he could see through the glass-panelled door.

There were two men inside.

Both were gazing pale-faced with fear at the stern deck. One was the helmsman. He had one hand on the wheel and a knife in the other. The second, Perez, was holding a pistol in either hand. Crouching outside, Mamkinga watched them for an instant. Then he dived at the wheelhouse door. He smashed it with his shoulder, and plunged through the splintered wood and shattered glass.

The two men whirled round. The helmsman let go of the wheel and jumped back. Perez lifted his guns.

'Cristos!' he whispered, terrified. 'The animal!'

His fingers snatched at the triggers. Mamkinga sprang at him. He knocked Perez's arms aside as the guns' hammers came down, and the two bullets went wide.

Perez reeled away.

Mamkinga leapt on him again. He seized the little man by his belt and his tunic, and swung him up into the air. Perez screamed and wriggled like a netted fish. Mamkinga carried him across the wheelhouse and hurled him through the window on the far side. Perez's body arched into the air, dropped on the far side of the shipboard rail, and vanished into the sea.

Mamkinga whirled on the helmsman. In terror the man jumped back from him. He leapt down on to the deck and sprinted away. Mamkinga stepped over to the open doorway and looked down.

What Mamkinga saw below chilled him.

The slaves had chosen the perfect time to attack. When they broke out, half the crew were up in the rigging setting the sails. Most of them were still aloft, trapped unarmed and helpless in the darkness. It left barely twenty sailors to try to crush the rising. Outnumbered ten to one and facing attacks from two directions, the crew might have been overwhelmed within minutes. But the sailors were well fed and had guns. The slaves were weakened by fever and starvation, and they were almost unarmed.

The mate had gathered a dozen sailors round the mainmast. Six of them were facing the bows, and six the stern. Whenever a slave tried to run forward, a shot cut through the night air and another silhouette crumpled on the deck. The deck was already littered with bodies. Each time a new one fell the others retreated further away from the deadly gunfire.

Staring down on the scene from the wheelhouse, Mamkinga knew the battle was almost lost.

Even in the darkness the crew had taken up an impregnable position. Dawn was only a few hours away. When the sun rose they would be able to slaughter any slave on deck at will. There would be nothing left for the rest to do except throw themselves overboard into the sea.

A wave of fury swept over Mamkinga. There had to be something. His eyes quartered the decks, the raised roofs of the centre-board cabins, the tangle of rigging. The rigging.

Mamkinga's gaze swung upward.

Running up from the gunwhale to the first yardarm on the mainmast was a rope ladder. It was used by the crew to reach the yard when they went up to set the sails. The ladder passed the wheelhouse door ten feet away. Mamkinga could just make out its cobweb of plaited hemp angling up above the deck. He crouched on the top step and waited until the next shot was fired below. Then in the confusion which followed he jumped blindly into the darkness.

His outstretched fingers scrabbled at a length of rope. He caught it and gripped tight. For a few seconds, swinging loose, he dangled by his arms above the deck. The smells of tar and cordite filled his nostrils. Then his foot found one of the ladder's loops. He anchored himself, pulled himself on top of the ladder, and scrambled up to the yard. There was no one on the traverse rope beneath the wooden arm.

Hauling himself hand over hand, Mamkinga moved along the rope until he reached the mast. He stepped on to the little platform that circled it, and looked down. Below him the two groups of sailors were facing in opposite directions. The mate was standing between them giving orders. He was directly beneath Mamkinga.

Mamkinga bent his knees. He leapt off the platform and plunged down like a leopard springing from a branch.

The distance to the deck was twenty feet. Mamkinga landed on Gomez's shoulders. The impact broke the mate's spine and killed him instantly. It also broke Mamkinga's fall. He tumbled across the deck, rolled away, and bounded up again.

'Now!' he bellowed. 'They are finished! Attack!'

Mamkinga bent and seized up an axe dropped by the ship's carpenter. Still shouting, he lifted the axe above his head and charged the sailors – slashing maniacally to left and right.

Mesmerized by the appearance of the giant who had dropped out of the darkness, and terrified by the whistling axe blade, the sailors fell back. They fired a few futile shots. Then they turned and ran. As they did they were engulfed by waves of their attackers.

Within minutes the battle was over. There were sailors above in the rigging, but they were impotent now. As soon as they came down they would be pitched overboard to the sharks who were already circling the ship's planks.

The command of the *San Cristobal* had changed hands.

When the sun finally lifted over the horizon Mamkinga made his way wearily towards the stern. He'd remained by the mainmast, axe in hand, ever since he'd plummeted down on Gomez and scattered the sailors who'd been inflicting the carnage. Mamkinga's daring had won them a victory that had seemed impossible.

Now Mamkinga wanted to greet the one person

whose courage had been even more important than his in achieving the victory. Aldoa.

He saw her as he approached the stern. She had gathered a group of women and children who had been penned in the rear hold. A slaver needed to carry ten times as much water as an ordinary merchantman. The *San Cristobal*'s supplies were stored on deck in large wooden casks. Aldoa had tapped one of the casks and was ladling out water to the dehydrated slaves.

'Aldoa!' Mamkinga called to her.

She looked up. Then she got to her feet and walked towards him, smiling shyly. Aldoa stopped in front of him.

'Pula!' she said. 'The ship is ours.'

'Pula!' Mamkinga replied. 'It is ours because of you.'

Mamkinga stretched out his hands to her.

Suddenly there was the shattering explosion of a gunshot fired very close. Aldoa lurched forward and fell against him. As Mamkinga gripped her he looked round, appalled.

A sailor was crouched in the rigging a few yards away. In his hand was a pistol. He must have hidden aloft and crept down when there were only women and children at the stern. One of the ship's lifeboats was nearby. The man had been trying to reach it when Mamkinga appeared. He'd fired at Mamkinga and hit Aldoa.

The sailor tried to fire again but the pistol jammed. He frantically scrambled upwards again. Mamkinga gently lowered Aldoa to the deck. His hands were covered with blood from the wound in her back. He got to his feet and snatched up the axe which was still with him.

Burning with rage and grief, Mamkinga ran to the foot of the rigging. The sailor was twenty feet above him. Mamkinga set off after him. Then Mamkinga stopped. He dropped back to the deck. The rigging was raised aloft on two running sheets. Mamkinga swung the axe savagely and cut both the sheets at their blocks. The rigging sagged and parted from the yard above.

For an instant the sailor hung screaming above the

water. Then, tangled in rope, he plunged into the sea where the sharks were crowding round the keel.

Mamkinga went back and knelt by Aldoa on the boards. He lifted her head and held it cradled in his arms.

'Pula!' he whispered, repeating the word again and again as tears streamed down his face. 'Pula, little Aldoa, pula!'

She tried to smile at him again. The effort and the pain were too much. Her face stiffened. A moment later her jaw went slack, her eyes closed, and her head fell against his chest.

Mamkinga was still whispering to her when he felt a tug on his arm. He shook the tears away and glanced up. The same grey-haired slave who'd taken the keys from him in the hold was bending down over him.

'The wind is rising and we are moving,' the man said. 'The horizons are empty and there is no shore. How do we guide the ship back to land?'

It took an instant for the question to sink in. Mamkinga shook his head helplessly.

'I do not know,' Mamkinga answered.

The *San Cristobal* tilted then as a gust filled its sails. The ship shuddered and drove forward, ploughing into the heaving sea.

Mamkinga lowered Aldoa to the deck and stood up. Through the spray he could see the foam-flecked ridges of the running waves. Mamkinga knew nothing about navigation. He had no more idea than any of the other slaves aboard where they were heading, how to change direction, or what course they must take to bring them back to Africa.

The *San Cristobal* had become a rogue elephant on the ocean – running blindly and wildly out of control before the rising wind.

'What's that?' Rachel asked.

At the camel's bridle Toomi paused. A cheer was rippling back towards them from the head of the caravan. As Toomi listened the waggons and animals in front began to bunch and come to a halt. Men started passing them at a run.

'I think we are there,' Toomi said.

Rachel slid off the camel's back and they hurried forward.

Toomi was right. After three months' travelling the caravan had finally reached Kano. Mohamet Asa, the caravan master, had halted on a low ridge above the city. Kano was spread out below them in the late afternoon light.

Toomi and Rachel narrowed their eyes against the setting sun, and stared down.

The city was still two miles away on the plain below. Oval in shape and almost fifteen miles at its greatest length, it was enclosed by a high wall of clay set at intervals with wooden gates clad in iron. Within the walls hundreds of sheets of stagnant water gleamed like beaten steel in the fading light. Many were no more than pools, others as large as small lakes. On the higher ground threading the pools and lakes were clusters of houses, barns and fortified buildings.

Innumerable plumes of smoke lifted towards the sky and even at that distance the air vibrated with the calls and bellows of huge herds of livestock. Kano was an awesome sight. Neither Toomi nor Rachel had ever seen anything like it.

In fact on that day in 1853 the city was one of the largest trading centres in Africa, with a population of over forty thousand people. It was, as it had been for centuries, the major caravan crossroads for the northern third of the great continent. Far to the south at the continent's tip the fertile lands of the Cape were being colonized by Europeans and blacks alike. But they were recent settlements and cut off from the north by the impenetrable forests, jungles and savannas of central Africa, still largely unknown and unexplored.

It was the north that had always mattered and Kano was far older than the settlements of the Cape.

It lay at the limits of Africa's penetration by Phoenician and Arab traders from the ancient Mediterranean world. From its marshy hub for two thousand years or more the radiating spokes of the caravan routes had carried goods of every description backwards and forwards across Africa. The caravans travelled north to the Mediterranean, west to the Atlantic, east as far as the Indian Ocean. On their return they were laden with spices, silk, pearls and gold.

Increasingly over the past hundred years the caravans also carried slaves.

The old man in Galla had advised Toomi wisely. Tracing Mamkinga after all this time was probably impossible. But for someone setting out to search for a child-slave from the kingdom of Malinda – the caravans passed through there and Gondar on their way to the Indian Ocean –Kano was the best place to start.

As Toomi and Rachel looked down from the ridge, Mohamet Asa rode over on his horse.

'You have never been here before?' he asked.

Toomi shook her head.

'I'm making camp at the Haraji well on the plain outside the walls,' Asa went on. 'If you're sensible, you'll camp there too. The stink from the drains and the water inside is unbearable. You've paid enough to camp with me until I leave. If you want to go on with me afterwards, we will have to negotiate again.'

Toomi nodded. 'We will camp with you.'

'I'm going into Kano tomorrow at first light. You may accompany me if you wish. Masu'r can show you round the market.'

Masu'r, a white-bearded but lean and energetic Berber, was Asa's clerk.

Toomi inclined her head. 'We are grateful.'

Asa studied the two for a moment. He rode off.

As he rode he thought about the two youths. There was something puzzling about them. Three months ago when they'd asked to join the caravan at the ford, Asa had been wary. They had no servants and only one ageing camel. Their trading stock, the bolts of cloth, was to his experienced eye saleable but nothing more. He'd been inclined to dismiss them as two youthful adventurers who'd stolen some of the plunder from the battle, and were trying to insinuate themselves into his protection until they could sell it.

When he saw the gold they offered him in payment, Asa changed his mind.

The gold was the finest quality – and he'd taken an exorbitant amount from them. The youths were clearly naïve, but their story suddenly rang true. They could only have acquired the gold from their father. Zanzibar merchants did indeed send their sons out on expeditions like the one behind the Galla army to give them experience of African trade – he'd done the same with his own son a few years before.

During the journey the two young men kept their own company. Asa found that puzzling too. It was usual for all the merchants in a caravan to eat together at night. Apart from a handful of occasions the two had eaten alone by their own fire throughout the three months.

As he dismounted, the Arab decided to tell his clerk, Masu'r, to keep an eye on them. It would be interesting to see what they got up to in Kano.

Toomi slept fitfully that night. Long before dawn she was up and moving restlessly round the little camp. By the time the sun rose she had woken Rachel, saddled and loaded the camel, and was waiting impatiently for the rest of the caravan to assemble. They moved off just as the light flooded over the plain.

They stopped briefly to unload and make camp at the Haraji well outside the walls. An hour later they entered Kano.

The original settlement had been built to one side of what long ago had been a conveniently placed marsh, whose slow-moving but clear streams provided the villagers with water. Then as the town grew it spread out to encircle the marsh. Waste began to drain into the water and soon the network of streams became a murky and foul-smelling swamp. The stench was made worse by the fumes rising from the endless stagnant pools Toomi and Rachel had noticed the evening before.

The pools had been created by the digging out of clay for the houses which stood between them. Now all of Kano's drinking water had to be brought in from springs outside the town. The first sounds that greeted Toomi and Rachel as they passed through the gates were the raucous cries of hundreds of women, hawking fresh water from leather containers along the streets.

Sticking close to Mahomet Asa and the white-bearded Masu'r they pressed through the throng until they came to the market.

The market was held daily on a neck of dry land between the old main marsh and a newer smaller swamp to its south. Gondar's metalware was famous throughout central Africa, and Asa's business that day was to dispose of a consignment he'd bought from the plundering Galla soldiers. Leaving Toomi and Rachel in the care of Masu'r, Asa disappeared in search of a wholesale merchant.

'Where would the young masters like me to take them?' Masu'r asked as Asa vanished.

'To the slave market,' Toomi said.

Masu'r bowed. 'We must cross to the other side.'

Masu'r set off through the crowd. Toomi and Rachel glanced round them as they walked behind him.

The market was divided into sections. Round the outside were pens containing livestock – sheep, goats, bullocks, horses and camels – and stores for bulky commodities like wood and bean straw. Then there were separate areas for the smaller goods. One group of stalls dealt in earthenware and indigo. Another in different kinds of bread. A third in fruit and vegetables such as yams, sweet potatoes, musk melons, lemons, mangoes, dates and cashew nuts.

All the transactions, the young women noticed, were carried out in cowrie shells which the stallholders counted with bewildering speed.

'Very fine currency,' Masu'r commented as he saw Rachel pause to watch a purchase being made. 'They are accepted everywhere and they are impossible to forge.'

Rachel remembered the hundreds of tiny shells which had helmeted her hair on the day of her baptismal feast. She had thought they were nothing more than traditional decoration. In Gondar coins and bars of salt were the currency. Now, she realized, the shells would have had another significance for any foreign guests at the banquet.

As they walked on Masu'r explained how the market was run.

'It is under the control of the sheik of Kano,' he said. 'The sheik rents out the stalls each month and fixes the price of everything on sale. He also collects a small commission on the transactions. Part of the rents and the commissions he keeps for himself. The rest goes to the governor –'

Masu'r pointed at the governor's palace to their left. It was like a separate village within the town. Above the wall that enclosed it Toomi and Rachel saw the dome of a mosque and several tall towers.

'The governor has final authority over everything but he leaves the market to the sheik,' Masu'r continued. 'It is run very strictly and fairly. Often people far away instruct a dylala, a broker, to buy goods for them. The goods are transported to wherever they were ordered. If the buyer finds they are unsatisfactory, he sends them back. The dylala returns them to the seller, and the seller must refund the entire purchase money. It can take months but the buyer is always protected.'

The slave market was at the far end of the main market.

It consisted of two long sheds, one for males and the other for females. Following Masu'r, the girls entered the first shed where men and boys were on sale.

The slaves were seated in rows with their owners, or one of the owner's trusted slaves, squatting behind them. All of them had been scrubbed and dressed in their owners' finest clothes to show them off to their best advantage. Prospective purchasers were strolling up and down. From time to time one would stop and examine a slave closely, peering at his teeth, his tongue and his eyes, and then making him cough to check whether he had a rupture.

Each time it happened, Toomi shivered. The examinations brought back with chilling vividness the occasion when she and Mamkinga had undergone the same humiliating experience.

'The buyers have three days,' Masu'r said. 'Within that time any slave can be brought back and his price refunded. After three days the buyer must keep him and send back the owner's clothes. But I'm sure you know that.'

Toomi swallowed and nodded.

'Is there anything else you wish to see?' Masu'r asked after they had toured the women's shed.

'I wish to talk to the manager of the slave market,' Toomi answered.

'That is simple,' Masu'r said. 'He is one of the sheik's sub-agents. We know him well. Come!'

He led Toomi and Rachel to a small covered enclosure between the two sheds. Another white-bearded Arab was seated behind a table with a clerk at his shoulder. The two men greeted each other. Then Masu'r introduced his companions.

'These two young men have travelled with us,' he said.

'They are the sons of a great Zanzibar merchant. Sheik Mohamet Asa commends them to you.'

The two greeted the white-bearded Arab. Then Toomi turned to Masu'r.

'Thank you,' she said. 'For the moment we have no further need of your services.'

Masu'r bowed and left the enclosure.

'How may I help you?' the slave-market manager asked.

Toomi took a deep breath.

'Ten years ago two Malindan child-slaves, a boy and a girl, were stolen by the Oye-Eboe from our father while he was travelling,' she said. 'He recovered the girl, but the boy is still missing. Our father paid much for him and he is still very angry. He is offering a handsome reward to anyone who helps us trace him.'

'Ten years!' the Arab wrinkled his face. 'That is a long time.'

Toomi nodded. 'The Oye-Eboe sold the boy in a village market far to the east. He was bought by a woman. She had a slave and a child of the boy's age with her. That is all we know.'

The Arab thought.

'It is unusual for a woman to buy slaves,' he said after a moment, 'that is men's business. If the woman was alone she was almost certainly a widow. Maybe the child with her was her son. Perhaps she wanted your father's slave as a companion for him. I have known that happen often.'

It was Toomi's turn to think. The Arab's suggestion was convincing. Toomi remembered the fat woman dragging the boy forward, and the boy nodding sulkily as he gazed up at Mamkinga.

'I ask guidance from the wisdom of your white hairs,' Toomi said. 'The boy-slave will be a man now. So will the widow's son. If what you say is so, what might have happened to the slave then?'

The Arab laughed. 'It is not my wisdom you need, but the Prophet's himself.' He paused. 'Maybe the woman kept him to work in her house. Maybe she had no further use for him and sold him. If she sold him, perhaps it was to one of the caravans.'

Toomi frowned.

She was certain Mamkinga hadn't remained in one place all the years they'd been parted. There had been long periods when her silent communication with him, her instincts about what was happening to him, had faltered and almost dried up. Then Toomi felt Mamkinga was at least safe. But for months now the anxieties, the unexplained wakings at night and the sudden stabs of pain, had troubled her again.

'The caravans pass through Kano,' Toomi said eventually. 'If the woman did sell him, then surely it is likely he was sold again here?'

'Not every caravan trades at Kano,' the Arab replied. 'With slaves many traders go direct to the coast. Whether that was so with this one, I know no more than you. However I am obliged to keep records of every sale so the sheik may take his commission. We shall see — '

He spoke to the clerk. The clerk opened a ledger and began combing through it. A few minutes later he murmured something to the Arab.

The Arab lifted his hands and spread them regretfully. 'No Malindan slave has been sold here for years,' he said.

Then as he saw a look of despair cross Toomi's face he added, 'I can think of only one other possibility. There are private traders in Kano who do not use the market. Maybe one of them will know something. They gather at the teashops every morning. Come back tomorrow and try them.'

He stood up and bowed. Toomi thanked him. With heavy hearts the two girls made their way back to the camp beside the well.

— 61 —

For the next two weeks Toomi rose in the darkness and walked into Kano so that she was at the slave market before it opened.

Every morning she watched the slaves being brought in by their owners and set out on display. Then she settled down to wait.

The Arab traders began to arrive at the start of business. They would inspect what was on offer that day, make their purchases, and retire to one of the nearby teahouses. There, over tall glasses filled with steaming water, sweetened with cane sugar and flavoured with sprigs of fresh mint, they would discuss their business. They gossiped, argued, and haggled, often re-selling their acquisitions or exchanging them for something that suited them better.

Toomi quickly learnt the morning's routine.

As soon as the traders drifted off, she followed them. When they were seated in the teahouse, she toured the low tables. Her story was the same as she told the slave-market manager. A young Malindan slave had been stolen from her father ten years before. Her father was offering a large reward for his recovery.

Could any of the traders help her?

None of them could. Over the two weeks Toomi spoke to about forty. The composition of the gathering in the teahouses changed daily as some merchants left Kano with their caravans and others, arriving in the town, took their place. But the answers were always the same.

Malinda was distant and Malindan slaves were rare. None of the traders had ever bought one.

Increasingly dispirited as the days went fruitlessly by, Toomi returned exhausted each evening to the camp. She would sit slumped by the fire as Rachel prepared their supper and tried to comfort her. Then she would fall asleep for a few hours before rising and setting off again.

Only one incident interrupted the monotony.

Every day one or more specially fattened bulls were brought into the market to be slaughtered. Their horns were dyed red with henna and drummers accompanied them through the crowds to advertise their arrival. As soon as they were dead the bulls were butchered and the meat sold. Most of the meat went to private buyers, but a dozen women, who ran kebab stalls near the slaughter area, bought part of the carcasses.

The women sliced the beef into thin fillets. They grilled the fillets on wooden skewers over open fires, and sold them to market-goers with horn mugs of ground-gussub water. On her third morning in Kano Toomi wandered back into the main market and strolled through the kebab stalls. As she passed one of them her attention was distracted by the arrival of a caravan.

Peering through the crowd to see if it was led by a slave trader, she stumbled against the grill and knocked a row of sizzling skewers into the coals.

Without thinking Toomi apologized in Malindan. 'Ekvama,' she said, 'ekvama vale.'

Toomi knelt and began to help the stall-owner to put the skewers back on the grill.

The woman, who was kneeling too, stared at her. 'You speak Malindan?'

Toomi nodded. 'My father trades there. I grew up in Malinda,' she answered, confused.

'Welcome, young man, welcome.' The woman beamed at her. 'It is far too long since I have heard my native tongue.'

She waved away Toomi's further apologies. 'Sit down. You are my guest.'

The woman had grey hair and a kindly, deeply wrinkled face. She produced a little stool.

443

Toomi sat down opposite her, and the woman began to talk.

Her name was Ayeshi and she came from a village near Malinda's western border. Thirty years before Ayeshi had been captured as a child in an Arab-led slave raid and brought to Kano, where she was sold to a rich farmer with lands to the north of the town. One of the farmer's herders, a free man, had fallen in love with her and asked the farmer's permission to marry her. The farmer agreed and as a wedding present he gave Ayeshi her freedom.

Ten years later Ayeshi's husband was killed by a crocodile as he was watering the herd in the river. Ayeshi left the farm and moved with their only child, a son, into Kano. She bought a small house in the town with her husband's savings and set up in business as a kebab-seller.

Ayeshi had worked in the market ever since.

'Kano is my home now,' she finished. 'But always I have promised myself that one day I would return to visit Malinda again. Lately there are stories about terrible things that have happened there. The caravans report the Galla have conquered the country, and Gondar too. Is it true?'

She looked at Toomi anxiously. Toomi nodded. 'All the three kingdoms are under the rule of King Culembra and the Acab Saat.'

Ayeshi's eyes filled with tears. 'It is so long ago but I remember so much. Now I fear I will never see Malinda again.'

She sat for a moment in silence, her face creased with pain. Then she brushed away the tears and shook her head.

'I should not complain,' she said. 'I have a good life. I have my son, my house and my business. It is enough for anyone.'

At that moment there was a rolling drum-beat on the other side of the market. A bull was about to be slaughtered. Ayeshi stood up.

'I must collect my order,' she said. 'Soon my customers

will be here. It was good to talk in my own tongue. Come back whenever you wish and let us talk some more. I treat you as my own countryman and you will always be my guest.'

Ayeshi smiled and walked stiffly away.

From then on Toomi visited Ayeshi's stall every day before trudging back to camp. Once she helped Ayeshi to carry the grill back to the old woman's house, and stayed to eat a meal with her. It was one of the few enjoyable experiences of her time in Kano.

As the two weeks drew to an end Toomi's mood darkened.

She'd known the enormity of her task from the beginning, but when they reached Kano she'd been filled with excitement and optimism. Walking through the town gates in the sunlight next day, her optimism had turned to confidence. Somewhere in Kano, Toomi had been sure, she would pick up Mamkinga's trail.

She was wrong. Aside from the slave traders, no one else in Kano had ever come across a Malindan who remotely came close to fitting Mamkinga's circumstances. Toomi took to touring the town and questioning passers-by – other merchants, local citizens, even slaves themselves. Finally she went to the governor's palace. After hours of waiting she gained an audience with the governor's secretary. His answer was the same.

'I cannot help you,' the secretary said. 'I have served His Excellency for nine years. I have no knowledge in all that time of any Malindans being sold in the market. I can only suggest you try the other great markets in Timbuck-toom and Garoua.'

Sick at heart, Toomi walked back to camp and dropped to the ground beside the fire. She had been there only a few minutes when Asa's clerk, Masu'r, appeared.

Masu'r bowed. 'My master leaves tomorrow for Garoua,' he said. 'He wishes to know if you will be travelling with the caravan.'

Garoua.

The name of the second great central African market

town had come up again and again since their arrival. It was not as large as the third, Timbucktoom, but it was on one of the routes to the Atlantic coast, and so a place much favoured by the slave traders.

Toomi thought for a moment. Kano had failed her. Toomi knew she had to go on and try Garoua. It would mean leaving Rachel – she couldn't ask Rachel to accompany her any further – and somehow finding a way of paying Asa. Perhaps she could work for the caravan master. Toomi didn't know. All she knew was that she had no choice.

She turned to tell Rachel. Before she could open her mouth, Rachel answered Masu'r.

'Yes,' Rachel said. 'My brother and I will travel with you. We will come over to your master's tent shortly to discuss terms for the journey.'

Masu'r inclined his head and left.

Rachel turned to Toomi. Still without giving Toomi a chance to speak, Rachel continued.

'Of course we go on,' she said. 'And if we have to travel further from there, even if we have to go to Timbucktoom, we shall do it.'

Toomi tried to protest. 'Garoua is far,' she said. 'The journey will take us another two months. We will be moving even further from Gondar. And we will need more of your gold.'

Toomi buried her head in her hands.

Alone, Toomi would have faced any journey, taken on any burden, paid any money. She was not alone. She was with Rachel. She could not allow Rachel to come with her. Yet without Rachel, as she thought about it now, she was helpless.

Torn and miserable, Toomi lowered her head to her knees. She sat hunched in silence by the flames. Then she felt an arm round her shoulder. She looked up. Rachel was kneeling beside her.

'Am I not your sister?' Rachel asked quietly.

She was smiling. Toomi tried to smile back.

'Yes,' Toomi began, 'but there is a limit to what any sister can ask of another – '

Rachel cut her off. 'There is no limit. You saved my life. My life is yours now. Your brother is my brother. All I have is ours between us.'

Toomi put her arms round Rachel. Tears filled Toomi's eyes and ran down her cheeks.

An hour later the two girls crossed the campsite and were ushered by Masu'r into Asa's tent. The merchant was sitting on a cushion smoking from a rosewater-filled pipe. He stood up and greeted them warmly.

'Masu'r tells me you wish to travel to Garoua,' he said. 'I am glad. May Allah give us all a safe and swift journey. Be seated.'

'How much will it cost us?' Rachel asked several minutes later after they had exchanged the traditional courtesies.

The Arab frowned. He clicked his teeth worriedly and shook his head.

'Garoua as you know is many miles from Kano,' he answered. 'The country we cross is hard and barren. Many areas are infested by bandits. I have had to hire double guards, buy extra camels, lay in special stores – '

He spread his hands out. 'It is a sorely expensive business. But for you two, because you are young and I know I would have respect for your father, I will charge only thirty shells weight of gold.'

Asa beamed at them benignly.

'We will give you eighteen – and you will be well paid,' Rachel replied.

Rachel stared at him levelly.

Since they reached Kano she had learned a great deal. While Toomi had haunted the slave market and the teahouses, Rachel had explored the town – talking, questioning, but above all listening. Within the first few days she had discovered that Asa had overcharged them outrageously for the journey from Gondar. She had also established the current price for the protection of a caravan to Garoua.

Asa opened his mouth to protest and bargain. Something in Rachel's face stopped him. He looked at her and his eyes dropped. Asa muttered to himself, then he conceded.

'Out of friendship, then, and for the love of Allah I will agree,' he said. 'You do mean gold, of course?'

'Of course,' Rachel answered.

For gold, Rachel knew, she could have demanded a lower price still. The journey was too important to Toomi to risk anything by haggling.

Rachel reached into the pouch at her waist. As soon as she had learned the relative values of the various trading currencies in Kano and discovered that gold was by far the strongest, Rachel had taken her store of treasure to an official weighing officer. He had put every piece in the scales and, for a small charge, had told her its weight and its value.

She handed Asa one of the rings she had brought with her from Gondar. The weighing officer had weighed it at the equivalent of eighteen cowrie shells filled with gold dust.

The Arab held the ring up and examined it in the light of a taper. He lifted it to his mouth to test its texture with his tongue. Finally he placed it in his own balance and weighed it for himself.

Asa smiled.

'May Allah give us all a safe journey,' he said again. 'We leave at midday.'

'For the last time,' Toomi said. 'There's been a new caravan every day. Maybe another came in during the night.'

Rachel was doubtful. It was almost dawn and neither of the girls had been able to sleep.

'Are you sure you can get back in time?'

Toomi nodded. 'It is only an hour each way. We don't leave until mid morning. I'll be back long before then.'

'What happens if you get delayed? Asa won't wait.'

'I won't be delayed,' Toomi said. 'I'll just check the slave market. If there's no one new I'll return immediately –'

She paused. 'Garoua's two months away. Think what it would be like if we left Kano and missed the one person who did know something.'

Rachel frowned.

Toomi was right, of course. A trip to the market and back from the camp would only take a few hours. Over the past two weeks Rachel had grown used to Toomi setting off on her own each morning. There had been no reason for Rachel to accompany her and there was none now.

Unaccountably Rachel was fearful. She stared at Toomi's face, lit by the still-glowing coals of the fire. Then she made up her mind.

'I am coming with you,' she said.

'There's no purpose,' Toomi objected. 'There's nothing you can do that I can't do on my own. You'd be much better here getting Amulet ready for the journey. Why do you want to come too?'

'I don't know, but I am,' Rachel said stubbornly.

Toomi looked across at her. Then she shook her head and smiled. Toomi had long since recognized that among the many characteristics they shared was a streak of obduracy.

'Very well, my sister,' Toomi said. 'Let us go.'

The two dressed. Leaving Amulet – as they had named the camel – tethered, they set off towards the town.

Halfway there they were passed by a group of horsemen riding in the opposite direction. Like the young women the men were dressed in Arab robes. As they crossed, the men raised their arms in greeting. Toomi and Rachel returned the salute.

Then they walked on. The men had been riding fast. For several minutes afterwards the young women coughed in the swirling dust left behind by their horses' hoofs.

'Yes,' Asa said. 'I recognize the marks.'

'You are sure?' the man demanded.

Mahomet Asa held the medallion up to the torch and examined the marks stamped in the gold again.

There were five men standing before him. Asa had just finished dressing for the day when he heard the clatter of their arrival on horseback outside, and voices asking to be taken to the caravan master. Moments later Masu'r had shown them into the tent.

Their leader, the man who had just spoken, had introduced them as agents of the deputy of Gondar, the high priest Acab Saat. Gold had been stolen from the Gondar treasury, the man explained, by a young woman-servant at the palace. It was thought the young woman might have used some of the gold to buy protection from a caravan heading west after the battle.

They had been sent to trace her. They had ridden to Kano and obtained the governor's permission to visit all the caravans which had arrived in the city since Gondar fell. They were looking for gold that might have come from the stolen treasure.

'The gold itself is of no importance,' the man went on. 'If any has been given you, you will have taken it in good faith. You are welcome to keep it. But the Acab Saat is determined to capture and punish the thief. He has offered a reward of one thousand shells of gold to the person who brings the young woman to his justice.'

Asa's eyes flickered. One thousand shells of gold was a fortune.

'Naturally I have no reason to disbelieve the honoured Acab Saat,' he said. 'But is there evidence of the reward?'

The man pulled a roll of sheepskin parchment from his waist pouch.

Asa examined it. Below the royal seal of Gondar was inscribed the promise that one thousand shells of gold would be paid to whoever secured the capture of the thief.

Asa reached into his own money belt.

'I believe this is part of the theft,' he said, producing the ring Rachel had given him. 'It bears the same marks.'

The man seized it.

'Where did you get it?' he demanded after only an instant.

'Here in my camp,' Asa replied. 'It was given only last night in payment for passage with my caravan to Garoua –'

The Arab paused. 'But it was not given by a young woman. It was given by two youths.'

'Youths?' The man looked surprised. 'What youths?'

'The young men of my own race,' Asa answered. 'They asked to join my caravan not far west of Gondar. They said their father was a Zanzibar merchant and they had been following the Galla battle column. They told me they were travelling to Kano to find their father's agent. I noticed something strange about them from the start. Since we got here I have had them observed. One of them has visited the slave market often, but they have made no inquiries about the agent.'

'Where are they now?' the leader of the Acab Saat's agents demanded.

'In their tent, I assume,' Asa said. He paused. 'If I take you to them and they lead you to the young woman, the reward is still mine?'

'You have my word on behalf of the Acab Saat,' the man said.

Asa nodded.

With the five men pressing behind him he led the way across the campsite to Toomi's and Rachel's tent. The tent flaps were pulled back, their camel was tethered, and the fire was burning, but the two had vanished.

As Asa glanced round, puzzled, the leader of the men swore.

'Where have they gone?' he shouted.

Asa thought for a moment.

'Each day one of them has gone into Kano. Maybe they have made a last visit to get supplies before we leave. They will be back. They have paid for the journey and left everything – '

The man was no longer listening. He remembered the two Arab youths he had seen heading for the city barely an hour before.

'Kano!' the man bellowed at his companions as he ran for the horses.

Toomi walked out of the slave market shaking her head disconsolately.

There was no one new inside or in the teahouses beside it – only the group of traders she had questioned the day before. She rejoined Rachel in the square. It was a clear bright morning and the sky above the town was a dazzling blue. For once the night breeze had swept away the stench of Kano's drains and the air was fresh.

'Never mind,' Rachel said as she took Toomi comfortingly by the hand. 'We'll buy some spice for the journey, have a kebab as soon as the stalls open, and get back to camp. And when we reach Garoua we'll find him, I promise you.'

Side by side they set off down the street.

A moment later they heard the drum of cantering hoofs

behind them. They both checked in mid stride. In spite of its clamour and bustle Kano was a tranquil slow-moving town, which went about its business to rhythms that Toomi and Rachel were now well used to.

The urgency in the drumming hoofbeats was new and alien.

The girls turned. Five horsemen were advancing swiftly along the middle of the street. All were wearing Arab robes and their leader's face was switching from side to side as he scanned the passers-by. Silhouetted against the climbing sun, they looked dark and menacing.

'Run!' Rachel called suddenly.

Her fingers tightened over Toomi's and she dragged Toomi forward.

Rachel had no idea why she reacted as she did. The sense of unease and foreboding, of an unknown threat to them both, had been with her ever since Toomi had proposed the final visit to Kano. Now the threat had suddenly and chillingly materialized.

She didn't know who the horsemen were or what they were searching for — but with utter certainty she knew it was one of them.

An instant afterwards, as Toomi stumbled bewildered alongside her, Rachel was proved right. There was a shout behind them. The cantering horses were spurred into a gallop, and the men raced forward.

The street ended in a junction. As the girls reached it Rachel glanced left and right. There seemed to be no difference. In both directions other streets stretched away. An hour later the streets would have been thronged and almost impassable to the horsemen. Now it was still too early. The men could gallop down the empty spaces of baked mud as fast as if they had been in the open country.

At random Rachel plunged to the left.

For a brief instant the sound of the hoofs was dulled by the intervening houses. Then the horsemen reached the junction too. The noise grew louder and closer again. Gasping and straining, their robes tugging awkwardly at their ankles, Toomi and Rachel raced on. Gaining on them with every stride, the men started to shout. Rachel turned her head and looked back. The leader had drawn his sword.

The blade glittered in the early sunlight and dagger points of light leapt from the hands of his companions.

'Here!'

Toomi had suddenly recognized their surroundings. She hurled herself ahead and dragged Rachel into an alley that ran away to their left. Pulling Rachel after her, Toomi pressed on.

The alley was narrow and shaded from the sun. Off it on either side ran other alleys, all of them equally dark and winding tortuously down towards the marsh. On the street the galloping horsemen clattered to a halt. They turned, burst into the alley, and began to thread their way in single file down the zig-zagging lane in pursuit.

Toomi glanced left and right, frantically searching for the door. It was painted a faded blue, she remembered that, and there had been a terracotta pot of marsh violets outside.

'This one!'

Spotting the flowers and the sun-bleached paint, she stopped and hammered furiously on the wooden panel.

There was an agonizing pause. Across the roofs, growing closer and closer all the time, came the calls of the horsemen. Then Toomi heard steps inside. The door opened and Ayeshi's face appeared.

'Pula!' Toomi said.

Without giving the old woman a chance to reply she pushed her way inside, dragged Rachel in behind her and kicked the door shut. Then she raised her finger to her lips.

In the silence the three heard the men ride down the alley and head on, still shouting angrily, towards the marsh. As the sounds faded Toomi turned round. She lifted her hand and placed it in greeting on Ayeshi's forehead.

'I am Toomi, daughter of the Embrenche of Malinda,'

she said. 'As your countrywomen, my sister and I ask you for sanctuary.'

Without waiting for the astounded Ayeshi to reply, Toomi unbuttoned her robe and let it fall to the ground. Beside her Rachel did the same. The robes slipped down and the two girls stood naked in the darkness of the hall.

The old woman gazed at them. Then she lifted her hands and held them out.

'You are my daughters,' she said quietly. 'My home is your home. My family is your family. All I have is yours.'

Ayeshi stepped forward and folded them in her arms.

— 63 —

Jamie stared out across the sea. The day was hot and humid, and the ship rocked gently beneath him as it cut swiftly through the light swell.

The *Forerunner* had made good time.

The Bay of Biscay had been free of storms and the packet slipped quickly past Cape St Vincent. She left the Canary Islands behind her, made the long swing south down the African coast, and then headed east towards the Gulf of Guinea. She had entered the gulf two days ago. Now she was only the same time from her destination of Lagos.

Jamie was on the bridge with Captain Culglass. They were, Culglass had told him, hugging the coast. Cloud and a strong haze had kept the shore hidden so far but if the haze thinned, Culglass went on, Jamie would get his first glimpse of Africa that morning. Jamie strained his eyes, scanning the horizon to the north.

It was Jamie who spotted the other ship first.

'What's that?' he asked.

Culglass raised his eyeglass and trained it in the direction where Jamie was pointing.

'Well, it's a craft sure as hell,' Culglass said. 'But she's flapping like my old mother's washing line. I fancy there's something very much amiss with her.'

Culglass wiped the lens on his sleeve and lifted the eyeglass again.

'A slaver,' he grunted after a moment. 'No doubt about it. Look at the water casks, dozens of them all over the deck. That's what our naval frigates look out for. Always gives a slaver away, however she's trying to hide herself. Here — '

He handed Jamie the eyeglass as the other boat came closer. 'You've got sharper eyes than mine. See if you can make out the name.'

Jamie took the glass and peered through it across the intervening stretch of sea.

The ship was lurching and wallowing aimlessly. Occasionally a current of air would fill one of the sails and the bows would be tugged round. Then the breeze would drop and the boat would swing back to lie with the run of the waves. He could see the ranks of water casks on the main deck, but there didn't seem to be any sign of life on board.

He trained the glass on the stern and spelt out the letters of the ship's name, painted in black and gold across the transom.

'The *San Cristobal*,' Culglass said. 'Portuguese and probably out of Rio. It'll be a cargo for the Brazilian sugar plantations.'

'What happened?' Jamie asked. 'I can't see anyone. It just seems to be drifting.'

'Maybe the whole crew's gone down with the fever,' Culglass answered. 'That happens often enough on sailings out of the Bight. If it's not that, I'd guess the slaves have broken out. They sometimes take over a ship, but they don't know a damn how to handle it. They just drift until they beach or everyone dies.'

He took the glass back from Jamie.

'We'll go closer and find out,' Culglass added, scanning the *San Cristobal* again.

Ten minutes later the two ships were only fifty yards apart. Until then what there was of the breeze had been behind the *Forerunner*. As Culglass signalled for the engines to be reversed to bring the packet to a halt, the wind changed and blew back in their faces. Instantly a poisonous stench that seemed to blend the fumes from charnel house, abattoir and sewer billowed over their faces.

Choking, Jamie covered his mouth and nostrils with his hands.

'What is it?' he gasped.

'Like I said, it's a slaver,' Culglass answered grimly, searching the San Cristobal's deck with the glass. 'That's the way they stink. She seems to have been taken over by the shipment. There's no white men around, but there's dead or dying niggers lying all over. There's nothing we can do. We'll go on.'

He snapped the glass shut and pulled the engine-room instruction lever to forward. The screws throbbed and the Forerunner began to pull away. Jamie watched in bewilderment.

'Ye can't leave them like that, man,' he protested.

'I certainly can,' Culglass said curtly. 'That ship's festering with disease. Its crew's been butchered. Most of the slaves are dead, the rest soon will be. I've got a healthy boat here, and I'm going to keep it that way. If I touch the San Cristobal I put everyone at risk. And for what – ?'

He glared at Jamie. 'I don't like slavery any more, no doubt, than you do, Mr Oran. But I'm not going to hazard the Forerunner for a bunch of dying Africans.'

The Forerunner was just passing the San Cristobal. Suddenly there was movement on the slaver's deck. A negro woman with a baby at her breast dragged herself to her feet. She waved feebly at them, and held out the tiny child in her arms. Another child, an emaciated little girl, stumbled towards her and clung sobbing to her knees. The two ships were so close that Jamie could see the sunken cheeks and weary listless eyes of all three.

An image of his grandmother and his two sisters rose from the depths of Jamie's memory. Somehow he was seeing them in the moments before they died – in the moments when, if he had been older and stronger, he might have saved them.

'For the Lord's sake!' Jamie burst out. 'We can't go on. It's inhuman. There must be something we can do.'

Culglass shrugged, his mouth set in a tight line.

'How far from shore are we?' Jamie insisted.

'Maybe forty-eight hours.'

458

'That's nothing. If we got a line on her, we could tow her in. At least they'd have a chance on land.'

Culglass shook his head stubbornly. 'I'm not putting any of my men on that ship.'

'You won't have to risk your men,' Jamie said. 'I'll go myself with my friends.'

Culglass's head snapped round in astonishment. 'You? Don't you understand what it's like on board? That ship's a deathtrap!'

Jamie's face was implacable. He couldn't rid his mind of old Mrs Oran with Jeannie and Morag in her arms, lying in the shallow cellar beneath the burnt-out croft.

'I've known enough folk die needlessly,' Jamie said. 'I'm no leaving them to do the same.'

Culglass stared at him. Confronted with Jamie's relentless gaze, he shrugged again and turned away.

'There'll need to be more than one of you to belay a line that's going to hold,' he said. 'And once you're there, you stay. I'm not having anyone who's boarded that fever-bed back on the *Forerunner*.'

'There'll be three of us,' Jamie said. 'We'll remain on the ship until we reach shore. Ye can lower us any supplies we need to a dinghy. Stop the engines and I'll get the others.'

Without giving Culglass a chance to reply, Jamie ran out of the wheelhouse. As he climbed down to the deck he heard the sound of the engines change. The ship began to slow.

Farquarson and Wolf were clustered with the other passengers against the starboard rail. Everyone was gazing at the *San Cristobal*. Farquarson was holding a scented silk handkerchief to his face. As Jamie approached he could hear Wolf haranguing the others about slavery being the inevitable consequence of capitalism.

Jamie interrupted him. He drew both Wolf and Farquarson back, and explained what he was going to do.

'You're mad, Jamie – ' Farquarson said.

He wrinkled his nose and coughed into his handkerchief as the smell from the slaver reached them again.

'I wouldn't board that hulk if it was carrying all the virgins from the harems of every sultanate in Araby. It's a floating coffin.'

Wolf nodded in agreement. 'Equality in life does not presuppose equality in death. Be sensible, Jamie,' he pleaded. 'The pox lies on that boat like a whore's nightshift. Once you're inside it there's no way out. We can't help those poor souls.'

'Maybe not – '

Jamie looked at them levelly. 'But how would ye feel if ye changed places with them – if ye were on board and dying, and they sailed on?'

He paused. 'Your minds are your own to fix. But if ye wish to see me again, it's yonder you'll find me.'

There was silence for a moment. Farquarson spat into his handkerchief again and shook his head despairingly.

'Mad,' he said. 'Mad as a dormouse in a witch's drawers.'

Wolf glanced across at the drifting slaver and back at Jamie. He threw back his head and laughed, his long grey hair lifting in the breeze and his pale yellow eyes suddenly alight with challenge.

'You're more contagious than the fever, Jamie,' Wolf said. 'We're all mad – so let the insanity take its natural course.'

Jamie smiled.

64

Fifteen minutes later Jamie, Farquarson and Wolf were rocking in a dinghy beneath the *Forerunner*'s stern.

At Culglass's order a heavy rope had been fastened to the stern stanchion. As the dinghy pulled away with Farquarson and Wolf manning the oars, Jamie guided the rope through his hands while a sailor on deck paid it out to him.

They reached the *San Cristobal* and Jamie gazed upwards as the dinghy bumped against the sheer sides of the slaver. For a moment he couldn't see any way of boarding the ship. Then he noticed a tangle of rigging hanging down into the water by the stern. They rowed round until they reached it. Jamie gripped the rope and shinned upwards. The breeze had been behind him until then, but as he rolled over the rail on to the slaver's deck it dropped and the fearful stench welled into his nostrils again.

Jamie shuddered and glanced round.

The woman he'd seen from the *Forerunner* tottered towards him. She was holding the baby to her shrivelled breast. With a shock Jamie realized that the tiny creature was dead. The other child appeared. She was so thin she looked like a bundle of twigs wrapped in skin. She put her hand in Jamie's and pointed to her mouth.

Jamie reached into his pocket for a biscuit and gave it to the child. Then he hoisted her on to his shoulders. Farquarson and Wolf climbed up over the side with the tow rope.

'Get it fastened at the bows,' Jamie said. 'I'm going to look round.'

He set off with the little girl still on his shoulders.

There were bodies everywhere. Many, curled on their sides or lying splayed motionless on their backs, appeared to be dead. Others lifted their heads as he passed. They looked at him despairingly and slumped back on the boards. Jamie lifted the lid of a water cask and glanced inside. The cask was still half full, but supplies of food must have been exhausted long since. The few survivors were sliding inexorably towards death from starvation.

'Effendi!'

The child was tugging at his hair and pointing. Jamie walked across the deck towards a shadowed space beneath the steps to the wheelhouse.

'Effendi!' the child said again.

Effendi. Leader. It was one of the words in common use throughout central Africa, which Mrs Livingstone had taught him as he lay in bed in the Blantyre room. Jamie put the child down.

He knelt and peered in under the steps.

A man was lying on a straw mat in the shade. About the same age as Jamie, he was tall, broad-shouldered, and powerfully built, although his body had wasted away from sickness and lack of food until the bones protruded like knobbed sticks from beneath his skin. His eyes were open and he was staring upwards. For several moments he paid no attention as Jamie knelt beside him.

Then the man moved his head and looked at Jamie. His eyes, deep-set in his emaciated face, were steadfast and defiant. He was on the point of dying, Jamie realized, and yet, had they been slavers, he would somehow have raised himself from the mat and tried to fight them off.

The little girl touched Jamie's arm. 'Effendi Mamkinga,' she said.

The courage and dignity in the man's face were dauntless. Involuntarily Jamie reached out and took the man's wrist.

'We will take you back to land,' Jamie said.

'You are British?' the man asked.

Jamie started. To his astonishment the man had spoken in English.

'Yes,' he said. 'You speak my tongue?'

The man gave an almost imperceptible nod. 'One of your people taught me. He said you do not take slaves.'

'That is true. We are trying to stop slavery everywhere.'

'Good. I will trust you then.'

His head rolled away and he gazed upwards again.

Jamie stood up and went back into the sunlight. Farquarson and Wolf had already made a tour of the ship. They were standing by the mainmast with handkerchiefs pressed against their nostrils, trying to shut out the smell.

'Food,' Farquarson said, coughing. 'That's what they need. There's water in plenty but the food appears to have run out days ago. There are corpses all over the place.'

'The whole ship needs a damn great clean-up,' Wolf added. 'If we can dump the bodies, sluice it down, and get something into the bellies of those who are still making any sense, we may be able to save a few yet.'

Jamie thought for a moment. The *Forerunner* was still idling fifty yards away with the tow rope floating on the waves between the two ships.

'Is the tow rope safely fixed?' he asked.

'We've got it treble knotted,' Farquarson answered. 'It'll take a storm to shift that.'

'Then we'll run the dinghy back, and collect some stores. As soon as we're on board again, Culglass can get going.'

They rowed back to the *Forerunner*. Jamie shouted up a list of what they needed and the supplies were lowered down. Half an hour after they first boarded her the three were back on the *San Cristobal*. Jamie signalled across to Culglass. The *Forerunner*'s propeller churned, and the two ships began to move in procession towards the east.

When they set off it was late afternoon. It was a further ten hours before the three Europeans on the slaver were able to rest.

As the *San Cristobal* got under way, Jamie called the other two together and assigned them their tasks. Wolf was in charge of cleaning up the ship, disposing of the dead slaves, and getting some order into the stinking chaos that littered the decks. Farquarson was to clear out the holds, assemble the living – mainly women and children – quarter them away from the sun, and distribute food to them. Jamie himself would try to get the billowing sails under control and stabilize the ship.

The three set to work.

Wolf encountered the first problem. As he tugged a dead slave across the deck and prepared to heave his body over the rail, two gaunt women threw themselves on him and clawed him frenziedly away from the corpse. Staggering back, blood oozing from his face, he beat them away and shouted for Jamie.

'For God's sake!' Wolf bellowed. 'If you can't call these harpies off, I can't even begin.'

Jamie hesitated. Then he went back to where the big slave was lying in the shadow under the bridge.

'Mamkinga,' he said. 'We must bury the dead in the sea. If we don't, the disease will continue to spread. Will you tell your people to stop hindering us?'

'They are all Bantu,' Mamkinga answered. 'The dead must be buried on land. Their spirits cannot swim. They will drown in the sea.'

'Then everyone's spirit will drown,' Jamie said. 'Because everyone will die before we reach land, and the ship will be cut adrift again.'

Mamkinga was silent for what seemed a long time. Finally he spoke to a young woman who was kneeling by him, bathing his face. She went away and returned with a dozen of the slaves who were still on their feet. Mamkinga talked to them in his faint husky voice. They muttered among themselves. Then they nodded and dispersed.

'You may put the dead in the sea,' Mamkinga said to Jamie as they shuffled away. 'They know I am a king's son. I have told them that where I go, water becomes land. The spirits will not drown. They will walk on the waves.'

'Thank you.'

Jamie returned to Wolf, who was angrily scraping the dried blood from his cheeks.

'Ye can go ahead,' Jamie said. 'No one's going to object now. Our friend back there has used a little magic.'

'What magic?' Wolf demanded.

Jamie grinned. 'A politician's magic. It's not sea out there – it's been declared good solid earth. The voters believe him. You'd better do the same.'

Wolf stared at him suspiciously but when he dragged the next body towards the rail, one of the slaves came forward and helped him to roll it over the side.

Jamie looked up at the masts.

There were three of them. When the mutiny broke out most of the sails must have been set. Since then a few had broken loose from their sheets at the top or bottom of the yardarms, but the majority were still rigged. A light breeze was blowing from out of Africa to the east. Combined with the movement of air generated by the *Forerunner*'s tow, it had the effect of an anchor – filling the canvas and slowing their progress.

Jamie searched through the detritus on the deck.

He found a mariner's double-bladed axe, dropped by someone, he guessed, in the confusion of the fighting. There was another lying close to it. He glanced round for someone to give it to, but abandoned the idea even as he looked. No one on board was capable of climbing with him up into the rigging.

Jamie draped the axe round his neck on its leather loop, gripped the nearest rope catwalk, and began to pull himself upwards. When he reached the first yard he worked his way across, slashing through the sheets as he moved. Then he climbed to the next and repeated the exercise. Afterwards he climbed again. Each time he went higher the swollen-bellied curves of canvas emptied. They shrivelled like punctured balloons, and tumbled to the deck below.

It was a slow and dangerous business.

Under tow the *San Cristobal* pitched and tossed unpredictably on the waves. The slashed ropes writhed and snapped like snakes round Jamie's head. The plunging sails seared his hands as he guided them away from his body. Swinging blocks cannoned against his ribs, the yardarms juddered and bounced, the spidery catwalks rose and dipped as he crawled up them.

Jamie cleared the mainmast and made his way back to the deck. He paused there, panting and shaking, to catch his breath. Then he set off to strip the other two masts.

In all it took him almost five hours. When he finally lowered himself wearily to the deck again, dusk was falling. Jamie looked at the bows. Fifty yards ahead he could see the *Forerunner*'s navigation lamps against the darkening sky. Now that they were no longer hampered by the drag of the *San Cristobal*'s canvas, both ships were running more swiftly and evenly.

Jamie glanced round.

Wolf wasn't in sight but he'd done a good job. The reeking corpses and festering mounds of rubbish had been tipped overboard, the tangled ropes had been coiled, and the scattered and upended water casks had been placed back in their mounts. Four of the slaves had been set to work washing down the boards with sea water and lime which Wolf must have found somewhere below. The terrible stench hadn't vanished altogether, but it was less noticeable than before.

Jamie set off in search of Farquarson. He found the Scot emerging from a stairwell down to the holds. Farquarson's ruddy freckled skin was obscured by grime, and a glistening layer of dirt had turned his sandy hair almost black. His face was grim.

'Fifty-three,' Farquarson said. 'That's all that's left. Eleven men, twenty-nine women and thirteen children. Plus the big fellow under the bridge. The ship must have sailed with well over four hundred – I did a count of the manacles in the holds – but almost ninety per cent of them are gone already.'

'What about the survivors?' Jamie asked.

Farquarson shook his head. 'We'll lose some more yet. There's at least one girl and maybe three youngsters who won't see the night out. I've handed anyone capable of working over to Wolf. The rest I've fed and quartered in the crew's cabins. There's nothing I can do with the holds. The filth and stink down there, it's unbelievable. You get giddy just putting your head inside.'

He took several deep lungfuls of air. Then he turned and disappeared back into the stairwell.

Jamie headed for the bridge. He found a lantern, lit its wick, and ducked under the arch below the steps. Mamkinga was still lying on his back on the boards.

Jamie peered down at him.

The slaves' leader was even taller than Jamie had realized. Before the mutiny he must have been a magnificent figure of a man. Now he was a husk. Dehydration and lack of food were part of the reason, but he was desperately sick with fever too. His face was running with sweat, his chest rose and fell in quick weak flutters, and his skin was almost translucent in the lantern's glow. Jamie spoke to him. This time Mamkinga didn't answer. His eyes were closed and he appeared to be unconscious.

Jamie looked up. Across the space beneath the steps the young woman was kneeling and weeping. Like him, Jamie thought, she knew Mamkinga was close to death.

Jamie studied Mamkinga again. Draped across his chest was a length of dirty cloth. Jamie lifted it off carefully and his face tensed. The cloth covered a massive suppurating wound in the left armpit. Across Mamkinga's chest, over his shoulder, and down his arm the flesh was putrid and rotten. Maggots which had been feeding in it wriggled away from the light and another foetid smell spouted into the air.

Jamie recoiled.

Then he collected himself. There was something familiar about the corrugated flesh, the stench and the coiling worms. He thought back. Suddenly he remembered. Years before he'd accompanied Dr Cameron

467

on a call out to a shepherd who'd been brought down from the hill pastures in summer. The man had broken and lacerated both his legs in a fall, and lain undiscovered on the tops for a week. The maggots had got to him too.

'Gangrene,' Dr Cameron said as he examined the shepherd. 'Shock and fever as well. We'll start by cutting away as much of the putrefaction as we can. Then we'll apply mercury-chrome and salts of soda.'

As always Dr Cameron talked as he worked. Jamie had listened and watched. Now it came back.

Among the supplies he'd collected from the *Forerunner* was a satchel of medicines. He opened it and found a scalpel, a jar of mercury-chrome, and some soda salts. Jamie took the scalpel and began to shave away the rotten flesh. After a few moments blood began to appear and he knew he'd cut back to the living tissue.

He stopped and started again on another section of the infection.

By the time Jamie had finished the entire infected area was running with blood. The wound looked worse than when he'd begun. Disregarding the young woman's anguished protests, he painted the wound with mercury-chrome and then sprinkled a layer of soda salts over the top. Jamie covered it all with a clean length of sail-cloth, winding it in a crude bandage separately round Mamkinga's chest and his arm to keep them apart.

Afterwards Jamie sat back on his heels.

The shepherd had recovered but he had only been wounded for a week. The area of putrefaction was much smaller, and the shepherd hadn't had Mamkinga's terrible fever. Mamkinga, Jamie guessed, had already lost a quarter of his body weight. The infection had probably been eating into him for much longer. And the fever was the worst Jamie had ever seen. Mamkinga's skin was puddled with sweat and constant convulsions racked his body. In spite of what he'd done, Jamie doubted whether Mamkinga would last through the night.

Unaccountably – for a man he'd only known for a few

hours and with whom he'd exchanged barely a handful of words – the thought filled him with anger and sorrow.

He cast round in his mind for anything else he could do. There was nothing. He had applied treatment for the gangrene. But the fever was Africa's – and Africa was still the unknown.

Troubled and frustrated, Jamie got to his feet. Then as he began to turn away he saw Mamkinga's eyes open. Mamkinga gazed up at him for a moment.

'Thank you,' he said in a whisper. 'If we meet again, I will remember.'

Before Jamie could reply, Mamkinga had slipped back into unconsciousness.

65

The African coast came into sight soon after midday the
following morning. Two hours later and less than half a
mile from shore, the *Forerunner*'s engines stopped and
the rope between the two ships went slack.

Jamie had been standing on deck ever since the shore
appeared. He saw a boat being lowered from the
Forerunner. The boat made its way across the gap
between the two ships and pulled to beneath the *San
Cristobal*'s bows.

'Are you there, Mr Oran?' a voice shouted up.

Jamie looked down. It was Captain Culglass.

'Aye, captain,' he said.

'How are you and your friends doing?'

'We've cleaned up a wee bit,' Jamie replied. 'There
aren't many left, maybe fifty out of the four hundred that
started. I want to get them ashore and find some food and
water.'

Culglass nodded. 'We've made landfall just south of
Lagos on the Bight of Benin. I'm taking my ship a little
north to dock at Lagos itself. I'm going to drop you here. I
can't risk taking you into port.'

'For God's sake,' Jamie protested. 'How are we going
to reach land?'

'The tide,' Culglass answered. 'It's making hard. An
hour or two and you'll be aground. Belay a sheet round a
couple of trees and you won't move when it ebbs again.
You're not the first.'

Culglass gestured at the shore. Jamie glanced round. A
dozen hulks, he saw now, were beached on the sand
beneath the fringing trees.

'They reckon it's safer against the fever,' Culglass went on. 'They could be right, but that's not my problem. If you're not infected a month from now, you'll be welcome in Lagos. Until then stay out of the port or you'll have the militia on you. I'm sorry, laddie, but I have to notify the governor. My ticket's at risk if I don't. If the fever gets in, it could wipe out the settlement. Good luck.'

He waved and the boat pulled away. Jamie watched it being hauled back aboard the *Forerunner*. The tow rope was cut, the *Forerunner*'s screw engaged, and the packet disappeared to the north.

Jamie looked back at the shore.

Culglass was right. An hour later the Atlantic tide had carried the *San Cristobal* in to land. The bows butted against the sandy beach, and the ship lurched to one side. Then it began to press up the shore at an angle as the waves drove it in from behind. Jamie called to Wolf and Farquarson. The three of them scrambled down into the water and swam ashore, pulling the cut tow rope behind them.

On land they knotted the rope to another length of hemp and ran it round a clump of palm trees standing high above the beach. For the next two hours, as the tide continued to carry the *San Cristobal* in, they hauled the rope in. Finally at slack water they made the rope fast and walked back down the beach to the ship.

She had come to rest wedged between two groups of rocks. The rocks had punctured the planks on both sides of the keel but their support had the effect of stranding the ship in an upright position. When the tide came in again, Jamie realized, water would pour into the lower hold and then out again without moving her. She was useless as a vessel but her beached hulk was still fully serviceable as living quarters.

Farquarson had reached the same conclusion.

'How long did Culglass say – a month? Well, we've just got ourselves lodgings somewhere between land and sea for the interim.'

They clambered back on board.

During the two hours they'd been ashore most of the surviving slaves had fled the ship. The entire coast, as they must have known, was under the control of slavers but after their month of hell at sea the land held few terrors. Even the risk of recapture was insignificant. Nothing could be worse than what they had gone through. The only ones left were a couple of men too weak to move, the young woman, and Mamkinga.

Jamie looked down at the unconscious body of the huge negro.

Twice during the night and once that morning Jamie had re-dressed Mamkinga's open flesh with mercury-chrome and soda salts. The gaping wound seemed to absorb them like a sponge sucking in water. So far there was no apparent improvement, but Jamie's trust in Dr Cameron's skills remained absolute. Within a few days, he was sure, the wound would begin to heal.

Whether Mamkinga would still be alive for the healing process to start was another matter. Jamie had nothing for the fever and it continued to ravage Mamkinga unabated.

With a heavy heart Jamie knelt down and began to bathe Mamkinga's face.

— 66 —

In Kano, Toomi and Rachel waited anxiously in the house of the old Malindan woman, Ayeshi.

It was two hours since they'd taken refuge there from the horsemen. Ayeshi had gone out to see what was happening in the town.

'There are horsemen everywhere,' Ayeshi said when she returned. 'Many more than the five who spotted you. They must know you are still here and they are watching everyone. Tonight they will guard the gates. For the moment you are safe, but tomorrow – '

She shook her head. 'They will go to the governor and ask his permission to search the houses. They will bribe him well and he will agree. It has happened before. Then they are bound to find you – '

Tears in her eyes, Ayeshi gestured helplessly round the bare little house. 'There is nowhere for you to hide.'

The two young women were silent.

During Ayeshi's absence they had tried to work out how they had been discovered. The Arabs were agents of the Acab Saat, there was no doubt about that. They could not have known about Toomi, but they had spotted Rachel instantly in spite of the Arab robes. It was Rachel who guessed.

'The ring I gave to Mohamet Asa,' Rachel said. 'It was stamped with the mark of Gondar. Every piece of gold in the palace carries the same mark. The Arabs who passed us must have questioned Asa and seen the ring. They offered him a reward and he told them where it came from.'

She hammered her hand on the table in anguish at her stupidity.

Toomi covered Rachel's fingers with her own. 'I could have done the same,' she said. 'It does not matter. At least we know how we stand.'

They knew all the better after Ayeshi's return. From her description fifty or more of the Acab Saat's men were patrolling Kano. Fifty armed men on horseback were more than enough to seal the gates of the walled town. If tomorrow they got the governor's permission to comb the houses, Rachel and Toomi were doomed.

'We must get out tonight,' Toomi insisted. 'Ayeshi, surely there is a way!'

Ayeshi clasped her hands to her face, the wrinkles on her forehead deepening into trenches as she thought.

'Hadji,' she muttered. 'Hadji will know what to do.'

'Who is Hadji?' Toomi demanded.

'My son,' Ayeshi answered. 'He has been readying a caravan this past week. He is camped near the Oxal well. Yesterday he came in to bid me farewell. He leaves this evening, he told me, but perhaps I can find him before he goes – '

Ayeshi drew herself up. 'Hadji has great blood in him,' she said proudly. 'He will help us.'

Ayeshi was away all day. She returned as dusk was falling over Kano. The light was draining from the sky and beyond the tiny open windows the evening clouds were beginning to gather. The door clicked open and Ayeshi appeared. Behind her was a man.

'My son,' the old woman said smiling. 'Hadji.'

The girls stared at him as he came forward.

Hadji was about thirty. Tall and sinewy, with copper-coloured skin, he was dressed in an Arab jellabah. His face was craggy and scarred, but his eyes were shrewd, bright and humorous. An ancient musket was slung over his shoulder and a curved broad-bladed sword hung from a cartridge belt at his waist. Standing in the little room there was something exuberantly debonair and piratical about him. Hadji radiated confidence and daring.

Both Toomi and Rachel felt instantly comforted by his presence.

'My mother tells me you have problems,' he said after greeting them. 'Let us see if we can do something about them.'

Hadji produced a bag. 'First change into these. They belong to two Touregs who are with me at my camp. My mother chose them to fit you.'

Rachel took the bag and glanced inside. It contained two pairs of the hide leggings, jute sandals, long black capes and beaded headdresses worn by the desert Toureg camel-riders.

'But they know my face,' she said. 'If we try to leave by the gates, they will recognize me.'

'There are other ways out of Kano apart from the gates.' Hadji grinned. 'Just do what I tell you and trust me.'

Rachel and Toomi looked at each other. There was no need even to discuss the matter. They had no choice. They retired into Ayeshi's tiny bedroom and changed into the Toureg clothes. When they returned Hadji was speaking urgently to his mother.

He broke off and turned to inspect them.

'Very good.' He nodded approvingly. 'Even at this short distance you could pass for Touregs. But it is only a precaution and you should not be put to the test. Listen carefully – '

Hadji advanced towards them.

'From now on you do exactly what I say. It is already almost dark. In a moment we will leave. Stay close behind. It will take us half an hour to reach the walls. By then the men will be guarding the gates. We will arrive between two of the northern gates where a sewer tunnel runs out – '

He grinned again. 'In the circumstances I don't think it will bother you. Soon after we reach the sewer there will be a disturbance at the gate to the west. Mother!'

Hadji glanced at Ayeshi.

'I run shouting to the guard captain,' Ayeshi said, repeating Hadji's instructions. 'Two youths dressed as Arabs came into my house and robbed me. I chased them to the walls and saw them trying to climb over.'

Hadji nodded and turned back to the girls.

'It should draw the men away. But whatever happens we leave through the sewer. My camp is four miles off. We go there as fast as possible. If we are challenged, leave the talking to me and say nothing – the Touregs cannot speak any tongue used here. I am taking a load of cloth to the northern markets and I have employed you as ox-drivers. Is that clear?'

Toomi and Rachel nodded.

'Then we go now.'

Ayeshi embraced Rachel and Toomi, holding each close to her breast. 'Go, my daughters,' she murmured. 'You travel in safe hands.'

The four of them left the little house.

Outside Ayeshi turned left and headed down the street towards the western gate under the fitful light of the torches that burned for two hours after sunset. Hadji, with the two young women behind him, set off in the opposite direction. Fifty yards further he left the street and slipped into an alley.

The alley was impenetrably dark. There were no torches. The houses pressed so tightly together that an arm's span separated the facing walls, and the moon hadn't yet risen. Only a dim gleam from fragments of starlight overhead and the occasional glow of dying coals from a cooking brazier put out to cool gave any illumination at all.

To Hadji the blackness was immaterial.

He walked with the silent sure-footed certainty of a cat, following the first alley and then threading his way through a maze of others. Occasionally they came across a prowling dog. If the dog's hackles bristled and the animal began to growl, Hadji would calm it with a soothing whisper and a hand brushed along its spine. Once they startled a woman emptying slops. Several times scurrying children squealed and cowered back against the walls. Hadji stilled them all with a few murmured words and a reassuring chuckle.

Eventually Hadji stopped. Toomi, who was following immediately behind, bumped into his back. As she stumbled she felt Hadji's hand grip her wrist.

'Look,' he whispered. 'The sewer.'

At their feet the starlight was reflected from the oily surface of a sluggish stream. The stench rising from the water was so rotten and foetid it was almost overpowering.

'It runs out through the arch.' Hadji pointed ahead as the two girls gasped for breath. 'As soon as we hear the noise we step in and wade through. Make yourself ready.'

The three waited.

Five minutes later there was a distant protracted wail to their left. Ayeshi had reached the gate and begun to complain. Shouts were exchanged along the wall. Then, to their right, they heard the muffled thud of hoofs on sand.

On the far side of the barrier of blackness above them, horses galloped past.

Hadji's teeth flashed white as he smiled.

'Now.'

He swung his legs over the bank and slipped down soundlessly into the stream of filth. Toomi and Rachel followed. The garbage and faeces-laden water rose to their waists. The smell from the putrefaction as the acids bubbled to the surface and erupted into the air made them choke. Gasping and panting, they stumbled on.

For several minutes there was nothing except the stench, the flow of garbage, and the arched brick roof of the tunnel intermittently bumping and dripping its slime against their heads. Then a crescent of starlight appeared ahead. Wading in Hadji's wake they struggled towards it. The crescent grew larger. Suddenly it became the canopy of the night sky. The tunnel had vanished and the air above the water was clean and chill.

Dizzy and swallowing great lungfuls of fresh air, Toomi and Rachel followed Hadji and pulled themselves on to the bank beneath the town's walls. Hadji, unaffected by the torrent of sewage, lifted his head and listened.

'No one,' he said in a whisper. 'The horsemen have gone. We can head for the camp.'

Hadji stood up and set off at a steady loping run.

They were on the plain. The earth was rutted by the passage of thousands of animals and then baked hard by the sun. Toomi and Rachel trotted behind him, their sodden britches slapping against their legs.

For the next two hours, alternately jogging and walking, they travelled north. The plain was dotted with dozens of fires marking the sites of little settlements or the tents of caravans which had pitched camp outside the walls. Hadji carefully circled them all. Finally they climbed a narrow defile and came out on to a plateau strewn with large boulders.

Hadji stopped and whistled. The shadowy figure of a man carrying a musket materialized in the darkness. Hadji spoke to the man softly and beckoned to the young women.

'We have arrived,' he said.

Toomi and Rachel followed him forward.

Hadji's camp, they realized immediately, was unlike any they had passed earlier. They could just make out the shapes of thirty or forty men moving about but there were no fires, no dogs, no tents, and no noise – even the smallest task was being carried out in silence. Hadji led them between two lines of oxen being loaded ready for departure. He stopped by a clump of rocks where he spoke to another armed man.

The man reached down.

He tugged at something, and an oval of orange light spilled out over the ground. Toomi and Esther blinked at the sudden brightness. The light came from the coals of a closed clay oven which had been built into the rocks. The man had opened the oven door. Behind it rows of flat maize bread were toasting on an iron grill.

'Eat quickly,' Hadji said. 'We have little time.'

The smell of the freshly made bread was rich and

enticing, and the girls suddenly felt ravenously hungry. They took the loaves the man pulled out for them and squatted on the ground beside Hadji.

'Listen again,' Hadji instructed them between mouthfuls. 'In a few minutes we leave. My mother has entrusted you to my care. I will protect you as best I can. You have my word. But from now on you must work as we all work. Two oxen have been loaded for you. You will take your places in the column and lead them. They and their loads are now your responsibility.'

'You mean the cloth?' Toomi asked.

Hadji paused with the loaf halfway to his mouth. 'Of course,' he chuckled.

Ten minutes later, with Toomi and Rachel each leading one of the laden oxen, the column was under way. Hadji rode on a horse at the head. They wound down through the defile and set off across the plain. They were no longer travelling north but almost due west.

They travelled without stopping for the rest of the night. At dawn Hadji called a halt. Toomi and Rachel had started off together, but Toomi's ox was slower and older than Rachel's and by the time they stopped, Toomi had fallen to the back of the column. She hobbled the animal wearily and walked forward to find Rachel again.

The sun was rising and the plain's insects were just beginning to return to life in the warming air. As Toomi moved, an early caddis fly settled on her ox's lower lip and bit it. Maddened by the sudden stab of pain the animal bucked and bellowed. Toomi swung round. The plunging ox, trapped by the hobble, lurched and fell on to its side, spilling its carefully packed load from the panniers.

One of the calico-wrapped bolts bounced away and split open. Toomi stared at it wide-eyed. There was no cloth inside the wrapping.

Clattering across the baked earth were guns.

Taking only the briefest halts for food and sleep, Hadji kept the column on the move for the next three days.

Rachel and Toomi had no idea of the reason for the urgency or what Hadji's business was – except it was certainly not taking cloth to sell in the northern markets. Even if the package on Toomi's ox hadn't split, the composition and behaviour of the caravan would have told them that something very different from trading was involved.

Apart from themselves there were no women in the party. Even more puzzling, there were no slaves among the forty heavily armed men who made up their companions. All shared equally in the camp chores. Whenever they stopped, the oxen were hidden in thickets of thorn. By night fires were forbidden and by day they could only be fuelled with bone-dry branches that produced no smoke.

The two young women had few chances to talk together. Although the column didn't travel fast – the measured pace of the heavily laden oxen prevented that – it seemed to be almost constantly pressing on. While they were moving, the dust by day, the cold by night and the vagaries of their own beasts – the one pulling on and the other drifting back – made conversation difficult. Whenever they paused they were both so hungry and tired all they wanted to do was eat the thin stew prepared by the cooks, and slip into sleep.

Twice they managed to corner Hadji and tackle him. Where were they going and why? On both occasions Hadji was evasive.

'You come with me at my mother's warrant,' he would say. 'If you trust her, then you must trust me. Besides – ' He gave his engaging grin. 'Are not the stars more appealing here than they would be seen through the bars of one of the Acab Saat's prisons?'

The girls retired frustrated to a brief few hours of sleep on the sand before the column set off again.

Early on the third morning after they left Kano everything changed.

They had spent the night travelling along a game track through mopane woodland. As dawn broke they saw water gleaming ahead between the trees. They were approaching a river. A hundred yards from the river's banks the column came to a halt. Toomi and Rachel saw Hadji dismount and speak to a group of his men at the front of the caravan. The men scattered into the trees. The chief ox-herder took the bridles of their animals, and led them and the other animals back into the woodland.

Toomi and Rachel waited alone on the track. Hadji walked back to them. Until then his musket had always been slung on a strap round his shoulders. Now it was in his hands.

'You have done well,' he said. 'We have been travelling fast and the journey has not been easy. I am pleased. Now listen to me again, for the time has come for me to tell you – '

He squatted on the sun-dried grass beside the path. The girls dropped to their haunches in front of him.

'We have been moving to overtake a caravan that left Kano before we did,' Hadji went on. 'They had almost a day's advantage on us and they were able to travel fast. That is why we had to hurry. Now we are ahead of them. Very soon they will come to where we are. They will have to cross the river at the ford here – '

Hadji gestured towards the shallows through the trees.

'The caravan has many slaves. We will attack it as they cross the water. My men are already in position.

481

The slaves will be released and we will take the caravan's goods. Your duties are to see that my men are kept supplied with ammunition – '

He indicated two bulky satchels of cartridges which one of the men was dragging towards them along the track.

'You' – he nodded at Toomi – 'will look after this side. You' – he glanced towards Rachel – 'will take the other side. If any man needs you he will whistle and signal with his arm like this – '

Hadji revolved his own arm in a circular motion.

'Take him a dozen shells, using the bush for cover. Then return to your satchel and keep alert for the next one. Understand?'

The two young women nodded.

'Good.' Hadji got to his feet. 'Pick up your satchels and I will take you to your positions.'

Ten minutes later Toomi and Rachel were in place.

Toomi was placed upstream of the ford on a thorn-covered knoll. Rachel was given a site a hundred yards away downriver on a reed-fringed bank. Neither could see the other but, peering through the foliage, both had a clear view of the shallows.

The place Hadji had chosen for the ambush was a sharp bend in the river's course.

The water was already forming an ox-bow that would soon become a shallow lake. Pouring down from the north, the torrent collided with a steep embankment and swirled away into a series of rippling shallows before plunging on again. As a crossing point the shallows had been used by caravans for years. Deeply trenched tracks, imprinted with the feet of animals and the wheel-bands of waggons, led down on either side, and the surrounding bush was pocked with the grey smudges of dead campfires.

The sun lifted in the sky and the air began to warm. Marsh flies rose in clouds from the reeds. Pied king-fishers, wing feathers flashing black and white, hawked the surface. A martial eagle, trawling its shadow across the stream, patrolled the thermals high overhead. Once an antelope came down to drink, stepping out from the bushes only yards away from where Toomi was lying.

Toomi held her breath as she watched it.

The antelope was a majestic male roan with a burnished chestnut coat and two spiralling horns that lifted above its head like lances. The animal was nervous and unsettled. It pawed the ground uncertainly. Something on the light gusts of river breeze was unfamiliar and menacing. It was the faint scent-spores of the waiting men.

The roan sniffed the air, trying to find where the traces of the disquieting smell were coming from. Twice it wheeled away and vanished back into the undergrowth with a clatter of hoofs.

On both occasions the antelope returned. Its thirst was stronger even than its fear. It snorted defiantly and stepped into the water. The hairs along its spine bristled with tension as it lowered its head to drink. The roan took a few rapid gulps. Then it suddenly bellowed and lashed out with its hind legs, raising a screen of spray high above the river's surface. Within an instant it had disappeared at a frantic gallop. This time it did not come back.

Toomi let out her breath. Her heart was pumping wildly. Slowly she calmed herself. As she did, quiet returned to the river again. Then towards the middle of the morning a rhythmic creak and rustle crept into the scatter of sounds that overlay the ford.

Lying on the knoll upstream, Toomi heard the noise first. She lifted her head and stared east. There was a slow-coiling trail of dust above the trees. The sound grew louder and separated into distinct elements –the grate of wheels, the rustle of leather, the tramp of feet, and then, closer still, the murmur of voices.

The caravan was winding down to the ford.

Toomi tensed. The morning breeze was blowing from behind the column of men, waggons, horses and camels. As they came closer she could smell the odours of sweat, oil and hide. A rider appeared and cautiously made his way down to the ford. Toomi squirmed round on her belly to watch him. The horseman examined the shallows and the bushes on either side of the river. He rode out into the stream and checked again.

Apparently satisfied, he called out to the column behind him. Four other horsemen came through the trees. A dozen camels, led by herders, followed them. Behind the camels the first waggon came into Toomi's sight. As soon as she saw it Toomi's eyes widened.

The waggon was unmistakably one of Mahomet Asa's. It had a particular red-and-black striped awning and an off-set front wheel which she remembered vividly. A second waggon appeared, then a third and a fourth, and she recognized them all.

It was the caravan they had travelled with from Gondar.

A moment later Mahomet Asa himself appeared on his horse. He rode into the water at the head of a dozen armed riders. At Asa's command, the men split into two groups and took up positions in the centre of the shallows fifty yards apart. Asa shouted another order and the column began to splash down into the shallows.

Hadji, hidden at another vantage point in the bush, waited until the head of the caravan was halfway across the ford. As the oxen pulling the leading waggon slowed at the point where the water was deepest, he suddenly shouted.

'Velama!'

A volley of musketfire rang out. Instantly the scene at the ford, which a second before had been an orderly progress of men, carts and animals, turned to violence and confusion.

Two of Asa's guards, hit by bullets from the hidden marksmen, toppled into the river. A herder screamed, fell forward, and began floundering in a spreading pool of blood. Several oxen, struck by the gunfire, bellowed and plunged frantically. A group of terrified camels bucked off their riders, shed their loads, and struggled against their traces. A waggon slewed round, lost its wheels, and submerged. Two lines of yoked slaves started to wade towards the far bank. A third line turned back. A fourth stopped and stood frozen with terror in the water.

At first with surprise, concealment and a larger force, the advantages were all on the side of Hadji's men. But Mahomet Asa was fearless. He was a veteran of caravan ambushes, and he had a large part of his fortune locked up in the stock that was being raided. Within moments of the opening volley he had begun to fight back.

'Close on me in a line!' the Arab bellowed.

The two groups of guards fanned out in a line with Asa at the centre and rode towards the attackers.

Asa had fewer men than Hadji, but they were better armed and more experienced. They were no longer stationary targets, but solitary weaving and swaying individuals who fired back as they drove their mounts forward through the spray. They reached the sand. Then they drew their swords and kicked their horses behind Asa's up the bank and into the bush.

Crouching on the knoll, Toomi saw what the Arab was doing.

He had thrown all of his men against the upper part of the ambush, cutting Hadji's forces in two. On land in the dense bush the Arab's men were stronger. Mounted, with swords in their hands, they had every advantage over men on foot. If they could overwhelm the ambushers here, they could turn their attention to the others lower down the stream.

None of Hadji's men had called for ammunition yet. If they did now, Toomi knew it was too late. No one could reach them through the cordon of horses sweeping through the thorn trees.

Her mouth dry and her heart pumping, Toomi knelt and waited.

Fifty yards away but hidden from Toomi's sight, Hadji also realized what had happened. He had counted on the first volleys felling Asa and enough of his men to demoralize the rest and drive them back to the far bank.

The plan had gone appallingly wrong. Hadji had taken Asa as his own target. As he fired, the Arab's horse sidled and he missed. Only two of Asa's guards had been killed. Now the speed and determination of the Arab's counter-attack had taken Hadji by surprise.

Cursing, Hadji got to his feet. He stood listening.

The crescent of Asa's horsemen was heading towards him through the bush. Branches cracked and thorn scrub splintered as they came forward. If they broke through now and attacked his men lower down the river, the ambush would end in disaster. There was only one way to stop them. That was to cut them down man by man in the undergrowth. It was not something Hadji could do on his own.

Hadji drew his dagger. He gave a high fluting whistle like the call of the crested lark. He repeated the whistle three times, changing its pitch at every repetition. Then he continued to whistle, using the bubbling song of the lark's mating call.

Within moments three of his men appeared from the scrub. They knelt beside him. Each had answered his own call, while the lark song had told them where Hadji was.

'Daggers,' Hadji whispered, tapping his own.

The men needed no further instruction. They had done it before and they knew exactly what Hadji meant. They drew their daggers and spread out in a tight semi-circle round him.

Hadji led them silently through the bush towards the sound of the horses.

As they moved there was a shot followed by a crashing in the undergrowth. A sword slashed down and a voice cried out. The voice died away in a choking cough. Hadji recognized the voice. It belonged to Larad, one of his best men. Larad must have fired at a horseman. His bullet had gone astray in the trees, and the horseman had charged him and cut him down.

If he wasn't swift, Hadji knew it would happen to all of them. He pressed on.

They came on the first of the Arab's men almost

immediately. The bushes parted in front of them and the horseman towered overhead. Hadji and the three men hurled themselves forward. They tackled the man and his mount with the speed and sureness of a well-drilled team. Hadji leapt for the horse's bridle. He halted the animal and dragged its head down. The men separated and attacked the rider.

One slashed at him from one side while the other two attacked him from the other. Twisting and turning between them the horseman slipped from the saddle. As he fell Hadji dropped the bridle. Hadji's dagger pierced the horseman's neck almost before he touched the ground.

'On,' he whispered again, barely pausing to wipe the blood from the blade.

In the next few minutes they slaughtered four of Asa's guards, springing on them without warning from the bush as the horsemen combed the thicket. Two of Hadji's men were wounded in the attacks. One had his arm sliced almost off by a sword cut, and fell back. Another was caught by a blow across his head. With half his scalp flapping over his neck but still able to fight, the man plunged on after Hadji.

They came to the rim of a clearing, and paused.

Until then they had been able to pick off Asa's men one by one. Now it was different. From the sounds in the bush ahead not one but three horsemen were approaching them. Hadji hesitated. He gestured for the men to draw back, but it was too late. The horsemen broke through the scrub into the clearing. They spotted the three ambushers, and galloped forward.

Their leader was Mahomet Asa.

'Attack!' Hadji shouted.

It was a desperate call. His men were already turning. At his command they swung round and threw themselves forward.

Before they could move the horsemen were on them. Hadji jumped for Asa's bridle. Asa was vastly more experienced than the other guards and his horse was in full gallop. The Arab was also filled with murderous rage at the ambush. He swung the musket and clubbed Hadji across the head before his fingers tightened on the leather. Hadji dropped to the ground, stunned.

As Hadji lay motionless, Asa brought the horse rearing to a halt a few yards away. He turned and drew his sword.

'You dog!' Asa shouted.

As he kicked the horse forward again, Toomi launched herself off the bank.

Toomi had watched everything from the knoll a few yards away. She threw herself forward now without conscious thought. Unheard in the confusion, she raced towards Mahomet Asa from behind. The Arab had stopped his horse above Hadji's body and was raising his sword in the air.

Toomi gathered herself and leapt up, reaching high above her head for the gun-sling across the Arab's back. She caught it and pulled down with all her strength.

Caught by surprise, Asa toppled backwards. As he fell he dropped the sword and twisted round, trying to save himself by grasping for the pommel. He caught it and pulled against her. For an instant they were balanced, Toomi clinging like a wildcat to the gun-sling and Asa straining desperately away from her. Then the girths began to slip under the lopsided weight. The saddle tilted.

Suddenly, before the saddle revolved completely and threw them both clear, the gun sling broke.

Toomi dropped on her back. The fall knocked the breath out of her and she lay staring upwards. Heaving and scrambling, the Arab managed to right himself in the saddle. He glanced round. Hadji was climbing to his feet with his dagger in his hand. Another of Hadji's men was closing on his horse from the other side. Mahomet Asa had lost both his musket and his sword. He was weaponless and the men were too close.

Asa grabbed the reins and drove his spurs into the horse's flanks. As the animal moved he looked down. He saw Toomi's face and recognized her as one of the two youths who had ridden with his caravan from Gondar. His eyes narrowed with fury. He cursed and spat down.

Then before Hadji could get to him, Asa was gone. He broke through the bush and galloped back into the shallows, calling his men after him. Abandoning the caravan, they crossed the ford under another volley of bullets, and vanished on the far bank.

The battle was over.

68

'I owe you thanks I can never repay,' Hadji said.

Toomi smiled. 'Then we are equal because we owe the same to you.'

Darkness had fallen and Toomi and Rachel were sitting with Hadji by his fire. They were still by the ford where the battle had taken place. For the first time on the journey the flames were open to the night sky.

'No.' Hadji shook his head. 'We are not equal. I gave you help when you faced difficulties. You saved my life when I faced death. Difficulties and death are not equal in the balance. What can I do to make the weights sit more evenly?'

Toomi glanced at Rachel. Without speaking Rachel nodded. There was no need for the girls to exchange words. Their lives had become inextricably entangled. Their destination now, wherever it lay, was the same.

'Help us to get to Garoua,' Toomi said.

'Garoua?' Hadji looked at her in surprise. 'Garoua is two months away. The road is bad and dangerous. There are many bandits along the way who rob and kill travellers.'

'We have discovered that,' Rachel said, smiling.

Hadji grinned. Then he shrugged.

'What happened today was different.' He waved his hand deprecatingly. 'I am speaking of truly bad men. Even if you succeed in passing them, what will you do in Garoua? You have nothing to sell. You have no money. You cannot hire yourselves out for work – people use slaves for their labourers. Also, as women you will be exposed all the time to assault – '

'No.' He shook his head firmly. 'Garoua would be madness. For me to help you get there would be repaying you for what you have done by sending you to your deaths. I cannot do it.'

'With or without your help, Hadji,' Toomi said quietly, 'we are going to Garoua. Nothing will stop us.'

Hadji stared at her in the firelight. He turned to look at Rachel. Both the girls' faces were obdurate. He sighed.

'We will go from here to Quilombo,' he said. 'If you still wish to proceed to Garoua, I will escort you myself. It is the least I can give in return. But before you finally make up your minds, I ask you to stay with me in Quilombo first.'

Toomi frowned. 'What and where is Quilombo?'

'You do not know?' Hadji smiled. 'Ten days from now I will show you – '

He paused. 'Once you have seen Quilombo, I do not think you will wish to travel further.'

As Hadji had said they travelled on for a further ten days.

The first seven days were spent pushing west across the plain. They moved parallel to the ancient caravan route between Kano and Timbucktoom, but they used hidden tracks known, it seemed, only to Hadji. Then at the end of the week they turned north and climbed through ranges of low hills.

Toomi and Rachel were no longer ox-drivers.

They had been given two of the horses rounded up after the ambush, and they rode at will wherever they chose in the column. Hadji also assigned them servants from the slaves who had been captured. The servants, an elderly man and a willing young woman barely older than they were, cooked their meals, washed their clothes, saddled and unsaddled the horses and took care of all their needs.

The puzzle to both girls was that the two carried out their tasks as servants and not as slaves. The difference between service and slavery was vast. A servant was a free person who worked for hire. A slave was a human

491

chattel. The old man and the girl had joined the caravan as captured slaves. Overnight their condition changed. They were servants but they were free.

The same applied to all the other slaves from Mohamet Asa's caravan.

Their wooden yokes were sawn in two and their manacles cut through. They were as free to move about the column as any of Hadji's own men. Several of the men among them, after Hadji had questioned them, had even been issued with muskets from the stock the oxen were carrying. They now stood guard round the camp at night with the veterans who had ridden from the well beyond Kano.

Rachel and Toomi had been accustomed to slavery all their lives. Neither had ever seen slaves freed and treated as these were. The puzzle lasted throughout the ten days. Although the urgency had gone out of the journey, the caravan was still travelling swiftly. There were few pauses when they might have questioned Hadji. On the rare occasions when they had the chance, he seemed to distance himself.

Hadji was always courteous, but he surrounded himself with his own people as if he were seeking protection in a crowd.

'I think he wants to surprise us,' Toomi said speculatively one night. 'He is holding something back because he believes if he can show it to us all at once, its effect will be stronger.'

Rachel agreed. 'He is like a man with a bird in a sack. The bird is rare and strange. He is dragging the sack across the ground towards his walls. Once he is there he will open the sack and show us the bird's splendours. Then we will think the splendours and the walls are the same.'

'Maybe.' Toomi smiled. 'Yet he has fine clear eyes.'

Rachel glanced at her thoughtfully. They were both in Hadji's hands. For once Rachel did not give her own opinion on someone who concerned them both equally.

69

'Are you going to sleep all day, Jamie – ?'

A hand was shaking Jamie's shoulder. He opened his eyes and blinked. Farquarson was standing above him. Behind Farquarson's head he could see a group of black faces.

'On your feet, laddie,' Farquarson went on. 'Wolf and I have been up long since. We've been ashore and made a friend, a Mr DeWitt. He's hired us this bunch of the local peasantry to clean up the boat. But if we're going to be billeted here for a month, there's plenty more to be done.'

Yawning, Jamie climbed to his feet.

It was 8.00 a.m. and the sun was already high. The last thing he remembered the night before was asking Farquarson and Wolf to help him to carry the huge unconscious negro into the captain's cabin. Jamie had been swaying with tiredness, but he knew he had to get Mamkinga into the shade before day broke. Even in the well beneath the steps to the ship's bridge the bars of sunlight were sucking moisture from his skin.

Between them they had heaved Mamkinga into the cabin and placed him on the padded bench that followed the curve of the ship's stern. Jamie remembered squatting down beside the bench. That was all. He must have toppled over and fallen asleep. Farquarson or Wolf had pushed a cushion beneath his head, and left him where he was.

Mamkinga was still lying on the captain's settle.

His breathing was so shallow his chest barely moved. Jamie had to put his hand on Mamkinga's heart to reassure himself that the slave was still alive. He felt a faint palpitation and changed Mamkinga's dressing. Then Jamie went outside.

Last night in total exhaustion he'd dimly registered the darting fireflies on the shore, the calls and screams of the hidden birds and animals, and the clammy night heat. Apart from that he'd hardly been aware he'd reached Africa at last.

Now in broad daylight Jamie really saw the continent for the first time.

The tide was out and the ship was beached on a great sheet of white sand. The sand shelved up from the water's edge to a dune thirty paces from the *San Cristobal*'s bows. The dune was crowned with clumps of palms. Behind the palms were other dunes rising towards a dense belt of trees. The trees were tall and dark and coiled with vines. Occasionally a brilliantly coloured bird dived out of them. The bird traced a flare of turquoise and scarlet across the air, and vanished into the canopy again.

Stirring gently in the treetops were heavy clouds of water-laden mist. Higher up, the mist grew thinner until it became a grainy haze which was still strong enough to screen out the direct rays of the sun. In spite of that the air was already suffocatingly hot and sweat was streaming down Jamie's skin. He wiped his face and glanced round.

The beach was part of a vast bay.

Stretching away into the distance on either side were other beached hulks. Some had been abandoned and were rotting away, but the majority were inhabited. There were lines of washing hanging over the sides, and figures moving about on the decks. Columns of smoke from cooking fires rose into the sky. An ox-waggon trundled down the dune. It stopped by one of the wrecks and two Africans started heaving sacks of supplies on board under the direction of a white man.

Jamie swung round and looked out to sea.

Three merchantmen were lying at anchor half a mile out, waiting for the tide to come in. Behind them on the horizon another ship was making laboriously for the shore, its sails almost slack in the thin breeze. Jamie turned back and stared inland again, his eyes drawn irresistibly by the line of trees.

The trees marked the start of the African jungle that Mrs Livingstone had read to him about all those years ago. Gazing at them, Jamie felt quick darts of excitement in the pit of his stomach. The forest looked lush and peaceful in the hazy light. Beyond it lay the whole immensity of the dark continent – the rivers, mountains, forests and scorching deserts he had dreamed about since childhood. Hidden somewhere among them was the source of the great river itself.

The river might still be thousands of miles away. Somehow it suddenly seemed so close that Jamie felt he could see the sunshine playing on its surface. He could taste the coolness of its waters in his mouth. He could smell the warm moist scents on its banks at dawn and hear the calls of the birds as they swooped above it.

'Ahoy, *San Cristobal* – !'

Jamie's head jerked up at the shout.

'Is there anyone on board?'

Jamie walked to the rail and looked over.

A white man was standing on the sand staring upwards, his hands shading his eyes from the sun. He lifted his arm in greeting as he saw Jamie and began to climb the rope ladder. A moment later the man swung himself on to the deck.

'Jesus, man, you got some cleaning to do here!'

The man wrinkled his nose at the still-lingering stench of the holds. Then he held out his hand.

'Cornelis DeWitt,' he said. 'Met your friends ashore earlier. Pleased to make your acquaintance, man.'

Jamie introduced himself and shook hands.

DeWitt was a paunchy man of about forty with a rugged face and a bushy grey beard. A sweat-stained leather hat was pulled down over his long grizzled hair. He was carrying a heavy knob-headed stick, and a pair of long-barrelled pistols was tucked into his belt.

'Any idea what happened to Gomez?'

DeWitt spoke with a thick nasal accent. Jamie frowned.

'Little Bartolomeo Gomez, the mate,' DeWitt went on. 'I saw him in Lagos only a few weeks before he sailed.'

Jamie shook his head. 'We didn't find any Europeans.'

'Poor bastard! They must have slaughtered everyone. Man, they're a wicked bunch if they get loose, those savages.' DeWitt paused. 'So you're from the *Forerunner*?'

Jamie nodded.

'Your friends told me you'd taken the *San Cristobal* in tow.' He looked at Jamie between narrowed eyelids. 'First trip?'

Jamie nodded again.

'Where are you bound?'

'Lagos and then inland,' Jamie answered. 'But it seems we'll have to spend a month in quarantine here first. Captain Culglass said we'd be run out of town if we came in any earlier.'

DeWitt grunted. 'True enough, man. The governor's a stickler over that. Not that it worries me. When you've been here as long as I have, you get like the niggers. The pox doesn't touch you.'

DeWitt glanced round the deck. He strolled over, lifted one of the hatches, and peered down.

'Doesn't look as if you've struck lucky,' he said, dropping the hatch back into place.

'Lucky?'

'Gomez always took a load of cotton if there was space. I came over to see if you wanted to shift it. But she's empty as a nigger's coffin. And how about the niggers? I'll take any healthy young bucks and up to a dozen fillies if their teeth are sound.'

Jamie understood.

DeWitt thought they'd picked up the *San Cristobal* for salvage. Jamie hesitated. DeWitt could well be useful to them. If he knew their reason for boarding the ship, it would be the last they'd see of him. British opposition to slavery had made Britons the most hated race on the coast. For the moment DeWitt had taken them for young adventurers —and there were still a number of them — who didn't share their country's view. He might as well go on thinking that.

'Most of them were dead,' Jamie said. 'The few still alive we turned loose. They weren't worth the keeping.'

'It happens.' DeWitt nodded. 'Still, the boat's worth a few dollars. I'll see if I can find you a buyer. There's some around but you've got to know where to look. Fifteen per cent, that's my terms, and you won't find fairer. Why don't we get out of this cursed sun and have a drink while you think it over?'

Jamie led the way down to the wardroom next to the cabin. He uncorked one of the bottles of brandy that Farquarson had found in the captain's stores.

Over the drink Jamie learned that DeWitt was a South African. He'd owned a freighter trading between the Cape and Lagos. The freighter had been holed and driven ashore a hundred yards along the bay from the *San Cristobal*. Since then he'd set himself up as a general dealer, living in the hulk and buying or selling whatever came his way.

'There maybe thirty of us doing the same,' DeWitt said. 'Some of them you want to watch. But on the whole they're not a bad bunch. They're all white, for Christ's sake. We got to stick together, I tell you that, man. In this goddamn country with the bloody savages all round we got no choice.'

DeWitt splashed another measure of brandy into his mug.

'So you're here for a month,' he went on. 'Ever done anything like this before?'

Jamie shook his head.

'You could do with a few tips, I've no doubt.' DeWitt leant back expansively. 'I've taken a bit of a shine to you, young Oran. You play fair with me and Cornelis DeWitt will see you right. First off you'll need a couple of good boys and a woman for the cooking and washing. As luck would have it I can fix you up with them cheap. Then you'll have to lay in some stores and fix yourself an oven – '

It was an hour before DeWitt left. By then Jamie had formed a fairly clear idea of what they would need over the next four weeks.

'Anything else you want, man, feel free to call on me any time,' the South African said as he stood up. 'If you can't find me at the boat, de Souza will know where I am.'

'De Souza?' Jamie frowned.

'Christ, you really are green, man, aren't you!' DeWitt chuckled. 'De Souza's the best bloody bloke on the coast. It's mainly niggers for de Souza but he deals in everything else too. Runs a general store and warehouse a few miles straight inland from here. You'll get all you need from him – but say I sent you.'

As DeWitt left, Jamie called Wolf and Farquarson together.

'We've got four weeks,' Jamie said. 'Let's get organized.'

70

'One more brick!' Jamie called.

Farquarson heaved another brick over to him. Jamie tapped it into place. He stepped back and inspected his handiwork with a critical eye. Sweat was pouring off him.

'Considering I haven't wielded a trowel in twelve years or more, it's nae so bad,' he said. 'We'll light a fire and see how she draws.'

Jamie beckoned to Ben, the young African hired to them by DeWitt as a camp boy. Ben ran forward and started to lay a fire in the oven's base.

It was mid morning on the day after the South African's visit. As well as Ben, DeWitt had provided them with another African boy and a girl. At that moment the girl was washing their clothes in a stream that ran down to the shore. DeWitt had also rented them an ox and cart. Wolf had left early with the cart to visit the store of the trader, de Souza, and buy the supplies DeWitt had suggested.

Wolf was due back soon.

Meanwhile Jamie had spent the morning building an oven out of coarse clay bricks in the shade of the clump of trees to which the *San Cristobal*'s mooring rope was fastened. He built it to the design of the old bread oven in the Oran croft on Iona. Jamie remembered every detail of the oven as vividly as if he'd seen it yesterday. Twice each year he had helped his father to repair it, cutting out the worn bricks and replacing them with new ones. Three times a week throughout the year either his mother or his grandmother would bake in it.

Watching the fire kindle and flame now, Jamie remembered the rich warm smell that would fill the croft as the oatmeal cakes crisped. The green turf and white sands of Iona with the curlews calling above them sprang to his mind. He felt a sudden aching sense of loss.

Jamie gritted his teeth.

It was no time for regret. There was much more work than building an oven to be done. At least the skills of his childhood had found a use here in the blazing African sun.

'Well, she certainly draws like a bitch,' Farquarson observed as the thin smoke from the fire ran straight and true up the little chimney. 'Maybe you're not just a pretty Highland face after all, Oran.'

'Wait until ye try my oatmeal cakes,' Jamie said.

Jamie got his chance to make them a few minutes later when Wolf returned with the ox and cart. The tide was high so they had to wait to take the cart down the shore and unload the stores on to the ship. Jamie lifted off a bag of ground maize, a bar of salt, and a leather jug of fresh buffalo milk.

As Jamie set to work, kneading the maize with the water and milk, Wolf described his visit to de Souza's store.

'I've met pigs in the Viennese police and veritable swine in the Paris gendarmerie,' Wolf said. 'But I tell you, that man tops the lot. De Souza's a monster. He's got this damn great store at the front where he sells everything to anyone. Then out at the back he's got these pens. He took me round –'

Wolf shuddered.

'He must have forty or fifty slaves waiting to be sold. They're crammed together like cattle in a market. They're all manacled to each other so when one moves, everyone has to move too. He feeds them out of troughs and there isn't a single privy. They just do their business on the ground. The place stinks almost as bad as the *San Cristobal*. There's almost no shade and it's like a furnace –'

He shook his head.

'I suggested he might put up some rush awnings. De Souza just laughed. "Niggers like sun," he said, "they're used to it." And all the while those poor bastards were lying panting on top of each other in the few scraps of shade they could find. If Karl saw what I've seen today, he'd pack in writing and pick up a gun. The revolution's waiting to happen here and now.'

'You could always lead it yourself,' Farquarson suggested mischievously.

'I'm an analyst of society,' Wolf answered. 'Not a catalyst.'

Farquarson chuckled.

Wolf moved away and sat down on the trunk of a palm blown down by the wind. He produced a knife from his pocket and began to whittle at a piece of wood.

'Right,' Jamie said. He slipped an iron tray covered with the cakes he'd made into the oven. 'In half an hour we'll see how they compare with good Highland scones.'

Leaving Farquarson and Wolf in the shade of the trees, he walked down the shore to the sea. He waded into the water, swam the few yards out to the *San Cristobal*, and climbed on board.

Mamkinga was still lying on the leather-padded settle in the captain's cabin. Jamie knelt and changed the dressing on the wound in his armpit. Then he got to his feet and stood looking down at him.

There'd been no change in Mamkinga's condition since they'd boarded the ship and Jamie had first dressed the wound.

Mamkinga hadn't recovered consciousness for almost forty-eight hours now. He lay very still on his back, a simple loin cloth over his waist and his once-majestic body resting limply on the worn leather. At the places where his joints pressed down on the leather, at his shoulders, hips and ankles, there were little puddles of sweat which dried and then glistened again as more moisture flowed out of him.

The soda salts had driven the worms and maggots from

the wound, and the mercury-chrome seemed to have checked the festering. At least the open tissue was raw and clean, not putrid and oozing pus as it had been when Jamie removed the filthy wadding. But Mamkinga was still sinking.

The fever ran backwards and forwards across his body like a tide. For hours he would lie in a torpor. Then he would start to twitch and shake. His teeth chattered and his wasted muscles clenched, standing out beneath his skin as tight as drawn bow-strings. For minutes on end as the convulsion gripped him he jerked and twisted. Sweat sprayed from his skin like raindrops and he moaned as he fought to suck air down his throat.

Afterwards he sank back into comatose stillness again. Each time he seemed to sink deeper, to move further away from life. Each time his breathing was shallower and the beat of his heart slower.

Jamie stared at him in anguish.

There was nothing more he could do. He had only the most basic medicaments in his satchel and he had tried everything he knew. Now he could only leave the outcome to the defences Mamkinga harboured in his own body.

Bleakly Jamie knew they wouldn't be enough.

The negro's natural strength and resilience must have been immense. Against all Jamie's expectations Mamkinga had survived for two nights since he'd boarded the ship. They could not protect him much longer. At the most he had only a day or two left before the fever finally overwhelmed and destroyed him.

Jamie went up on deck. He plunged over the side into the sea, already falling as the tide withdrew. The hot sweat that clung to his skin seemed to be as much Mamkinga's as his own. He tried to wash it off in the cool salt water. For a while it seemed to work. He broke the surface refreshed, struck out for the shore, and climbed up the beach.

'In your own wee way you're a genius, Jamie,' Farquarson greeted him beaming as Jamie reappeared.

'I'll wager not even the kitchens at Invergordon could match these. Try one for yourself.'

Farquarson had pulled the metal baking tray out of the oven.

The scones lying on it were plump and firm. Jamie took one. The scent that reached his nostrils as he lifted the scone to his lips was the same as he remembered from so long ago in the croft on Iona, floury and mouth-watering. He sank his teeth into it hungrily. Suddenly as he ate he saw Mamkinga's face, hollowed and pain-racked, with his eyes sunk so deep into his skull he might already have been a corpse.

Jamie choked and spat the scone out.

71

Mamkinga's crisis came two nights later.

By then Jamie, Farquarson and Wolf were comfortably installed in the hulk. The holds which had housed the slaves had been scrubbed with lime and their hatches nailed down. The last lingering traces of the terrible stench had vanished. The officers' quarters had been cleaned and each of the three had his own cabin. The galley was functioning again and Farquarson had decided to make himself responsible for their provisions.

Under Farquarson's instruction Ben, the young African servant, was proving an enthusiastic cook. Farquarson had discovered that there was an African market two miles along the coast. Every morning he set off early with Ben and returned a few hours later with their purchases.

'Feast your eyes on this!' Farquarson cried triumphantly when he came back after his first visit.

He held up a sea turtle which the fishermen had caught during the night. The creature was still alive, switching its grey scaly neck and flippers slowly from side to side.

'The chef at Massey's Chop House in the Strand would turn green just thinking about it.'

Farquarson carried the turtle into the galley with Ben trotting happily behind.

Wolf divided his time between exploring the surrounding countryside, and lying sprawled on the afterdeck in the shadow of an awning, whittling away at lengths of African hardwood. He was carving a chess set. Dexterous with his hands, he had already made the board, veneering a piece of teak from the ship's carpenter's workshop with alternating squares of ebony and palm. Now he was making the pieces.

Jamie barely found time to eat, let alone for anything else. As Mamkinga's remaining strength ebbed hour by hour, Jamie stayed by his bedside in the stifling cabin, reluctant to leave even for a few minutes.

'For God's sake, man, you must get some sleep!' Wolf protested.

It was long after midnight.

Wolf and Farquarson had gone to bed much earlier. Something had woken Wolf. He'd walked along the deck in his nightshirt and seen a candle still burning in the captain's cabin. Jamie was sitting beside Mamkinga as he'd sat for the past three nights. The young Scotsman's face was haggard and there were dark pouches under his eyes.

Jamie stood up wearily as Wolf came in. He walked over to the lantern window above the stern. The tide was in and the slow rolling waves below glittered with plumes of yellow-green phosphorescence.

'I canna sleep,' Jamie said.

Wolf glanced down at the great gaunt frame on the leather-covered settle. Even in the coolness of the night the leather was steaming from the evaporation of the sweat falling from Mamkinga's skin.

'You've done everything you can –'

Wolf brushed his long grey hair from his face and looked at Jamie with concern.

'Give it a rest, Jamie. It's up to him now. You won't help him by breaking yourself too.'

Jamie shook his head stubbornly. 'He may need me yet. I'm staying until the end.'

Wolf stared at him. He shrugged helplessly. Then he went out and walked back to his cabin.

Jamie stood gazing down at the sea.

'He called you Jamie. Is that how you are named?'

Jamie froze.

The question was barely a whisper. It had come from the settle. Jamie turned from the window. Mamkinga's eyes were open. They were dull and filmed with the hot mucous of the fever, but somewhere deep inside them a spark burned like the brilliant phosphorescence which tipped the waves.

'Aye,' Jamie answered.

'It gives me gladness to have your name. You have cared for me well. I owe you much. I will take what you have given with me – '

The voice, so faint and thin it might have been the night call of a young animal, wavered and faded. Then briefly it seemed to recover.

'I am Mamkinga, son of the Embrenche of Malinda. I have a sister, Toomi. Find her for me. Tell her she is my sister and my life and that I go to the spirits with her name on my lips. Wiil you do that?'

Mamkinga's eyes were fixed on Jamie's face. He tried to lift himself. The effort was futile. He hadn't even the strength to lever with his arms. He collapsed limply on the bench.

'It is over – '

Mamkinga's voice was hardly audible now and his chest was heaving from the effort it had cost him to frame the words.

Jamie's tiredness suddenly vanished. He hurled himself across the cabin. He dropped to his knees by Mamkinga's side, and seized his wrist. Mamkinga's eyes had closed. He had lapsed into unconsciousness again. Jamie searched for his pulse. Tremulous and uncertain, it was still beating.

Jamie racked his brain.

He thought he had tried everything. As he knelt by Mamkinga's bed something surfaced from the dimmest recesses of his memory. He was a child and he had been out with Dr Cameron attending one of the doctor's patients. The patient was a woman. She had given birth to a child after a long and difficult labour. After the birth her heart stopped beating.

Dr Cameron had made the delivery. When the woman's heart failed for the second time, Dr Cameron reached into his bag for a small black bottle.

'Extract of digitalis,' he said to Jamie. 'It is reduced from the common foxglove on the hill. Unless used with the greatest care, it is a powerful poison. But on occasion and in extremis digitalis can save a life.'

It had saved the woman's life then. Filtering into her bloodstream, it had shocked her nervous system into reaction and started her heart pumping again.

The very last phial Jamie had packed into the satchel he had brought with him from the *Forerunner* was the same digitalis extract.

Jamie leapt up. He searched frantically through the leather bag and found the phial. With the tiny bottle in his hand he hesitated. Dr Cameron, as far as he remembered, had given the woman a few drops on the tip of her tongue. 'If ye miscalculate the dosage,' Cameron had warned him, 'ye might as well stick a knife through the patient's heart. It's as deadly as adder venom.'

Jamie poured some of the liquid into the phial's cap. It no longer mattered if the dose was too strong. Mamkinga's life was balanced like a feather on a whirlpool. If the digitalis pulled him under, it would only do so moments before the ebbing currents of his vitality did the same.

Jamie lifted Mamkinga's head. He pulled down Mamkinga's jaw and tipped the capful of liquid into his mouth. Jamie washed it down his throat with half a tumbler of water. Mamkinga heaved and spluttered but seemed to swallow. Then his head lolled back.

For fifteen minutes there was no reaction.

Mamkinga lay as if dead. Only the sweat breaking from his pores and the occasional weak flutter of the heart beneath Jamie's hand as it rested on his chest told Jamie he was still alive. Then suddenly Mamkinga's back arched. His mouth opened in a scream of agony. His limbs churned, legs flailing against the hard wood of the pallet. He tossed from side to side. His muscles contracted into throbbing knots of flesh. His tendons stood out and vibrated like cords stretched to breaking point by drying sea-spray.

Jamie caught both his hands. He threaded his fingers through Mamkinga's and clenched them together. The digitalis poison was flooding Mamkinga's body. It would either kill him or shock his system back from the brink of death into life.

Jamie tightened his grip. He closed his eyes and began to pray.

Beside him, welded to him by their locked hands, Mamkinga fought and heaved like a spring salmon gaffed on a river in spate. Sweat showered into the clammy air. Groans and choked cries rang through the cabin. The cushion beneath Mamkinga's head whirled across the floor and burst open against the table leg, scattering a cloud of feathers over the floor. Mamkinga began to howl. He lashed out with his leg and a panel beside the settle crumpled, the wood caving in as his heel struck it in frenzy.

Still Jamie clung to him and prayed.

Jamie didn't see the curving roof beams of the cabin, the lantern hanging above the *San Cristobal*'s afterdeck outside, the myriad African fireflies, drawn by the ship's glow, that had swarmed out from the shore. He saw instead the ancient burial ground beside Iona's abbey. He saw the Celtic crosses above the graves he had dug for his grandmother and sisters. In his mind's eye he saw the all-powerful and all-seeing God of his childhood, Who had watched above him as he laid them to rest and Who had gathered them from their rough turf-strewn beds into His arms.

Long before they harvested kelp, Iona's people were fisher-folk. Beyond the green grass and the white sands of their home, their territory was the sea. Each time they sailed from the little island they placed themselves in God's hands.

Jamie had found Mamkinga on the ocean. His eyes shut, Jamie asked the Almighty to heal and safeguard Mamkinga as He had cherished and protected the Hebridean fishermen of Jamie's past.

Jamie clung to Mamkinga and waited.

An hour went by. Then another. Mamkinga's frantic convulsions dwindled. The rivulets of sweat pouring off him slowed to a trickle. His eyelids drooped and closed. His fingers, which had gripped Jamie's like claws, went limp. His hands dropped by his sides. His chin slumped on to his chest and the frenzied pumping of his lungs steadied to a measured rhythmic beat.

Jamie reached out and felt for Mamkinga's heart. It was still very quiet but it rose and fell beneath his fingers like a steadily chiming bell.

Jamie stood up. He went out on to the deck. The Atlantic tide was at full flood and the ocean was washing around the ship. Stars glittered overhead and the waves were brilliant with phosphorescence. Jamie stripped off his clothes and plunged overboard into the sea.

He surfaced and expelled his breath in a great roar of laughter. Stars or phosphorescence – he didn't know which – cascaded down his shoulders. Jamie didn't mind whether he was being showered with falling constellations or Atlantic foam.

All that mattered was that Mamkinga was alive. He had survived the crisis and he would live.

72

Hadji pointed ahead between the ears of his horse.

'Quilombo!' he called proudly.

Toomi and Rachel rode beside him towards the village as the rest of the waggons lumbered up the slope behind. It was exactly ten days since they had left the river ford where they had ambushed Mohamet Asa's caravan. As they rode the young women looked round.

Quilombo was a walled and fortified settlement of some five thousand people. It was set on a broad saddle in the wooded hills that rose up from the plain. Outside the village an area of land had been cleared of trees and scrub, and placed under cultivation. The earth was fertile and well watered. The ripening crops were strong and healthy, and there were rich pastures for sheep and cattle.

As they entered the village both Toomi and Rachel were struck by its prosperity and cleanliness. The baked earth streets were swept. The unblocked gutters ran with clear water. The people were well fed and well dressed. There was no sign of beggars – almost a phenomenon in an African town. Even the scavenging dogs looked plump and sleek.

Hadji led them towards the centre. Following him, Toomi and Rachel noticed something else unusual. The houses in every settlement they had ever seen, from towns as big as Gondar and Malinda to tiny villages, were built in the same style. Here there was no uniformity. Some dwellings were simple conical huts, some were grouped in compounds, some were built of brick in the elaborate Arab fashion, some were reed-walled and roofed with leaves.

Toomi shook her head in bewilderment. 'It's as if they've collected houses from everywhere,' she said.

'But look at the people,' Rachel pointed out. 'They're just the opposite. Almost everyone's dressed the same.'

Mystified by the strange rag-bag of buildings, Toomi hadn't taken in Quilombo's inhabitants until then. Now she saw that Rachel was right. It was even stranger.

Except in very remote areas most African villages housed people of several different nations and cultures. In trading centres like Kano dozens of races would be represented. The architecture would be the same, but the inhabitants kept their own customs and, most noticeably, their own dress.

Here it was the reverse. The buildings were wildly, bizarrely different from each other but the people were dressed the same. Everyone – men, women and children – wore robes striped in blue and white. And yet, as Toomi looked at them more closely, they had the same almost extravagantly different features, physiques and colourings she had seen everywhere else on her travels. They seemed to come from every tribe and race in the continent.

They rode on until they reached a wide oval of open ground between the houses.

At its centre was a council chamber, a large open-sided structure raised on stripped tree trunks and roofed with layers of palm fronds. Three long benches were arranged beneath the roof. Thirty or forty men, most of them with greying or white hair, were seated on the benches. As they approached the men stood up.

Hadji turned to the girls.

Throughout the journey, at camp, in battle at the ford, and later when he had withdrawn from them, Hadji had clearly been the caravan's leader. At the same time he had never been more than a soldier – the first among equals.

As they approached the village something changed. The armed and mounted guards, until then the companions he had laughed with over the fire, drew themselves upright in their saddles. They clustered tightly round him, and rode at his side with eyes fixed unswervingly ahead. Hadji himself sat taller in the saddle. Crowds had gathered at every street corner and people bowed and applauded as he passed.

It was almost as if a king had returned to Quilombo.

'I must report to the council,' Hadji said. 'I have ordered that quarters be prepared for you. With your permission I will visit you at dusk to eat with you.'

He raised a hand and two men ran forward.

'They will show you to the dwelling,' Hadji added. 'I look forward to seeing you when my business here is finished.'

He dismounted and walked into the council chamber. The men took the bridles of Toomi's and Rachel's horses and led them away.

The quarters Hadji had assigned them turned out to be a spacious two-storey house. It was built of brick in the Arab style, with an open courtyard at its centre and an arched balcony running round the upper floor. From its size and position – it was only a hundred yards from the council chamber – the house was evidently kept for the use of important visitors.

At the door Toomi and Rachel were met by a group of female servants. The women escorted them upstairs and showed them to their rooms. Each had a large airy chamber, and these were connected by a brass-studded door. The floors were tiled with mosaic. There were deep beds with mattresses filled with soft dry moss, and the arched windows looked out over Quilombo into the valleys beyond.

'Your arrival left us with little time to prepare,' the oldest of the women said. 'Water is being heated for your baths. When it is ready we will come to collect you. Meanwhile we wish you peace and comfort.'

She bowed respectfully. Then with the other servants following her she withdrew.

Toomi threw herself down on the mattress. She closed her eyes in delight. She had never known such luxury in her life – not even in the distant lost years in Malinda.

'Can you believe it?' she called out. 'For three months we've slept on sand beneath the stars. We've bathed, when we could, in streams. We've cooked our meals, washed our clothes, looked after our animals, tramped and travelled, rode and run. And now this – '

She swept out her arm at the clean sweet-smelling room, the wax-polished furniture, the bunches of fresh-cut flowers on the tables and the newly laundered robes laid out on the couch.

'Who is he, Rachel?' she demanded. 'Where are we and what's happening to us?'

Rachel had been looking through the arched window in her own room over the roofs of the village. Beyond there were hill slopes, valleys, and very distantly the presence of mountains. Somewhere, much farther still, was Gondar.

She turned at the sound of Toomi's voice and walked through into Toomi's room.

'We will find out tonight,' Rachel answered.

73

Hadji arrived as dusk was falling.

An hour earlier a group of men had appeared in the central courtyard. With them they brought several crates of provisions and a number of live animals. Among the animals Toomi noticed two vervet monkeys, a large lizard in a basket and a young goat. They built a fire. Then they slaughtered the animals and put their carcasses to roast on an elaborate iron spit. Afterwards they set out the courtyard with cushions and tables.

By the time the old servantwoman came up to announce Hadji's arrival, Toomi and Rachel had bathed in hot scented water and dressed themselves in new clothes. They were the same long robes of fine cotton everyone else in Quilombo wore, but with one difference. They were dyed bright saffron yellow instead of blue and white.

When they walked downstairs the house was filled with the enticing scents of herbs, roasting meat and vegetables cooking in gourds. Hadji was waiting for them by the fire. Like the young women he, too, was wearing a yellow robe.

'It is my privilege and pleasure to offer you Quilombo's hospitality,' he said, smiling. 'Please be seated.'

They sat down on the cushions. Hadji clapped his hands and a male servant appeared.

'Is everything prepared?' Hadji asked.

The man inclined his head. 'It is ready,' he replied.

'Then let us eat.'

For the next two hours the three were served with what seemed to be an endless succession of dishes.

They started with roasted slices of the young goat, cut from its flanks as it hung above the fire. After that there were cutlets of gazelle on beds of rice. Following the gazelle came the two monkeys. They were presented upright and cross-legged on great metal salvers in a sauce flavoured with their livers. The lizard, stewed in a cauldron of peppers, came next. Then a platter of roasted crocodiles' eggs was brought to the tables, the shells charred and flaking and the flesh inside pale, rich and rubbery.

Later there followed cuts from a haunch of smoked elephant, saucers of fried locust, and bowls of specially fattened land-crab, grilled and served in their shells. The bowls were removed with their empty shells and a cauldron of manatee brought forward to replace them. Only the breasts of the manatee, the sea-cow or mermaid as the European sailors called it, had been cooked. They floated, twin islands of tender sweet-smelling fat, in a lake of herbal soup.

Finally a dish of the hearts of cabbage palm was produced.

'Have you ever tasted this?' Hadji asked as the palm hearts, stewed in a white butter sauce, were placed before them.

The young women shook their heads.

'It is a great delicacy and very rare,' Hadji explained. 'The tree dies when its heart is cut out. The ordinary people are forbidden, on pain of severe punishment, to take them. Even among the chiefs they are served only at great feasts on great occasions.'

Toomi's and Rachel's eyes met.

As so often they knew what the other was thinking. The palm hearts could only mean that Hadji was a chief. What the great occasion might be they had no idea, but the feast was in their honour – there was no doubt about that.

Already gorged, they forced themselves to try the palm hearts. A moment later they were eating the hearts as if they were famished. The dish, sweet and soft and juicy, fragrant with herbs and sharpened with wine, was the most delicious they had ever tasted. When they finished they sat back, their bellies distended and their minds dazed.

Toomi had attended celebrations given by her father, the embrenche, in Malinda, Rachel even more lavish ones in the palace at Gondar. Neither had ever eaten a dinner like the one that night. It was the finest, largest, most succulent meal they had ever had.

'You have fed us like queens,' Toomi said as the last dishes were being carried away. 'You have done us great honour. We are deeply grateful. Yet we wish to know what we have done to deserve this – '

Toomi paused. Then she added with her customary forthrightness, 'Tell us – who are you and what is Quilombo?'

Hadji sat for several moments in thought before he answered. Eventually he looked up.

'Quilombo is freedom,' he said quietly. 'It is also me and I too am Quilombo. I will tell you – '

He started to talk. The young women leant forward, listening intently.

The servants cleared the tables and retired. The constellations of stars wheeled up the night sky and hung glittering above the open courtyard. At intervals the fire burnt down and flared again as the single remaining guard fed it with fresh logs. Pearl-spotted owls, the tiny nocturnal scavengers of African towns they both knew so well, called beyond the roof. Jackals barked outside the town walls and once a distant lion roared.

Still Hadji talked on.

'Ayeshi calls me son,' he began. 'I call her mother. By now she may even believe it is so. It is not. I was born in the real Quilombo. Do you know where that is?'

Toomi and Rachel frowned. Neither of them had ever heard of it. They shook their heads.

'It is across the great ocean in Brazil,' Hadji said. 'It lies deep in the forests to the north of the January River – '

The settlement of Quilombo, he explained, was very ancient.

More than two hundred years ago, as the coast of South America began to be colonized by the Portuguese, groups of their imported African slave labour escaped from the new plantations and fled into the forest. Most were pursued and caught by their owners. They were marched back in chains to the work fields. But some evaded recapture and set up communities in the remote hinterland.

There the former slaves tried to recreate the style and patterns of their lost life in Africa. The communities were fragile. Many were destroyed by New World diseases. They were harassed by Indian tribes whose territory they had unwittingly invaded. They were attacked by vengeful expeditions sent out by the expanding colonialists. A few clung on. As the years passed their numbers were swelled by more fugitives from the plantations.

By the end of the seventeenth century at least one of them, Palmares, had become so large that rather than attempting to destroy it, the Portuguese acknowledged its independence as a vassal state within Brazil.

One of the main problems the communities faced was a lack of women. It was the men, housed separately, who escaped. Almost always they left their women still in captivity behind. To acquire a breeding stock for their settlements they were forced to raid the white farms on the shrinking forests' edges. Any male Portuguese they took was slaughtered. The women, whether white, Arab or Bantu, were carried back to their villages. There they bred with the fugitives.

Palmares grew too big to feed itself and collapsed. The soil in the fields cleared to grow its corn became at first sterile from over-use and was then washed away by the Brazilian rains. Other communities – at one stage there were more than thirty – lasted longer. In the end they too withered. There was one exception.

The Portuguese named the slave sanctuaries quilombos after the very first settlement of all. It was the original

Quilombo that survived. It was there, two hundred years after Quilombo's foundation, that Hadji was born.

'I do not remember my parents,' Hadji said. 'Later I was told they had died of fever when I was an infant. I was taken in and brought up by a family which survived the sickness. I looked like my foster brothers and sisters. We all had pale skins and Arab features. It was not surprising. Quilombo was not far from where the Arabs had colonized the coast. Many Arab women were taken in the early raids. The Arab blood dominated Quilombo's stock. We lived in African houses and followed African ways, but I can hardly remember a single pure Bantu face from my childhood – '

The settlement where Hadji grew up had known many assaults from the Portuguese over the two hundred years since its birth. It survived them all. But when Hadji was nine it suffered its last and fatal attack.

By the 1830s the Portuguese were expanding greedily into the Brazilian interior. Remote and isolated as it was, Quilombo was proving more and more of an irritation – a beckoning symbol of freedom for the slaves of the Portuguese settlers. Nine times in as many years there were slave uprisings in the coastal plantations. Under torture they revealed that they wanted to join their brothers in their new African home.

Eventually the Portuguese decided to crush Quilombo once and for all.

A heavily armed force was sent from the coast. Quilombo was taken. Together with the spreading network of villages round it, the town was burnt to the ground. The slaughter was fearsome. Eight out of every ten of Quilombo's inhabitants were killed. The survivors were marched back to the coast in chains and sold to help pay for the expedition's costs.

Hadji was among them.

A tall and well-built boy, he caught the eye of an elderly Portuguese sea captain. The Portuguese was a pederast who was looking for a cabin boy and a bed-mate. Hadji, he decided, would fill both roles. A month later Hadji found himself on board an ancient cargo ship slipping anchor in Rio de Janeiro.

By day Hadji worked in the cramped and steaming galley where the Portuguese officers' meals were cooked. By night he warmed the captain's bed. The ship's destination was the Bight of Benin. On the outward trip from Rio it was loaded with crude trade goods manufactured in Brazil. For the return voyage it was due to carry a cargo of slaves.

'But we never reached Africa,' Hadji said. 'As we approached the Azores we were caught in a terrible storm. We were swept north towards the mouth of the Mediterranean sea. When the storm died down we had lost all of our sails and two of our masts. We were helpless. And then a Barbary corsair found us –'

It was almost four hundred years since the North African Arabs had been expelled from their golden kingdom in Spain. Yet the memories of the lost paradise – they had called Granada the 'antechamber of Paradise' – were as vivid as ever. So too was the bitterness and resentment they felt towards their conquerors.

The Moors, as the Arabs were known in Europe, made no distinction between the Spanish and the Portuguese. To the pirates of the Barbary coast the Iberians were one race – and their blood enemies. They raided any ship whatever flag it flew. But when they found a vessel sailing under an Iberian ensign, their assault was fuelled by an ancient and still-burning hatred that outweighed even greed for plunder.

The Arab corsair circled the stricken Portuguese ship for three days before attacking.

When the corsair finally closed on its victim, the fighting was brief and bloody. The Arabs boarded the Portuguese ship and slaughtered its parched and exhausted crew man by man. Only four were spared. Three were half-caste girls who had been embarked to service the Portuguese officers. The fourth was Hadji.

All four owed their lives to the Moorish belief, inspired by the Koran, that it was foolish and wasteful to kill women and children. Women should be saved for breeding, children to be reared for work. The half-caste girls were handed over as spoils to the corsair's crew. Hadji was taken by the captain.

'Naturally, as an Arab, he was a pederast too.' Hadji shrugged and smiled. 'There was no difference. One day I was a cabin boy on a Portuguese freighter. The next on an Arab corsair. All that changed was the language – '

For the next ten years Hadji was constantly at sea.

The corsair operated out of Tangiers. It would be away from its home port for months at a time, scouring the African coast southwards or sailing far into the Atlantic in search of booty. When it had made a successful raid it would return to Tangiers with its plunder. After a brief spell ashore the crew would set sail again.

Over the ten years Hadji grew up. By the age of fourteen, already at almost his full height, he had been replaced in the captain's bed by another child. From then on Hadji served as an ordinary crew member. Intelligent, resourceful and brave, he was promoted two years later to assistant mate. At nineteen the captain, now an old man, promoted him again. Hadji was made second in command of the corsair.

Hadji's very first voyage in his new post also proved to be his last.

As so often before, the corsair headed south. For weeks it searched for a suitable prey. Then off the Bight of Benin it spotted a Dutch merchant ship becalmed and in difficulties – the crew had gone down with dysentery. The fight was quickly over. The corsair's captain supervised the placing of a tow rope on the Dutchman's bows. As he turned to tell Hadji to set sail for Tangiers, he collapsed from a heart attack.

Hadji found both ships were under his command.

'I did not sail back to Tangiers,' Hadji said. 'For ten years I had been a slave. Now I was free. I gathered the crew together. I told them what I was going to do. I offered them a choice – '

Like Hadji the crew were also slaves. Hadji told them

he was going to sail the two ships into an African harbour. There he would sell the Dutchman's cargo. Afterwards he intended to head inland. Those who chose could go with him. The others could take the corsair back to Tangiers.

'You see . . .' Hadji paused, frowning. 'All those years I had never forgotten Quilombo. How could I? It was all I had of the past, of my own, in my life. It was what I held to throughout everything. My Quilombo, the real Quilombo, had gone. But when the captain died and I became free, I realized I could make a new Quilombo in Africa. I had the Dutch ship's cargo to raise the money and the crew to join me.'

'Did the others join you?' Toomi asked.

Hadji nodded. 'Every one of them. But it was not as easy as we thought — '

He frowned again.

The port Hadji sailed the ships into was Porto Novo on the Guinea coast.

When he went ashore he quickly learned that the coastal region was a deathtrap for foreigners, and all the major markets were hundreds of miles inland. If he wanted to get rid of the Dutchman's cargo, he would have to mount a caravan and take the goods on a two-month journey west.

The destinations suggested to him were Kano or Garoua.

Hadji consulted his crew again. This time most of the men refused. The idea of a settlement on the coast near the ocean they knew was one thing. A two-month journey into Africa, into the unknown, was different. As he promised, Hadji turned the corsair over to those who had changed their minds. Then, undaunted, he bought camels, waggons, oxen and horses. He loaded them with the Dutch merchandise. Accompanied by the few who still wished to follow him, he set off into the interior.

Three months later the caravan reached Kano.

During the journey almost two-thirds of the men who set out had been lost. Some fell to diseases they contracted along the way, others were killed in ambushes when the caravan was attacked, others still gave up hope as day followed day of sapping heat, exhaustion and fear. They stole away into the bush and died.

Of the ninety souls who left the coast with Hadji, barely thirty gaunt and emaciated men trudged behind him into the walled market town of Kano.

There their luck changed. Few caravans had reached Kano for several months. Supplies of almost everything in the market were short. Prices were at record levels. Hadji sold the Dutchman's cargo for far more than he had ever hoped.

'We were able to buy everything we wanted,' he said. 'Tools, building materials, seed, animals, labour. All we needed was somewhere to settle.'

It took Hadji a further three months to find where he wanted. On the saddle in the hills ten days' journey from Kano he came across it. The small upland plateau had everything — water, fertile ground, thick surrounding forests for fuel and timber, a healthy climate, a remote and secure position.

Hadji set up camp and began to clear a space in the trees. The new Quilombo was about to be born.

'But that was ten years ago,' Hadji finished for the night as the fire began to gutter down and the girls' eyes filled with sleep. 'You have promised me a month. In that time I will show you what we have done.'

74

For both Toomi and Rachel it was the strangest month of their lives.

There was the luxury first. Toomi, captured at the age of nine, had never known the experience of being pampered. Comfort and security, not luxury, were what she associated with Malinda and had never forgotten. Yet they were childhood memories and long distant now.

Rachel's experience was different. She had grown up as a princess, as heiress to Gondar's throne. She was an adult when her world had been taken from her. The loss of Gondar was only months, not years, away, and her memories were quick and vivid. Yet she too knew little of luxury. Under Ras Michael's regime her life had been spartan and demanding. To her, living was a matter of hard beds, early risings, simple food, physical exhaustion and the company of soldiers.

Even to Rachel the world of Quilombo was bewildering.

Two days after they arrived the girls were transferred to an even larger house overlooking the town's walls. The new house was almost a palace. The staff who looked after them was trebled. The six women who greeted them on the first day went with them. To their number were added grooms for the stables, gardeners, cooks, guards and many more.

Hadji visited the house every morning.

'I want you to see all of Quilombo,' he said the first day. 'We will ride over our lands.'

There was a clatter of hoofs on the baked earth roadway beyond the gate. Hadji led the girls outside.

Two horses with scarlet leather saddles and bridles were waiting for them. Hadji got up on to his own mount as grooms helped Toomi and Rachel on to theirs. Then they set off.

Each day Hadji arranged a different expedition.

Sometimes, as on that first day, he came with them. On others, when Quilombo's business forced him to remain in the village, he provided them with guides. As day followed day the two began to learn about the strange community he had founded.

As in the original Quilombo every citizen, however humble, was free. Almost all the inhabitants were former slaves. Throughout Africa it was common for freed slaves to acquire slaves of their own. The institution of slavery was as common and widespread as the ownership of cattle. In Quilombo it was forbidden. Anyone could join the community but a price was demanded for leaving it.

'To survive we must grow,' Hadji explained one day as he rode with Toomi and Rachel through Quilombo's cassava fields.

'At the start we hid ourselves away here. No one knew of our existence and we were safe. I knew it would not last. Word would spread out of a small settlement in the hills. The slavers would learn about us. They would send a raiding party to see what they could pick up. We had to become strong enough to defend ourselves. That meant more people. They are still needed – '

He paused and pointed at a man gathering cassava heads.

'That man comes from the Niger,' he said. 'I know him. We freed him when we attacked a slave column from Kano to the coast in the winter. Now he wants to go home. Well, he can do so but first he must find two others to replace him here.'

Toomi frowned. 'How can he do that when he's working in the fields?' she asked.

'He must volunteer to join an expedition to ambush another slave caravan,' Hadji answered. 'He must fight. If the ambush succeeds and the slaves are freed, he must persuade two of them to come to Quilombo. He must bring the two before me and let them declare their wishes. Then I will let him go.'

'And if he doesn't want to fight,' Toomi asked, 'if he runs away, what happens then?'

'We will follow him wherever he goes,' Hadji said bluntly. 'We will find him and we will kill him. Quilombo's freedom is strength. Quilombo's strength is people. Quilombo's people are indivisible. We all accept that – '

The man from the Niger lifted his head and waved as they passed.

Smiling, Hadji waved back. 'He will not run,' he said. 'He has been a slave and Quilombo freed him. Home is a great prize, but freedom greater. He will pay his just dues for what he has been given.'

On another day Toomi and Rachel were out riding with one of the guides Hadji assigned them. They came to one of the little satellite villages which had spread out round Quilombo. Under a baobab tree at the village's centre a very old man with a wispy white beard was telling a story to a group of wide-eyed children.

As they reached the tree the guide dismounted. He went over to the old man and bowed. The old man chuckled and exchanged a few words. Then he waved the guide back to his horse and went on with his story.

The guide remounted and the three rode on.

'Who was that?' Toomi asked, looking back over her shoulder. 'And why is dressed as he is?'

With the exception of the council elders the old man was the first person they had seen – apart from Hadji and themselves – who wore a yellow robe.

'He is a chief of the Inyuki,' the guide answered. 'His whole tribe was captured by slavers. They were the very first we released after Quilombo was established. I remember it well – '

The girls' guide that day was one of the men from the corsair who had followed Hadji from the coast.

'We attacked the caravan and drove off the slavers,' he

525

went on. 'Hadji explained what we were doing. He asked the old man's people to join us. The old man told them they should do so. He and his people have been here ever since. They are part of Quilombo's foundations. He is brave and wise and much respected.'

'But why the yellow robe?' Toomi insisted.

'Because that is how we confer honour,' the guide said. 'Everyone, wherever they come from, has the right to make their own shelters in their own way. That is only natural – how else should a free man live except under the roof of his fathers? But to remind our people that they are also Quilombo and free, that they are all brothers and sisters, everyone must wear the same dress. Only those of the highest distinction are different. To them we give the yellow robe.'

The two girls exchanged glances. Both were thinking the same. Why had they been given Quilombo's highest honour?

Toomi voiced the question as casually as she could.

'We are deeply honoured that the robe has been given to us,' she said. 'We are a little surprised Quilombo feels we deserve it. Maybe you can tell us the reason?'

The guide glanced at her sharply. He frowned and opened his mouth to answer. Then he changed his mind. What he said next, it was clear to both of them, was different from what he had been about to say.

'Hadji and the council decide,' he said vaguely.

Then, moving away from the subject, the guide went on.

'The yellow is a dye which comes from the roots of the fayar tree and the bark of three other trees. When the extracts are mixed together they create a poison. The poison is so strong that if the cloth is worn too soon after being dyed, it enters the skin and causes death. But later, when the poison has dried, the dye has the opposite effect. It protects the wearer. That is why we give it to those we honour most – '

He broke off and gestured ahead. 'Now I will show you how we pasture our sheep. After the rains we keep them up here where the grass is long. As the grass withers we move them by levels down towards the valleys – '

With the guide still talking, they rode on.

'The guide did not tell us the truth,' Toomi said emphatically when they returned to the house that evening.

Rachel thought for a moment. 'You saved Hadji's life. Hadji is king here whatever name they give him. Maybe he told the council what you had done and the council decided as the guide said.'

Toomi shook her head. 'Hadji's life must have been saved many times in many battles. Who else have we seen wearing the yellow robe? No one except a few old men. Why us, Rachel, why us?'

Rachel was silent. 'He asked for a month. There are only five days to go. We will know before the end.'

There was no time for further talk. Almost every night Hadji arranged a banquet for them to attend. They were due at yet another in half an hour. The two retired to their rooms to prepare themselves.

On the twenty-eighth day, the day when the revolving moon would rise above Quilombo at dusk in its full shining splendour as it had done on the evening of their arrival, Hadji came to the house earlier than usual. He had warned them he would do so, and Toomi and Rachel were ready for him. As soon as he appeared they knew he was tense and elated.

'Today I have a surprise for you,' Hadji said, laughing. 'But to make it a surprise, I must have you out of the house all day. To fill your time until the surprise is ready, I am taking you hunting.'

Beckoning exuberantly, he led them to the door. Horses were waiting. The girls mounted and followed him out of the village on to the plateau.

They rode through the fields to the high rolling plains beyond. It was further than they had ever gone before. Waiting for them was a group of horsemen with dogs and hawks. Hadji spoke to the men. Then he turned to Toomi and Rachel.

'Ride, watch, and do as these men say,' he called. 'Above all, enjoy!'

He kicked his horse into a gallop.

The hounds bayed. The hawks rose and flared their wings. Dust lifted behind the drumming hoofs as the men launched themselves after him. Toomi and Rachel galloped behind.

It was a day such as neither of them had ever known. The morning air was sweet and fresh. The bush was green and laden with the night's dew. The grass shone like silk. The hill flanks were crisp and radiant with shifting bands of gold and violet, turquoise, ivory-white and dark quivering chestnut, the colour of a gazelle's faun in flight. Game rippled away in waves before them. Mountain, forest and plains game, a swirling cornucopia of animals – antelope and zebra, baboons and giraffe, lion, cheetah and trumpeting elephant herds.

At midday they rested in the shade of an ancient baobab. They ate wind-dried biltong, carried in the hunters' saddlebags, and drank herbal tea, brewed over a fire of bone-dry branches. They talked and laughed. Then, under the now searing sky, they were on their way again.

Finally, as the sun lowered and the soft evening breeze began to lift, they turned back towards Quilombo.

They rode back through fields past returning workers who were singing as they headed for home. As they entered the town the first stars drifted out across the evening sky. The animals and birds they had taken were draped over the horses' flanks. The largest game, an eland and two gazelle, had been butchered in the field. Hadji hunted not for the sake of hunting but, as Africans had always done, to eat. His men, his hounds and the hawks had killed as prey only the old and failing among the herds and flocks which had run or risen before them – and then only as much as they needed.

Across the saddle of Hadji's horse was slung a single

small gazelle. As the procession approached the house where Toomi and Rachel were quartered, he raised his hand.

'No,' he said. 'This evening you will bathe and change elsewhere. Come with me.'

To their surprise he led them away from the gate towards another house. Hadji ushered them in. Women were waiting to serve them. They went upstairs. Baths had been filled and clothes laid out. They bathed, changed and went down again.

Hadji was still waiting outside. He was unchanged and the gazelle was still lying in front of him on his saddle.

'Now I can take you home,' he said.

Hadji dismounted.

Leading his horse by its bridle, he took them up the street to their house. When they reached the entrance he stopped and knocked. Someone, unseen inside, must have been ready for their arrival. The gates swung back. Toomi and Rachel stepped forward.

Inside the courtyard they stopped and gasped.

75

Jamie swayed and his legs seemed to buckle.

His head was swimming. He stumbled and almost fell. Then he recovered and walked on, cursing the morning sun which seemed to be even hotter than usual.

It was the day after the crisis in Mamkinga's fever. When the crisis passed Jamie had slept for a few hours on the floor beside him. The sun was already high when Jamie woke. He took Mamkinga's pulse again. Its beat was steady and even. The illness was draining from him and he was sleeping peacefully. Jamie left him lying on the settle in the cabin and went ashore to check that the fire he'd left burning in the oven was still alight.

Now he was on his way back to the ship. A few minutes afterwards as Jamie climbed the ladder to the deck the giddiness overtook him again. His arms lost their strength and he almost toppled back on to the sand. With an immense effort of will he pressed himself forward and held on. The dizziness passed. He struggled weakly upwards and staggered down into the wardroom.

Wolf was inside unpacking a crate of stores. He glanced at Jamie as he entered. Wolf's face stiffened.

'What's the matter, Jamie?' he said. 'You're as white as a sheet.'

Jamie collapsed on to the bench. He was shivering now and his body was sheeted with sweat. He opened his mouth. Before he could speak a dark mist enveloped him and he fainted.

When Jamie recovered consciousness he was lying on the bench with a pillow beneath his head. He was shivering even more violently and a blanket had been draped over him. Farquarson had joined Wolf in the cabin. The two of them were gazing anxiously down at him.

'What happened?' Jamie asked.

His throat felt hot and dry, and his voice was a whisper.

'You passed out, man,' Wolf answered. 'You're sick, Jamie.'

'Get me some water,' he said.

As Farquarson fetched a mug, Jamie tried to concentrate. He was the only one of the three with any medical knowledge and he knew his life might depend on it.

Fuzzily he tried to diagnose himself.

Giddiness, fever, trembling, a raw and aching throat. They might have been the symptoms of almost any of the myriad African diseases to which the books had told him Europeans were particularly vulnerable. He'd certainly contracted one of them but, despairingly, Jamie had no idea which. All he could do was try the crude all-purpose remedies in the medical bag he'd brought with him from the *Forerunner*.

'There's some colchicum root in the bag,' he said as Farquarson lifted the mug to his lips. 'Also some powdered eringo. Give me three grains of each every four hours. If I – '

Jamie never finished the sentence.

His voice seemed to shrivel and die in his throat as another uncontrollable bout of trembling swept over him. For a terrifying moment he thought he was dying.

The last thing Jamie saw before the sickness engulfed him was Mamkinga's silhouette against the cabin window. The huge African must have heaved himself up from his bed under the awning outside and was watching him through the streaked, mosquito-spattered glass of the window.

Jamie's eyes met Mamkinga's and held them for a moment. Jamie heaved himself upwards and held his hand out towards Mamkinga. Then the young Scotsman fell back, sliding deep into the delirium of his sickness.

'It's useless,' Wolf said. 'The medicines do nothing. If anything he's getting worse.'

Wolf turned away from the bed, his fists clenched in frustration.

It was three days later. He and Farquarson were in the wardroom. They had moved Jamie from the bench to a makeshift bed. Every four hours throughout the three days they had dosed him as Jamie had instructed. Neither the colchicum nor the eringo had had any effect on the disease. Jamie remained unseeing, his body boiling with the fever, his skin clammy with the sweat which poured from his tormented body.

That morning Farquarson had gone to the hulk of DeWitt's freighter. Farquarson begged him to come over to the *San Cristobal* and see if he could give any advice. The South African had peered down at Jamie and shrugged.

'It's the yellow jaundice,' DeWitt said. 'Keep on giving him the preparation but I'm not offering you much hope, man. It's a killer, that one.'

DeWitt went away, shaking his head grimly.

'Pass me the colchicum flask,' Farquarson said, kneeling by the bed.

'For Christ's sake, man, what for?' Wolf rounded on him. 'It's doing him no good. Nothing's doing him any good. Jamie's dying, can't you see?'

'It's all we can do,' Farquarson said quietly.

Wolf was silent for a moment. Then his head slumped wearily.

'I'm sorry,' he said. 'Here, I'll bring it to you.'

He crossed the floor with the worn leather bag and pulled out the flask of colchicum. Farquarson poured some of the liquid into a spoon. He lifted Jamie's head, and trickled the medicine into his mouth.

Afterwards they both sat silently by the bedside. It was night and the cabin was lit by a single candle. In the small pool of light Jamie's face was sunken and yellow. His chest barely moved as he breathed.

In the captain's cabin along the passageway Mamkinga opened his eyes.

He'd been woken a few seconds earlier by a noise. Until then he'd slept uninterrupted for three days. His sleep had been quite different from when the infection was raging. Then it had been fitful and restless, filled with nightmares and broken by constant aching awakenings, when he had tossed deliriously. For the last three days his rest had been deep and still and nourishing. Now he felt fed. His body was weak but Mamkinga knew the sickness had gone. He was healed.

Mamkinga frowned and gazed up at the stars shining through the porthole windows. Something was troubling him. He concentrated on the sound that had woken him. The echoes of a voice were fading swiftly on the night air. Mamkinga realized it was Wolf's. There had been anger and anguish in the shouted words. The anguish seemed to hover round him in the darkness.

Suddenly everything came back.

Mamkinga's sleep hadn't been entirely untroubled. Once before, he remembered now, something had woken him and prompted him to rise. He had managed to heave himself to his feet, stagger along the deck, and peer into the wardroom. Jamie was lying on the bench. He had reached out his hand towards Mamkinga. Then he had dropped back and his eyes had closed.

Mamkinga had thought it was a dream. It was not. He was well and Jamie was sick. Jamie had been calling to him. Far down beneath the slow healing waves that had rolled over him as he slept, Jamie's silent cry had been ringing in his ears. As life had flowed back into Mamkinga like a making tide, it had been draining from Jamie.

Mamkinga got stiffly to his feet.

He walked across the deck and looked into the wardroom again. Farquarson and Wolf were curled up asleep on the floor near Jamie's bed. Jamie was lying motionless on his back. Mamkinga stared at his face. Jamie's skin had the colour and the cold waxy sheen of the yellow tallow candle burning on the table. The air in the cabin seemed to be filled with the sweet rotting presence of impending death.

Mamkinga went to the ship's side and heaved himself over on to the ladder.

As he climbed down he realized that the muscles of his arms were so weakened they could scarcely hold his weight. Grimly he clung on, moving foot over foot, until his bare feet touched the water. The tide was in and he had to wade ashore. Fountains of phosphorescence lifted round his waist and trailed in green plumes behind him. The breeze from the land felt cool on his skin as he left the water and began to climb up the shore. Mamkinga came to the top of the ridge.

A single palm tree, much taller than the others which lined the dune, stood apart from the rest.

The tree's roots ran deep into the sand. Its coronet of leaves was so high that the stars seemed to be turning between them. As the leaves brushed together their sound mingled and became one with the crash of the surf. Plunging down into the earth at one end and soaring up into the air at the other, the trunk linked the sky and the ground – a living vibrating umbilical cord between the two.

Mamkinga dropped to his knees beside the tree. He put his arms round the trunk and leant his forehead against the bark. The young white man who had saved his life was dying.

Mamkinga conjured Jamie to his mind and began to pray.

Jamie, Mamkinga knew, had found him sorely wounded, at the lowest darkest point of his existence. He had taken Mamkinga in his arms. He had dressed his wound. He had sat up beside him night after night through the long hours of darkness. Often Mamkinga had woken from his feverish sleep and been aware that watch was being kept over him by the anxious hooded blue eyes.

Night after night, hour after hour, Jamie had never moved from his bedside.

Throughout the torment those eyes – and the comforting touch of Jamie's firm cool fingers on his skin – had been the only fixed marks in the darkness. Mamkinga had had a brother watching over him. He had had a brother's care. That his newfound brother was a stranger, the offspring of a wild land many moons distant from the Benin coast, mattered not at all. Jamie had turned the hour-glass of his own life on its end and let its healing, saving powers pour into Mamkinga.

Now Jamie, as equally alone as Mamkinga, as equally a stranger in a foreign land, was dying. Mamkinga could not and would not let it happen. The bond between them had become too strong. As the stream of life had flowed into Mamkinga, so he could channel the stream back into Jamie. To help him do it and defeat the fever, Mamkinga needed the spirits. He needed them to speak to him, to give him their wisdom and their balms.

To make them talk he would have to reach for them, and offer himself up to their mercy.

The trunk swayed and throbbed in the night wind. The stars burst and cascaded through the leaves, showering him with a glittering silver light. The waves drove against the shore. They drained through the sand, and spent their filtered wetness over the palm tree's roots.

The spirits would not answer him.

In a frenzy Mamkinga conjured up his father, the embrenche, who was proud of his royal healing skill and who laid hands on the most sorely ill in Malinda's villages. He conjured up the professional healers, the grey-bearded old men who toured the countryside treating people and animals with their spells and medicines. He brought back the primitive mountain goat-herds who could restore a dying wild bird to the wing. He asked the spirits to speak to him on behalf of all of them.

Behind the rustle of the leaves and the pounding of the sea there was only silence.

Again and again Mamkinga called. He gripped the trunk until the bark tore his skin. He strained every muscle and sinew. He threw his mind across the years and the distance that separated him from Malinda, like one of the rope bridges that spanned the gorges in the Mountains of the Moon.

The hours passed and still there was nothing.

Towards dawn he unlocked his arms. They were stiff and bloodied and aching now. Mamkinga fell back on the sand. He lay huddled in a ball, his knees drawn up to his chest. He was so drained and exhausted that he was beyond even despair. He had tried and he had failed. The spirits had refused to answer.

The white man would die. There was nothing Mamkinga could do to save him.

The air cooled swiftly as the night ended and a heavy dew fell. Mamkinga felt a chill creep over his body. Instinctively, as he had done so often as a child in the Malindan winters, he reached out to pull Toomi towards him for warmth. His arms groped and found nothing. Mamkinga lifted his head.

The space round the tree, hazy now with the dawn mist, was empty but the unseen presence of his sister was so vivid and overpowering that Mamkinga felt he could touch her. He sat up.

Toomi.

For some reason he hadn't summoned her with the healing spirits. Now he remembered her kneeling by their nurse and pounding out a potion of her own. Once when he was hurt she had smeared it on his arm. The little lesion had healed almost as he watched it. Toomi could heal as well as anyone and Toomi was half his soul.

If Toomi was alive the spirits would speak through her.

Mamkinga turned back towards the tree. There was no need to embrace it, to clench and hug the bark as he'd done all night. To reach Toomi all he had to do was touch the trunk. Mamkinga reached out and placed his finger gently on the wood. Instantly the tree began to vibrate. The vibrations quickened to a pulsing song that entered his hand and ran through his body.

The exhaustion dropped from him like dust washed away by a waterfall. He sat up straight, alert and bright-eyed. The stars were fading and the sound of the surf was dwindling with the falling tide. Mamkinga saw neither the vanishing night nor the gathering day.

All he was aware of was a voice inside him singing. It was Toomi's voice. The spirits were singing with her.

76

The sun was high and the morning hot when Mamkinga finally stood up. Weak as he was he ran back down the ridge towards the shore.

As he came to the foot of the dune something shone gold on the sand in front of him. Mamkinga looked down. Seeking the warmth that would fill it with life, a snake, a West African king viper, had crawled out of the undergrowth on to the sand. The sun, glittering off the golden scales of its back, hadn't fully woken it yet, but it had already given the viper enough energy to raise its head and turn towards Mamkinga's footfall.

The snake gazed up at Mamkinga.

Its eyes were dark and fearless and unblinking, tiny almond-shaped chips of agate in a triangular head ringed with a jewelled collar of turquoise and emerald. Mamkinga stretched out his hand. He touched its back with the finger he had rested on the tree.

'Come with me, my brother,' Mamkinga said quietly. 'Help me to keep watch over our friend.'

The snake's tongue leapt out and flickered from side to side. Then the snake lowered its head tranquilly to the sand.

Mamkinga unknotted his loincloth and folded it into a triangle. He lifted the snake gently by its belly, laid it at the cloth's centre, and picked it up. Then he ran on towards the *San Cristobal*.

'An oven,' Mamkinga said to Farquarson as he clambered over the side on to the deck. 'A clay oven with bars above it to hold a pan.'

'An oven?' Farquarson looked at him, puzzled. 'We've got an oven. Jamie built it.'

'Not the sort I want. I want a new one, and I want it quickly.'

'For Christ's sake, man,' Farquarson burst out. 'You're talking about building ovens and Jamie's dying.'

'He's not going to die,' Mamkinga answered. 'He's going to live. I need an oven to help him.'

Mamkinga pushed Farquarson aside and stepped down into the wardroom.

Wolf was crouching above Jamie's bed. He'd been bathing Jamie's face with a damp cloth. As Mamkinga entered, Wolf straightened up. Mamkinga set the loin-cloth down on the floor and untied the knot. As the golden coiled band of the viper appeared Wolf stepped back, appalled.

'What the hell are you doing?' he cried.

Mamkinga tipped the snake carefully on to the boards.

Warmed from the journey, the viper lifted its head and gazed round the confines of the cabin. It straightened its body and flicked its tail, its eyes opaque and impenetrable. A beam of sunlight was slanting down over the floor where it lay. For a moment the snake absorbed the sun's heat. Then it slid out of sight into the layer of shadow beneath the bed.

'You're mad!' Wolf shouted. 'Get the creature out of here. If the sickness doesn't kill him, that beast will. It's deadly, you savage!'

Mamkinga watched the switching golden filament of the viper's tail disappear into the darkness. He looked up.

'The two are together,' he said. 'While the snake lives, Jamie lives. Guard it with your life, white man. It holds the spirit of your friend – '

Mamkinga paused. Then he snapped, 'Help the little man with the oven.'

The urgency in Mamkinga's voice sent Wolf stumbling out of the cabin and up on to the deck, where Farquarson was already stacking bricks from the galley oven.

'More!' Mamkinga instructed. 'I want it so hot it's white.'

As he turned away Wolf and Farquarson set to work with their axes again. They were shaving tiny chips from a dry hardwood trunk and piling them on to the glowing heap of coals at the oven's base.

Mamkinga wiped his face.

Like the others sweat was pouring off him. They were gathered at the foot of the ridge, where Wolf and Farquarson had built the oven. They had finished it at midday. Two hours later the heat from the fire was so intense it was melting the surrounding sand. For Mamkinga it still wasn't enough.

Mamkinga shook his head and blinked.

Then he went back to the mortar. He picked up the worn antelope thigh-bone he was using as a pestle, and hammered it down into the bowl. A wet slurry of juice and half-broken shells spurted up into his face. Mamkinga scraped the mixture from his cheeks. He dropped it back into the bowl, and pounded it again.

'Now!' He waved the other two aside.

The flames were shimmering white and the bricks were beginning to crack. Mamkinga poured the contents of the mortar into a shallow iron pan. He held the pan over the oven.

The mixture he had pounded together was a blend of the sliced roots of a cassis plant, yellow and fibrous, wrinkled nuts from a mopane bush, and an assortment of shore-dwelling herbs. The cassis and the nuts were familiar to Mamkinga. They grew all over the Malindan hills. The herbs he had never seen before. But as Toomi sang to him through the palm tree, her voice had told him exactly where and how to gather them.

Mamkinga had obeyed her without question. He plucked the leaves and mashed them together with the cassis root and the nuts. Now he simmered them over the flames.

The water evaporated in an instant, leaving a residue of root and nut steaming in the bottom of the pan. An aromatic smell from the charred herbs lifted into the air. Mamkinga tipped the mixture into a cloth and squeezed the remaining moisture from it. Then he hammered it with the bone once more until it was reduced to a dough. He peeled the cloth away and spread out the dough on a flat stone.

The dough dried within minutes under the fierce midday sun. As it dried it crumbled to powder and turned a bright saffron yellow. Mamkinga swept the powder into a dish. He stood up and stared round. A few yards away a stream, circling the tree beside which he'd prayed, was tumbling down to the shore. He picked up a jug and filled it with the clear foaming water.

Mamkinga set off for the ship.

Jamie was still lying unconscious on the bench. His face was sunken and the jaundice had turned his skin to the colour of old and dusty parchment. Apart from the shallow movement of his chest, he might have been a corpse. Mamkinga sat down beside him. He filled a mug with water and dropped in a few grains of the yellow powder. Then he lifted Jamie in his arms. He opened Jamie's mouth and poured the liquid down his throat.

Instinctively Jamie swallowed.

'From now on he has a mug of this every hour,' Mamkinga said to Farquarson and Wolf who had followed him in. 'His body's full of poison. This will wash it away. When it has gone he will be healed.'

Mamkinga carefully lowered Jamie. Then he crossed the wardroom and settled himself cross-legged on the bench opposite where Jamie was lying.

'When it is ready, bring me my food here,' Mamkinga added. 'I will not leave until he is well again.'

The other two went out. Wolf had been standing in front of the window. As he left, sunlight poured across the floor. The snake crawled out from the shadows and coiled itself on the boards.

Glittering, it lay with its eyes open and its head resting on its body at Mamkinga's feet.

Mamkinga barely moved from the wardroom for two days. When the others ate, food was brought to him. At night he slept on the bench. The rest of the time he remained cross-legged, watching over Jamie. Every hour without fail he crossed the room and poured a mug of the cassis-and herb-infused liquid down Jamie's throat.

At first the liquid passed straight through Jamie. Gradually as the hours went by his body began to absorb it. He took in more and more until the sunken hollows in his face seemed to be filling. As they did the colour of his skin changed again. It lost the dead waxy look of old parchment and took on the brilliant saffron hue of the cassis roots.

The change was frightening. It made Jamie look even closer to death than before. When Farquarson saw it he begged Mamkinga to stop.

'You can't do it to him,' Farquarson pleaded. 'No one can survive like that.'

'The poison is coming out,' Mamkinga answered. 'Soon it will begin to wash away. Look at the snake – '

The king viper was lying in its favourite place in a pool of sunlight on the floor. The sheen on its golden skin was sparkling and clean, and its dark eyes were bright and alert.

'That is the spirit of your friend. The spirit is strong and full of health. Soon Jamie will be too.'

Farquarson shook his head helplessly and went away.

That night Jamie began to sweat. Sweat had come off him throughout the illness. This was different. It poured from him in streams, so fast and thick it pattered down on to the boards like rain. Until then he had lain still and quiet. Now he tossed and moaned. Incoherent shouts broke from his throat. He sat up convulsively and struck out at the air with his clenched fists, as if he were fighting something. Then he slumped back on the bench, gasping and muttering.

Mamkinga poured more liquid into him, no longer at hourly intervals but every fifteen minutes. Jamie soaked the liquid up like a sponge. He held it inside him for a while. Then he expelled it from every pore, spraying it across the boards and soaking the leather upholstery until it steamed. His teeth chattered and all the while he jerked and howled.

The noise woke Farquarson and Wolf and drew them to the wardroom. They gazed down in horror as Jamie thrashed and shuddered in torment. Mamkinga waved them away.

'Let him be,' Mamkinga said. 'The spirits are washing him clean.'

They returned to their cabins and lay trying to sleep as the terrible cries rang through the ship.

Confident and impassive, Mamkinga sat in watch over Jamie. Beneath him the viper's tongue flickered between its lips. Each evening as the sun dipped and darkness fell, the snake had retreated into the shadowy space beneath the settle. That night it was lying out on the floor.

The moonlight sparkled off its collar of turquoise and gold, and its eyes shone as brightly as the stars wheeling outside.

Towards dawn Jamie at last fell silent. His limbs ceased their frenetic twitching and the sweat dried on his skin. His breathing became slower and deeper. Just as it had done with Mamkinga at the same hour, the crisis in his fever had passed. The toxins in his body had been sluiced away. He was whole again. For a while he slept, calm and untroubled.

Jamie woke as the sun lifted over the horizon.

A shaft of light filtered into the wardroom and brushed across the viper's head. The snake uncoiled itself. Then in the gathering warmth it began to slide across the floor towards the door.

Jamie opened his eyes.

'Where am I?' he asked.

'You are with me and you are safe,' Mamkinga answered.

Jamie turned towards the voice. He saw the huge gaunt frame of a young black man sitting cross-legged on the bench opposite him.

'Who are ye?' Jamie said, puzzled.

'I am Mamkinga,' the man replied. 'You found me and guarded my life. I have done my best to return the same to you.'

Jamie remembered now. The man was the slave with the suppurating gunshot wound he had found on the *San Cristobal*. Jamie had healed him. Then, it dimly came back to him, Jamie had fallen sick himself.

'How long was I ill?' Jamie said.

'Seven days and nights. Now you are well.'

'And ye are well too?'

It was all beginning to return to Jamie.

He had given Mamkinga the extract of digitalis, and gripped his hand as Mamkinga writhed and heaved while the powerful stimulant coursed over his body. Finally Mamkinga had fallen asleep. Jamie had gone out on to the deck. The sun had risen and he had plunged into the sea. He remembered the shock of the cool water and the taste of salt in his mouth, but after that nothing.

'We are both well,' Mamkinga answered. 'We have healed each other.'

'I gave ye digitalis,' Jamie said as more of the scattered jigsaw of the past week came together in his mind. 'It was very dangerous, but all I could think of. Ye felt no ill effects afterwards?'

Mamkinga shook his head and smiled. 'None.'

'I am glad.' Jamie stopped and frowned. 'I told the others to treat me with colchicum. Ye have been giving me something different. Colchicum leaves a bitter taste in the mouth. I have none. What have ye given me?'

Mamkinga hesitated. 'In truth I am not sure,' he said. 'My sister spoke to me. I gave you what she told me.'

'Your sister?' Jamie looked at him, puzzled.

Mamkinga stood up. He came over to the bed and stood looking down at Jamie. Then he smiled again.

'When you are rested I will explain,' he said. 'For now accept only that my sister spoke to me and your life is saved as you saved mine. You owe me no thanks. If thanks are due, they are due to her. She is your sister too now. I greet you on her behalf as my brother –'

Mamkinga paused. Then he placed his hand on Jamie's forehead. 'Pula!' he said.

Jamie had never heard the word before. It meant

nothing to him. He thought for a moment. Then he reached up and covered Mamkinga's hand with his own.

'Pula, my brother!' Jamie replied. He smiled. An instant later his eyes closed and he slept again.

Mamkinga gently replaced Jamie's hand beneath the blanket that was covering him. He stepped back.

The viper was nudging the door, its tongue flickering out from its mouth as it explored the crack through which the light of the rising sun was seeping into the wardroom. Mamkinga went over. He unknotted his loincloth and placed the snake inside. Mamkinga went up on deck. He swung himself over the side, and carried the snake ashore, holding it above his head as he waded through the waves.

Mamkinga walked to the start of the dune and slid the snake out on to the sand. For a moment it lay coiled, looking up at him through its fathomless eyes. Then the heat of the morning sun filled its body. The snake stretched out. Something, some possible prey, caught its attention in the bush beyond. Its head reared up, alert and pulsing with life. Its tail lashed, there was a dazzle of gold — so fierce and vivid it made Mamkinga blink — and the viper was gone.

Mamkinga stared down at where the snake had rested. Briefly the sand held the print of its coiled form like a snail shell pressed into the earth. Then the tiny ridges began to crumble and dissolve in the heat.

All that was left on the sultry morning air was the golden arrowing glitter of its passage.

Mamkinga was still gazing at the sand when Wolf appeared with the ox-cart. Wolf had visited Jamie in the wardroom as soon as he rose. He saw that at last the jaundice had run its course and Jamie was sleeping peacefully.

Wolf greeted Mamkinga buoyantly.

'You've done marvels,' Wolf said. 'When Jamie wakes he'll be as hungry as the poor beast who's pulling my waggon. We're getting a feast ready for him.

Farquarson's gone to the market. I'm off to see what de Souza can furnish us with.'

Mamkinga's head jerked up.

'De Souza?' he said. 'Who's that?'

'The trader we get our supplies from,' Wolf answered. 'He's a bastard who deals in slaves, but he runs the best store on the coast. Between Farquarson and de Souza, we'll come up with a meal fit for a king.'

The ox-cart trundled away up the dune. Mamkinga watched it disappear through narrowed eyes.

Mamkinga might forget many things in his life but the name de Souza, and the obscene presence of the man who had caused him to be beaten until he had almost died, was one that would remain engraved on his memory for as long as he drew breath. Mamkinga walked back to the hulk of the *San Cristobal*. For the first time in days neither Jamie nor even Toomi was on his mind.

Mamkinga was thinking of de Souza. Like the instincts of the king viper as it vanished into the bush in search of prey, Mamkinga's mind was fierce and hot.

77

'It is a dream,' Toomi said.

She shook her head in bewilderment. Beside her Rachel caught her breath and stood spellbound.

The house in Quilombo where they had lived for the past month had been transformed. While they had been out hunting with Hadji the courtyard pillars and arches, the two flights of steps leading upwards and the balcony above, had all been garlanded with thousands of flowers. The stone and brick had vanished. In their place was a dazzling tropical garden filled with rainbows of colour and scent.

The myriad blossoms gleamed in the torchlight, and the scents hung heavy and fragrant in the still night air.

The courtyard itself was covered with great mounds of fruits, vegetables and crops. There were piles of melons, pawpaws, oranges and mangoes. Bunches of grapes, bananas, figs and dates. Pyramids of yams, cassavas, eggs and coconuts. Stooks of maize, corn and cotton –fresh and golden as if they had just been harvested from the fields.

The girls gazed at the scene in silent astonishment. In their absence an immense cornucopia seemed to have been emptied over the house.

'It is not a dream,' Hadji said quietly. 'It is Quilombo.'

He stepped past them and threaded his way to the centre of the courtyard, where a small space had been left clear round the fire.

The gazelle he had killed was draped across his neck. Hadji laid it down on the tiles. He butchered the carcass quickly and expertly with his hunting knife. Then he began to grill the steaks over the flames. As the meat hissed and crackled, he beckoned the girls towards him.

'Please sit,' Hadji said.

The girls came forward and sat on stools by the fire. Soon the steaks were ready. Hadji removed them from the grill and handed them to Toomi and Rachel on thick pottery platters.

'The meat is mine,' he said. 'I share it with you as should any hunter who has been successful in the chase. The rest is Quilombo's – '

Hadji gestured across the floor. 'Take whatever you wish.'

Round them, amidst the stooks of corn and cassava, the yams and maize, were loaves of bread, pots of butter, jugs of palm wine. The day's hunting had started at dawn. It was eight hours since midday when they last had any food. Now the young women suddenly realized how famished they were.

The meal lasted an hour. When it ended and the one servant girl who attended them had retired, Hadji got to his feet. He stood in front of the fire, his feet apart and the jewelled dagger at his waist sparkling against his yellow gown in the light of the flames.

'I wish to talk to you,' he said.

Toomi and Rachel sat watching him. For once Hadji seemed to be uncertain and ill at ease.

'I asked you for a month,' he went on, 'from one moon's rounding to the next. You have given it to me. I am grateful. What I wanted in return was to give you Quilombo. I have done my best to do so. Now at the end I have brought Quilombo here to the house – '

He gestured round the courtyard.

'Quilombo is not fully secure yet, but almost so. Soon we will be strong enough to defy anyone. It has taken me ten years. It is, if you like, my garden. In the years I have been digging and tending it, I have been alone. I am still alone – '

Hadji paused.

'I am an educated man. My first mother told me I

should always learn. I have followed her advice ever since I was taken from Brazil. I have taught myself to read and write in Arabic and Portuguese. When I can, I read books. I listen when the storytellers speak. I like music. But my companions for the most part are not educated – '

He smiled wryly. 'It is not surprising. Those I know best are the slaves I free. You do not expect to find culture among slaves. But then I met you and I found something different – '

Hadji stopped again. He was having difficulty in speaking now and his face creased painfully as he searched for the words. He found them and they suddenly flowed out.

'I have given you Quilombo's garden,' he said. 'I ask you to stay here and share it with me. I ask you to be my wife. Both of you if you so wish, because I respect you both equally. Either one of you if you do not. But if you are agreed it should be one and I may let my heart speak, then I would ask you first.'

Hadji faced Toomi and knelt.

The two girls sat in stunned silence.

Neither of them had had any inkling of what was coming. All of their thoughts had been concentrated night and day on their different goals – Toomi's to find Mamkinga, Rachel's to return to Gondar. They had assumed – as much as they had assumed anything – that the month in Quilombo and the royal treatment they had been accorded was in return for Toomi saving Hadji's life at the river ambush.

Now everything fell into place.

The yellow robes, the rides, the tours, the feasts, the guides drawn from the members of the council who had changed day by day. Hadji must have told the council of his decision to take a wife. While the two young women had been shown Quilombo, the council members had been inspecting them. At the end, like the simplest and poorest African peasant wooing the girl who had taken his heart, Hadji had gathered the fruits of his garden and laid them at their feet.

The first great feast Hadji had ordered to be prepared for them on their arrival had been a banquet fit for chiefs. The simple meal they had just eaten was utterly different. Lovingly prepared with Hadji's own hands, it contained nothing except game that he himself had hunted and the harvest of his land. It was the meal of ancient tradition that a man of honour gave to his future wife.

Toomi stood up first. Like Rachel she was overwhelmed. She blinked away tears. Hadji had spoken first to her. Toomi knew she should be the first to reply.

'Hadji,' she said. 'You have done us more honour than I can say. We give you our deepest thanks and we return your love.'

'And you will be my consort?' Hadji asked gravely. 'You and your sister? Or your sister can live with us and I will give her any husband she chooses. It does not matter. For one or the other or for both, all Quilombo is yours.'

Toomi was silent.

Rachel got to her feet then. She came forward and stood by Toomi. Together the two put their arms round Hadji. Either could have said what came next, but it was Toomi again who spoke.

'We love you, Hadji,' she said. 'But neither of us can marry you.'

'Have I not offered enough?' Hadji gazed round. 'If there is anything more I can give, it is yours too.'

Toomi shook her head.

'It is not that. The smallest part of what you have offered would have been more than enough. We cannot marry you because we cannot stay in Quilombo. We must go on.'

'Go on?' Hadji looked at her, puzzled. 'Where can you go on to? You come from Malinda. Your country has been invaded and conquered by the Galla. There is nowhere for you to go. Here, you have sanctuary, a home, anything I can give you. If you leave Quilombo, you have nothing.'

'I come from Malinda,' Toomi said. 'Rachel does not. She is from Gondar.'

'Gondar? But she is your sister,' Hadji protested. 'You cannot come from different countries. And Gondar, too, is under the Galla's rule. What do you mean?'

Toomi glanced at Rachel. Rachel nodded. They stepped back and sat down.

'I will explain,' Toomi said.

She told Hadji their two stories. When she had finished he sat in silence for several minutes. Hadji was unable to speak.

From the start it had never occurred to him that they were anything other than two beautiful and educated young Malindan sisters, the daughters perhaps of some minor chief. Now he learned the truth. It was not the shock that silenced him. It was bitter and anguished realization that had they come from any other background, had they been the simplest of slaves, it would not have mattered.

Hadji had fallen in love with Toomi with all the intense and consuming passion of a mature man, who had long since accepted that his dedication to the dream of Quilombo had condemned him to a life of loneliness. He knew that one day he would have to marry to give Quilombo an heir. It would be a marriage of convenience to one of the freed slave-girls. Hadji had put off the moment again and again in spite of the urgings of the council.

Hadji did not want a peasant girl.

All through the years of Quilombo's making he had ached for an equal companion, for someone to share his dream with him, someone before whom he could spread out his garden like a bower. And then at the end, when he had given up hope, he had found Toomi. Beautiful, brave, cultured and wise, she was not just all he had ever yearned for but more. The council had approved her rapturously. So had Quilombo's people.

That Toomi had a sister she loved mattered not at all.

Rachel was just as lovely, she had just as many of Toomi's qualities. Out of normal courtesy Hadji had offered to marry her too. He had even offered to marry her alone. He knew intuitively that the sisters would not be separated and he would have done anything to keep Toomi with him.

Now he had discovered that, however closely yoked together, however almost incomprehensibly alike in their looks, they were not sisters. Toomi was the child of the embrenche of Malinda and Rachel the queen of Gondar. Somehow their destinies had become interwoven. They had met, they had joined their lives, and they had embarked on a journey together.

The journey led them inexorably away from Quilombo.

For an instant, in rage and despair, Hadji thought of keeping them there by force. The impulse died immediately. Glancing between their faces, Hadji knew nothing would stop them. When his gaze came to rest on Toomi shame flooded over him. In the firelight, her eyes steady and bright, she was more beautiful than anyone he had ever seen.

Hadji loved her then more than ever before. Loving, he knew, was to give and not to take. Whatever Toomi wished, it was his sacred duty to give her.

'You wish to go to Garoua,' he said, 'to see if you can trace your brother?'

Toomi nodded. 'He is my other self. I cannot rest until I find and free him.'

Hadji stood up.

He walked across the courtyard, stepping carefully between the piles of fruit and vegetables, the mounds of nuts and the sheafs of corn.

The day-blossoming flowers on the pillars had folded their blooms. Some of the vegetables near the fire were shrivelling in the heat from the flames. Some of the fruit was browning – the fruit had been there in the sunlight since the morning. It did not matter. The scents were still strong and fragrant. There would be other fresh offerings from his garden. What there would never be again was the presence of Toomi and Rachel.

He turned and looked back. The two sisters – Hadji

would never be able to think of them apart from each other – were standing side by side amid the fading bounty of his gift.

He gave them a smile that was compounded equally of dignity and immense sadness.

'We should leave at dawn,' he said. 'The last big market in Garoua before the onset of the rains takes place in four weeks. All the slave traders will be there. It will take us four weeks' hard riding to arrive in time. You will excuse me if I leave to organize the escort and the caravan.'

Toomi frowned. 'You were intending to leave for Garoua?'

'No,' he answered. 'But I am going there now.'

78

They left Quilombo as the sun was rising.

Riding down the same winding valley that had led them up there from the plain, Toomi and Rachel paused on a shoulder in the hills to look back. The rains came earlier to the hills than to the plain, and the morning sky was filled with dark cumulus clouds. Between the clouds, shafts of bright sunlight lanced down over the landscape.

One of the shafts caught the town and the fields that surrounded it.

Bathed in the clear early light the houses looked clean and neat, the fields rich and well tended. Distant cattle were lowing, waggons were lumbering out into the pastures, people were beginning to move about the streets. Dogs barked faintly. The air was full of bird calls and the scents of flowers as the dew lifted from them.

The clouds rolled on.

Somewhere rain must have begun to fall. Suddenly in place of the sunlight, a rainbow was resting on Quilombo. For a few moments the entire saddle was irradiated in blue and gold, crimson and green. Crisp, secure and sparkling, enveloped in the safe everyday sounds of a community's business, rooted safely in the hills, the fortress and garden shone against the blackness.

Then the clouds surged forward again. The rainbow and the beams of light vanished. Swirling mist covered the hill shoulder. The saddle disappeared. Shivering, Toomi and Rachel rode on. As they did they caught sight of Hadji at the head of the column. He too had been looking back, but not at Quilombo – he was intently watching them.

As soon as he saw they had noticed him, Hadji swung his horse round and cantered ahead.

It was a very different journey from the one they had made from Kano to the river and then on to Quilombo. On that occasion they had travelled with slow-moving ox-waggons. There had been fifty men in the column, and many more after the ambush, and they had moved at the pace of those on foot. Now the total strength of the caravan was only fifteen. Everyone was mounted on horses and they had with them a single light provision cart pulled by six strong mules.

Because of the growing heat on the plain as they headed west they rode only by night. They covered twice the distance during the hours of darkness as they had before in daylight. Every rider, including Toomi and Rachel, carried their essential equipment with them. Only the food from the cart was shared. They ate three times in every twenty-four hours – once at dusk before they set out, once midway through the night, and once at daybreak after they had made camp.

Hadji was no longer a presence among them.

Deliberately keeping himself apart, it seemed, he rode at the column's head flanked by two of his men. When the halts were called and the food prepared, he stayed away from the fire and ate alone, served by his personal servant. When they camped he slept at a distance from everyone else, dismissing the servant and taking his bedding roll, a quilted sheepskin cape, out into the bush.

All Toomi and Rachel saw of him was a dust-haloed figure on horseback against the stars, or a lonely silhouette walking away to lie down in a scoop on the sand as the sun rose. They both knew the reason and they grieved for him. Hadji had been wounded in the depths of his being. There was nothing they could do.

The road both Toomi and Rachel had to follow led inexorably away from marriage, family and security – from everything Hadji had offered them in Quilombo – back into the dark and dangerous heart of Africa.

On the twenty-seventh day after they left Quilombo,

the pattern changed. At dusk, just before they were due to start out, Hadji rode over to where the young women were standing ready to mount their horses. It was the first time they had seen him close at hand in almost a month. He dismounted and squatted on the ground.

His face was haggard, Toomi saw, and from the dark shadows under his eyes, he had not been sleeping.

'We are a few hours from Garoua,' he said. 'There is a house there where I lodge when I visit the town. The owner is a friend and a good man. If you will be safe anywhere, it is there. Yet I would ask you again to turn back now.'

'Why?' Toomi demanded.

'While you slept this morning a caravan from Garoua passed this way,' Hadji answered. 'I know the caravan master and I spoke to him. He told me the town is full of stories and rumours. Many strangers have arrived from the east. They are offering rewards for the return of what they say are stolen slaves – '

Hadji glanced at Rachel. 'I believe they are agents of the Acab Saat.'

Rachel sat for a moment, frowning in thought.

'Salama cannot be looking for me in Garoua,' she said. 'He heard of me last two full moons ago in Kano. If he is still searching for me, it will be there. He has no reason to suppose I have left Kano for Garoua.'

'The caravan master spoke of strangers and rewards,' Hadji said stubbornly. 'I can think of no other source but the Acab Saat – '

He paused. 'I beg you to change your mind. If I am right, it is not only you who will be in danger but Toomi.'

There was silence. The girls looked at each other. Then Rachel spoke again.

'Toomi will take the risk for her brother,' she said. 'I will take it for myself. We must go on.'

Hadji stared at the ground, his face furrowed in anguish. Then he stood up. He mounted his horse again and called to his men.

'Garoua!' he said, pointing ahead into the darkness.

They reached the town at midnight. The gates were barred but Hadji had been there often before and he knew the gatekeeper. Hadji called up. A torch flared, there was a brief conversation and the chink of coins being passed. Then they rode in. They wound through the deserted streets until they reached the house where Hadji lodged. The owner, a small fat Sudanese, rose sleepily to open the door. He saw Hadji and greeted him with delight.

A few minutes later the girls were shown to a room on the upper floor. They went to bed and slept until daybreak. Then there was a knocking on the door. Hadji was standing outside.

'I am going down to the market,' he said. 'Stay here until I return. I will make inquiries and see if I can find out the truth of the stories the caravan master told me.'

Hadji was away for several hours.

The girls waited impatiently as the morning light filled the sky outside the arched windows. Finally they heard Hadji's footsteps in the passage outside. They stood up anxiously. Hadji came in. Even before he spoke Toomi and Rachel knew his news was bad. Hadji's face was grim and the knuckles on his clenched hands were white.

'It is worse than the caravan master reported,' Hadji said. 'The Acab Saat's men are all over the town. He expects to find you and he has offered a reward of one thousand shells of gold to anyone who helps him.'

The girls looked at him in horror.

'I spoke to a merchant named Waziz,' Hadji continued. 'When we were building Quilombo I bought much from him. Over the years he has become a friend. He knows everything that happens in the market –'

Hadji sat down wearily.

'Waziz told me a caravan arrived here from Gondar last week. Its leader is a warrior-priest, one of Salama's men. He put out word he was searching for two young slaves who had stolen from Gondar's treasury. He said they were seen in Kano two full moons ago. They were making their way to Garoua with a group of bandits. As well as the reward, he has offered twenty times the worth of any of the gold they try to sell.'

'But how can he know?' Toomi demanded.

The answer came to her even as she spoke.

Before they escaped from Kano they had asked Mohamet Asa if they could continue with him to Garoua. The Arab had recognized her at the ford when she leapt for his arm. Asa must have returned to Kano and told the Acab Saat's agents what had happened and where they were bound.

Toomi shook her head in despair.

'Neither of you can remain here,' Hadji said. 'Salama's men are everywhere. The reward he has offered is huge. Garoua is not large. Word travels swiftly among the traders. If you start to ask about your brother, the men will know within hours.'

Toomi was silent. She felt trapped and helpless. Beside her Rachel was equally quiet.

'Listen to me,' Hadji implored. 'Tonight there is no moon. We can get out of Garoua and be far from the town before daylight. They will never know you have been here. Even if they do find out, you will be long on your way to safety – '

As he spoke Toomi sat very still.

Suddenly she felt dizzy. Something was pounding at her temples and pulsing in her wrists.

'I beg you.' Hadji's voice fell to a whisper as he pleaded. 'I will do anything for you. I do not even wish to take you back to Quilombo. I only want you to be safe. Garoua is a deathtrap. Wherever you wish to go, I will take you. But you must get away.'

Toomi barely heard him.

The throbbing in her veins grew stronger. It became a drum-beat, a drum-beat that was carrying a message. For an instant the message was blurred and confused, a tangle of sounds that rang in an incomprehensible cacophony inside her head. Then the uproar faded and the message reached her as clearly and plainly as if it were being chimed out by the cattle-bells in the high Malindan pastures.

Toomi blinked as if she were coming out of sleep. She stared blankly at Hadji. Her eyes focused, and Hadji's words swirled back into her mind.

'We cannot leave,' Toomi said. 'Mamkinga has been here in Garoua. Maybe he is still here now. I cannot go until I know.'

She reached out. Still in a trance she seized Rachel's hand.

Unhesitatingly Rachel threaded her fingers through Toomi's. Rachel held her tightly. Hadji's glance moved backwards and forwards between the two faces. He knew what he was confronted with. It had happened to him before. He was up against a joint force he neither understood nor had any power to control. He was helpless.

'Very well,' he said. 'But you cannot go down into the streets to ask about your brother. I will have to go for you.'

'You cannot go,' Toomi protested. 'If there is a watch for people asking about Malindan slaves, then you will be caught.'

'I know the Garoua market,' Hadji answered. 'You do not. I am a known merchant here. You are not. Above all I am a man. The Acab Saat is searching for a woman. Even if I am arrested and stripped, he will find little to interest him beneath my robes — '

Hadji smiled. For the first time in a month the bold confident look they had first seen in Ayeshi's house was back on his face.

'I will start in the morning,' he said. 'If your brother is here, we will find him.'

79

They stayed in Garoua for ten days.

Every morning Hadji rose early and left the house. He returned late, often as midnight was approaching. Whatever the hour Toomi and Rachel would be awake, waiting for him to come in. When they heard his footsteps on the stairs they stood, and watched as he entered the room. Always his expression was the same, bleak and tired. He would shake his head dispiritedly and throw himself down on his mattress. Then they too would lie down and attempt to sleep.

For Hadji at least the days were filled with activity.

For the girls there was nothing. Unable to leave the house, unable even to go down to the courtyard, for them the room was a cell. They woke, they ate the meals the little Sudanese prepared and brought to them, they visited the privy at the corner of the landing. Then they hurried back to the room again.

The hours passed. They watched the pigeons wheel against the sky. They timed the sun as it climbed and sank back again. They listened to the street sounds, the clop of mules' hoofs, the calls of water-sellers, the arguments of the washerwomen, the whining cries of beggars, the occasional raucous tumult of a brawl. They heard the summons of the muezzin and gazed at the sky as it filled with the darkness of evening.

Then, when the stars emerged and the moon began to rise, they settled back to wait for Hadji's return.

On the tenth night he came back even later than usual. Rachel had fallen asleep. Even Toomi, in spite of her anxiety, was drowsing. Toomi heard the grating of the door latch and struggled to sit up. She was still yawning and rubbing her eyes when Hadji crossed the floor. He knelt down by the bed and took her wrist.

'What is it?' she asked.

'I have found someone,' Hadji said.

'Mamkinga?'

For an instant she hardly believed that her tongue had formed his name. Hadji shook his head. The hope that had begun to soar in Toomi withered and fell.

'No,' he answered. 'But someone who may know something about him.'

'Who?'

'An old man, a Malindan, a slave. He arrived here from the coast only a month ago. He was owned by a trader who had a store near the shore. Last month his master was killed. The old man with the other slaves was sent back here where his widow lives. She has put them up for sale. I found him in the market stalls – '

Hadji paused. 'Dress and come with me.'

Hadji's return had woken Rachel too. The two young women scrambled into their clothes. With Hadji leading the way they crept out of the house and set off through the silent sleeping town.

Garoua's slave market was identical to Kano's.

The slaves were displayed for sale in a series of pens beside the stockades where the cattle and goats were gathered. At night most of the slave pens were empty. The slave traders brought their goods in each morning and removed them when the market closed at dusk if the slaves hadn't been sold. Occasionally they would arrange with the slave-market manager to leave them there overnight.

The Malindan slave Hadji had found was one of the few whose owner had quartered him in the pens for the night. He was an old man and he was sunk in sleep when Hadji arrived with Toomi and Rachel. Hadji prodded him with his stick and swore at him, using the slave traders' curses to wake him up.

Slowly and reluctantly the old man dragged himself

561

out of sleep. He heaved himself to his feet. He stood ankle-deep in the mud with his arms crossed over his chest and his head bowed.

'It is I,' Hadji said. 'We spoke before.'

'Yes, effendi,' the old man mumbled. 'I will work hard. I eat little. I have no diseases.'

He raised his bony arms to expose his armpits and spread his legs to show his crutch.

'Look, effendi, there is nothing.'

He coughed to show his stomach was not ruptured. Then he began to mumble again.

'I know of maize. I can hoe well in the fields. I am used to cattle – '

'Listen to me,' Hadji interrupted him. 'I was here a few hours ago. We talked of Malinda. Tell this young effendi what you told me.'

'Malinda – ?'

The old man licked away the saliva dribbling down his mouth.

'I am from Malinda.' His face quickened into life. 'What do you wish to know of Malinda?'

Toomi leant towards him.

'We are looking for a Malindan who was stolen and sold as a slave. Do you know of any such child?'

'Child, no,' the old man shook his head. 'Few Malindans are slaves.'

He started to murmur. Hadji prodded him again.

'But you told me you had met one when you were on the coast.'

'The young man? Yes, I remember him. How could I forget him? He came in with a caravan from the interior. He stayed for a week while the ship was due. We spoke together every time we could. I brought him his food. He was the tallest, the strongest young man I have ever seen. How can I tell you of him – ?'

The man's eyes were ringed with pale circles of age. He brushed them with his emaciated forearm. Then he lifted his head and peered at the two of them.

Until then Toomi and Hadji had been vague silhouettes

against the night sky. Now the old man focused on Toomi's face. He froze. He gazed at her, bewildered. Then he lowered his head and began to tremble.

'I did nothing to you,' he muttered, his voice barely audible.

'What do you mean?' Toomi asked.

'I did nothing,' the old man repeated. 'I only helped you. Why have you come back?'

Suddenly he was in a state of such terror he was hardly able to speak. Toomi frowned. No one had threatened him, no one had done anything to cause the panic which had overwhelmed him. She waited. Then it dawned on her.

Toomi reached forward and took his wrist.

'Look at me again,' she said. 'I am not his spirit. I am the man's sister. We are twins and we are separated. That is why I am searching for him.'

The old man huddled away, trying to bury his head in his arms.

Gently but firmly Toomi pulled him towards her until he was forced to look up. The old man blinked. He peered at her fearfully, wincing as if the sight of her face might cause him some terrible harm. Gradually, when nothing happened, he relaxed.

'You are his twin sister?' he said.

'Study me carefully,' Toomi answered. 'If I am not a spirit, can I be anyone else?'

'You have his features.' Still riddled with uncertainty, the old man continued to tremble. 'I am not sure.'

Toomi glanced at Hadji. 'Give me your dagger.'

Hadji reached for his belt. He pulled his dagger from its sheath and handed it to her.

Toomi drew the razor-sharp blade lightly across the back of her hand. A line of blood welled out from the cut. She lifted her hand and held it in front of the old man's eyes as the blood began to trickle down her fingers.

'If I was a spirit, would I bleed?' she said.

The old man lifted his manacled hands and touched the cut with his fingers. He raised his fingers to his mouth and licked at the blood. It tasted warm and salty. It was no mirage, no trick, no sleight of hand by some cunning demon. The blood had come from a human.

'You are truly his sister,' he said.

'Then where is my brother?' Toomi demanded. 'When did you last see him? Where is he now?'

There was silence for several moments.

'He came to the coast – ' the old man answered.

'It was two moons ago. He was in one of my master's caravans. The slaves stayed in my master's compound. They were to be loaded on a ship. While they were in the compound I fed them. I discovered he was from Malinda too and we talked. He told me he had been taken as a child and spent much of his life since on the plains – '

The old man looked up.

'He could speak many tongues. When there were difficulties of whatever sort, he resolved them. He was an embrenche, a leader. Everyone respected him, even the Arab's servants. Then the ship docked.'

Toomi was listening with an intensity that walled everything else from her mind.

It could only be Mamkinga the old man was describing. She did not recognize his physical description, the picture of a tall and powerful young man. In Toomi's mind she had only an image of a slender well-made boy. Nor had Toomi ever seen her brother as a leader. Yet he was the embrenche's son, and the years must have changed and hardened him.

Everything else the old man said had a ring of absolute truth.

'What happened when the ship came – ?' she asked.

The sky was lightening and she felt Hadji plucking anxiously at her sleeve. They had been there an hour. Soon the market would open and the Acab Saat's men would begin their patrols. She shook off Hadji's hand and persisted.

'Did he board it?'

'Of course,' the old man said. 'He was part of the cargo. My master saved him until the last. He wanted to impress the ship's owner. For the final week I was told to fatten the men up – I was given double rations to do so.'

'Where was the ship bound for?'

'Across the ocean to Brazil.' The old man paused. 'But they did not get there.'

'What happened?'

'Later it was towed back to the shore by a British ship. I was not there but I heard the stories. It seems the slaves rose against the Portuguese. Under your brother they took the ship, but they could not sail it. When the British found them, most had died from disease and thirst. Only a few women and children came back to land.'

'And my brother?'

The old man shook his head. 'He was not among them. He must have died at sea.'

Toomi didn't even have time to take the words in.

Hadji had been growing more and more agitated as the conversation continued. Sounds of the approaching day were already echoing off the walls outside. As the old man finished speaking Hadji heard the distant clop of horses' hoofs.

'We are leaving,' he snapped.

An instant later they were on the street. Without giving Toomi a chance to protest Hadji half-dragged and half-carried her back to the house. Finally, inside the room, he let go of her.

'Your brother may be dead,' he said bleakly. 'While there is breath in me, I am not going to allow you to die too.'

'Mamkinga is not dead,' Toomi replied.

Her face had the same trance-like look as before, almost a look of elation. She had pondered the old man's words. Toomi believed everything he had said up until the last.

Everything was true – except for the end. Mamkinga was alive. She knew it with the same utter certainty that had made her defy Hadji before and remain in Garoua. The pulse in her head and wrists that had beaten so strongly then was beating even more powerfully now. It was a song and it was being sung to her by a living body.

'My brother is alive,' she went on. 'He is somewhere close. The old man knows more than he thinks. We must go back and visit him again.'

Hadji looked at her in despair. He turned imploringly to Rachel. Rachel shook her head.

'Mamkinga is my sister's brother,' she said quietly. 'We must do as she says.'

Hadji raised his arms helplessly.

'Very well,' he said. 'The pens where the old man is being held will not be cleared for sale until tomorrow. We will go down there when night falls again.'

80

Salama walked quickly through Gondar's royal park.

Behind him, hurrying to keep up, followed a retinue of six robed and bearded priests, each with his acolyte. The priests went with him everywhere now. Outside the palace grounds their number was increased. Depending on the importance of the occasion there could be as many as a hundred. At times Salama seemed to move with an escort of a white-robed army.

The priests had no function except to emphasize Salama's position and authority.

Six months after the victory over Ras Michael, Salama was no longer just Gondar's Acab Saat, although he jealously retained the post he held when he was exiled. He was also archbishop and primate of the kingdom, and confessor to the nation. On Salama's orders Murabit, his bandy-legged lieutenant, had killed the former archbishop in the confused aftermath of the battle for the city.

There had been no need to slay Welorin, the previous confessor. The old man was senile. Salama had simply dismissed him and dispatched him to end his days in a monastery in the mountains. Then Salama had had himself enthroned in Gondar's cathedral-church. A terrified young bishop had confirmed and blessed him in the three posts. Salama had walked out to the drunken acclaim of Culembra's soldiers. The citizens of Gondar watched in cowed silence.

As he passed the palace Salama paused.

It was still early in the morning, but the same inebriated cheers that had greeted his enthronement were echoing out from the ground-floor chambers. The Galla warriors were celebrating again. The king, Salama knew, would be in their midst. The feasting and carousing had continued uninterrupted ever since the Galla's successful invasion.

The fabled kingdom of Gondar was a cornucopia. The Galla were like children who had captured a vast hive of honeycombs from which the stinging bees had fled. They would not rest until they had drained every last drop of honey.

Scowling, Salama walked on.

For the moment Culembra and his savages were welcome to Gondar's sugar. They would not taste it for long. The Galla had served his purpose well, but their time was running short. As soon as the last of Ras Michael's scattered armies had capitulated to the new regime and Salama's authority was unchallenged throughout the kingdom, the barbarian king would see a very different face to his one-time partner and ally.

Striding angrily across the dusty earth, Salama came to the steps that led up to the garden of the nightingales. At the foot of the steps he turned to the priests.

'You may leave me here,' he said. 'I wish to be alone. As soon as Murabit returns, send him to me instantly.'

The leading priest bowed and withdrew. The others shuffled away in his wake.

Salama climbed the steps and pushed his way through the lavender bushes to the parapet above the plain. With the infant river gushing out in plumes of spray below him, he stood looking down on the tawny gold and ochre expanse of land far beneath.

Much had changed in Gondar since the Galla's crushing victory over Ras Michael's forces. Galla contingents were in control of every market town, trading route, crossroads, pass and ford throughout the kingdom. Culembra's soldiers might be coarse and simple. They were also brutal and effective. With the menacing sanction of the Acab Saat and the dark shadowy cross of the church behind them, no one in Gondar had dared challenge their authority.

One by one Ras Michael's far-flung garrisons had made their way to Gondar, only to lay down their arms and swear an oath of loyalty to the new powers that ruled the city. Their commander, the Ras, was dead. The royal family was slaughtered or scattered. Confronted by Culembra's swordsmen and the chilling threat of the Acab Saat's pointed finger, they had no choice except to surrender.

Within days many of them were ordered back into the field.

This time it was not in defence of Gondar's borders, but to push those borders outwards. For years Salama had waited in angry frustration and impatience for Ras Michael to wilt and fall. Salama's hunger and rage had been fed by his exile. Now that the Ras was dead and Gondar was his, his ambition erupted like a pent-up torrent sweeping through a ruptured dam.

Some of Ras Michael's best troops were allowed barely twenty-four hours between their capitulation and being sent out again. They watered their horses in the river's springs. They ate at the city's food stalls, they drank in Gondar's taverns, they coupled with the prostitutes in the alleys. Then, under a different banner now, they rode down from the ridge in the mountains.

Their destinations were south and west. To the north were the lands of the Galla and the kingdom of Malinda – both now under Gondar's control. But at the other points of the compass the horizons, and the scope for conquest, were limitless. Like well-cast spears, iron-tipped and razor-sharp, Salama's armies were lancing deep into the savannas that fell away from the Mountains of the Moon.

Salama glanced up at the hill flanks above Gondar. A small cloud of dust was winding quickly down towards the city along a track. It would be Murabit. At the speed Murabit was riding he would reach the palace within the hour.

Salama drummed his fingers impatiently on the parapet. As he waited his face darkened.

In spite of everything Salama had done, he had still not captured Ozoro Rachel. Until she was in his power he knew he would never be entirely safe. For the moment the people of Gondar were dispirited and helpless. Salama had made brutally sure they were. But they were a proud and stubborn nation. Their loyalty to the royal dynasty and the river's child ran even deeper in their blood than their fear of the church.

If Ozoro Rachel found backing outside Gondar's borders and returned to claim the kingdom, not even Salama with all his arrogant confidence was sure he could fight her off.

Finding her had become Salama's obsession. Within a week of the battle he knew she had somehow slipped through the net of the Galla forces, and escaped from Gondar. The only route she could have taken, Salama was sure, was west along the caravan trails. He had sent out two hundred of his most trusted men in pursuit, promising to anyone who caught her riches for life.

For six months now Salama's men had been scouring the breadth of the continent, journeying even as far as the Atlantic coast.

In spite of the almost unimaginable size of the area, their task was not as impossible as it might have appeared. The immensity of the bush was no use to her. If Rachel planned to return to Gondar she needed support. Support could only be found in human settlements. There were only a small number of towns where she might find it, and an even smaller number of trails between them.

Systematically his men set out to search them all. They made threats. They offered lavish bribes and rewards. They interrogated merchants, village headmen, slave dealers, ferrymen and the masters of the Arab caravans — the great sources of intelligence about Africa's affairs.

Finally in Kano they came across Rachel's trail.

She was travelling disguised as an Arab youth. With her, according to the reports, was another youth also in Arab robes. Salama's men were within minutes of seizing them both when they mysteriously disappeared. Salama's rage at the news had alarmed even Murabit. Later, when the Acab Saat became calmer, Murabit had persuaded him it did not matter.

'We are close to the little she-jackal now, Acab,' he said. 'Kano is not safe for her. Where can she go from there? Only to Timbucktoom or Garoua. Timbucktoom is far and takes her away from Gondar. Garoua brings her closer to us. That is where we will find her.'

Still seething with anger, Salama reluctantly agreed.

Messengers were sent out from Gondar that evening, ordering everyone searching for Rachel to gather at Garoua. By now, almost two months later, they would have assembled in the trading town on the Benoue river.

'Murabit is here, my lord.'

Salama's head jerked round. One of the priests had climbed the steps to the nightingale garden. The priest bowed low as he made the announcement. Behind him Murabit came into sight.

The squat little mountain man's leather riding chaps were damp and white with foam from his horse. As he came forward he brushed the dust from his thick drooping moustache, and rubbed his eyes wearily.

'It is done, Acab,' he said. 'We stormed the fort eight days ago. We have been in the saddle ever since.'

Murabit had been sent out to subdue the last of Ras Michael's troops who had remained loyal to the old warlord. They were garrisoning an isolated fortress in the southern hills, and they had held out against Culembra's soldiers ever since the news of the battle reached them.

'Are they ours now?' Salama demanded.

'Those that are left, yes,' Murabit nodded. 'When they surrendered I gave them the choice. Two out of every ten were stubborn. A river runs below the fort. There are many crocodiles. We cut off the hands and feet of the ones who refused and threw them in the water. The crocodiles ate them alive as the rest watched –'

A smile crossed Murabit's dark scarred face. 'The others can now be trusted.'

'And the ones who were stubborn,' Salama asked, 'what reason did they give?'

There was no need to ask the question. Salama knew the answer. Somehow he felt impelled to hear it from Murabit, almost as if he deliberately wanted to goad himself, to inflame his anger even more.

'They claimed allegiance to the river's child,' Murabit said quietly.

'I want her, Murabit.' Salama hammered his fist impotently on the stone until blood ran between his fingers. 'I want her here before me in the palace. I want to choke the life out of her myself with my own hands – '

Almost incoherent, Salama broke off.

'Even now they will be seeking her in Garoua,' Murabit said. 'Do not distress yourself, Acab. The little jackal will be found.'

'It is not enough. There must be something more we can do – '

Salama glanced round and his eyes narrowed.

'The dwarf,' he said suddenly. 'That snake's dropping knows more than he has told us. We will beat him until he screams again.'

With Murabit following, Salama ran down the steps of the garden and headed across the park.

The palace cells were gouged out of the rock beneath the main chambers on the ground floor. Salama seized a torch from the guard at the entrance of the corridor which led to them. He paced along the tunnel until he came to a heavily barred door. The guard ran up and slid back the bolts. Crouching, Salama stepped through and lifted the torch.

The cell was little more than an arched vault.

The heat inside was stifling. The walls were covered with spatters of dried blood, and the stench of stale urine, vomit, raw excrement and putrefying flesh was so powerful that Salama reeled. He gripped the doorframe and steadied himself. Then he peered down.

Huddled in the corner on the bare stone was a tiny emaciated figure. It was Doho. His hair was white, and great suppurating sores covered his body. All round him, smearing the stone like the glistening tracks of snails, runnels of fresh blood from his wounds ran away into the darkness.

Doho's thickly filmed eyes blinked painfully up at the light and registered Salama's face.

'She has gone to the north beyond the mountains.' Doho's voice from the floor was so faint it was almost inaudible. 'It is all I can tell you. I know no more. She has gone to the north – '

Like a litany the words were repeated again and again. Holding his hand to his nose, Salama stepped forward and kicked the little body violently to silence it.

'Beat him, Murabit!' he shouted as a wave of nausea flooded over him.

Murabit stepped forward to Salama's shoulder and gazed down at the mutilated form on the stone beneath him.

'The little man has been beaten enough, Acab,' Murabit answered. 'What he needs now is a little encouragement. He carries too much flesh. He wants the attention of a knife blade to lighten his load.'

Murabit drew the razor-sharp curved dagger that hung from his waist.

He whetted its blade on the stone. Then he knelt beside Doho. He gripped the dwarf's shrunken penis in his hand and began to whittle it away as if he were sharpening the point of a stick.

As the tiny slivers of bleeding tissue built up in a mound on the floor, Doho twitched convulsively and moaned in agony. Salama leant down and thrust the torch in his face.

'Where did you hide her?' Salama bellowed at him.

Doho stiffened. He rinsed his tongue round his mouth and with a last defiant act of will managed to spit upwards. Then he rolled back unconscious.

81

'The knight.' Wolf nudged Mamkinga's elbow. 'Advance it along the bishop's file and you will have Jamie's pawn en prise.'

Mamkinga hunched himself forward and scanned the board, frowning.

Wolf was teaching Mamkinga to play chess with the set he had whittled from scraps of hardwood. Mamkinga in return was teaching Wolf to play ojukla, the ancient African game of draughts which involved moving groups of beans round little scoops in the sand.

Across the table under the awning on the *San Cristobal*'s afterdeck, Jamie watched him with quiet satisfaction.

It was two weeks since Jamie's recovery and the last day of their month's quarantine on the shore of the Bight of Benin. Neither Farquarson nor Wolf had contracted the fever and they were ready to continue. Long afterwards Jamie was often to remember the two weeks as among the happiest he had spent. If he hadn't been restless to press on, from the moment he could stand, he would have enjoyed them even more.

At the start both he and Mamkinga were still weak. Wolf and Farquarson were contentedly running the hulk and the shoreside camp with the African servants. There was little for the other two to do except rest and recover their strength.

That they had both come so close to death and recovered at each other's hands had forged a deep but silent intimacy between them. They had become brothers, yet Mamkinga was still wary of the white stranger. Taciturn and self-contained, he spoke little and sometimes even seemed to be avoiding Jamie.

Jamie guessed that Mamkinga's enslavement had been accompanied by some tragedy in his past. Jamie was naturally reserved too. He remembered his own dark days on Iona and did not press Mamkinga to talk.

Instead they both devoted themselves to restoring their wasted bodies. Mamkinga would run silently for miles along the endless grey-white beach, his thigh muscles straining as his bare feet sank into the soft sand. After a day or two Jamie began to run with him. He could keep up with Mamkinga for the first few miles, but as the sun rose higher and the mosquitos bit deeper he dropped behind.

Mamkinga never seemed to tire.

His stride remained steady even when he crossed the great swampy river mouth to the north of the encampment. As he ran Mamkinga would reach down and pick up bright seashells, tossing them in an arc high in the air ahead and leaping to catch them as they fell. When they reached the river Jamie would drop to the ground and lie watching through glare-narrowed eyes the strange birds and animals which thronged its banks.

All the wildlife of the forest seemed to congregate here. There were hornbills with raven-black bodies and gigantic scarlet bills, little lily trotters which crossed the floating leaves on delicate splayed feet, herds of deer and buffalo, grunting hippopotamus with great yawning mouths, and once a huge black-maned lion.

Jamie gazed at them all with wonderment. They were the illustrations from Mrs Livingstone's long-ago books brought suddenly and brilliantly to life. When the lion appeared Jamie froze. He remembered little Tau roaring at his bedroom door in the Camerons' house, and the story he used to make Mrs Livingstone tell him again and again of her husband's terrible encounter with the lion in the Kalahari.

Long after the great tawny creature had prowled back into the trees, Jamie went on staring transfixed at the spot on the bank where it had lowered its head to the water.

Often, as the sun dipped below the horizon, Jamie would throw off his clothes and plunge into the ocean, cleaving through the rolling breakers as the phosphorescence dripped in showers of green and golden sparks from his body. One evening when he came out of the sea he found Mamkinga squatting on his haunches by the waves' edge.

Mamkinga gave Jamie one of his rare hesitant smiles. 'If you teach me to run in water, I will teach you to run on land.'

Jamie looked at him in surprise. 'Can ye not swim?' he asked.

'I did so once in my life,' Mamkinga answered. 'It was many years ago. Then the spirits bore me up. Now I wish to do it on my own.'

Jamie gave him his first lesson next day.

Mamkinga was an apt pupil, well coordinated and fearless. Soon he was swimming almost as well as Jamie. In return he taught Jamie how to run balanced on the balls of his feet as the Malindan hunter-trackers did, how to lengthen his stride and steady his arms so that he was moving as swiftly and economically as possible.

The experience of exchanging skills created another bond between them. It was forged at the same time as their health and strength began to return. Gradually the instinctive trust which had brought them together in sickness reasserted itself. They started to talk. As they ran side by side through the dunes or floated on their backs in the steel-blue sea, Mamkinga at last told Jamie his story.

Mamkinga described his childhood with his twin sister in the embrenche's house in distant Malinda. He told how they had been captured by the Oye-Eboe, and then separated from each other when they were sold in the village market. He spoke of his life with the Widow Okuma, the long years with Ndele the goldsmith, his travels west with the Arab slaving caravan, and the terrible voyage on the *San Cristobal*.

Most of all Mamkinga spoke of Toomi, returning to

her again and again. It was a loss Jamie understood bitterly and well. Jamie too had lost sisters. He still could not think of them lying in his grandmother's arms without an ache in his heart, and the sound of the searing flames as the croft burned returning to crackle in his ears.

'Ye will find her again, I am sure of it,' Jamie said once when Mamkinga had fallen silent after talking about her. 'Ye may count on my help and support always.'

For a long time Mamkinga stared at him without speaking. Finally he nodded gravely.

'I believe it will be so,' he said. 'I have met few of your people and I know little of the white race. What I do know is that before the spirits we all stand equal. We are each one neither more nor less than what we are. That must be so in your land as in mine –'

Mamkinga paused and frowned. Something, Jamie sensed, was troubling him.

'I have your name,' Mamkinga went on. 'Every day I hear your friends use it. You yourself gave it to me the night my sickness was at its darkest. I was glad then. I am still. Yet in truth your name means nothing to me. Now we are both healed and together, I would you had a name from my own land.'

Mamkinga stopped again. He was looking anxiously at Jamie. Jamie realized that the African was waiting for his agreement.

'Ye may name me as ye choose,' Jamie replied.

'I have thought long,' Mamkinga said. 'On the mountain slopes in Malinda there are stones which stand upright in the watercourses. They are old and hard. The rains can do nothing against them and at night they catch the starlight. Our herders use them to navigate by when they are moving the flocks. We name them Umshebi – the guide-stones of the men among the rivers.'

As Mamkinga spoke, the image of the stone crosses beside Iona's abbey flashed across Jamie's mind. The crosses were ancient and strong. They too had stood firm against the storms and rains. For centuries they had guided other men, not Malindan herders but the Hebridean crofters and fisherfolk, on their journeys.

Jamie looked wonderingly at the tall African as Mamkinga continued.

'You came to me in the night,' Mamkinga said. 'From the cabin windows there was starlight on your shoulders. I saw you were strong. I knew if I trusted you, I would find my way back from the dark. I will name you now Umshebi. In my mind that is how you will always be.'

Mamkinga's dark powerful face was briefly lit by another of his fleeting smiles. He reached out and touched Jamie's forehead with the tips of his fingers.

'Pula!' he said.

Pula. Rain, as Jamie had come to learn the word meant. The greatest and most sacred blessing of the African continent.

'Pula!' Jamie replied quietly.

In Jamie trust grew from that moment. For the first time in his life he had found a companion to whom he could speak about things he had never entrusted to anyone, not even to Mrs Livingstone. Like Mamkinga he discovered that once the walls of silence between them had been breached, there was nothing he could not say.

He told Mamkinga of his childhood on Iona, the firing of the croft, and his burial of his grandmother and sisters in the royal graveyard. He described his years with Dr Cameron, the momentous visit of Mary Livingstone, and the dream that had formed in his mind as she read to him about Africa – a dream that one day he would come to the dark continent and find the source of the great river.

'I too will help you in your search,' Mamkinga said when Jamie himself had fallen silent. 'We have both stood and looked into the darkness. The spirits guided us back to the light. They have given us each our tasks and made us brothers so we may complete them together.'

Jamie looked at him thoughtfully, then he smiled. 'As a son of the kirk,' he replied, 'I would credit it more to the

Lord and a foul wind blowing fair. But maybe the Lord and the spirits together intended we should travel the same road.'

At first they spoke in English. Occasionally Mamkinga would use Malindan phrases to fill in some gap. Malindan, Jamie knew, was one of the chief tongues of the Abyssinian kingdoms, the region he was bound for to join Mr Walter Baimbridge's expedition.

Jamie asked Mamkinga to teach it to him. Mamkinga, with his own wide knowledge of other languages, was an excellent teacher, and Jamie an enthusiastic and quick-witted learner. At the end of the two weeks Jamie could understand almost everything Mamkinga said to him in Malindan, and speak it adequately himself.

'And that,' said Farquarson, who had watched the progress of the friendship with amusement, as he saw them talking earnestly together one evening, 'is surely enough companionship for any two men to give each other – and surely more than a woman to either of them would endure.'

The days passed. Finally the period of quarantine was over. They were ready to move on.

Mamkinga's only thought was to find Toomi. Lacking his sister's tenacity and decisiveness, he had never considered scouring Africa for her as Toomi had been doing for him. The task was too enormous, too daunting to enter his mind. All he could think of was to return to Malinda, and reunite himself with the embrenche and his family. Then they could jointly decide how to search for Toomi.

Mamkinga had no means of knowing that the Galla had conquered Malinda, and his father and family had all been slaughtered.

Abyssinia was Jamie's goal too. He had to travel there by way of Garoua to find out where he could link up with Baimbridge's expedition. Garoua, five hundred miles inland from the Bight of Benin at the head of the great Benoue river, was directly on the route of anyone heading east for the mountain kingdoms. Jamie had the funds needed for the journey. Mamkinga knew how to organize and provision it.

They would all travel together.

'We will hunt when we can,' Mamkinga said. 'But there will be many days when the river forest is too thick. We must take food with us.'

With the help of Jamie and the African servants, Mamkinga dug a deep pit across one of the hippo tracks that ran down to the river.

He set sharpened stakes into the base and covered the top with branches. That night Mamkinga waited in the fork of a tree above the trap. Towards dawn a large male hippo crashed down into it. Mamkinga leapt from the tree and dispatched the animal, which bellowed in agony beneath him, with a spear thrust through the brain.

The carcass was butchered and the strips of meat, rubbed with salt and spices, were spread out to dry on every bush within fifty paces of the camp. As the sun rose the meat was covered with a swarming, humming mantle of flies and insects.

Mamkinga inspected the bushes and shook his head unhappily.

'It is how we used to cure provisions for journeys in Malinda,' he said. 'But there the mountain air is dry and sweet. Here I fear the meat will rot.'

He frowned in embarrassment and frustration. In the Bight of Benin's cloying humidity, the old ways of his homeland had failed him.

It was Jamie who found the answer.

For some reason Wolf was a particular target for the mosquitos and other biting insects that plagued the shoreline. To protect himself Wolf had taken to spending the worst of the day in the drifting smoke of the cooking fire, puffing on a pipeful of pungent tobacco he had bought from de Souza. As Jamie glanced at Wolf huddled in clouds of smoke, a thought struck him.

'If we canna do it in your fashion let us do it in mine,' Jamie said. 'We will smoke the meat as my grandmother smoked haddies. The air in the Hebrides isna as damp as it is here, but it can be damp enough. And when it's damp, smoking is the only solution.'

A huge fire was built on the shore.

The fire was piled with green leaves. Racks made out of branches, with the strips of flesh hanging on them, were erected round it. Two days later there was enough smoked and cured hippo meat to last them for the entire journey up the Benoue.

Mamkinga negotiated the purchase of three broad canoes, hollowed from single tree trunks. Two were for the travellers and one, under Mamkinga's supervision, was packed with stores. From among the Africans in the camp, Mamkinga selected six strong young paddlers and a guide, a bright-eyed half-caste son of an Arab trader and one of de Souza's female slaves.

'The servant become master can surely recognize his own,' Farquarson observed smiling as he watched Mamkinga bargain shrewdly over the money the paddlers would be paid at the end of the voyage.

Supplies of salt fish, oil, dried fava beans and manioc were barrelled up and stowed in the provision canoe. Finally Wolf was sent with the waggon to de Souza's store to acquire trade goods – salt and pepper, pots, pans and tin cups, knives and spoons, reels of button thread, needles and combs, ribbons, beads, and a few lengths of brightly printed cotton cloth.

The expedition had no shortage of weapons. Jamie's last purchase before he left London had been a heavy shotgun. In addition the *San Cristobal* had provided them with an almost unlimited stock of rifles, pistols, and additional scatterguns to choose from. Farquarson, who had shot deer and grouse at Invergordon and claimed to be an authority on guns, equipped them all. When he finished they looked, in Wolf's words, like Turkish brigands.

Jamie settled the rifle Farquarson had given him round his shoulders, and adjusted the leather belt that supported a pair of pistols at his waist. They had transport. They were armed and provisioned. The sale of the *San Cristobal* hulk to DeWitt had supplied them with gold. They needed nothing more. At dawn next morning they would set out.

As they lingered over the remains of the evening meal in the wardroom that night, Farquarson raised his glass in a toast.

'To bold journeying and a sure bonny end,' he said.

'Will ye not provoke God nor the fates?' Jamie cautioned, frowning before he drank. 'The journey's long. Garoua's only a stage on the way. We must press on there fast. Afterwards we have far to go. The ending isna sure and only the Almighty knows what stands between.'

Farquarson laughed.

'A dark wee pessimist, *dhu* they'd call you in the Gaelic, you peasant's child of the isles,' he said. 'Will this content you – let the journey be bold and the Devil take the hindmost on the road?'

Jamie chuckled.

'I didna mean ye should switch the Devil for the Lord, but as ye've proposed I will drink.'

They all raised their glasses. Afterwards Mamkinga quietly left the table. He climbed down from the ship to the sand and walked up the dune into the trees. There was a broad well-worn path that led away from the shore.

His face set grimly and his eyes glittering, Mamkinga followed the path through the forest.

82

It was impenetrably dark.

There were two hours before the moon rose. The dank sea mist of the Bight of Benin was hanging heavily over the trees and the starlight was blotted out. The fruit bats were clinging to their roosts. Even the night-hunting cats, the lynxes and leopards, were lying up in the bush or waiting on branches above the game tracks for a glimmer to break through the fog and darkness.

Mamkinga never hesitated. It was the first time he had walked the forest trail. He had carefully avoided it until then, yet he might have been travelling it all his life. Each bush, each tree, each contour of the ground, seemed familiar.

The intensity of his anger and hatred carried him unerringly on.

The name of the Portuguese trader, de Souza, had struck and lodged in his mind like a barbed and poisoned fish hook from the instant Wolf had mentioned it weeks before. Mamkinga had waited patiently until his strength came back and they were ready to depart. Now the time had come.

The trees ended and a clearing spread out in front of him. The store stood at the clearing's centre. The tracks of waggon wheels ran towards it from every side, and a lamp was burning in a ground-floor window. Mamkinga walked towards the light. He peered inside.

A man was lying asleep in a hammock slung from the upright beams that supported the loft. He had black curling hair tinged with grey, a swollen belly, and a fleshy jowled face. It was de Souza. As Mamkinga watched, de

Souza belched in his sleep. He muttered and scratched his groin. Then he turned on to his side. His arm dropped down and he sprawled against the coir netting.

Mamkinga glanced round the room.

A young black girl was asleep on the mat below the hammock. Behind her Mamkinga could see the wooden serving counter of the store. At one end, hanging between slabs of dried fish and an assortment of iron cooking pots, were pairs of brass manacles, each with its own padlock. Mamkinga knew them well. They were used by slave traders to shackle newly-bought slaves together until they could be joined to a column.

Mamkinga went to the door. He lifted the latch. There was no lock and the door swung open. He stepped inside. As his foot touched the floor the boards creaked. De Souza didn't stir but the girl opened her eyes and sat up.

Mamkinga crossed the floor in two swift strides.

He placed his hand over her mouth. The girl cowered back. Mamkinga put his finger to his lips. He waited until she gulped and nodded. Then he went over to the counter. He took down a pair of the manacles and clamped one of them round his wrist.

The click as the bolt shot home made de Souza roll over and mutter again. He pawed at the netting and settled back into sleep. Mamkinga went over to the hammock. Gently he picked up de Souza's arm. He clamped the other half of the manacle round the man's wrist and snapped it shut, yoking the two of them together. The Portuguese grunted but didn't waken.

Mamkinga paused for a moment.

Then he pulled out his knife and slashed through the hammock's rope. De Souza tumbled to the floor. As he fell he was jerked round by the chain that bound him to Mamkinga.

'Cristos!' de Souza shouted.

He clambered to his feet, rubbing blearily at his eyes with his free hand. He tried to move away but something was restraining him. He turned and saw

584

Mamkinga. De Souza stared at him in a daze. He recognized the huge negro and his face froze.

'The animal!' he gasped.

He lunged wildly at Mamkinga.

Mamkinga's hand darted out and gripped him by the throat. Taller and immeasurably stronger than the Portuguese, Mamkinga squeezed de Souza's neck in his huge fist and shook him until his knees buckled. Choking, de Souza dropped to the floor.

'Stand!' Mamkinga dragged de Souza back to his feet. 'If you touch me again, I will break your neck.'

Terrorized, de Souza stood unresisting in front of him.

'Where are the keys?' Mamkinga demanded.

The Portuguese didn't need to ask which keys Mamkinga wanted. He pointed to a hook on the wall beside the slashed rope. Mamkinga pulled him over.

'Take them down,' Mamkinga said.

De Souza did as he was told. Mamkinga led him outside and round to the pens where the slaves were housed.

The mist was clearing and a thin watery light was filtering through the clouds. Mamkinga could just make out the slaves. Manacled together, they were lying in groups on the ground. Most were asleep but a few raised their heads at the sound of the approaching footsteps. Mamkinga reached the door to the enclosure and paused.

Carried to his nostrils on the night air was a terrible smell. Weaker but still unmistakable, it was the charnel-house stench of the *San Cristobal*'s holds. It was the smell of slavery. Mamkinga would never forget it for as long as he lived.

'Open!' he said.

De Souza fumbled with the keys and unlocked the door. Together they stepped inside.

Most of the slaves were awake now. They sat up and stared fearfully at the two figures in the darkness. Mamkinga clapped his hands and woke the rest.

'My brothers and sisters!' he called out. 'I am Mamkinga, son of the Embrenche of Malinda. I have come to free you. You were chained by a creature beneath humanity, beneath the kingdom of the animals. I have dragged him out from under his stone. It is proper that he who put on your bonds should also take them off –

'Unlock them,' he snapped at de Souza.

Mamkinga led de Souza from one group to another. As they reached each group he made de Souza kneel and open the padlocks. The slaves stood up stiffly, rubbing their arms and legs. When the last one was freed, Mamkinga went back to the centre of the enclosure.

'There is food in the store,' he said. 'Take everything you need and make your escape.'

One of the slaves came up to Mamkinga then. He was a middle-aged man with wiry grey hair. He looked at de Souza and his eyes narrowed in murderous hatred.

'Give us the creature,' he said. 'He raped my wife and let our child die in the sun. We will deal with him.'

De Souza backed away from him in terror. Mamkinga forced down his arm and made the Portuguese kneel again. Then Mamkinga glanced back at the slave. He shook his head.

'The creature is mine,' Mamkinga said. 'He has done as much to myself and those I care for. I will make him account to us all. Rest assured. You will be satisfied.'

The man nodded grimly and walked away. Mamkinga pulled de Souza back to his feet.

'Our business is not finished,' Mamkinga said. 'We are going to walk to the sea. Move!'

With de Souza stumbling beside him Mamkinga set off back along the forest trail.

An hour later they reached the shore. Mamkinga paused and looked round. Night lamps were burning in the beached hulks ranged round the bay, including the hulk of the *San Cristobal*. Mamkinga ignored them. He walked down to a wooden jetty, where a number of small shallow-bottomed craft were moored. The boats were used to ferry supplies ashore from the merchantmen which anchored out in the roads.

Mamkinga loosed one of the mooring ropes and curtly

beckoned de Souza to climb aboard. Cowed and shocked, the Portuguese obeyed him. Mamkinga picked up a paddle with his free hand and drove the boat away from the jetty. The tide was ebbing and the waves quickly carried the boat out into the bay. When they were four hundred yards from the shore Mamkinga dug the paddle into the water.

'Stand up!' he instructed.

De Souza rose uncertainly to his feet. Still chained by the wrist to Mamkinga, he balanced himself at the centre of the boat. Mamkinga sat below him with one arm lifted and the other gripping the heavy paddle.

'There was a young woman named Aldoa,' Mamkinga said. 'Do you remember her?'

De Souza, his eyes held by the ferocity in Mamkinga's, nodded weakly.

'You bought her and kept her in your house,' Mamkinga went on. 'You abused and violated her. Then you sold her like a bar of salt. You sold me and many others like bars of salt too. Aldoa died giving us freedom. We threw her body to the sharks because we had no choice. Remember her well, remember all of us well, when you meet the sharks now – '

Mamkinga tensed himself. He braced the arm that was manacled to de Souza against the gunwhale. Then he lifted the paddle and struck de Souza violently across the face.

De Souza screamed. Blood spurted from his mouth and he toppled overboard. Mamkinga bunched his muscles and leant against the pitching of the boat as de Souza's weight pulled it down. The head of the Portuguese surfaced in the water. He spluttered and screamed again in terror. His hand, still bound to Mamkinga's, flailed above the waves.

Mamkinga held out his own arm as stiff and as firm as a hardwood branch. He waited.

It took only a few moments. The bay was heaving with sharks attracted by the refuse from the hulks and the anchored ships. They caught the scent of de Souza's blood and felt the vibrations of his body thrashing in panic against the boat. Mamkinga saw a triangular fin cutting through the water. Behind it was another, then another, then a dozen more.

The first shark dipped as it reached de Souza. Mamkinga felt the jolt as it attacked the Portuguese from below, its teeth scything through his thigh. De Souza screamed once more. He gave a last imploring glance at Mamkinga. Mamkinga thought of Aldoa and the hundreds of others of his companions on the *San Cristobal* who had died.

He gazed back at de Souza with implacable, unforgiving eyes.

The rest of the sharks reached the boat then. The water churned and bubbled as they tore into de Souza from every side. His head vanished. A pool of blood stained the water black. The Portuguese seemed to disintegrate. Seconds later only his forearm, still chained to Mamkinga by the manacle, was left. Mamkinga unlocked the bolt. He tossed the manacle and the lacerated remnant of the arm into the waves. Mamkinga paused. Something was shining on the bottom of the boat. He leant forward and picked it up. It was a dagger which must have dropped from de Souza's belt. The dagger had a curving razor-sharp blade and a sharkskin handle. Mamkinga smiled bleakly and tucked it into his own belt. Then he dug the paddle into the water and headed back for the shore.

Behind him the pack of sharks, eighty or ninety in number now, circled and fought over the last scraps of flesh.

The three Europeans had risen and were moving about on deck when Mamkinga climbed back aboard the *San Cristobal*. It was still dark. Jamie peered across as Mamkinga heaved himself over the rail.

'Where on earth have ye been at this hour?' Jamie asked.

'There was a man to whom I had to bid farewell for my companions who sailed with me. They could not do it themselves. I have done so for them.'

Mamkinga smiled.

'We must hurry. If we catch the tide early, we will be well on our way up the river when the sun rises.'

— 83 —

The journey up the Benoue took them a month.

That first morning they set out in thick white mist. Gradually as the sun climbed the mist began to churn and clear. The outlines of huge trees, their branches trailing vines, came into sight on either side through swirling clouds of vapour. The mist clouds parted and the surface of the river spread out before them, dark and oily and shining.

The paddlers chanted as they heaved, and the boats drove forward through the water.

By midday the river had become a canyon threading through towering green walls laced with the gold and vermilion blossoms of climbing plants. The water was burnished silver-white and the sun dazzled off the ripples. Parrots, hornbills and kingfishers spun in arabesques of colour above the reeds. Iguanas and crocodiles thronged the banks. Monkeys tumbled chattering through the treetops. Herds of antelope and the occasional black-maned lion or solitary elephant tusker, towering among the silver leaves of the thickets, came down to the creeks and inlets to drink.

As the light faded the landscape changed again.

Mist began to smoke on the water once more. The trees retreated into darkness. Orange and lemon and deep smouldering scarlet flooded the sky. The moon appeared. The call of hunting owls rang through the cooling air. Then night pressed down over the river. The last glow of the day was blotted out, and constellations of fireflies irradiated the banks.

As the days passed the journey settled into a routine

with a steady and purposeful rhythm of its own. The paddlers' blades carved through the flat water. The sun rose, traced its arc through the sky, and fell behind the forest. The expedition slept beside the fire's glowing embers beneath the African stars.

Before daylight they were on their way again. To Jamie the whole journey was a dazzling echoing experience of the wild, soaked in heat and sweat and sun and water, that filled his body and mind and eyes by day, and his dreams by night.

Every evening as dusk fell they made camp in a clearing on the river's banks, where the roots of great trees overhung the water. The twisted root canopy provided mooring posts for the canoes and shelter against the rain which periodically fell over the river. Under Wolf's supervision the paddlers gathered dry brushwood for the cooking fire.

In spite of his passionate adherence to the philosophy of his mentor, Karl Marx, Wolf had a natural facility for organizing a workforce. As he shouted out his orders the Africans would obey him with good-natured tolerance. When they were carrying out the other tasks that Mamkinga gave them – stripping and weaving acacia fibres to replace worn ropes or making minor repairs to the boats – Wolf would watch them with earnest concentration.

The young guide hired by Mamkinga had a smattering of English.

Using the guide as an uncertain but enthusiastic translator, Wolf would occasionally lecture the paddlers on the dignity of labour and the evils of capitalism. The paddlers, delightedly recognizing a storyteller, listened eagerly. Interpreted and embellished by the guide, Wolf's grim accounts of coal, pit children, and sweatshop factories were transformed into dazzling fables of black wood that could be mined like gold, and palaces where young girls could weave enough cloth in a day to cloak a king's army for a year.

As Wolf came to an end the Africans would sharply

clap their hands once to express their pleasure, and beg him through the interpreter to continue.

'I think I'm winning them,' Wolf remarked to Farquarson after a particularly eloquent session. 'I doubt even Karl has had quite such a committed audience. I'll make brothers of them yet.'

While Wolf set up the evening camp, Jamie and Farquarson scoured the surrounding forest with their shotguns and rifles for game. There seemed to be an almost infinite variety. There were francolins, tree ducks, spur-winged geese, doves and pigeons, endless monkeys, rodents and small forest deer, and sometimes long-quilled porcupines which Farquarson encased in clay and baked in the fire's embers.

Best of all in Farquarson's view were the flocks of slate-grey, red-wattled guineafowl.

'Stewed with sweet yams they will eat as fine as plump young grouse,' Farquarson said one evening as he expertly gutted and plucked a pair by the fire. 'Indeed, were I to serve them to my cousin Argyll, I think His Grace would be forced to concede they were as tasty as any bird that ever came off his moors.'

Mamkinga hunted too, but he used the ancient slower techniques of his homeland.

He would spend hours trawling a still pool for catfish, or set a trap and squat on his haunches in the nearby shadows, half sleeping and half waking, while he waited for the prey to spring it. When Jamie went with him into the forest Mamkinga made Jamie remove his boots and walk barefoot through the undergrowth. Fearful that he might tread on a snake or a scorpion, Jamie began by tiptoeing awkwardly beside him.

'Let your weight rest on the ground,' Mamkinga instructed. 'You must feel the dry twigs under the curve of your foot. Then you will not snap the branches and waken the forest. How can you read the warmth of the soil and print of the spoor with heavy boots between you and the earth?'

The most common and persistent of the animals they met along the river were the Benoue's baboons.

Within an hour of their making camp, the surrounding trees would be thronged with a pack of the yellow-toothed dog-faced monkeys, all of them coughing and barking and calling. Insatiably inquisitive, they would steal everything that was not tied down. Once Wolf's treasured copy of Marx's writings was seized from the ground beside him by an aggressive young male. The book was only recovered after a furious chase through the trees with Farquarson firing into the air above the baboon's head.

As the sun set every evening the baboons came down from the trees to drink. Jamie never tired of watching them. Close to their chosen drinking place there would always be a waiting crocodile, lying motionless and almost submerged in the river. Usually the baboons would spot the danger and the air would echo with screams of warning and the frenzied shaking of branches.

Occasionally the vigilance of the pack would waver. An incautious young baboon would taste the water and venture deeper into the stream. Suddenly there would be a surge, a flurry of ripples, the churning of arms and legs between immense toothed jaws, and a terrified howl. The howl would be silenced abruptly as the victim was dragged beneath the surface and drowned in the depths below the bank.

Afterwards a few smears of blood floated upwards.

The baboons were not the only victims of the river. Three-quarters of the journey was complete when tragedy struck the expedition. It was early in the morning. They had camped overnight in one of the Benoue's rare bays. A hundred yards away a long spit of sand ran out into the water. The canoes were loaded and everyone was ready to leave, but Farquarson was still out hunting somewhere in the nearby forest.

As they waited for Farquarson to return, the young guide wandered round the bay and walked out along the spit. A few moments later Jamie, Mamkinga and Wolf, relaxing on the ground by the boats, heard a fearsome trumpeting scream. They all leapt up and gazed across the bay.

The guide was standing frozen at the end of the spit, staring back at the forest.

To his horror Jamie saw that a huge bull elephant had come out of the forest on to the sand. The elephant was standing between the young man and the trees. It ears were spread wide and its trunk was raised. The black tulip of its nostrils scanned the air for the unseen intruder in front of it.

The elephant registered the guide and trumpeted in rage again.

'It is an old rogue bull,' Mamkinga said quietly, his voice grim. 'They are the most dangerous animals in the forest.'

As he spoke the elephant put back its ears and lowered its trunk. Then still giving out the terrible chilling screams, it charged. The three watched helplessly.

In spite of its vast size it moved more quickly than any animal Jamie had ever seen. The little guide had no chance. The water behind him was full of crocodiles. In any event he couldn't swim. Like a great grey wall of death the elephant reared up in front of him. The elephant lowered its tusks and tossed him high into the air.

As the guide fell back to earth, the elephant folded its front legs and knelt, trumpeting, on his body.

It was a sombre and silent party which set off up the river half an hour later after Farquarson's return. The paddlers' faces were shuttered and fearful. For once they did not sing or chant all day. That night Jamie heard them muttering among themselves as they huddled in the darkness beyond the fire.

Mamkinga listened. 'They think the spirits of the forest are angry with us,' he said. 'I fear we will have trouble.'

Jamie sat up alone and late by the fire.

That Africa was full of menace and perils was not new to him. He had known it as a child almost from the first moment Mrs Livingstone started reading in the Blantyre house. But that the perils could strike with such terrible speed and ruthlessness, with such a crushing finality, Jamie was unprepared for. The fastest, strongest and boldest man alive would have been as helpless as a child before the elephant's enraged charge and its scything tusks.

Jamie had seen the river and the forest sparkle and gleam. Now behind the fresh clean gold of the African sunlight he suddenly realized that the continent's darkness was always only seconds away. On a pleasant peaceful morning death had come to the little guide like a lance hurled out of the night. The Benoue was a great river, but it was not the river of life.

If the Benoue harboured lances of death, what would that other much mightier river be harbouring on its banks to protect its mysterious source?

For the first time the confidence that had sustained Jamie for eleven years wavered. He had come to Africa to redeem his promises and fulfil his dream. Now he wondered how many of the promises Africa would allow him to keep, and how much of the dream to realize.

Jamie shivered as the sparks flew upwards.

Then he shook off the mood of doubt. He threw more logs on the fire and lay down to sleep, firmly shutting out of his mind any lingering image of the immense creature which had raged forward across the sand like a towering and foam-flecked Atlantic breaker.

In spite of all his efforts, Jamie's sleep that night was troubled.

The next morning Mamkinga was proved right. All the paddlers had vanished. Without waiting to be paid, they had taken one of the canoes and headed back down the river towards the coast.

The cut mooring rope of the missing canoe was still dangling in the water. Mamkinga held it in his hand for a moment. Then he threw it away.

'We have strong muscles and stout paddles,' he said. 'Let us put them to use.'

*

Exactly four weeks after they left the Benoue's mouth they reached Garoua.

The river was much narrower and faster-flowing here close to its headwaters, and the settlement spilled over both banks. Mamkinga instructed them to moor the boats to one of the many jetties that angled out into the stream. Then he led the party into the town.

It was close to nightfall. They found lodgings in a house belonging to an Arab merchant off the street where most of the trading stores were grouped. After dining they went to bed and slept for the first time in a month on firm straw palliasses beneath a roof.

Jamie woke as soon as it was light. He dressed. Leaving the others still asleep, he went out on to the street. In spite of the earliness of the hour a group of guides, escorts and agents had already gathered outside, waiting to hire themselves out to any merchant who wished to use their services. Jamie walked among them until he found one who could speak English.

'The British consulate?' he said.

'Right at once, effendi.'

The guide Jamie had chosen was a young Sudanese. He led Jamie through the winding streets of Garoua until they reached a tree-lined avenue.

'Here, effendi,' said the young man. 'Very wealthy, very generous people, the British people.'

Jamie smiled dourly and handed the young man a small coin. Then he glanced up.

The British consulate was a square European building, built of brick and standing sturdy and uncompromising in the middle of a line of ornate Arab villas. A sun-bleached Union flag hung limply from a pole on the roof and the royal coat of arms glistened on a plaque set into the wall by the door. Jamie's guide knocked and a Waziri houseboy appeared, smartly dressed in a scarlet fez and white tunic.

The houseboy saw Jamie and drew himself up stiffly. 'Yes, sir,' he said looking straight ahead.

'I wish to see the consul,' Jamie said.

'Yes, sir.'

'He is able to receive visitors?'

'Yes, sir.'

'Then will ye take me to him, please?'

'Yes, sir.'

Jamie made to step forward but the houseboy didn't move. He remained stiff and motionless in the doorway, gazing over Jamie's shoulder. Puzzled, Jamie glanced back at his guide, who was squatting on his haunches in the shade.

'I think maybe is only words he knows,' the guide volunteered.

Jamie thought for a moment. Then he produced the envelope and held it out. The houseboy took it warily.

'Yes, sir,' he repeated, still without looking at Jamie.

The houseboy disappeared.

A few minutes later he returned and stood aside to let Jamie in. As Jamie followed him up a flight of stairs he saw that only the façade of the building was European. The interior was Arabic in style with an arched court-yard at the centre and a gallery round the upper floor.

The houseboy opened a door and beckoned Jamie through. Jamie stepped inside. He found himself in a large dusky room with windows shuttered against the sunlight. A European was seated behind a mahogany table with a large faded globe almost obscuring his face. He stood up as Jamie came in.

'Mr Oran – ?'

The man came forward and held out his hand. He was small and trim, with a tanned sunken face, jet-black hair and pale staring eyes. He was dressed in military uniform and knee-length leather boots gleaming with polish.

'Skinner, Her Majesty's Consul, pro tem, at your service, sir.'

Jamie shook a dry claw-like hand and sat down in the chair Skinner offered him.

'Always a pleasure to see a fellow countryman,' Skinner went on. 'We get few enough of them through here. God knows, they've every reason to avoid this benighted spot. So what can I do for you, Mr Oran?'

'You've read the letter from the Royal Geographical Society?' Jamie said.

Skinner nodded.

'I'm trying to join up with Mr Baimbridge,' Jamie went on. 'The society said you might know his last position, or at least be able to put me on his track. It's most important I find him. I have a letter for him from the society.'

There was silence for a moment. Skinner was looking curiously at Jamie.

'I doubt he'll have much use of letters now,' Skinner said.

Jamie looked at him, puzzled.

'Mr Baimbridge is dead, sir,' Skinner continued flatly. 'He and his party were ambushed by savages four months ago. Everyone perished.'

Jamie shook his head. 'But he can't be dead –'

'The fate is not unknown elsewhere.' Skinner smiled bleakly. 'In Africa it is the rule for the white man rather than the exception. The news of the tragedy reached us last month. I sent notification to the society immediately. No doubt it arrived after your departure.'

Jamie sat quite still. He felt cold in his stomach.

'And what happens to the expedition?' he asked at last. 'Surely it will set out again?'

'There is no expedition,' Skinner replied. 'Every member is dead. In due course I imagine the society may mount another. You will know more about that than I. It will naturally take time. There are men to be recruited, transport to be arranged, the rains to be considered – let alone the question of finding someone able and willing to lead it. I would hazard a minimum of two years.'

'Two years?' Jamie's voice was bitter.

'I am sorry, young man. You had obviously set your heart on joining Mr Baimbridge. Unfortunately there is nothing I can do.'

Jamie thought for a moment.

'Can you at least tell me where it happened?'

'Within a hundred miles or so.' Skinner revolved the globe. 'As you know, Baimbridge was searching for the source of the Nile. The Benoue's source has never been charted. Baimbridge told me he believed the river's headwaters might be as distant as the Abyssinian highlands. In which case he thought the Nile might originate there too – '

Skinner's little stick-like finger reached out and touched an area of the dense green and brown which marked Abyssinia.

'According to the report of the tragedy he was travelling up a tributary of the Rahad river. He made camp somewhere in the forest near a ford. There he was attacked by local tribesmen. The reason is not clear, but it seems they may have mistaken the expedition for a slaving party. That is all I know.'

The consul paused.

'I regret what happened, deeply,' Skinner went on. 'But I have to say, sir, that I warned Mr Baimbridge. The highland kingdoms are strange and powerful. Baimbridge had set his heart on reaching Gondar, the most ancient and in my view the most dangerous of all. I urged him to consider what Mr Mungo Park wrote about Gondar more than half a century ago. You are no doubt familiar with his writing, Mr Oran?'

Jamie nodded.

'Since then,' Skinner continued, 'by report much has happened to Gondar. Of late there are further stories of great disturbances within its mountains. It is, in my view – and, I would hazard, the opinion of any authority on Africa – the last place on this great continent for a European traveller to venture into. Only a stubborn and misguided man would consider it. Mr Baimbridge – '

Skinner did not finish his sentence. He shrugged and stood up. Jamie shook hands and turned to leave. Then he checked and glanced back.

'You say everyone died,' he said. 'How did the news reach you then?'

'Forgive me,' Skinner replied. 'You are quite correct. By everyone I referred to the European members. What happened to the porters no one knows. But there was one survivor, Mr Baimbridge's personal servant. He returned and gave me the news himself. His name is Bakulu. He is an Abyssinian and a very reliable man. I have no reason to doubt him.'

'Where is he now?'

'Here in Garoua, I should imagine,' Skinner said. 'If he is, you will be able to find him by asking in the market. I fear he won't be able to tell you any more than I can.'

Jamie walked slowly down the steps.

By the time he reached the street the numbing coldness of the disappointment had drained out of him. In its place was a burning determination. All of Jamie's life had been dedicated to reaching Africa. He had achieved it. He had already travelled almost a quarter of the way across the continent. Jamie wasn't going to be thwarted in his search for the great river now.

Though Baimbridge was dead, he would go on alone.

'Bakulu?' Mamkinga said. 'Are you sure?'

'Quite sure,' Jamie nodded. 'He was Mr Baimbridge's personal servant. He somehow escaped the massacre and made his way back here with the news. And he's Abyssinian.'

Mamkinga frowned. 'One of my father's herders was named Bakulu. It is not a name I have heard since I left Malinda.'

'Then he may even be a Malindan,' Jamie said excitedly. 'You could tell him who you are. Maybe he knows things he hasn't told anyone else. He'd talk to you – '

'Wait, Umshebi, wait,' Mamkinga interrupted. 'We do not even know where he is yet. We have to find him first.'

'The sooner we start looking the better.'

For two days Mamkinga scoured the Garoua market without success. Then he found a Herero woman who sold toasted maize cakes. The Abyssinian had bought his morning meal from her stall and she remembered him talking about the expedition. Bakulu was trying to hire himself out as a boat-man in a fishery, she said. When he didn't appear one morning she assumed he had found a job and left for the river.

Mamkinga and Jamie set off on foot along the river bank.

The fisheries were tiny settlements scattered at intervals along the Benoue. Each had a circle of huts, a rickety wooden jetty, and a number of canoes. They found the Abyssinian in the fourth one they visited. The fishery's owner pointed at the water's edge where a man in a loincloth was threading slabs of dried carp on to a plaited cord.

'Pula!' Mamkinga said as they walked up to him.

'Pula!' the man replied.

Bakulu was tall and spare-framed. He had tight-curled greying hair and a patient thoughtful face. One of his shoulders was hunched higher than the other and his head was set at an awkward angle to his neck, giving him a clumsy stork-like appearance, but his hands were quick and skilful as he worked.

Mamkinga spoke to him in Malindan.

The man answered in the same tongue and the two began to talk. Jamie stood beside them listening. Bakulu was indeed from Malinda. He had been born on the western border of the kingdom. Although it was many years since he had been back, he remembered vividly the landscape of his childhood.

As they spoke Mamkinga leant forward and embraced him. Then Mamkinga glanced at Jamie.

'This is the first of my countrymen I have met in eleven years,' Mamkinga said. He shook his head wonderingly.

'What can you tell us about Mr Baimbridge and the expedition?' Jamie asked eagerly as Mamkinga stood in silence.

Jamie repeated the story he had been told by the consul. Bakulu nodded.

'It is as the consul told you,' he said. 'When we were attacked I managed to escape and hide in the forest. I came back at night after the attackers had gone. Everyone was lying dead in the shallows. They had been stripped of everything. I pulled the bwana Baimbridge ashore and buried him in the sand. I wished to do the same for the others, but I heard sounds as if the men were returning. I ran away again. Next day I started back for Garoua.'

'Do you know where Mr Baimbridge was heading?' Jamie said.

Bakulu nodded again.

'He was looking for the true birthplace of the great river. He spoke about it much. Another white man, he said, believed he had found it in the kingdom of Gondar. Bwana Baimbridge said he was wrong. The birthplace was in Gondar but higher in the mountains than the other thought. That is where we were bound.'

Jamie thought for a moment.

It was exactly as Sir Roderick Murchison had described it to him. The other white man was the great explorer, Mungo Park, whom Skinner had referred to two days earlier. Park claimed he had found the Nile's source in the foothills of the mountain kingdom. Like other explorers since, Baimbridge believed there was a single permanently flowing stream that sprang from the rocks higher in the mountains.

'If we paid you well,' Jamie said, 'could you take us on from where you were attacked to the place Mr Baimbridge was making for?'

Bakulu frowned.

'I could take you there,' he said cautiously. 'But I doubt whether the Galla would permit you to enter their lands.'

Mamkinga had been listening intently to the conversation.

'The Galla's lands are to the north,' Mamkinga said, puzzled. 'It is not necessary to travel through Galla territory to reach Gondar.'

Bakulu glanced at him in surprise.

'You do not know?' Bakulu said. 'This year after the rains ended the Galla invaded Malinda. The Acab Saat of Gondar marched with them. They killed the embrenche and marched on Gondar. They took Gondar too. Now Culembra sits on Gondar's throne with the Acab Saat guiding his sword arm, and all the lands of the Mountains of the Moon are theirs.'

'They killed the embrenche?' Mamkinga's voice was a whisper.

Bakulu nodded. 'The embrenche and all his family are dead. Malinda's people are slaves. The country is a fief of the Galla now.'

Mamkinga said nothing.

For a moment he looked slowly and unseeingly from

one to the other. His eyes were blank and his face was a stony mask out of which everything had ebbed, all interest, all awareness, all life. Then, moving like a sleepwalker, he stepped into the river. He waded out until he was standing waist-deep in the water, and stared sightlessly at the far bank.

Astounded and alarmed, Jamie waded out after him and tried to pull him back. Mamkinga hurled him roughly away.

Mamkinga lifted his face to the sky and began to howl like a mortally wounded animal.

'For God's sake, man!' Jamie shook Mamkinga's shoulder. 'Ye cannot give up. Ye must pull yourself together. We're going on.'

Mamkinga didn't reply.

Frozen and stiff, he sat with his head lowered, gazing numbly at the floor. Jamie glanced up helplessly at Wolf and Farquarson who were standing behind him. Both of them by now knew the story of Mamkinga's past.

Wolf frowned. 'I think all the years he was a slave, he held on to the hope he'd one day escape and return to Malinda and his family. Now the poor bastard's discovered there's nothing to go back to. He's lost everything. His family are dead and his country's been conquered. He just can't take it. He's in a state of shock.'

Farquarson nodded in agreement. 'The wretched man's mind has caved in. Maybe the journey will restore his sanity,' he suggested.

Jamie looked back at Mamkinga in despair.

In spite of all Mamkinga had told him, Jamie had sensed there were areas of the giant African's life and mind he didn't know about – perhaps that, even Mamkinga himself did not understand. For most of the time he seemed to be confident and resolute. On the river and in the forest he was more than the match of the three Europeans. Wise, practical and decisive, he was their master.

Yet at intervals in the Bight of Benin and on the journey

to Garoua he had unaccountably lapsed into dark moody silences. Sometimes they lasted for hours. Mamkinga would sit huddled apart from the others, his head sunk on his chest and his eyes distant and clouded. He was incapable then of making any decision, almost incapable, it had seemed to Jamie, of speech.

Until now the paralysing cloud which intermittently seemed to haunt and stifle him had always lifted. This time it was different. Mamkinga's private darkness had overwhelmed him. There appeared to be no way out. Like one of the bodiless spirits of the forest which the paddlers claimed terrorized them by night, Mamkinga had become a ghost.

Jamie knew little about twins except that the relationships between them could be so strange and intimate they touched on what Dr Cameron used to refer to with distaste in long-ago Blantyre as the unnatural. Dr Cameron was a dour Glasgow man, a hard-headed practitioner of science and medicine. He had no time for what he termed superstition, vanity, and nonsense.

Jamie was different.

Jamie was a child of the Hebridean isles. His early years had been spent in the ancient Gaelic world where dreams and portents and spirits were as familiar and real as Iona's green turf and white sands. It was a world in which twins, too, moved as effortlessly between the boundaries of magic and reality as the island's otters between the sea and the shore.

Jamie felt deeply and acutely for Mamkinga as the African sat locked in numb silent anguish. If there were one key which would unlock the dark shutters that had walled in Mamkinga's mind it was held, Jamie guessed, by his lost sister Toomi. Whether Mamkinga would ever find his sister again, Jamie had no idea.

What Jamie did know was that there was no chance at all while Mamkinga remained an automaton in the Garoua lodging house.

'We'll have to take him as he is,' Jamie said, getting to his feet at last. 'Give me a hand.'

Together they heaved Mamkinga to his feet and propelled him towards the door.

It was the evening of the following day. Jamie had eventually got Mamkinga away from the river and back to Garoua. There Mamkinga slumped down on his bed and lay silently with his face to the wall. He hadn't spoken in the twenty-four hours since.

The night before Jamie had held a council with the other two. Bakulu, Baimbridge's Abyssinian servant, had agreed to leave the fishery and travel with them to the borders of the Galla's newly enlarged lands. Then, if the Galla gave them safe conduct, he would guide them up into the Mountains of the Moon along the route Baimbridge had intended to follow.

The Benoue had been mapped as navigable to its source a hundred miles further east. Afterwards they would have to travel across land. Meanwhile they could continue by water. They had guns and boats. They could buy more stores in the market, and hire other paddlers.

Jamie was determined to go on.

Were the other two, Jamie asked, prepared to continue too?

'You've stretched me for the gallows as a lamb,' Farquarson said. 'Harebrained as your scheme is, Jamie, I'm damned if I won't see how my neck fits the noose as a sheep too.'

Wolf nodded in agreement.

'In the words of your bardic countryman we seem to be stepped in so far, returning were as tedious as go o'er.' Wolf flicked his long grey hair out of his eyes and gave his yellow-toothed smile. 'Let us march on and see what lies along the trail.'

They had spent the morning restocking in the market and negotiating for new paddlers. Jamie had intended to leave Garoua at noon, but the day was so oppressively hot and the air so humid and sultry he put off their departure until dusk. They would travel for a couple of hours, Jamie decided, to get clear of the riverside settlements. Then they would make camp and continue at dawn.

As they bundled Mamkinga along the jetty and into one of the boats, Jamie glanced up at the sky.

The sun was setting and the light was fading quickly. Normally then the air began to cool. That evening it was as torrid as at midday. A fierce glare seemed to linger in the gathering darkness and sweat was pouring from him as Jamie lowered himself on to his seat. Clouds of mosquitos swarmed round him, whining and stinging him so violently that within moments every inch of his skin was covered with swollen red blotches.

Jamie raised his arms and frantically tried to brush them away. They were everywhere – clogging his nostrils, humming in his ears, attacking his eyelids, biting him even between his closed fingers. His head was aching from the charges of static electricity in the air, and his eyes blinked painfully from the reflections off the water.

Jamie waited impatiently for the others to climb aboard. Then he shouted a command. The boats swung out into the river. They passed the settlements beyond the town and headed upstream. A few minutes later there was a shattering thunderclap.

Bolts of lightning flared overhead and a tropical rainstorm burst over them.

— 85 —

Twenty-four hours earlier, only a few streets away from
the lodging house where Mamkinga was lying in silent
numbness on his bed, Toomi had waited fretfully for
darkness to fall.

Her belief that Mamkinga had been in Garoua, that he
might be there even now, had become a burning un-
shakable conviction. She had sensed his presence first
after her visit with Hadji and Rachel to the old Malindan
slave. Since then something had happened to her brother.
Toomi had no idea what it was. He hadn't been
physically hurt, as so often in the past, she was sure of
that. Long years of experience had taught Toomi to
recognize the pains that ran through her when Mamkinga was beaten or wounded.

This was different.

Something dark and troubling, a black cloak of misery,
seemed to have wrapped itself suffocatingly about him. It
was as if Mamkinga's very being had been lanced and the
vital spirits were seeping out of him. Somehow, Toomi
felt, Mamkinga had suddenly and inexplicably surrendered to despair, and his hold on life was slipping
away.

Toomi had always been stronger than Mamkinga.
Now more than at any other time since they were
separated, more even than during her own worst
moments of misery and fear, she wanted to put her arms
round him. She wanted to hold and comfort him. To pour
the warmth of her body into his. To cherish and nourish
him and restore him to life.

Toomi paced up and down the floor in anguish and

frustration as daylight waned and dusk filled the windows. Watching her, Rachel knew that for once there was nothing she could do. Finally Hadji appeared.

'It is dark enough,' he said. 'We may go.'

It was a moonless night and Hadji led the way with a torch.

The slave pens were ten minutes' walk from the house. By day there was a guard at the door, but at night there was no one. With Toomi and Rachel behind him, Hadji walked between the rows of cubicles. Some of the slaves, caught in the passing torchlight, were lying asleep on the ground. Most were awake and the night air was full of a cacophony of shouts, cries, voices talking and the rattling of chains.

Hadji came to the cubicle where they had visited the old man. He stopped and lifted the torch high in the air. Toomi and Rachel came to his shoulders.

As the light flared over the inside of the cubicle all three froze.

'In the name of Allah,' Hadji whispered.

The old man was lying spreadeagled on his back in a great pool of blood. He was dead. Before he died he had been tortured and mutilated. His hands, feet and genitals had been chopped off. His eyes had been gouged out, and his head battered to pulp with a club. Hadji bent down and dipped a finger in the blood. It was still sticky.

Hadji stood up. Toomi and Rachel were staring at the ground, their faces shocked and disbelieving.

'They were here less than an hour ago,' he said grimly.

'Who?' Toomi asked, dazed, her mind still struggling to take in the barbarity of the scene in front of them.

'The Acab Saat's men,' Hadji answered. 'They discovered someone had been talking to him. They must have tortured him to find out who it was and what he'd told them.'

'But how – ?'

'It doesn't matter,' Hadji cut her off. 'We must get out of Garoua now. The old man will have talked before they killed him. They know you are here and I am with you. At daylight they will search the town. It is only by the grace of Allah they did not think we might come back tonight. We cannot even be certain about that.'

As he spoke Hadji was unwinding his turban.

He sliced off a section of the cloth with his dagger, wound the cloth round the burning head of the torch and extinguished the light, stamping out the sparks on the ground.

The space round the cubicle was plunged into darkness. All that was left was the stench, the clamour of the slaves, and the terrible image imprinted on Toomi's and Rachel's minds of the old man lying butchered at their feet.

'Stay close as my shadow,' Hadji ordered.

He set off through the pens. This time he turned away from the door that led out to the market. He moved towards the wall at the back. In spite of the darkness he walked swiftly and unhesitatingly. They reached the wall and he pulled himself on top of it. He drew the young women up behind him and the three dropped down on the other side.

Then they set off again.

Half an hour later they stopped. They were, Toomi and Rachel sensed, close to Garoua's town walls. For a moment they thought they were about to repeat their experience of escaping from Kano through the sewer. Then they saw Hadji begin to climb. He beckoned them to follow him.

'I have shown you the underground drainage,' he whispered. 'Now we are going to use a drain in the sky.'

His teeth shone as he smiled. Hadji continued to climb upwards.

Following him the young women found they were mounting a steep and narrow flight of stone steps that zig-zagged backwards and forwards up a tower. As they approached the top they heard the rustle of flowing water. When they reached the final platform Hadji was waiting for them on hands and knees.

They knelt beside him.

Peering round, Toomi saw they were kneeling on an inspection platform for one of the aqueducts that brought Garoua its drinking water. In Kano drinking water came into the town by hand to be hawked about the streets by the hundreds of water-sellers. Garoua had dealt with the problem by copying the ancient Roman settlements to the north.

Stretching away from them was a brick-walled channel supported on a series of arches. The channel ran down from a reservoir in the marshes of the Benoue river. Hadji rolled over the retaining wall and slid into the water. Stooping low to prevent his silhouette showing above the brickwork, he began to trudge away against the flow.

The young women followed him again. The water reached to their waists. On the platform it had appeared deceptively tranquil and slow-moving. In the channel it surged violently against them. They grabbed at the parapet to prevent themselves being swept away. Then, hunched over like Hadji, they began to wade forward.

They were in the water for an hour.

At last, chilled, buffeted and exhausted, they came to another platform above the reservoir. Hadji heaved himself out of the channel. They climbed out too and descended a second stone staircase. Finally they arrived, panting, on the ground.

'It will be easier now,' Hadji said. 'We are in the marshes. There are paths raised on dykes through them. I left one of my men with the horses six miles to the east. The journey will take another two hours. By then it will be close to daylight. I do not think the Acab Saat's men will be out here but many caravans use the marsh islands as campsites. It is possible they will have posted guards among them. We will remain at the camp throughout the day. When darkness comes again we will take the horses and leave.'

Within moments they were on their way again.

Hadji strode ahead, his body, silhouetted against the faint starlight, bending and swaying as he threaded his way along the winding paths between the dense thickets of reed and papyrus. On either side the night rang with the booming of frogs, the churr of startled nightjars and the occasional frantic splashing of a water antelope as it bounded away across the swamp before them.

Apart from that there was nothing except the rhythmic pad of their feet on the dry earth of the tracks, the incongruous mixture of dust and water scents in their faces, the endless soft brushing of the reeds against their legs, and a gathering, almost overpowering sense of tiredness in Toomi's and Rachel's bodies.

Then, with the first faint shell of dawn starting to life over the horizon, Hadji stopped and turned.

'We are here,' he said.

They had reached one of the little islands in the marshes. The almost-dead embers of a fire glowed in front of them. Beside it a man in a goatskin cape was getting to his feet. Behind the man the horses that had carried them from Quilombo to Garoua were grazing the wiry swamp grass.

Hadji went forward and greeted the man. Then he glanced back at the girls.

'Sleep,' he said. 'I will wake you when it is time to leave.'

The young women stumbled forward. Limp with exhaustion, they threw themselves down by the fire. Within moments they were both asleep.

Toomi woke to the feel of Hadji's hand on her shoulder. She sat up. It was dusk again. Toomi realized she must have slept for twelve hours. She glanced round and saw Rachel was sitting too.

Hadji raised his finger to his lips in a gesture for silence. He was frowning and his nostrils flared as he sniffed anxiously at the air.

'Something is wrong,' he whispered. 'Stay here. Make no sound until I return.'

Hadji slipped away into the reeds.

86

Toomi crawled over and knelt beside Rachel.

Both of them strained their ears to try to pick up what had disturbed Hadji. They could only hear the evening bird calls, the murmur of the rippling water, the stir and rustle of the marsh plants. The air was chokingly hot and humid in spite of the onset of evening. Glancing down, Toomi noticed her clothes were drenched in sweat. Apart from the tormenting insects nothing seemed strange or different.

Five minutes later Hadji reappeared.

He moved soundlessly on his belly. Neither of the young women was aware he had come back until the reeds parted and his face emerged only inches above the ground. Hadji slid himself round until he was lying between them. He glanced back in the direction from which he'd come.

Mist was rising over the reeds with the approach of darkness. In the dusky half-light that was beginning to filter through the mist Toomi saw that Hadji's face was taut with anger.

'The Acab Saat's men are riding towards us,' he whispered. 'They are combing the camps in the marshes. I never calculated they would be so thorough – '

Hadji swore silently between his teeth. 'I am known in Garoua. Once they learned someone was asking about an escaped Malindan slave, it was not difficult to find out it was me. Then it was just as easy to discover where my camp was.'

He cursed again.

'Can't we slip back into Garoua?' Toomi said. 'We could hide in the house again.'

Hadji shook his head. 'There are horsemen on all the paths to the town. Nor can we stay here. There is only one thing we can do – '

He raised himself on his knees. 'We will take the horses and try to get past them to the west. If we get through, we can turn back north for the hills.'

Hadji whistled quietly. The man in the goatskin cape crept over. Hadji whispered in his ear and the man crawled away.

A few moments later three of the horses were saddled. Hadji beckoned the girls to mount. He vaulted up on to the leading horse and led them away from the island.

The marshes near the head of the Benoue were patterned with a web of meandering dykes and banks. The tracks along them linked the little low islands and led down to Garoua. Hadji had used his campsite for years. He knew every one of the embankments that radiated from it – which was so narrow it could only take men in single file on foot, which was broad enough to carry an ox-drawn cart, which was safe for a galloping horse.

He set off now heading west along the hidden lanes through the reeds and papyrus. As minute followed minute and no one appeared before them, Hadji became increasingly confident they had evaded the Acab Saat's men. He was wrong.

Hadji's horse broke through a reed bed and checked. A rider was blocking the path ahead.

'Ride!' Hadji shouted.

He kicked furiously at his horse's flanks and the horse surged forward. Behind him the mounts of Rachel and Toomi broke into a gallop. With the young women clinging to their necks, the horses followed Hadji's.

Hadji swerved to the right and headed along another dyke. Moments later he was brought to a halt again. A second horseman was blocking the way ahead. Hadji drew his sword and prepared to ride him down. Then he hesitated. He could see other silhouettes behind the horseman and he heard the jangle of bridles. On his own he could have dealt with the first rider and possibly the others at his back. With Toomi and Rachel to protect it was impossible.

Cursing, Hadji swung his horse round. He rode back into the reeds. Seconds afterwards he was blocked for the third time. Again he cut away from the path and broke through the papyrus on to another track. He rode along it for fifty yards.

Then he reined in his horse and paused. For an instant he sat still in the saddle, thinking furiously.

The Acab Saat's men had somehow found a guide who knew the marshes as well as he did. They had barricaded the tracks that led across the swamps to the west — towards the plain and safety. South there was only Garoua. The town was inevitably a trap now. North lay the immensity of the upper swamps. Even Hadji did not trust himself to navigate through their perilous waters.

The only way out was to the east.

Two tracks ran eastwards. Both led to the Benoue river. They reached its bank at a point where the river was still narrow but already deep and fast-flowing. There was, Hadji remembered, a tiny settlement and a ferry that was occasionally used by caravans from the coast, when heavy rains had flooded the marshes and closed the usual routes into the town. It was possible Salama's men were guarding the ferry. Hadji thought it unlikely. The spring rains had been light and the river was low.

In any event it hardly mattered. With the tracks north, south and west blocked or impassable, it was their only chance.

'We'll head for the river,' Hadji whispered over his shoulder.

He set off through the reeds again.

As the minutes passed it seemed as if Hadji had gambled successfully. The shouts of the horsemen faded behind them. No one appeared in front to block their path. On either side there was only the constant rustle of the papyrus and, beneath them, the quiet clink of the horses' hoofs on the baked earth of the track.

They reached the river. Hadji turned to the left and

rode along the bank. The ferry was only a few yards in front of them. There were boats moored to the jetty and no one in sight. He glanced back and beckoned Toomi and Rachel towards him. As they spurred their horses to his shoulder, a cry rang out ahead.

Hadji's head jerked round.

Three riders were galloping towards them along the path that stretched away on the far side of the ferry-point. Hadji had been wrong again. Salama's men had cordoned the river crossing, but they had positioned themselves upstream of the track he had chosen to reach it.

Hadji narrowed his eyes. He calculated the horsemen's speed against the length of the path. It would be thirty seconds before they got to the jetty.

'Dismount!' Hadji shouted. 'Take one of the boats. Paddle upstream as fast as you can. The forest closes in a hundred paces from here. Once you get there you will be safe. If you need me again I will be waiting in Garoua!'

Toomi and Rachel flung themselves off their horses.

They raced to the jetty. Rachel tore at the mooring rope of the nearest boat and threw the rope clear of its stanchion. Toomi jumped into the bows. She knelt on the keel, and picked up the paddle. At the stern Rachel did the same.

The two drove the paddles into the water and the boat surged away from the jetty. As they arrowed into midstream Toomi turned and looked back.

The three horsemen were only yards away from Hadji. Before he left his island camp he had buckled a long sword to his belt. He had drawn the sword now and was holding it out in front of him as he crouched in his saddle, waiting for Salama's men. Hadji lifted the sword and its blade flashed in the starlight.

To Toomi it seemed to be raised in salute to them.

As the riders clashed the ferry-point was hidden by a bend in the river. Toomi turned and the boat swept on into the darkness.

They paddled for an hour. At the end of it they had

passed the last of the settlements that reached upriver from the town. The night was increasingly dark and dank. Sweat flowed from their skins and the air was charged with strange disturbing currents of fluctuating energy. The nightly noises of the river had been extinguished and the only sounds were distant growling rolls of thunder.

Toomi lifted her face to the sky. The stars had been blotted out and thick clouds were piling above them.

'There will be a storm,' she said. 'A bad storm. We must make for shore.'

Moments later as she peered through the gathering murk Toomi spotted a broad shelving bay on the river's southern bank.

'Here,' she said.

She and Rachel drove the boat ashore.

They pulled it out of the water, turned it upside down, and propped up its bow and stern with driftwood logs. As they crawled beneath it, thunder roared above the trees. Lightning dazzled and the skies spilled over with cataracts of rain.

Lying beneath the curved wooden canopy with the water drumming down and Rachel curled against her, Toomi suddenly felt she had never been so close to Mamkinga since her childhood. The feeling was so vivid, so intense, she sat up expecting to see him in front of her. Her head struck the boat's keel. There was nothing there before her except the blinding cascading sheets of water.

Toomi lay back. She put her hands to her ears and tried to shut out the tumult of the storm.

87

'We'll have to get ashore!' Jamie shouted above the tumult. 'If we don't, we're going to sink.'

Farquarson was in the bows of the leading boat. He peered ahead through the rain and darkness.

'There's a bay on the right!' he bellowed back.

With the other boats following, Farquarson headed for the bank. They ran the boats aground and pulled them up on to the land. Jamie gripped Mamkinga by the arm and led him to the partial shelter of an acacia bush. Farquarson and Wolf joined them, and the four of them squatted on the ground.

The rain continued until dawn.

Mamkinga was used to tropical deluges, but even he had never experienced one like this. To the other three, at the centre of an African storm for the first time, it was a terrifying experience.

The water fell in vertical cataracts. The drops were as thick and heavy as hailstones. They hammered down, stripping leaves and branches from trees and bushes, crushing the grass to a pulp, bruising and chilling the skin. The accompanying noise was deafening. There were no thunderclaps or wind-roar now. Instead a monotonous unbroken drumming battered the ears and numbed the mind.

The surface of the Benoue was in turmoil. The water was torn and fragmented as if by endless raking volleys of gunfire. On the banks the rain sliced through the vegetation, and jetted back from the earth in explosions of mud. A dry leaf leapt on one of the plumes. It was shredded instantly to powder, and vanished as if it had never existed. Birds and insects were pulverized. Animals huddled cowed and sodden under tree roots.

It was impossible to hear and impossible to see. There was nothing except an impenetrable roaring darkness sheeted with great steely curtains of water.

The men crouched together in a circle, arms shielding their heads. The bush under which they had tried to shelter had long since been reduced to a tangle of broken twigs. It was too dark and the assault of the battering rain too powerful to find anywhere else. As the hours passed they remained where they were, shoulders hunched, faces sunken, eyes shuttered – all of them chilled and sodden.

The storm ended as abruptly and dramatically as it had started.

One moment the deluge and uproar were as violent as ever. The next a grey watery light spilled over the bank. The rain thinned to a spray, and the cataract of sound faded. Moments later the clouds parted. The early sun crept over the bank, and a tentative morning chorus of bird and animal calls filled the suddenly still air.

Mamkinga got to his feet.

The others had rolled, exhausted, on to their sides and were lying in a torpor of sleep. Mamkinga was tired to the bone too, but something was plucking insistently at the edges of his mind. For the first time in two days he became aware of the world outside the wall of grief and despair that enclosed him.

Mamkinga gazed round.

The rain-flattened vegetation was wreathed in a dense low mist. On the river kingfishers had already started hunting. He saw the green and gold flicker of a malachite kingfisher and heard a tiny splash as it speared into the water. A jackal called warily. A troop of wart hogs, tails raised and tusks flashing, trotted across the grass, and flights of emerald-breasted doves passed overhead.

Mamkinga slowly stretched his arms and legs, like a great cat awakening.

Life was returning to the Benoue and its banks. The air was growing warmer every second in the rising sun. He stepped forward. It wasn't the life and warmth and light that had lifted him from his misery – it was something else. Something was calling to him, something as clear and vivid as the song that had come to him out of the palm trunk when he touched it with his finger.

Mamkinga walked on. Then he stopped with his foot poised in mid air. Fifty yards away a figure had appeared through the mist. It was a young woman and she was walking towards him. She came forward until she was standing in front of him.

She was almost as tall as he was. She had the same dark eyes, the same fine-boned face, the same long lustrous hair. Mamkinga barely saw her. He was only aware of a shining physical presence before him in the coiling mist. The song grew louder and louder until his entire body was quivering.

'Mamkinga,' she said quietly.

She reached out her hand and touched his forehead.

'Toomi,' he answered.

He lifted his own hand and placed it on her cheek. As he felt her skin a sensation of such peace and completeness surged over him he swayed and almost fell. Mamkinga's head dropped.

'Let us sleep together,' he said.

They lay down side by side on the sodden grass and put their arms round each other. The sun was rising and its heat was drawing scents from the soil.

Within seconds they were both asleep.

— 88 —

Locked together, arms and legs entwined, Mamkinga and Toomi slept throughout the day.

When they woke the afternoon light was draining from the sky and the first stars were approaching. They sat up. They gazed at each other and smiled. For the first time then Mamkinga saw his sister as a person rather than a presence. It was a profoundly strange and unsettling experience, at once deeply familiar and utterly new. The newness was because he'd last seen her as a child, unformed and fragile-boned. Now she was a mature woman with full breasts, rounded hips, and a face that was already setting into the strong clear lines of maturity.

The familiarity was even more bewildering.

Toomi was a woman, grown and changed. Yet she was also and equally unaltered, the child he had known from his birth. The tilt of her head, the smiling shift of her eyes, the candour when she gazed at him, the restless play of her hands – they were all as Mamkinga had always known them.

The two, the remembered and the new, blended and became one – the one that was half of his soul.

Mamkinga lifted Toomi's hand to his nose and smelt her skin. Then he smelt his own hand. The smells were the same. They had been lying together and each was impregnated with the other's sweat. But they would have smelt the same, they had always smelt the same, even two thousand miles apart.

Mamkinga smiled at Toomi through the tears that flooded his eyes. 'Tell me – ' he began but Toomi went on, 'What happened when you left me on that log in the village?'

Toomi finished the question for him in the very words that were formed but unspoken in Mamkinga's mouth. It had always been so between them. They had been separated for eleven years and nothing had changed.

Mamkinga nodded. 'In the time before you went to war. That came later, was it not so?'

Toomi nodded in return. 'That started when you were working with the fire and the metal. What was the metal?'

As she spoke images of the golden birds and flowers and animals that came to life under the fingers of old Ndele, the goldsmith, came to Mamkinga's mind. He had no need to answer her, to tell her. Toomi knew without him speaking, just as he knew about her service with Tamule.

'Gold.' Toomi had been frowning. Her face cleared. 'So that was it. I knew it came from the fire, that it had the colour of the fire. I knew you were making things with it, but I could never see what it was.'

'Yet before that you came to me as an owl,' Mamkinga said. 'I was in the tree and you brought me food.'

'I had many dreams of owls when I was with the war woman.' Toomi wrinkled her face in thought again. 'Once when I was on a hillside with her, she asked me why I was asleep in the night and yet she saw my eyes open. Maybe it was then.'

'Of course it was then,' Mamkinga replied firmly. 'I too dreamed often of owls.'

Toomi laughed. 'There were always owls with us. You ran away first when you lost my owl, remember?'

Mamkinga smiled and nodded. 'And the wars?' he asked.

Mamkinga had no means of knowing Toomi had been to war, but the awareness of battle and bloodshed, the shock of armies meeting and the clash of weapons, had been as vivid to him as part of his sister's life as if he had fought beside her.

'They were very bad at the start,' she said.

Mamkinga wrinkled his forehead, remembering things he had no means of remembering.

'There was an old man,' he began.

'No, an old woman,' Toomi cut him off. 'The old man was yours, the man who beat you across the legs. Aiee, it hurt.'

Toomi rubbed her calves, wincing at a memory that was not hers either.

'But the old woman beat you too,' Mamkinga said. 'Here on the shoulder and with her hand on your face. And then sometimes she held you and you were warm – '

He broke off.

They were joined in time and space for eternity. Separated they had been living each other's life blind-folded. Now they were putting faces and names, colours and smells, hardness and softness, to each other's existence. They were taking a monochrome map of the past they had travelled apart and filling it with colour.

'Tell me about her,' Mamkinga said.

'Tell me about him,' Toomi said.

They spoke at the same time. They both laughed and started again. They stopped and laughed once more. Then they began to talk.

An hour later both of them had filled in the eleven years each had missed. For both Toomi and Mamkinga the eleven years had been crowded and turbulent. They spanned the major part of the outward personal history of their two lives. The years had also encompassed vast changes in the internal lives of each – from childhood to adolescence to maturity. Toomi and Mamkinga had parted as children. They had met again as adults.

Yet one hour was enough.

It was enough because they could communicate whole periods of time, of experiences and people, in a single word or phrase. Toomi would say 'The old woman, Tamule, had servants and many times we went into battle', and she had no need to say anything more. The wealth of images and sensations behind the words passed across her memory as she spoke. As they passed they entered Mamkinga's mind, sharpening and illuminating the images that had reached him long since.

It was the same when Mamkinga spoke to her. He would say 'The Arab put me with the women, we marched, it was always hot,' and Toomi had the entire three-month journey of the slave caravan before her. Sometimes she would remember incidents he had forgotten.

'There was a girl then,' Toomi would say. 'You were hurt by the chains. I felt it each night before I slept. She tended you. Who was she?'

Mamkinga would have to think back. Then it would come to him.

'You mean Zia? They tied me next to her. She often gave me her food and held me at night when it was cold.'

Toomi nodded. 'I felt her warmth for you.'

As children their nurse had played a game with them. She would smooth a space of sand and use a sharpened bone to stipple it with a pattern of dots. Then she would give them the bone and make them join the dots with lines until a picture of an animal emerged.

Both of them were unconsciously playing the ancient childhood game now. The dots were the punctures that the years had made on their lives. The lines they were drawing in the questions and answers were the veins and tissue that made the picture complete.

The hour finished. The pictures were finished. There was something more.

'Who is the other that has been added?' Toomi said.

'Who is the other that joins with you?' Mamkinga's question was an echo of her own.

Toomi lowered her head. She wrinkled her face and drew abstractedly with her finger on the ground.

'I have found a sister,' she said.

'But not a sister of mine?' Mamkinga asked.

Toomi didn't answer.

She went on drawing in the earth, sketching with her nail until suddenly a flower took shape and grew. The flower seemed to give her confidence. Toomi lifted her head and gazed at him. Then she faltered once more.

'I do not know, Mamkinga,' she said. 'She came with me to find you. Now she is a part of your life as I am a part. Love her for me.'

Mamkinga paused. 'You have both been searching for me since you escaped?'

Toomi nodded. 'We have done nothing else.'

'Why?'

Toomi thought again. 'In part for the same reason that you would search for me. That we should be together. But there was something more. I am you, Mamkinga, and I am also different. I knew our father, the embrenche, was slain, our family dead, Malinda conquered. I was grieved to the deepest river-pools of my spirit. Yet I knew I could still survive. I could still be alive – '

Toomi's voice was even softer now. She was speaking almost as if she were talking to herself.

'I was not sure you would go on living,' she went on. 'That you could bear what I could bear. In the body and the fashions of men's thinking, maybe the years have made you stronger than I. But in the mind and the other ways of living, it is I who am stronger, much stronger. I had to find you to give you back courage and hope, for yourself and for Malinda. My sister joined me in the task. I am glad. You will always need me. Now, if I am not with you, she will be there in my place. I said love her for me –'

Toomi looked up and smiled. 'I would have better said love her for yourself.'

Mamkinga nodded gravely. 'I will do as you ask,' he said.

The two were kneeling opposite each other. For a long time there was silence. Then Toomi shook her head and laughed, as if to break a spell cast round them.

'And you?' she asked.

'I have a – man – as a friend, a new friend – '

The old uncertainty, the old childhood lack of confidence, made Mamkinga hesitate and fumble for the words. Toomi had always been able to declare herself, to speak forthrightly and openly. Mamkinga drew back and prevaricated.

'He is a stranger, a white man,' Mamkinga went on. 'I know him little but – '

'He saved your life,' Toomi interrupted. She smiled. 'I knew that. Of course, how could I not? And in return you saved him. I know that too. You called to me at night through the trees. I heard you and I sent you the knowledge of the Galla. They are a wandering people and skilled with herbs from all the mountains and plains. I learned much from them. You cured this white man and now he is your brother.'

Mamkinga frowned.

He tried to speak, but the words dried in his mouth. Toomi was right. As he had declared to the white man, Jamie was indeed his brother. Somehow he found it difficult to make the acknowledgement to Toomi. For a reason Mamkinga could not fathom, a small slender shadow seemed to have passed between himself and Jamie.

Mamkinga remained silent.

Toomi stared at him for a moment. Then she looked up at the sky. The light was fading fast. Soon dusk would close in over the Benoue. The kingfishers had stopped hunting. Flocks of sand grouse were flying home to their nestlings with water stored in their feathers. Distant jackals were giving night calls to their mates.

Toomi reached over and twined her fingers through his.

'I will make a fire,' she said. 'There is wood I kept dry beneath the boat and maize for gruel. I will make a fire and prepare food. Bring your brother and your companions to eat with me.'

Mamkinga looked up as she spoke. 'And you?'

Toomi smiled. 'I will bring my sister to you.'

89

Toomi had made camp a hundred yards upriver from where the men had dragged the boats ashore.

When Mamkinga led the others towards her fire, night had fallen again. The sky was still and cloudless. A full moon had risen, and the stars were bright. Like Mamkinga the others had slept throughout the day. When they woke they discovered that the paddlers they had hired in Garoua had vanished. Terrified by the storm, they must have slipped away when the rain stopped and scuttled back to the town.

Disappearing paddlers, Jamie reflected, were clearly one of the hazards of African travel. At least this time they hadn't taken one of the canoes with them. Garoua was still close enough to be reached on foot through the forest.

Jamie strode on towards the flames.

Mamkinga walked ahead, with Farquarson and Wolf following at Jamie's shoulder. Their Abyssinian guide, the grey-headed Bakulu, remained behind by the boats. As they approached the fire Jamie saw that two figures were standing waiting for them.

Mamkinga stepped into the circle of light cast by the flames.

'I give you my brother Jamie,' Mamkinga said. 'Also his companions and now my friends too, Farquarson and Wolf.'

'I give you my sister Rachel,' Toomi said in reply.

Beckoning to Jamie, Mamkinga stepped round the fire. He placed his hand first on Toomi's forehead and then on Rachel's. Jamie did the same. Following him so did Farquarson and Wolf.

The two young women gravely made the same gesture in return to the men.

'We have met,' Toomi said. 'Let us share food.'

A metal cooking pot was hanging on a tripod over the flames. Toomi placed the pot on the ground. Everyone sat down in a circle and began to eat. It was twenty-four hours since their last meal. Jamie was as famished as any of them. Yet while the rest gulped down the maize gruel, Jamie barely ate a mouthful.

Jamie sat mesmerized by the two young women opposite him.

They were both beautiful, more beautiful than any women Jamie had ever seen. Toomi was the mirror image of her brother, but a mirror image transformed by her sex. Mamkinga was sculpted out of African hardwood, dark and powerful. Toomi was made from the springtime saplings of the fever tree — supple and shining and graceful. They shared features, a voice, a way of moving and laughing. But where Mamkinga exuded physical strength, Toomi had a certainty and a strength of the spirit that was stronger still.

Jamie looked at the sister and then at the brother. Always his glance returned to the third, to Rachel.

Toomi had presented her as her sister. If Jamie hadn't known from Mamkinga that she was a sister in name only he would have accepted her as that — a full-blood child of the same parents. She was not. Hard as it was to believe, Rachel came from different stock.

Watching Rachel intently as the firelight played over her face, Jamie began to see where the differences lay.

She had Toomi's bright direct eyes, but Rachel's were even more shining, even more alert. Both were wearing the Arab robes of their travels, but they had cast aside the turbans. Their hair had long since grown out. Rachel's hair was finer and paler. Her face and body were Toomi's but the bones were straighter, the planes more chiselled, the muscles firmer and yet more slender.

More than anything there was a restlessness about her, a yearning and a dreaming Toomi did not have. Toomi would be satisfied with small contentments. The reunion with her brother was a vast one – and it fed her to the core of her being. Rachel, Jamie sensed, wanted nothing less than the distant stars. Rachel was a woman who would dream of the sources of great rivers and would not rest until she found them. Rachel, he saw too, had loss and grieving in her.

Jamie stared at her. She caught his eye and gazed back at him. Her eyes were level and candid. A half-smile edged her mouth, hiding the sorrow that had been there moments before.

Confused, Jamie looked away.

When they finished eating Mamkinga stood up.

'We will go back to our camp to sleep,' he said to Toomi. 'In the morning we will hold a council to decide what we shall do.'

Toomi nodded. 'May you all return to our table whenever you wish,' she replied.

The men returned to what Mamkinga called their camp. It was only four hollows in the rain-beaten grass round the wreckage of the acacia bush. The water had evaporated in the day's sun and the hollows made adequate beds in the warm night. Jamie lay down. He said goodnight to Mamkinga, but Mamkinga didn't answer. Soon the others were asleep.

Jamie could not sleep.

Turning his head he could see the glow of Toomi's fire. Beyond it he could make out two silhouettes in the darkness. From time to time, as the flames sank, one of the silhouettes would rise and materialize into a moving figure. Logs would be tossed on to the smouldering embers. The fire would blaze again, and the figure would settle back on the ground.

Jamie had no idea which of the young women it was. Each time the figure moved behind the glow his mind put a shape and face to it. The shape was tall and slender. The face was bold and steadfast, with a full mouth and dark thoughtful eyes framed in silken hair. Its gaze was both sad and resolute.

Jamie fell asleep at last.

Before he slept he heard a fish owl call. The calls of the barn owls which colonized the eaves of Iona's crofts had been the most familiar sounds of the Hebridean nights of his childhood. In his grandmother's stories their cries were the bells tolled by the handmaidens of the Scottish queens.

'For sorrow and for joy,' his grandmother used to say. 'For the birthing of the royal bairn, and his carrying away in the oaken shroud at the end. Across from Salen to the head of Loch Na Keal. From there down the loch past the other sacred isle, the wee one of Inchkenneth. And from Inchkenneth to the grey sea's mouth to bring him home to Iona – '

His grandmother would pause.

'Oak to cradle him, oak in his saddle to send him out, oak in the water to bear him back. And the owl's cries that will follow him to speak for his grieving mother. Hear an owl, Jamie, and you hear the footsteps of a queen behind.'

The raging storm of the night before had kept the Benoue's owls perched on the branches of their trees. Now, after twenty-four hours without food, they were hungry and eager to hunt.

All the night long their calls troubled the air.

Jamie woke with the first light.

A small breeze was blowing from off the river. He sat up and glanced instinctively at where the flames had glowed in the darkness. The fire was dead but a tiny coil of smoke was rising from the ashes. Low-lying mist covered the ground and he could see neither of the young women.

Jamie got to his feet.

Mamkinga was already up. He was standing with his head lowered, gazing into the river. The turbulent water of the day before had stilled to a mirror-like calm. Jamie walked up and stood beside him. Mamkinga had plucked an ear of wild wheat. He was shredding the grains between his fingers.

The dark paralysing depression had lifted from Mamkinga the instant he found his sister. Yet now, Jamie knew, something else was troubling him. The reflection of his face, brilliantly clear on the river's surface, was furrowed and thoughtful.

'Rachel is the Queen of Gondar.'

As if Mamkinga were answering a question, he spoke before Jamie had time to say anything.

'The Queen of Gondar?' Jamie repeated in amazement. 'Gondar is far to the east. It is where I am bound for, where Mr Baimbridge was searching for the Nile's source. Gondar is a thousand miles distant. If she is Gondar's queen, what is the lassie doing here?'

All Mamkinga had told him the evening before as they walked towards the fire was that Rachel was Toomi's sister in spirit but not in blood.

Now Mamkinga repeated the story he had heard from Toomi.

Rachel was Gondar's hereditary queen-empress. She had escaped from the city during the battle when the forces of Culembra and the Acab Saat had overwhelmed Ras Michael's army. Rachel had encountered Toomi in the wake of Gondar's defeat. The two young women had travelled west disguised as Arab youths. Pursued by the Acab Saat's agents they had made their way first to Kano and then to Garoua.

Near Garoua, escaping from the Acab Saat again, they had taken to the Benoue. The storm that had forced Jamie and Mamkinga ashore had also grounded the young women.

'Why did ye not tell me this last night?' Jamie said as Mamkinga finished.

'Because I saw that you love her —'

Mamkinga used the Malindan term for an over-powering emotion that even the spirits could not control. It signified a feeling so powerful that it could divide kingdoms, sunder families and set brother against brother in feuds that lasted beyond death.

He looked at Jamie, his face furrowed with a mixture of anger, resentment and sorrow.

'You love her and it will come between us.'

Mamkinga tossed some grains of wheat on the water. The reflection of their two faces was blurred by ripples.

Perplexed, Jamie shook his head in denial.

'How could I possibly love her?' he protested. 'I met her only last night. I do not even know her.'

'You are my brother and I know,' Mamkinga said stubbornly. 'You looked at her across the fire and decided she was your woman. If you do not love her yet, it will come to you. I watched your eyes and I know.'

Jamie tried to argue but Mamkinga cut him off.

'Let it be as it will be,' Mamkinga said. 'We have other matters that must come first. We must go to the council.'

Mamkinga set off across the grass towards Toomi's camp. Jamie lengthened his stride so that he was walking beside him.

Bitterly Mamkinga pushed him back.

90

The council took place in the morning sunlight round the rekindled fire.

It must have been, Jamie reflected, one of the strangest and most forlorn gatherings in Africa's history. Brought together by the accident of the raging storm on the Benoue were the three hereditary rulers of two of the continent's most ancient kingdoms. They were far from home. Their countries had been enslaved by a tyrant. All three –Rachel, Mamkinga and Toomi – were young and in exile.

They did not have a servant, let alone an army, between them. All they had were the clothes they wore, and a belief that they could somehow return and claim their inheritance in the mountain kingdoms of Abyssinia.

Then there was Jamie himself. Jamie too had a kingdom to win and a promise to redeem. His kingdom was of the mind not the earth, but the promise he had made in Iona's royal churchyard to his dead grandmother and sisters was just as binding. Jamie had the river's source to find. The Nile rose, Jamie had come to believe after all his reading in the Royal Geographical Society's library, somewhere in the lands the others had lost – the lands Mr Walter Baimbridge had been searching.

Jamie had come to Africa. In Mamkinga he had acquired a brother. Mamkinga had given him Toomi as a sister too. Because of Toomi he had met Rachel, the exiled queen-empress of Gondar and Toomi's own adopted sister. The lives and hopes and fortunes of all three were bound together. So were his now with their own.

Jamie's quest and fate, he knew, had become inextricably entwined with the distant mountain kingdoms.

It was Toomi, always more practical and decisive than her brother, who opened the council.

'Let us like a prudent merchant take measure of our stock,' Toomi said. 'The Acab Saat rules with Culembra in Gondar. Malinda was their stepping stone on the way. Now, together with the Galla's own lands, it is part of a much larger kingdom. That we know for certain. From hearsay we think Salama may be adding other territories to his empire. We shall only find out the truth when we return. Meanwhile – '

Toomi paused.

'Here, we are far away. We must get back. We need boats for the river journey. After the river there is much land to be crossed. We will need stores, porters, horses. Those require money.'

'We still have the last of the treasure I brought from Gondar,' Rachel put in.

'It will help but it is not enough,' Toomi said. 'We have many miles to travel. We will need more.'

There was silence for a moment. Then with considerable hesitation Jamie spoke.

'I am bound the same way,' he said. 'I and my friends are purposed for the kingdom of Gondar too. Between us we have a small stock of gold. It is not much, but Mamkinga tells me it is enough for our carriage and our needs on the journey.'

He glanced at Mamkinga. Mamkinga nodded in confirmation. The two of them had discussed the matter as they walked to the fire.

Rachel stared at him. Her eyes were narrowed in puzzlement.

'You are coming with us?' she asked.

'If you will have us as your companions, yes,' Jamie replied.

'But we do not journey for the journeying's sake,' Rachel went on. 'Nor do we have safety at the end. We are going to war.'

'Then you will need soldiers,' Jamie answered. 'We have weapons and we can fight.'

Still frowning, Rachel turned questioningly to Mamkinga.

'Umshebi is my brother,' Mamkinga said. 'I have kept nothing from him. He knows how stands Malinda and Gondar. He knows of the Acab Saat and Culembra and the evil they have wrought in the mountains. Yet he and his friends wish to march with us. Jamie is searching for a river. His quest follows the same spoor as ours.'

Rachel turned back to Jamie. She looked at him with the same candid unwavering gaze of the night before.

Now there was something else in her eyes.

'Then it is very proper you should ride with the river's child,' she said.

A brief uncertain smile crossed Rachel's face.

Jamie looked back at her uncomprehendingly. Before he had a chance to work out what the smile and the enigmatic statement might have meant, Toomi continued.

'If that is so,' she said, 'we have companions and gold. We are doubled in number. We have the means to reach the borders of Malinda and Gondar. But once there, what do we do? We are six. Against us there is the Acab Saat, Culembra, and the thousands they command. What then?'

Mamkinga spoke for the first time. He had been squatting on his haunches listening intently. Now he glanced up.

'When Umshebi and I set out from the shore,' he said, 'I thought only of returning to Malinda so I could search for my sister. Two days ago I learnt my father and family were dead, and the Galla had made of my country a burial ground. In truth then my heart and spirit failed me. I no longer thought even of Toomi. I wished only to die. Now I have found my sister. My heart, my spirit, have been returned to me –'

Mamkinga paused. Toomi gazed at him across the fire.

She understood more vividly than ever the cause of the

sickness and desolation she had sensed enveloping her brother as she paced the floor of the Garoua lodging house. As she looked at him a realization came to her, a realization both puzzling and frightening. It was almost the same perception she had voiced when she and Mamkinga were reunited twenty-four hours earlier on the river's banks barely a hundred paces from where they were gathered now.

Toomi knew that the flaw in Mamkinga's troubled spirit was deeper, darker and more intractable than she had ever imagined. Mamkinga had been healed once by his new-found brother Jamie, and a second time by herself.

Had they not been there, on both occasions he would have died.

Mamkinga was vulnerable to sickness and despair in a way she was not. He would be vulnerable for as long as he lived. He would always need someone to save and heal him. Toomi had offered him, almost laughingly, Rachel in her place. Now, gazing at his stern but tormented face, Toomi wondered if even Rachel could draw Mamkinga back from the abyss that constantly seemed to open before him.

Toomi prayed silently to the spirits that she would never be parted from him again.

'Now Toomi and I can go home together,' Mamkinga continued. 'That Malinda has been conquered by the Galla does not in itself give me fear. We are the embrenche's children and the spirits will look after us. The lands are ours. Malindans are not slaves. There will never be a slave in Malinda again. When we return the people will rise for us. We can win our country back. But we are not fighting for Malinda alone – '

Mamkinga traced his fingers in the dead ash at the fire's edge as he assembled his thoughts.

'Malinda has been made a province of an empire. To win Malinda while Salama rules in Gondar means nothing. Gondar has always been larger, richer, stronger. Now it is more powerful than ever. From

Gondar the Acab Saat can always return to conquer us – '

Mamkinga lifted his head.

'We can only win and hold Malinda,' he added, 'if we first destroy Salama in Gondar. Toomi and I can raise an army among our people, but it can be for one purpose only – to attack Gondar. Gondar must be our goal.'

Rachel was kneeling opposite Mamkinga across the fire. Her brow had been furrowed in concentration as she listened.

'I am Gondar,' she said.

Rachel spoke very softly but with absolute assurance.

'My people obey two powers. Their church and their monarch. They have done so from the beginning of Gondar's time. From the time of Sheba, from times long before that, maybe from the start of time itself. Today the church is Salama, but I am their queen. The Acab Saat is strong. I am stronger. Faced with a choice between us the people will follow and obey me – '

Rachel turned towards Mamkinga.

'You are right in all you say,' she continued. 'For Malinda to be free, Gondar must be free. Then we can live as good neighbours with good fences. Let us start in Malinda. Let us raise an army there. Then let us march on Gondar. The people will rise for me as they will rise for you. But for both of us to be free the Acab Saat must be brought down. Let us go to battle together. May God and the spirits give us victory.'

Mamkinga nodded in agreement.

He reached out his hand and gripped Rachel's wrist. It was Toomi, inevitably, who anchored the discussion firmly back on earth.

'You both talk of armies,' she said. 'Armies need more than soldiers, they need commanders. Otherwise they are a headless rabble. Who is going to command the armies?'

Mamkinga rounded on her resentfully.

'I will lead the Malindans. Do you think I cannot fight? Who led the uprising on the *San Cristobal*? Ask him!'

Mamkinga paused and looked at Jamie.

'It is true enough,' Jamie said. 'There was a sore battle for yon boat. Only a brave man could have won it.'

'I can also fight,' Rachel added. 'It is what I have been trained to do all my life by Doho and the soldiers Ras Michael sent to the palace. If the need comes, I am ready to die for Gondar.'

Toomi shook her head stubbornly.

'I am not talking of bravery. I mean who is going to command – to prepare for battle, to plan, to direct, to organize. Listen to me – '

Toomi's voice was urgent.

'Since I was taken as a child all my years have been spent with soldiers. Women soldiers, maybe, but soldiers all the same – and better than any man. I have seen more of fighting than both of you together. I know war is a profession, a trade like any other. I know that without Tamule's long years of experience the Lendama could have done nothing. I know we need a general like her, and it is neither of you – '

Like Mamkinga Toomi turned in appeal to Jamie.

'Is that not so?'

Jamie had barely spoken to Toomi since they'd met.

Suddenly she, like Mamkinga, had made him the arbiter in an issue which involved Rachel just as profoundly as Toomi and her brother. The matter was crucial. On it might turn the entire success or failure of what they were setting out to do.

It was also deeply sensitive. For both Mamkinga and Rachel the command of the armies of their peoples was a matter that touched on the well-springs of their pride and authority. To deny them the right to lead was to challenge their very being.

All three pairs of eyes were fixed on Jamie. He took a long slow breath and stared at the fire.

'I come from far away,' Jamie said. 'We have wars there too, declared and undeclared. The better part of my folk died in an undeclared war. I was but a child when it happened. I have read and thought much since. There is nae difference between the two sorts of war. For the winning they both need generals. It has always been so. Had we had a general, a strong hard man experienced in the ways of battle, we would have won. Our lands would be our own and my folk would be alive – '

Jamie lifted his head. He gazed steadily at Rachel and Mamkinga.

'I side with the sister to the both of ye,' he said. 'She speaks sense. We need a man of battle. With such we shall win. Without him we place all in the hands of God. God looks more kindly on those who follow guid counsel and take sensible precautions. Let us help God to help ourselves.'

There was a long silence.

It was the most difficult speech Jamie had ever made.

Jamie had no idea what the other two would say, but he knew that Toomi was right. Even if they completed the arduous journey to Gondar, before them lay a difficult and dangerous campaign against an entrenched enemy and almost unimaginable odds. To stand any chance of victory they needed what none of them there on the banks of the Benoue could provide. To have denied that would have been the worst betrayal of all.

Mamkinga and Rachel confronted his gaze.

Unflinchingly Jamie stared back at them. For minute after minute the three were held locked together in a contest of wills. Finally the other two gave way. Mamkinga switched his eyes to the river and Rachel to the flames.

'You are right,' Mamkinga said.

'For Gondar, I agree,' Rachel echoed.

Jamie slowly let out his breath.

'Yet there is one thing more,' Rachel added. 'If we need a commander for our armies and none of us can do the task, who is it to be? Where can we find such a man?'

'We have found him – ' Toomi said.

Her face opened in a smile like the blossoming flower she had drawn in the earth when she found Mamkinga again.

'He is cunning, skilful, experienced and brave. He has

planned battles and led men in war for many years. Furthermore he is our loyal friend and ally. Have you forgotten him so quickly – ?'

She put her arm round Rachel's shoulder. Toomi's smile welled up into laughter.

'Hadji will lead our forces.'

Jamie walked slowly back to the men's camp beside the upturned boats.

Farquarson and Wolf were waiting expectantly for him. Unable to speak Malindan, they had remained behind while the council took place. Jamie dropped to his haunches opposite them. He glanced from one to the other. His face was pensive and clouded.

Both of them had come with him of their own free will. They had cheerfully risked disease and, according to Captain Culglass, death in boarding the *San Cristobal*. They had helped him to clean and ground the slaver. They had kept the camp on the Bight of Benin when first Mamkinga and then Jamie himself had almost died of fever. They had made the long journey with him up the Benoue. They had survived the storm. Now they were squatting smiling in front of him in the wilderness on the river's banks.

Jamie looked at them again.

Farquarson, the dissolute little laird of Invergordon, with his ruddy face, deeply tanned and freckled now after the glaring sunlight off the river, his thinning sandy hair, his love of food and hunting, and his irrepressible good humour. The grey-maned hawk-faced Wolf with his agate eyes and crumpled black serge clothes, sardonic and angular and as passionate about his philosophy and his chess as Farquarson was about his meals and the chase.

They had proved as bold and trustworthy companions as Jamie had guessed, when he agreed at the start they could come with him. Yet what lay ahead was different. Until now the journey had been an adventure.

From now on it would be an odyssey with war, battle,

bloodshed, and undoubtedly death at its end.

For Jamie it was a road he was unhesitatingly prepared to follow. He had the great river's source to find. He had become yoked inextricably to Mamkinga, Toomi and Rachel. Their fortunes were his. All their entwined destinies lay in the towering Abyssinian mountains.

For Farquarson and Wolf there were no such ties or obligations. They had no promises to keep, no bonds of newfound kinship to honour. If they went on, all that lay before them would be hardship, struggle and the likelihood of a shallow grave somewhere in the plains or hills of the desolate landscape of eastern Africa.

Jamie shook his head. The time had come for the three of them to part.

'They are destined for war,' he said. 'Since the journey advances me towards the region Mr Baimbridge was exploring, I have agreed to go with them. There is no sense nor purpose that ye should come too – '

Jamie related what had been discussed and agreed at the council.

When he finished there was silence for a moment. Then the little Scotsman burst out laughing.

'Are you seriously proposing we turn back?' Farquarson demanded.

'Aye.' Jamie nodded gravely. 'I foresee sore and bloody business ahead. It will be no concern of yourself or Ferdinand.'

'Listen to me, you peasant from the isles,' Farquarson said as he leant forward. 'When your distant ancestors were trying to work out how to cut turfs, mine had been riding to battle in defence of the poor Highland swine for upwards of a thousand years. Do you think a son of those famous warriors, as I may modestly claim to be, will ride quietly home and leave a veritable clodhopper to carry his sword?'

'Aldred, ye must hear me out,' Jamie began. 'There is far more matter, deadly matter, in yon cause than ye might think – '

'Furthermore,' Farquarson disregarded him and

continued, 'what of Wolf? His forebears, if I may hazard, clad in iron and wielding Prussian axes, were laying most of Europe to waste when even we were only beginning to raise our eyes towards Hadrian's wall. What of this Teuton knight? Is he going to limp cravenly back as you head for the skirmish?'

Farquarson glanced at Wolf in appeal. Wolf flicked his hair out of his eyes and rubbed his jaw with his long bony hand. Then he frowned and looked at the ground.

'In principle, of course, I agree with you,' Wolf said. 'We came with Jamie for better or worse. But from what Jamie has described the affair has changed beyond measure. We are no longer searching for Jamie's river. We are asked to embroil ourselves in a war between savages, and a doomed war at that – '

Wolf raised his head. Jamie saw that his face was harrowed and unhappy.

'My weapon is the pen, not the sword,' Wolf added. 'It would be more prudent for all three of us to leave the others to the carnage in which this will surely end.'

For a moment Farquarson gazed at him astounded. Then he burst out.

'Principle? Prudence? Pens?' Farquarson shouted. 'When was a war ever won with such women's nonsense? For God's sake, man, what's happened to your stomach? You heard Jamie. He goes on. I go too. What of you? Do you abandon us now?'

There was silence.

The little Scotsman was still staring at Wolf. On Farquarson's face was an expression of mingled anger, shock, and distress. Farquarson, Jamie realized, felt a deep and wounding sense of betrayal. Faced with the prospect of battle, his trusted friend and companion on the long journey had let him down. Wolf had no heart for a fight.

Jamie's eyes swung round to the Austrian.

Looking down at him, Jamie saw a Wolf he had never seen before. His eyes were haunted and miserable, his mouth twitched uncertainly, his fingers kept plucking in anguish at his head. Wolf was a thinker, a writer, a revolutionary of the intellect who used words and ideas instead of bullets and swords. At the thought of the gunfire and bloodshed ahead his nerve had failed him.

Wolf glanced up and looked at him imploringly. Jamie had felt profoundly for Farquarson. Much more now, watching the fear and misery that flickered over Wolf's features, he felt for the Austrian.

'Ferdinand's right,' Jamie said to Farquarson. 'It is no quarrel of his. Let the man go his own way – '

'Let the man answer for himself,' Farquarson cut him off bleakly.

Farquarson waited a moment longer. The little Scotsman's face was as austere and unforgiving as granite. Wolf said nothing. Farquarson turned and began to stride off.

'Wait – !' Wolf called after him.

Farquarson checked and glanced back. Wolf stood up.

'You are right, Aldred.' Wolf smiled wanly. 'The sun must have touched both my head and my stomach. We embarked on this together. Let us finish it together. From what I hear of these bandits who have taken Malinda and Gondar, they are not better – indeed, they may be worse – than the brigands who enslave your own farmlands, shipyards and factories. A working man could have many a more ignoble fate than in finding his grave opposing them.'

The little Scotsman gazed at him. 'You are coming with us after all?'

Wolf nodded.

Farquarson's face widened in a beam of pleasure. His friend had returned to sanity. Impulsive and generous-hearted, as ready to forgive as he had been to blame, Farquarson stepped back and embraced Wolf.

'Didn't I tell you?' Farquarson glanced at Jamie. 'The man has the sand of his ancestors in his belly. He will bear arms as steadily as the rest of us. In the name of God and Madame Belle the three of us will complete this as we began.'

Farquarson gripped Wolf's hand and shook it exuberantly. He turned and put his arms round Jamie.

For a moment Jamie, smiling, held the little laird by the shoulders. He reached for Wolf's hand and shook it too. Then the smile left Jamie's face. The ceremony was the same as when the three of them had left London. This time there was a difference.

In London only unknown Africa had lain before them. Immense spaces of the unexplored continent still lay ahead. Yet now as they journeyed on, they would also be travelling towards Africa's most ancient battlegrounds.

The battles they would have to fight there, Jamie guessed, would be the bloodiest the Mountains of the Moon had ever seen.

91

'We should be back before darkness falls tomorrow,' Mamkinga called. 'Keep the fires burning high to guide us in case we are late.'

As the boat headed out into the river Mamkinga picked up a paddle and drove it into the water. Bakulu, the Abyssinian guide who had come with them from Garoua, was already paddling at the stern. Toomi was sitting between them at the canoe's centre.

Jamie lifted his arm and waved from the bank. Carried quickly downstream by the flow of the water, the boat vanished round the river's bend.

It was still early in the morning.

Mamkinga, Toomi and the grey-haired Bakulu were returning to Garoua in search of Hadji. Jamie had little idea of who Hadji was. From Toomi's description Hadji had Arab blood. He was, according to Toomi, a bold and quick-witted soldier of fortune who had forged his own kingdom in the hills, and he had long experience of leading men in battle.

He was also, Jamie had privately concluded as he listened to Toomi, almost certainly a bandit like one of the Highland thieves from his grandmother's tales of Jamie's childhood. It did not matter. The Highlands had bred some of the finest warriors that ever came down from the hills. For an attack on Malinda and Gondar, as Jamie had argued by the flames, they needed such a man. He trusted Toomi's judgement. Rachel and Mamkinga had agreed. For Jamie it was enough.

Jamie turned from the river.

Farquarson and Wolf were standing behind him on the

bank. The camp needed provisioning and they were being dispatched to find food. As it was a hunting trip Farquarson was in charge. He was carrying a shotgun and rifle while Wolf had been given the ammunition and Farquarson's gamebag.

'Don't fash yourself about dinner, Jamie,' Farquarson said as he hefted the gun. 'We'll eat like kings tonight. Given the position of our lady companion, maybe that's no more than appropriate.'

Grumbling, Wolf slung the gamebag over his shoulder.

'In the jungle no man's a king, nor woman a queen,' Wolf said. 'We are equal born and equal die.'

'Wrong, you grim revolutionary,' Farquarson answered, chuckling, elated by the prospect of the chase. 'Here in the forest we are all kings and queens.'

Arguing with each other they set off along the bank.

Jamie glanced round. Rachel had been standing behind him watching the boat head out into the stream. Now she had vanished. He looked back towards Toomi's camp.

Rachel was kneeling by the fire. Jamie frowned and hesitated. Every yearning in Jamie urged him to approach her. Yet her self-containment was so absolute he felt fearful. He turned away. He studied the eddies and whirls in the water as the kingfishers splintered the surface in their dives for fish from the far bank. He lifted his head to the air, and rubbed his face thoughtfully with his hands. Then he glanced back.

Rachel was in the same position.

Jamie set out to walk towards her.

He took one step. The next he turned and headed back for the circle of scoops in the sand where the men had slept. Jamie squatted beside them. He felt wary and tongue-tied. He remained there for several minutes. Finally he gathered up his courage again. He stood up and walked over to where Rachel was kneeling. Jamie stopped by the fire, flushed and sweating.

'I was wondering whether ye would care to walk with

me,' Jamie said. 'I am learning the Malindan language. I would be grateful if ye would tell me the correct names for some flowers and animals.'

He had memorized every phrase in the Malindan tongue, and the words came out in endlessly rehearsed groups. Rachel looked up at him. She smiled. Then laughter rippled quietly over her body.

'You speak my language to perfection,' she said in English. 'No Jesuit priest – from whom I learnt how to speak yours – could have phrased it better.'

Jamie stared at her in astonishment. 'Ye speak English?'

'Isn't that what I'm speaking now?'

'But how did ye learn it?' he stammered in confusion.

'Did I not just tell you that too?' Rachel was still smiling. 'The Jesuit priests. They came to the court in Gondar and they taught me. I also learned French, Arabic, Portuguese and many African tongues. But of them all I like English best. Except – '

She wrinkled her face thoughtfully.

'I do not think you are English. I believe you are Scottish. There were traders who came to Gondar and they spoke with your accent. They taught me that if I saw a handsome boy to call him a bonny loon. Am I right?'

Jamie was dumbfounded. The young woman not only spoke English. She had recognized his accent and she knew phrases of Gaelic.

He opened his mouth but nothing came out. Rachel came to his rescue. She stood up.

'We will walk by the river,' she said. 'I will tell you the Malindan name for every plant and animal we see. When we have finished with them we will move on to the birds and bees. The Scottish traders told me what they signify too.'

Rachel smiled mischievously.

Jamie closed his eyes in disbelief. Then his shyness and his embarrassment vanished. He burst into laughter and set out with Rachel along the bank.

They walked together until midday. Occasionally

when a bird or animal came into view, Rachel would point and tell Jamie its name in Malindan. If the name varied for Gondar, she would give it to him in the language of her own kingdom too. Jamie would say the word after her, repeating it again and again until Rachel, satisfied, nodded and smiled.

Mostly they walked in silence.

The raging storm had cleansed the Benoue's airs, and the day was still and jewel-clear. A strange calm and stillness lay over the mighty river. Animals that even Rachel had seldom seen stepped fearlessly out of the trees and walked down to the bank to drink. A splay-footed lechwe, the forest's shyest and most elusive deer, passed confidently in front of them on its way to the water.

A rhino cow and her calf trotted past them, the two lumbering creatures, seemingly sculpted among the dinosaurs of prehistory, unaware as they snuffled by of Jamie's and Rachel's presence only yards away. A sinuous hunting otter pawed a rounded golden fish from the stream. A leopard, as fugitive and dark as the racing night clouds above the Benoue, briefly nuzzled the waters. A great solitary elephant strode into the river and trumpeted in defiance at the sky.

To Jamie it was a morning of magic unlike any he had ever known.

He had been fearful of Rachel, the dark-eyed enigmatic young woman who was Gondar's queen, and more fearful still of words. Slowly as they walked Jamie discovered there was no reason for fear. Apart from the occasional whispered phrase, there was no need for talk in the shining green and golden sunlight of the Benoue's banks.

Nor, Jamie found, was there anything to be frightened of in the young woman at his side. Her beauty, her bold shining eyes – sometimes quizzical and laughing – her flawless skin, her slim erect body, still dazzled him each time he glanced at her. But when she spoke to him, when she gave him the name of the animal or bird before them, her voice was as blunt and knowledgeable as any of

Iona's shepherds describing one of the beasts in his flock on the hill above.

Her world, her background, her history and her people might be as remote from Jamie's as the life on another constellation. Yet in her presence Jamie felt secure and at ease. And when she smiled at him, when laughter irradiated her face and she flung back her head in delight towards the sky, his heart leapt.

Towards midday Rachel paused and glanced up.

'The sun is high,' she said. 'We will stop and rest here – '

They had followed the game tracks along the Benoue. Jamie guessed they were five miles from where they had started. Rachel had a short machete knife tucked into her belt. She used it to make a tunnel-shaped clearing in the undergrowth.

'Gather some frangi leaves and lie down,' she instructed him.

Jamie used his own knife to cut some of the broad springy foliage of the frangi reeds. He piled the leaves inside the tunnel, and settled down on his back. The bed of vegetation was soft and comfortable, and the bright sun was filtering softly through the tree canopy above.

'Hold my hand – '

Rachel slid into the tunnel beside him. She too lay on her back, and threaded her fingers through his.

'With our hands like this we have a double warning of danger,' Rachel said. 'Whichever receives an alarm signal, the other learns of it immediately too by the squeezing of the fingers. It is how the hunters lie. Learn from me as you would learn from your brother, Mamkinga. Like him I am teaching you the ways of Africa. Now sleep. We are safe together.'

Within seconds Jamie knew from Rachel's breathing that she was sleeping. He stayed awake for several minutes. Then he also slept.

They woke in the late afternoon.

Jamie opened his eyes to feel Rachel's hand squeezing his. He heard the sound of rustling near the bush. The rustling was followed by tremors in the ground as if something immensely heavy were moving close at hand.

Jamie raised himself and peered through the screen of twigs. Only feet away a huge crocodile was moving cumbersomely towards the water. The creature must have been sleeping beside the bush. It was passing so close that Jamie could smell the carrion on its breath and see the sky reflected in the tiny bright eyes of the oxpecker birds perched on its skull. The crocodile lurched into the river and was gone.

Sweating, Jamie glanced to his left. Rachel was looking at him, alert and smiling. Her face was haloed by the lowering sun.

'You see,' she said. 'If you hold hands you can sleep in safety.'

They walked back with the sun behind them.

By the time they reached the camp Farquarson and Wolf had returned from their hunting expedition. Farquarson had shot a small dama gazelle and six guinea fowl. The guinea fowl were hanging by their necks from Farquarson's belt, and the gazelle was draped over Wolf's shoulders.

'My God, you should have seen the game, Jamie!' Farquarson cried ecstatically. 'With a loader apiece and some foreknowledge of the ground, we could have stocked the larder for months.'

Wolf heaved the gazelle to the ground and slumped down in exhaustion.

'Tomorrow I carry the gun,' Wolf said, 'and you do the porterage.'

'Ignore our political firebrand,' Farquarson said contemptuously. 'The man's neither the heart nor the head for hunting. If he brings the same passion to his vaunted revolution, it will have all the flair and brilliance of a crofter's peat fire in the November rains.'

The little Scotsman dragged the gazelle towards the flames.

'Maybe the wee lassie can butcher it for us,' Farquarson added. 'One of the haunches would make a bonny stew for tonight.'

Farquarson made signs to Rachel with his hands to show her what he wanted done. Jamie looked at Farquarson, appalled, but Rachel spoke before Jamie could say anything.

'I think you will find the shoulder more tender,' she said in careful but fluent English. 'Perhaps you can leave the choice to me. I promise you will eat well.'

She smiled. Then, as Farquarson gazed at her astounded, Rachel pulled out her knife and expertly began to quarter the animal.

Rachel cooked the gazelle over the fire that now burned beside the men's camp. They ate as well as Rachel had promised. Afterwards she stood up and gravely shook hands with them in turn. Jamie was the last. When Rachel came to him she paused. She said nothing but she gave him another of her fleeting radiant smiles, before she turned and walked back to her own fire.

As Farquarson lay down he gave a soft contented whistle.

'I'll say this for the lassie,' he remarked drowsily. 'She has a bonny hand with the skillet. She can butcher a beast, too, as neat as any Highland ghillie I ever saw. Keep your eyes on her, Jamie, lad. She may be a queen, but she'll be sore useful at dinner time in the days ahead.'

Jamie lay down too.

The harsh warning cries of the fish owls rang out again all through the hours of darkness. That night Jamie barely heard them. For a long time he lay once more gazing at the glow of the distant fire. Then he slipped into a deep untroubled sleep.

92

'Do you remember me?' Toomi asked.

The fat little Sudanese bowed. 'Of course. You were here until two days ago with your friend and Hadji.'

'Is Hadji still here?'

Toomi held her breath as she waited for the answer.

The last she had seen of Hadji was a silhouette on a horse, his sword blade flashing in the air before the galloping riders, as the canoe swept round the river's bend.

The Sudanese nodded. 'He returned yesterday – '

Toomi's eyes closed in relief.

'At the moment he is out somewhere in the town,' the man went on. 'Do you wish to wait for him?'

'Please,' Toomi said.

The Sudanese showed her up to Hadji's room. It was the one he had occupied before, next door to the room she had shared with Rachel. Toomi sat down and waited.

It was mid afternoon. Toomi, Mamkinga and Bakulu had arrived in Garoua an hour earlier. Accompanied by the other two Toomi had gone straight to the lodging house. She had changed from her Arab robes into the long gown of a Garoua woman. It was not her the Acab Saat's agents were searching for, but in view of her resemblance to Rachel Toomi barely paused at the door before going inside.

'This I must do alone,' Toomi had said to her brother. 'I will meet you tomorrow.'

Mamkinga nodded. He and Bakulu left and made their way to the house where they had lodged with Jamie and his companions.

Hadji returned at dusk.

He opened the door and saw Toomi standing against the arched window with the evening sky behind her. Her face was in shadow. For an instant he paused. Then he crossed the room in two quick strides and seized her by the shoulders.

'Are you safe and well?' he demanded.

Toomi nodded.

'And your sister, too?'

'Yes.'

'Allah be praised!' Hadji pressed Toomi to him and held her for a moment. Then he stepped back.

'And you?' Toomi asked.

Hadji laughed. 'There were three at the river and one more who came from behind. I did not see the fourth. Allah was teaching me a lesson. He guided the scoundrel's sword – '

Hadji took off his turban.

Toomi reached out and felt his scalp. A long weal ran down from the crown of his head to his ear. When she took her hand away there was fresh blood on her fingers.

'It is nothing.' Hadji was still chuckling. 'Allah was reminding me to watch my back. It was a very small lesson compared to the one I gave the man who struck me, and the others too. The crocodiles fed well.'

Hadji sat down on the bed. He parted his legs and rested his arms on his knees. Then he looked up at Toomi, his head tilted to one side and his eyes keen and inquiring.

'What happened?' he asked. 'What brings you back to me?'

The laughter had gone.

Hadji was once again as Toomi remembered him on so many occasions in Quilombo. No longer the hard-riding brigand who attacked caravans and plundered their cargos, but a speculative thoughtful man who had nourished a childhood dream of a state without slaves, and made the dream real in the saddle in the hills. The man who had taken such delight in showing her and Rachel what he had wrought.

The man, more than anything, who had declared his love for her and her sister.

Toomi knelt opposite him on the floor.

'Much has happened,' she said. 'I will tell you.'

Toomi told him of the storm on the Benoue, of her reunion with her brother, of the white companions travelling with Mamkinga. She described the council by the fire that morning. She told him of their decision to cross Africa to the borders of Malinda. To raise an army there and march on Gondar. To defeat the Acab Saat, Culembra and the Galla, and to free the kingdoms of the Mountains of the Moon.

'To do all this,' Toomi finished, 'we need a man experienced in the arts of war, a warrior, a general to lead our forces. That is why I am here.'

Hadji looked round him in bewilderment.

'I know of no such man here in Garoua. I know of no such forces,' he said. 'Why have you come to me?'

'Our forces are as yet in the mind,' Toomi answered. 'They are the armies of faith. But when Mamkinga and I reach Malinda, when Rachel rides into Gondar, they will rise on every side like wheat from the earth. Men and women, children even, they will become soldiers in truth. And as for the man to lead them – '

Toomi paused. 'He is in this room. You are that man, Hadji.'

Hadji was silent. For a long time he stared at Toomi. Then he stood up and crossed the floor. He leant over the window's sill and gazed out at the night sky.

'I loved you and your sister,' he said at last. 'I love you both still, perhaps more than ever. You I love above all. I wanted you to live with me in Quilombo. You refused. I understood. Yet now you ask me to join you in a distant war. Why?'

Hadji had spoken very quietly. Toomi answered equally quietly.

'There will be gold,' she said. 'Much gold. If we succeed, and with you we will succeed, there will be more gold than you have ever dreamed of. That will be the prize of victory. But that is not the true reason – '

Toomi paused again.

'In Quilombo people are free. In Malinda and Gondar they have been made slaves. If we win, *when* we win, they will be free too. I ask your help in freeing them.'

'I do not want gold,' Hadji answered, his voice a whisper. 'I do not even want the freedom of people I do not know, although, as Allah is my witness, I wish it for them with all my heart. All I want is you.'

Toomi thought for a moment. Then she got to her feet.

'You have listened to me and I thank you – '

She moved towards the door.

'I am myself. I cannot barter myself for gold or even for freedom. We will fight without you.'

Toomi opened the door and stepped on to the gallery above the courtyard.

As she did Hadji turned from the star-blazoned window. He looked at her. Then he lifted his head and laughed.

His laughter was joyous and unrestrained, the same buoyant fountain of pleasure Toomi remembered from the day they had hunted the upland plains of Quilombo, when the game had surged away before them and the hawks had flared, their wings beating in tawny bars of chestnut and gold, above the wrists of the falconers.

'I will lead your armies,' he said, 'not for gold, not for freedom, not for your body. I will lead them for you, for yourself alone.'

Toomi stopped.

She came back into the room and closed the door behind her. She lifted the Arab jellabah from her body, tossed it away and stood naked in front of him.

'For what you would do for nothing,' she said, 'you have won everything.'

Toomi smiled at him. She drew Hadji over to the bed and pulled him against her, kissed his face and held his hard stiffening body tight to hers.

'We have a mighty journey before us,' Mamkinga said.
'Let us ask the spirits for their protection on our travels.'

It was the following evening. Everyone was gathered
again round the fire on the bank of the Benoue river. They
lowered their heads as Mamkinga spoke.

Toomi, Mamkinga and Bakulu had returned with
Hadji from Garoua at dusk. They had spent the day in the
town buying more stores and acquiring another two
boats. Hadji had brought three of his best men with him.
With the paddlers who were accompanying them to the
river's end, the party that set out next day would be
fifteen strong.

For weeks to come they would be travelling, and
travelling hard. As Mamkinga had said, a mighty journey
lay before them. Even that was only the beginning. At the
journey's end would be the battle for Malinda and
Gondar. Beyond that still was Jamie's quest for the
source of the great river.

It was all vast and perilous and uncertain. For an
instant Jamie was daunted. He shivered. Then he
clenched his hands until his knuckles whitened. He had
his promises to keep and his companions to guard. It was
no time for a faint heart. It was time to put the steel of a
Hebridean sword blade into his soul.

Jamie lifted his head resolutely and glanced round the
fire.

The eyes of the others were closed in prayer. Toomi
and Mamkinga to the spirits of the Malindan hills and
woods and skies. Hadji to Allah and his prophet
Mahomet. Rachel to the God of Gondar's ancient

Christian church. Even the pagan and libertine Farquarson seemed to be asking the blessing of some Highland deity. Only Wolf was scowling open-eyed.

Jamie nudged him with his foot. 'Pray, ye heathen, pray,' Jamie whispered.

Wolf's scowl darkened. 'I do not hold with superstitious nonsense,' he whispered back. 'It is the deluding opium of the enslaved masses.'

'You're not among the masses,' Jamie said. 'You're in the company of queens and chiefs and warriors. Show a wee morsel of companionship with the common cause.'

Wolf cursed him under his breath. Then slowly he grinned. For a moment Wolf, too, closed his eyes.

Jamie prayed to his own God.

As he prayed an image took shape in Jamie's mind. It was the Celtic cross which stood above the graves of his grandmother and sisters beside Iona's abbey. The cross was immensely old and carved from granite. Winter snow whirled round it, spring rains lashed down across it, the summer sun baked it dry, the rowan leaves of autumn tormented and shrouded it. Unmoved, unchanged, the cross kept guard above the royal tombs as it had done for centuries, as it would do for centuries more.

The cross was the symbol of their journey and the battles to come. The cross had endured and survived. So would they.

Jamie looked up again. The prayers had ended and everyone was standing. As Jamie watched, Mamkinga drew a short dagger from his belt. The dagger had a razor-sharp blade, curved in the Arab style, and a worn sharkskin handle. Jamie remembered noticing it first at Mamkinga's waist on the day they set out from the Bight of Benin.

Mamkinga thrust the dagger's point into the fire until it was glowing white with heat. Then he lifted it from the flames. Rachel was standing opposite him. She was gazing steadily at his face. Mamkinga stared back at her. Rachel raised her arm and held it out towards him with the underside of her wrist exposed.

'May Malinda and Gondar be joined in battle against a common enemy,' Mamkinga said.

He took hold of Rachel's hand and drew three quick lines with the dagger's tip on her skin. There was a hiss of burning flesh and the smell of scorching rose into the night air.

'May it be so,' Rachel said without flinching. 'May the kingdoms together restore peace to the mountains.'

She reached up and pressed her wrist against Mamkinga's forehead. The three incisions left a thin imprint of blood like the veining of a leaf on Mamkinga's skin.

Mamkinga scored the underside of his own arm with the same knife-marks. He touched Rachel's forehead and the same imprint appeared. Mamkinga replaced the dagger at his waist.

'The battlefields may yet be far,' he said, 'but from this moment on we are at war.'

Toomi stepped forward then. She placed her hand first on Mamkinga's forehead, and then on Rachel's. Toomi's face was radiant. Round her wrist, Jamie noticed, was an ebony bracelet studded with emeralds she hadn't been wearing when she left for Garona.

'Pula, my brother!' she said. 'Pula, my sister! Let the spirits guide us to victory!'

Toomi nodded at Hadji and the three Europeans.

All four had been waiting uncertainly for her guidance. Now they gave the same benediction as she had done, invoking the ancient sacred prayer of pula – rain – to bless their endeavours. Jamie was the last. When he raised his hand to Rachel's forehead, he saw that the print of the blood-mark was not so much like the veining of a leaf as the forked tongue of a snake.

For an instant he stared puzzled at the V-shaped emblem. Then he touched his fingertips to Rachel's skin.

'May you sleep well,' he said.

'May we venture boldly,' Rachel replied. 'May Malinda and Gondar be free!'

She touched his forehead in response. Then she put her

arm round Toomi's waist. Her smile as the men walked away was radiant with confidence but somehow, to Jamie's eyes, forced and troubled.

The men returned to their own camp. On the way back Jamie walked beside Mamkinga.

'The mark ye made to signify that the kingdoms were joined as allies in battle,' Jamie said. 'What does it represent? I thought first it was the veining of a falling leaf. Then it seemed to have the form of a snake's tongue. Is it either or something else?'

Mamkinga glanced at him sharply.

'You have keen eyes, Umshebi,' he answered. 'It is indeed the sign of the snake. The two arms of the fork stand for the separate kingdoms. The root for what binds Gondar and Malinda together.'

'But why a snake's tongue?' Jamie insisted. 'Serpents are creatures of venom and ill omen. Surely their mark does not augur well for our success?'

Mamkinga gave a short harsh laugh.

'You think with the ways of your own plains and hills. You are not among those pastures now. You are in Africa. Here the snakes are holy. In your sickness you were cured by one. There is sickness in the mountains. The serpent's mark will cure that too.'

As if determined not to be questioned further, Mamkinga strode swiftly ahead into the night.

Jamie stood and looked after him, frowning.

The giant African was his brother. It was Mamkinga himself who had declared as much. They had both travelled to the rim of darkness and set foot on the last cliff edge above the abyss. Each had hauled the other inch by inch back into life. They were welded together as no two other men could ever be.

Yet now a shadow had fallen between them. Something strange and bewildering seemed to be severing the trust they had in each other. A grim and hostile blackness was enveloping them. They were friends and brothers still, but drops of acid poison were trickling down upon the bonds that joined them.

Perturbed and uneasy, Jamie walked on. He lay down in the hollow in the ground as the others settled round him. Then he lifted his head. He looked back at the fire.

A figure was standing silhouetted against the flames.

Rachel was still wearing the Arab robes of her journey. For once Jamie could tell it was her that he was seeing and not Toomi. Rachel was gazing in his direction as if she were seeking his face. There was something puzzling in the way she was holding herself, something awkward and hesitant as she leant forward above the fire. It was almost as if Rachel had had a premonition and were trying to communicate it to him, as if she were asking for his comfort and reassurance.

Jamie lifted his arm. Then he realized she couldn't see him in the darkness. He touched his fingers gently to his lips. Afterwards, as the flames dipped and the silhouette merged with the darkness, he lay back and slept.

For the third night in succession the banks of the Benoue echoed to the calls of the hunting owls.

94

'Further!' Salama shouted. 'There is an hour yet before darkness. We can reach the next ravine.'

Without giving Murabit a chance to reply, Salama spurred his horse down to the river. Lashing the animal with his whip, he drove it chest-high through the foaming water. Then he cantered out of sight up the bank on the far side.

Murabit turned and beckoned to the column behind him.

Wearily the priests and soldiers — there were more than fifty of each — urged their mounts forward. Murabit led the way across the river. On the far side he set off behind Salama. He followed the deep plunging hoofprints of Salama's horse first in the sand and then in the leaf mould of the forest.

By the time they caught up with the Acab Saat the sun had set. The evening air was chill with the approach of night and stars were flooding the sky. As Murabit rode up to him, Salama pointed at the rising moon.

'In an hour it will be high,' Salama said. 'With its light we can still ride on.'

'No, Acab,' Murabit replied bluntly. 'It is time to make camp. The men have ridden all day. They are at the end of their strength. We will stop here.'

This time it was Murabit who denied Salama the chance to answer.

The little mountain man wheeled round his horse. He rode back to the column behind them, and ordered the men to make camp for the night. Bowed with exhaustion, they slipped off their horses. They spread out their bedding rolls, and lit fires in the gathering darkness.

Salama walked back and squatted down opposite Murabit beside one of the fires. He picked up the haunch of a gazelle that was roasting in the flames, and gnawed at it hungrily. His eyes were hooded and his gaze vacant as he ate.

'You are defying me, Murabit,' he said. 'You halt my travels and turn me back. Why?'

'I halt nothing, Acab,' Murabit replied. 'I make sure only that you and your escort sleep by night so that you may ride by day.'

Salama was silent. Murabit sank his teeth into a piece of flesh which he too had plucked from the fire. Then he stared back at his master.

The Acab Saat's wanderings had become a source of deep disquiet to his lieutenant. Salama had taken to rising early in the palace and insisting, without warning, that he wanted to ride out into Gondar's countryside. An escort of priests and soldiers would be hurriedly assembled. Then the procession would set off with Murabit at its head.

There was no purpose to the journeys. They were wild, random and unfathomable. Sometimes they would come across a village and Salama would order that every living creature within it was slaughtered. The men, women and children, together with every family's livestock, would be herded into the main square and put to the knife.

The carnage was horrifying.

Sometimes even the brutal Murabit was sickened by its pointlessness. When the procession continued even the robes of the priests would be stained brick-red with blood. The priests would wash their garments in the river they camped by that night, but for days afterwards the robes reeked of the slaughter. Not even repeated washings could take the stench away.

'It is a message that will be carried on the wind,' Salama would say as they rode away from the now-silent houses. 'Wherever the little she-jackal is, the word will reach her. This is what awaits her too if she dares return. She will stay away, Murabit, she will stay away!'

Murabit did not answer. Like everyone else in the column his clothes were wet and the smell of death hung heavy in his nostrils.

Madness, the mountain man knew, had begun to take possession of his master. Its source was fear. Murabit knew too where the fear was rooted.

'Let me speak true to you, Acab – '

Murabit tossed away the bone he had been gnawing and leant forward.

'Your thoughts are overmuch on the river's child. It is not well for your mind's health. She is not a spirit. She is a woman such as you or I could crack like a nut in one hand. Without an army she is nothing more. She has no army. If she had, we would have known these many weeks since. But from far beyond the borders there is only silence.'

Salama reached out and nudged the ashes of the fire with his booted foot. When he answered it was as if Murabit had not spoken.

'She was mine in Kano,' Salama said. 'We lost her. She was mine again in Garoua. We lost her there too. Each night she is in my dreams, but I cannot see where she hides herself. Where can I find her now? Tell me that, Murabit.'

'Let her hide herself until her hairs are white,' Murabit replied stubbornly. 'It is no matter to us. Consider instead your own armies. They advance everywhere. Soon Gondar will run to the western ocean and southwards further than any man has ridden before. That should be the matter of your dreams, not this weak and hunted child-woman who runs in the darkness like a faun before the storm.'

For a moment the mention of Salama's invading armies brought the Acab Saat back to life.

It was true.

His forces were thrusting out on every side of the

kingdom. Every week galloping messengers brought back news that another great swathe of countryside had been subdued, another tribal nation conquered, another town or trading centre taken. The pace of his armies' advance was breathtaking. Already the lands under Gondar's rule had been doubled. By the time the first crescent moon of the new year rose, Gondar's territories would be six or seven times the size of those he had wrested from Ras Michael.

Salama had dreamed of an empire that would reach to the seas on either side of the continent. Within months of the battle for Gondar the dream was becoming a reality.

Salama smiled. Then his eyes filmed again with the brooding suspicion and anger that had come to disturb Murabit more and more.

'We must seek her out, Murabit.' His voice was a whisper now. 'We cannot rest, either of us, until we find her. She is of Sheba's line – and Sheba's blood, the old men say, is immortal. Let us prove them wrong. Let us give her to the crocodiles as I did that peasant who sired her. Then we can sleep.'

'Yes, Acab,' Murabit answered shortly.

Leaving the Acab Saat staring into the fire, the mountain man got to his feet and walked away to his bedding roll.

Murabit lay down and pulled the heavy woollen cape round him. His master was welcome to stay awake all night, torturing himself with fantasies about the fugitive girl ruler of Gondar. Murabit had ridden all day. He was tired and he would sleep until dawn, whether Sheba's blood line was hanging over his dreams or not.

Murabit did not sleep until dawn.

In the early hours he was woken by a blood-curdling shout. He sat up abruptly and saw Salama running towards him in the moonlight. The Acab Saat knelt down beside him and shook his shoulders.

'She is coming, Murabit,' he said hoarsely. 'I slept and I saw her riding for Gondar. There were seven horsemen at her side. I could not see their faces. All like hers were hooded, but the thorns and the rivers parted before them as they rode. They came to the city walls and called my name and then – '

Salama paused.

He shook his head in anger and frustration. 'I do not know. I woke and they were gone. But she is coming. We must go back. She has spirits with her and she threatens Gondar.'

Murabit brushed the sleep from his eyelids. He was wide awake now and he stared intently at the Acab Saat.

'If the jackal's cub has hidden her face,' Murabit said, 'how shall we know her?'

A chill brutal light flared over Salama's eyes.

'We both know her well from the palace, Murabit,' he replied. 'A young woman with long dark hair. Let word of such a woman go out to every soldier who bears Gondar's arms. Let them be ordered to slaughter every woman in the kingdom of her description – '

Salama kicked exultantly at the pile of coals which still glowed beside Murabit's sleeping place.

'Hooded or not she will be swept up in the net! And when she is, when the knife crosses her throat, all Gondar will learn that the line of the river's child is ended for ever!'

An hour later the column was riding furiously back through the night towards the city.

Cantering steadily behind Salama's shoulder, Murabit knew more surely than ever that his master's mind was stricken. After what the Acab Saat had said, the realization gave the mountain man no comfort. The mad, Murabit knew, could see further and more clearly than other men.

They saw best of all in their dreams.

If Salama had seen the river's child and the seven horsemen riding towards the city, he had surely seen the truth. They could slaughter every young woman in the kingdom. But until Ozoro Rachel's severed head was raised on a spear, the days of triumph were over.

Gondar under the Acab Saat's rule was in peril, and battle lay before them again.

95

As Mamkinga had prophesied the journey to the Mountains of the Moon was indeed a mighty venture.

It lasted for three months and it took them more than a thousand miles across the centre of Africa. When the Benoue's navigable waters came to an end they took to the land. They bought ox-carts and set off east through the great savanna grasslands and forests of Chad and the Sudan. For day after day vast plains teeming with animals spread out round them. Then for weeks they would find themselves in dark forests where elephants moved like huge grey cloud shadows between the trees.

After the forests there was more savanna.

They swung south to avoid the marshy wilderness of the Sudd, where the waters of the Nile spread out to flood thousands of square miles of swampland. They reached the Nile's banks and for the first time Jamie saw the western arm of the great river. He gazed in awe at its dark mud-flecked surface, remembering Mrs Livingstone telling him of the millions who depended on its waters for life.

As Jamie stood on the bank Rachel came forward to join him. She too stared down at the ripples of yellow and umber foam coiling beneath them. Then Rachel walked on down the bank. She knelt beside an inlet where the reeds had filtered the foam away, and the river ran clear.

Rachel lowered her head and drank. Afterwards she cupped her hands. She scooped up some of the water, and walked back to Jamie.

'You have never drunk from the great river?' she asked.

Jamie shook his head.

'Drink now,' Rachel said. 'Then for always you may say that when you drank its waters first, you did so from the hands of the river's own child.'

Jamie stared at her.

They were both standing waist-deep in the rippling summer grass that covered the river's banks. The grass was dry and golden. It surged and rustled round the young woman like ocean surf. The wind pressed her robes back against her and Jamie saw the outline of her body etched beneath the thin cloth, her small uplifted breasts, the curve of her slim waist, the long firm lines of her thighs.

Jamie dipped his head and sipped from Rachel's outstretched hands. The water was sweet and warm. It was flecked with tawny shreds of vegetation like the fragments of peat and bracken which turned the Hebridean burns of Jamie's childhood into streams of bronze.

Jamie wiped his mouth and looked up.

Rachel's face was grave. Her eyes were gazing into his but they were seeing something else, something far beyond where he stood. She tossed away what was left of the water. Then she put her hands to his cheeks and drew them slowly downwards, transferring the drops of wetness to his skin. Afterwards Rachel walked away.

As Jamie turned to watch her go, he saw another figure was standing higher up the bank looking down at them. It was Mamkinga. He stood very still at the head of his horse, his towering frame silhouetted against the sky. Jamie couldn't see the expression on his face, but there was something strained and troubled in the way he held himself.

Rachel passed him without a word or a glance, and vanished. Jamie strode up the bank to speak to him. As he came closer Mamkinga suddenly vaulted into his saddle. He swung his horse round and cantered silently away. Jamie walked back to camp alone.

That night, after the others had lain down to sleep, Jamie questioned Mamkinga by the fire.

'Twice now,' Jamie said, 'Rachel has spoken to me of being the river's child. What does she mean?'

Mamkinga stared into the flames.

'She is of Gondar and I of Malinda,' Mamkinga answered. 'She does not know the lore of my land, nor I hers. So in truth I cannot tell you. Yet there are stories that all the peoples of the mountains know. It is said that Gondar's ruler is not seeded by man, but by the river. How that is so, no one knows. Yet she is Gondar's queen and therefore the river's child –'

Mamkinga shifted restlessly on his haunches.

'Let her be, Umshebi,' he added. 'These are not matters for you. They will bring only discord and unhappiness. Leave the affairs of the kingdoms to those who belong to the kingdoms.'

Mamkinga stood up, frowning, and piled more logs on the fire. Then he walked away abruptly and lay down to sleep.

For a long time Jamie remained where he was. For reasons he couldn't understand the shadow he had sensed on the Benoue's banks had fallen between them again. Finally, disquieted and puzzled, Jamie lay down too. His disquiet passed as soon as he fell asleep.

Jamie's dreams that night were filled with the sweet warm taste of the river's waters, and the fugitive image of a young woman whose sun-warmed body shimmered behind an almost transparent robe as she retreated in front of him amidst a sea of golden grass.

Next morning they crossed the Nile and headed east. There were more grass plains, more forests, more thorn scrub and palm. Now at last they were approaching the foothills of the Abyssinian mountains.

For Jamie the entire journey was richer and more dazzling than anything he had ever imagined.

For three months Africa folded itself round him like a cloak of dreams. Its sun and winds burnt and tanned his skin. Its heat made him pant and sweat, its icy frosts at night made him huddle for warmth towards the fire. He saw the rolling crimson splendour of its sunsets. He smelt

668

the freshness of its dawn air, fresher, cleaner and sweeter than even the air of a Hebridean summer morning.

Jamie watched Africa's animals as they streamed away from the little caravan on every side. Herds of wildebeeste and antelope, stately galloping giraffes, lumbering rhinoceros, prowling hyenas, hunting cheetahs like bronze arrows on the dry grass, majestic prides of lion, the occasional solitary leopard — the cornucopia of the living wild was inexhaustible.

He saw the kaleidoscope of Africa's peoples, too, shaken out in constantly changing patterns of dress and feature, of skin colour and language, in the myriad villages they passed through. He heard the night-long beating of drums and watched the silhouettes of chanting warriors as they leapt and danced beside their fires.

Most of all Jamie felt Africa's grandeur, its vast age and wisdom, its ferocity and innocence.

Everything here was starker, bolder, more barbaric and merciless, and yet purer and more radiant. Here, Jamie sensed, beneath the vast African skies which stretched from horizon to horizon, life — all life — had been rocked and cradled from the beginning. Jamie finally understood what Mrs Livingstone had meant when she spoke of the great river as the river of life.

If the river of life had its source anywhere, it could only be under African stars in this ancient, pitiless and fecund landscape.

Although the journey was long and arduous, it was interrupted seriously only once. The interruption was caused by the little Scottish laird, Farquarson.

Farquarson was a passionate hunter. From the first day on the Benoue's banks, when he had shot the gazelle and the guinea fowl, he had demanded to be given the task of provisioning the expedition. Whenever they needed meat it was Farquarson who set out to find it. Sometimes he took with him a reluctant Wolf, sometimes one of their paddlers or porters. Occasionally he left on his own.

One morning, as they were travelling through the forests of southern Sudan, Farquarson set out alone.

'Give me an hour,' he called to Jamie who was beginning to strike camp for the day's journey. 'I'm going to try for some venison for supper tonight.'

Jamie waved back at him and Farquarson set off through the trees.

The forest abounded with game and normally Farquarson shot what he wanted within fifteen minutes of leaving camp. That day something must have disturbed the animals. Farquarson walked for well over half an hour before he saw any creature at all. Then as he rounded a bend in a narrow winding game track he stopped and froze.

Fifty yards ahead of him was a magnificent young kudu bull antelope with spreading horns and pale stripes down its glossy blue-grey flanks.

Farquarson was downwind of the antelope and the kudu hadn't heard or scented him. He lifted his rifle and fired. The kudu lurched but didn't fall. Instead it wheeled away and set off at a slow painful trot, dragging what was clearly a broken foreleg. Farquarson swore. He'd aimed at the heart but the bullet must have come low and shattered the leg just below the animal's shoulder.

Farquarson reloaded and began to run after the wounded animal.

The kudu could do little more than hobble and Farquarson gained on it quickly. Twice he stopped to fire again but both times another bend in the sinuous track took the antelope out of sight among the bushes before he could squeeze the trigger. Although it was early it was hot and humid. Sweat flooded Farquarson's eyes and he started to pant. If he didn't manage to kill it within the next few minutes, Farquarson knew he would be forced to abandon the chase.

Farquarson ran faster. He saw the blue-grey flanks only fifteen yards in front of him. There was one more bend and then, as he glimpsed the path through the thorn branches, the track seemed to straighten. Farquarson put his finger round the trigger and hurled himself round a jutting bush.

At the same instant he plunged downwards. The rifle went off with a shattering roar and something crashed against Farquarson's face, gashing his forehead. For several minutes he lay stunned. Then he lifted his head. Blood was pouring down his face, almost blinding him.

Farquarson brushed it away and peered round.

Dizzily he saw that he was lying on top of a dead rhinoceros at the bottom of a game pit. It was the rhino's horn which had split open his forehead as he plummeted down. The pit must have been dug by some forest-dwelling tribe. In his hurry to catch up with the kudu, Farquarson hadn't seen it before him. The rhino had died impaled on sharpened stakes like those Mamkinga had set for the hippo in the Bight of Benin. If the rhino hadn't fallen in first, Farquarson would have been impaled himself.

Farquarson tried to stand. As he put his weight on his right leg, he felt a jolting spasm of pain and his ankle buckled beneath him. He realized he must have broken it in the fall. He levered himself up with the help of his rifle and reached for the rim of the pit. It was just out of his reach.

Farquarson twisted and hopped and stretched. Whatever he did the rim remained stubbornly beyond his grasp. Finally, covered in sweat again, he gave up and sat down on the rhino's back.

Whoever had dug the trap would be back to inspect it. Until they returned he was trapped where he was.

The hours passed and the sun climbed.

The rhino must have died during the night. By mid morning its body was already starting to decompose in the torrid heat. Flies and beetles were attracted to it first. They descended on the pit in great humming swarms. Farquarson tried to beat them away. It was useless. They gathered on the carcass in their thousands, their green and black wings flashing iridescent in the sunlight as they buzzed tormentingly round him.

Soon afterwards vultures and maribou storks appeared. Farquarson heard a flapping above him and glanced up. Several branches overhung the pit. Perched on the lowest was a large ungainly bird with a bare ugly neck. It was a black vulture. Within minutes it was joined by another and then a third. A group of maribou storks spiralled down and drove the vultures off the branch, forcing them higher up the tree.

An hour later every branch Farquarson could see was laden with the scavengers. The huge birds bobbed their heads and clattered their beaks as they watched him with opaque hungry eyes.

Later as the light began to fade there was a scuffle in the bush somewhere close to the pit. A moment later a shadow fell across Farquarson's face and he heard the sound of snarling. He looked up again. A hyena was staring down at him. Its tongue was lolling from its mouth and its great jaws were dribbling saliva. A second hyena appeared beside it and then seven more.

The pack spread themselves out in a circle round the pit so that wherever Farquarson looked he could see nothing but their heads, their massive humped shoulders, and their yellow eyes even colder and hungrier than the vultures'.

'Get away, you bastards!'

Shouting furiously, Farquarson hauled himself up on his one leg and clubbed at them with the butt end of his rifle. Growling, the hyenas backed off, but as soon as he sat down again they returned.

Snarling and giving out fearsome screaming cackles, they began to prowl round the rim. The vultures were still perched in the trees, and from somewhere close Farquarson could hear the howling of jackals.

For the hundredth time since he'd plunged into the pit Farquarson checked that his rifle was loaded and the safety catch was off. Then, grimly, he too continued to wait.

The first indication that someone was approaching the trap came at dusk. The jackals' cries faded, the vultures flapped away from the surrounding trees, and the hyenas vanished. Farquarson clambered up on his one leg again. As he peered into the gathering darkness a small black face suddenly materialized above him. Instantly it was surrounded by fifteen or twenty other faces.

They stared down at him in astonishment.

'So what kept you, you ignorant savages?' Light-headed by then, Farquarson shouted at them in delirious relief. 'Pull me up, for God's sake! Can't you see a scholar and gentleman in sore need of assistance?'

Farquarson pitched his rifle up on to the ground. Then, one leg tucked like a stork's beneath him, he balanced himself on the rhino's back and raised his arms into the air.

A moment later he was lying on the ground above.

Free for the first time in twelve hours from the claustrophobic enclosure of the trap and the stench of the rhino's decaying body, Farquarson lifted his head and gulped hungrily at the evening air. Then he glanced round.

He was surrounded by not twenty but forty or fifty of the smallest people he had ever seen. Wiry and slender, wearing only pouches of leaves at their groins and with bows slung across their backs, they had ebony-black skins and watchful darting faces like tiny jungle animals.

Farquarson reached in his pocket. It was full of the bright glass beads and copper coins the expedition had been using for barter on the journey. He scooped out a handful and tossed it on the earth.

'If ever good folk deserved the laird's penny,' Farquarson said, 'it is surely you, my friends. Pray accept my bounty.'

Farquarson beamed at the silent bemused faces. As he opened his mouth to speak again, the stress, dehydration and exhaustion of the day overwhelmed him.

Farquarson fainted.

At the expedition's camp, only a few miles away, the day passed in growing anxiety.

By nightfall Farquarson had still not returned. It was useless to look for him in the dark, but next day a search was mounted. Rain had fallen during the night and they had no trackers. Combing the forest and thorn bush for a solitary missing hunter, most likely wounded and perhaps unconscious, was an almost impossible task.

Four days later there was still no sign of him.

Sorrowfully that evening Jamie agreed with Mamkinga and Hadji that the little Scotsman must have met with an accident, almost certainly caused by some animal he'd been pursuing. There was nothing more they could do. By then Farquarson was probably dead. Wounded or crippled, as Farquarson must have been, no white man would have survived for more than forty-eight hours in the tropical forest. As soon as his bullets ran out the predators would have got to him.

With heavy hearts they decided they would continue the journey the following morning without him.

They had struck camp next day and the carts were ready to move when Mamkinga heard a faint sound through the trees. He called for silence. Everyone lifted their heads and listened. A distant voice was coming towards them, singing. Jamie strained his ears. To his astonishment he recognized the song. It was a Highland ballad. The singer could only be Farquarson.

A few minutes later Farquarson came into sight.

His right leg was in splints and he was being carried in a litter of woven vines by a group of pygmies. Jamie stared at them in disbelief. They were evidently fully grown, yet they were no bigger than children.

'They are Wazan,' Mamkinga said softly to Jamie as the party approached the carts. 'Your friend has fallen among the small people of the trees. I have never heard of them ranging this far towards the rising sun.'

As Mamkinga frowned, perplexed, the pygmies put down the litter.

With the help of an improvised crutch Farquarson heaved himself to his feet. He limped forward. His pink and freckled face beamed with pleasure as the others greeted and embraced him in relief.

'I am mightily glad to find you still here,' Farquarson said. 'God knows, it was close run whether I should return at all. I have adventures to tell that will keep you late at the fire for nights. Without my new-found friends the hyenas would have feasted handsomely off my haunches on the day I left you.'

Between them Jamie and Mamkinga lifted Farquarson and placed him in the leading ox-cart. The pygmies, at least forty in number, clustered protectively round the cart, refusing to abandon their charge. Hadji shrugged and the expedition, quadrupled in size now, at last set off again.

As they travelled Farquarson told them what had happened.

'May God send fire and ashes over Edinburgh and tend his roses in the Highlands!' Farquarson uttered the old Highland imprecation as he came to the moment where the Wazan appeared above the pit. 'But was ever a man more glad to see his fellow creatures!'

Driven from their forest home to the west by the depredations of the slave traders, the pygmies had ranged deeper and deeper into the Sudanese savannas. When they came across Farquarson they were three hundred miles from their ancestral territories. Having rescued the little Scot from the hyenas, they put splints on his broken ankle and hoisted him in a litter.

The next day, firing from the litter, Farquarson shot another kudu, larger even than the one he had wounded at the start of the disastrous hunt which had plunged him into the Wazan's trap. This time he killed the antelope with a single bullet. The Wazan had never seen a gun. As trade goods the beads and copper coins Farquarson had given them were treasure, but to the hungry pygmies the kudu was priceless. The rhino trap had taken three days to dig. The kudu had been felled in a fraction of a second.

The white man who could kill such an animal from a

distance with his smoking stick was nothing short of a god.

'At which point they seemed to adopt me,' Farquarson said, smiling happily. 'I indicated I had friends I wished to rejoin. There was the considerable formality of the feast to be gone through first. When that was dealt with, we set out. They're canny wee buggers, I can tell you that. They picked up my hunting spoor although it was three days old. Then they brought me back.'

As the weeks passed Farquarson's ankle healed but the pygmies stubbornly refused to leave the expedition.

They were formidable hunters themselves and their bows were lethal. Yet to them nothing could match the power and magic of Farquarson's rifle. From the moment he first fired it and felled the kudu, the little Scot became their talisman. Exiled by the slavers from their own lands and constantly hungry as they roamed the forest, they would allow nothing to separate them from their provider of food.

Late one afternoon Mamkinga was riding at a distance ahead of the column when Jamie saw him rein in his horse.

Mamkinga sat for a moment. Then he raised his arm and beckoned. Jamie spurred his own horse forward and joined him.

'Malinda,' Mamkinga said.

He spoke so softly that even at his shoulder Jamie could barely hear him.

The day had been unusually cool and still. Now, towards dusk, the great herds of zebra, giraffe, wildebeeste and antelope, together with all the myriad other animals which thronged the golden summer plains on every side, were making their way to water. A cluster of cumulus clouds, as bold and rounded as the wind-filled sails of an ocean schooner, raced across the horizon.

Early stars were glittering and a late hunting falcon hung against the sunset sky.

'Malinda,' Mamkinga repeated, his voice still almost a whisper.

They sat side by side, utterly still in their saddles. Jamie wiped the sweat from his face and gazed forward.

They had been riding all day. To Jamie the landscape was no different from the one they'd travelled through since morning. Occasional clumps of pine lifted on either side, and the ground beneath them was littered with porcupine quills. The quills gleamed black, umber and white in the fading light, and larks were calling in the bushes.

They had seen the same earth and sky and animals for days now. Suddenly for some reason it was different. Mamkinga turned in his saddle and called urgently for Toomi.

'Malinda!'

This time it was a shout, a joyous explosion of sound that scattered the larks and brought Toomi galloping towards them.

'How do you know?' Jamie asked as the sound of hoofs came closer.

'Because I have come home,' Mamkinga answered.

Toomi halted beside them.

'What is it?' she said.

Without speaking Mamkinga swung himself off his mount and knelt by the stirrup. He slid his fingers through the dust, letting it trickle between his fingers. Then Mamkinga spat on his palms. He coated them with the deep ox-blood-coloured earth and got to his feet.

'Malinda,' he said again.

Mamkinga reached up and pressed his hands against Toomi's cheeks, coating her skin with the soil.

Toomi stared down at him. She raised one hand, scraped off some of the earth, and licked it from her fingers. Then she plunged from her horse and threw herself into her brother's arms.

The two clung together, holding each other so tightly they seemed to be trying to wrest each other's life away. After eleven years of slavery and wandering Mamkinga and Toomi had come home. Jamie tugged at his horse's bridle and turned aside. He might be their adopted brother, but it was not his home.

Jamie dismounted. As his foot touched the ground he thought of Iona.

Images of the sacred island, with its dazzling white shores, its green pastures, its mourning curlews and its ancient abbey, had crossed his mind endlessly since he swam across the sound all those years ago. There had hardly been a night when he had not fallen asleep with the sound of the Hebridean wind in his ears, or woken in the morning with the dazzle of the sun from the grey Atlantic breakers behind his eyelids.

Never before had Jamie felt its presence so vividly as he did now standing under the lowering African sun. The wind off the distant Abyssinian hills was harsh in his nostrils, a bateleur eagle stooped from a shimmering sky, somewhere in the bush a pack of hunting dogs bayed at the approach of evening. Jamie was further from Iona than he had ever been. Yet because of Mamkinga and Toomi he was also closer.

Their long exile was ended. They had come back to their ancestral hearth. The sun was its fire, the trees its furniture, the evening air and the star-bright sky the walls and roof of their childhood. They had come home.

Jamie put his arm round their shoulders. As the three of them stood silently together, Jamie noticed Rachel. She too had ridden forward and dismounted, but she was standing apart. Rachel's home was still far.

Jamie lifted his head and looked at her grave thoughtful face. Her dark eyes stared steadily back at his.

96

They made camp before darkness in a clearing by a watercourse a mile further on.

The watercourse was almost dry at the summer's end, but a trickle ran over the bare bleached stones at its centre. As soon as he saw it Mamkinga ran forward. Cupping his hands, he scooped up a mouthful and raised it to his lips. As soon as he tasted it he let out another shout of delight.

'Malindan water!' he called. 'Come, everyone, and taste! It has run all the way from the Mountains of the Moon, but it still has the flavour of the snow where it was born.'

Toomi was the first to join him.

She sipped the water and embraced her brother for the second time that day. It was a quieter gentler embrace this time but somehow even happier, even more fulfilled.

Mamkinga had known they were in Malinda when, riding tall and urgently in his saddle, he'd seen the distant whale-backed humps of the foothills of the Mountains of the Moon on the far horizon.

'When you can see the mountains,' he told Jamie that night, 'you know you are in Malinda. It was the first lesson we ever learned. But to taste the water that gives Malinda its life, that is something different. Then you are tasting life itself.'

Jamie thought of Iona's tumbling burns, shot with golden peat-flecks in the autumn spate or running silver-grey and silent as the clouds in spring, and his heart ached.

They made a fire and ate. As darkness fell Mamkinga became more and more restless.

He paced round the flames, pausing often to gaze east. All day the air had been hazy and the wind had blown from behind their backs. Without smells or sounds or even signs of human habitation, the landscape in front of them might have been deserted. Now the wind veered round. The air cleared and suddenly the night was filled with the presence of people.

Fires sparkled on the plain, marking the sites of villages. Smoke drifted back on the wind. Far-off cattle bellowed. Occasionally distant voices called. In spite of the Acab Saat's rule in Gondar, the first impression given by the evening's activity was that life in Malinda was continuing. Whether it was true or not only a visit to one of the villages would prove.

The closest village fire was a mile away. Mamkinga was eager to go there immediately himself. Hadji dissuaded him.

'Think with your mind, not with your desires,' Hadji said. 'Malinda's earth may lie beneath our feet but we do not yet know what that earth bears. The Acab Saat may have put a garrison of his men in every village. You could walk straight into them. One of us shall go. It can be me or even Toomi, or best of all Bakulu. But not you – you are our standard here, not a hostage to be hazarded to fortune.'

Reluctantly Mamkinga agreed. The grey-haired Bakulu set off into the darkness. Twenty minutes passed and they heard a chorus of dogs barking as he reached the village. They sat waiting uneasily for his return.

As they sat Jamie glanced round the fire.

Rachel was next to him. Her face was alert and eager but composed. As always now when Jamie looked at her his heart lifted and he felt a constriction in his throat. As they had drawn closer to Gondar she had become, it seemed to Jamie, ever more beautiful, ever more filled with a haunting loveliness. They had spoken little on the journey, although day after day they had ridden for many hours together.

Silence for Jamie had been enough. He had no need to speak. Rachel's presence at his side, the easy balance of her slim body in the creaking saddle, the ripple of her hair as the wind tossed it back from her face, the occasional glance she gave him, warm and smiling and candid, they were all and more than he wanted.

She was the queen-empress of Gondar and she had made herself his companion. Solitary and wary, hardened by the bitter experiences of his childhood yet still driven by the dreams that had haunted them, Jamie's heart was filled simply by her nearness.

Jamie's gaze travelled on.

Next to Rachel was Toomi. Beyond Toomi was Hadji and at Hadji's shoulder there was Wolf. Over the long weeks and the long miles of the journey, the three had formed a strange alliance. Hadji adored Toomi, Jamie had seen that from the start. The Arab warrior – and Hadji appeared to Jamie to be every bit as suited to his task as Toomi had claimed on the Benoue's banks – worshipped the ground Toomi trod.

Wolf's involvement with the two of them puzzled Jamie at first. Then one evening Wolf explained.

'Our Arab friend is one of the most interesting men who's ever come my way,' Wolf said. 'He's done what Karl and I have been arguing for years. He has created a community without slaves where all men are equal and property is shared. He has named it Quilombo and he wants Toomi to join him there when this is finished. I intend joining them too. There are one or two ideas I can contribute which will make the society more equal still.'

Tall and hollow-cheeked, his long grey hair straggling down over his gaunt face round his pale agate-yellow eyes, Wolf drew thoughtfully on a cheroot.

Jamie chuckled. 'Providing ye concentrate your mind until we're through with the matter in hand,' he said, 'ye can socialize all Africa afterwards with my own fair blessing.'

Jamie's eyes moved further round the fire.

Sitting next to Wolf was Farquarson. Behind the

freckle-faced little Scotsman, his skin the vivid scarlet of autumn rowan berries now and his sandy hair bleached almost to whiteness, the Wazan pygmies were squatting patiently in the darkness.

Their allegiance to Farquarson was deep and strangely touching. To Jamie's surprise Farquarson returned it. He chased and chivied the silent little men, he shouted orders at them, he communicated with them in abrupt and often irritable gestures of command. Yet if anyone else complained about them, as Hadji sometimes did when the Wazan raided the expedition's stores, Farquarson leapt instantly to their defence.

'They're my own folk,' he would say. 'Each one is a full bonneted, plaid-wearing blood member of the clan. Whoever touches a hair of their bonny wee heads plucks a strand from my own balding pate. Now, what is your ill-founded quarrel with my brothers, you Muslem cattle thief?'

Faced with Farquarson's wrath, Hadji would shrug and turn away.

From time to time Jamie would come across Farquarson sitting alone with the Wazan. Farquarson would be talking to them, not in the arrogant hectoring tones of the Highland landlord and kelp millionaire, but softly and earnestly. As he described the fish traps of the west coast crofters or the Argyll method of rabbiting with ferrets, his voice would slip back into the burr of his own childhood.

The pygmies would be gazing at him intently. Whether they consciously understood one word that Farquarson said, Jamie doubted. Yet as Farquarson's hand drew pictures in the air or sketched with a stick in the dust, Jamie knew the little laird was speaking to them as vividly and comprehensibly as if he spoke in their own language.

Watching him then, Jamie knew that Farquarson had changed almost beyond recognition.

Farquarson had come to Africa on the same madcap impulse that might have led him to scatter his money across a new brothel, or wager it drunkenly on the nose of a racehorse. The dark continent had altered him. It had strengthened him, tempered him, forced him to confront and overcome the challenges and hazards of day-by-day living in the wilderness.

Most of all it had returned Farquarson to his roots. He had gone back to his past, he had rediscovered his old skills, he had learned to live with his companions as equal people again. He would always be a laird but he had found a clan. That the members of his clan were naked stone-age pygmies with blue-black skins and hunting bows across their backs, mattered nothing.

In the clan the laird and the poorest crofter ranked equally.

Jamie's gaze returned to Wolf.

If Farquarson had changed, so had the sardonic grey-haired revolutionary Jamie had first known when he played chess with him in the Marxes' apartment, and then rescued from the police. Wolf had also come to Africa almost on whim and because he had little choice except to flee from London. If the experience of the voyage, the weeks on the Bight of Benin, and then the long journey east, had not affected him as obviously as Farquarson, it had none the less changed him too.

Wolf was still as fanatical and partisan a disciple of Karl Marx as he had ever been. But his exposure to the rhythms and patterns of Africa, above all to its people like Mamkinga, Hadji and Toomi, was beginning to alter the way he too thought. He could still be as dogmatic as ever, but the articles of his faith were no longer engraved on tablets of stone. They were written now on the continent's shifting rivers and sands and winds.

Wolf was learning the harsh and painful lessons of ancient peasant economies, where cowrie shells stood for gold and men themselves could be bought and sold like cattle. He did not like the knowledge he was acquiring, but at least he had the grace to chuckle now as he witnessed the transactions in the village markets.

'Karl and I will change it all,' he would say to Jamie as they stood beside the pens where the slaves were corralled for sale. 'All men will be equal, and the world will be new and fresh and shining. Although sometimes, God help me, I am forced to wonder quite how and when.'

For the first few weeks Jamie had watched Wolf closely, but there'd been no recurrence of the apprehension which had briefly seemed to paralyse him before they set out. Outwardly at least he was the old Wolf of the voyage up the Benoue – buoyant, argumentative and energetic. He had either conquered his fear, Jamie thought, or it had somehow been exorcized by the journey. Even now on the point of entering Malinda he showed no sign of strain.

Jamie glanced at his gaunt enthusiastic face. Wolf was lecturing Toomi over the flames. Jamie smiled. His companions might have been wished on him by Providence, but Providence had served him well.

Then Jamie lifted his head and listened. Someone was approaching the fire. He turned. It was Bakulu. Two hours had passed since his departure.

Now at last they would find out how matters stood in Malinda.

97

Bakulu entered the rim of the firelight and squatted by the flames.

'It is just a small village and we are still far from Malinda itself,' Bakulu said. 'But it is bad even here. All the young men have been taken to fight in the Acab Saat's wars. Many of the young women are gone too as slaves. Soldiers came and rounded them up in the spring. That is not all –'

His face was sombre.

'All Malinda has been divided into districts. Each district must produce so much maize and cattle to feed the armies. The amount leaves nothing for the villagers. Worse, it is more than the soil can bear. Yet if the supplies are not provided, children from each village are executed –'

Bakulu shook his head.

'Here on the plain at least the people are hiding just enough to survive. But I met a man, a herder from nearer to Malinda. He had been sent with cattle bound for Gondar. He managed to escape. Round Malinda he says it is terrible. People are starving, the pastures are dying from over-use, and still the children are being killed.'

As Bakulu talked Mamkinga's face had tightened with a mixture of anguish and rage. Toomi's eyes filled with tears. Rachel, her own face pale and angry, put her arm round Toomi's shoulders.

The rest sat in grim silence.

Salama was turning Malinda into a wasteland. He was enslaving the country's young women to reward Culembra and the Galla warriors, conscripting

Malinda's men to satisfy his own greed for conquest, and murdering its children for failing to fill his armies' larder. Worst of all the Acab Saat was committing sacrilege against the earth. He was forcing the Malindans to bankrupt their life-giving soil.

Starvation, Jamie realized, would be Salama's deadly legacy for the generations to come.

'These armies the people are being made to produce food for – '

Hadji's level practical voice cut through the silence that had followed Bakulu's story.

'Do we know where they are now?'

Bakulu nodded. 'In part at least. In that I was fortunate. To the villagers even Malinda means little. Gondar is just a word. Beyond Gondar might lie the moon. But the herder had served as a young man in the embrenche's bodyguard. Also he is intelligent – '

Bakulu had indeed been lucky with the companion he'd found in the village. The herder had travelled with the embrenche – Mamkinga and Toomi stiffened with pain at each mention of their father's name – and visited not only Gondar, but the country to the west. It was the country over which Salama was casting his net.

Bakulu repeated what the man had told him. Hadji nodded with increasing satisfaction. When Bakulu finished, Hadji looked up at the twins.

'We have heard many bad things,' he said. 'To listen to them fills me like you with sorrow. Yet for us and our purposes they may also be good. Consider what Salama is doing with the plunder of men and food he is robbing from your country – '

Hadji knelt. He smoothed out a bed of ash at the edge of the fire and began to draw with a pointed stick.

'Here is Malinda,' Hadji said. 'Here the lands of the Galla and here Gondar. The Galla's lands we can ignore. They are remote, a mountain fastness for hungry wolves. For the Acab Saat they have served their purpose. He has fed the wolves and led them south. If he were wise, they and Malinda's men and stores would be in Gondar. But they are not, are they?'

Hadji glanced at Bakulu for confirmation.

Bakulu shook his head. 'No,' he said. 'The Acab Saat has moved them all south and west to the watered lands beyond Gondar.'

'The lands the Acab covets?' Hadji urged him again. 'The territories where he sees his empire growing?'

Bakulu nodded. 'So the herder told me. I believe him.'

'What does your friend say of Culembra?'

'The word from Gondar is that the Galla's king is mad. That the Acab feeds him raw meat and fresh women daily, and that he grows always madder.' Bakulu shrugged. 'He talked not of Culembra, but of Salama. The Acab Saat holds the power.'

Hadji drew a network of lines in the ash ranging south and west from Gondar.

The lines were like the veins on a young leaf – growing with the spring rains and then withered by the sun. They all started from the same point, they surged impulsively forward, then they faded into nothing.

'Both our enemies are mad.' Hadji addressed the others, his eyes keen and confident. 'Salama alone matters. Culembra's wits have gone. The Acab Saat has his mind still but it is diseased. He is ill with ambition. His sickness has led him into folly. He has committed his forces to the enlargement of his empire. It has stretched the veins of his vision so tight they throb with his own over-confidence. If we can cut them, we cut his lifeblood. Gondar is his heart. With the veins to Gondar severed, he dies.'

'What does this mean?' Jamie asked, frowning. 'To win what we are all gathered here to win, how do we engage and defeat him in battle?'

'We raise our flag here in Malinda now,' Hadji said. 'Mamkinga and Toomi must rally what forces they can. With them we shall ride against such garrisons as Salama in his vanity has left to guard his rear. Then we ride swiftly on Gondar. In Gondar we depend on Rachel. Of her alone is the Acab Saat truly afraid, for only Rachel can challenge him for the people's allegiance. With her before us we shall approach and take the city – '

Hadji glanced at Rachel.

'You are our banner,' he finished quietly. 'You are our victory.'

The flames flared up and lit Rachel's face. She was sitting very still. For several moments she stared silently into the darkness beyond the fire. Then, gravely and slowly, she inclined her head.

'If battle must come to Gondar,' she said, 'I shall be the sword blade at our armies' head.'

98

They rode on at daylight.

Before they left Jamie made a rapid count of their number. With Wolf and Farquarson together with Hadji and his three men, the original forlorn little group who had gathered on the Benoue's bank had grown to ten. All of them were armed and mounted. Then there were the forty or more Wazan pygmies. The pygmies too were armed with their bows. They would prove, Jamie guessed, ferocious little fighters.

In all the force that set out from their camp on Malinda's borders totalled over fifty. It was hardly an army but it was stronger than any of them would have dared hope for three months earlier.

That night their numbers had doubled.

The Acab Saat, it seemed, was so confident that Malinda was cowed and terrorized, he had left the country almost ungarrisoned. As they rode through village after village they were told the same story. The Galla soldiers had marched the young men and women away. The soldiers only returned now to enforce Salama's edict and collect the quota of food the Acab Saat demanded from them.

'You were right, Hadji,' Mamkinga exclaimed as they entered yet another unguarded hamlet. 'The Acab Saat has miscalculated. His vanity will be his destruction.'

Hadji frowned. 'Either I am right, or I have under-estimated his cunning. If it is the last, then messengers have told him of our approach and he is deliberately withdrawing before us. In which case it can only be for one reason. Salama is leading us into a trap.'

Hadji shook his head with foreboding as they rode on.

Not all the young men and women had been enslaved. Some had fled at the Galla's approach. They had hidden in the bush and escaped the raiding parties. That evening the column made camp by a river. Before the evening fires were lit, Mamkinga gathered a dozen of the young men who had joined them and rode down to a grassy shelf by the water's edge.

There they held a tournament, using lengths of fresh-cut acacia branch in place of swords but otherwise clashing on horseback with leather shields to defend themselves as they did in battle. It was an ancient ceremony among the Malindan people, and one they practised twice a week when they went out to war.

At the end of the contest Mamkinga, with his vast size and strength and his now burning will to defeat the Galla, had easily vanquished all the others. Toomi proclaimed him the Malindan champion. Then with the young women who had also joined them gathered round her, Toomi started to sing the traditional Malindan songs of victory in her brother's honour.

Until her capture by the Oye-Eboe, Toomi had sung the songs from her earliest childhood. Now, as she led the others, Toomi embroidered and changed the words of the old chants. The young women followed her.

'Out of the darkness a new champion has come!' Toomi sang. 'He is both young and old. Young in his strength and bravery that no enemy can match. Old because he has returned to his people and his birthplace. The seed of the great embrenche was lost in the pasture. After long years the spirits have blown the seed back on the wind, living and grown and strong – '

Toomi lifted her head to the evening stars. She sang on.

'The night is over. The sun rises and the seed bears fruits. The fruits are warriors. The warriors ride to battle and the enemy flees and falls before them. Now light shines on the plains and the mountains and the villages. For with the champion from the river's side, Malinda is free!'

The song ended. Toomi turned to the young women and urged them back into the countryside from where they had come.

'Go from village to village,' Toomi ordered. 'Sing the song everywhere. Let the people know who has returned to Malinda at last. Tell them of the strength he bears to lead them to victory.'

The young women vanished into the darkness.

By the seventh evening the band had doubled in number again. The story of the embrenche's lost twin children had long since become a legend in even the remotest Malindan village. Their magical reappearance was greeted with rapture. It was a sign from the spirits that the dark time of the Galla's rule was over. People flocked towards the column from every side. Every time Mamkinga and Toomi appeared the air rang with a clamour of acclamation.

At the end of the third week the force numbered several hundred. It might have been much larger, but every evening Hadji ruthlessly pruned the volunteers who had joined them during the day. The only ones he allowed to remain with the column were men armed with their own weapons, who in Hadji's opinion were also capable of finding their own food. Everyone else was turned away.

'We ride to war,' Hadji said. 'Our battles lie ahead. When we come to fight them, we must be as lean and self-reliant as lions in winter. Only the bold and the taloned and the hungry shall travel with us.'

That night they made camp in the hills midway between the town of Malinda and the border with Gondar. As dusk fell a cluster of fires suddenly began to blaze on a hill flank several miles in front of them.

Jamie noticed the glow of the beacons from his tent. With Farquarson and Wolf behind him, he walked forward to join Hadji, who was already studying the flames with Rachel, Mamkinga and Toomi at his side.

'Whose fires are they?' Jamie asked.

Hadji frowned. He peered forward into the darkness.

Then his fingers began to tap uncertainly on the hilt of his sword.

'Our guides say the hill where they burn is barren,' Hadji answered. 'In which case they can only mark an encampment. But I do not like it. The fires are too evenly spaced, and they glow too brightly. There is no movement of men or animals between the flames. I think they may be a trap. Someone wishes us to believe an army confronts us. They wish us to send out scouts so they may capture one and learn what we are doing.'

Rachel wrinkled her face.

'We are still too far from Gondar for the Acab Saat to have learned of our approach,' she said, puzzled. 'There is no one else who would challenge us.'

'Perhaps I am wrong,' Hadji answered. 'Maybe after the turmoil of the Galla invasion, one of the hill tribes has decided the moment is right to make a raid into Malinda. Possibly the fires are theirs – '

He paused. For a while the drumming of his fingers on his sword handle continued. Then the sound stopped. Hadji turned and smiled at the others.

'I have been too long in the saddle with a sword in my hand,' he said. 'I am starting to see the leopard's shadow behind every bush on the track. Rachel is right. If Salama is in Gondar, he cannot know yet of our approach. I do not know who lit those fires, but when daylight comes tomorrow we will send a bold man forward to find out. Meanwhile – '

Hadji chuckled. 'Let us all sleep without ghosts of the priest inhabiting our dreams. The Acab Saat will get a welcome to singe the hair in his nostrils if he tries to visit us here.'

Hadji walked back down the hill.

Jamie followed him with Farquarson and Wolf still at his shoulders. As they reached their tents the three separated. Just before he ducked under the flap that led to his bed, Jamie heard Wolf's voice.

'Hadji will send a scout out tomorrow to find what lies round those fires?' Wolf said.

692

Jamie withdrew his head from the tent and nodded.

'Aye,' he replied. 'The smoke will still be rising. We'll learn the spoor of the scoundrels who raised them.'

'But it will not be easy, will it?' Wolf went on. 'The scout will have to ride alone into the hills. God knows what he will find there.'

Jamie laughed. 'Dinna fash yourself, Ferdinand. Ye are right. It will no be an easy task. But Hadji will pick a good braw man to do it. By the time we come to eat at midday, we will know the explanation. Sleep ye well on that.'

Jamie clapped Wolf affectionately across the shoulder. Then he vanished into his tent. Wolf walked away. He reached the tent he shared with Farquarson. Instead of entering it he sat down on the dew-laden turf outside.

As the stars wheeled across the night sky he gazed, intent and frowning, into the darkness.

99

A bank of cloud had swept down from the mountains during the night, and the early morning light was dull and flecked with occasional splatters of warm rain.

Wolf rode as quickly as he could.

He had risen while it was still dark and the others were still asleep. Stepping quietly across the wet grass he had saddled his horse and set off into the hills. Until two months ago he had never even mounted a horse. Since then he had learned the rudiments of horsemanship, but he had never ridden except in line with the others across the level expanses of the savannas.

This was very different.

There was no other horse for his own to follow, and instead of open plain he was travelling through steep winding gullies. He lurched awkwardly from side to side. Occasionally his horse's hoofs slipped on the loose stones underfoot, and he plunged forward across its neck. Once on a steep bank above a dry watercourse the horse shied suddenly and swerved away. Wolf was almost thrown from the saddle. He clutched frantically at the horse's mane and managed to pull himself upright.

Sweating and shaking, he kicked the animal on. Always ahead to guide him were the five pillars of smoke lifting into the sky above where the fires had blazed in the darkness the night before. They hung there tantalizingly, sometimes seeming to retreat before him and sometimes suddenly appearing to swing closer.

Panting, Wolf brushed his long white-flecked hair back from his face.

The columns of smoke might be as chimerical and

deceptive as rainbows, but he was blindly, grimly determined to track them to their source and return with the news of what surrounded them. He gathered the reins clumsily in his hands and urged his horse forward.

Wolf first realized something was wrong two hours after he had left the camp. By then he had travelled for eight miles, and the sun had risen in a hot hazy glow behind the clouds. He had been riding through a winding ravine when its shelving walls abruptly opened on to a long flat saddle. Wolf tugged at the horse's mouth and stopped.

On the far side of the saddle the hill flank rose again. Dotting the summer-dry grass of the slope in front of him were the remains of the five fires. The smoke was still lifting from their embers, but there was no one in sight. There was not even the smallest sign of a horse or a tent or a waggon.

The fires might have been lit on the empty hillside by ghosts who had vanished in the night.

For an instant Wolf peered ahead through narrowed eyes. Then he drove his heels into the horse's flanks and dragged the animal violently round in its tracks. As icy darts of acid ran through his stomach, he realized Hadji had been right. No one was camped on the hill. The fires were nothing more than a lure to draw Malinda's invaders out.

Fighting against the panic that was beginning to flood his body, Wolf lashed the horse with the reins and spurred it back up the ravine. The rocks clattered and tumbled away behind him. The walls reared up on either side, dark and oppressive and claustrophobic. He could see the cloud-veiled beacon of the sun hanging, a fierce and menacing orange-red, overhead. His head was pounding and the dry sour taste of fear filled his mouth.

At a gallop Wolf rounded an angle in the ravine.

As he did he dimly registered that five other horsemen were gathered shoulder to shoulder in a group blocking his path. Wolf's horse saw them instantly. Snorting with fear, it reared up and swung back. Wolf was thrown out of his saddle to the ground. His ribs struck a boulder and the air jetted out of his body.

Heaving and gasping, he managed to stagger to his knees.

Wolf's rifle was slung across his back. Desperately he reached for the weapon and tried to pull it towards him. As he fumbled for the stock, one of the men leapt from his horse and raced up to him. The man was short and bandy-legged. He had a thick drooping moustache and cold sadistic eyes. He stared down. Then he gripped Wolf by the neck and began to tighten his powerful stubby fingers round Wolf's throat.

Weakly and still half-stunned, Wolf struck out at the man's face. It was useless. The man's fingers contracted inexorably like a vice. As Wolf's horse continued to plunge and scream in fright behind him, the reins now tangled round its forelegs, Wolf choked and fell forward unconscious.

'Who are you – ?'

Wolf opened his eyes.

A hand, its knuckles clenched, was jabbing painfully at the underside of his jaw. He trembled uncontrollably at the repeated violence of the assault and a wave of nausea rippled over him. He managed to heave himself up and he vomited. Then he slumped back again.

'Who are you? Dîtes-le-moi, dîtes-le-moi!'

Harsh and angry, the voice was shouting at him again, switching now between English and French.

Wolf blinked. He was lying on his back. Sweat and saliva were running down his chin. He could see the sky overhead. The clouds had passed, and the air was white and shimmering with heat. Between him and the sun was a dark lowering shape. He wrinkled his eyes and the shape came into focus.

It was the head of a man who was leaning over him. The man was wearing a white robe and a white cowled headdress. He was bulky and heavily muscled and his face was bronzed and fleshy, with glittering almost fever-bright eyes, heavily shadowed and sunk deep in his cheeks, and a great curving hawk's-bill of a nose. Dangling from his bull-like neck was a golden cross.

The intensity of the hatred and urgency in the man's gaze was so strong that Wolf recoiled as he looked up at him.

'You are a northerner, a European. Do not deny it! Your skin betrays you!' Anger flecked the man's lips with foam. 'I speak all your tongues. Tell me which one you use and who you are!'

His hand speared brutally into the top of Wolf's throat again. As he gasped for air, Wolf's head rolled to one side.

Above the white-robed figure who was kneeling over him, Wolf glimpsed the short bandy-legged man with the heavy moustache who had almost throttled him. Gathered behind him were twenty or thirty other men, all of them heavily armed and with grim predatory faces.

'You may speak to me in English,' Wolf gasped. 'My name is Wolf, Ferdinand Wolf. I travel with an expedition with no other purpose except peace and exploration. We seek the source of the great river.'

There was an instant's silence. Then with a ferocity for which Wolf was utterly unprepared the man drew back his hand and hit him across the mouth.

'You lie!' The man's voice thickened with rage and menace. 'You have come here with the jackal's whelp and you seek to take Gondar!'

The man hit him again and then again. His fingers were laden with rings. Each time his hand slashed across Wolf's face, Wolf's skin was torn and blood welled out from the lacerations.

'Where is she now?' the man shouted. 'Tell me, tell me!'

Wolf's head was buffeted from side to side. The pain was agonizing. Blood and sweat filmed the air on every side of him. Wolf grunted and moaned but kept his silence.

'I can tell you no more,' he whispered when the hail of blows stopped. 'I travel with an expedition in search of the source of the great river. That is all.'

There was a moment's silence.

The white-robed man – through the miasma of pain that enveloped him, Wolf had finally realized he could only be the Acab Saat of Gondar – glanced across at the stocky moustached horseman. The horseman nodded. Hanging from his waist was a long rhinoceros-hide whip. He drew the whip from his belt and beckoned to two of the riders clustered behind him.

As the three men stepped forward Salama suddenly raised his hand. He looked down at Wolf's haggard and bloodied face, and then back at the bow-legged horseman.

The rider who had almost choked Wolf to death was Murabit.

'He is made of dry reeds,' Salama said contemptuously. 'We shall reap more seed from him by shaking the stalk, than by winnowing it.'

Murabit glanced at the prisoner. He stroked his moustache.

'The pit is dug and the animal penned,' he said.

'Put him inside,' Salama ordered.

A moment later Wolf found himself being heaved to his feet.

With arms gripping his elbows he was bundled across the floor of a gully that led off the ravine, until he was standing above a deep trench dug in the ground. The trench was bisected by a crudely fashioned wooden gate. Without being given a chance to see what lay on the far side, Wolf was pushed forward.

He tumbled into the trench. Winded and staggering, he stood up. He stared round. The top of the trench walls was beyond his reach. At one end was a vertical plane of earth. At the other, the wooden frame of the gate. On the far side of the gate something was grunting and snuffling.

Stumbling and swaying, Wolf lurched down the trench to the wooden barrier. He peered through.

On the far side a small stocky animal was running in rapid unending circles round the already muddied and compacted earth of its pen. Thickly coated with fur, the animal had a huge broad head, a pale grey back, a dark belly and heavy muscular legs. As it moved it gave off a dense musky odour that seemed to fill the entire trench.

Wolf had never come across an animal like it before. All he knew, as he gazed at it through the slats of the wooden partition, was that it had the most powerful jaws and teeth of any creature he had ever seen.

'It is a ratel, a honey badger –'

The voice, thickly accented, came from somewhere above. Wolf's head jerked up. Salama was gazing down at him over the rim of the trench.

'It is the most dangerous animal in Africa,' Salama went on. 'More dangerous than a lion, a buffalo, even than an elephant. Cornered, it will attack and destroy anything in front of it. It has the mouth of a hyena and the courage of a wounded leopard –'

In Salama's hand was a plaited hemp cord.

He jerked it and the partition lifted fractionally from the ground. As it rose the ratel hurled itself forward, savaging in a frenzy at the wooden bar. Wolf recoiled.

'This ratel is cornered and tormented,' Salama continued. 'Let loose, it will attack the groin of whatever confronts it. It will rip out the genitals and its enemy will bleed to death. Nothing on earth can stop it. And as its prey dies, it will begin to eat it alive.'

Salama tugged at the cord again. Once more the creature threw itself murderously at the gap and fought to get through to Wolf.

Wolf swayed. Fear poured over him in sickening waves. It seemed to clog his throat and his nostrils, and leave him gasping for air. Sweat poured down his face and his knees buckled. For a moment he thought he was going to faint. He reeled backwards until he cannoned into the wall of the trench. He stood there propped against it, trembling and heaving.

The partition dropped back to the earth.

'The next time I will raise it fully and let the ratel through,' Salama shouted. 'Where is the woman they call Ozoro Rachel? Answer me!'

Wolf closed his eyes.

The animal's raw feral stench enveloped him like a foul-smelling cloud. He could hear the scuff of its paws and its quick enraged grunts. In his mind he could see its massive jaws and its scarlet tongue flickering between its yellow-stained teeth. Above him Salama cursed. There was a rustle and a creak. Wolf realized he was pulling on the cord again.

Wolf could take it no longer. He opened his eyes and leapt forward.

'No!' he screamed. 'I will tell you!'

He stood for an instant staring up at Salama, his face tormented with anguish and humiliation. Then sobbing uncontrollably he dropped to his knees.

'The reports are true,' Salama said to Murabit five minutes later. 'It is the jackal's whelp beyond doubt. She rode into Malinda two weeks ago with the embrenche's lost children and a group of companions. They have already raised an army of several hundred men. Every day it grows larger. As I saw in my dream, she is heading for Gondar.'

Salama swore savagely.

He and the mountain man were standing on the rim of the trench. In the pit below them Wolf was slumped, beyond caring, on the ground.

With Murabit and an escort of fifty men Salama had been out restlessly quartering the lands of Gondar when word reached them of an uprising in Malinda. They were close to the Malindan border when the messengers arrived. Travelling day and night, they had ridden towards the insurrection. Then they had set a trap in the hope of capturing an enemy scout and discovering the cause of the disturbance.

'What do we do now, Acab?' Murabit asked.

For several moments Salama stood in silence, his forehead trenched in thought.

'There is a garrison of Culembra's Galla at the village of Imaligre,' he said eventually. 'The village lies next in their path. Go there with half the men we have here. The garrison is our last strong force between the vixen and Gondar. Organize the Galla to fight. When she arrives, try to crush her there. If you fail, fall back on the city.'

Murabit nodded. 'And you, Acab?'

'I will return straight to Gondar,' Salama answered. 'If she cannot be stopped at Imaligre, we must draw her forward to the city. Gondar is impregnable. Beneath its walls she will bleed to death. I will call back the regiments from the borders. When they return, her days and the days of all the dogs who run with her will be ended.'

Salama swung away and headed for his horse, his robe flaring out behind him. As he strode off Murabit called after him.

'What of this one?' Murabit gestured down at Wolf. 'Do I let the ratel through to finish him?'

Salama checked. He shook his head.

'Leave him where he is,' he replied. 'The creature is a shadow. The ratel will keep him safe. Whatever happens at Imaligre, return and collect him afterwards and bring him to me. There may be more meat on him yet.'

Salama rode off at the head of a group of his men. A few minutes later Murabit galloped away too with the other half of the escort.

As the drumming of their horses' hoofs faded, silence fell over the little shelf in the hills and the trench at its centre.

Wolf clambered unsteadily to his feet.

On the far side of the wooden barrier he could hear the ratel snuffling and grunting as its feet pattered endlessly on the bare earth. He tried to shut the sound out of his ears, and the rank smell of its body from his nose. He looked up. Above the rim of the trench the morning sun was climbing swiftly. It was already suffocatingly hot and his skin was running with sweat.

Wolf shook his head and wiped his face. Then he forced himself to think.

The Acab Saat and his men had obviously gone. Before they left Wolf had heard voices talking above him. He had no idea what they were saying, but they must have been discussing what he had told Salama. At the thought, his gaunt sallow face flushed with bitterness and shame. The memory of what had happened on the Benoue's banks months before, of Farquarson's shocked and contemptuous face, had haunted him throughout the journey.

Wolf had panicked then. He had betrayed the trust and confidence of his friend. Although the generous-hearted little Scotsman had forgiven him instantly, Wolf had never forgotten it. The wound inside him was still unhealed. In setting out that morning to track down the mysterious fires, he had been determined to redeem himself.

Instead he had betrayed them all. This time it was infinitely worse. At the threat of the ratel his mind had caved in in hysterical terror. Under the Acab Saat's brutal questioning he had revealed everything. Now the lives of everyone – of Rachel, Jamie, Farquarson and all the others – were in jeopardy.

Distraught at his own weakness, Wolf ran his hands wildly through his hair. He gnawed at his knuckles until his hands were running with blood. Then he somehow managed to control himself again.

He stared round the trench.

It had been dug deep enough so that in spite of Wolf's unusual height, even he – jumping with his arms raised above his head – could not reach the rim. But that was only in the section where he was imprisoned. Beyond the wooden partition where the ratel was penned, there had been no need for the diggers to go so far down. There the floor was at least three feet closer to the surface of the ground.

If Wolf could get through to the other side he would be able to haul himself out without any difficulty. All that stood in his way was the maddened animal with its slashing teeth and its bone-crushing jaws.

Wolf looked at the partition. The ratel was nuzzling it with its snout. The animal gave a deep chilling bark and another wave of the hot musty stench gushed through the slats as it contracted its scent glands in fury.

Wolf shuddered and closed his eyes again.

At that moment, he guessed, the Acab Saat and his men, armed with the information Wolf had given them, would be riding to prepare an ambush for Rachel and his other companions on the journey. If he did nothing else in his life, even if he were killed by the hideous malevolent animal only a few inches away from him, he had to try to warn them.

Very calmly, his breathing steady, every trace of fear now gone, Wolf removed his tattered shirt. He wound it round both his hands and held it out like a frayed rope in front of him. Then with his knee he nudged the sliding gate of the partition upwards.

What exploded through the gap was worse, was more violent and destructive and terrifying, than even Wolf had been prepared for.

A bristling muzzle probed at the opening. A massive thickly boned head splintered the wooden frame. Teeth slashed to left and right. Then, grunting and snarling, the animal was at his waist.

Talons ripped open Wolf's arm from his elbow to his wrist. He felt a searing pain at his thigh as its teeth tore into his leg. Then the jaws were butting and snapping at his groin as they sought his genitals. Somehow Wolf drove the coiled rope of the shirt down over its neck. He pressed and heaved and levered the animal away between his legs.

The ratel shot out behind him. It collided with the wall at the end of the trench. Squealing with rage it whirled round and hurled itself back. The thick grey and black fur of its face was dripping with blood. As the animal launched itself at him again, Wolf squirmed under the partition and slammed down the wooden gate.

He stood up dizzily.

There was a great jagged gash from the ratel's teeth in his thigh, and another laceration in his arm where the animal's talons had raked his skin. Blood was welling out from both wounds. He reeled from the pain and felt himself begin to fall. With an immense effort of will he forced himself to remain upright. He unwrapped the remains of his shirt and bound the wounds with rough bandages. Then he reached for the rim of the trench. He clambered out and staggered to his feet. Beneath him the ratel was tearing great splinters out of the partition in a frenzy of blind malign destructiveness.

Wolf glanced down at the animal and shuddered.

He turned away. His horse was tethered to a thorn tree only a few yards off. The Acab Saat, he guessed, must have been confident he wouldn't be able to escape, and had intended to return to collect him.

He found he hadn't the strength to mount the horse. Desperately, he urged the still-tethered animal a few steps until it stood beside a boulder. With this as a mounting block he scrambled into the saddle.

Then he set off back up the ravine he had ridden down that morning.

By the position of the sun it was almost midday. The expedition was heading due east. According to Hadji, if Wolf remembered correctly, the next large village they would pass through was named Imaligre. Imaligre. The named seemed familiar not just because Hadji had mentioned it, but for some other reason.

Wolf shook his head and tried to think.

Then he remembered. Huddled at the bottom of the trench after his interrogation by the Acab Saat, he had heard Salama and his men talking above him. He had not known what they were saying, but the word Imaligre had been repeated again and again.

Wolf stiffened in the saddle. Tense and fearful, fearful now for his companions, he spurred his horse on.

100

'Imaligre!'

Hadji reined in his horse and pointed at the village in front of them.

Jamie came forward to his shoulder. They had ridden all morning and it was early in the afternoon. It had been a busy and eventful day. They had risen early to find Wolf had vanished with his horse. Casting round, Hadji's scouts soon picked up his tracks. From the direction Wolf had taken it was clear he had set off into the hills in the direction of the fires that had blazed the night before.

Jamie remembered his conversation with the Austrian outside the tent in the darkness.

'The idiot!' he said bitterly. 'He's trying to prove himself a hero.'

Jamie swore. At his side Farquarson shook his head grimly.

'He has chosen a bad time and place to do it,' Hadji replied. 'If it was a trap, then he will have ridden straight into it.'

They waited for two hours but Wolf didn't return. Eventually Hadji decided they could wait no longer.

'I will send a small search party after him,' Hadji said. 'It is all I can do. There is word there are Galla ahead. We must ride on. Every hour gives them more time to prepare for our coming.'

Silent and apprehensive, the column continued. Now they were within sight of Imaligre.

The reports about the Galla were true. The village was garrisoned by the largest number of Culembra's soldiers they had yet encountered. The Galla had obviously been given warning of their approach. The settlement had been ringed with weapons and the enemy were gathered in readiness behind them.

Hadji studied the position thoughtfully. Shielded by the waggons, the Galla were shouting and chanting and stamping. Occasionally one of them would rush forward, leap high in the air, and shake his spear in defiance at the column.

'We must win every battle we fight,' Hadji said. 'But this one, because it is the first, we need to win most of all. If we succeed here word will travel before us. In Malinda and Gondar the people will know we can truly defeat the Acab Saat and Culembra at the end — '

Hadji glanced back.

By then the forces at his command totalled some four hundred men. A little under a quarter were mounted. The rest, carrying swords and spears, were on foot. In number they were about equal to the Galla, but the Galla were entrenched defensively and Hadji's men were in the open. For an attacking force to be confident of success, as Hadji knew from long experience, it needed to be four or five times the size of the defenders.

They would have to fight the Galla man for man on equal terms.

Hadji's gaze swept over Jamie and Farquarson.

'I need every man we have,' Hadji said.

Jamie gave a quick hard smile and lifted his gun. 'We have not travelled a thousand miles to watch others do the work. Ye may count on us.'

'I am glad,' Hadji answered. 'Let everyone listen to what I say.'

Rachel, Mamkinga and Toomi were also in the group at his side. Swiftly and incisively Hadji outlined his plan. Minutes later the Malindan force began to advance on the village.

The horsemen trotted ahead with the foot soldiers jogging behind. When they were fifty yards from the Galla position and the clamour of the enemy was almost deafening, Hadji shouted an order, his voice soaring over the tumult. The horsemen broke into two groups. Spurring their horses into a gallop, they swung left and right, circling back to attack the waggons from the rear.

As the riders launched themselves on the enemy, the Malindan foot soldiers broke into a run. They surged forward and attacked the Galla head on.

Jamie was in the left-hand group of horsemen with Mamkinga and Rachel. Farquarson and Toomi were with Hadji on the right. As he galloped Jamie was aware only of the searing choking dust lifting from the hoofs, the ferocious cries of the Galla warriors, and the flash of sunlight on the spear heads raining down round them.

'Now!' Hadji shouted. 'Ride in and cut them down!'

They were behind the crescent of waggons. Hadji wheeled his horse and rode in between the wheels. Jamie followed him.

On either side he was aware of Mamkinga and Rachel doing the same. Rachel was mounted on a white stallion. Flowing back from her shoulders in the mountain wind was a warrior's leather cloak, dyed the deep turquoise of the Abyssinian monarchs. One hand guided the reins, the other rested on the handle of the short keen-bladed fighting sword she had been taught to wield since childhood.

For an instant Jamie glimpsed her face. Clear-eyed and radiant, it seemed to shine above the dust clouds. Jamie's heart turned over inside him. Then he was among the enemy.

A Galla soldier reared up beside his bridle. Jamie swung his gun and shot him at point-blank range in the throat. A sword slashed past his arm and glanced off his thigh. Jamie fired again and another of the Galla fell back. He reloaded and fired half a dozen times more. The Galla fought back stubbornly as the horsemen plunged among them, but the ferocity of the attackers seemed to unnerve them.

Suddenly the enemy were falling on every side. Confused by Hadji's tactics, the Galla abandoned the waggons and tried to escape. Fleeing at their head was a group of riders who seemed to have been directing the battle on the Galla side. The riders burst past Jamie and vanished, but for the ordinary Galla soldiers on foot there was nowhere to run to. Hadji's horsemen were behind them, the Malindan infantry ahead. Not one of the Galla force who were caught in the village survived.

The battle was over.

Sweating and panting, Jamie rode over to Hadji. Hadji was nodding approvingly in the smoke and dust of the aftermath. The Malindans were slaughtering the last of the enemy soldiers and the village streets echoed with the screams of the dying.

'They are tasting blood,' Hadji said. 'It is good they should do so. Ahead lies Salama's fortress in Gondar. Only blood will dissolve Gondar's chains.'

Hadji glanced at Jamie's thigh. Blood was running down Jamie's leg. In the heat of the battle he hadn't realized the sword had cut him.

Jamie reached down and felt the wound. Then he shook his head.

'It is nothing,' Jamie said. He looked round. 'Are the others safe?'

Hadji followed his gaze.

Apparently unharmed, Mamkinga, Toomi and Farquarson were all in sight between the huts and the waggons. Jamie frowned. There was no sign of Rachel.

Jamie's glance swept the space beyond the waggons. With a sudden icy chill in his stomach he spurred his horse forward. On the far side of the village the ground opened out into a stretch of plain. Half a mile away he could see a galloping horse and rider.

From the flaring turquoise cloak at the rider's shoulders, Jamie knew it was Rachel.

Just in front of her was a group of running men. They were Galla soldiers who had somehow managed to flee from the waggons. Jamie realized what she was doing. Rachel was trying to prevent them from escaping with their weapons. As he watched the men suddenly stopped and turned. A moment later they had surrounded her horse and were slashing up at her with their swords.

Horrified, Jamie began to gallop towards her.

As he rode he saw Rachel lurch and begin to slip in her saddle. One of the enemy soldiers had caught her arm and was dragging her down. Frantically Jamie urged his horse on. Suddenly another horseman burst out of a hidden ravine beside the struggling group. The new horseman seemed to be unarmed but he charged straight into the Galla and struck out with his hands. The man who had almost pulled Rachel to the ground let go of her, and the others scattered.

As the Galla streamed away, one of them paused. He was holding a heavy throwing spear. He raised it and hurled it at the horseman. Jamie saw it plunge into the rider's chest. The man slumped and toppled to the ground. An instant later Jamie reached them.

Jamie glanced first at Rachel. She shook her head to indicate she was unhurt, but she pointed in anguish at the figure on the earth beneath her.

'It is Wolf!' she cried.

Jamie slipped from his saddle and knelt to the ground.

Wolf was lying on his back. For some reason his shirt had vanished and he was bare to the waist. The spear had entered his chest just below his ribs. The tip had missed his heart but it had lanced deep into his body. Wolf's hands were locked round its shaft. His gaunt face was white beneath his tan and his eyes were unfocused.

'Ferdinand, it is me,' Jamie said softly.

He reached out and touched Wolf's cheek. The skin was cold and sheeted in sweat. Wolf was dying.

At the sound of Jamie's voice Wolf stirred. He coughed, spitting out blood. He blinked painfully and registered Jamie's face. Then he managed to force a smile.

'Would you believe it, Jamie,' he said, his voice so quiet Jamie could barely hear him. 'After everything Karl and I have always stood for, I manage to get a spear in my belly protecting a queen!'

He paused as he coughed up blood again. Jamie wiped his mouth.

'Ye saved a noble young woman,' Jamie said. 'Whether your revolution comes or not, that will always be worth the doing.'

'Jamie, Jamie, I hoped to do so much better by you,' Wolf went on, his face grey and puzzled. 'I wanted to find what lay round those fires for all of you. Instead they caught me. The Acab Saat was there.'

'The Acab Saat?'

Wolf gave a faint nod. 'He threatened me with an animal. I could not take it. I told him everything. Now he knows Rachel is with you and you are coming for Gondar. I escaped but I have failed you all.'

'Ye failed no one,' Jamie replied. 'He would have known of our approach within days in the event. Ye fought here as a brave man. To do that is enough for any of us.'

Wolf unclasped one of his hands from the shaft of the spear. Weakly he reached out and took Jamie's hand. He held it for a moment and smiled for the last time.

'Tell Hadji to keep faith in Quilombo,' he whispered.

Wolf began to cough again then. His chest heaved and shuddered, and more blood flecked his lips. Then his head rolled aside. His long grey hair fell down across his face and he lay still.

Jamie glanced up. The others had gathered beside Rachel now. All their faces were strained and pale, and Farquarson was shaking his head bitterly.

Hadji looked down from his saddle.

'You spoke rightly,' Hadji said. 'It was not his cause, but he fought and died a warrior. He shall be sent on his journey in the place of honour among the best and bravest of those who did the same today.'

Hadji gave an order. A group of Malindans ran forward.

'Wait – !' Rachel called out.

She swung herself down from her horse and undid the clasp that held the cloak round her neck. Beneath the cloak she was wearing a white silk shirt. Rachel stripped off the shirt, leaving herself naked to the waist. Then she stepped forward and placed the shirt over Wolf's chest.

'Let him be dressed in this before you send him on his way,' she said. 'It lies only in the gift of the Ras of Gondar. It signifies that now and for always this man is of Gondar's nobility. I, Ozoro Rachel and now Ras, give it to him. Let there be drums before him too when he leaves.'

Rachel buckled the cloak round her neck again.

The men picked up Wolf's body. Then they carried it away to be laid out for the vultures with the others who had fallen in the battle.

— 101 —

They made camp that night on the high ground above the village where the Galla had been routed.

In the village itself the feasting and celebrations of the Malindans lasted until the early hours. The Galla dead had been stripped under Hadji's supervision and their weapons – their leather shields, their swords and spears, and a number of matchlock guns – issued to the Malindan soldiers. The Galla horses too were commandeered.

The rest of the plunder the Galla had looted and stored came from the surrounding villages. It belonged to the villagers and Hadji ordered that they should be allowed to reclaim it. Much was in the form of bars of salt, the chief and most valuable currency in Malinda. The Galla had accumulated huge quantities. It was nothing less than a treasure trove that the victorious Malindans shared out.

In the camp the mood was dark and sorrowful. Wolf had been with them from the start. He had always been an energetic and cheerful companion. In different ways his death had affected them all deeply.

By then the arrangement of the nightly camp had altered. As the following behind them grew and different tasks and responsibilities came the way of each, they started to build separate fires. Hadji had one of his own where he would hold discussions with the gathering band of Malindan headmen who had joined them. Mamkinga and Toomi had another fire to themselves where they could welcome, comfort and encourage their countrymen.

The three Europeans, three as they had been until the battle, had a third. Rachel a fourth. All now slept by their own fires. In the darkness each of the four fires were shrouded with silence and regret. Restlessly Jamie got to his feet beside the blaze he would share now only with Farquarson.

Jamie tossed a log on the flames and glanced down at the little Scottish laird.

Farquarson was sitting staring sadly into the embers, his head propped on his hands. For months Wolf had been his closest friend and companion. Of them all Farquarson's loss was the most acute. Jamie rested his hand in sympathy on the Scotsman's shoulder. Farquarson gave a gruff grunt of acknowledgement, but didn't speak.

Jamie left him and walked out into the night.

Three of the four fires were close together. The fourth, Rachel's, was at a distance apart from the others higher up the hill. Jamie could see the outline of her body as she knelt behind the flames.

Jamie stood in thought for a moment. Then on a sudden irresistible impulse he strode up the hill towards her. Rachel heard him coming. As Jamie stepped into the firelight, she lifted her head and gazed up at him. Her face was pale and grave but tranquil.

'The words have been said.' Rachel's voice was quiet. 'He was a brave man and he fell as the brave should. I owe him my life. I shall never forget him.'

'Would it had been I,' Jamie replied.

Rachel stared back. 'If God intended you to walk along the paths of my life,' she said, 'it was not to safeguard me from a Galla spear. God has other deeper matters in mind.'

Jamie stood in silence. For a long time he looked down at her.

Over the long months of the journey from Garoua they had been together often. Day after day, seated in the canoes or riding across the plains and through the forests, their shoulders had been pressed against each other's. For hours on end they had travelled wearily in silence. But from time to time, very occasionally at first and only later with growing frequency, they had talked.

Slowly and carefully Jamie had told Rachel about Iona and his childhood and the austere difficult years as he grew up in Dr Cameron's house.

In interrupted fragments – sometimes with days between them – he described Mrs Livingstone reading to him from her old and worn leather-bound books. His dream of exploring Africa and finding the great river's source. The border fairs where, battered and bruised, he had earned the golden sovereigns which had eventually paid for his journey south and his passage on the *Forerunner*.

In return Rachel had spoken of her life in Gondar.

Rachel too had been diffident at first. Somehow the companionship of the journey, the shared hardships and dangers, the constant unavoidable intimacies and the rare moments of laughter, broke down Rachel's own reserve as it did Jamie's.

She told him of the life of the court, of little Doho, Ras Michael, and her old servant Kalima. The soldiers and merchants and scholars among whom she had lived, and whose skills and languages she had acquired. The terror that greeted the invasion of Culembra and the Acab Saat, and her wanderings with Toomi since her escape.

It did not come easily to either of them.

They were speaking of the past, of experiences and images and memories precious and vivid, and sometimes wounding, to them both. Both were sensitive and wary. Both, at different stages of their lives, had faced loss and pain and death. Yet both were dreamers and yearners, seeking something different from the turbulent and troubled histories each had inherited.

They came from worlds so distant and apart they might have been different planets. Jamie, the crofter's son from the green white-shored island of Iona cradled in the Atlantic waves. Rachel, the queen-empress of the ancient and fabled mountain kingdom of Gondar, the rightful heir to Sheba's throne.

Yet now, Jamie knew as they faced each other in the firelight, the differences did not matter.

He had known Rachel as a sturdy partner on their great journey, drenched in sweat, fly- and mosquito-haloed, stinking of marsh mud and bleeding from saddle sores, bowed with exhaustion at the day's end and yet as ready as any of them to search with an aching body for firewood, and then to laugh as the flames lifted into the night sky. He had loved her then with a desire that made his blood race each time he saw her breasts shaped by the windblown lines of her simple cotton robe, or glimpsed her stooping to bathe naked in the half-hidden bay of some river.

Today he loved her more. Today Jamie had seen her ride as a queen among the dust and spears.

He had caught her face resolute and shining among the swords. He had seen the white stallion beneath her, her imperial turquoise cloak flowing out in the wind, her hair rippling back from her head. He had watched her strip the silk shirt from her back and lay it on Wolf's chest, standing unconcernedly half-naked among the common Malindan soldiers because she knew it was her due tribute to the man who had saved her life.

Rachel was, Jamie realized suddenly, the young woman who had walked towards him amidst the Celtic crosses and the gravestones of the Scottish kings in Iona's royal burial ground on the night when he put his grandmother and his sisters to rest.

Only queens walked the royal graveyard. Rachel was a queen. Even that was no longer important. All that mattered was that they were together and a spark had flared between them.

Jamie gazed down at her in wonderment. Then because he knew it was right and appropriate, because in his grandmother's stories it was what the Highland princes had always done, he knelt.

'I love ye,' he said simply.

Rachel reached out her hand towards him. 'I give my heart to you too,' she replied.

They stared at each other in the fire glow under the African sky.

The empty space at the centre of Rachel's life had been filled just as it had been filled in Jamie's.

Rachel had known it the moment she had first seen the young Scot with his proud angular face, his curling red hair, and his shuttered blue eyes, intense and cat-like, as he walked towards her at Mamkinga's shoulder by the fire on the Benoue's banks.

He was a solitary man, she knew instantly, a solitary man and a dreamer. Rachel was solitary and dreamed too. Their solitudes were different. Jamie's had been imposed on him by the loss of his family. As he grew up he had lived inside himself privately and alone. Rachel's life had always been thronged with people. They had crowded her everywhere. A few, a very few like Doho and old Kalima, she had loved deeply.

Yet even with them she too had been alone. Rachel had known loneliness throughout her childhood. She had felt it most acutely when Kalima dressed her for her baptismal feast. She had become a woman and she was clothed not just as a woman, but as a queen.

As she had turned inside the billowing robes, feeling anxiously for the reassuring touch of her body against the silk, Rachel knew something was missing.

The gaze of Kalima and the other servantwomen was on her. They were all applauding and their eyes were filled with tears of happiness. Rachel did not want their clapping hands or their tears. She gazed in the mirror in her bedchamber and she wanted the eyes of a stranger to see her. A stranger who would be a friend and companion and fellow dreamer.

Above all a stranger who would look at her and love her as a woman.

Rachel had found her stranger. He had come to her out of the darkness, out of the great storm that had tormented the banks of the Benoue. Mamkinga brought him to her fire. She had walked with him by the river. She had talked to him and laughed with him, and they had rested together holding each other's hands as the hunters did. She had woken him, many months ago now it seemed, at the sound of the crocodile's passage.

Now at last, unprompted and unasked, he had come to her side. He was sorrowing for the death of his friend. Wolf had saved her life, but Rachel was no longer thinking of him. She saw only Jamie.

As the flames lifted on the night air and soft-winged moths circled the fire, Rachel felt fulfilled and at peace in a way that had never happened in her life until then.

'Sleep beside me as you did before,' she said.

Jamie was rising to leave, but Rachel caught his hand and pulled him down.

Jamie's arms enfolded her. He pressed himself against her body. His lips moved across Rachel's face. He kissed her eyelids, her cheeks, her mouth, her neck. They clung fiercely together, kissing each other hungrily. Desire flooded over Jamie until he was shaking.

Very gently, Rachel disengaged herself and pushed him away.

'Be still,' she said. 'The time will come. It is not now. I am the river's child. The coming together is not with me as it is with other women. Lie close and hold my hand as we did once.'

Jamie rolled away. He lay beside Rachel holding her hand, his fingers threaded once more through hers. Gradually the pounding of his blood ebbed.

The river's child.

It was the third time Rachel had used the phrase. The strange enigmatic words chimed in his mind like the haunting church bells he had woken to on his childhood Sunday mornings in Blantyre. Jamie had asked Mamkinga what the words meant, but Mamkinga's answer had been vague and elliptical. Jamie's African brother was a Malindan, not a citizen of the much more ancient kingdom.

Mamkinga did not know.

Jamie turned to question Rachel, but the eyes of Gondar's queen-empress were closed and her breathing was slow and rhythmic. Jamie gently kissed each eyelid in turn. She smiled and murmured in her sleep. Jamie settled himself on his back.

They had won a great victory. Malinda was already almost theirs. But ahead lay Gondar, the Acab Saat, Culembra and the core of the murderous Galla army.

Jamie lay very still as the forest and the mountain cold crisped the hides of their night capes with crystals of whiteness.

Tomorrow they would ride on for the fabled kingdom in the hills.

102

A week later the column crossed the border between Malinda and Gondar. It entered the mountain fastness and began to climb through the ancient lands of Sheba's kingdom.

Like a rolling wave it swept triumphantly on again. Now it was Rachel who was its guiding star. If Mamkinga and Toomi had been greeted with rapture, Rachel was greeted with frenzy.

Rachel rode at the column's head on her white stallion.

Her eyes were steady and bright. She was young. She was beautiful. She was queen in a land where queens had been revered from the beginnings of human time. Most of all Rachel was the river's child – the daughter of Sheba and the heir to the world's most ancient throne.

Gondar's people thronged to see her. The crowds choked the streets of every village she rode through. They screamed and cheered and threw themselves down before her. They cut vine and palm leaves and lined the roads in front of her with a carpet of soft green foliage. They piled the communal village fires with herbs and filled the air with fragrance.

At Rachel's approach the Galla seemed to melt away. They had briefly defied Mamkinga and Toomi in Malinda, and they had been savagely routed. This was different. A queen was moving among them. Against her spells they were defenceless.

The progress was triumphal but it was not always happy or untroubled. Every day their advance was shadowed on the distant horizons by prowling groups of horsemen. The riders never approached the column and whenever Hadji sent parties out to confront them, they melted away into the gullies and ravines. Yet like the circling vultures they were a constant menacing presence as the army moved forward.

'They are the Acab Saat's eyes and they never leave us,' Hadji said as he watched a far-off cloud of dust where one of the mounted squadrons was galloping along a hill flank. 'Every step we take, every band that joins us, every waggon that brings us grain, the word of it goes back to him by nightfall. It is as if he is clearing our path towards a feast – except the tables are being prepared for him to dine off.'

The circling bands of Salama's scouts were not the only shadow that hung over the journey.

Within days of entering Gondar stories began to reach them of a terrible campaign of slaughter that Salama had instituted. On the Acab Saat's orders every young woman in the kingdom of Rachel's age and appearance was being put to the sword. Mothers would come forward to greet Gondar's queen, and turn away weeping as they looked on her face and remembered their own lost daughters.

To Rachel it was the most haunting and harrowing experience of her return. Day after day as she saw the grief of the sobbing women, her own eyes would fill with tears.

'If Salama is not killed swiftly,' she said once to Jamie, 'then I beg you to see that I die soon so their children may live.'

'We ride to the death of the Acab Saat,' Jamie replied bluntly. 'Your own coffin does not travel with us.'

His words were no comfort to Rachel. She spurred her horse and cantered away from him. For the rest of the day she rode on her own, abruptly waving away anyone who approached her.

The wave of the column rolled on. It surged higher through the foothills, throwing patrols of outriders like spray before it, and spread over the plain that lay beneath Gondar. Finally late one afternoon the column rippled forward to the foot of the ridge on which the citadel city was built.

Rachel as always was riding at the head of the army. Hadji was at her shoulder and the others a short distance behind. Rachel reined in her horse. She shaded her eyes against the westering sun and looked up.

It was the first time Rachel had set eyes on the city in almost a year. The year had encompassed so much – the defeat of Ras Michael's forces, her escape, her wanderings with Toomi across Africa almost to the western coast, her meeting with Jamie, Mamkinga and the others, their long journey back, then the campaign through Malinda – it might have been half a lifetime.

In the interval nothing seemed to have changed.

The cliff reared up almost sheer above her, cloaked with its savage acacia thorn and threaded by its narrow precipitous paths. The little houses clung like swallows' nests to the ledges. Gondar itself was still draped over the towering rib of rock like a majestic woven tapestry of tawny gold, shining umber, and snow- and wind-beaten bronze, the colours as rich and ancient as the hill flanks themselves.

She could see the battlements that encircled the royal park, clustered with darting swallows. The coils of wood smoke lifting from the houses. The domes and turrets of the palace, and the arched roof of the covered market beyond.

She could even see the tiny shadowed shape of the garden of the nightingales hanging, as she had envisioned it from childhood, like a raft anchored between the air and the clouds. In her mind she smelt the scent of lavender, she heard the fluting song of the birds, she saw old Kalima's face furrowed above the worn brick paths where they had walked and talked together.

Most vividly of all she saw the wind-thrown plume of the river, shot through with the evening light and cascading down from the cliff.

For a moment Rachel sat in her saddle spellbound. She was the river's child and its soaring plunging water was hers. She had come home.

She turned to Hadji.

'It is my city,' Rachel said. 'How do we take it back?'

Hadji was silent. He glanced up at the towering cliff and then back at the earth his horse was pawing beneath him. Hadji was frowning and his eyes were hooded.

The wave of their advance, Hadji knew already, had spent its force. Hadji had been right about the Acab Saat's greed and vanity. Salama had committed his armies to Gondar's borders and beyond. Yet once he had learned of Rachel's approach, he had acted boldly and cunningly. He had withdrawn his garrisons in the path of their approach.

Salama wanted to lure them forward.

The Acab Saat had made the road through the mountains easy. Now they were encamped below the city with perhaps one quarter of the strength they could have gathered had they taken their time. With the forces at Hadji's disposal, Gondar was impregnable. All Salama had to do was wait until he had recalled his own armies. Then he could destroy Hadji's forces.

Hadji opened his mouth to reply to Rachel. Without speaking he wheeled his horse away and rode off.

Hadji had no answer to give her.

'The she-jackal has fed on the poisoned meat, Murabit,' Salama said. 'She has taken it in her mouth and chewed it well. Now let the poisons spread.'

Salama chuckled. At his side Murabit nodded.

The two of them gazed down from the battlements that ringed the royal park of Gondar's palace.

Ozoro Rachel's army was encamped on the plain below the cliff. Messengers, as Hadji guessed, had brought word of their approach to Gondar days before. Salama had been enraged, but not dismayed. He had guessed the impact that Rachel, Gondar's queen-empress, would make on the superstitious villagers.

It did not matter.

Confronting him below the walls was nothing more than a rabble. The old rock-clad city was invulnerable to any threat they might have posed. Salama had enticed them on to the plain, just as he had goaded old Ras Michael out to face him. He had made the same mistake as the Ras, Salama knew, but unlike Ras Michael he had time to put it right.

Salama's armies were scattered. He had called them back. As soon as the armies returned the rabble would be crushed.

Crushed, too, would be the young woman, the fruit of Esther's womb, whose very existence had tormented Salama more, had caused him more frustration and anger, than even her mother. As soon as he knew of Rachel's approach, the Acab Saat had told Culembra she was returning to avenge her mother's dishonour. The Galla king had summoned Esther before him and slaughtered her with his own dagger in the palace throne room.

'A granary for giants, you promised me, Acab!' Culembra shouted as he wiped the dagger in fury on the glowing Arabian carpet that overlaid the floor. 'You did not say the whelp of cane rats would try to burrow amongst my corn.'

Salama looked at the now gross and constantly drunken king in anger and contempt.

Controlling himself, Salama walked away without a word. His priests shuffled after him nervously as Culembra's warriors raised their swords. Before the messengers from the Malindan plains, Salama had been on the point of ending Culembra's days. Now, with Ozoro Rachel's force below the walls, he would need the Galla army and their king for a while longer.

All Salama needed was time.

The time was not long. In its brief passing he was safe inside the citadel. When it was over, when the moment came, he would butcher Rachel as brutally and swiftly as the pagan king of the Galla had slaughtered her mother. Salama would stamp on the she-jackal's belly until not one seed of the Sheba's line would ever root again.

The image of violence that accompanied the thought

made Salama pant. His blood quickened and his chest heaved. He controlled himself.

'Give me the dispositions and the routes again,' he snapped at Murabit. 'Where are they coming from and when do we expect them to arrive?'

The bandy-legged mountain man stroked his moustache and glanced at the dried sheepskin scroll in his hand.

The scroll had been lettered by the Acab's personal servant, Jacob. The writing on it meant nothing to Murabit. He could not read. It did not matter. Murabit carried in his head the positions of the armies that had been sent out from Gondar better than any scroll could record.

'The first to reach us will come from the south, Acab,' Murabit began. 'The force you sent towards Imbali will have been held up by the rains – '

As Murabit continued, Salama rested his arms on the parapet wall.

Below on the plain the fires of the encamped army blazed in distant pinpricks of light in the darkness. Salama's powerful heavy-shouldered body shifted restlessly as he listened, and his eyes stared out into the night.

Half of the Acab Saat's mind was concentrating on what Murabit was saying. The rest was dwelling on what he would do to the little she-jackal, the elusive tormenting child-woman he had hunted across Africa.

As her face came to Salama's mind, he caught the stone parapet and gripped it until his fingers bled.

The door of the cell creaked open.

The Galla soldier who entered had a small bowl of gruel in one hand and a wooden mug of water in the other. Stooping under the low roof, he crossed the floor, wrinkling his nose at the stench of filth which rose to his nostrils. On the far side he bent down. He placed the bowl and the mug on the ground, and picked up the now-empty ones from his visit the day before.

The soldier went out.

He didn't even bother to glance at the little creature

lying huddled motionless on the stone at the back. For all the soldier knew or cared the dwarf might already be dead. If he wasn't yet, he soon would be. At the Acab Saat's insistence the dwarf was still being fed, but no one – man or animal – could survive the treatment he was being given for much longer.

The soldier locked the door behind him and walked away down the passage.

Doho wasn't dead. As the footsteps faded he lifted his head. He had been watching the soldier closely for a week now. The man was new and he wasn't as experienced as the one he had replaced. Each time he bent to put the bowl and mug on the ground, he did so with his back to the dwarf.

The man had done the same today. The movement swung the blade of the dagger at his waist forward, and left its handle protruding above his hip at the rear.

Doho pushed himself painfully to his feet.

His face was crusted with dried blood, and dark festering weals covered his body. Trailing one leg behind him – his knee had been wrenched and almost broken during one of the beatings – he limped across the floor. He forced himself to eat the rancid gruel. Although his stomach rebelled, Doho knew he needed the food to conserve what remained of his strength.

Afterwards Doho squatted and sipped at the water. As he gazed into the darkness his eyes were fierce and calculating.

103

'Nothing?'

Jamie asked the question only to break the silence.

Hadji shook his head wearily.

'Unless you count a caravan of three waggons of wheat,' he said. 'We caught them last night on a track from the south. The drivers have been pegged out on the hillside for the vultures. I doubt it will teach anyone a lesson. The town is as porous as a sieve – '

Hadji leant forward from the saddle and spat at the ground. Then he wheeled his horse round.

'I will check the other patrols to see if they have fared any better,' he added.

Hadji galloped away, his shoulders bowed dispiritedly.

Jamie stood on the plain looking up at Gondar.

It was early in the morning. The sun was behind him and every battlement stood out clearly in the bright clean light of the mountains. Jamie could see the Acab's soldiers moving about on the walls. Smoke from the cooking fires in the streets and squares lifted into the air. He heard the distant hum of the town going about its business as if it were unaffected by the army encamped at its foot.

It was the fifteenth day of the siege. Gondar looked more impregnable than ever.

Jamie scuffed his booted foot in the summer-dry earth of the plain. He watched the slow-moving coils of dust rise into the air. As a child reading the books in Dr Cameron's library, Jamie had been puzzled at how long it had taken medieval armies to subdue some garrisoned fortress that stood in their way. The armies might be mighty and the fortress tiny. Yet months or even years could go by before the defenders surrendered.

Now Jamie understood all too well.

Gondar could have been any of the fortresses he had read about. Under the Acab Saat's leadership it was fiercely and well defended. They had discovered that when their first assault had been almost contemptuously repulsed. Since then they had been forced to mount a siege.

Like any medieval citadel, Gondar could survive a siege almost indefinitely. It had water. It had sources of provisions in the surrounding countryside. It was gripped by a reign of terror which had cowed its citizens into submission.

Nor was that all. Apart from Gondar's mighty walls and the towering ramparts of the cliffs, the besiegers faced other problems.

When the siege began the attackers outnumbered the garrison inside the walls. Two weeks later they still outnumbered Salama's forces, but the difference shrank every day. The reason was a simple matter of food and water. It was high summer. The few rivers that crossed the plain were drying swiftly. Some had already failed altogether.

It was the same with food. There was no cattle pasture for miles around. From the beginning grain had to be brought in by waggon from distant villages. Now both meat and grain came from further and further away. Each evening Hadji was forced to dismiss more of the village companies that provided the backbone of the armies. There was nothing to feed them with.

Well before the summer's end, and that was not long now, the balance would have changed. The garrison inside Gondar would be larger than the attacking force without.

'Your horse, effendi.'

Jamie turned.

A groom had saddled and brought forward his mount. Jamie swung himself up into the saddle. He cantered alone towards the west. Then he reined in the horse and scanned the horizon.

In the distance he spotted a small cloud of dust. It swung from side to side as the hidden riders it enclosed followed the course of the dried-out wadis. Hadji, Jamie knew, would be at the group's head.

Jamie rested on his pommel.

Hadji was still attempting to quarantine Gondar. The attempt was doomed. The hill flanks and valleys which fell westwards from the Mountains of the Moon needed not groups of men, not even an army, but a multitude to cordon.

They did not command a multitude. Hadji's efforts were futile. Yet every two days he set out from camp smiling and apparently confident.

Hadji's trips, Jamie was starting to understand, were born of frustration and anger. Hadji was a soldier. In his own country on open ground he was a superb tactician. He knew where an enemy would concentrate his resources, where the enemy was vulnerable, where a few bold and inspired men could wreak havoc out of all proportion to their numbers.

To enlist him and bring him with them, to give him command of the armies had been the right decision. Only under Hadji could they have achieved what they had done so far. Malinda had fallen. So, with the exception of the city of Gondar, had all of Gondar's lands. Without him the campaign would have faltered long ago.

Now Hadji was out of his depth. Gondar was a nut that defied the cracking. All of Hadji's brave sorties and smiling words of encouragement were no more than bravado. He was lost. Hadji knew it, and his patrols along the mountain tracks were nothing more than a frenzied camouflage for his bewilderment.

Jamie turned back.

He headed sombrely for the tents where the leaders of the expedition would be gathered. The whole bold thrust of their invasion had lost its momentum. The campaign was floating on a slack tide. Soon the water would begin to run against it.

When the ebb tide gathered force they would be doomed.

Jamie dropped to the ground. He stepped into his own tent and washed himself sparingly from the bucket that had been left ready for him. Water was already becoming a luxury. He changed his rough cotton shirt and went out again. It was time for the evening council meeting. He crossed the arid space of earth that led to Rachel's tent and went inside.

Rachel, Hadji, Mamkinga, Toomi and the chief captains of the Malindan and Gondar armies were gathered round the clay model of Gondar and the surrounding hills and mountains which stood at the tent's centre. The model had been made at Hadji's orders on the day after the first unsuccessful attack on the city. It showed the dispositions of both sides, and acted as a focus point for the evening's deliberations.

The council was already in progress. Jamie slipped in and found a place between two cavalry captains. Hadji was speaking. The news he had brought back from his tour of the patrols was bleak.

'The waggons are getting through,' Hadji was saying. 'We expected that and at least we are stopping some of them. But there are messengers travelling the other way. They are carrying bribes – '

He lifted his head and snapped his fingers.

The tent flaps parted and two of his men appeared. They were dragging a prisoner whose outspread arms had been lashed to a branch. The prisoner had been savagely beaten. Clots of dry blood clung to his skin and he stumbled almost unconscious between his guards.

The guards brought him to a halt. They propped him upright and jabbed a sharpened stick under his chin. The man lifted his head and opened his eyes.

'Tell the council who you are,' Hadji instructed.

'I am Krakos Mustafa, a grain merchant of Gondar,' the man said dully.

'You were caught on the road to Faran,' Hadji went on. 'What were you doing?'

'The Acab Saat sent me,' the man replied. 'My brother is headman of the village of Faran. The Acab told me to see that he gathered thirty armed men from the village and went to the ravine near the river. There he would meet with other groups of men. They were to march under the Acab's orders to Gondar.'

'And what would your brother gain from this?' Hadji demanded.

'My brother would be granted salt-trading rights over all the area round his village.'

'And if you failed to do what the Acab instructed?'

'He would kill my wife and children.'

A small fire of camel dung was burning at the tent's centre. Hadji walked slowly round it until he was standing in front of the prisoner. The man, his arms looped over the branch, watched him in terror.

'You are frightened of the Acab Saat, are you not?' Hadji said.

'Yes, master,' the man answered.

'Because he is the most powerful man in Gondar?'

'Yes.'

Hadji frowned. 'Is there not one even more powerful than he?'

'I do not know of such a one.'

'You do not?' Hadji suddenly gripped the man's hair and jerked his head back. 'Is there not a queen of Gondar? Is she not more powerful than anyone – even the Acab Saat? Answer me!'

The man squirmed in agony. 'There was a queen,' he whimpered, 'but she is dead.'

'Yet if she lived,' Hadji went on remorselessly, 'would it not be truly worth dying to cast your eyes on her just once? Would not your wife and children die happy that you had done so? Would it not be worth spurning the Acab Saat for that?'

Hadji levered the man's neck against the branch. The man's voice rose to a shriek.

'If Gondar's queen lived I would die happy!'

'Then you shall die happy – '

Hadji let go of the man's hair. He swung the prisoner round until he was staring across the fire at Rachel.

'Look on your queen,' Hadji said.

The man stared at Rachel. His eyes widened. He opened his mouth. Then he fainted.

'Take him outside,' Hadji ordered the guards. 'He has had his wish.'

The guards dragged the prisoner from the tent. As the flaps fell back there was the dull crack of a sword blade biting deep into living bone. A scream followed by a choking splutter filled the air. Then there was silence.

Hadji stepped back from the fire and glanced round at the council.

'My patrols caught him,' he said. 'There are others, many others who escape them. Salama is sending messengers out from the town all the time. They all carry the same instruction – '

Hadji positioned himself above the model of Gondar and the surrounding countryside.

'North is Malinda.' His fingers touched the model as he spoke. 'East the Mountains of the Moon. Malinda we hold because of Mamkinga and Toomi. The mountains harbour few. But west and south? What of Tigre? What of Shiha and Massowa? There are people, valleys, villages, plains and plenty. They are the lands beyond Gondar's borders. They have become provinces of the Acab's empire. Make no mistake, they owe allegiance to no one but him – '

Hadji drew himself up. 'The Acab Saat is now calling that empire to him. He is offering bribes and inducements. The tide has turned. Soon soldiers, weapons and supplies will be pouring into his stronghold. If we cannot break Gondar, we are lost.'

Hadji stepped back out of the firelight.

Jamie's eyes followed him. He knew Hadji was exhausted, but the exhaustion was more than physical. Hadji was fighting a battle he could not win. He had led the army against Gondar and the citadel had driven him back. He had tried to encircle it and choke it into defeat, and the fortress town had defeated him. He had used every wile, every stratagem, every trick he knew. None of them had worked. Gondar was impervious.

The realization caused Hadji shame and humiliation. He had been unmanned before those he had loved best and wanted to help most.

Hadji retreated into the tent's deepest shadows.

There was silence. Jamie glanced at Rachel. She was the council's leader and it fell to her to speak. But Rachel, Jamie knew, had nothing to say. Nor had Mamkinga, the great brooding and distracted presence at her shoulder. Nor had his sister Toomi, nor any of the captains.

Unless Gondar could be captured they were all doomed.

Suddenly the grim silence was broken by raised voices from the darkness beyond the closed flap of the tent. Everyone inside the tent swung round. Mamkinga's hand was on his sword and Hadji moved out of the shadows. The shouts were nearer now and punctuated by the clatter of weapons.

Across the leather wall flickered the glow of lanterns.

Hadji and Mamkinga started for the entrance. Before they reached it the flaps were hurled aside and a dirty, dishevelled figure, as small as a child, tumbled into the tent. Jamie, who had immediately placed himself between Rachel and the doorway, gazed down at the intruder.

With a shock Jamie realized it was not a child. The face which stared wildly up at him through eyes sunken into dark sockets, its head covered with matted white hair and its hands bloodstained, belonged to a dwarf. The gap behind filled with the shapes of the guards. Swords flashed and lanterns flared.

Before anyone could touch the dwarf Rachel pushed Jamie aside.

'Stop!' she cried. 'Touch a hair of his head and you die at my hand!'

Rachel's eyes blazed over her drawn sword. She advanced across the floor. As she reached the dwarf she let the weapon drop from her hand. She knelt and gathered him in her arms.

'Doho,' she said softly. 'I have come home. You are safe now.'

Crooning to him as if to a child, Rachel cradled the dwarf against her body.

104

'Is it truly you, my queen?' Doho whispered.

'It is indeed I, little man,' Rachel answered. She bathed his forehead with a damp cloth. 'Try to rest.'

The dwarf shook his head. 'I have had time for sleep in the priest's dungeons. Soon I will have eternity to rest. Now I wish to talk. Where had I reached?'

His hand tightened round Rachel's fingers. Rachel smiled and bent over him. Toomi was sitting in the shadows behind her.

'The night you hid me with the servant girls,' she prompted.

'I was pleased with that.' Doho managed a faint smile. 'But soon afterwards the priest found me. The Acab beat me with his own hand at first, he and that devil's acolyte who shares his thoughts. When I would tell him nothing, he had me given to Culembra's women soldiers – '

Doho closed his eyes and shuddered.

'What they did to me I cannot tell you, queen. For days and nights without cease I was their plaything, a rock-rat in a den of she-hyenas. Often I thought I would die. I longed for death every moment, but always they stopped just short of the final knife-twist. When I opened my eyes they would still be there, and I knew I was still in hell. But they got nothing from me.'

Rachel stroked his cheek. 'You are the bravest of the brave, Doho.'

'I am a soldier.' The little man tried to hold himself stiffly. 'I fought at Ras Michael's shoulder. You are my queen. I know my duty.'

Rachel's eyes filmed with tears.

'What happened then?' she asked.

'In the end they realized it was useless,' Doho answered. 'They knew my mind or my body would die before I would speak. The Acab did not want a corpse. I knew more about you than anyone. He was determined to find you. He wanted me alive in case one day I could be of use to him in that.'

The torture ceased. Doho was taken away and imprisoned in one of the cells beneath the palace. He was given food and water and left until he had partly recovered. Then he was beaten again until he lost consciousness once more. For months the same continued.

'The Acab was trying to break my spirit and my will,' Doho said. 'Sometimes he would be absent for weeks. Then he would come back and kick me and scream at me, hoping I had been destroyed and I would talk. But I knew what he was doing. I fought against it. I survived.'

Tears came to Rachel's eyes again as she looked at him.

Doho might have survived but he had paid a terrible price. His once-strong body was fevered and bone thin. His skin was marked everywhere with bruises, scars and lesions. His hair was white, his face emaciated, his eyes sunken and dull, and every few minutes his limbs were convulsed with trembling.

'How did you escape?' she said, stroking his cheek.

'I knew things about the palace the Acab didn't.' Doho forced another smile. 'When I first came there with Ras Michael I was young and I liked going with women. I liked one a night, more if I could afford it.'

Rachel smiled back at him affectionately. Doho's appetite for women had been legendary throughout her childhood.

'In the old days in the palace, when the Ras retired I lay down outside his door. As soon as he was asleep I rose. All the palace doors were barred and guarded. But I discovered the drains. They run all over Gondar. If you are as small as am I, you can use them to take you anywhere. I used to go right from the heart of the palace to the market.'

'And you used them to get out?' Rachel asked.

Doho nodded. 'After your forces attacked, the guards were taken away. The Acab wanted everyone for the walls. The cell door was still locked, but a man came down every night to feed me. I knew if I was patient the moment would come.'

Two weeks after the siege was mounted Doho got his chance.

The guard Doho had been watching stumbled as he placed the bowl and the mug on the cell floor. His back was towards Doho and the handle of his dagger was protruding into the air. Doho leapt on the man. He plucked the dagger from its sheath, and drove its blade into the soldier's neck.

A moment later Doho was out of the cell. He limped upstairs and slipped into the drainage system he had used so often in the past. Using the warren of tunnels that ran below Gondar's streets, he worked his way down to one of the outlets below the walls.

'Afterwards I climbed down the cliff,' Doho finished. 'I reached the plain and found your tent. Now I am here where I belong – with my queen and ready to do whatever she commands of me.'

Rachel gathered him in her arms. She was weeping and so was Doho now.

They held each other tightly, the ravaged and lacerated white-haired head resting against the smooth young skin of the queen's face, as the tears poured down both their cheeks.

'Doho! Doho!'

The quiet insistent voice that interrupted the sobbing was Toomi's.

Toomi had said nothing as the dwarf had told his story. Now, in response to her repeated calls, Doho looked round. He gazed at her uncertainly.

'Who is this?' he said to Rachel. 'She is so like you – '

'She is Toomi,' Rachel said. 'She is my sister.'

'Sister? You have no sister. You are the child of the river – the river's only child.'

736

'Yes,' Rachel agreed. 'But she is my sister all the same. We have gone through much together and now we are one.'

'What do you want?' Doho asked of Toomi.

. The worry had gone from his voice but the confusion was still there.

'You escaped through the sewers, Doho,' Toomi said. 'If you could do that, could not other people use them to enter Gondar?'

Doho's face wrinkled as he tried to take in what Toomi was asking him.

'Yes,' he replied eventually. 'Of course they could. But only if they were like me, as small as I am. But you cannot think of taking Gondar like that. You would need an army of children – and children could not fight against the Acab and his men.'

'But if we had such an army,' Toomi went on, 'and if they could fight, you could tell them how to use the sewers?'

'Of course I could. There may be a thousand tunnels in Gondar, but I know them all. I have had a woman at the end of every one,' the dwarf said proudly.

Toomi glanced away from him and looked at Rachel. Rachel was watching her, puzzled.

'We do not have an army of children,' Toomi said. 'But we have enough and they can fight. The Wazan people, the pygmies, who found Farquarson. If they can open Gondar's gates, the army can do the rest.'

Rachel held the dwarf Doho in her arms.

For several minutes she was silent in thought. Then her heart began to quicken in excitement.

105

The council met again at midnight.

It was a very different gathering from the one earlier in the evening. Then the mood had been apathetic and listless, almost despairing. Now everything had changed. The atmosphere was charged with excitement and hope. Glancing round, Jamie could see the difference on every face.

The pallor had gone from Rachel's cheeks and her eyes were bright. Mamkinga had thrown off the sullen resignation and anger which had clung round him before. He listened eagerly as the others talked. Hadji was striding up and down. The exhaustion had dropped away from him and his shoulders had lifted. Even the captains looked resolute and confident again.

'And you are sure they can do it?' Hadji said to Toomi.

Toomi nodded. 'I have talked long with the Wazan's leader. He is content. They are warriors and ready for battle. If we succeed I have promised him salt and corn for every man and his dependants as long as they live. I will go with the Wazan. Doho says I am slim enough to travel through the drains. The dwarf has told us all we need to know about where they run.'

'We will attack tomorrow in the dark before the dawn,' Hadji said. 'The Wazan will be in two groups. They will open the south and west gates when the dog star is in the moon's shadow. Outside the west gate I will be waiting with one half of the army. Mamkinga will lead the other half through the south gate – '

Hadji glanced at Mamkinga. 'I will be ready,' Mamkinga said.

'We will come together at the palace,' Hadji went on. 'The dwarf says Culembra has his lair there. Where the Acab Saat has based himself inside the town, it seems no one knows. But we must find him and kill him. Until we have done that the task is not completed – '

Hadji paused. He looked now at Rachel.

'You are the tree of spring from which all our forest grows,' he said. 'But as it was with Mamkinga and Toomi in Malinda, so it is with you here in Gondar. The Acab Saat, Culembra, the Galla, they have all their world to lose. Even if we storm the gates, the fighting will be fierce. We cannot risk that they should cut you down. You will enter as Gondar's queen when the battle is over.'

Rachel was silent. She lifted her head and looked at the tent's roof. Her eyes seemed to pierce the hide awning to gaze at the stars beyond.

'I have been trained as a soldier all my life,' she said. 'Not to fight now for my people and my kingdom would be to betray everything I have been taught to believe in. Yet I know what you say is true. I am Gondar's queen. There is none to follow. Until the river has given me a child, I must live – '

Rachel looked down.

Watching her, Jamie saw that her face was anguished. She wanted desperately to fight beside the others. Yet Rachel knew her life was too vital to Gondar to be put at hazard.

'I will make a bargain,' Rachel went on. 'A bargain with myself and my people and with you who are here with me. I will enter Gondar by the river's womb, as Gondar's kings and queens have always come to the city. The Acab Saat has sealed the passage down to the cavern in the grounds beside the palace. Doho has told me so. Storm the gates, take the city, open the passage to the cavern. Leave me the palace – '

Rachel paused.

'The palace is mine. I will return to it as queen and take it back with my own sword.'

Hadji was silent for a moment. If the gates fell and

Gondar was taken, the chief dangers to Rachel should have passed. Whether they had or not, Hadji knew he could not argue with her.

Hadji shrugged. 'Very well,' he said. 'I will go there straight from the gate and open the passage myself.'

'There is one thing more,' Rachel said. 'Jamie has ridden with us from the start. I wish him to accompany me.'

Jamie frowned. Then he burst out in protest.

'I rode with ye to help ye win Gondar back,' he said. 'There's fighting to be done now. That's where I'm needed, up where the swords clash. Not skulking beside ye in the bowels of the earth. Any servant can look after ye there.'

Rachel turned and gazed at him. Her eyes were as dark and deep as the moonless mountain sky.

'You are in Gondar,' Rachel said quietly. 'You stand before Gondar's queen. You will do as I say.'

Jamie looked at Mamkinga for support. Mamkinga was staring at the ground. Deliberately he avoided Jamie's eyes.

Jamie swore under his breath. He unbuckled his sword. Jamie threw it at Rachel's feet and strode from the tent.

Seething with anger, Jamie walked back to his own tent. Farquarson was waiting for him inside. Curtly Jamie told him what had happened. Seeing Jamie's distress, the little Scot clapped an arm round his shoulder in sympathy.

'Don't fash yourself overmuch, Jamie,' he said. 'By the day after tomorrow you may well be shovelling earth on top of me, and thanking the merry Lord He's chosen you for other tasks.'

Jamie looked at him in astonishment. 'You're not intending to go with them?'

Farquarson grinned sheepishly. He ran his hand through his thinning sandy hair and wandered to the far side of the tent.

'Those wee savages, the Wazan, they saved my life,' he

said. 'I owe them a modest quittance for the commodity. I've never been one for heroics, but maybe a gun judiciously levelled tomorrow can help square the account. I'll be with Hadji outside the western gate.'

Jamie stared at Farquarson for a long time. Finally his anger drained away and he burst out laughing. Jamie shook the little Scot by the hand.

'We have travelled far together,' Jamie said. 'Now as we come to the nub of the business, ye, the dilettante, will be in the thick of things while I will be penned underground like a rabbit in the dark. Let us drink to the guid Lord's sense of humour and that He laughs enough to let us drink together again.'

There was a jug of wine on the low table. Jamie filled two horn tumblers. He and Farquarson lifted the tumblers and drank to tomorrow.

106

'Here,' Doho whispered back over his shoulder. 'The path slants to the right. Grip the boulders on either side and follow me.'

The dwarf scrambled upwards.

Behind him Rachel began to climb again. Jamie wiped his face. In spite of the height and the cool night air he was sweating. He blinked and peered up into the darkness. He waited until Rachel was securely balanced on the next ledge. Then he continued upwards too.

It was two hours after sunset.

The attack on the gates was due to take place in the early hours of the morning. By now under the cover of darkness everyone would be moving into their positions. The two parties of Wazan pygmies would be approaching the drains that funnelled up into the city near Gondar's western and southern gates. Toomi was with them. Hadji, accompanied by Farquarson, was circling the walls towards the western gate at the head of half their forces. Mamkinga was making for the southern gate.

If all went well the pygmies would attack the gates from inside the walls at the same moment. They would overwhelm the guards and haul the great hardwood doors open. Hadji's and Mamkinga's soldiers would pour in and take the Galla by surprise. In early morning blackness they would surge through the city to the palace, and Gondar would be theirs.

If all went well. Jamie gritted his teeth and climbed on.

Jamie had put his bitterness behind him. The insult he felt at being denied the chance to take part in the assault still cut him to the quick. So did Mamkinga's silent refusal to come to his support. They would rankle, Jamie guessed, for as long as he lived. But there were more important matters at hand. Rachel was Gondar's queen. However much she meant to him, to her kingdom she was beyond price.

At least Jamie would be with her, at least he could help to protect her, when Rachel entered her city.

Jamie stretched for a boulder and pulled himself up again. Above him he could hear Doho whisper encouragingly to Rachel as the dwarf scrambled on. Doho amazed Jamie. The dwarf's spirit was indomitable. Twenty-four hours earlier the tiny figure, beaten and bruised and gasping, had seemed on the point of death. Somehow he had recovered. When he learned that Rachel was going to enter Gondar through the ancient caverns in the cliff, Doho had insisted he was her guide.

'Is there anyone else who can lead you up through the rocks?' Doho demanded. 'No one, I can tell you, no one! Nor if there was would he have the right to bring his queen back such as I have —'

Doho brushed the white hair from his sunken and bruised face, and stretched out his misshapen body on the couch where he was lying.

'You need me, little princess,' he said. 'You need me now as you needed me when I sat you on your pony Armit and taught you to ride. As much as when I carried you down from the owl's nest in the crag. Only I know the caverns where the river runs. Only I can take you home.'

Rachel had looked down at him.

Doho was seeing her, she knew, not as the woman she had become but as the child he remembered. It did not matter. Doho was right. Only he and perhaps a few other old servants in the palace who had attended her mother and her grandmother too, knew the labyrinthine twistings and turnings of the river's passage through the rock.

'You shall guide me,' Rachel said quietly. 'Now sleep, Doho.'

Doho had slept with a smile on his lips. When he woke

he was a man changed, a man rejuvenated. The beatings, the torture, the nightmares of the months in the Acab Saat's cells, belonged to the distant past.

Doho had the greatest task of his life to perform. He had his queen to lead back to her home.

'Now there is no more difficulty – '

Jamie heard the dwarf's voice above him again. He clambered over another shelf of rock and found himself on level ground. Jamie clambered to his feet and walked forward.

Until then there had been the faint glow of starlight above and behind him. Suddenly the darkness was impenetrable. Jamie realized he had entered a cave in the cliff face. He waited. There was the scrape of a flint, and a torch flared.

Jamie blinked and peered round.

He was in a chamber hollowed out of the rock. From somewhere ahead he could hear the sound of falling water. Rachel was a few yards in front and Doho, with the torch in his hand, further ahead still. Their escort, fifty of what Hadji had decided were the best and most reliable soldiers who had joined the campaign, blocked the chamber's mouth behind Jamie.

Doho beckoned.

The dwarf disappeared into a tunnel that led upwards. Rachel set off behind him. Jamie followed.

They climbed for what to Jamie seemed like an eternity, although he knew that in the meandering darkness of the caverns time was impossible to measure. They passed through great vaulted grottos. They crawled along low passageways. They came suddenly into caves where the echo of their footsteps chimed like bells off the rock, and the light of Doho's blazing torch was not strong enough to reach the roof.

Occasionally Jamie glimpsed paintings drawn on the rocky walls.

There were hunting scenes, groups of warriors gathered round a kill, the representation of a fire, stiff elongated animals streaming away across a plain. In almost every scene there was the childlike figure of a woman in a blue robe. The blue of the robe had faded with the years and the damp, but the woman was somehow familiar. Each time, Doho's torch moved on round another bend in the rock before Jamie could recollect her face and remember where he had seen her last.

Jamie shook his head, puzzled, and hurried on.

Finally the dwarf stopped. He raised the torch and looked back. They had reached a large and airy chamber in the cliff. The night air was fresh on their faces and the sound of falling water was louder than at any time since they'd entered the caverns.

'Beyond is the chamber of Sheba,' Doho said. 'Above that are the caves that lead to the palace grounds. You would do well to rest here where the winds blow and it is cool. I will continue to the cave below the palace. When Hadji unseals the entrance I will return to bring you up.'

'Are there tapers in Sheba's chamber?' Rachel asked.

Doho nodded. 'There are always tapers.'

'Light them for me, Doho.'

As the dwarf scuttled on, Rachel turned to the soldiers who had gathered behind her. She ordered them to remain where they were until she summoned them. Then she looked at Jamie.

'You too will stay here until I call for you,' she said. 'Then you will come to me.'

Rachel vanished up the passage behind Doho.

Jamie settled down to wait. He had no idea how long he waited but eventually he heard his name being called distantly from somewhere ahead. He stood up. The soldiers were squatting on the ground round him. Jamie stepped between them and walked forward. For a time the passage was in darkness and he had to feel his way with his hands. Then he saw a gleam ahead. The gleam grew brighter as he approached it.

Jamie turned a corner in the passage. Light suddenly flooded over him, and he stopped, momentarily blinded.

He had come out into another cavern, into what he

knew from Doho must be Sheba's chamber. The cavern was vast. It was lit by thirty or forty torches ranged round the dark walls, their flares darting among the crystals embedded in the rock. The roof, high-vaulted as a cathedral, reached into darkness. At the far end of the chamber a stream jetted out from a tumble of boulders and fell foaming into a pool. The water swirled among clusters of golden lilies and then vanished somewhere underground.

Standing beside the pool was a young woman.

She wore a long gown of sheer blue silk. It swirled round her body like the morning mist that clung to the high snowdrifts on the Mountains of the Moon. Jamie stared at her transfixed. Suddenly he knew why the woman in the rock paintings on the walls had been so familiar. She was the young woman who had come to him in his vision in Iona's royal graveyard so long ago.

Warily Jamie stepped forward.

He saw that the young woman was Rachel. When she left him she had been wearing the leather riding cloak and flared trousers of a royal Abyssinian horseman, the uniform she had worn from the day they entered Gondar. Now Jamie realized that not only Rachel and the young woman who had appeared out of the Hebridean night but also the queen in the flaking paintings were one and the same.

Jamie crossed the cavern's floor. He leapt the stream and stopped before her on the bank. Rachel held out her hands. She smiled.

'You have seen me in all manner of guises,' she said, 'from the Arab youth on the banks of the Benoue to the dust-stained traveller of our journey. I wished you to see me as I can also be. I am a queen. I am also a woman.'

Jamie stared at her. Then he glanced round. The torchlight sparkled off the falling water and the stream's murmur was like a song.

'It is here where the river is born?' Jamie asked.

Rachel nodded.

'We call it the river of life,' she answered. 'Between

746

here and the sea the river feeds all of creation – all that walks or runs or crawls or flies or swims. Before Sheba and since Sheba, it has always been so. Many other rivers join to serve it. The greatest, they say, rises further to the south still. I do not know. I know only that this is the true river and that men have always sought to find where it was born and you are the first of your race to know – '

Rachel paused. 'When you told me you were searching for its birthplace, I knew I could give you what you sought. I also knew I would have to give you myself. I and the river are the same.'

Jamie was silent. Rachel's long hair gleamed as dark and shining as the rocks down which the water flowed.

'I am the river's child,' she continued. 'From the beginning, Gondar's rulers have been sired by the river. Gondar's queens have always come down here to Sheba's chamber where the great queen lay with Solomon. The river takes many forms and the wise king of the Israelites was only one of them. I too was sired here – '

Rachel stopped again.

She gazed at Jamie with the dark candid eyes that had held him spellbound from the moment he first saw her face across the fire after the great storm on the Benoue.

'When you searched for the river,' Rachel smiled gently at him, 'you were searching for me. And I and the river sought you. We have found each other.'

She let go of his hands and stepped back. A moment later she reached down. She caught the hem of the shining blue robe and lifted it lightly over her head.

Rachel stood in front of him naked.

In her hand she was holding a white flower, a single acacia blossom on its stalk of thorns. For an instant Jamie closed his eyes. The great river and the young woman before him seemed to blend into one overpowering sense of desire in his mind and blood. Jamie opened his eyes again. He saw the smile on her lips, the golden sheen on her skin, her up-tilted breasts, her long slender legs with the soft curve between them.

Jamie caught her in his arms.

He kissed her as fiercely as on the night when they lay together on the cold star-strewn hillside after the battle in Malinda. Then Rachel had pushed him gently away. Her kisses now were as hungry and passionate as his. Jamie knew she would never turn him away again.

They dropped slowly to the bank at the water's edge. Together they lay on the soft green grass, cool and damp against their burning skin. Their arms twined round each other like the strong roots of the heather. In Jamie's nostrils Rachel's body seemed scented with herbs like the wild thyme on the hill.

Her breasts were firm and yielding under the press of his body. Jamie sensed them binding together thigh to thigh like silver salmon joining in a soaring leap as they mounted a cascading waterfall, their mouths touching and tasting as sweet as the dew-laden sphagnum moss on Iona's moors.

Behind and beyond their interlaced bodies, the waters of the source of the Nile rustled and flowed inexorably onwards. The child of the river had become the river itself. Jamie tossed and surged in its depths.

When at last it was over, Jamie lifted himself above her. As he did he felt a tiny stab in his leg. Jamie glanced down. Rachel traced the fine line of blood with the tip of her finger. She touched it to her lips and smiled.

It was only one of the thorns on the stem of the acacia blossom.

107

Toomi paused and raised her head.

She was three-quarters of the way up the cliff. It was a brilliant star-filled night. High above she could see the black imprint that the city's walls made on the sky. The walls turned this way and that, following the contours of the rock. Above the fretted line of their battlements were the distant constellations. Below, there were circles and oblongs of warm golden light and the occasional wavering flare of a torch on an open terrace.

Toomi glanced to her right.

Pota, the pygmies' chieftain, had been following behind her up the narrow zig-zagging path. Now he climbed to her shoulder, pulling himself up on the tufts of wiry grass that had colonized the almost sheer face of the cliff. Further down in a silent ant-like chain were his men. Each of them was armed with a short stabbing sword, a hunting bow and a quiver of poisoned arrows. The pygmies, black-skinned and wearing only dark leather aprons, were invisible in the darkness.

Pota raised his face to the night air and flared his nostrils, sniffing the light wind.

'Avala,' he whispered.

He lifted the fingers of one hand and pressed them towards his thumb until only a tiny space separated them. Pota had picked up the smell of the drain. They were very close.

Toomi climbed on.

Fifteen minutes later she smelt the drain herself. In Gondar drainage smells were rare. The fierce sun and the action of myriad birds, animals and insects swiftly broke down any refuse. Someone must have thrown a load of rubbish into the drain after sunset. It had spilled out of the vent in the darkness. Beetles, grubs and insects would already be raiding it, but the smell was strong enough to reach Toomi's nostrils.

She heaved herself over a ledge and clambered on to a sloping funnel-shaped space of earth. It was the tip. The smell had vanished beneath the swirling scents of mountain wildflowers which had seeded in the fertile earth.

Pota scrambled up beside her. He peered upwards. Above them was a circle of blackness set into the cliff. It was the mouth of the drain. Moving like a spider, Pota climbed the shelf and vanished inside it.

'Monna! Monna!'

Pota's face reappeared from the drain. He whispered and beckoned Toomi towards him. As she crawled upwards, the shelf behind her filled with the small black shapes of Pota's men.

Toomi reached the drain's mouth and groped in the blackness with her hands. Her fingers touched the vertical plane of a step. Above it was another and then a third. The steps were dry. She pushed herself off the shelf, squeezed her head and shoulders into the drain, and began to climb. Above her she could hear Pota encouraging her upwards.

Thirty feet higher Toomi saw a square of starlight.

As she approached it the drain broadened behind her back. She heaved her body on to a platform and paused for a moment. The platform was beside a ventilation shaft. Beneath her the tunnel sloped away in thirty-foot sections. The blocks of stone were vast and immensely old, but the engineers who had constructed the system had been extraordinarily skilful. There was barely a trace of slime on the rock-falls and no more smell than on the shelf below.

'Monna!'

Pota was calling again. Toomi pushed herself off the platform and continued upwards. Below her she could hear the soft mice-like scrabble of the pygmies climbing behind.

Toomi had no idea how many sections she climbed.

It could have been fifteen, twenty, twenty-five. She lost all count in the effort of getting from one platform to the next. She would settle herself on one rock shelf, and rest panting for breath as she gazed at the tiny frame of stars. Then Pota would be urging her on again. Toomi would lever herself wearily up and go on.

Finally she felt Pota's hand on her head in mid climb. She stopped and twisted her face round to look up. Pota was poised above her. Directly above him she could see the sky. They were within feet of the drain's mouth in one of Gondar's streets.

Pota edged higher.

The silhouette of his head appeared outlined against a cone of light. It hovered there for an instant. Then he ducked and the silhouette vanished. Toomi heard the sound of voices. Shadows cut off the light, someone laughed, and a thick stench swept down the tunnel. Instinctively Toomi buried her face against her chest. A load of refuse came tumbling down. Bones struck her shoulders, vegetables splattered across her arms, urine and excrement cascaded over her body.

The shadows and the voices vanished. Pota peered up again.

'Vau! Vau!'

Pota was holding his finger to his lips. He gave a final wriggle and disappeared.

Toomi brushed off as much of the garbage as she could and followed. Her head came out above the lip of the tunnel. A wave of fresh air swept over her face, and she blinked in a sudden glow. A hand caught her wrist and tugged urgently. She half-fell head first off a circular stone platform and crouched in the shadow beneath. Pota was squatting beside her.

Toomi looked round.

They were huddled under the overhanging ledge of a fountain-like structure at the centre of a square lined with houses. It was exactly as Doho had described. The encircling buildings, the raised stone parapet on which the people of Gondar rested their buckets before tipping the contents downwards, the tapers burning at the square's corners.

Toomi could even see the dark narrow alleyways where Doho had taken his pleasures.

According to the dwarf the square was close to Gondar's southern walls. Toomi couldn't see the gate – it was hidden by a curving street – but she knew it must be near. She could hear the murmur of the guards talking and an occasional whiff of tobacco smoke drifted across her face.

The windows of several of the houses were lit by lanterns, but apart from a pack of scavenging dogs the square was deserted. As Toomi scanned the half-darkness there was a scuffing noise on the ledge above. A tiny black shape appeared and dropped soundlessly to the ground, then another and another until they became an unbroken black ripple.

Pota's men were emerging from the sewer.

The pygmies gathered round the fountain, spreading out until they covered the square for yards on either side. They waited as silently as a flock of roosting starlings.

Pota spoke to them in a whisper, gesturing as he talked. He made a signal and one of them slipped forward. Toomi recognized the pygmy's face. He was the leader of the second group, the group who would be attacking the west gate. Pota produced a circle of bone from the pocket in his apron. The bone, so fine it was translucent, had been shaved from the thigh bone of an elephant. The second pygmy had one too.

The two bone wafers were punctured with pinpricks. Each pinprick represented the position of a star or a planet. Held to the eye against the night sky, the discs were the pygmies' ancient timekeeping and navigational instruments. Pota checked that they were both using the same constellations to time their movements. Then he put his thumb to his mouth. He revolved his nail and blew softly. Across the square floated the churring call of a male mountain nightjar. Pota's lieutenant answered softly with the same call, but lower pitched.

The two men nodded and pressed their palms together. They were satisfied. They knew exactly the moment at which they would both attack and how they would communicate with each other.

The second pygmy stood up.

He was so small that even upright his head barely reached the stone ledge. He nodded to his group. They set off at a silent trot, heading in the direction that would take them to the western gate. Within seconds they had vanished. Pota touched Toomi's hand. They stood and Toomi towered over him as they moved to cross the square.

Pota took two steps. Then he stopped so abruptly Toomi almost tripped over him.

Toomi steadied herself. Pota raised his head and turned his ear towards the darkness ahead. Toomi strained her own ears. Faintly she could make out the sound of footsteps approaching from one of the alleyways.

Pota gave a low whistle and the pygmies vanished back into the shadow round the tunnel's mouth. Toomi knelt beside him again. As they watched a man came into sight. From his leather tunic and the sword at his waist he appeared to be a soldier. He had evidently been drinking. He lurched as he walked and the occasional slurred fragment of song lifted into the air.

For a moment it looked as if the man was making for the street that curled away to their right, the street that led to the gate. Then he turned and headed straight for them. Toomi tensed. The man came on, clutching his stomach. To her horror Toomi realized he had decided to vomit into the drain. It would bring him on top of them.

Toomi glanced frantically at Pota.

The pygmy raised his finger to his lips. He waited, utterly still, until the man was barely a yard away. Then he moved. In a single leap as swift and silent as a hunting cat, Pota sprang into the air. For an instant he seemed to hang level with the man's chest. Something flashed in the faint light. The man clutched his throat. He gurgled, and began to crumple.

As the soldier sank to his knees Pota caught him. The knife flashed again and suddenly there were three more pygmies at Pota's shoulders. They stripped the man of his sword. Then they heaved his body up on to the ledge and rolled it into the tunnel. There was a light thump as it hit the bottom of the first shaft. Afterwards there was silence again.

Pota wiped his knife on his apron and glanced round.

There was no one else in sight. He whistled and set off again. The whole incident had lasted only a few seconds. Closing her eyes briefly in relief, Toomi followed.

Moments later they arrived within sight of the southern gate. They rounded an angle in the curving street and the gates were immediately ahead across another smaller square. Pota didn't even need to whistle. The pygmies saw him check in mid stride. Like a flock of birds instinctively obeying the commands of a leader they dropped back into the shadows.

Pota and Toomi flattened themselves against the wall. Then they peered cautiously across the square.

108

The gates were set into Gondar's walls between twin towers.

Mounted on great hinges and supported by wheels, they were secured at the centre by an iron bar. For the gates to be opened the bar had to be raised and revolved until it was upright. Then the two wings had to be pulled inwards from the walls. They could be moved either by ropes fitted on pulleys or by the brute force of men's shoulders.

What Doho hadn't been able to tell them was the strength of the defenders the Acab Saat had posted to guard the gates.

Toomi scanned the scene.

At a rapid calculation they were faced by about a hundred men. Directly ahead were two groups of fifteen soldiers. Each group was responsible for one of the wings. They were supported by two more parties of the same number, waiting in reserve across the square. Then there were the towers. Toomi made a rough head count of the shadows which passed behind the torch-lit windows. There were at least another twenty soldiers in each tower.

Pota spread out both his hands and dabbed the ground ten times with his fingers, printing a shell-like abacus in the dust. Toomi nodded in agreement.

It would be the same at the other gate. At both gates one hundred of the Acab's best soldiers would be confronted by twenty barefoot and almost naked pygmies equipped only with their bows and short swords. Pota appeared undaunted. He slipped away.

Toomi was aware of his compact shadow flitting between the pools of darkness where his men had hidden themselves. Pota was giving his men their last-minute instructions.

Pota materialized at Toomi's side again, his face imperturbable. He felt in his waist pouch for the crescent of bone and held it up to the sky. Pota moved it gently from side to side until he had the pattern of stars he wanted revolving through the punctures. Then his lips moved rhythmically as he began to count.

'Dhu!' The sound was as soft as the wingbeat of a moth.

The moment had come.

Pota tucked the bone away. He put his thumb to his mouth and gave the nightjar's call. The call faded. There was silence. Then an answering call echoed distantly, it seemed to Toomi, far to their right.

The second call died away. Pota licked his lips. He waited for five beats that he tapped out with his hand. Suddenly he opened his mouth wide and screamed. The terrible howl rent the darkness. In the distance Toomi heard the echoes of another scream.

Pota erupted from the shadow. Behind him the Wazan, firing their bows and filling the air with their war screams, burst from their hiding places. Toomi was swept along with them.

At the gate there was an instant of shocked confusion. Then the soldiers panicked. Dawn was close, the night watch was almost over, the guards were tired and sleepy. They believed Gondar was impregnable. If the city were to be attacked at all, it could only be from outside the walls. Suddenly they found themselves attacked from behind, from Gondar's heart. And not merely attacked but overwhelmed by a tide of screaming black furies. The tiny squat figures, the murderous noise, and the whistling arrows were images from a terrible nightmare.

Most of the guards broke and ran. Their howls of terror mingled with the pygmies' shouts and added to the pandemonium. A few, too stupefied to run, drew their swords and out of some blind instinct tried to fight back. Instantly they became targets for the next volley of poisoned arrows. One by one they began to stagger and fall. In less than a minute the gate was undefended.

Pota reached the gate and whistled again. Shrill and piercing, the sound soared above the clamour. The Wazan separated into three bands and the second wave of the assault began.

Two of the bands encircled the towers on either side of the gate. Hiding themselves in the shadows across the little square, they began to rain arrows down on the battlements and through the windows. As they fired they kept up the fearsome screams. The arrows' tips were coated with the deadly toxins that had felled the guards below. The soldiers in the towers had seen what had happened to their fellows on the ground. Bombarded by the terrifying cries and the clusters of humming thorn-tipped fletches, they flung themselves face down below the parapet.

The third group raced for the gate itself.

The massive locking bar had to be raised from its horseshoe seats to allow the wings to push forward. Under Pota's direction five of his men threw themselves on the chain that lifted the bar, and began to haul. The others formed a human ladder from which the man on top could guide the bar clear of its mounts.

Toomi's eyes quartered the shadows, searching for movement. Behind her the grinding of metal told her the bar had begun to lift.

As the little men strained on the pulley the bar rose. It cleared the wide horseshoe mounts and hung wavering above them. The pygmies below began to push the two wings of the gate outwards. Normally the wheels on which all Gondar's gates were mounted were greased every night. Since the siege started they hadn't been touched. The wheels rolled an inch in their grooves and ground rustily to a halt. The two groups, the one on the pulley, the other using their shoulders, heaved again. They gained another inch. Then the wheels stuck again.

Toomi held her breath, her heart pounding and her ears straining into the darkness.

One inch more and it would be over. The bar would clear its metal seats and fall free. Whatever happened then the gates could be pushed open from outside. Toomi could already hear the shouts of Hadji's men beyond the walls. Pota's men gathered themselves for a final heave. They chanted, the pygmies hauling the pulley joined in, the gate wings started to grind back again.

As the pygmies gathered themselves for the final heave, the square was suddenly flooded with light and noise.

From every approach soldiers ran forward, blazing torches held high in their hands, spears flashing in every leather-bound fist. Toomi swung round on her heel, her short sword in her hand. She stiffened. The familiar monkey-skin cloaks which swung from the men's shoulders were the feared emblem of Culembra's body-guards. The Galla's king was at their head.

Culembra took in the scene at a glance.

The human ladder of the Wazan, momentarily frozen by the sudden blaze of light, heaved frantically at the bar. From outside the walls, Hadji's soldiers bellowed their encouragement. Culembra leapt forward.

All of Pota's men had put down their weapons to wrestle with the gates. Helpless now before Culembra's sword, they gave way. The human ladder collapsed. The pygmies rolled aside in the dust. As they did the bar began to teeter and fall.

Toomi threw herself out of the shadow and raced for the gates.

As the bar dipped back to the level of the mounts from which it had been painfully raised, Culembra's shoulder crashed against the gates. They juddered but instead of sealing they suddenly seemed to swing back towards him. A crack opened between them. At the same instant a pair of hands appeared through the gap at their top.

Slowly, their knuckles bloodied, the wrist muscles shaking with effort, the almost-crushed hands inched the gap wider. With a shock Toomi realized that the hands were pale and freckled. The bar settled on the iron brackets. It quivered. For an instant it could have fallen one way or the other. The straining hands gave an immense final push. The bar crashed down safely outside the brackets. Creaking and groaning with rust, the gates swung inwards.

The doors to Gondar were open.

As Hadji's soldiers shouldered the gates back and the torchlight poured into the darkness beyond the walls, a figure dropped down from the gates' top. It was Farquarson. The little Scot's hair was dank and his face was sheeted with sweat. His chest was heaving and his arms were trembling, but he was grinning.

'Pota!' he called as Hadji's men began to surge past him. 'Where's Pota?'

The pygmies' leader had been slashed by Culembra's maddened sword blade. He was crouched in the lee of the gate, his arms clenched over the gaping wound in his belly where the sword had caught him.

Farquarson ran forward and knelt by Pota's side.

'Pota!' Farquarson gently touched his face. 'Don't worry, old fellow. I did that just for you. We Highlanders must look out for each other.'

Toomi was still watching them.

She had forgotten about Culembra. The Galla's king had retreated from the gates and gathered his bodyguards round him as Hadji's soldiers swarmed through. Now, enraged once more as he saw the white man who had breached his kingdom, Culembra charged the tide of the incoming forces again.

He cleaved his way through Hadji's soldiers until he was standing above the still-kneeling Farquarson. Culembra lifted his sword. Howling like the wild dogs from whose hunting grounds his people came, Culembra stabbed his sword down into Farquarson's neck. The little Scot fell forward and died on Pota's chest.

As Farquarson collapsed Toomi shook her head, dazed. Her own sword was still in her hand. She raised it and ran towards Culembra.

Toomi burst through the press of the soldiers.

Her eyes were on the Galla king's face. Culembra saw her coming. He stared wildly at her. In Culembra's own eyes Toomi saw all the horror and disorder which had lain like a bleak and suffocating shadow over her years with Tamule. Culembra had taken the simple peasant woman and turned Tamule into a monster in his own image. Toomi had survived like a stunted plant deprived of the spirits' rain under the dark skirts of Culembra's creation.

Toomi raised her sword and slashed at Culembra.

Culembra parried the blow and hit back with manic force at her. Toomi warded off his thrust, but she was standing in the pool of blood that was flowing from Farquarson's neck. She slipped and fell to her knees. Culembra lifted his sword again.

Culembra lunged and buried the blade in Toomi's body.

As Culembra struck, Hadji appeared on his horse through the gate. His eyes swept the scene in front of him. He saw his own soldiers surging forward. He saw the occasional tiny black figure of the Wazan pygmies swept along like flotsam on surf among them. He saw the guttering torches and the fleeing Galla guards. Then he saw Toomi lying on the ground with Culembra standing above her.

Hadji narrowed his eyes.

Furiously he spurred his horse on, threading his way between the soldiers. Hadji was carrying a spear. As he reached the Galla's king he drove it deep into Culembra's chest. Culembra was lifted by the spear's thrust and thrown backward until his weight brought Hadji's charge to a halt.

Hadji dismounted with the king's body beneath his feet. He threw his horse's bridle to one of his soldiers and ran back to Toomi. She was still alive. Hadji gathered her in his arms and held her to him.

'Find my sister,' Toomi whispered. 'Tell her the gates are open and Gondar is hers again.'

Hadji nodded. 'I will,' he said quietly.

'Tell her, although you have no need, that I love her,' Toomi went on. 'I love her and my brother Mamkinga, and Jamie, the white man, the newfound brother to us all. Give them all an embrace from my heart. Tell Jamie that his friend, the little one with the marks on his face, died valiantly. Without him there would be no victory.'

'I will tell them as you say,' Hadji answered. His eyes blurred as he looked down at her.

'And for you, Hadji,' Toomi whispered. 'We had our time. I held you in my arms and slept by your side. Take my heart back with you to Quilombo. Plant it there and gather the flowers that grow round it. They will be my heart, they are yours.'

For a moment Toomi gazed up at the sky. Then her head slipped to one side and she lay still.

Gently Hadji lowered her to the ground. He got to his feet. His soldiers had gathered in a circle round him. They were standing shoulder to shoulder in ranks that stretched back to the edge of the square. Their faces were sombre and the points of their drawn swords were resting in respect on the dust.

'To the palace!' Hadji shouted. 'She will not sleep in peace, nor these brave Wazan who fell with her, until Gondar is wholly ours!'

109

Outside the other gate, at the southern entrance to Gondar, a twisting track ran up the steeply shelving hill flank that lifted to the walls.

Mamkinga stood by the head of his horse on the slope below.

The horse lifted its head. It flared its nostrils nervously against the night air. Mamkinga patted the animal's neck comfortingly. The horse's bridle had been silenced with plaited ribbons of cotton, and its iron-shod hoofs muffled by wrappings of woven hemp. The other half of the forces that had rallied to the standard of Gondar's queen-empress were gathered round Mamkinga in the darkness.

At first it seemed the southern gate would be easier to storm than the western one. The guards, a detachment of Culembra's mountain men, had found a cache of fermented honey wine in one of the storehouses beneath the tower. Unused to the strong liquor, they were in no state to fight back when the fierce little Wazan attacked. The few Galla who escaped the initial slaughter ran dizzily away into the darkened streets.

Pota's lieutenant, Haik, crept up the stairs into the watchtower. A lone soldier slumbered in one corner. Haik slid his knife expertly between the man's ribs. The soldier died without waking.

Haik leaned over the parapet. In the shadow of the wall, light glinted on metal as Mamkinga and his men moved quietly into position.

'Dhu, brother!' Haik called softly.

Mamkinga stared up into the shadows against the

night sky. 'We have the watchtower,' Haik went on. 'Now we go for the gate.'

Haik ran back down the narrow stairs, wiping his knife on his loincloth.

Back in the courtyard, he examined the great iron-studded gates. Unlike the western gates they were barred not only by two heavy wooden poles, but also by a massive chain secured to the stone pillars of the gateway and held in position by a huge padlock. Each link of the chain was as broad as a man's arm.

The poles came easily out of their cradles. Haik ordered two groups of the pygmies to push them through the chain, and use them as crowbars in an effort to part one of the links. For an eternity of precious seconds, the Wazan heaved and strained at the unyielding metal. Then one of the poles suddenly snapped.

Frustrated and powerless, Mamkinga listened intently with his men outside the gates.

Mamkinga knew they had minutes at most before the alarm was raised. A thin crescent moon came out from behind a wisp of cloud. In its light the mortarless stones of the tower sprang into relief. Mamkinga peered upwards. With a quick surge of hope, he glimpsed triangular dark shadows etched at intervals in the stone. The ends of the beams which supported the tower's staircase protruded slightly from the wall. It was just possible they might provide a ladder to the parapet.

Tossing away everything except for his sword and his leather jerkin, Mamkinga leapt upwards and began to climb.

The exposed ends of the beams were so narrow that Mamkinga had to support his entire weight on his fingertips and his toes. The strain made every muscle in his body quiver and ache. At almost every step he thought his grip would slip, and he would plunge downwards. Somehow as he climbed all the strength and agility he had honed in the goldsmith's workshop seemed to flood back into his limbs.

Slowly Mamkinga inched his way upwards. Finally,

sweating and trembling, he heaved himself on to the parapet. He stood up and gazed down inside the walls.

The streets radiating away from the square below were still dark and empty. Across the roofs to the west Mamkinga could hear the clamour of the battle for the other gate. His mind churning, Mamkinga thought for a moment. Then he threw himself down the stairs. As he reached the ground Haik swung round to greet him. The pygmy's teeth were clenched with frustration.

Haik's men were still heaving frantically at the remaining pole, but the great links of the chain refused to yield. Haik shook his head grimly.

As Mamkinga stared at the pygmies his mind went back to Ndele's workshop. Once more Mamkinga saw himself struggling to weld the little golden nipples to the tiny statuette of the woman. Time and again the hot iron had seared through the shining body.

'Break up the poles!' Mamkinga ordered. 'What will not yield to force will yield to fire.'

Swiftly, under Haik's direction, the Wazan's knives splintered the poles into kindling. Mamkinga piled the tinder round the base of the great wooden gates. The clamour from the western walls was rising. Mamkinga lifted his head and listened. The shouts were coming closer.

Haik squatted down beside him. The pygmy pulled a flintstone from the leather pouch at his waist, and struck it against Mamkinga's sword blade. A shower of sparks sprayed over the wood and a flame crackled upwards.

At the same moment, the first of the Acab Saat's white-cloaked guards erupted into the courtyard.

As the fire began to eat into the dry wood of the gates, the Wazan turned and hurled themselves at the guards who were streaming forward from every side now. Calmly Mamkinga swung back to the flames. He stripped off his heavy hide jerkin and wrapped it round his arm. Bracing his foot against the stone doorjamb, he started to heave at the red-hot links.

The heat of the chain burnt through the leather. The

smell of scorching flesh, his own flesh, filled Mamkinga's nostrils. He disregarded it. Mindless too of the pain, he threw his weight on the chain again, the sole of his foot no longer braced against the stone but on the glowing metal itself. His long years in Ndele's forge told Mamkinga the links were close to breaking point.

The Wazan were giving way before Salama's soldiers and retreating in a ring towards him. A spear scythed past Mamkinga's shoulder and buried itself in the burning wood. A pygmy crumpled and died at his feet. The air rang with screams and war cries and the clash of swords. Still Mamkinga strained against the metal cordon. His muscles stood out in great rippling knots and sweat showered off him.

Suddenly there was a soft wrenching hiss and the chain snapped. His hair charred and his body singed with heat blisters, Mamkinga reeled back. The gates burst apart and the men outside poured through.

Mamkinga steadied himself.

He ripped two pieces of leather off what remained of the smouldering jerkin, and used them to grip the now-free length of chain. Then, dragging his injured foot behind him, Mamkinga sprang forward. Whirling the still-glowing links around his head, he began to lash out at Salama's soldiers.

The metal flail glittered and whistled in the firelight. Slashing through the air at the end of Mamkinga's great arms it cut down the guards in groups of two and three, searing flesh and crushing bone. Faced with the terrible weapon and the giant who wielded it, Salama's men checked. The Wazan, in full retreat by then, rallied behind Mamkinga.

Mamkinga surged on.

Before him the guards wavered and began to give way. He beat them down as if he were scything wheat at the summer's end on the common outside Malinda. The pygmies' arrows whirred past his head and their victory screams lifted again. Suddenly the enemy soldiers broke and ran.

As they fled, for an instant Mamkinga found himself face to face with a heavily built man in a white robe. Mamkinga glimpsed a fierce predatory nose and cold fanatical eyes above a golden cross. The man must have been at the centre of the fighting. His robe was torn and stained dark, and the sword in his hand ran with blood.

Mamkinga raised the chain to strike him down. As he lashed out, the man turned and vanished. The heavy links clattered harmlessly against the earth. Heaving and panting, Mamkinga stared into the empty darkness.

The man in the white robe, Mamkinga realized with a shock, could only have been the Acab Saat.

It was an hour before Mamkinga and his soldiers joined forces with the others who had stormed the west gate.

The fighting at the two gates had been fierce and bloody, but both had fallen to the attackers. Now the Galla were in retreat and the armies of Gondar were sweeping victoriously through the town. Hadji had ridden with his men to the royal park and opened the entrance of the tunnel that led down to the caverns. Doho led Rachel and Jamie out.

Followed by Rachel's bodyguards they ran across the park towards the palace, ready to storm it at sword point. News of Culembra's death had already reached his garrison there and his soldiers had fled. Now Rachel was standing with Hadji and Jamie under the torchlight in the forecourt.

'Salama was at the head of his men when we broke through the gate,' Mamkinga said as he came up to them. 'I saw him there myself. When he saw we were too strong for them he disappeared. We have searched everywhere. There is no trace of him – '

Mamkinga leaned panting on the cross-haft of his huge sword. He gestured at a prisoner his soldiers were holding.

'We caught this one hiding in an alley near the gate. One of my men says he saw him standing behind the Acab in the fighting. I have beaten him but he will not tell us where the priest has gone to ground.'

Hadji swung round towards the prisoner.

The man was a smooth-skinned Abyssinian with an intelligent face, bloodied now after the blows Mamkinga had struck him, and tightly curled greying hair.

'Who is he – ?' Hadji began but Doho interrupted him.

'I know the creature well,' Doho said. 'His name is Jacob. He is Salama's personal servant.'

'His servant? Then if anyone knows where Salama has gone, it will be him –'

Hadji pulled out his dagger. He gripped Jacob's hair and jabbed the dagger's point against his neck.

'Speak!' Hadji shouted. 'Tell me where the Acab is, or you die now.'

The prisoner stared back at Hadji with an expression of fatalism and defiance. He remained silent.

In frustration Hadji pressed the dagger harder. It lanced Jacob's skin. Blood began to flow down his throat, but still the man refused to speak.

'Wait!' Rachel called out. 'Let me talk to him.'

Hadji moved aside as she stepped forward.

Rachel gestured to the men who were holding Jacob to let him go. The soldiers stood back. Exhausted, Jacob fell to his knees.

'Look up at me,' Rachel said.

Jacob slowly raised his face. He recognized her and his gaze turned from bewilderment to terror.

'The Acab said you were dead,' he whispered. 'That an imposter had come to deceive us.'

'Kiss my hand,' Rachel commanded.

She held out her hand. Jacob bent his head and touched her fingers with his lips.

'You see, I am not dead. My flesh is living,' Rachel went on. 'Nor am I an imposter, for you have known me all my life, Jacob, and you know me now. I am your queen. I am Gondar. I am head of the Acab's church, but I am older and stronger than the church or the Acab. I am the river's child. Tell me what I need to know.'

'I will tell you all – '

Tears ran down Jacob's cheeks and he spoke between choking sobs.

The Acab Saat's servant was not a brave man except in his loyalty to his master. There Jacob was unflinching. He had been loyal to Salama ever since he was a youth and he would have died readily rather than betray him. But Jacob had a greater loyalty. He was a citizen of Gondar. Its earth and streets and water were his ancient home.

Gondar's river was his mother and its child his queen. To her he could deny nothing.

'The Acab has gone to the old fort.'

'The old fort?' Surprise crossed Rachel's face. 'It is a ruin.'

Jacob shook his head. 'No longer. After the battle when the Acab took Gondar and you escaped, he had it rebuilt. He feared Culembra, he feared most of all that you might come back and the people rise against him. So he made a fortress for himself. It is now the strongest citadel in the town.'

'But what good will it do him?' Rachel asked. 'We have taken Gondar back. We hold the city. I can starve him out of the fort. It needs only time.'

'The Acab believes time is on his side,' Jacob answered. 'His armies outnumber yours. Most of his forces were away when you attacked. He has called them back. Soon they will be here again. If he is alive to lead them when they return, he believes he will defeat you whether you hold Gondar or not. And in his fortress he knows you cannot touch him.'

'You know all this from the Acab himself?' Rachel said.

Jacob nodded. 'Together with Murabit, his master of horse, I am his most trusted servant. As God is my witness it is true.'

'Take him away,' Rachel instructed the soldiers. 'Give him food and keep him safe. He has told the truth.'

As the soldiers led Jacob off, Hadji asked, 'Where is the old fort?'

'At the western end of the town,' Rachel answered. 'At the highest point of the cliff above the plain.'

'Take us there,' Hadji said curtly.

Rachel turned. Her bodyguards gathered round her, and they set off.

Striding beside Hadji, Jamie saw that his face was bleak and tense. Jamie knew all too well why. It was what they had all feared. Salama and his armies together formed a monster. The Acab Saat was the monster's head. Without him the monster was helpless, it lost its brain. But Salama alive and free was almost as powerful a symbol and rallying point as the queen.

If his armies returned to the city and the Acab was there to direct their assault on the walls, Gondar would become a killing yard for everyone who had joined the queen — including Rachel herself.

His face as sombre as Hadji's, Jamie hurried on.

Here and there flames licked a roof. In the first light of dawn, the flies would begin their attentions to the bodies huddled on the battleground by the gates. The stench of death hung in the air already. Soon the vultures would begin to circle overhead on the thermals of the morning.

The streets were full of fearful scurrying figures. Mothers clutched their screaming children under tightly wrapped body cloths. Old men shuffled silently into doorways. A riderless horse, its broken reins tangled in flying hoofs and its jaw wide with terror, plunged from a dark alley. It careered wildly across the roadway, scattering people and howling dogs before it.

A small girl, too slow to escape, was caught between its flailing legs. She died instantly as the hoofs pounded down on her body. Crazed with fear, the horse galloped on. A woman ran out of the shadows and knelt weeping above the tiny mangled corpse. Only a few yards away a dog whined and tugged in puzzled frenzy at the lifeless remains of its master.

A patrol of Rachel's soldiers, their torches flickering against the shuttered houses, erupted through an archway. They saw the hurrying group and drew their swords. Then they recognized the queen among the royal bodyguards and fell back respectfully. By the marketplace a group of Mamkinga's men had slaughtered an ox and were butchering it for the fire. The beast's discarded innards mingled on the earth with the debris of the battle.

A pack of half-wild dogs snarled and howled over the spoils from the carcass of a donkey which, stiff-legged and blank-eyed, blocked the shaft of one of Gondar's many wells. A pair of gaunt mules ploughed past. Behind them careened a watercart, its iron-ringed wheels spraying dust. A young boy clung to a pile of earthernware water jars. The driver's waist cloth was ripped and bloodied, and his fists were clenched tightly round the mules' reins.

As the group moved upwards through the town, the houses began to press in. The towering spur of rock on which Gondar was built rose and narrowed like the bows of a ship towards the west. Over the centuries buildings had spilt out from the centre of the spur towards its point. Finally the houses and the increasingly narrow alleys came to an end.

The bodyguards halted.

Ahead was a track along a ridge with the hillside falling sheer on either side. At the end of the track on a final soaring pillar of rock was a massive fortified tower, its foundations bedded like deep-set roots in the cliffs that plunged down beneath it.

Rachel gasped as she stared forward. 'It is the old fort,' Rachel said. 'I have known it all my life, but never like this. It was just a crumbling ruin.'

Hadji and Jamie came forward to stand at her shoulder. Hadji sucked in his breath.

'If it was a ruin,' Hadji said, 'it's been rebuilt brick by brick, and stone by stone. It's a citadel now.'

Mamkinga limped up and joined them.

The track running in front of them ended before an iron portcullis. Behind the portcullis was a second iron grille, equally massive. Beyond that, set in an arch, was a mahogany door studded with metal bolts. Above the door lamp light shone from windows, all of them protected by heavy bars. Many of the windows were arrow slits, angled to cover the ground where the track reached the portcullis.

Mamkinga rubbed his face grimly. He opened his mouth and closed it without speaking.

The same thoughts had been running through his mind as through the minds of the others. A frontal assault on the fort was out of the question. The soldiers would be cut down on the track before they could penetrate even one of the three defences. An attack from the sides was equally impossible. There was no means of approaching the fortress up the cliff walls that surrounded it. They could not even set it ablaze with torches strapped to arrows. The fortress was built of brick and stone.

'Do they have water?' Mamkinga demanded eventually.

'Gondar is built on the river's cradle,' Rachel answered. 'There are springs everywhere.'

'They will have water,' Hadji said bleakly. 'Salama would not have made it his eyrie otherwise. They have water and food and time to wait us out.'

Hadji cursed and kicked savagely at the ground. Dust rose as his foot struck the stone beneath.

Hadji swung his head, searching the darkness. There was nothing to see except the wheeling stars and the falling black folds of the cliffs. Daylight would yield nothing more except ravens soaring over the now-hidden crags. Salama had chosen his refuge with care. The old fort was impregnable except against time. Time was what they lacked.

'By the bones of my ancestors,' Hadji swore again. 'It would take the king of the eagles to pick the priest from that nest.'

110

As Rachel, Hadji and Mamkinga stood gazing at the fort in silence Jamie stepped back.

He slipped through the ranks of Rachel's bodyguards and walked to the edge of the track. A path sloped downwards along the flank of the ridge. Jamie followed it. Ten yards later the path came to an end above a precipice. Jamie stood and looked down.

Beneath him there was a drop of a hundred feet to a shelf which the inhabitants of the upper town evidently used as a dumping place for garbage. Jamie could hear the stir of scampering rats and a thin smell of refuse rose to his nostrils on the night wind. He glanced to his right. In the starlight he could see that the rock face was studded with lumps of granite. He stretched out his hand and touched the stone. It was rough and warm.

Jamie reached out with his other hand and felt the hold. With one foot anchored on the path he swung the other foot clear and probed for a ledge. He found one. He manoeuvred his foot into place until he was supporting himself with three points of his body. Then he began to move sideways along the face just below the rim of the track.

Half a minute later Jamie stopped. He retraced his steps. He put his foot on the path, pushed himself away from the granite outcrops, and walked back up to the track.

The others were still staring up at the dark outline of the fortress. They were silent and their faces were frowning and strained. None of them had noticed Jamie's disappearance.

'Get fifty of your best men,' Jamie said to Hadji. 'Bring them here and hold them ready just this side of the light.'

Hadji glanced at him in astonishment. 'What for?'

'I'm going into the fort,' Jamie said. 'I doubt the windows at the back will have bars on them. If I can get inside I'll open the doors for ye.'

'How can you get there?'

Jamie smiled. 'As a bairn I climbed the Griben cliffs for gulls' eggs more times than ye've ridden to war. I reckon I can climb the scarps of Gondar. Give me your sword.'

Hadji handed Jamie his sword.

Jamie buckled it on. He stooped, pulled the dagger from his stocking, and tucked it into his belt. He stripped off his leather jerkin, kicked away his riding boots, and removed his stockings. As a child he'd always climbed with bare feet. The soles of Jamie's feet weren't as leather-hard as they'd been then, but they were hard enough, he guessed. He trusted himself better with the old ways.

Jamie straightened up. He was wearing only tweed britches and a light shirt. If he'd had a kilt instead of the britches, he might have been climbing the Griben cliffs of his childhood again. He was ready.

He turned to find Rachel. The young woman had vanished.

'It is her kingdom,' Mamkinga said. 'She will climb with you. She has already started.'

Jamie glanced at the sloping hill flank behind him. Somewhere in the darkness he heard a pebble bouncing downwards over rocks. He looked back at Mamkinga. Their gaze met. They stared at each other, grim-faced and anxious.

'Go with the spirits,' Mamkinga said.

'I want the queen to sleep in peace in Gondar,' Jamie replied. 'If the spirits wish that too, they will climb with us.'

Mamkinga touched Jamie's forehead.

'Pula!'

Jamie gave Mamkinga the salutation in return.

Mamkinga, Jamie sensed, wished to say something more but the words would not come. The huge Malindan shook his head and limped away. Jamie turned to Hadji.

'My men will be waiting here in ten minutes from now,' Hadji said.

Jamie nodded.

He walked back down the path and swung himself out on to the rocks. Swiftly Jamie started to climb again. He did not see Rachel until he almost stumbled over her outstretched leg. The young woman was huddled back against the rock face only a few feet from the end of the path. She was staring down into the sheer drop below as if she were hypnotized.

Jamie put his arms round her. Rachel's shoulders were shaking and her hair was soaked with sweat. She stared up at Jamie, her eyes bright with terror.

'I am sorry,' she whispered. 'I wanted to climb with you, but I should have known. It happened to me once before when I was little and the eagle owl took my gazelle. Doho rescued me then.'

Jamie reached out and touched Rachel's forehead with his fingertip. Her skin was throbbing in fear. Gently he picked her up and carried her back to the path.

'May there always be men when you stand in need of them,' Jamie said. 'For now, reign as queen and leave the hill to me.'

Jamie turned back to the plunging wall of rock.

This time he moved with a steady deliberate rhythm. As before he kept three of his points anchored while he probed for a secure hold for the fourth. Then, fitting his speed to the surface of the traverse, he swung himself forward again.

At first it was simple and he moved quickly. He was working his way round Gondar's old foundation walls and the ledges in the ancient blocks were riddled with hand-and-foot holds. Then the walls ended and Jamie came out on to the open rock face. Within moments the spill of light from the track had vanished, and he was suspended silent and alone in the star-filled darkness.

Now it was much more difficult.

The fort was somewhere immediately above him. Jamie couldn't climb up and work his way round the fort's masonry for fear of being seen by a guard from one of the barred and lighted windows. Instead he had to circle the prow of the crag on which the fort was perched until he got to its far side. Only then could he tell whether, as he guessed, the pinnacle windows above the sheer fall to the plain had been left undefended.

The crag was formed of limestone. In places, where the limestone had been pitted and eroded by rain, it was almost as easy to traverse as the walls. But for most of the way the stone flanks were flat and unbroken. Sometimes Jamie had to search for minutes on end before finding some tiny crevice he could use. At others he had to turn back. He had to retrace his path, and try again from another angle or another level.

In spite of the coolness of the night air Jamie began to sweat.

Every muscle in his body ached. Several times, as he paused to gather his strength, he glanced down. The drop was terrifying. Beneath him for more than three thousand feet there was nothing. Even the village fires on the plain below were so small they might have been reflections of the stars. The wind swirled round him. An owl called softly from the crags. Fragments of stone clattered down, their sound fading long before they crashed against the earth.

Jamie climbed on. He was like a spider inching round the rim of a bottomless abyss. Never before in his life had he climbed as high and never at night. Yet in spite of the strain and tiredness and the dizzying void beneath, he felt calm, almost exhilarated.

Throughout the siege he had felt a growing and eventually humiliating sense of frustration. Rachel, Mamkinga, Toomi and Hadji were all deeply and actively involved, each of them had his or her part to play. Jamie did not. He was a stranger in a land not his own. Their war was not his war.

If anything the sense was made more acute by what had happened in the river's cavern.

He loved Rachel with a feeling that filled his entire being. He knew she felt the same. She had shown it by giving herself to him in Sheba's chamber. He longed to be able to offer her a gift in return, something as valuable as she had given him. For Rachel that could only be Gondar. Jamie had wanted above all to fight for the city. Instead with a heavy heart he had had to stand aside while the others went into battle.

Now everything had changed. Gondar's fate hung not on the siege or the storming of the gates, but on taking Salama's lair. And that only Jamie could do.

His exhaustion melted away. The wind raked through his hair, drying his sweat and cooling him. Beneath his confident fingers the limestone felt firm and safe. A nightjar, one of the mountain birds whose call the pygmies had used, churred close to his face and flew startled away.

Jamie laughed. Then he swung on.

Several minutes later he stopped and took his bearings. According to the pattern of the stars above him he had completed a half-circle traverse of the crag. The northern face of the fort should be immediately over his head. He began to climb up. Thirty feet higher his hands touched hewn stone blocks. Jamie climbed on. A gleam of light appeared. The light was obviously spilling out of a narrow window.

Gingerly Jamie pulled himself up to the window ledge and looked in.

The room was empty but to Jamie's surprise the window itself was barred. Other lights glowed above him. Jamie hauled himself further up the wall. All the lights inside came from tapers. The rooms were empty like the first, but to Jamie's increasing alarm all the windows were also barred.

Grimly Jamie climbed on. It seemed his guess had been wrong. The Acab Saat hadn't trusted in the defence of the precipice below the fort's northern wall. Out of paranoia he'd barred even the windows above the void. Jamie passed the second-but-last glow. He paused, panting, and glanced up. He was almost at the top of the fort.

He could see the saw-toothed rim of the ramparts against the sky. Only one last gleam of light remained between him and the stars. He wedged his foot in a crack and began to lever himself up. Then he stopped. Suddenly he could hear voices, coming from above. Jamie edged sideways along the run of the limestone blocks until the light was falling to his right. Then he cautiously climbed higher.

A moment later Jamie was peering into a room on the fort's topmost level.

It was a large attic room with a gabled roof. As Jamie stared through the window, relief cascaded over him. It had no bars. Inside the room was a rough-hewn table with a vellum chart spread out across it. Two figures were standing over the chart. One, an eager feline-looking young man with a slate in his hand, appeared to be a secretary. The second was short, broad-shouldered and stocky. He had bulging arms, a heavy moustache, and a brutal heavily scarred face with small unblinking eyes.

From Doho's description he was Murabit, Salama's master of horse.

A heavy curtain hung over the far end of the room. As Jamie watched, the curtain was abruptly pushed aside by the opening of a heavy brass-studded door behind it. The man who entered then could only have been the Acab Saat.

Gazing at him Jamie felt an icy knot form in the pit of his stomach. Salama was wearing a white robe and a cone-shaped white hat embroidered with a golden cross. A curved jewelled dagger was hanging from a cord at his waist. As a young man Salama must have been immensely strong. He still had a powerful body and his wrists were thick with muscle, but his neck had slackened and a heavy paunch distended the front of his robe.

What appalled Jamie, what provoked the coldness in his own belly, was Salama's face.

Stern and hawk-nosed, with hollow cheeks and restless fever-bright eyes, it was the most malign face he had ever seen — a face infected and wasted by sadistic madness. The madness was frenetic. Salama stabbed at the chart. He cursed the secretary. He swore at the impassive bull-like Murabit. He paced the room. He whirled round and strode back, talking unceasingly in a half-whispered mixture of oaths and instructions.

Jamie positioned himself more securely.

He leant forward, trying to hear what the Acab was saying. Salama was speaking in Malindan but so fast, in such a tangled torrent of words, Jamie found it impossible to understand. Suddenly Salama stopped. A smile spread over his face, a smile of extraordinary charm and warmth. He put his arm round Murabit's shoulder. For a few moments Jamie heard him clearly.

'I am sorry, old friend,' Salama said. 'That she-witch and the pirates she has bought with Gondar's stolen gold unbalanced my mind. But I was ready, never let it be said I was not, for her worst treachery. The armies are called back. It will be a matter of days only. We are secure here until their return. And when they return — '

The Acab Saat lifted his head and laughed.

'You will have pasture and horses, horses, mark me, Murabit, such as you have not dreamed of. And even you.' Salama turned to the secretary. 'What for you? Ten warehouses full of corn? A harem of young virgins? Twenty villages to pay you taxes? Whatever you wish, it will be yours. You have my word. And as for Ozoro Esther's dropping, this child of the river, I will do to her — '

The Acab Saat shook his head and broke off. Rage and incoherence overwhelmed him again.

In the darkness outside Jamie balanced himself on his toes.

The shock and coldness had gone. Jamie knew now that Salama was not only sick, ill with the insanity of a rabid dog. He was also cruel and violent and dangerous. He hated Rachel with a consuming hatred that passed all reason. While the Acab Saat lived neither Gondar nor its queen would ever be able to sleep in peace.

Jamie slipped the dagger from his belt. He balanced it in his hand, and tightened his fingers round its sharkskin handle. He scanned the room again, taking in the disposition of the three men and in a fraction of a second assessing them in terms of his own priorities. Then he gripped the window frame.

Jamie pivoted on his hips and leapt inside.

He landed on his hands and knees. The squat heavy-shouldered Murabit was nearest to him. Murabit's back was to the window. As Jamie jumped Murabit whirled round. Before Jamie could get to his feet Salama's bow-legged master of horse was crouching and reaching for his own dagger. Jamie knew Murabit would be the most dangerous of the three.

What Jamie hadn't anticipated was the speed of Murabit's reactions.

With the same momentum that had carried him through the window, Jamie gathered himself on his haunches. Murabit was facing him. His eyes were on a level with Jamie's and only inches away. His dagger was already in his hand. Jamie's dagger was held a fraction higher. He threw himself forward, driving the dagger before him and knocking aside Murabit's blade with his free hand. The blade entered Murabit's chest and Jamie's weight drove it in up to the hilt.

Murabit toppled sideways and died.

Before his body reached the floor Jamie had pulled the knife clear and leapt to his feet. Salama had pulled his own long dagger from its sheath and was backing towards the doorway. The secretary, dazed and frozen, hadn't moved. For the moment Jamie wasn't concerned with Salama. Jamie had drawn up his own order of battle. His priorities were graven on his mind as if on tablets of stone.

Salama's secretary was next.

The secretary was gazing at him, wide-eyed with shock and terror. Jamie put his free hand under the table. He upended it and hurled it forward. The table cannoned into the man's ribs. He reeled away and began to fall. The table had shattered under Jamie's assault. He vaulted the wreckage and stabbed downwards into the secretary's back. The man gave a scream as the dagger plunged into him. Then he collapsed, choking and moaning, on the floor.

Jamie withdrew the dagger again.

With one part of his mind Jamie felt sickened at what he'd done. With the other he knew he'd had no choice. Everyone who surrounded Salama was part of the man himself, was infected with the same terrible illness. Until the illness was rooted out and destroyed, no one would be safe.

Jamie jumped to his feet for the second time.

He kicked away the broken table and swung round to face Salama. To his bewilderment the Acab Saat wasn't there. The space on the floor where Salama had been standing moments before was empty. The door behind Salama had been closed until then.

Now it was swinging open.

— 111 —

Jamie gulped for air.

Behind the curtain through which the Acab Saat had first appeared the door stood ajar. Jamie slipped through it and pulled the door shut behind him. In the darkness he fumbled for the bolt, found it and shot it home. Above him the winding stair led upwards towards a faint patch of starlit sky.

Cautiously Jamie crept forward, all of his senses tingling with alertness. The wound across his knuckles was beginning to throb, but he barely noticed it. No door barred Jamie's way as he stepped out on to the ramparted roof.

At first sight the great turreted parapet which crowned the fortress was empty. Jamie's eyes quartered the moonlit walls.

'Who are you and what do you want of my kingdom?' The voice was low and close.

Jamie swung round. In the shadows beyond the entrance from the stairwell he could see a white-robed figure. It was the Acab Saat.

'My name would mean nothing to ye,' Jamie said softly. 'I come from far. There were long years in the making of my journey. I am here to see that the river's child sleeps quiet in her bed.'

Salama stared at him for an instant, his face shrouded in darkness.

Then he leapt across the space between them and slashed wildly at Jamie with his sword. Jamie raised his arm to parry the blow. The blade cut into his flesh. Jamie rocked back. Instinctively he raised his arm and licked at the blood that was beginning to pour from the wound. Salama was standing close to him. The Acab Saat was panting and his chest was heaving in frenzy.

Salama raised his weapon again. Jamie smiled. His other arm speared out and his clenched fist struck the flat surface of the descending blade. The sword spun away from Salama's hand. As it fell moonlight flashed from its silver hilt and sparks showered up from the rocks beneath.

Jamie faced the priest. 'Now we are equal,' he said.

Salama sprang at him.

His long fingernails raked the young Scotsman's face. Jamie recoiled for an instant. Then his fist jabbed out again. Salama staggered as the blow glanced off his jaw. Turning with the speed of a leaping gazelle, Salama jumped backwards.

A line of battlements curved away behind the Acab Saat's back. Springing from one to the other, Salama began to retreat. Jamie followed him. Far below him as he moved Jamie glimpsed the narrow causeway leading to the fortress gates.

When Jamie had stood on the causeway last – it was less than an hour ago although now as the sky began to pale overhead it might have been days – the precipitous path was deserted and the square beyond empty. Suddenly both the causeway and the square were thronged with people. Word of the appearance of Gondar's queen had reached the town's inhabitants, and they had streamed out of their houses to see her.

A huge rippling tide of figures filled what before had been the emptiness beneath. Jamie drew in his breath in astonishment as he glanced down. The crowd, churning and milling and shouting, filled the streets for as far as he could see.

The Acab Saat registered their presence at the same instant.

'Listen to me, people of Gondar – !'

Salama had positioned himself on the highest of the turrets that rose at intervals among the battlements. As he bellowed down, his white robes flared out round him and the golden cross at his neck glittered in the moonlight.

'An imposter walks among you claiming to be your queen! Disregard her for she is a monster of the night! With the dawn she will be gone! Heed only me as the leader of your church – !'

Salama raised the cross from his breast and swung it backwards and forwards across the darkness.

'To whoever listens to me, I promise salvation! Whoever ignores me will be damned and I hereby excommunicate them!'

Salama tore the cross from its chain and hurled it into the night air. As it fell, the surging crowd cried out and began to retreat in fear.

Suddenly there was a stir at the head of the causeway. Jamie peered down. A white horse appeared beneath them. On its back was Rachel. Riding bareback and wearing the turquoise leather cloak that had been draped round her shoulders from the moment they entered Gondar's lands, Rachel guided the horse through the throng and out on to the path which connected the town with the fortress.

At the centre of the path she stopped. Rachel lifted the horse's head and turned the animal, rearing on its haunches, back towards the crowd. The horse's hoofs pawed the air above the blackness of the drop on either side. It was the most brilliant, breath-taking display of horsemanship Jamie had ever seen.

Unconcerned Rachel gazed back at her people.

'The Acab Saat may lead our church,' she called out, 'but I am the river's child. You and the land are mine. Let us together cast out our fear, and take back what is rightfully ours!'

Rachel spun the white horse again.

Behind her the crowd swayed in momentary confusion. Then, caught up by her call, it began to flow forward across the causeway. As she galloped towards the gates of Salama's fortress, thousands of Gondar's citizens poured after her.

On the battlements high above, Jamie's glance returned to Salama.

The Acab Saat's face was foam-flecked and crazed. He looked down at the racing crowds. Then his eyes lifted towards Jamie's. Murderous and unseeing, Salama reached for the dagger that still hung from his waist. He pulled it out and leapt from the turret towards the Scotsman.

At Jamie's belt was the skean dhu he had carried with him all his life. Before Salama had even moved Jamie hefted it in his hand. Then he cast it into the night as he had thrown it so often before at a salmon lying in a Highland river.

The point of Jamie's knife caught Salama in the neck.

The Acab Saat raised his hands to his throat. He choked and stumbled. Reeling to one side, his legs struck the rim of the battlements. Toppling over, Salama fell outwards. With his white robes swirling round him he plunged down towards the plain.

Jamie turned and ran back down the stairs. Salama's soldiers were still thronging the flights that led to the hallway.

'Your queen stands outside!' Jamie called to them as he ran. 'If you value your lives, make ready to greet the river's child as her rank demands!'

Jamie reached the floor of the fortress and walked forward.

He unbolted the locks and revolved the wheel that opened the portcullis. Then he stepped out on to the track that ran into Gondar.

Rachel was mounted on her horse in the darkness beyond the light that spilled forward from the lanterns. Surging round her were the waves of Gondar's citizens who had defied the Acab Saat and accompanied their queen to the entrance of the fortress.

As the doors swung open and Jamie appeared on the track, Rachel slipped out of her saddle and ran towards him.

'The Acab Saat is dead,' Jamie said. 'Gondar is yours. May you now sleep well.'

Exhausted, Jamie fell against her.

— 112 —

'It is over,' Mamkinga said. 'Culembra is dead, Salama is dead. The Galla have fled. No one offers resistance. Even the women warriors have surrendered.'

They were back in the palace.

The last of the Acab Saat's soldiers had laid down their arms in the old fort, and the city was theirs. Rachel reached for a jug of wine and handed it to him.

'Drink and rest for a while,' she said.

Mamkinga took the jug of wine and drank, but he shook his head at the thought of rest.

'We still do not know what forces may be marching on Gondar,' he said. 'There is nothing they can do now, but I must see the gateways are safely guarded – '

He put down the jug and glanced at Jamie. 'Because of you the queen may rest safe in her city.'

'Ye have taken the city for her,' Jamie answered.

'They were both labours for men,' Mamkinga said. 'Each could have done the other's task as well.'

There was silence.

This time it was a comfortable silence. The tension which had existed between them, from the moment they set out on the great journey from the Benoue, had gone. Jamie was not sure why. Perhaps the victory over Salama, he thought, had dissolved it. The reason did not matter. All he knew was that in the shared grief for Toomi's and Farquarson's deaths and the shared triumph in Gondar's freedom, there was no room for jealousy or bitterness.

The two men embraced. They held each other closely. The warmth that flowed between them was stronger than it had ever been. Then Mamkinga turned and strode away.

'I wish to walk in the park,' Rachel said. 'Come with me, Jamie.'

Outside in the palace grounds, darkness still blanketed the courtyards and gardens, though a shell of light was spreading over the western sky.

Beyond the walls flames were flickering upwards. Some of the houses which had caught fire in the fighting were still burning. There were still sounds of running feet, confused shouting and the occasional scream. But even as they walked the noise began to die down.

Mamkinga was right. The battle for Gondar was finished. Sheba's city had been returned to its rightful queen.

The earth was fresh with the night's dew and the air, sharpened with a small breeze blowing from off the Mountains of the Moon, was cool. Rachel and Jamie walked westwards between the trees. The summer was almost over and the leaves were already beginning to fall. As one floated down, a flare of light from a distant burning roof touched it, outlining its veins and shining off its bright red-gold.

Rachel bent and caught the leaf before it reached the ground. She glanced at Jamie, smiling.

'Kalima, my old nurse, taught me to do that,' she said. 'For every leaf you catch before it reaches the earth, you will have one moon-span of happiness in the year ahead. Take my arm, Jamie.'

Jamie slipped his arm through hers. She pressed him against her and went on.

'I wanted to walk with you here because the park is very important to me, the most important place in my life. This is where I grew up. The trees, the lanes between them, the sky above, the wind, the mountains over there.' Rachel swept out her hand. 'They all mean something. Doho taught me to ride here. Do you remember me telling you about my first horse, Armit the firefly?'

Jamie nodded.

They had been standing on the banks of the Benoue and he had seen Rachel's face light up with pleasure as she described the little pony.

'This is where I first rode him,' Rachel continued. 'After him there were others, but Armit will always be my favourite. It was here I learned my languages. Here the soldiers used to come to teach me about war. Here the women in the palace would bring me on the hot days to sit in the shade and instruct me in what I should know as a woman. Here Ras Michael came to see how I was progressing. Look – '

She turned and pointed back towards the palace.

'Do you see that room high up on the right, the one with the lantern burning in it?'

Jamie looked back. 'Yes, I see it.'

'That was my bedchamber. Sometimes at night I would climb through the window and down that tree. I would run over here – '

Rachel let go of Jamie's arm and began to look for something in the darkness. They were close to a pair of old magnolia trees whose roots had reared up from the ground and tangled into a writhen bundle of wood, tendrils and flowers.

'This is it,' Rachel said delightedly. 'I would tuck myself in and go to sleep here with the wind in my face and the stars above and the scent of the flowers all round me.'

Jamie glanced down.

Two of the roots had twisted into an arch. Beneath it on the ground was a scooped-out hollow just big enough to hold the sleeping body of a child.

'I ran here. I rode here. I learnt here. I fought here. I slept here. I dreamed here. But when something very important happened, the most important things in my life, I was brought to where we are now.'

They had reached the end of park.

The palace was far behind them, hidden now by the trees. In front was a flight of steps leading up to a little walled and terraced garden. Jamie climbed the steps behind Rachel.

She moved away from him again and he heard the rustle of foliage. A moment later the rich fragrant scents of geranium, penny-royal and chamomile filled the air. It was a herb garden, Jamie realized, and Rachel had been crushing the plants' leaves to release their smells.

She settled herself on the parapet wall.

'Sit beside me,' she said.

Jamie swung himself up on to the wall and sat facing her.

The dawn light was widening swiftly on the sky. Beneath them the cliff plunged down almost sheer in its fall. Near its foot a cascade of water jetted out from the rock and dropped to the plain, where it tumbled and meandered away in a bright stream. Birds were beginning to call. The morning wind was crisp and clean, but constellations of stars still glittered above the distant mountains – their highest peaks mantled with ice-white drifts of snow.

'This is where I first walked,' Rachel said. 'It is the garden of the nightingales. Doho brought me here. He spun a top across the terrace. Without knowing, I was on my feet trying to catch it. That evening Doho brought Ras Michael to see what I could do. They both laughed and laughed – '

Rachel laughed too at the memory. Then her face became grave.

'On this terrace Doho told me that one day I was to become queen. It was here I learnt about Gondar. He showed me the villages on the plain and made me learn their names. It was here I sat alone before my baptism in the river and the feast which the Acab Saat's invasion ended – '

She paused. 'It was here I discovered I was the river's child and the river would give me a child too.'

Perplexed for reasons he could not understand, Jamie sat gazing fixedly at her.

Rachel had shown him the park. It was her background, her history, the 'garden of my life' as she had called it once on the journey. He knew that. He was glad and proud to have walked through it with her, to have been shown the most secret places of her childhood like the tree where she tethered Armit and the hollow where she had slept when she climbed down from her room.

Yet Jamie sensed, with a premonition that chilled him, that there was another reason for what she was telling him.

Jamie could not think what it was. He loved her and she loved him. They had held each other in their arms. They had made vows to each other that could never be broken – that they would live together for ever and cherish each other until they died.

Cold in his stomach, Jamie fixed his eyes on her.

'What are ye telling me?' he asked.

'That I love you,' Rachel answered. 'That I have loved you from the first moment I saw you across the fire. That I have never loved another man and never will. That you are my stranger in the mirror of my bedchamber. That you are all I want and need and have prayed for. You are my life, you have completed my life. That is what I am telling you. Also – '

Rachel took a deep breath. For an instant she closed her eyes in anguish.

'That I have brought you to my garden to bid you farewell. It is my will, and that of my people, that I wed Mamkinga.'

Jamie sat very still.

He felt stunned and disbelieving. It was as if someone had taken an axe and cleft his life in two. Behind him was the living part, the laughter and hope and delight. Ahead was the emptiness, dead and cold and deserted.

'Mamkinga loves you,' Jamie said. 'Of course he does, so would any man. But ye don't love him. Ye love me. Ye said so yourself. Rachel – '

Jamie reached out and gripped her hand. 'We are well together. Let us be together.'

Rachel held Jamie's hand tight. She patted it comfortingly as if she were soothing a child.

'No, Jamie,' she said. 'We cannot be together. I am not like other people, one person among many. I am a queen. Like the honey bees, the life of the hive depends on me. If I am lost, the life of the hive is forfeit. Gondar needs me for its life. Gondar too needs Malinda for peace and security. If I am wed to Mamkinga I can give the hive its safety –'

She broke off.

'I have known it since we all stood together and prayed beside the fire, so long ago it seems now. Mamkinga cut the sign of the snake's tongue on my wrist. I could have refused the knife and drawn my arm away. I did not for I knew he was right. I joined my kingdom to his then and they are still joined.'

Between her fingers Rachel was still holding some of the geranium leaves she had pulled from the garden. She crushed them and another wave of scent billowed into the air.

'Until tonight I thought I could find some way of being a queen, of safeguarding Gondar and yet staying with you.' Her voice shook as she went on. 'Now I know I cannot. It is not only a matter of kingdoms and great issues. It is a matter of those others who loved me. Toomi died tonight. I had made her my sister. She died for me and for Gondar, and for Mamkinga and Malinda. Without Toomi, Mamkinga's life is incomplete. The loss and the wound are unhealed. I can give him myself, whom he loves, for Toomi. I can bring our countries and peoples together. I can bring him myself for the healing of himself and our lands –'

Rachel paused. 'Do you understand what I say?'

Jamie thought for a moment. With a terrible burdening sense of loss he nodded.

He longed to fight against her, to argue with her, to deny and contradict everything she had said. He could not. Mamkinga was his own brother and Toomi his sister. Toomi had lived for Mamkinga. When Mamkinga's spirit had been broken, she had given life and courage back to him. She had made him fight for their kingdom and their people.

It was not only Gondar which Toomi had helped to save from slavery – it was Malinda too.

The rim of the sun lifted over the mountains and a great wave of light flooded over the plain. It was autumnal light, clear and crisp as the night wind.

'Kiss me,' Rachel said.

Jamie held her in his arms. He pulled her tight against him. He buried his mouth on hers, and tasted the sweetness of her lips.

As the sun rose Jamie saw through a mist of tears the palace of Gondar, the falling leaves in the royal park, the strands of Rachel's hair drifting across her face, and the lingering flames in the burning houses beyond. Everything – the queen, the seasons, the great journey, the battle and his enduring love – was gathered in that single moment.

'You could stay,' Rachel whispered. 'I have considered it. I could give you whatever you wanted. You could be Master of the Horse, my Chamberlain, anything. At least you would be near me.'

'Near ye? Knowing that at night ye slept in another man's arms? That the children ye bore were his?' Jamie smiled bleakly. 'Did ye really believe I could live like that?'

'I had hoped so. But, no, in my heart I did not believe it.'

Rachel was weeping too.

She collected herself. She brushed her hand across her eyes and stepped back. Then she stared at him. In her face Jamie saw an overpowering sense of loss and grief mingled with a radiant expression of certainty and love.

'I would never have you live like that. You must leave Gondar, Jamie. It will be my order. You will have nine days from now to cross the border.'

'Ye are ordering me away – ?'

Jamie stared at her. 'Ye are ridding yourself of me? I canna believe it. What have I done – ?'

He broke off, the words dead on his lips.

Rachel backed away from him across the terrace. She

was very pale and although the sadness had gone from her face, the radiant confidence was still there.

'You spoke of me bearing another man's child,' she said quietly. 'I shall never bear another man's child. Only the child of the river. And the father of the river's child must either leave Gondar or die.'

Jamie could barely take in what she was saying.

'But it was only last night.' Jamie fumbled for the words and the meaning he was trying to find in them. 'Ye canna even know – '

'I am a woman before I am a queen,' Rachel said. 'I know when the seed is planted. I know when the seed has taken root.'

'For the love of Christ!' Jamie protested. 'Ye could be wrong – '

'I am not wrong,' Rachel cut him off again. 'I know and I am going to announce from the palace balcony that you are banished from Gondar after nine days from today on pain of death. And everyone who hears it, from one end of the kingdom to the other, will know what I am declaring.'

'Including Mamkinga?' Jamie said.

Rachel nodded. 'He is your brother and he will be my husband. If he loves us both as I believe, he will accept what I have declared. He will also cherish and protect the river's child.'

Jamie shook his head.

He was silent, overwhelmed by what Rachel had said and her implacable confidence in saying it. Rachel stared at him. Her face was dauntless but triumphant. Then she began to smile.

An acacia tree was trailing its long leafy fronds over one corner of the terrace wall. Rachel leaned over and plucked a spray of its white blossoms. She slipped it into the neck of Jamie's bloodstained shirt.

'You have my heart in your heart,' she said. 'I have your child in my belly. This flower stands for them both. The heart and the child will live long. The flower, whose thorn has already pierced you once, will not live long.

With wine and water, a week maybe. Gondar's borders are only two days' riding on a good horse – and you will have the best. That leaves us, like the flower, a week – '

Rachel took his arm again and pulled him towards the steps that led down to the park.

'We have the span of seven moonrises – and I am not married yet!'

In the rising sun they at first walked and then ran laughing through the trees towards the palace.

113

'Water – seven gourds and five tubs on the waggon. Grain – five sacks and two bags here already milled. Powder and shot, they are both measured and sealed in waxed paper – '

Mamkinga was muttering to himself as he checked the stores.

It must have been the twentieth time Mamkinga had done it, but he still went through the list with the same meticulous care.

'Biltong. Well, I'm not even going to count the coils. They're the very best too, I saw to that myself. You've got enough to last you from one end of Africa to the other – '

'Mamkinga!' Jamie protested. 'For God's sake, man, ye've equipped me with enough to take me to the moon.'

'Be patient!' Mamkinga frowned and lifted his hand. 'I want to be sure.'

Jamie raised his shoulders in a shrug of resignation. He stood back.

Jamie, Mamkinga, the waggon train and the fifty armed Malindan soldiers Mamkinga had insisted on sending with him as an escort, were gathered somewhere on the imprecise border that divided Gondar from the sloping lowlands which led to the sea.

They had left the capital forty-eight hours earlier. They had ridden throughout the night and the day that followed. Now at dusk they had come to the end of their journey together.

On the day that followed the fall of Gondar to Rachel's forces, Jamie had seen Toomi and Farquarson buried side by side with the other heroes of the assault on the city's gates in the royal graveyard near the palace. Pota, the Wazan pygmies' chieftain who had died the same night, was laid to rest beside his idol, the little Scottish laird.

Among Farquarson's belongings was the chess set Wolf had whittled from the scraps of hardwood he'd found on the shore of the Bight of Benin. Unbeknownst to Jamie, Farquarson must have come across it after Wolf was killed in Malinda, and kept it as a memento of the Austrian. Now the chess set was packed away in Jamie's baggage on the ox-cart in front of him. So was the gift Mamkinga had given Jamie.

In the days between their victory and Jamie's departure, Mamkinga had found a smithy inside the palace walls. He had the fires lit and the metal implements cleaned. Then with his own hands Mamkinga had cast and polished a golden snake. He presented it to Jamie, smiling, as they left the city.

'You watched over me when I was sick,' Mamkinga said. 'The snake watched over you. Life came back to us both. May it always be so. May the snake remind you of the healing spirits of Malinda. May it guard you now and for ever.'

Now on the barren track Mamkinga finished his count of the stores. He stepped back and gazed at Jamie.

'It is done, Umshebi,' Mamkinga said. 'You are ready to leave.'

Jamie walked over to him.

He put his arms round Mamkinga's shoulders and held him tight. Tears blurred both their eyes, but neither could speak. Jamie turned away. Without looking at the towering Malindan again, Jamie mounted his horse and spurred it towards the lowering sun.

The ox-cart laboured after him.

Hidden deep inside Jamie's baggage on the cart's swaying boards was a fold of coarse paper. Nestling beside the paper was the ebony bracelet studded with emeralds Toomi had worn on her wrist from the day she went to find Hadji in Garona. The bracelet had been a gift to Jamie from Hadji. Lodged alongside them was another

gift from Mamkinga, the sharkskin-handled dagger he
had borne at his waist from the morning they left the
Bight of Benin.

Yet it was on the paper that Jamie's thoughts dwelt as
the small procession wound down from Gondar's hills.

The paper had wrapped the phial of the extract of
digitalis he had brought with him from Britain. The
digitalis had saved Mamkinga's life. Between the paper
now was the fading blossom of the flowering acacia. The
acacia bloom might be dying. In Jamie's nostrils its scent
was still as keen and fragrant as when Rachel had picked
it in the garden of the nightingales.

He had left his heart behind him in the rambling golden
palace in the mountains, but he had found the river's
birthplace and the queen in the blue robes.

Jamie's promises were kept.

He spurred the horse's flanks and rode down towards
the distant sea.

114

'Hold him, my child,' Kalima said.

Rachel reached out and took the baby.

For a moment she was too tired even to look at the infant. Her labour had lasted all night. Now at dawn, minutes after the delivery, she was more exhausted than she had ever been in her life.

Rachel blinked wearily in the wavering candle light.

The stars were paling outside the windows and the sun was starting to rise over the mountains. She lay back on the couch and held the child cradled in her arms.

It was nine months after the fall of Gondar. Much had changed since the defeat and death of the Acab Saat. There was a new Guardian of the Sacred Fire, a wise and compassionate old priest whom Rachel had chosen herself. Mamkinga sat on the throne as her consort. Malinda's lands had been joined with Gondar's. At her side Mamkinga, as she knew he would, was proving a just and valiant ruler of the joint kingdoms.

At Mamkinga's instigation the institution of slavery had been abolished. No longer could any citizen of Gondar staff his house or work his lands with captive and manacled labour. No longer could the Arab slaving caravans wind through the kingdom to the coast, or roving bandit traders like the Oye-Eboe haggle to buy convicted criminals.

Rachel had supported everything Mamkinga proposed. In her name, as the river's child and queen-empress, they had been made law. Yet she had done more than change the customs and political geography of the Mountains of the Moon. In a smaller way she had changed the habits and practices of Gondar's court. No longer was the birth chamber thronged, as it had been when Rachel was born. Now in the great dark room on the first floor of the palace there were only herself, old Kalima, and Doho the dwarf.

Doho was sitting cross-legged on the floor.

Soon he would go back to sleep in his favourite place on the lintel-stone of what had once been Ras Michael's chambers and now were Mamkinga's. The difference meant little to the dwarf now. He was old. His hair was white. The beatings and torture he had endured at Salama's hands had shattered his body and wrecked his health.

Yet Doho was indomitable. He had survived. If God and the spirits of the mountains chose, he would continue to survive for more years yet. His beloved queen, the bold and dark-eyed child he had taught and guided and cherished, was back on Gondar's throne. It mattered nothing to Doho who she had taken as consort.

Nor did it to Kalima, older still than Doho. Yet the white-haired servantwoman who had attended Rachel's mother, Ozoro Esther, and her grandmother too, the Dowager Empress Iteghe, had other matters on her mind. The river had given birth to a new child.

The child needed nursing and it needed its sleep.

'Kiss your baby, my little one,' Kalima said to Rachel. 'Then give him back to me. It is time the child slept.'

Rachel raised herself on the couch.

She looked down at her son. The new child of the river was a strong well-formed boy with the fine features and the pale glowing skin of the Abyssinian race. Unlike any other Abyssinian infant Rachel had ever seen, his hair was red and curling and he had blue-grey eyes, as dark and unfathomable as the waters of some cold and distant ocean.

Rachel kissed his cheek softly. She handed him back to Kalima.

Rachel lay back on the couch and gazed at the wheeling stars beyond the open window. In Gondar it was night.

Somewhere thousands of miles away the same stars would already be fading as a spring dawn spread over a tiny green-turfed and white-shored island.

Yesterday the swallows had been gathering on the palace roof, anxious to be away as winter gathered over the Mountains of the Moon. Long ago she had asked Doho where the swallows flew. Doho hadn't known. Rachel had at last found out. She knew now where they went and where they nested.

As a crescent moon rose above Gondar the young queen-empress smiled.